SOURCE OF A RIVER

SOURCE OF A RIVER

A NOVEL

GARY MORSE

BOOK I

ICE FISHING

John was trying to sleep, but he heard footsteps thumping down the hallway. The wooden floor beneath his bedroom doorway creaked. He closed his eyes tight, hoping his eyelids wouldn't flutter, and praying that he looked dead asleep to his mother.

This was the third time she had come in since putting him to bed. The last time she caught him with eyes wide open. "John Louis Anderson!" she had said then. "If you don't get to sleep, you can't go tomorrow. Do you hear me?"

John's head itched but he forced himself to lay still, pretending to be asleep. The itch burned, begging to be scratched, but he thought of the ice fishing trip. John wanted to go but he didn't want to make his mom upset. He bit down on the inside of his lip, squeezing a small ball of his flesh between his teeth. Finally, he heard his mother walk away, her feet pattering back down the hallway.

John opened his eyes and glanced at the empty doorway. He ran his fingers through his buzz cut and found the itch came from a mole on his scalp. He scratched it until it hurt. He'd gone with his dad to the barbershop the past weekend but Bubba, his regular barber, had four men waiting, so John got his haircut from the new barber, Frank. Frank kept pushing his short, pudgy fingers against John's head, telling him to hold still. When John and his dad returned home, his mother laughed, saying it was his shortest haircut ever and she could see moles all over his scalp. She rubbed her smooth hands across his fuzzy, brown head. He still looked handsome, she told him, before exclaiming that the moles on his head formed the shape of the Cross. "It's a sign you'll be a priest," she said. "Or maybe even a saint."

John scratched his mole again and then reared up to look at the small clock on his bookcase. The tiny blue bulb from his aquarium cast enough light that he could make out the clock's hands. Still eight hours before they would leave in the morning. He flopped back against his fluffy pillow.

John pictured himself on the frozen lake with his dad. They were bundled in thick coats and their fishing lines disappeared through the hole in the ice, the bait sinking deep into the lake. John felt a huge tug and his pole bent almost in two, but he held on. He yanked the pole and a huge red-and-blue fish sprang out of the ice water. His dad grinned and patted John on the shoulder, saying he was proud.

The clock hands were stuck in about the same places when John checked again. He sighed, glancing across the room at the poster taped to the wall of Willie Mays in his San Francisco Giants uniform. His best friend, Danny, had given it to him in August for his eighth birthday. He sniffed a stinky odor again and was upset with himself for spilling a big pinch of smelly fish food onto the rug when he'd fed them dinner. Beneath the glossy image of Willie's cleats sat a twenty-five gallon aquarium where two black-and-white angelfish nudged the front glass, their small fins waving gently at John. He looked past the angelfish, searching unsuccessfully for his favorite, the kissing gourami. The gourami, John figured, was hiding again in the ceramic cave in the corner of the tank—it had become the fish's regular spot since the other gourami that it used to kiss had died. His father had flushed the dead fish down the toilet while John watched its limp body swirl around the white bowl before it disappeared. It was selfish to cry because dead people had gone to a better place, his dad had said once. John slipped away from his dad after the bowl emptied and cried alone in his room.

John flopped over on his mattress and buried his nose into his pillowcase. He listened for the dishwasher—its gurgling and surging helped John fall asleep most nights, but his mom didn't have it running and he heard only the dull vibrations of his fish tank pump.

John worried his mom would come back so he decided to count sheep. He imagined a huge flock, white and fleecy. The first sheep jumped over a stone fence. And then the next sheep jumped and so did the next one. Seventy-eight sheep hopped over the fence, one after another, but John was still awake. The sheep disappeared from his mind, but the stone fence remained, just floating in space. How far did space go? He imagined being an astronaut on a mission exploring the outer reaches of the universe. The big, black sky spread past thousands of stars. He zoomed through space, looking for its edge. There it was! A huge stone wall. John grabbed onto the stones, pulled himself up, and peered over the wall. For as far as he could see, there was more darkness.

How could space go on forever? John wondered. But how could it just end?

"It's too cold and too dangerous." His mother's words carried down the hallway.

"Hon." His father's voice sounded higher pitched than usual. "It'll be fine. We'll dress warm."

"You could catch pneumonia." His mom's words held a nervousness that John recognized. "I don't want John going," she said. "Maybe next year when he's older."

"I was younger than John when I went with my dad."

"That was thirty years ago in Vermont." His mother sounded like she was scolding John.

"I should have taken him and my dad last year when I first thought about it."

"Maybe it would have been okay then with two adults."

"John and I are going tomorrow," his father said.

"If you're fool enough to go, then the hell with you. But you can't take John."

"I'm taking my son with me," his father's voice boomed. "Do you hear me?"

John turned over and faced the bedroom wall. He pulled the covers over his head. He liked how the sheets felt cool against his ears but his stomach suddenly hurt. He felt sick. He thought he should tell his mom and dad. He pictured them taking his temperature instead of arguing. He pulled the covers off his head and listened closer. He could no longer hear their voices.

His dad had said ice fishing was the best time of his life. John craned his neck toward the door. He heard only the hum of the fish pump.

He looked again at the clock—10:20—and then peered at the crucifix hanging above his bed. A wilted strand of palm drooped over Jesus' outstretched arm. He had said his prayers when his mom had put him to bed but that seemed like hours ago.

"Dear God," John whispered, "hear my prayer. Our Father who art in Heaven, hallowed be thy name." He recited the Lord's prayer again, then added, "Please Father, look after my parents and make them not argue anymore, and let me get to sleep and let me and Dad go tomorrow and catch some big fish." A thought about his maternal grandmother came in nearly the same breath as his parents: "And especially please look after Nona. Thank you very much, God." He then remembered and added to his prayer, as if his mom was listening, his mom's dad, Grandpa Shea, and her grandmother, Mama Clara, who had both died during the last school year, and then her grandfather Papa Marco, who had died before that. When he had handed the note excusing him from school for the last funeral to his teacher, she had exclaimed, "Your poor mom. Is she okay?" John had said yes, even though his mom cried every day.

"And look after Grandpa Anderson in heaven too," John said quietly to end his prayer.

After he prayed, John's stomach didn't hurt as much, yet he still couldn't sleep. He remembered Sister Cecil saying during first-grade catechism that God always was, always is, and always will be.

He hadn't dared ask her, but the question still came to him: Who created God?

John was dreaming of his grandfather when he woke to his dad rubbing his back.

"Son, wake up. It's time to go fishing."

John sat up and rubbed his eyes. His father loomed over him.

"Are you awake?"

The foggy image of John's burly grandfather calling him still floated in John's mind. "Yes."

His father stood up, stretching his six-foot-four frame to full height. "Good boy. Get dressed and we'll go."

John put on the long underwear, jeans, flannel shirt, and dark blue wool sweater his mom had laid across his dresser. He used the bathroom, brushed his teeth the way his father had shown him when he was little, and walked into the kitchen, which smelled of coffee and cigarettes. His mother sat at the steel-and-Formica table in her long, green velvet robe, the black hair of her bangs wrapped tight in two pink curlers. She cupped a coffee mug in her left hand and a cigarette dangled through the fingers of her other hand. John hardly ever saw his mother smoke. She stared blankly into the dining room before her eyes transfixed on John.

His dad pulled a big, brown sack from the refrigerator. "There you are." He grinned at John. "Ready to catch some fish?"

Through the small, square kitchen window, John saw it was still dark outside. He nodded and then noticed his mother's face was creased in a frown. His dad had told her on their anniversary last week that she was a beautiful woman, and he had admitted then that John, with his dark hair and facial features, looked more like her. Yes, his mom had laughed, they both had long, pointy Italian noses.

"I heard the weather report, Hank," his mother said. "It's supposed to be very cold today. It'll be bitterly cold in the mountains."

"Your thermos of hot chicken noodle soup will keep us nice and warm." His dad swooped down to kiss her, but she turned away and his kiss glanced off her cheek. A strange expression slid across his father's face, but he shook his head and then winked at John. "And if chicken noodle soup doesn't do it, this other thermos of hot chocolate that I made will definitely do the trick."

"Why don't you go in a few weeks when it's a little warmer?" his mother asked.

"Hon, think about it. In a few weeks it *will* be warmer and then there won't be any ice fishing."

"I don't know why you can't just go fishing around here like other men." His mother fidgeted with her coffee cup, plate, and spoon, nudging each of them an inch or so, back and forth, as if trying to find the perfect order. "You never go fishing—and now you have to go ice fishing?"

"Liz, we have fished here before—"

"One time."

"*Today*," his father said, "we're not going to just mope around the house again. We're going ice fishing like I did with my dad when I was a boy."

John thought his mom was pretty, but the corners of her mouth sagged. He remembered his dad teasing her once that she had a huge frown like an upside-down U when she was upset. Now she puffed on her cigarette, and then beat the ashes against the glass ashtray. John worried he had ruined his nighttime prayer for them to stop arguing when he wondered: who created God? "I felt sick last night," he said.

"What?" his mother asked.

"I felt kind of sick last night. My stomach hurt."

"Ah, shit," his father said. He rolled his eyes and yanked a pack of Winstons from his shirt pocket, before shaking out a cigarette.

His mom pulled John toward her. She clamped her hand tight against his forehead. "You can't go." She looked at his dad. "He's sick."

"Here." His father brushed away her hand and placed his own across John's forehead. "You're not hot."

"It was his stomach, Hank."

"Son, how's your stomach feel this morning?"

John looked from his dad to his mom and then back to his dad. "I don't know."

"What you mean you don't know how you feel?" his father asked. "It's a simple question of fact. Do you feel sick or not?"

John hunched his shoulders. He was confused. This wasn't what he expected and suddenly he felt bad, but not in his stomach.

"He shouldn't go if he doesn't feel good," his mom said.

His father glared at her and then at John. "You're not sick, John. Now get your coat and get in the car."

"He's sick," his mom said. "Why can't you be sympathetic?"

"Don't pull this on me. Not this goddamn time." His father's voice rose in pitch. "You're not sick."

John felt his lips quiver. His dad usually spoke softly but lately he'd been yelling more and even swearing sometimes. John was afraid that his dad would start yelling now at him or his mom or both of them. This wasn't what he'd wanted. He felt tears welling around the sides of his eyes, but he blinked the tears back.

"Listen you two," his father said. "I'm going ice fishing, with you or without you." He pointed a long finger at John. "You can stay here all day with your mother, if that's really what you want, but if you do, there's no TV, no going outside, and no having Danny over. You'll stay in your room all day until I get home. Do you understand me?"

"Hank, you can't punish him for being sick."

"Damn it! He's not sick." He sucked a deep drag from his cigarette. "John, I'm going to ask you one last time. Do you want to go ice fishing with me today or not?"

John looked again at his mother. She stared at him with big, desperate eyes, and he knew without words being spoken she wanted him to stay.

"John?" his father said.

He wanted to go. "I don't know." Tears slipped from his eyes.

"Go to your room," his father said. "Go on—get back to sleep."

His father snatched the brown bag and thermoses from the counter and brushed past John. John watched him twist the doorknob to the garage.

The tears broke through, but John managed to yell to his father. "I want to go ice fishing with you."

His dad spun around and smiled. He stepped back toward John. "Well, good." He leaned down and wiped tears off John's cheeks. "That'll be great."

"But your stomach?" his mom asked.

"Last night I felt kind of sick. But I feel better now."

His mother looked shocked and John was surprised he'd spoken the words aloud, though they were true. His mother's mouth sagged again, but he turned toward his dad and grabbed his coat.

John woke to a bright light. He peered over the maroon dashboard of his father's old Mercury, blinking twice at the sun that squatted between gray clouds and a range of mountain peaks that looked like vanilla ice cream cones in the distance.

"Look, Dad, there's snow in the mountains."

"Yup. Plenty of it." His dad grinned at him. "Did you have a good nap?"

"Yes."

"Good. We had an early morning wake-up call—it must have tired you out. How's your stomach feeling?"

"Good—I can go ice fishing with you."

His dad laughed. "Very good because that's exactly where we're headed."

They had been to the lake twice before for summer vacations. John remembered lots of blue water and playing with his toy dinosaurs on a big sandy beach, but they had not been back to the lake in a few years.

"How much longer?" John asked.

"About an hour and forty minutes. So, are you feeling well enough to eat a chocolate bar?"

"Yes!"

His dad reached into his coat pocket, rummaged about, and pulled out a Nestlé Crunch.

"That's my favorite."

He handed the candy to John. "That's why I bought it this morning when I gassed up."

John thanked his dad. He smelled the chocolate through the wrapper. "Can I eat it now?"

"Yup. Plus, look at this." His dad pulled out another Nestlé Crunch. "This one's for when we're fishing."

John tore open the wrapper and bit off a small chunk. The crisped rice crackled between his teeth. He sucked the sweetness of the chocolate against the edge of his tongue. John bit off another chunk and asked his dad if he wanted some.

His dad declined and dug back into his pocket, pulling out a Snickers bar. "Bought my favorite, too. Want a bite?"

John tore off a piece of the Snickers with his hands; the caramel stretched gooeyness across his fingertips.

His dad glanced over. "Sorry if I got cranky this morning."

His father had been a lot grouchier than usual lately. "It's okay, Dad."

"The short night of sleep must have tuckered me out too."

Another piece of Nestlé Crunch melted in John's mouth. "I dreamt about Grandpa last night." He searched his dad's face for a reaction. He hoped it was okay to talk about his grandfather even though he had died.

"You did? What did you dream?" His dad sounded excited.

"Me and you were fishing on the ice and then all of a sudden we're on a river in a forest and there was Grandpa. He was calling me to climb up the hill to where he was." John saw his dad smile. "Then these huge red fish jumped out of the water and Grandpa just reached out and grabbed this big pink fish in his hand—"

"A salmon. What happened next?"

"Then he asked me if I wanted to go fishing."

"Then what?"

"I woke up."

"That's a good dream, John. I wish I'd have a dream like that." His father stared at the empty highway lanes ahead. "It would have been Dad's birthday today."

"I know." John savored the chocolate on his tongue. "Grandpa told me last summer he knew where there was some gold."

His dad nodded. "He probably did. Your grandfather did a lot of prospecting in his day."

"Do you know where it is?"

"Can't say that I do."

"He said it was way up in the mountains. He said I was supposed to keep it a secret, but that when I was old enough—when I was a man, he said—we'd go there and pan the river and find the gold together."

"He would have loved that," his dad said.

"He said he'd been waiting years to get it, but he'd wait a few more for me to get bigger." John watched St. Christopher jiggling on the dashboard as they drove. "Why did Grandpa die?"

"He had a heart attack."

"But why did he die?"

"When you have a heart attack, your blood stops circulating. You need your heart to live. It's your body's motor."

"I wish Grandpa could have gone back and gotten the gold." John's mom had said it was terribly unfair that Grandpa Anderson had died so soon and hadn't been able to enjoy his retirement.

"Me too." His father was silent and John worried he had upset his dad. When his father pursed his lips, though, John knew that meant his dad was still think-ing. "But your grandfather loved ice fishing and that's exactly what we're going to do today—for him and for us. And he had a more adventurous life than anyone I know. There's no man I admire more. He lived without regrets."

John slowly ate the last of his candy bar. "I don't want you to die, Dad."

His dad looked at him. "Don't you worry about that now."

"I don't think I'm going to die."

His dad started to speak, then paused. "Hey," he said, "I've got one more bite of my Snickers. Want it?"

John thanked him and took the last bite.

"Did I tell you I'm really proud of your report card?" his dad asked. "Straight As, and A-pluses in math and science. You can be a fine engineer or scientist someday. Your Grandpa was an engineer of sorts, but mostly self-taught. That would be a good life, even if you never find that gold. I'll be proud of you. So would Grandpa."

It was eleven o'clock when they caught their first glimpse of the lake. His father pointed to a flat expanse of ice wedged between the mountains and forest. The ice glistened a silvery sheen, and then disappeared as they dipped into a long descent. His dad guided the old car down a steep, curving road. When they reached the valley floor, a wall of snow packed taller than a man rose from the edge of the road and blocked John's view. After a few minutes, they turned into a cleared parking lot at the public boat launch area and rolled to a stop between an outhouse and the only other vehicle in the lot, a red-and-white pickup truck.

His dad pointed ahead. "Beautiful, huh?"

The lake looked like a gigantic ice rink to John. Everywhere he could see, ice shone a milky gray. The lake seemed huge—it was three miles long and a half-mile wide, his father said—but it was barren except for two men in black coats ice fishing more than a hundred yards out. Pine trees sprinkled with snow surrounded the lake on three sides. Across the lake, huge mountains covered with pines, boulders, and snow vaulted toward a sky of broken clouds. Halfway to the ridge, train tracks crossed the face of the mountain like a child's braces.

John grabbed the blankets, a thermos, and folding lawn chairs that his father told him to carry. He followed his dad across the lake's edge. He hesitated, tip-toed lightly on the ice, took a few steps, and then saw that large black-and-white, oval stones speckled the lake bottom beneath the milky ice.

"Dad." He started to point out the rocks beneath him, but his dad was already a dozen steps ahead. "Where are we going?"

"About fifty paces this way."

"Mom told me yesterday we should stay next to the shore."

His father spun around. "Mom said that to you, huh? Do you know what we'll catch if we stay next to the shore?"

"What?"

"Nothing." His father adjusted his grip on the faded khaki duffel bag slung over his shoulder. "Come on."

John ran after his dad, but his feet slipped. His toes flew up and his bottom smacked against the ice. The metal lawn chairs slipped from his hand and rattled against the frozen lake.

"Are you okay?"

"Yeah." John rubbed his butt.

"Good." His dad stepped toward John and extended his huge hand. "You can't run on ice. Too slippery."

John followed his father until he stopped nearly across from the other two men, but the length of a ball field away. From the duffel bag, his father pulled a hammer, a stake, and an ax. John watched his dad drive the stake a couple of inches into the ice, pull it out, reposition the stake a few inches away. He pounded the stake again, pulled it out, and repeated the process until he had outlined a small circle. His father grabbed the ax and struck short, powerful blows to the ice until it cracked open. His father scooped out the big chunks of ice with the fishing net while John stared into the hole, hoping to see a fish. All he saw were pieces of ice and gray water. His dad set up their fishing lines, which they lowered into the lake.

The sun played hopscotch with the clouds over the next hour, warming John's checks when it shone. John and his dad fished into the afternoon without a bite. Three times, John thought he had a fish, but each time there was nothing on his hook but the soggy cube of cheese bait.

A gust of wind blew across John, ruffling the edge of the brown wool blanket that his mother had told him to lay over his chest and lap. The clouds thickened across the sky and John could no longer see or feel the sun. His toes burned.

"Getting cold with the wind gusting, eh?"

John nodded.

"Yup, colder than a witch's teat in January." His father winked and then looked embarrassed.

John had seen the other fishermen pull two blue-and-red fish—rainbow trout, his dad said—from beneath the ice. His father said a river flowed into the east end of the lake and John thought the fish must be hiding in the river or near the middle of the lake. He wanted to ask his dad if they could try one of those spots, but instead he sniffled and wiped his running nose.

"Are you warm enough?" his dad asked.

"I'm okay." His teeth chattered.

His dad poured him more hot chocolate.

The other fisherman packed up their gear. After they walked off the lake to the parking lot, his father asked if John wanted to try a different fishing spot.

"Yes."

"Where shall we go?" his father asked.

John thought of the river. He wanted to go to where the river met the lake or to the middle of the lake. He pictured schools of large rainbows, hiding just beneath the ice at both places, waiting to be hooked. It was the sort of adventure his grandfather would do, and John longed to do the same thing, but he remembered his mom telling him not to venture far from the shore. He suddenly felt bad. "I don't know."

"Let's try close to where those other guys were fishing," his father said.

John scuffed over the ice with his father. He watched his dad cut open a new circle and he peered through the ice. They fished for what seemed like a long time to John. His stomach growled loudly, and his dad twisted off the red cap to the soup thermos; it was the last of their food. Earlier, they had finished off the hot chocolate, eaten two salami and Swiss cheese sandwiches, and gobbled down their second candy bars. Noodles plopped from the thermos into the cup, splattering spots of yellow against the ice.

His dad handed him the cup. "Here, this will fill you up."

John sipped the soup but it tasted cold and smelled too much like the old chicken sandwich he'd left in his lunchbox last week. He slipped off his gloves, rubbing his hands together to make sure he could still feel his fingertips.

"Look, Dad." John pointed halfway up the mountain. Three black train engines pulled a long train. John and his dad counted eighty-seven cars before two pink cabooses wound around the curve. The train chugged west, its whistle hooting. The sound rolled across the mountains. John loved train whistles. When he stayed at Nona's house, he listened to the sounds of trains while he fell asleep. He watched the train until it disappeared into a tunnel, its hooting fading to the whisper of an echo.

John heard voices and twisted around in his lawn chair. The two other fishermen were walking back across the lake.

"Are they going to be mad at us for taking their space?" he asked.

"Of course not." His father's words sounded sharp. "We opened a new hole and there's still three miles of lake for them."

The men stayed to the right of John and his father by fifty yards. His dad waved and they waved back. Forty strides past John, the men stopped and punched a hole in the ice with a funny-shaped pole that his dad called an auger.

Within five minutes, John heard shouts. One of the men's poles was bent way over. John watched the man churn his reel for a long time before pulling up a huge white fish. The man held it up, the fish dangling from the man's shoulders to his waist. He flopped the fish onto the ice. The man's laughter reverberated across the frozen lake.

"What kind of fish was that?" John asked his dad.

"I don't know. A big one."

John felt his line tug. It pulled again. "I think I got one!"

His father examined the pole. "No."

"I felt it pull. Two times."

"You can check it, but there's nothing."

John rapidly reeled in his line. The yellow glob of cheese bait clung to his hook, dripping water.

His father gave him fresh bait and John let his line sink again. He heard the other fisherman laughing again and turned to look. This time they reeled in a rainbow.

A bright spot in the sky that looked like a huge cross or a plus sign to John glowed a luminous yellow through the clouds. His father said the sun was trying to break through the clouds again. They watched the sky until the glow slipped behind the peak of the mountain and the world became gray.

His father looked at his wristwatch and shook his head. "Damn it, we might be out of luck today. When I was a kid, we always caught fish." His dad sounded strange, like he was sad.

"Is it late?"

"4:06."

"Dad, can we try just one more place?"

His father glanced again at his watch and frowned.

"That's okay," John said.

"We have time for just one more spot. Where do you want to go?"

John thought again of the place where the river joined the lake, but he worried they didn't have enough time and he was afraid his father would tell him no. He pointed instead toward the center of the lake. "Can we go out there?"

"That's a good idea. There's probably more and bigger fish near the middle."

They packed their gear and started across the lake, crossing paths and nodding at the other two fishermen, who were again leaving.

"Is Mom going to be mad if we're late?" John asked.

"I told her not to hold dinner for us. We'll stop for burgers in Sacramento. And for dessert, we can grab another candy bar."

John worried his mom would be mad at him when they got home. She wouldn't yell at him, but he pictured her with that frown on her face and not saying anything. "Can we get a candy bar for Mom? Nestlé Crunch is her favorite too."

His dad nodded. "That's not a bad idea."

"Look." John pointed to a protrusion of ice. It was cylinder shaped, sticking an inch or two above the surface of the frozen lake. "That's neat. What is it?"

His father stooped down for a closer look. A stream of clear bubbles was trapped inside the cylinder of ice. "Some water bubbled up and got frozen, but I'm not exactly sure how."

"Dad, how is ice made?"

"Water freezes at 32 degrees Fahrenheit. When it gets that cold, the water molecules lose energy. They just sort of stop dead, frozen in their tracks."

"Really?"

"Yup. Now, come on if we're going to fish." His father repositioned his grip on the fishing poles and took long strides toward the center of the lake. John carried the folding lawn chairs and followed his father. They walked past the other men's fishing hole by fifty yards, and his father announced it was a good spot.

"Dad?"

"Yeah?"

"If we catch a fish, do we have to eat it?

His father looked askance. "If we keep a fish, we're going to eat it. Otherwise, it would have died for nothing."

"If he's little, can we throw him back?"

"If he's little, we'll throw him back. If he's a big one, he's Sunday's supper. Now here, move back." His father positioned the stake against the ice and smacked it with the hammer, but the stake plopped over onto the frozen surface of the lake. "Damn it."

"Is it hard to do?" John asked.

"The ice can be tough to crack. But it's not so hard to do. Want to try?"

John shook his head.

"Come here. You should know how to do this."

John listened to his father explain again how to hold and swing a hammer. His father held the stake against the ice and John swung easily but missed the stake. The hammerhead slapped against the ice.

"Remember to concentrate, John. Aim right for the head of the stake."

John swung again and hit the top of the stake, but the hammer bounced off onto the ice.

"That's better."

"But it didn't do anything."

"Keep trying. But harder this time."

John swung again, and then four more times. All he could see was a few small chips in the ice. Frustrated, he reared back and swung hard. The hammer glanced off the stake and landed on his dad's hand.

"Goddamn it!" He waved his hand as if he was trying to shake away the pain.

"Sorry! Dad, I didn't mean to."

"I'm okay."

"Dad." Tears rolled from John's eyes.

"Stop crying."

John tried to stop but he sniveled more tears.

"Jesus, sometimes you sound just like your mom." His father shook his head.

"I'm sorry."

"Just . . . don't worry so much, okay?" He held out his hand. "See? No blood. I'm fine. It just hurt for a second."

"Sorry."

"Let's forget about it. Here, I'll tell you what. Let me get this ice open and we can start fishing before we have to go. Okay?"

John wiped his cheek, the tears stung in the cold, and nodded.

"Now, hand me the hammer."

John obliged, and his father tapped the stake into the ice.

"Do you want me to hold it for you?" John asked.

"No."

His father struck a few quick, short blows to drive the stake firmly into the ice. He pulled out the stake, moved it a short distance away, and repeated the staking and hammering until he made the shape of a circle.

"Not exactly the tools that we had back in Vermont, but that's loosened her up. We got her now." He grabbed his ax.

He reared back, farther back than any time before, and swung. The ax pounded the ice and John heard a sharp crack like a gunshot. John's feet wobbled and he felt himself slipping. The ice, the lake, the mountain—all of it turned sideways, then upside down.

A burning wetness encircled John. Freezing water seized him, sucking at the breath in his lungs. He felt himself sinking. He wanted to scream but he couldn't. He was beneath the surface, coldness ripping through his body. His head bobbed above the surface.

He gasped but felt no breath. He coughed, spat water, and tried to scream for his father, but the words came out weak as he gasped again for air.

"John! Here!"

John turned to see his father thrashing in the water behind him. His dad splashed forward. He gripped John's shoulder and pushed him toward the edge of solid ice. "Grab onto the ice," his father yelled.

John reached for the ice. A chunk broke off in his hand.

His father gulped a deep breath, and then disappeared into the water. John felt his father shove him by his bottom and John rose up in the water. John reached again for the solid ice, but he slipped out of his dad's arms and back into the lake.

Water splashed over John's head. It was dark. He couldn't see. His head bobbed above the surface and he gasped again for more air. Something that felt like a thousand cold knives pierced his chest. He didn't see his father. "Dad!"

John's body burned. He tried to scream but no sounds came out. He was overcome by terror, and then grew numb, not yet thinking he would die but afraid his father already had.

BOOK II

SEX, RELATIONSHIPS, DEATH

PART ONE

CHAPTER 2

Sleep wrapped itself tight around John's mind as he struggled to wake up. He felt himself slipping back toward a comfortable void, and then he startled, remembering he should be awake.

"Shit," he murmured, seeing the red numbers of the digital clock shine 9:47.

He thought Joanie was already up but when John rolled over, he saw his wife's short black hair sticking out from under the covers at the far side of the mattress. He considered waking her but figured she needed the extra sleep. He stepped onto the carpeted floor and tiptoed to the bathroom.

When he used the toilet, he peered out the small bathroom window; frozen crystals of ice caked the glass, obscuring the view. After he showered, he brewed the morning coffee, listening for a moment to the coffeemaker gurgle, before ambling toward the sliding door to the apartment balcony and pulling back the drapes. He was greeted by more ice crystals creeping along the edges of the sliding door and his own fuzzy image in the center of the glass. He peered beyond his reflection to the slate gray sky and tried to remember the last time he'd seen the sun. He searched for a patch of blue in the clouds, but the gray was solid like the underside of a stone slab. The weather, he hoped, would be better in Tennessee.

John's stomach cramped but he tried to ignore the tightness. Their apartment was on the top floor of the building, atop a small hill that faced west. He looked over the other apartment buildings, across their tar-and-gravel flat roofs spotted with patches of snow and tightly rounded air conditioning units that looked like beehives. He remembered when he and Joanie had moved into the complex from California three-and-a-half years prior. They'd arrived before the moving van, and for three nights they'd slept on the floor in front of the balcony door, each night watching with novelty the crooked fingers of Midwest lightning splinter across the black sky. Those initial three nights without TV—before the start of his psychology graduate school, before her MBA program, before her job at the bank—were his favorite memories since moving to St. Louis. He hoped today's trip to the Smoky Mountains would become another memorable experience he could savor.

His stomach cramped again and he felt exhausted. He smelled the French roast brewing. He swallowed, craving a cup of coffee, but he heard the coffee pot still dripping and realized he needed something more than coffee. He needed some adventure—no matter how brief—away from the ordinary. Winter seemed to last forever in St. Louis. By February, he was sick of the cold, the gray skies, the blahs that the Canadian Clippers blew in.

Behind him, he heard feet patter across the living room carpet. "Good morning, Joanie," he said.

Her canary yellow nightgown covered her short, thin frame. She plopped onto the sofa she had picked out as a wedding present from John's parents four years earlier. "Morning."

He bent down to kiss her and she met him with dry lips that pecked against his own. He brushed his lips across the nape of her neck. Her skin was still warm from bed. "Happy Anniversary and Happy Valentine's Day."

She stretched and yawned. "Actually, our anniversary was last week and Valentine's Day is this coming week."

"But this is the weekend we're celebrating." They were married four years prior in early February. John had wanted to celebrate with a nice, long vacation that spanned the interval from their anniversary to Valentine's Day, but Joanie had argued it wouldn't be practical; with their limited money and time, the best they could do was a three-day weekend over a bank holiday. "How did you sleep?" he asked. "I was dead asleep this morning—I couldn't believe how late it was."

She shook her head. "It's really late. Too late, really."

"We should get going." John strode to the kitchen, pulling a metal travel mug from the cupboard. "Do you want coffee now or a mug for the car?"

She gave him a sideways glance while shaking her head, as she often did when dismissing one of his ideas. "This is silly."

"What?"

"Driving so far for two nights."

"You were the one who wanted to go for only two nights." He heard his voice rise, a byproduct of incredulity and frustration, but then he tried to speak softer. "Joanie, when we were in college, I used to drive farther to see you just for a weekend."

"I've got a ton to do on the strategic plan by Wednesday and it would be great if I could meet with Steve again."

"We've planned this trip since Thanksgiving—and now you don't want to go?"

"Plans need to be flexible and adapt to the changing circumstances. All the business strategic planning materials say that. You have a dissertation proposal meeting Wednesday, too, right?"

John bit the inside of his cheek to check his impulse to snap back. Since her new assignment at the bank, she was constantly quoting business planning principles to him. "It'll be good for us to get away from everything for a couple of days, including this lousy St. Louis weather."

"It's too long of a drive. We can celebrate here with dinner and a movie and still have time left over."

He clanged his cup onto the countertop. "Maybe we should just forget the whole damn thing."

"John, don't get mad."

"If you don't want to go, let's just forget it."

"We'll go," she said.

"It doesn't sound like you really want to."

"I'm feeling really pressured with work." She brought her hand to her mouth, gently pinching her upper lip between her thumb and forefinger as she tended to do when she was stressed. "But let's go. I don't want you to be all mad and sulking."

"Joanie, you can work as much as you need while we're there—really. I just want us to get away. It'll be fun, okay?"

"Let's go then." Joanie stood up, and he stepped next to her, encircling her shoulders in a hug and bending down to kiss the top of her head. At five-foot-three, she was a foot shorter than him. She wiggled out of his arms. "I'm taking a shower, and then we'll go."

He watched her walk away, the bare flesh of her legs barely visible beneath her nightgown, before she disappeared into the bathroom.

The smell of baked garlic wafted across the table. "How's your shrimp?" John asked.

"Wonderful." Joanie lifted a goblet of chardonnay to her full lips. "I don't think I've ever had such plump shrimp."

"You know, you look so attractive in your gold earrings and with your beautiful smile." He still remembered her smiling at him ten years before from across the room at a party after a regional high school basketball tournament. Before the night was over, they had made out and started a long-distance romance—she lived ninety miles away—that had given him the strength to refuse his mother's intermittent pressure to go into the seminary instead of college.

"Why, thank you, Mr. Anderson, for being so complimentary. Don't you love this place?"

John nodded, glancing around the lodge dining room, which was constructed from thick pine timbers and decorated with photographs of the meadows, rivers, and peaks of the Smoky Mountains; a bearskin rug hung over the hearth. Joanie said something about how her parents could never afford a weekend away. "But here we are, able to travel even while you're still in graduate school," she said. "Just wait until you're finished and I'm promoted."

"How's your work going?" John had hoped for a long hike along the mountain stream, but it had been rainy and cold and he didn't want to press Joanie, who had worked most of the day in the cabin.

"There's still a ton to do but it's going well. I'm working on the environmental scan, identifying threats and opportunities now and over the next five years. I think I'm getting the material, and Steve promised to massage the draft plan with me when we get back."

She spoke about competitors and regulatory changes, but John lost the particulars. Joanie was a natural for developing the bank's five-year plan. Since their marriage, she had mapped out their lives in five-year increments. They were late in the final phase of their first five-year plan that called for finishing their education and launching professional careers. John's semiannual evaluations from the doctorate program had been glowing and he had been awarded a fellowship given to the program's most promising graduate student, but he knew he was still well behind Joanie, who often reminded him of their timeline. She'd finished her MBA in eighteen months. After a stressful experience of being let go from her first management job as part of layoffs at McDonnell Douglas and a brief period of unemployment and despair, she was now throwing herself with passion into the world of banking. She had said during the second five-year period they would buy their first house and have their first child while advancing in their professional careers. Joanie's goal was to be a bank president by age thirty; John was to be firmly established in his private practice as a psychologist. Joanie described the third stage as transitional: she would have their second child but continue her career without prolonged interruption while securing an executive position within the corporate office, and they would buy a larger house. John wasn't sure what came next, and he wasn't particularly interested in asking.

"How's your steak?" she asked.

"Real tender. And it's nice to feel full, rather than, you know, cramping or something."

"Aren't you relieved that the doctor said there isn't anything seriously wrong with your stomach?"

"Yeah, but I'll be glad when we know for sure what's going on." He reached for her hand under the table. She pulled away and dabbed a napkin to her lips.

"At least you know you're not dying of cancer."

John winced. He had known that was highly unlikely, but the thought that he was dying of cancer had worried him since his stomach had been hurting again over the past six months. A friend's cousin had died of stomach cancer a few years before, and so had his own great-uncle. He had mentioned the fear only once to Joanie, but he felt foolish whenever she brought it back up. "I'm sure there's nothing seriously wrong, but I'll be glad when Dr. Wolff gets the lab results back."

"What did he say he thought it was? Irritable Bowel Syndrome?"

"Shhh." John felt his face flush with warmth, and he was afraid he was blushing. He glanced at the next table where a gray-haired couple ate in silence and looked his way. "I hate that term," he whispered to Joanie.

"I see your point." She sipped more chardonnay.

After she finished a slice of strawberry-glazed cheesecake and paid the bill, they followed the path from the lodge to their cabin. The rain had stopped and John considered hiking the mountain trail to the waterfall, but he decided it would be foolish to try in the dark.

"I wish we could sit in the hot tub for a while," he said. "It sucks that the heater's broken."

"I should work a little longer tonight anyway."

John smelled the strong, sweet scent of pine while entering the cabin. He watched Joanie change into her jeans and a Washington University sweatshirt. She slipped on her reading glasses and bent over a legal pad and a stack of file folders on the wood table that she'd claimed as her workstation.

John sighed at the thought of more studying, but not knowing what else to do, he jammed two pillows against the headboard, pulled himself and his backpack onto the bed, and sprawled his research folders across the bedspread. He flipped through a file of papers on a psychological scale that he was considering using in his dissertation. The test was straightforward: a one-page self-rating of psychological symptoms that could be used with adolescents as well as adults, and the results yielded a profile of a person's psychopathology. John expected that Dr. Graf, his dissertation chairperson, would ask if he had piloted the measure.

"Hey, Joanie. Do you want to take a one-page inventory of your mental health?"

"No." She scribbled on her legal pad without looking up.

John wasn't surprised. She had hated feeling anxious and depressed when she'd been unemployed, and she wanted to put that period and her feelings about it behind her without looking back. He grabbed a pencil and a copy of the questionnaire and slumped deeper into the pillows. The first question asked how often he felt low on energy: "never, a little bit, moderately, quite a bit, or all the time." He debated whether to mark moderately, a little bit, or quite a bit, before settling on moderately. He read and answered each of the remaining fifty-six questions. He rummaged through the folder for the scoring key, tabulated his answers for each of the nine types of mental health disorders, and plotted the results on the graph.

"Shit," he mumbled. He stared at his test profile, which was flat, well within the normal range, except for mountain peaks on two of the nine scales: somatization and depression. Those two scores rose above the broken line of the ninetieth percentile, which indicated a need for outpatient mental health treatment.

He considered the somatization score. That was explainable, he thought, because of his stomach problems. He remembered reading that people with actual medical problems scored high on this scale. The irritable bowel syndrome, or whatever the hell it was, was the likely culprit.

He was less sure about the depression score. Perhaps it was just the winter blahs. Or maybe it was the consequence of three-and-a-half years of hard work in graduate school. The program's a good one, he told himself—interesting, satisfying, and necessary—but a hell of a lot of work. The workload would leave anyone feeling a little flat, he thought, especially with his wife working so much.

"Joanie? Want to go for a walk? Or go look at the stars?"

"In a few minutes, maybe."

"I'll be outside. He stepped onto the cabin porch. He told himself not to worry about the depression score. It was probably a statistical anomaly, or just the weather. Or maybe it wasn't even anything personal, but just part of the American malaise that President Carter and the media had been talking about not so long ago. A puff of cold wind fluttered across his cheeks. John shivered, but he stepped off the porch, hoping to see a mountain sky chock-full of stars. He saw only a grayish haze, the underbelly of a cloudy night. The screen door to the cabin slapped shut behind him.

"John?"

"Yeah?"

"It's cold out here."

"Yeah, it is."

Joanie stepped next to him. "Can you see any stars?" She yawned.

"No, too cloudy," he said. "You tired?"

"Yes." Her shoulder brushed against his. "I worked a bunch today, but I got a lot accomplished."

"So, do you want to open presents?"

"Absolutely!"

She scurried back into the cabin, John following. From his backpack, he pulled a large white envelope and a small box wrapped in shiny red paper. "Happy Anniversary," he said.

"You already gave me a card last week." She cupped the present in her petite hands.

"I know, but I wanted to give you another."

Joanie slipped the card out from its envelope and read the inscription. "That's sweet."

John tried but couldn't remember exactly what he'd written, other than signing the card, "Love Always," as he always did. He thought he'd scribbled something about how much she meant to him and all the past good times they had shared over ten years together. When he'd written the card, he'd been feeling nostalgic about the summer before they married when she had an apartment on Franklin Street in San Francisco. He remembered their picnics after ferry rides to Angel Island and rollerblading in Golden Gate Park on Sundays. His best friend Danny had teased John that they seemed like a boring, middle-aged couple. John hadn't disagreed, but there was something fun as well as comfortable about being together then, and there had been both an ease and romantic passion to Joanie which he still missed.

Joanie neatly unwrapped the gift—she always tried to save and reuse the paper—and lifted the lid off the small white box. She pulled out a silver necklace with a diamond chip pendant, and a simple note, "Love Always, John."

"John, it's beautiful."

"You like it?"

"Love it." She smacked a dry kiss against his lips, and then glided to the mirror, fastening the chain around her neck. "This will go perfectly with two—no, three—of my work outfits."

"Well, good." He had been imagining how it would look against the skimpy nightgown he'd bought for her Christmas.

"Here." She reached into the closet, pulling out a garment covered by a plastic bag. "I gave you the card last week, but here's your present."

"Hmm, looks like one of your long dresses all wrapped up."

"Maybe so. Better open it and see."

Beneath the plastic, John found a long, tan men's overcoat. "This is nice. Thank you."

"It's a London Fog." Her toothpaste commercial smile cracked wide. "Expensive, but worth it. You'll look very professional. Here, put it on." Joanie held out the sleeves, showing him the wool lining as she did so, and he slipped into the coat. She turned him around, smoothed out a wrinkle in the back, and straightened his collar. "*Now* you look like a doctor."

He leaned down to kiss her. He smelled the garlic on her breath as she stepped back and yawned.

"Sorry, I'm suddenly so tired," she said.

"Do you want to go to bed?"

She nodded.

"Since that hot tub isn't working, I'm going to take a nice, hot shower first. Want to join me?"

"No."

"Okay." He kissed the white skin of her forehead. "See you in bed, soon."

John quickly washed himself, but when he opened the bathroom door, the rest of the cabin was already dark. "Joanie?" He slipped naked between the sheets and found her lying near the far side of the mattress. "There you are."

He scooted closer, slipping his hand beneath her nightgown—it was the long, cotton one, not the silky, sexy one he'd given her at the holidays. He inched closer, cuddling her body, finding her lips with his own. He kissed her softly and whispered into her ear "Happy Anniversary, Happy Valentine's Day."

Joanie yanked her legs up toward her stomach, her knees jutting into his groin.

"Joanie, are you okay?"

"I feel really pressured."

"About what?"

"Work, of course. The whole strategic plan has to be completed and distributed to the entire management team in five days."

He had the sinking, dismal sense that her feeling pressured was about the prospect of them having sex, too, even if her work was the bigger—and easier to talk about—issue. He patted her shoulder. "Joanie, if anyone is capable of doing a good job on the strategic plan, it's you."

"I don't want to do a 'good job.' I want people to read it and think it's a great plan."

"I bet it will be great. Plus, it's not just your responsibility, right? Isn't Steve involved too?"

"He's wonderful, but I'm the lead and everyone keeps telling me, 'it's your baby.' It's a lot of pressure."

"Sorry it's so stressful." He rubbed deeper into her shoulder for a minute. "You know, I can think of one thing we can do to help relieve your tension."

"Not tonight, John."

John felt the silence stiffen between them. He knew he should say something, but he didn't feel like talking.

Joanie finally spoke. "John, it's late and I'm too tired. And I've got to get up early before that long drive back. Sorry."

"I understand. I was kind of kidding anyway."

"Maybe tomorrow night."

"Here, I'll give you a good back rub," he said.

"For real? I feel bad."

He had suddenly felt guilty, too, for pressuring her. He figured the back rub would be a good penance. "Yeah, for real. Roll over."

Her shoulder blades protruded in bony ridges as he rubbed her back. He laid his hands together, spanning the width of her small back. She had always been thin, but he was sure she had lost weight in recent months. She loved her new job even if she felt overwhelmed sometimes by the responsibilities, and the stress seemed to be changing her. He rubbed the back of her neck, feeling its tightness. Her muscles relaxed beneath his massaging fingers.

"Feels good," she murmured. "Relaxing."

"Good."

"I think I can fall right asleep now. Thank you."

"Sure." He flipped onto his back. His own body felt tense. He fidgeted, trying to find a comfortable position.

"John, do you want me to touch you?"

He remembered her hand pulling away from his at dinner; they had once held hands under the table at every date. "No, that's okay."

She released a deep exhale, her body relaxing into the mattress.

John wished he would fall asleep quickly, but he was tired, not sleepy. He felt an ache in his stomach.

Joanie's breathing became slower. He imagined her wide awake instead of falling asleep, making love with him to celebrate their anniversary and Valentine's Day. He remembered his great-uncle Henry talking to him at their wedding reception. "Now, the first year you're married, put a jellybean in a large, empty pickle jar every time you have relations," he had told John. "By your first anniversary, the jar will be brimming full. Then, each year after the first, take out a jellybean every time you have intercourse. When you get to your fiftieth anniversary, have sex one more time—if you still can—and by then you should be taking the last bean out of the jar."

Not even the first year of marriage was like his great-uncle promised. John still wondered why. He remembered how different things had been before they were married. They'd waited a year, until their last semester of high school, before having sex. Back then they would have filled up a pickle jar in the six months. As undergraduates, they had gone to different colleges: John in California, Joanie in Oregon. John had detested the distance, but their get-togethers were amazing. Even when John had stayed as a visitor in the men's dorms in a separate building, she would sneak into his room and they would make love every night, every morning, and most afternoons. It seemed then like she couldn't get enough sex. But each year since they had been married—and especially after she'd started her new job—their sex life had diminished, and in the past few months, their lovemaking had become almost nonexistent, save for a few occasions late at night, usually after Joanie had been drinking at an after-work social event.

But it wasn't just the sex, he told himself. High school had been full of fun dates, and in college John loved taking trips together, especially to the mountains and Oregon's waterfalls. Proxy Falls had been his favorite. He had climbed through green ferns high up the mountainside. Joanie had stopped, saying she couldn't go any further, but he kept climbing. He found a spot where he maneuvered around the ferns and rocks to the waterfall's edge. Something about the place—watching the clear water cascading, hearing it crash against the rocks below, feeling the spray of mist on his face—had mesmerized him. But then Joanie had called out to him, breaking the spell.

They had camped that night in a state park. They had only one sleeping bag and no tent, and the campground was crowded. They waited until their neighbors had doused their fires and were quiet in their tents before having sex. John woke later, sometime in the middle of the night. Dew had dampened their sleeping bag and clung to his face, but pressing tight against Joanie, he found himself again erect and wanting her. He woke her with kisses and soon they made love a second time, moving slow and deep, then faster into each other. Joanie soon quivered in spasms beneath him, and after her orgasm, she fell dead still. Somehow she had gone suddenly back to sleep. John was still inside her, aroused, wanting to climax, but she lay motionless, so he simply held her for a long time before he returned to sleep.

Joanie's leg twitched against him in the cabin bed. He hoped she was awake, but he realized, peering through the darkness, that it was an involuntary movement. She was asleep.

The cramping in his stomach returned. He tried to ignore the sensations, but he felt a slow tightening and aching of his insides, a spasm contorting his gut and bowel. When he could stand it no longer, he threw back the covers and trudged toward the toilet.

A milky grayness covered the sky, except for the western edge where a thin line was visible between the clouds and terrain. John drove toward the horizon without much thought, following the narrow strip of asphalt that rose and fell in small swells across Southern Illinois. He had driven five hundred miles since morning, finding the drive neither difficult nor boring, yet his stomach cramped as they approached St. Louis.

An orange flame torched the corridor of open sky. John watched the color deepen, orange burning into red, before its intensity faded. The grenadine remnants of the sunset grew pale, turned the color of ash, and disappeared.

"Beautiful sunset," he said.

Joanie glanced up from the work papers spread over her lap, her legs crossed Indian-style in the passenger's seat. "Was it? There's not much sky for a sunset."

"It was just a narrow band, but it was beautiful.'

"Uh-huh."

"I almost wish we could just keep driving." He glanced from the highway to his wife. "You know, keep going west back to the mountains. Remember when we camped at Rocky Mountain National Park on the move out?"

"Yes."

"That was great."

"After you finish and get a real job, we'll vacation some summer in Colorado. Steve says both Estes Park and Breckenridge have awesome resorts."

He hesitated, but the enthusiasm in her voice about Colorado had encouraged him. "I've been thinking—when I'm finished with the dissertation, maybe we could take some time off and just travel. Take, say, a summer and just drive around the country. Imagine: not being on a schedule, not worrying about the demands of daily life, and just going wherever we wanted. We could go back to Oregon, to the mountains and waterfalls. Doesn't that sound like fun?"

"Sure," she said in the flat tone she used for sarcasm. "Fun. Meanwhile, by that time we'll be $87,500 in debt with student loans to repay."

"But it would be an adventure," his voice trailed off. "Just for a couple of months, or even six weeks or so."

"You're not being practical." She looked back at her papers.

John watched the last of the charcoal light drain from the evening sky. He checked the glowing green fuel gauge on the dash and told Joanie they had to stop for gas.

"I can switch with you and drive the rest of the way home," she said.

"*Wow!* That would be about seventy-five miles after I drove eleven hundred miles on this trip." When he looked over, he saw her lips pursed tightly together, and he knew his sarcasm had aggravated her. "Actually, that would be great, thanks. I'm suddenly exhausted."

After they used the restrooms and John had pumped the gas, Joanie climbed into the driver's seat. She shoved the throttle toward the floorboard the way she did when she was annoyed and merged back onto I-64.

"Thanks for driving."

She nodded.

"I'm really tired," he said.

"Why don't you take a nap." She said this more as a statement than a question. "It might do you good."

He was drowsy but not wanting to fall asleep. He watched acres of farmland coated with a vanilla snow roll by until it was too dark to see beyond the highway. He closed his eyes, thinking the cold, rainy weather had been shitty for their trip. He wished they could have hiked more, soaked in the hot tub, made love—but then he told himself it was still good just to get away.

His head drooped then jerked erect. He opened his eyes. It was dark, except for taillights glistening ahead.

"You doing okay driving?" he asked.

"Fine. Go to sleep."

His eyelids fluttered closed. This had been his first trip to the South. It was good to see new places, parts of the world that he'd never been to before. There'd been pastures with cattle and sheep spread between antique-white steeple churches. Eventually, the ranchlands gave way to mountains and pine trees—it was almost like the Sierras. He remembered how the road cut deep into those mountains, into layered rock, rock that had somehow bled water that froze on the face of the boulders and now the ice and stone looked like wax melted on a candle.

Waxy cascades of ice. The image stuck in his head as he tumbled toward sleep. And then he remembered, way below the mountain curve, a river frozen in winter.

John woke to a crack like a gunshot.

"What?" he shouted.

Tires screeched and John lurched toward the dashboard.

Two cars, hinged together at the bumpers like Siamese twins, slid in the lane ahead.

"Stop Joanie!" he yelled.

She braked harder while the two cars pirouetted. The silver car unhinged, falling away, but the red car twirled across the lanes like a spinning top.

"Goddamn it! Stop Joanie!"

Joanie's car slid right, swerved back, and then straightened. The red sedan pivoted to a stop, its headlamps pouring light into John's eyes. Joanie's car halted inches before the red car's shiny metal grill, and John stared into the terrified faces of a man and a boy in the other car.

"Thank God!" Joanie yelled.

More tires squealed from the rear. Two cars skidded to a stop right behind Joanie's car and a flood of headlights poured inside their cab from the back.

"Go! Hurry!" John yelled. "Before we get smashed from behind."

"Don't yell!"

"Goddamn it, Joanie—before we get killed—go!"

Joanie's engine had died. She was crying but restarted the engine and followed John's directions to inch backward and then pass the red car on the highway shoulder.

"We shouldn't be leaving the scene of an accident," she told him while driving away.

"We're not. *We* weren't in an accident. And—"

"There was too an accident," she said.

"Not involving us—but if we had just stayed there like sitting ducks, like you were doing, we would have gotten plowed into from behind in a thirty-car pileup."

"You always know best, don't you?"

"No." The self-righteousness in her voice infuriated him. *She* was the one always acting like the know-it-all. "But for once, I'd love it if you just did what I asked."

"For once? Why do you think we were even out here in the first place? You're the one who insisted we go on this ridiculous and expensive long trip."

"Ridiculous? It's ridiculous to want to celebrate an anniversary?"

"Which we did last week." Her voice was squeaky, defensive.

"Yeah, a quick dinner at home after you were late once again from work."

"Somebody's got to be making the money while you're still in school taking out more student loans."

He felt like screaming but bit the inside of his cheek instead. "Just stop, Joanie. Will you please just fucking stop?"

She said nothing more. He waited a minute and asked her to take the next exit so he could call the accident into the police. After he made the call from a pay phone and returned to the car, he found her sitting in the passenger's seat.

"You're driving the rest of the way," she said.

They said nothing until John could no longer stand the pout on her face. "That was too close of a call; it made things pretty stressful for both of us."

"You were yelling and swearing at me," she said. "That was worse than the accident."

"I wasn't yelling and swearing at you." He glanced over, but she still frowned. "Well, maybe I was yelling and swearing, but it wasn't about you—I just didn't want us to get rear-ended. Anyway, I'm sorry. It was just a total shock. I was asleep and dreaming or something—and then boom: I woke up to the crash. I just had to get the hell out of there as soon as possible." He looked over but she said nothing. "What happened anyway?"

"The red car tried to change lanes, but he didn't see the other car until they almost hit. He suddenly tried to swerve away then, but he . . . what do you call it? When the car swerves back and forth?"

"Fishtailed?"

"Yes. The red car fishtailed and slid right back into the silver car. Their bumpers hooked and they were stuck together for a few seconds. I slammed on the brakes right away, but I was afraid we were going to slide right into them—I could see the man and the little girl staring right at us. They both look terrified."

"It was a man and a boy," he said

"No, it was a girl."

"Whatever. Was the highway icy or something?" he asked.

"A sudden patch, I think."

John steered their car into the apartment complex parking lot, braking slowly to an easy stop in front of a mound of blackened snow. He carried their luggage up the three flights of stairs to their apartment and began unpacking. He had accomplished little despite the hours of study over the weekend and was annoyed. Although he didn't feel like doing so, he started reading. Joanie soon interrupted him, saying his father had left a message on the answering machine to call him back as soon as possible.

When John called back, his father answered on the first ring. He asked where John and Joanie had been, and then mentioned his own trip to the Smoky Mountains after World War II.

"Charlie Brewer and I drove a '32 Ford back from California" he said. "The radiator kept springing leaks so we had to put pepper in to plug the holes every hundred miles or so, but it didn't keep us from making the trip. Actually, we went first to Iowa. There were a thousand WAACs there during the war but by the time we got there they had been discharged so we just kept going to see the Smokies."

His dad loved to reminisce, and most of his stories were about when he was young and single and gallivanting around with his brothers or friends. He could go on for a long time about their escapades and though John liked his old stories, he had heard most of them multiple times and he felt pressed now to get back to his research. "I remember you telling me before," he said. "So, how are you and mom?"

"I need to tell you some bad news."

"What?" John asked.

"Grandma passed away."

"No!" A strong sensation surge through his body, but he was unsure if it was shock or sadness or some mixture.

"The nursing home called early this morning. She passed away late last night."

"Dad, I'm sorry. What happened?"

"I guess her heart just gave up. She's had so many things wrong with her for so long, it wasn't a big surprise."

"That's sad," John said. "How are you feeling, Dad?"

"It's for the best. She really hasn't been living for years. The dementia destroyed her mind long ago. You know what she's been like—trapped in her body without her mind. It's better this way."

"Hank, I don't know how you can say that." John's mother's voice echoed from the background. He could picture her: pastel, flowered apron wrapped around her slightly bulging belly, hand propped against her hip, hovering next to his father who sat at the round kitchen table. "She was alive, and she was your mother, for God's sake."

"Hon, the quality of her life had been terrible for years. In fact, for the last half-dozen years, it's been nonexistent. It's better this way."

"A life is a life, Hank," his mother said.

"That's not living. There's no thinking, no working, no accomplishing anything in life. To want to keep someone alive in that state is selfish."

"That's for God to decide." His mom said this with authority.

"God did decide. Her heart stopped." His father's voice rose in pitch. "Now will you let me finish talking to my son about the death of my mother?"

John knew his mom would get his dad back later for his shortness, either by a critical comment or withdrawing or most likely by both. He hurried to fill the brief pause between his parents, saying he was sorry both that his grandmother had dementia for so long and that she died. "I can come home for her funeral, if you want."

"There's no real point," his dad said. "Better to stay and put the time into your studies."

After they had hung up, he filled Joanie in on the details. She had never met this grandmother—she had been in the nursing home for almost a decade—but she told John she was sorry. "How's your dad taking it?"

"Pretty good, I think. He's stoic to begin with, and I don't think he was that close to my grandmother. We always spent a lot more time with Nona, but I'm sure he loved his mother. He was always really nice to her, though, especially after she was in the nursing home." John pictured his dad spoon-feeding his grandmother as she sat babbling, strapped to a nursing home bed. "But I don't think he ever completely forgave her for leaving my grandfather and marrying Feltman."

"But wasn't that a really long time ago?"

He nodded. "About twenty years, I think."

"That seems overly harsh."

"I didn't know it when I was little, but my mom told me later that Grandma had a flagrant affair with Feltman for years before my grandparents divorced. And then when they finally split up, my grandfather died a few months later. I think on some level, my dad blamed her for his father's death."

"That's not fair." She frowned.

"Probably wasn't." He wasn't sure how much his grandmother had cared about what anyone thought though. By all family accounts, she had been a lifelong rebel and adventurer who followed her own path over social conventions, even in romance.

Joanie asked if John was going to fly home for the funeral, then shook her head at his response. "I think you should go. I can't because of the strategic plan, but you should."

"My dad said to keep working on the dissertation. I'm behind now, and it's probably better this way. In fact, I should get back to reading tonight."

"I still think you should go." There was an edge to Joanie's urging.

Joanie was pushing him, which annoyed him, as she wasn't willing to go herself and she didn't even know his grandmother. "I have too much to do." He retreated to the spare bedroom that doubled as his study and spread journal reprints across the walnut-papered desktop. He tried to understand the intricacies of a multivariate statistical procedure that he was considering using for his dissertation, but his mind wondered. He thought of his grandmother, remembering not only the short, white-haired woman with the crinkled face, but also her horses, especially the giant chestnut stallion standing in the dusty road next to the stable that smelled of hay and manure. Two of his younger cousins sat in the saddle while Grandma led the horse around by its darkened brown leather reins. When Grandma announced it was his turn, his own mother suddenly said he was too young to go. John cried and Grandma told him when he was older, she would take him on an overnight ride to Mount Diablo. It was her favorite trail, she said, and you could see almost every mountain peak in California from there. But they never went. John didn't know why and now she was dead. He was sad he had never gone with her, but at least she had traveled often and, even more, lived her life as she desired, without regrets or regard for social opinion. He wondered if it was worth it for her—he imagined that it was—and he hoped God would forgive her marital transgressions.

He considered flying back for the funeral. But what was the point? He knew if it had been Nona—his favorite grandmother by far—he'd be on the plane in a heartbeat, but he told himself to not even think of that possibility. She was about a decade younger than Grandma, and he could not even imagine losing her.

John searched for his place on the page in the statistics article. He felt nauseated, as he had intermittently for months. He had read somewhere that everyone had some organ that was predisposed to problems. For whatever reasons, he had trouble digesting things. No big deal, he told himself.

He looked for his place on the page again. He gripped his yellow highlighter tight between his fingers and thumb and plowed a yellow line through an obtuse sentence explaining the meaning of unstandardized beta coefficients. He looked back at the start of the sentence, still trying to understand exactly what it meant.

"Goddamn it!" He hurled the article against the white wall. The pages fluttered like a bird with a broken wing before smacking against the plaster and falling to the carpet.

He found Joanie in bed, pillows propped up against their oak headboard that was molded like a setting sun. Her chin drooped over the legal pad on her lap.

"Good, you're still up," he said.

"Barely." She shuffled her papers off the down cover to the nightstand. "I'm really sleepy."

John peeled off his clothes and dropped them onto the chair in the corner of the room. He slipped into bed while Joanie flicked off the nightstand lamp. He scooted closer to Joanie, leaned over, and kissed her.

"Good night, John."

He rolled back to his half of the mattress. When he closed his eyes, the two cars were colliding on the highway. He saw them twirling together like two ballet dancers before the red car spun away and fell to a stop, its headlights glaring into his eyes.

He worried about the man and boy in the car but told himself they were fine.

John flipped over and took a deep breath. He hoped to stop thinking, to just fall asleep, but his dad's call about the death of his grandmother resurfaced in his mind. He had nodded in agreement when his mother had said multiple times in years past how terrible his grandmother had been to have carried on an affair and then to have left his grandfather, but now John felt something more like admiration rather than condemnation. She obviously had loved Feltman more than his grandfather. It was difficult to imagine—they were old—but he guessed she and Feltman must have shared an intense passion to have carried on an affair for years while losing family approval. He sensed, thinking about it for the first time this way, she had exercised courage for the love and life she wanted. It was a very different path than for most people, including his parents. His mom and dad had earned social respectability with a marriage going on twenty-nine years, and as far as he knew, they no longer had major arguments like when he was little, but they had seemed to have settled for a semi-peaceful yet passionless coexistence. He stopped himself then from being too critical. His parents were probably not much different than 90 percent of married couples, though he felt an uncomfortable stirring for wanting more.

His ruminations left him agitated, his body tense and with longing. He debated with himself, hesitating at first, but then he reached for Joanie, rubbing her shoulder, and then stroking her short hair. He inched closer, pressing a kiss against her cheek. She flinched and then buried her face in the hollow of his neck. "Joanie," he whispered, "do you want to make love?"

"Too sleepy." Her nose nuzzled deeper into his neck. "Sorry."

"It's okay." He held her, his arm stretched across her body. Her breathing slowed. After a few minutes, he knew she was sleeping. Finally, he rolled over, his back to Joanie, and exhaled deeply.

He felt himself drifting, and then he startled, realizing he was falling toward sleep. He told himself it was okay and felt his body relax deeper.

He woke to the sound of a bang. His heart pounded as he recalled his dream about the red car spinning off the road, followed by Joanie's car sliding off too. The front bumpers of the two cars collided, and the boy and man had stared at John for an instant before there was a crack like thunder and the red car disappeared through broken ice into a frozen lake.

John checked the clock: 12:32 shone back at him. Just a crazy, bad dream he thought. He looked toward Joanie, but she lay motionless. He rolled over. There was nothing to worry about. He should fall back asleep.

He lay on his side until 12:57, flopped onto his back, and closed his eyes, but pictured again the boy and man in the red car spinning out of control. He hated being awake late at night. For a moment, he wished he could pray like when he was a child. But that was a long time ago, before college, before philosophy classes, before his doubts. He placed more stock now in Nietzsche than the Church: God *is* dead. No, he reprimanded himself, don't say that. The ultimate sin is to deny God—that dooms you to Hell. God isn't necessarily dead, he thought, but at the least, He's on sabbatical.

John scooted back toward Joanie, snuggling her close in her sleep. He wished she would awaken and make love to him, like camping in Oregon. But Joanie didn't move. He rolled over once more, trying to find a comfortable position. Nothing felt good. The clock radio shone 1:06.

He cursed his insomnia, threw back the bed covers, and returned to his study. He read statistics for an hour while fending off intrusive thoughts about his grandmother, his depression score, and the near-car accident. By 2:13, he felt exhausted.

He fell back into bed, wrapping the warm sheets tight around him, and soon felt himself slipping away from consciousness.

His body pressed against hers. She nudged back. He felt his hard penis pushing against her, and she pressed back. He surged into her, feeling her body matching his own, their lips joining.

He felt exhilaration, one of wondrous passion, of sexual drive rising through dreamlike sleep. He felt underwear being wrestled off, his and hers, and the pressing flesh of bare legs, abdomens, and genitals. He realized he and Joanie were having sex.

It is a wonderful pleasure, he thought, feeling the grinding of their bodies— of thrusting into her, of pulsating and melting, and of still being half-asleep.

CHAPTER 3

Two drops splashed against the library tabletop. Instead of beading up, as John expected, the water soaked into the oak wood, leaving a mark. Phil reached for his bottle again, and John withdrew his papers from the middle of the table.

Phil slurped more water, wiped his sleeve across his mouth, and shoved the bottle into his fluorescent orange backpack. He rustled his papers together, stuck them in a binder, and stuffed the binder into the backpack. "See you tonight."

"I think so," John said.

"What do you mean, 'you *think* so?'" The corner of Phil's lips puckered beneath his neatly trimmed mustache.

"I'm not feeling that great."

"What's the matter?"

"My stomach's feeling kind of sick," John said.

"Take a couple of Tums." Phil slung the backpack over his shoulder. "But don't leave me alone with Dr. Whitson tonight. I want this party to be fun."

Phil walked through the brightly lit lobby and out the doors. John absently skimmed over his notes for a few more pages before cramming his papers into his backpack.

A cold wind pushed John backward as he left the library. Joanie had taken his old parka to the dry cleaner the day before, and the gusts whipped through the new overcoat that Joanie had given him for their anniversary, jabbing a long, icy finger at his insides. His ache was higher than normal, more in the solar plexus than the intestines. He reminded himself that the doctor had said there was nothing seriously wrong with him, but he questioned that assessment as a dull but painful spot, like a nascent cavity, grew inside him, and the wind tugged at its soft, crumbling edges.

He veered from the main path leading back to the psychology department, taking the walkway to the left. Pellets of dry snow blew across the concrete. As he'd hoped, the cafeteria was deserted. He dug cold fingers into his pocket, fumbled with the coins within, and then dropped a quarter into the slot of the pay phone.

"Joanie Anderson," she answered after the first ring. "How may I help you?"

"How are you?" John asked.

"Busy."

"Let me guess—with the strategic plan."

"No, follow-up calls and paperwork all afternoon after the loan committee meeting. I'm just getting to the plan now."

"Bummer," he said.

"It's stressful, but it's part of the job."

The sound of tapping echoed across the phone line. John visualized Joanie thumping the end of her pen against a pad of paper, as he'd witnessed a hundred times before. For a long time, he'd thought it was nervous energy, but now he realized it was as often from impatience as much as stress. "Do you want to meet for a quick dinner?" he asked.

"Can't," she said. "I've got way too much to do on the plan tonight, and Steve's already called for pizza delivery."

"I was hoping we could talk."

"About what?"

"Just talk," he said. "Get a chance to connect and catch up."

"If the team gets a lot accomplished today and tomorrow, you and I can see a movie Saturday night. But the entire plan *has* to be finished and distributed to the whole management team by Monday."

"I know."

"So, how was your day?" The beat of her drumming pen quickened.

"I saw Dr. Wolff today for the follow up," he said.

"What did he say?"

"My blood work came back normal—"

"So it's nothing?" Joanie asked.

"It's the irritable bowel syndrome. Dr. Wolff said he sees it a lot in graduate students—stress can trigger it. But it's not serious."

"That's what I thought," she said. "It's good it's not serious. John—people are waiting for me in the conference room. I have to go. Sorry."

"I'll try to slip away from Dr. Whitson's and Phil's stupid class party before it gets too late so I can see you before bed."

"Stay and have fun at the party," she said. "I'm going to work late and then go straight to sleep. I'll be exhausted."

Darkness had overtaken the sky and the air felt colder to John on the walk to the psychology department. He imagined coming home: Joanie curled up, her back toward him, asleep on her side of the bed. He remembered the other night, the two of them wrestling with underwear, groping for each other while having sex in their semi-sleep. He had wanted to make love with her the entire trip, but that wasn't the way he'd imagined it. They were like two animals, like rabbits, he thought, screwing to be screwing. No fervent kissing, no whispers of love, just screwing. He hated acknowledging it, but he realized their sex that night really wasn't so different than a couple of other times in the past few months when Joanie had avoided his romantic advances for weeks and then arrived home late at night after a work party or happy hour, climbed into bed tipsy, and they had impulsively fucked while falling asleep. He'd hoped to talk with Joanie about wanting their lovemaking to be something different, something more, but how do you bring up something like that, especially over the phone?

The wind blew fiercely at the bottom of the hill, near the frozen campus pond. His fingertips were numb and he cursed himself for forgetting his gloves. The dim light from a streetlamp reflected off the ice.

The first winter John had lived in St. Louis, he'd watched a fourth-year graduate student standing at the edge of the pond, chucking snowballs against the ice. Dave Herman had heaved one snowball, then another and another; each one splattered against the ice, bits and pieces of snow skittering off. Herman had glanced at him, and John had waved but he felt uneasy, like he was intruding, even as he wondered if this was what happened after four years of graduate school. Now the pond was still, except for traces of snow that the wind scattered across the ice. An impulse overtook John to throw snowballs against the pond, but he dismissed the idea as foolish and hurried his pace to his office.

John waited for a pause in the banter between Phil, Felice, and Claire, his three remaining classmates sitting in the living room, to interject that he needed to leave. He'd say the party was fun, and while that was an exaggeration, he'd found it a pleasant diversion. But now the cavity in his solar plexus ached again, and he wanted to go home. He waited for Phil to deliver the punch line to a joke. Instead, the wood floor creaked and Branham lumbered down the hallway, pulling on his faded green Army field jacket. John silently cursed himself for letting Branham beat him to the exit.

"No way," Phil told Branham. "Ten thirty, the professor finally just cleared out after she drove away half of our class, and now you're headed home?"

"Responsibility calls." Branham zipped up his jacket. At a husky six-foot-six with shaggy brown hair and a fuzzy beard that crept far down his neck, he looked more like a bear than a man. "There's that little matter of the minority mental health paper that you, me, and Anderson still have to write for Carter's class."

"Bullshit," Phil said. Branham was a half-generation older than most of the graduate students, but he loved to party. "What's calling you is the new divorcee you've been seeing. What's her name—Judith?"

"A gentleman never discloses a lady's identity," Branham said, bowing slightly and winking at Felice and Claire. "You can trust me on that, ladies. But for now, good night." He glanced over his shoulder and nodded at John. "Anderson."

John struggled to get up from the beanbag chair.

"Don't bother." Branham extended his mammoth hand, which smelled of cigarettes mingled with the lingering odor of cologne.

Once Phil shut the apartment door behind Branham, he pivoted on his toes and clapped his hands together. "Our numbers are small, but our spirit is strong. Time to party!"

John feigned a disappointed frown and glanced toward the door. "I really should get going too."

"Fuck that shit," Felice said.

John laughed anxiously—Felice was always using that expression when the professors weren't present—and Phil whirled toward him too.

"Come on, man," Phil said. "Almost everybody has left and we wanted to party—not listen to Whitson's intellectualized soliloquy over wine and cheese. Jesus, I thought she'd never leave. John, be a buddy, help me out here."

John hesitated, watching Phil's upper lip quiver. He wanted to leave, and then Claire stepped past Phil. "Stay." Her words were inviting, not begging or whining like Phil's, but self-assured. Earlier in the evening, he had heard her proclaim to Felice and Branham, "I want to experience it all." He wasn't exactly sure what she meant—he had been engaged in a different conversation across the room, but he imagined from her language and the fervor of her pitch that she longed for a wealth of new experiences and for adventure; in any case, her words had rung clearly through the noise of the party as if she had called out his name and now her statement resurfaced in his mind. "All right," John said. "I'll stay for a while."

"Now you're talking." Phil fiddled with the stereo system on the bookcase constructed from cinder blocks and wood planks. "I made a great tape for dancing. I just have to keep the volume reasonable, since the last time I had a party the old lady who lives upstairs called the police saying it was too loud,"

Felice stepped forward, snapping her fingers to the emerging sounds of Marvin Gaye. "This works." A thin Black woman from the South Side of Chicago, she was nearly as tall as Phil.

Phil grinned at her. "Shall we dance?"

Claire stepped closer to John's beanbag, extending her arms. From their first meeting three-and-a-half years before, she had reminded John of the actress on the 1960s TV show, *The Farmer's Daughter*—tall and blond with prominent cheekbones and dimples. Claire had always been warm and friendly, but she socialized very little outside of class. She usually ran off, explaining she was older than most of the class and needed to be home for her two sons and husband, who was a public defender downtown. Claire exuded innocence and wholesomeness, and this too reminded John of the nanny on the old television show. But a rumor had recently surfaced in the graduate psychology program that Claire's marriage was on the rocks with her husband having an affair. Tonight, dressed in a tight-fitting black top, jeans, and knee-high boots, she seemed like anyone but the Farmer's Daughter.

"Dance with me," she said, yanking on John's hands.

John stood up to oblige, but Claire was already dancing. Her body pulsated with the music—her hips, her chest, her legs—her entire body seemed synchronized with the sound of soul. A rhythm, an ease, flowed through Claire that John contrasted with his own stiff and reserved feelings. He stepped side-to-side, trying to see his reflection in the window. He hoped he was dancing okay, but he noticed that Claire wasn't watching him. Her eyes were closed, the fine muscles across her face straining, as she sang the lyrics with Marvin Gaye.

The artists changed but Claire kept dancing, moving seamlessly from one song to the next. Sweat dribbled down John's rib cage. He smiled, enjoying the music and Claire's dancing even more than his own.

The song ended and Claire let out a whoop. She leaned against John's shoulder as she yanked off her black leather boots. She tossed the boots next to the sofa, leaned over the coffee table, and plucked a cube of cantaloupe from the half-eaten food platter. Claire plopped the cantaloupe between her full lips, sucking on the fruit, before taking it all the way into her mouth. "Umm, delicious," she said. "Thick and juicy. Want one?"

John couldn't help himself from enjoying the erotic image of oral sex that popped into his mind, though he immediately felt guilty. "Sure."

Claire plucked another chunk of cantaloupe and brought it to his mouth. Her fingertips felt soft against his dry lips. John bit down, and the fruit squirted sweet juice against the side of his tongue.

"That's good," he said. "I don't think I've ever tasted cantaloupe so fresh."

The twanging beat of Credence Clearwater Revival filled the room and Claire began dancing again. She closed her eyes, but her body came alive, picking up the rhythm. Her forehead creased, straining with the sound; she seemed oblivious to everything but the music, as if in a trance. "Rollin', rollin'," Claire sang, "rollin' on a river."

John stepped closer, dancing next to her, forgetting about his reflection in the window. Claire drew out the last chorus while John wished the song wouldn't end.

CCR's rock was replaced with the soft tempo of "Hey Jude." Phil and Felice slipped into a slow dance. John looked at Claire but hesitated. She gazed at him with an expectant look, and then stepped forward, wrapping her arms around his shoulders.

"I love to watch you dance," he told her. "You move with so much freedom and feeling."

"I love to dance. It's how I lose myself."

"Do you dance a lot?"

"Shh," she whispered. She nuzzled her face against his cheek.

John held her, dancing in silence. Her hair smelled sweet, almost like orange blossoms, and he imagined her lathering her long hair with fragrant shampoo. She edged closer, pushing her chest against his. She wedged her thigh between his legs.

"Your hair," he said softly. "It smells so good."

She shifted positions in his arms, her face turning inward. He felt then a warm, almost moist breath, as she blew in his ear. He said nothing, both embarrassed and exhilarated. He squeezed her tighter.

Claire leaned back and gazed into his eyes. John glanced at the floor.

"Don't be shy." Her fingers pressed against her cheek, repositioning his face toward her. "Look at me."

Her eyes were a steel blue, like the reflection of water on a cloudy day.

Claire pursed her lips. She then blew a long, slow breath across his face.

John blinked. Startled, he didn't know what to do. He watched her as she blew a second slow breath that fluttered across his cheeks, his nose, his eyes. He closed his eyes, imagining a light caress. He smelled something sweet, like the German wine they had been drinking.

Another warm breath swept over his face and down his neck, stirring something inside. The sensation flickered, and then soared, leaping forward, reaching the aching cavity inside him. Warm and light, the sensation rose again, swelling through his chest. His ache, he realized, had given way to a different feeling, something much more alive.

John opened his eyes. He stroked her hair, and then the small of her back. She blew another breath that rippled across his cheeks and lips.

He held Claire tighter in his arms, and then he leaned down to kiss her. Her lips were warm, moist. Her mouth opened, her tongue twirled with his tongue.

John savored the warmth of her kiss, the firmness of her thigh pressing between his legs. This, he thought, was the way to lose himself.

Claire broke away. The music had stopped, John realized.

"Excuse me," she said. "I have to use the bathroom." She glanced at Felice.

"As do I," Felice said.

Phil followed Felice out of the living room, and veered off into the kitchen, returning with two German beers. He thrust a cold bottle into John's palm.

"Drink up," Phil said. He clanked his bottle against John's beer, grinning. "So, what's up with you and Claire?"

"I don't know—things just started happening suddenly." John pictured Joanie curled up in their bed, covers pulled high over her face, and his mix of passion and confusion became further complicated by guilt. "This looks bad, I know. Shit, I've never done anything like this before, not since I've been married anyway."

"Hey, I'm not judging."

"We were just dancing and she started blowing on me."

"Blowing on you?"

"Yeah, first she blew into my ear, and then she looked into my eyes and blew a long breath slowly across my face."

"That's hot." Phil grinned.

"Yeah, and just like that, I was kissing her. I didn't plan it, and I don't really understand what happened."

"Better to just go with it. Us psychologist-types can get all wrapped up in our heads, trying to figure everything out, instead of simply flowing with the moment."

Phil frequently digressed to psychobabble while referring to them as psychologists, even though they were still only graduate students and his future was iffy after failing a statistics course and falling far behind in his research. His presumptive arrogance usually annoyed John, but this time he thought Phil had a point. John raised the cold beer to his mouth, remembering the warmth of Claire's lips, and he again felt a stirring within.

"Felice is hot tonight too," Phil said. "If it goes that far, you can use this room with Claire while Felice and I go to my bedroom."

John's stomach tightened. "I don't know about that." Despite the intensity of his feelings while kissing Claire, he couldn't imagine actually having sex with anyone other than Joanie.

The bathroom door squeaked.

"We've got to go," Claire called from the hallway.

"Yes," Felice added. "I've got a paper to work on tonight to clear up a delayed grade."

"Stay awhile," Phil said. "The paper can wait until tomorrow."

"Not really," Felice said. "The paper is long overdue for Dr. Whitson's advanced psychotherapy seminar. When she walked in tonight, I was surprised that she didn't demand that I leave immediately to go work on it, but did you see that look she gave me? She's a pro—doesn't have to speak a word with that guilt-inducing icy stare. I thought psychologists were supposed to alleviate guilt, not trigger it?"

"Come on," Phil said. "There's some cool dance songs on the next tape. They're very therapeutic for assuaging guilt."

Felice rummaged in the closet for her coat. "I need a cure, not palliative treatment."

Claire grabbed her boots.

"How about a couple of more dances?" John asked her

"It's late." Claire pulled on a boot without looking at him. "I need to get home."

"Just one more dance?" John asked.

"No," she said. "I need to go, now."

CHAPTER 4

John thought he saw Claire—it was only a brief glimpse, a bounce of blond hair, a black bootheel lifting off the brown-speckled linoleum floor—before the woman disappeared into the restroom. Since he'd arrived on campus twenty minutes before, he'd been searching for Claire. But few of his classmates were in the building this evening, and no one had seen Claire.

John slumped over the water fountain across from the restroom. He let a cold stream run down his throat, wiped his mouth dry, and waited. Soles clacked hard against the floor. The statistics professor pivoted around the corner, his black trench coat sullied at the hem by the milky ash of melted snow and dried rock salt.

"Dr. Zuckerman," John said, "working late in the lab?"

The professor, a man in his late fifties with sunken cheeks and a sallow complexion, cocked his head, fixing a hard stare at John. Even from a distance, Zuckerman smelled of chain smoking and coffee. "And what are you doing—loitering in the hallways?"

"Thirsty." John pointed at the water fountain. "It's good water—nice and cool."

Zuckerman squinted.

John mumbled a good evening, and then self-consciously trudged back toward his office, glancing over his shoulder on the way. "Asshole," he muttered. Zuckerman was the least friendly of the faculty and he prided himself on that repetition. John doddered in his office, and then returned to the water fountain. He wanted to see Claire, though he wasn't sure what he'd say. Without knowing why, he suddenly felt uncomfortable, or maybe it was unsafe. He considered leaving for his apartment but felt torn between being home and finding Claire. The hallway clock showed 6:27, and he wondered now if it was even Claire that he'd glimpsed, or if she had left the restroom when he'd wandered back to his office. He decided he'd try to talk with her if he found her before 6:30. Otherwise maybe it wasn't meant to be, and he'd go home.

The bathroom door swung open, revealing Claire.

"Claire, hi!"

"Hi." Her smile looked forced, more like a grimace.

"Do you have a few minutes?"

"No." She walked past. "Sorry, a client's waiting."

Claire slipped around the corner. John returned to his tiny graduate student office where he thought again about leaving for his apartment. But Joanie had said she needed to work late again, and Claire's voice—cheery, animated, warm—echoed from the therapy waiting room as she greeted a client. Her door, just around the corner, shut tight. John decided to wait.

He shuffled through mimeographed memos from his campus mailbox, flipped absently through the table of contents and the first chapter of a new library book, and then called home. He told the answering machine, and perhaps Joanie if she beat him home, that he was working late on campus. He hated telling Joanie a half-truth. When he'd arrived home Friday night from Phil's party, Joanie was dead asleep, knees curled up in a ball, just as he'd imagined. He was careful not to disturb her when he slipped into bed, and even though he had turned and twisted much of the night thinking of Claire, Joanie had slept without waking. They had spoken few words in the morning, not because she was mad, but because she was rushing to get into the office early on Saturday, as was her routine recently, while John was still trying to rouse himself from sleep.

He told himself he should be driving home, but his watch showed that Claire's therapy session would be over within fifteen more minutes. He remembered Phil's party: Claire's intense eyes, her full lips pursed, her breath blowing across his face. Initially, he'd felt surprised and embarrassed, but his awkwardness being with Claire had quickly transformed into something enlivening that he still didn't understand, but which he longed to experience again. Maybe it was crazy, but he needed to talk with Claire.

After Claire's door creaked open, after her lyrical voice provided her client with a warm goodbye, after his intestines pinched again, John approached Claire's office. She leaned over her desk, writing in a chart. John knocked on the half-open door.

"Hi, Claire."

"Hey." She glanced up without a smile, a serious, maybe even guarded look in her eyes.

"Do you have a few minutes?"

She nodded, pointing to the blue reclining chair in the corner of her small office. At the center of Claire's desk sat gold-framed photographs of towheaded boys, one grinning, the other boy's shy smile lined with the silvery crisscross of braces. A third photo showed younger versions of the two boys standing next to Claire and a scruffy, bearded man—he figured it was her husband—alongside a canoe on a riverbank. Most mothers would display a contrived photo of their family next to the hearth, but the river and canoe seemed fitting for Claire.

"I thought it was important that we talk about Friday night." John worried that his voice, high-pitched and rushed, made him sound nervous, which he was hoping to mask. He tried to lower his voice and spoke the next line that he'd rehearsed in his office. "I think we should talk about what it meant and how we feel about it."

"Okay." Her lips were full, and he remembered how they'd pressed hotly against him when they'd kissed. She peered at him now, her eyes more of a gray rather than the steel blue he had perceived in Phil's living room. "I agree," she said. "What does it mean to *you*? How do *you* feel about it?"

"Well, I don't quite know. I mean it doesn't fit well with my marriage—I've never done anything like that before, and I didn't plan on us kissing. It just happened, but it felt nice, good, you know?" He sounded like he was starting to babble, so he stopped. He found simply looking at her helped his nervousness. She was attractive, but in a different way than Joanie. Claire was approaching her mid-thirties and at least a half-dozen years older, and though faint crow's feet cornered her eyes, she still looked young and he couldn't help himself from imagining what the rest of her body looked like. She also conveyed a maturity and confidence that Joanie lacked. He was physically attracted to her, yes, but there was something more—a spark of energy, a connection of personality or spirit or something—he wasn't sure—that tantalized him even more.

"You're unhappy in your marriage, aren't you?" she asked.

"I don't know exactly." He hadn't anticipated her question, and he felt flustered. "Why do you ask?"

"You kissed me, right?"

"Yeah, but—"

"But what? We were dancing and you kissed me."

"Claire, *you* blew on my face."

"And *you* kissed me."

He didn't understand where she was coming from. How could she not see how she had seduced him, blowing in his ear and then on his face? He started to argue the point, but he noticed how her jaw tightened, a frown beginning to set around her chin. He decided not to upset her any further even as he felt embarrassed and too exposed. "I'm sorry if I offended you. I didn't mean to."

"Oh, you didn't." She gazed at him, looking comfortable with the following silence.

She confused him. He didn't know what to say next. He decided he didn't want to disclose any more without knowing how she felt. "So, Claire, how do you feel about Friday night?"

"I enjoyed it, but I was surprised too." Her facial muscles relaxed, and a wry expression seemed to quickly cross her face. She opened the metal desk drawer and draped her long, slender fingers around a package of smokes. She tapped out a cigarette and lit it. "I'm in a crazy place. Ted had an affair. I don't know, maybe he still is. We're talking about whether to stay together or separate."

"I'm sorry, Claire. That must hurt."

"Yep."

She looked sad. He had an impulse to reach for her hand. "I feel for you, Claire."

"John, listen to me." She straightened in her chair. "I'm not going to have an affair with you."

"What?" He felt himself flush and worried he was blushing.

"I like you. I have since we first started the program. You're very nice, very smart, very handsome, and sometimes I've felt a warmth toward you as if you were a younger brother—much younger. But I've never, ever fantasized about having an affair with you, and I don't plan to start now."

"Claire, I wasn't asking you to have an affair. I'm not sure why you would even say that."

"Tell me: Why are we having this conversation, alone in my office at night, after you kissed me?"

He was wishing he could rewind the conversation to the point where he'd never approached Claire and had gone home to Joanie instead. He felt put on the spot as well as embarrassed by Claire's questions. He really hadn't been planning to ask Claire for an affair. To cheat on Joanie would be too shameful, and to consider leaving her unthinkable. "Claire, I wasn't proposing an affair. I just thought it was important that we talk about Friday night, instead of letting it drift away as if nothing had transpired. That would have felt dishonest and crazy to me."

"I appreciate that." She nodded, muttered okay, and then twiddled her cigarette between her fingers before taking another long drag.

"I didn't know you smoked."

"Just started a few weeks ago. John, listen, I don't know why we danced and kissed like we did at Phil's party, but I'm not going to have an affair. Ted and I have been married for fourteen years, and I need to figure out what's going on and what I want. I don't know where we're headed, but I need to focus on my marriage and my own feelings."

"I understand. And I respect you for that."

"Thank you."

John thought she looked proud. Not haughty, he thought, but she exuded something else, strength, dignity; he wasn't sure. He realized the moment presented an opportunity to bow out gracefully, that he could simply announce he needed to get home, but he felt compelled by some vague urge he didn't understand to be closer to Claire. "That's what I need too. Time to figure out my own feelings and marriage."

Claire nodded.

"You know, though." He waited for her to make eye contact with him again. "I've realized that we don't really know each other that well. I mean, we've had lots of seminars together, and I've liked you since that first day of graduate school when Dr. Whitson made each of us introduce ourselves in the group therapy room—remember?"

"Not really."

"Anyway, you've always seemed like such a good person, Claire. I'd really like to get to know you better—as a friend. How about you?"

"We can be friends, not lovers." A sad, half-smile passed over her face. "Besides, can you imagine what people would be thinking if they saw us kissing, even if we weren't married to other people?"

"What?"

"What's he looking for in that older woman? A mother?"

He had not understood it before, but he'd often wondered why Claire had always associated with two middle-aged mothers in the graduate program, even though there was a greater age difference between them, than with Phil, himself, and the other twenty-something grad students. "Claire, you're maybe seven or so years older than me, I think—not twenty-seven years older."

Her expression sagged, like she was tired. "I feel so much older."

CHAPTER 5

Claire skipped a stone against the Missouri River, the rock bouncing twice before plopping into the brown water.

"That's great," John said, biting his tongue so he didn't add, *for a girl.*

"Years of playing softball growing up," Claire said. "You try."

John found a slender, flat stone exposed between patches of snow and the river's slushy edge. He hurled it with a sidearm delivery, the rock hopping four times, dribbling once more, then disappearing beneath the surface.

"Show off," Claire said.

"Years of playing softball—and baseball."

Claire threw several more rocks, none skipping more than once, before John handed her a stone the size and weight of a silver dollar that smelled faintly of fish. She skipped it three times, then turned from the river, her boots crunching through the icy crust of old snow, and hoisted herself onto a large boulder. She wiped her wet nose against her black gloves and patted the boulder, motioning for John to sit next to her. They sat beneath a patchwork of gray and blue sky, watching the Missouri's milky brown water—the color of coffee and cream— swirl downstream.

"It's beautiful here," John said. "Thanks for bringing me."

"I love this place," she said, looking not at him but over the river.

"I'm glad you suggested here instead of a restaurant for lunch again." Actually, Claire had *insisted* they go to the river. Earlier in the week, they had gone to lunch and while that was nice, Claire said she didn't want to get caught in the typical rut of going to a restaurant to meet like most friends. She wanted something different, something unique and natural.

Claire smirked, and then laughed to herself.

"What?" he asked.

"I was picturing again that look on Dr. Whitson's face when she saw us getting into the car together."

"I know." Whitson had been driving through the campus parking lot and when she spotted John and Claire, her eyes grew large, and then she flashed an impish, knowing smile, as if she understood something was happening between them; affairs between graduate students were not uncommon. John had felt guilt churn in his stomach, but he told himself it was innocent enough. They had not *done* anything improper—no more kissing, certainly no illicit sex—but had only gone to lunch once and been hanging out together each day on campus. True, he hadn't told Joanie of their lunch, but then again Joanie went out to lunch most days with coworkers or customers and she rarely told him the details. At worst, he was guilty of a menial sin of omission, not commission. "For a second, she made me feel like I was a kid in trouble when she stared at us."

"Not me," Claire said. "Most of my life, I probably would have, but these days I try not to care what other people think."

He nodded. "That's good. I probably could benefit from more of that attitude."

Claire turned her gaze from the river to John. "You're not very happy in your marriage, are you? Why did you get married so young?"

"Wow, that's kind of abrupt, isn't it?" He was surprised by her question, and his reflex was to divert the topic.

"You've asked me earlier about Ted and my marriage, and I've shared a lot." Claire had told him that as a good Mormon girl of nineteen at the time, marrying a returning missionary was fulfilling expectations, including by immediately getting pregnant. "You're great about asking questions and being a good listener, but you don't talk much about your own feelings. Are you happy?"

"I don't know."

"If you don't want to talk about it, then don't," she said. "Just be straight about it with me."

He gave her a faint, twisted smile. "It sounds terrible to say, but no, I'm probably not very happy."

"Why did you get married so young?"

"I don't know."

Claire squinted at him.

"Actually, I didn't really want to get married when we did. Joanie had suddenly become depressed our last year of college and she was really anxious about the future, about whether we'd even stay together during graduate school—she got another offer from USC that had a better financial package that she was seriously considering because of the money. We talked once about living together here instead, but both of our parents would have disapproved—my mom in particular would have thrown a fit about 'living in sin,' as she puts it—and Joanie didn't really like the idea either. She wanted more certainty, I guess, more definite plans about the future, especially since she was giving up the USC offer. I really loved her—I still do—and I thought we'd get married someday, anyway, but I didn't really want to get engaged then. I didn't feel ready. When I told her that, she got even more depressed. So, anyway, one night, when she was crying and really upset about the future—she looked so sad and unhappy—I asked her to marry me. I thought it was a small sacrifice to make someone I love happy."

"Has it?"

"What?"

"Made her happy?"

"I don't know." He felt uncomfortable, maybe even inadequate, knowing down deep that Joanie wasn't happy, but that was hard to admit.

Claire said nothing but just looked at him like she was not going to let him slide off the question.

"At first, she was thrilled. She really got into planning the wedding, even though that turned out to be stressful." He picked a pebble off the boulder and threw it toward the river, but it fell short. "But I don't know how happy she is now. She feels really pressured, and worries a lot about her job, even though she's good at it, and she worries about getting promoted."

Claire scooted off the boulder. She scanned the shoreline, then leaned over to pick up a small rock. With a sidearm delivery, she sent the stone skimming the surface, touching the water four times before sinking.

"Nice throw," John said.

"Yep." She shoved her hands into her coat pockets. Her expression had become serious, maybe stern.

"You okay, Claire?" He wondered if he had somehow upset her, though he was realizing she had a way of suddenly switching moods, and acting serious, maybe even dramatic, when she wanted to make a point.

"Why?"

"You aren't mad, are you?"

Claire marched back through the snow, stopping less than a foot in front of John.

"Tell me," she said. "If you felt free instead of worried about taking care of others, if you could do whatever *you* really wanted to do in life—anything at all—what would it be?"

"Hmm." Her questions had a way of taking him back, but he liked that she made him think. His fingertips were nearly numb. He tugged on his gloves and wiggled his fingers, warming them against the fuzzy glove lining as he tried to think through a void to what he wanted. "I'm not sure."

"Time to figure it out, isn't it?" she said.

He laughed, but she just stared at him. "I'd step off the treadmill for a while, I guess. I don't really know. Maybe I'd take some time, maybe a whole summer, and just travel around the country or maybe even Europe, without any deadlines."

"Anything else? Anything you've ever really dreamed about doing?"

"Sounds kind of silly." He glanced at the river. "But like a lot of guys, I'd love to play professional baseball—you know, just for one season. That would be fun. Does that sound juvenile to you?"

"No. Sounds tame, typical guy stuff, but fun. But the important thing is if it's what *you* want to do."

"And what about you? What do you really dream about doing?"

She spoke without hesitation: "I'd spend time in the mountains. I'd just go and not worry about being back in a week or two or even a month. I'd step away from school, from work, from family—from everything. Just go, and I'd come back only when I felt ready."

"What would you do there?"

"I'd just be in the mountains. I'd camp out wherever I'd want, in places of solitude without anyone else around."

"Not campgrounds?"

"Definitely not campgrounds." Claire's upper lip curled. "You *are* a city boy from California. No campgrounds. I'd stay where I wanted—high up in the mountains in a forest or alongside a river or lake. I'd have a canoe and put in for a good, long stretch. Camp each night where I felt like it."

"Sounds great—actually, a lot better than great." Her dream intrigued him, and he realized he longed for something similar, even though he hadn't words for it before. Without intending it, the image of he and Claire sitting together alongside a mountain river appeared in his mind. "Who would you go with?"

"No one but myself."

"Really? Have you ever done anything like that?"

"I'd go with my dad when I was a girl. We'd go into the mountains, camping, canoeing sometimes—just put in on a river, but only for a short time. I used to hate when Sunday afternoons came and we'd have to go home." Claire climbed onto a fallen large, white tree trunk—it was either a sycamore or whitened from drifting in the river for a long time—that was propped against higher ground. She lowered herself to a sitting position on the trunk and pulled her heels up next to her bottom. "And once I brought Ted and the boys, but Ryan and Josh were too little and Ted felt pressured to get back to work, so we didn't go very far."

"Canoeing is a dream of mine, too, though actually I've only gone once, and that was as a little kid," he said. "My dad and uncles took my grandpa for his retirement celebration on a fishing and floating trip on the Stanislaus River, and my boy cousins and I went, although I almost didn't get to go."

"Why not?"

The truth embarrassed him, and while he considered telling her something different, he decided to be honest without providing a full disclosure. "My mom. She was worried I was too young—I was just turning eight—but then she's always worried something bad is going to happen." This was an understatement, but he didn't want to get into the severity of his mom's mental health problems when he was a child. Besides, his mom was a lot better now—sure, she was still anxious and high strung, but not like when he was young, and he was grateful and relieved about that. "Luckily, my dad insisted—it was an all-males trip for the Anderson clan to celebrate his dad's retirement, he said, and he wanted me to go. So, eventually I got to go, my mom's fears notwithstanding, though the terms for my trip included a life vest strapped around my torso for every minute and my dad needing to be at my side at all times. But it was great. It was beautiful there— at least it used to be. The Army Corps of Engineers built a dam since then, so God knows what they did to the river. There were steep canyon cliffs, water trickling down the face of the stone, and the water was crystal clear. I remember seeing a big fish right next to the raft like he was in front of my nose in an aquarium."

"Sounds beautiful. Why didn't you ever go back?"

"We were supposed to." He flipped up his coat collar against the cold wind. "It was going to be an annual event with my grandpa, but he died suddenly of a heart attack about a week later. He was just sixty-five."

"I'm sorry."

"Me too. I don't remember that much about him. But I do remember looking up him—and so did my dad and uncles. He was a big, strong, proud man." In his memory, his grandfather was the size and shape of a grizzly bear. John flipped another rock into the river, and then sat next to Claire on the tree trunk. "It would have been a fun trip every year." The next summer his dad wanted them to go again with his brothers, but John's mom threw a huge fit and his dad acquiesced. He'd found out a couple of years later from his cousins that they and his uncles still went on a float every summer, but it was probably for the best that his dad gave in and that they didn't go again, after the ice fishing accident and all of his mom's problems. "Anyway, maybe because of that trip, I've always had an interest in rivers. In fifth grade, I did a paper on the Mississippi. 'The Mississippi: North America's Mightiest River,' I think I titled it. Corny, huh? Anyway,

I developed this dream of floating all the way down the Mississippi. I wanted to start at its headwaters and float all the way to the Gulf. And then I saw a TV show about these guys who did exactly that. I told Danny—he's been my best friend since first grade—and the two of us talked about taking a trip down the Mississippi after high school graduation. We'd take the whole summer and float from beginning to end, and party along the way at places like St. Louis and New Orleans."

"What happened?"

"We never went," he said.

"Why not?"

"We chickened out." He gave a furtive, sideways glance and saw what looked like disapproval on Claire's face. "No, actually our parents were dead set against it." His mom, of course, had been most opposed to the trip, which bothered but didn't surprise him, and his father backed his mom. That wasn't so surprising, either, as his dad had come to invariably support what his mom wanted, at least if she became very upset.

"How come?"

"Our parents were scared—not just my mom who's scared about every-thing, but even Danny's folks, who were normally carefree." He hadn't thought of it before, but now he wondered if his mom had talked with Danny's parents, persuading them not to let Danny go either. "They were afraid we'd get mugged in some strange town or capsize and drown. Danny and I protested, but to be honest, their horror stories scared us a bit, plus we worried about having enough money and time to complete the trip before college started. So, we compromised. They bankrolled us a hundred dollars each—probably it was a bribe—and we went instead to Spokane, where Danny had an offer from Gonzaga to play base-ball, and then to Yellowstone, and took side trips along the way to Redding and Idaho Falls to visit girls we'd met at high school basketball tournaments. It was a lot of fun, but it wasn't a journey down a long river. We missed out on something really special, I'm afraid."

Claire nodded. "I've never floated the Mississippi, but mountain rivers are remarkable. When you're on one, alone, or maybe just with a partner, there's a feeling of nature's power that's awesome. Your problems feel so insignificant—there's a sense of calm, like you fit in the universe. It's special. I hope you go. You and Danny should still take that trip."

"We've talked about it. But it seems like the older you get, the harder it becomes to set aside the time for a special dream; you get too caught up with day-to-day commitments. But we've talked about going, although we've joked it may not be until we hit age sixty-five and it'll be for retirement, instead of graduation."

"Hopefully you don't die first at sixty-four."

"Hopefully not." He gave her a quizzical look. "That's a strange thing to say, eh?"

"You have to think about those things."

"You may—I don't."

"You never know what happens in life," she said. "*Carpe diem*, right? No regrets; live what you dream."

"Are you?"

"I will. I'll get back to the mountains and a wild river long before I die."

The afternoon sun glanced off her high cheekbones. She looked back over the river and then turned toward John.

She was beautiful, John thought. Something about her desires, about going to the mountains and canoeing a wild river, felt synchronistic and enticing, though he couldn't say precisely why. He remembered their dancing together, her blowing her breath slowly across his cheeks, and he felt himself again connect in some deep, unspoken way with Claire. He wanted to kiss her again, even though he knew it was wrong. He sensed she was feeling their connection, too—she seemed to lean slightly toward him, and so he swayed toward her, planning to kiss.

Claire jumped onto the snow instead. "We'd better go."

CHAPTER 6

John steadied his right hand, trying not to spill the Tab he'd bought for Claire as he quickened his pace. Her office door was ajar, and he noticed himself smiling. He hadn't seen Claire since before the weekend, and he hoped for a few moments alone together before the departmental research colloquium.

He knocked, there was no answer, and he knocked again, calling out her name. He waited, and then pushed her door half open. Claire slumped in the recliner, her vision transfixed on the photos of her sons on the desk.

"Hey, Claire. About ready for the colloquium?"

She was still.

"Claire? Are you okay?" He offered her the cup of soda, but when she made no motion, he placed it on her desk. "What's wrong?"

"I don't know if it's worth it."

"What's not worth it?" He worried she was going to say they needed to break up, though he realized that made no sense, as they weren't really together.

"All the pain."

"What happened? Are you okay physically?"

She looked at him for the first time, but with a sneer.

"Claire, talk to me, please. What can I do to help?"

"Nothing."

John peeked at his watch. They should be taking their seats in the seminar room. He considered encouraging Claire to gather pen and paper and to walk to the colloquium. He said, "Let's get out of here."

She blinked.

"We can go to the park and talk," he said.

"I don't want to talk,"

"Then we can go for a walk, or just sit in the car, if you want."

She said nothing but looked angry. Then she rose to her feet without speaking and grabbed her coat.

Pellets of a snow and rain mixture—the St. Louis weatherman had called it "snain"—pinged off the windshield. Claire was silent, her complexion pale, her face expressionless, almost like she was in a trance. He tried to engage Claire in simple conversation, talking about the weather, rambling on about winter refusing to relinquish control and his longing for spring. After they arrived at the park, they watched from the parking lot inside the car as gusts of wind whipped falling sheets of sleet across the empty softball field.

"Sorry, it's gotten too crappy for a walk," he said.

She gave a slight shake of her head. "It doesn't matter."

"Claire, how are you? What's going on?" He'd never seen her so uncommunicative and he was reminded of a patient he'd seen once in the hospital in a vegetative depression. Claire wasn't responding to any of the questions, which worried and frustrated him, though he wanted to be supportive. "I don't know what's going on, and I wish you'd tell me. But whatever it is, I know things will get better."

"Stop!" She yelled.

"What? Geez!" He checked himself, and feigned a contrite half-smile, though it was confusion and irritation he felt. "Sorry if I offended you."

The door latch clicked. She sprang from the car and ran onto the field. Icy snow droplets pelted her. John hesitated, and then flung his door open.

"Claire!"

She walked further away.

He hurried after her. "Claire, for God's sake, come back before you catch pneumonia."

She ran.

John called her again, and then he chased her. Cold pellets bit against his cheeks. On the outfield grass, he caught Claire from behind, pulling on her shoulders, slowing her down. "Claire, will you stop?"

She whirled about, her fist clenched like she was going to strike him. She paused, her eyes glaring. Tears slipped down her cheeks.

John hesitated, wanting to say something but his words had only seemed to make things worse. On impulse, he reached out, wrapping his arms around her shoulders. He gently squeezed her in a bear hug. She struggled for a second, became still, and then sobbed. He held her face against the nape of his neck, his cold hands shielding her damp hair from the icy rain. "I'm sorry you hurt so much."

She cried harder, and he patted her back. He held her for a long time until her sobbing subsided.

After they returned to the car, John handed her a gym towel from his back seat. She patted herself dry.

"Thank you," she said.

"It's okay. I'm here for you."

"Ted's not," she said. "He moved out on Saturday."

"Oh, Claire," he said. "That's huge—I'm sorry."

"For now, it's a separation but we could end up getting divorced," she said. "But whatever happens, my marriage and family will never be the same."

"God, that's hard."

"You know what my mom said?"

"What?"

"She said this is what happens when you focus too much on school instead of your family and church. She told me I should try harder and do everything I can to get him back as soon as possible."

"Ugh," he said. "That's not what you needed. Sorry she blamed you—that must have hurt."

"She's always been quick to lash out under stress." Claire pulled a cigarette out of her purse, lit it, rolled down the window a crack and took a long drag that she exhaled into the cold. "But in some ways, she's right about how important family is. Since I left my mother's house at nineteen, my marriage has been the center of my life. I loved Ted, love my boys, love my family above everything, and that was my foundation—they were always there for me, no matter what else happened. But that's been shattered. It was naïve and innocent, I know now, but it has been what I believed in, and it was comforting. No matter what Ted and I decide, it can never be the same again."

He shook his head. "That sounds like a huge loss."

"It's a death."

John started to speak, but again being unsure of what words to utter, he put his arms around Claire instead. Her body felt stiff across the car console, but she sniveled, then rubbed her face against his damp collar, and relaxed into his upper body.

On the drive back to campus, Claire thanked him. "It meant a lot to me that you just listened and held me," she said. "You're a great listener."

His mom had often told him something similar when he was a boy. "You're such a good listener—unlike your father," his mother used to say when he sat in the kitchen listening to her complaints. His mom's praise pleased but confused him when he was younger, as most evenings his parents sat around the kitchen table drinking highballs after his dad got home. But by the time he got to junior high, he realized his dad enjoyed droning on in great detail about some engineering issue, taking his pencil out of his pocket holder and drawing a diagram as he spoke, or railing incessantly about the government bureaucracy. His mom often interrupted, wanting to talk about herself, and soon his dad would disappear to his woodworking shop in the garage. "You'll make some woman very happy someday," his mom would tell John when she finished talking at him (though this was also confusing as at other times she talked about his becoming a priest). He felt bad he was no longer making Joanie happy. When they were first together, she used to talk to him all the time, especially about how her own mother—a woman with a plethora of somatic complaints—didn't understand her and hurt her feelings with critical comments. "Nothing I do makes her happy," Joanie used to tell him. He felt sorry for Joanie. At least he knew he pleased his mom, even if her happiness never lasted long and required constant feeding. But these days Joanie rarely talked to him about feelings, and when she did, John (he hated to admit this to himself) felt distant while she blathered on about chronic work stresses, which she was overreacting to out of insecurity (*that* interpretation she didn't take kindly to, even when he said it in a gentle form) or some material thing she wanted someday. He told Claire: "I really care about you. I'm glad you trusted me with how you're feeling."

"Usually, I'm the supportive and nurturing one in relationships," Claire said. "But you're even better in that role than I am."

"It's easy to be that way with you. I'm happy that you let me in."

"It felt really nice."

"It did feel nice," he said. "It feels, feels *intimate*."

A look—he couldn't decipher if it was fear or embarrassment or maybe even attraction—quickly passed over her face. She glanced out the passenger's side window.

He worried he might upset her, but he took a deep breath. "I feel a deep connection with you, Claire, like there's a special bond between us. Do you feel it too?"

"Yes," she said, still looking away.

▶ CHAPTER 7

The next evening, after working late at his part-time job at the state hospital, John returned to Claire's office, hoping but not expecting to see her. The curtains to her small window were pulled open, and she sat at her desk, looking over a morass of papers. Her blond hair fell onto her shoulders, and from the profile, he noticed the shapeliness of her breasts and long legs. She glanced over—as if she could sense she was being watched—and smiled at him, waving him into her office.

"Hey," he said. "What are you up to so late?"

"Trying to catch up on an assessment. Plus," she pointed toward the empty reclining chair, "I thought I might see you here tonight after your work."

"That's sweet." He caught himself grinning. "How are you?"

"Better now."

"Great." The energy he often heard in her voice had returned, and she looked both relaxed and beautiful. "What changed?"

"Last night it hit me that I've been living my life in limbo. For months, I've been waiting for Ted, waiting to see what he would decide about the marriage. You know what I decided once I realized that?"

"What?"

"To follow Felice's saying: 'Fuck that shit.'"

He laughed. "Well, good."

"Really. Since last summer when I found out Ted was having an affair, I've been holding on to what we used to have, hoping Ted would eventually say he still wanted the marriage. And then I realized last night that I've still been just passively waiting, wishing Ted would say he still wanted me—even now while he's moved out and openly dating other women. That's bullshit and I'm tired of living like that."

"Sounds like a good move for you." He leaned toward her. "So, do you know what that means? I mean, what will you do?"

"I don't know exactly what that means, but don't you see?" She rolled her desk chair closer to the recliner. "I feel free now. I'm not going to wait around to hear what Ted might want tomorrow. I'll make decisions because it's what I want."

She lifted her chin and there was some mixture of fierceness and passion in her expression that he'd seen before at Phil's party and at the river's edge. She sat less than an arm's length away, and he again felt the stirring inside his solar plexus. He imagined kissing her, and then, without intending to do so, he pictured them making love.

"I need to go." She stood up. "The boys are at home with a sitter and it's late."

It was irrational, but still he wondered if she had sensed his feelings? He felt guilty, then, both because he didn't want to make Claire uncomfortable, and because to have sex with her would be a betrayal of Joanie. He felt bad for a moment, and then he remembered Jimmy Carter telling *Playboy* magazine a few years earlier he had lusted after women in his mind. If the president could admit to such feelings, perhaps his own desire was only natural?

Claire wheeled her ten-speed bike out of her office, planning to pedal to her house, but she eventually agreed to let John pack up her bike and drive her home. They first stopped in the psychology department office to check their campus mailboxes. John's box was cluttered with memos that smelled fresh with purple mimeograph ink. When they turned around, Branham towered at the doorway over Claire's bike.

"You ride this back and forth to campus, don't you?" Branham asked.

"Most days," Claire said.

"I thought so." Branham bent way over, leaning his face to the bicycle seat. He passed his nose along the seat, inhaling a deep and slow breath, as if savoring the aroma of a fine cigar. "Ahh."

"Branham!" Claire slapped him on the shoulder. "You're incorrigible."

"That's what my high school teacher used to tell me, too—at first. Want to hear what she said later?"

"Spare me."

"Bet sometime you will want to know." Branham rubbed his hands together. "Just let me know when."

"Don't hold your breath."

On their way to the parking lot, John checked over his shoulder to make sure Branham wasn't within earshot. "Branham's pretty unbelievable sometimes, huh? That was especially bad."

"He's flirted with me since our first year when we shared an office together— he was pretty obnoxious on occasion and I had to put him in line once in a while," Claire said. "But he's a friend, too, and I just don't take him seriously."

But Branham was serious, John thought. He knew Branham would hump her in a heartbeat, but he realized he was more uncomfortable about it than Claire, so he said nothing more about Branham as he drove the short distance to Claire's neighborhood. He turned left onto her side street and parked just up from her house. The street was dark, save for faint moonlight that fell across the bridge of Claire's nose. She thanked him for the ride.

"Glad to help," he said. "I'll get your bike out."

"You asked earlier how I want to live now, without Ted?"

"Yes?"

"I want to live with passion as well as freedom. No more moping around as the passive victim, grieving Ted."

"I've never thought of you as a victim. And, Claire, you *are* a woman of passion. That shows, and I love it."

She leaned across the car console, raising her hand to his cheek. John scooted closer to kiss her.

"Wait." She scanned his face, and then she pursed her lips and blew a long, warm breath across his eyes, his cheeks, and onto his lips. She lifted his chin, and pressed her warm, moist lips against his. He felt again warmth swell inside himself, like the time they had kissed at Phil's party; he had hoped he would feel that way again. He kissed her back with intensity until Claire pulled away. She then brushed her lips across his mouth in light, teasing strokes. He wrapped his arms tight around Claire, stroking her hair, savoring the intense feeling—it was like he was waking up and feeling truly alive again—that grew again inside him.

"Umm." She leaned away. "This living with passion—I like it!"

"I love it." He leaned forward, wanting to kiss again, but she touched a fingertip against his chin.

"Got to go," she said, opening the car door. "I want to see my boys before their bedtime and I'm already late."

From multiple comments it was clear she not only loved her boys but was sensitive to their emotional needs and wanted to be present for them, and he appreciated this about her. "I know. I don't want you to go, but I understand." He pulled her bike from the trunk.

"Thank you—for everything." She wheeled her bike onto the sidewalk.

"Good night." He shivered in the cold and retreated to the driver's seat.

Claire rode toward her house, and then turned at the neighbor's driveway, making a U-turn loop. She pulled up to John's car on the driver's side, and he rolled down his window.

She swooped across her bike frame, leaning toward him, and John stretched toward the window to kiss her again. Claire paused short of his lips; she blew another slow breath that fluttered across his face, and she rode to her porch.

On Friday when John parked his car outside of Claire's he let himself wonder for a moment about the question he had anxiously relegated to the back of his mind: was passionate sex what Claire had on the menu for their lunchtime rendezvous? This was the first time she had invited him into her home, and given it was the middle of the day during the school week and she would be alone, he thought she must at least be contemplating taking their relationship to a more physically intimate level. He fumbled with his key while trying to lock the car door, and he took a deep breath to try to settle the jumble of excitement and nervousness, longing and guilt, that churned in his stomach. He'd dreamed last night of Claire—of their kissing and making love—and as much as he delighted in the fantasies, he felt terrible when he considered the possibility of cheating on Joanie. He was morally opposed to extramarital affairs—it was ingrained into him by Catholicism and his mother—but his attraction for Claire was strong and growing. He immediately corrected himself: it was more than attraction— though he was anxious to admit it even to himself—it was an inexplicable sense of intimate connection and love, the intensity of which surprised him, that had suddenly overtaken him. He was unsure how he'd respond if Claire wanted to take him to her bedroom. He wished he could talk with someone, but he worried about his friends in the program because graduate students love to gossip. He'd thought, too, of trying to call his best friend Danny back in California, but for now he decided to push away the worries, figuring he would know what to do in the moment, if Claire did try to seduce him. He knocked on her front door.

He heard her voice call out, though he couldn't make out what she was saying over the din of two barking dogs. After a moment, the door swung open, revealing a brown-haired boy. From photos, John recognized him as Claire's oldest son, though his hair had turned darker while growing longer and mop-like, and his face a mixture of rounded, plump cheeks and small pimples breaking out across his nose and forehead; he looked like a boy blossoming into adolescence. "Are you my mom's classmate?" he asked.

"Yes, I'm John. And you must be Ryan." John smiled and extended his hand, which Ryan limply shook while two dogs, a beagle and a tawny hound mix, sniffed his shins. "And who do we have here?" John glanced at the dogs.

"Bart the beagle and Serendipity."

"Cool names." John saw a glimmer pass quickly in the boy's eyes. "Good dogs, too, I bet?"

"Yeah."

"So, Ryan, did you get a day off from school?"

"My mom gave us a mental health day. Josh was having another temper tantrum—my mom calls them meltdowns—this morning, and she let him stay home. I was supposed to go to school, but I said that wasn't fair, so she let me stay home too."

"Got it. A nice fringe benefit for you," John said, while trying to figure out whether his own feelings about Claire's boys being home represented disappointment or relief or some incongruous mixture.

"Yeah." Ryan waved his hands as he spoke, probably more from nervousness than an animated personality. "Mom's talking to him again in the sunroom. She asked me to answer the door, but I'm watching TV upstairs."

"You probably want to get back to your show."

Ryan blushed. "She said you could go on back."

John thanked him, saying his mom had talked a lot about him and that it was good to meet him in person. Ryan scrambled up the stairs.

At the far side of the house, across the living room and dining room, an entryway opened into an enclosed porch room. As John entered the room, he saw Claire sitting on a worn loveseat, holding her other son who sat awkwardly, perched on the edge of her lap. Josh was fourteen months younger and significantly smaller than Ryan, but he still looked too big for his mother's lap; he wiggled off when he saw John. Claire squeezed him around the shoulders as she looked up.

"Ah, sorry for interrupting." John sensed he was intruding.

"Josh," Claire said. "This is my classmate, John."

"Nice to meet you, Josh," John said.

Josh gave him an abrupt head nod—his eyes were red—and looked away.

"John, will you give us another minute? There's a teakettle on the stove that's on low." She pointed toward the small kitchen off the dining room. "Turn it to high."

"Sure," he said. "Sorry if I interrupted. Take your time."

From the kitchen, he watched in quick, intermittent glances as Claire talked softly to Josh. John couldn't make out the words, but her tone was soothing. She gave Josh a long hug, and though her son initially tried to pull away, he soon relaxed into her arms.

"Have a seat in here," she called out to John after a few minutes. "I'm going to walk upstairs with Josh and check on Ryan. Be right back."

John sat on the loveseat, closest to the black, potbellied wood-burning stove that radiated heat from the corner of the room. Bart immediately sauntered over, plopped himself down, and shoved a cold, wet nose against John's hand. John rubbed the beagle behind his floppy brown-and-tan ears. Serendipity cautiously sniffed at his knee, and John offered her an open palm.

The teakettle whined a low whistle and Claire pattered into the kitchen. "Do you want lemon and honey with your tea?" she called out.

Usually, he didn't drink tea, but he said yes, as he looked around her sun porch, which reminded him of an arboretum. The glass windows ran floor to ceiling on three sides, and philodendrons and asparagus ferns cascaded from ceiling hooks to the tile floor. At the far end of the room, a miniature orange tree grew in a wooden tub, and petite oranges peeked out from between green leaves. The sweet scent of citrus wafted through the air. "Claire, I love this room with the big windows," he called to her. Next to the orange tree, two finches tweeted in a long bamboo cage. "And all the plants and animals. There's a lot of life here."

Teacups clattered in the kitchen. John figured this was probably the best outcome for now—with her boys home, they wouldn't be tempted to cross the line into a sexual tryst, at least today, and yet he took satisfaction in the thought that sex was probably exactly what she had intended when she'd invited him over, before Josh's meltdown. The boys would probably be with her Friday night and maybe Saturday, too, and he was glad for that, too, as he'd been feeling anticipatory guilt about abandoning Claire over the weekend since they'd been seeing each other every day during the week. Perhaps he could ask Claire if she wanted to meet Saturday to study together and for lunch—he could get away with that rendezvous, as Joanie would be working up to the last minute on her strategic plan presentation for her bank management retreat. He'd have to leave with Joanie on Sunday afternoon, however, for the opening cocktail hour and dinner for the executive team and their spouses before the work meetings began in the morning.

When Claire strode into the room, he said he was sorry if he'd interrupted. He thought he'd invite her to his intramural championship basketball game Monday night while Joanie was still at her retreat. "It was a privilege to see how you were with Josh."

"What do you mean?"

"You were so tender and caring. It touched my heart to see you like that—such a sensitive mother."

"Ah, thank you. That's good to hear."

"What's going on with Josh—is this about the separation?"

"Yep." She handed him a teacup.

"I'm sorry. That's got to be rough."

She nodded, sat in the green rocking chair at a diagonal from John, and looked him in the eyes. "I need to stop seeing you."

"What?" Something like panic swelled through his chest. "Claire, why?"

"Because you're married."

"I've been married this whole time, plus we're friends anyway."

"Friends who kiss." She rested her teacup onto the coffee table. "John, be honest with yourself and with me."

"I know—and I feel guilty because of Joanie." He felt bad because of his mom and God, too, but that was too uncomfortable to say aloud. He fidgeted, shifting his hips to try to find a more comfortable spot on the sagging loveseat cushion. "But it's been nice, Claire. There's a connection between us. You feel it too."

"There's something sexual happening. You know that."

"Yes, I feel that. But I also just feel close to you as a person." He reached out toward her with open palms, speaking with his hands, though now they seemed too large and awkward. "It feels like we have this special bond together."

"It's more than that." She shook her head. "You're unhappy in your marriage, and you're emotionally vulnerable, but I'm not going to have an affair with you."

"Claire, I'm not asking you to have an affair." Bart nudged his wet nose against the back of John's hand.

"Not in words, but in actions," she said. "We're kissing, we're spending lots of time together, including off campus and at night—we've been one step from ending up in bed together. When Ted and I were together, he slept with another woman, and that was terribly painful for me. I'm not going to do that to Joanie or any other married woman. That's *not*," she drew out the word, "who I am."

"And I respect that about you, Claire—and I'm not trying to get you in bed." Though his sexual fantasies of Claire had delighted him, he could forgo actually sleeping with her but not their sense of closeness. "I care a lot about you, as a person, and more than anything, I want to be your friend."

"You've been a good friend to me, John. I'm going to miss that."

"Miss it? Why? *No*," A swell of desperation overtook him as he sensed her withdrawing. "It doesn't have to stop."

"For now it does."

"Claire, no. That makes no sense."

"Don't tell me I'm not making sense." She pointed a finger at him, as if she was scolding a child.

Bart flopped his chin onto John's lap. John rubbed both of the beagle's long ears. "I'm sorry. I don't mean it that way, but Claire, why?"

"We're both vulnerable. I'm just separated and you're unhappy in your marriage. We're both searching for something, but it needs to be something deeper than an affair."

"Being friends means something. We can still get together and talk."

"I'd like us to be friends." She stood up and pinched off a brown leaf from a hanging philodendron tendril. "That feels like the right fit between us."

"Good." She was too nonchalant in her response. "I want us to be friends. You're important—very important—to me."

"Right now we have to be careful about the situations we put ourselves in and the time we spend together." One of the finches fluttered wildly in its cage. "We should take a break from seeing each other."

"Claire, no!"

"Why not?" she asked.

"Because when I'm with you, I feel alive." He peered into her eyes, but she said nothing. "And because I love you."

"That," she said, "scares the shit out of me."

"Why?"

"Because you're married and I've just separated. And we really don't know each other that well."

"We can make things work, Claire." His own words frightened him, though he didn't know what they meant. He was married to Joanie and leaving her was unimaginable. But Claire's expression seemed to soften, and he had the sense that she was on the verge of disclosing her love too. He had no idea what would happen next, but he wanted to hear her speak the words. "I know it seems impossible, and I don't know what it will all mean, but I do love you already, and Claire, I think you feel it too, don't you?"

She walked to the wood burning stove and unhinged its iron door. Orange and gray embers glowed in the belly of the black stove. Claire stoked the embers, shoved a log into the stove, and slapped shut the door. "It's time for you to go."

"Why?"

"I need time alone now."

"Let's talk this through."

"No. Come on."

"Claire?"

"I need space."

Only Bart walked him to the front door.

CHAPTER 8

Joanie's bank president was the dullest speaker John had ever heard. Glenn Bond, standing stiffly at the head of the long dining table in the lodge's banquet room, spoke in monotone at the opening group dinner about the bank's assets, liabilities, balance sheet, and other things that John didn't understand or care about. Still, Mr. Bond was an interesting fellow in other ways, being in his late fifties with black, thick-framed glasses and a comb-over, and a young, curvaceous, blonde wife who smiled knowingly at him. She had to be at least twenty-five years younger.

John's attention drifted to the last forkful of blackberry cobbler that he slid into his mouth. The blackberries, sweet and tart on his tongue, were his favorite part of the sumptuous banquet for the bank directors, management staff, and their spouses. The dinner was intended to be a general kickoff to the bank retreat, and John winced as Bond continued to drone on, plodding through the introduction of Joanie and Steve. Bond spoke in dry, halting phrases about how excited he was that Joanie and Steve would unveil the draft of the bank's five-year strategic plan at this year's annual management retreat. He called Steve and Joanie to the head of the table to give an overview of tomorrow's meeting for the executive management team, which would include an in-depth presentation of their strategic plan.

Joanie looked professional. She had asked John's opinion about several outfits before deciding against his advice and choosing a red business suit with a crème, cowl-neck blouse. It was a businesswoman's power suit, she had told John, but he was glad she also wore the necklace he'd given her for Valentine's Day, which added a touch of femininity and softened her appearance. Steve, with slicked-back, black hair and dressed in a suit that Joanie had whispered earlier was a Christian Dior, said he'd recently opened a checking account at a branch office of their major rival, just to keep an eye on the competition.

"Now, I don't want to slander our competition by saying their customer service is bad." Steve spoke in a strong, self-assured tone, and then paused as if for effect. "But when I went in yesterday and asked the teller to check my balance, she leaned over the counter and pushed me." After the laughs, Steve lavished praise on Joanie, who stood at his side, citing her dedication, hard work, and professionalism in developing the strategic plan. "Never before," Steve said, "have I seen such a dynamic combination of commitment and intelligence in such a young officer: Joanie Anderson, the true genius behind your strategic plan."

Joanie's face flushed with the clapping. "I have been so incredibly fortunate to work with Steve on this project," she spoke in a fast, high-pitched voice. "As you know, he is as intelligent as he is funny. Thank you, Steve, for all of your amazing mentoring and support—I have learned so much from you and our plan is the labor of a true partnership."

Joanie went on about the organization of the plan, the environmental scan, the analysis of the bank's strengths, weaknesses, opportunities, and threats. Her hands flailed as she talked. In his mind, John reminded her to take slower, deeper breaths—she hated public speaking. John had given her a long back rub on Saturday night to help her relax and he'd also bought her a half-dozen roses, saying the flowers were to celebrate her completing the strategic plan, though he realized in the back of his mind they were also his covert attempt to assuage his guilt for kissing Claire.

He told himself their flirtation had only been a temporary thing, anyway, and a small transgression. They hadn't had an affair; they were just friends. But he still felt rolling waves of some vague, sickly feeling in his stomach, and it disturbed him that he'd thought of Claire almost constantly over the past three days. He'd wanted to call her several times. He'd restrained himself, but he felt a lingering sadness and emptiness, the depth of which both surprised and scared him.

Joanie stumbled over the phrase "regulatory ramifications," having to pronounce it twice, before turning it back to Steve to describe the planning process. It had been Steve's idea, Joanie had told him earlier, to take turns presenting, going back and forth like local TV news anchors, to help her feel more comfortable. She looked up at Steve as he spoke confidently. John tried to pay attention to the particulars of their presentation, but his mind wandered, wondering what Claire was doing. He imagined the boys were now with their dad and she was alone in her house, feeling sad. For all of Claire's courageous words, he knew it was hard for her to be without her boys and that she was still grieving the loss of her family. He wished he and Claire could spend more time together. He imagined them together next summer, floating in a canoe on a pristine river through a pine forest high in the mountains. Claire sat in front of the canoe, her blond hair golden in rays of sunlight. The applause startled him, and he realized Joanie's presentation was over.

John left the bar early, after only three beers, having to extract himself from the rest of the psychology department team, especially Kevin and Dennis, both hardcore drinkers, who wanted to celebrate late into the night after winning the university's intramural basketball championship. But John needed to call Joanie, hoping to hear how she felt about her strategic plan meeting. He'd left the Illinois lodge where the bank was holding its retreat early in the morning for the hour-plus drive back to St. Louis, telling Joanie he felt guilty that he wouldn't be back for dinner—spouses were invited for the evening meal, and, indeed, most of the wives of the bank's executives had stayed over at the lodge. Joanie had waved him off, saying she'd probably be super busy, anyway, reviewing the day's feedback and planning the wrap-up group sessions for the following morning.

The night air was frigid. Did alcohol make the temperature feel colder? No, it was probably another Canadian Clipper blowing through St. Louis. His breath was visible inside the car, and tiny crystals formed a lattice of ice inside the windshield. He swore under his breath at the cold and decided to call Joanie from the university; his office was closer than the apartment, plus he hoped to bump into Claire.

While John was unlocking his office door, he heard the echo of Claire's laughter from somewhere inside the building. He scurried into the main hallway and saw Claire walking out of the psychology department's office. Branham's burly body hovered close to her. Her laughter vanished when she saw John.

"Claire?"

"Good evening, Mr. Anderson." Branham nodded, a half-smile twisting across his face.

"John, hello," Claire said. "What are you doing here?"

"Just stopped by the office for a few minutes after the basketball game."

"Did you win?" she asked.

"Yep." He peered at Claire and then Branham, trying to figure out what they had been doing.

"Congratulations," she said.

"Thanks. So, what are you two up to?"

"Trying to finish up that evaluation report for Dr. Lerner's court project," Claire said.

"In fact," Branham said, "we're done, just locking up the barn now, and I'm giving Ms. Evers a ride home. Congratulations on the basketball, Anderson. Have a good night and give my regards to your missus."

Claire smiled, but the skin pulled taut across her cheeks, as if she was forcing the expression. She said good-bye and walked away with Branham, who winked at John as they passed.

After watching them disappear out of the building, he returned to his office. He picked up a folder and slammed it back onto the desktop, swearing aloud as he imagined Branham driving Claire home: he would sweet-talk her, invite himself in for a drink, ply her with alcohol, then maneuver her into the bedroom to earn another notch on his penis. And Claire could fall for his ploys—she was lonely and vulnerable.

He slammed his door shut and found himself calling his best friend, Danny, in California, instead of Joanie.

"Hey, what's happening, Big Andy?" Danny, who barely measured five foot six when he stood straight, still often called John by his childhood nickname.

John told him about the intramural basketball championship, and Danny said his work team had won their three-on-three industrial league, though a fight had nearly broken out in the final minute.

"So, how's Julie doing?" John asked. She'd been Danny's girlfriend since they were high school sophomores, and they'd been living together for the past three years.

"She's good. Joanie?"

"Okay, I guess."

"That's not very convincing," Danny said. "What's up?"

"Nothing, really. She's just really into her job, always working hard with lots of long hours, but I guess I spend a lot of time with graduate school crap too."

"Doesn't sound like much fun."

"Nope." John jiggled his leg, his knee rattling the bottom of his small metal desk. "Something's missing, Danny."

"What? Sex?"

"That, too, but it's more than that." He debated how much to share but pushed himself. "It feels like things are dead with Joanie—sometimes it feels like I'm half-dead too."

"Are you fucking someone else?" Danny asked.

"What?" It bothered John that he was talking about something deeper and Danny cheapened it by going immediately to sex, but he lost that thought in the worry that somehow Danny already knew about his feelings for Claire. He tried to reassure himself that was impossible.

"Are you?"

"No. I'm not. Why do you ask?"

"Just wondered. Sometimes it causes problems, but sometimes it helps," Danny said. "Believe me, after you've been with one girl for a long, long time, it feels good to know there's someone else out there who will fuck you, but it can complicate things too."

"I haven't been sleeping with anyone else, but there's a woman in the program, Claire—I've gotten real close to her."

"So fuck her."

"You're hopeless, you know?" Danny had a one-track mind about sex, and John questioned himself as to why he'd even called him. His thoughts strayed then to Branham and Claire, and he had a horrible image of them having sex.

"I'm just kidding—sort of." Danny chortled. "What's she like?"

"She's blonde and beautiful and smart. Plus, Claire's got this depth to her, this passion for living."

"Passion's good."

"I really care about her. You know," John hesitated, not sure he wanted to tell Danny what he'd only recently let himself even consider. "I've even thought of leaving Joanie to be with her."

"Whoa! Be careful, big guy," Danny said. "That's a huge step."

"I know. It's scary as hell, but I think about Claire all the time, wishing I could be with her." He heard the tension—it almost sounded like desperation—in his voice. "It feels almost like something I have to do for myself, you know?"

"Not really."

"It feels important."

"All I'm saying is that it's really risky—you've got a lot to lose. Yeah, it seems exciting to be with this new girl right now, and it probably would be for a while. But is it going to last? Probably not. Pretty soon you'll be arguing over whether to leave the goddamn toilet seat up or down. And then if it blows up, where are you going to be? Who's going to be there for you every night, like Joanie is now? Go—have sex with this Claire, if you want, but don't start by separating from Joanie."

"I don't want to be sneaking around, having some cheap affair. That doesn't feel right." The words were true, but they sounded distant, as if spoken by someone else. And then the idea of leaving Joanie for Claire—someone he'd only been attracted to for a few weeks—seemed ludicrous.

"So, you'd leave your wife for a woman you've never even had sex with? Your mom definitely took you to Catechism for too many years. Come on, John, don't go crazy on me."

"I'll do whatever I need to do." John felt better, then, pushing back at Danny for the sarcasm instead of worrying about his own self-doubts.

"I know. And I know you get as stubborn as a jackass if you think someone is trying to tell you what to do. I'm not. I'm always behind you a hundred percent. I just don't want to see you get hurt, brother."

"I know," John said. "I appreciate it."

"Listen, I'll call you in a few days. Just make sure we talk again before you do anything rash, okay?"

"Don't worry. I'll be okay."

But John worried. Danny's words about Joanie being there for him every night replayed in the back of his mind while he drove home. The steering wheel moaned in the frigid temperatures every time he turned a corner, and his fingers grew numb inside his gloves. Despite their problems, Joanie *was* there for him. She had been for ten years. But Claire? He felt something for her—a deep longing, even love—but that was only a few weeks old. Leaving Joanie to be with Claire now seemed like a crazy idea.

He fumbled with the key to his apartment, his fingertips cold and clumsy, before opening the door to darkness. The bulb in the lamp nearest the doorway had burned out, and he stumbled across a pair of shoes he'd left in front of the sofa. He flipped on the overhead light in the kitchen.

The message light on the answering machine blinked red at him. He expected a message from Joanie, but there was only the hum of a dead dial tone before the next message.

"John? John, are you home?" The voice of Nona, his maternal grandmother, boomed from the answering machine. "You must be out. How are you, my dear boy? We just got back from Pebble Beach. We brought our sticks and played a round—oh, I played terrible, but you should see Emerson hit that little white ball. Like a pro!"

John laughed. They'd been married more than a dozen years, but Nona still seized every opportunity to make Emerson sound like a real catch, though he was a bit of an odd and indifferent character. When he and Nona would come to his parents' house for a weekend dinner, he'd often trudge immediately to the other room and park himself with nary a word in front of the TV to watch a golf tournament, all the while emitting an air of arrogance without any real credentials to back it up (until it folded, he owned a very small trucking business with one semi and a trailer—a "one-horse operation," his mom called it). If anything, Nona's lavish praise only reinforced John's mother's opinion that Emerson was a big asshole, though that was probably harsher than what he deserved.

Nona's message continued in her animated if somewhat shaky voice. "We stayed overnight at the Del Monte Lodge and had a delicious dinner, steak and crab legs. I'll send you a little check so you and Joanie can take another nice trip. It's good to get away together."

"Emerson," she called. "Do you want to say anything to John?"

John pictured Emerson in his regular perch, leaning way back in the large recliner in the corner of the living room, facing the TV. To talk on the phone, he'd have to sit up and lean over toward the phone on the end table next to the sofa, and John couldn't imagine Emerson putting forth that much effort for a conversation. Emerson was a bump on the log, his mom often said, unless he had a few drinks under his belt.

"Tell him," Emerson's native Oklahoma drawl was distinct even though he wasn't on the phone, "he's a good boy."

Nona used the "good boy" expression for John so frequently that Emerson liked to rib them both. When John was a boy and Nona and Emerson first married, he initially disliked Emerson, but mainly because his mother detested her new stepfather. Of course, his mom hadn't liked Nona's second husband, either, though she grew more positive about him after he had died of lung cancer a year into their marriage, and after Nona married Emerson. Emerson had reportedly insulted his mom on their first meeting ("I thought you'd be beautiful and outgoing like your mother"). His mom was one to carry a grudge, and she also took exception to Emerson being much younger than Nona (a decade, his mom used to say with ridicule while Nona always immediately corrected her that it was only eight-and-a-half years).

Nona repeated Emerson's "good boy" message over the phone, which made John smile—it seemed like a good-natured teasing between the three of them. At times Emerson displayed a sharp though often sarcastic wit, which John enjoyed though he remained generally agnostic about his step-grandfather, especially when speaking to his mother

"Good luck with your studies," Nona added. "Work hard but don't study too much and take time to go out for a good dinner. I sent you a care package today with a few treats and some dinero, and don't forget to take the multivitamins. Okay, I love you, my dear boy. Now call me when you get the package so I know it didn't get lost in the mail."

John called the lodge, asked the front desk for Joanie's room, but her phone rang without answer. He figured she was out working, plotting the final retreat activities for the next morning. Or maybe they were all celebrating, taking the night off to relax over drinks after unveiling the strategic plan. He hoped the day had gone well for Joanie. She'd worked awful hard.

The Canadian Clipper had chilled the apartment and John pulled on his favorite sweater with earth-tone colors and a Navajo design. He warmed his hands in the deep side pockets, and his right hand struck cold metal. He'd forgotten to turn his room key into the lodge. He flipped the oversized, golden key over in his fingers. Maybe it was a sign, he thought, that he should go back to the lodge? Like Nona said, it was good to get away together.

John thought about Claire, and it scared him that maybe he'd been living in his own little fantasy world. He barely knew her. Yeah, they'd kissed and had a few good talks together, but they'd never slept together, and now she didn't even want to see him. She was separated and—what? Off messing around with Branham? And he was married but sitting at home, missing Claire, while his wife was celebrating the most important day of her career.

He decided the right thing to do was to try—to *really* try—with Joanie. The marriage needed some work, he thought, and it needed time and attention, not fantasizing about another woman. He figured he needed to talk with Joanie, to get her to really listen to what he wanted in the relationship. He remembered the waterfall in Oregon and camping out under the stars in the dewy night. And the summer before they married she had an apartment in San Francisco. They'd go to bars along Franklin Street, hold hands together under tables and talk, and then go back to her apartment a little tipsy and make love in a dreamy state. That was fun. That was what they needed: more fun, more sex, more intensity.

Yes, they needed to talk about all of that, he thought. But not tonight. Don't spoil her celebration. Go be with her, drink together, make love tonight. Another day, sometime soon, talk with her.

John collected clothes for the morning, walked back to his freezing car, and drove to Illinois to surprise her.

He followed the two-lane highway north of Afton. The Great Rivers Road paralleled the Mississippi, and then, after the confluence, the Illinois, but he could no longer discern the river in the darkness at night. His watch showed it was a few minutes after 11 p.m., and he wondered if Joanie would still be awake. After rounding a bend, the lights from the lodge reflected across a field of snow. On impulse, he made a quick left, into the parking lot to the boat launch into the

Illinois River. He parked adjacent to the river, stepped into the cold, and stared back at the lodge. Most of the rooms were dark, but yellow light glowed from the great room in the center of the lodge. John turned and stepped closer to the river, snow crunching under the soles of his basketball shoes.

The river was frozen solid. He had noticed the ice cap on Sunday afternoon when he and Joanie had first arrived from the retreat. Kent, the bank's elderly senior-vice president who sat next to John at the opening dinner, explained that the Illinois stayed frozen longer than the Mississippi since it was narrower, shallower, further north, and surrounded by country rather than concrete. As far as John could now see, the dull gray of ice stretched into the night. He glanced around. The road was barren and no one was visible. John inched closer, toeing the shoreline, though the boundary between the snow of the land and the frozen river was hard to discern. Coldness spread across his cheeks.

A loud but dull sound rose from the ice and John jumped back. He stared at the river, examining the ice, while straining to listen. The ice emitted another low moan, like the haunting song of a diving whale. The ice was breaking apart, he thought. His heart thumped hard. His impulse was to run, but he forced himself to stand at the river's edge. The ice near the shore was thick, perhaps a foot deep, though he couldn't tell for sure. The river groaned another low rumble. The ice wasn't cracking apart, he realized, it was thickening as the temperature dropped, and moaning as it expanded.

His breath froze solid against his mustache, and he told himself that he needed to go be with Joanie. Six months, John thought, give the relationship six months to improve. That was the right thing to do.

He wondered about Claire. What would she be doing in six months? She could be divorced and in a new relationship, even committed to someone else.

He turned his back on the river, crunched his way through the crusty snow to his car, then heard the ice whine again. An impulse to pivot and run across the ice seized him. The feeling swelled from his stomach into his head.

Crazy, he thought, *fucking crazy*. But the feeling overwhelmed him.

He clambered behind the steering wheel of his car. His fingers trembled, trying to slip the key into the ignition. The engine cranked over and an image overwhelmed his mind: shove the accelerator to the floor and speed across the ice.

He shook his head and told himself not to lose control. He felt crazy and ashamed, and he had scared himself. He made himself back up the car and drive carefully to the lodge.

John parked in the lot at the south end of the lodge—their room was the second from the end—and fingered the cold metal key to open the side entrance door. He hesitated at the door to Joanie's room, took a deep breath, and convinced himself to yell, "Surprise!" He croaked out the greeting; the room was dark and quiet. He worried he was waking Joanie up—she was irritable when awakened—and tiptoed to the bed. Though it was nearly dark, he saw the bed was still made and barren. John twisted on the lamp. Her room was tidy—that was Joanie, even with maid service—but empty.

He checked the clock: 11:39. It was late for Joanie to be awake, but he took it to be a good sign that the presentation of the strategic plan had gone well, and they were all still celebrating and relaxing. Or perhaps the meetings had gone poorly, and she was sequestered in a conference room, plotting how to salvage the retreat in the last meeting? He decided he should go discover the verdict and help her celebrate—or offer support in what might be an overwhelming disappointment.

John turned off the lamp and stood in the dark. The windows were mere slits set high on the outer wall. He peered out, wondering if he could see the river, but there was only darkness. A terrible design, he thought. It was impossible to see the river even on tiptoes. Only a few rooms on the second floor, which flanked the great hall, had a scenic view of the river—this according to Joanie, who had exclaimed after a tour on Sunday that Steve had an awesome overlook on the second floor.

John wandered down the hallway toward the great hall in the center of the lodge. He hesitated at the threshold and looked about. The room was empty, save for Joanie sitting with Steve at a table for two next to the window. John instinctively stepped back into the hallway where he was hidden, although he could still see them.

Steve spoke in a booming voice, arms waving, telling a joke perhaps, and Joanie laughed. Her smile glistened white; brightness gleamed in her eyes in a way that he hadn't seen in a long time. She laughed again, leaned forward, and touched Steve on the knee. Joanie's knee rested inside Steve's leg, pressing the inside of his thigh. John watched them for a few minutes, feeling both jealous and somehow like he was intruding, as they laughed some more, and then talked in softer tones. Steve leaned forward, whispering. Joanie raised her cocktail glass, an apricot brandy sour, her favorite drink, and swallowed. She nodded. Steve twisted around, glancing over his shoulder, and John ducked even further back into the hallway.

John listened to their footsteps echo across the hardwood floor of the great hallway. The steps pounded louder, and then faded. John peeked around the corner. Joanie's hips and legs were visible, ascending in unison with Steve's legs, up the staircase to the second floor. Her hand clasped Steve's hand then, and she intertwined their fingers.

John waited in the dark in Joanie's room. He was sure she was having sex with Steve—the look in her eyes, the pressing of her knee against his thigh, the interlocking of their hands: he remembered all of that romantic body language from years before when he and Joanie had dated. She'd bring him back to her apartment in San Francisco after a night of dinner and drinks, and they'd become lost in lovemaking. And now? Now she was probably fucking Steve with abandon.

No wonder they hadn't been having sex, John thought. All of those late nights and weekends working together on the strategic plan—ha! She'd been sleeping with Steve. And he'd played the fool—the supportive sucker husband, believing it all.

He thought of going to Steve's room and kicking in the door. And then what? Seeing Joanie on top of Steve, fucking his brains out? Smell sweat, sex, semen?

Claire. He'd wanted so much to be with her. But he'd held back because of his marriage, because of Joanie. Meanwhile, Joanie had been banging her bank vice-president.

The clock shone 12:37 a.m. She'd been with Steve for almost an hour. Was she going to creep back into her room sometime soon, smelling and dripping of sex? Or was she going to spend the whole night with him and sneak back early in the morning before the other bankers were up? John stood up and walked around her room. None of her clothes were visible. She'd hung them all up in the closet or put them away in drawers. Her room was more than tidy; it was barren.

He sat back on the bed. What was he supposed to do now? Wait there all night while she was in Steve's arms? Without wanting to, he imagined them having good-morning sex.

He leaped from the bed and slammed the door shut on the way out.

John sped away from the lodge and hit the Mustang's brakes just before the boat ramp to the Illinois River. The screeching car skidded to a stop on the icy pavement. He popped out of the car, looked about, grabbed two handfuls of hard snow, and patted them into a ball. He heaved the snowball toward the Illinois; it slapped hard against the ice and he watched it break into a thousand particles. He flung another snowball that splattered against the frozen river. He chucked one more snowball, and then another and another, and laughed.

Maybe it was for the best. He was free now to be with Claire—if she wasn't with Branham. He was free to really live as he wanted.

He shaped and patted together more icy snow, reared way back, and threw the ball deep into the river. The snowball smacked the ice and scattered in broken pieces across the frozen river.

"Fuck it." He laughed and grabbed more snow and threw the ball as far as he could. "Fuck it, fuck it, fuck it." He forced one more laugh, and then found himself crying.

CHAPTER 9

The aroma of chicken baking with white wine sauce wafted across the room when John entered the apartment Tuesday evening. The dish was one of his favorites.

"Hi," Joanie glanced over her shoulder as she called from the kitchen.

"Hey." All afternoon he had been working himself into a knot of self-righteous anger, looking forward to the moment of confrontation when he could explode and then walk away from Joanie—but now he felt sickly. He wished he could slink back out the door.

She met him in the living room and planted a dry kiss on the corner of his mouth. She peered into his eyes. She quickly looked away when he stared back.

"So," John stepped back, sat in the rocker, and motioned Joanie toward the sofa while he tried to steady his resolve. "Tell me all about your retreat. I want to hear *everything*."

"The review of the plan went great," she said. "They loved it. Absolutely loved it."

"That's just great."

"Do you know how hard it is to get a bunch of bankers excited? But they were—we got so many compliments. Mr. Bond even wants Steve and me to present our strategic plan to corporate headquarters—can you believe it? Now *that* makes me nervous."

"Wow. Congratulations."

"It's going to take a lot more work. Not just prepping for the corporate presentation, but now we have to implement the plan, and Mr. Bond appointed Steve and me to be coproject managers. We're going to be super busy."

"I bet," John said. "A lot more late nights?"

"Yeah." She cocked her head and paused. "Probably some."

"I can imagine." He felt the anger return—he'd been hoping it would—but he wanted to play out the conversation methodically and not just explode. "So, what did you do last night? How'd you celebrate?"

"We had a fun dinner with lots of drinks," Joanie said. "I had jumbo shrimp Creole. And Steve ordered champagne for the whole table."

"He's such a great guy, huh?" John said. "What else did you do?"

"Later we had a follow-up planning meeting. Just Mr. Bond, Kent, Steve and me."

"That's it?"

"Pretty much. I was really, really tired. I went to bed kind of early."

"I bet you did."

Joanie flushed. "I did," she said with a wave of her hand. "What? Are you mad because we didn't talk last night? I left that message for you at home about 10:45 saying I was planning to go to bed soon, but you didn't answer. Where were you? Oh, your basketball game—I forgot to ask. I'm sorry—did you win the championship? Were you out celebrating with the guys?"

"Earlier, but then I went to celebrate with you."

Joanie blanched. "What do you mean?"

"I drove back out to the lodge last night. I got there around 11:30 and saw you and Steve talking and drinking in the great hall."

"He called with an idea for this morning's meeting."

"I bet," John said. "And I bet I know what idea he had in mind."

"Really." She nodded but avoided his gaze.

"Bullshit, Joanie! I saw you leave together, headed for his room."

"He'd left some papers in his room and we went to review those."

"Don't lie!" He slammed his hand against the chair armrest. "I saw you—the way you looked at him, your leg pressing against his and holding each other's hands when you left."

"I was tipsy walking. I'm sorry."

"Joanie!"

"I had too much to drink—you know how champagne goes to my head. But nothing happened in his room. We looked at some papers and planned this morning's meeting, and then I fell asleep, drunk and exhausted, on his sofa. I'm sorry."

"You know, your lying is worse than your sleeping with him. Just tell me the fucking truth, will you? You slept with him, didn't you?"

Her eyes teared. She gave the slightest nod of her head and cried as she did.

"Joanie, goddamn it." He hated when she cried—he felt bad and like he should do something to make her feel better—but he tried to focus on being mad.

"I feel horrible," she said. "I was tired and I was on this high from how great the presentation went and I drank way too much. I didn't intend it—it just happened."

"How long has this been going on?"

"First time." Her lips quivered.

"After working all those late nights and weekends with him for months? I find that hard to believe."

"You have to believe me." Tears gullied her makeup.

"Do you love him?" For an instant, he debated what answer he wanted to hear. It might hurt more, but he hoped she would say yes. It would make his plan easier.

"That's an unfair question." For the first time, she sounded angry.

"Tell me—what do you feel for him?"

"John—"

"Tell me."

She shook her head. "He's funny and sophisticated and successful and we have a lot in common as bankers, but that's not really the point. John, we need to put this behind us."

He hesitated. Even though his wife had slept with her boss, even though he was hurt and angry, he still found it hard to speak aloud what he wanted for himself. "I'm sorry, too, but we need to separate."

"*What*? John, no!"

"We need to separate. I'm sorry."

"*No.*" She shook her head. "Don't throw everything away we've been planning—a house, careers, nice vacations, a child."

"I don't even know if I want those things anymore."

"Don't be crazy." The narrowing of her eyes made her look angry as well as frightened. "I made a big mistake, but don't let it destroy everything we've been working for."

"Something's wrong with us, Joanie. It has been for a long time." He had been wishing he could rewind the whole conversation, but now it felt good to speak the truth and he couldn't stop himself. "It's like we're sleepwalking through our marriage."

"That doesn't make any sense," she said. "We've just been super busy. We just need to spend more time together. That's all."

"We tried that on our anniversary. But we couldn't even connect then."

"That's not fair." She pointed her finger at him, the way she did when she got really mad. "I was overloaded with work on the strategic plan. I told you before we left, but you still insisted we go. You even told me to work as much as I needed—you just wanted us to take a trip together."

"Do you realize the only time we ever make love anymore is in our sleep? That's a serious sign, Joanie."

She waved her hand. "Don't do this to me!"

"I'm sorry."

"Why can't you forgive me? What will people think—your family, my family? That I'm some adulteress, some whore?"

"They don't need to know the details." His mom would be dead set against a separation. He was tempted to tell her about Joanie sleeping with her boss, but images of kissing Claire filled his mind and he knew he'd feel too much like a hypocrite to blame Joanie. "Besides, I'm not saying it's all you. I've realized I'm not very happy in our marriage, and I haven't been for a long time."

"Goddamn it. This isn't what I want." She broke into sobs again.

John moved next to her on the love seat. The sickly feeling in his stomach swelled. He took her hand.

"I'll be so unhappy," she said. "I don't want to be a divorced woman at twenty-seven."

"I'm not saying I want a divorce." He patted her hands. "But we need some time apart to figure out what we really want."

"Separating isn't what I want." She lifted her head, her chin raised, pointing at him. "I can tell you that right now."

"It's what I need, at least right now, I think."

"You're only 50 percent of the decision," she said. "I definitely want us to stay together and work this out."

"I know you do." He had felt so sure about needing to separate before the conversation, but now the possibility of actually leaving Joanie seemed unthinkable.

"I'll be so unhappy if you leave. I'll be absolutely miserable. Why can't you forgive me? I feel awful."

She cried harder. John gently squeezed her hand. "It'll be okay."

She pulled away, screamed, and scratched violently at her cheek. A short trail of blood sprang from her fingernails and trickled down her face.

"Joanie, stop. Please." The moment—Joanie crying, scratching herself until she bled, the talk about leaving—felt surreal, and a fuzzy image surfaced of his parents arguing loudly once when he was little. When he went to their bedroom, his mom was yanking his dad's clothes out of the closet and throwing them on the floor, yelling like a crazy woman. His dad had walked John out of the bedroom and closed the door behind him.

"Don't leave me," Joanie said. "I don't want to be alone."

He remembered Danny's words from the night before: *Who's going to be there for you every night?* John nudged his nose against her hair. He grabbed a tissue from the coffee table and patted the tiny beads of blood on her cheek. "Oh, Joanie."

She frowned a deep grimace. He'd never seen her look so sad.

He thought of giving in. He could do that for her; he loved her. He could make her happy if he just stayed.

"Will you stay?" she asked.

His mom had asked him to stay with her one Sunday morning when he was a boy and his father had left with two suitcases, saying he had a long business trip. His mom told John she wasn't feeling good, but he already knew this before she spoke. John had a ticket to go with Danny and his family to the Giants' game—they were playing the Dodgers and he wanted to see Willie Mays hit a homer off Koufax—but he stayed home with his mom. He even made his mom laugh that day while playing Crazy 8s, and Willie only hit a single anyway. "Maybe," he mumbled.

"Stay," she said.

It wouldn't be so bad, he thought. All he had to do was say he wouldn't leave and she'd be happy again. He should tell Joanie he'd stay. But then his chest felt tight. He gulped for air.

"John?"

He felt like he couldn't breathe. He inhaled rapidly, trying to catch his breath.

"What's the matter?" she asked.

He heard himself sucking for oxygen in a succession of desperate, short breaths. Terror overwhelmed him. He thought he was dying.

"John, stop."

How could he stop? He was dying. He wanted to tell her, but he couldn't even breathe, much less speak.

"It's just an anxiety attack." Joanie had gone through a few of her own after she'd gotten her layoff notice from McDonnell Douglas.

Hyperventilating, he thought. Yes. That's all. He tried to fight the panic with this thought, but the anxiety attack was refusing to relinquish its control. He saw himself sitting on the sofa next to Joanie, gasping for air, but now he felt like he was watching from far away.

Yes, he could stay. He remembered having sex in their sleep. It wasn't so bad—being half asleep, like in a hazy dream. The feeling of dying—not imminent and intense, but slow and sure—returned.

Phil's party floated back into his mind: Claire stepping up to him, pulling him up by his hands, her hair smelling like orange blossoms as they danced. She had looked deeply into his eyes, pursed her lips, and blew a long, warm breath gently across his face. He closed his eyes now, trying to tighten his hold on the memory. He felt again the way her breath had caressed his flesh and stirred his spirit. His breathing became slower, deeper. The hyperventilating passed.

"John?" Joanie poked his shoulder. "John?"

He kept his eyes shut, visualizing Claire dancing. He felt her breath flutter across his lips and seep into his lungs.

When his breathing returned to normal, he opened his eyes and told Joanie he was sorry, but she'd be okay.

He was leaving.

CHAPTER 10

John parked his car in the side lot and cut a diagonal across the campus toward the psychology building. The evening air felt warmer—the Canadian Clipper had blown eastward with fierce winds, and a warm front had finally moved in. He stepped through the slush of melting snow pocked by scattered brown goose droppings and stopped at the small wooden deck overhanging the pond. He checked his watch, saw it was ten after seven, and calculated that Claire would be finishing up her weekly Tuesday evening therapy client in twenty minutes.

A slow, intermittent patter murmured beneath his feet where melting ice dripped from the deck face board onto the thinning sheet of pond ice. He was no longer short of breath, nor tense, and this pleasantly surprised him. He thought he'd call Phil when he reached his office and ask if he could stay a few nights on his sofa until he found a place of his own. He thought again of Claire, imagining himself telling her about Joanie and Steve and his own decision to separate. He pictured her listening, her blue-gray eyes intent, as she reached out and embraced him in a warm hug. In the past few weeks, she had become his most trusted confidante. Perhaps they could grab a bite for dinner tonight after talking? He wondered if her children were with Ted—and then he imagined spending the night not at Phil's, but with Claire.

After she ended her therapy session, he met Claire in her office. He told her about finding Joanie with Steve and then confronting Joanie at his apartment. He said he made the decision to separate but neglected to share how his initial resolve had quickly faded into a sickly feeling of doubt when he had faced Joanie.

"I really don't feel very hurt anymore," he said. "It's strange, but it's almost a relief. It's like I realize now that I'm not right for Joanie and she's not right for me."

As he expected, Claire stared at him, her elbows propped up on the arms of her desk chair, a half-smoked cigarette propped between her fingers.

"It's hard." He decided not to tell her about his panic attack and almost staying with Joanie. "But it feels freeing. I want something more."

"It hurts for a long time when your spouse has slept with someone else," Claire said. "But then you're not exactly innocent, either, are you?"

John cocked his head. "What do you mean?"

"Our relationship."

"I care a lot about you, but we haven't slept together."

"John—be honest. You've been having an emotional affair with me."

Her words sounded strange, as if the feelings were one-sided. "You and I—we've become good friends. Yeah, we've gotten close—but that's a good thing, and we didn't cross any lines into a sexual affair."

"You should go back and work it out with Joanie."

"*What*?"

"Separations are too painful." Claire crushed the cigarette butt into the ashtray. "I can't change my decision now—it's too late for me. But you can. Save yourself the pain."

"I can't believe you." He had expected Claire of all people to understand. "This is something I need to do."

"There's so much to lose."

"Even before I knew about Steve, I felt like I was drowning with Joanie. I want something more than plodding half-dead through the motions—I want a relationship that's passionate and authentic and alive. And Claire," he paused, waiting for her to look up and into his eyes. "I want that with you."

"No."

"Claire—why?"

"I'm in no place for a romantic relationship."

An empty feeling, like he hadn't eaten in days but was no longer even hungry, gathered inside. "We can take things slow."

She shook her head.

He sensed a growing disbelief—even horror—come alongside the emptiness inside himself. He'd gone through the turmoil of telling Joanie he needed to separate from her, not really because she had sex with Steve, but because he hoped to sleep with Claire. "I'm a patient person."

"I don't want a romantic relationship with you."

Despair reared up on him. He shook his head. "No, Claire."

"I don't mean to hurt you," she said. "But you should know how I feel."

He thought of Joanie, wondering if he could go back to her, but he knew there was something bigger—that somehow his happiness, his best chance of ever feeling truly passionate and alive, rested with Claire. He shuffled his feet, searching for the right words or expression that would move Claire, but he could think of nothing.

"Claire," he said after a long pause. "There's something between us—a special connection. You've even said that."

"More like a brother, I said, not a lover. Besides, it's not a good time for me to be with anyone."

John thought of walking out right then, of cutting his losses and slamming the door behind him. He suddenly felt like a fool, and the idea that he should return to his apartment and Joanie flooded his thoughts. He looked intently at Claire. She seemed different. She looked older, harder.

"What's the matter?" he asked.

She shook her head.

"Something's wrong, isn't it? This isn't like you. Please talk to me."

"You should be talking with Joanie—not me—trying to work things out."

"You're the one I want to talk with."

"I don't have anything more to say." She shoved a book and several folders from her desk into her backpack.

"Stop," he said. She had always been warm, supportive, caring. The way she was acting—so detached and cold—was inconceivable. "Why are you being so cold?"

She slung the backpack over her shoulder. "I need to go."

"For God's sake!" A welling of emotion—he wasn't sure if it was sadness or fear or hurt or some conglomeration—rose up inside him. "I'm going through a goddamn separation and probably a divorce. Where's your empathy?"

He tried to stop himself, but he started to cry. He wanted to hide his pain, but to his horror he heard himself sobbing, like a scared, hurt child. He was not even sure what he was crying about—leaving Joanie, or not being with Claire—which seemed worse? Yet he was dimly aware of a shadow of something deeper and more pervasive, but its nature was unclear. He struggled to figure out his feelings, even as he tried unsuccessfully to stop crying. He remembered with self-disgust a spell of crying every day in first grade. When his teacher had asked him in front of the entire class why he was crying, he said he missed his mom. She had gone to Nona's house for a week to rest her nerves, but even after she was back, he still cried for her at school. His teacher must have been disgusted by his daily crying, for she told the rest of the class, "Let's all say 'boo-hoo, we miss our mommies.'" The class complied. He felt almost as humiliated now, crying in front as Claire, as he did then, but her arms encircled his shoulders. Claire squeezed next to him in the recliner and tightened her hug. He smelled her scent—it was a deep, earthy smell mingled with the faint scent of perfume—and he began to feel better.

"It's good to cry now," she said, pulling his head snug against her bosom. "It's sad to lose a marriage."

He struggled for an instant, feeling uncomfortable, swaddled against her, like he was going to suffocate. He tried to pull away, but she held him, and he gave himself over to her. He cried harder, sobbing into her chest. He remembered her holding Josh in her porch room, and he felt both embarrassed and comforted.

"Sometimes I feel like a motherless child," she sang the words softly in a rich voice, and then hummed a melody. Her breasts, soft and full, pressed against his face. He remembered Joanie years before in California, before they had married, dressed in a Minnie Mouse T-shirt and short-shorts, cutting his hair. As Joanie had leaned forward, cutting his hair on the top, her braless breasts had bobbed in his face. Through Minnie's face, he had seen Joanie's nipples, and he had leaned forward, kissing her breasts through the Disney T-shirt, and he had felt happy. He wanted to tell Claire, but how do you explain that memory? He sobbed again. A torrent of weeping overtook him. He felt small and scared, as if the tears were stronger than his will.

After a period of sobbing—he was unsure if it was a very brief time or many minutes—he felt better, but without knowing exactly why. Somehow, the grieving over Joanie had passed, like a thunderstorm that gives way to blue skies.

Claire still held him tight, humming in a deep-throated voice. He felt her breasts rubbing against his face, almost pressing against his lips. To his surprise, a swell of sexuality surged within him. He nudged his face tighter against her breasts, and he sensed a nipple close to his mouth. He kissed her breast through her blouse and reached his hand to caress her other breast. He reared up then, wanting to kiss Claire on the lips.

She met him with a firm hand, pressing her fingers against his lips. He gazed up at her eyes.

"You need to go." Her softness had evaporated, replaced with a stern frown.

"Claire—"

"Now," she said.

CHAPTER 11

John searched for but couldn't find Claire the next day on campus. He wondered if she was avoiding him, and he worried that by kissing her breast he had irrevocably broken the relationship. It was an obsessive worry, he recognized, but one that might well be true and it scared and saddened him. He realized—and it seemed odd to him intellectually but true emotionally—he was far more upset about the possibility of losing his new relationship with Claire than he was leaving his marriage of four years with Joanie.

He spent another aggravating night trying to sleep on Phil's sofa and returned to campus early the next morning to find Claire alone in her office. He knocked lightly at her open office door.

She glanced up from her desk. "Good morning."

"Can I come in?" He tried to lean casually against the doorjamb but miscalculated the distance and stumbled slightly in the doorway.

She looked him over, and then nodded.

He gently closed her door and slipped into the recliner. "Claire, I'm sorry about the other night."

She waved her hand. "Don't beat yourself up about it."

"No, really," he said. "I crossed a line."

"You were upset and vulnerable," she said. "I get it. When men are hurt emotionally, they want sex."

He felt himself flush. Perhaps that was true but it was embarrassing. "In any case, I'm sorry, Claire, for going too far."

"Thank you." The tight lines around her eyes relaxed. "It means something to me that you apologized."

"Well, good," he said. "But then I felt like a big baby, crying like that—"

"Don't," she said. "Your soul needed a good cry."

It had been a long time since he had thought in terms of what his soul needed, but he knew immediately it wasn't crying—he wanted Claire's presence and affection. He felt understood and emotionally supported by her in a way that he had never experienced before. But it was more than that, as his fantasies of being with her soon morphed into sex. He also knew he shouldn't speak those words. "Anyway, it felt good—the way you held me. You're such a good friend. I don't want to lose that."

"I accept your apology." She flipped closed a therapy chart and pushed away from her desk. "I know how grief and loss after a separation can get the best of us. And, the truth is, I realized I wasn't being a very good friend to you at first either. I was being pretty shitty, given you had just separated from your wife."

"Well, thanks." He was surprised but pleased she acknowledged acting badly; it gave him a sense of hope.

"So," she said, "how are you?"

"I'm okay. You know, a little tired as it's been hard trying to sleep."

"John," she drew out his name slowly, as if his name had a double vowel. "Really—how are you?"

"Really, I'm okay." He fidgeted, thinking he shouldn't tell her that he had lost more sleep over her than Joanie and had worried to the point of feeling desperate and panicky about what he'd do without a romantic relationship with Claire now that he'd separated. "I mean, you know, it's sad and upsetting, but there's actually some sense of relief."

"Separations are so painful." She rubbed her face in her hands for a moment. "Did you go back to Joanie?"

"No." He heard the edge of indignation in his voice, even though he had wrestled mightily with the same possibility. "I told you, we're done. I'm staying with Phil for a few days until I find a place of my own."

"I wasn't a hundred percent sure," she said. "It would have been easy for you to go back."

"No." He knew it would have been easy—too easy. "That's not what I need now."

"I respect you doing what you need to do," she said. "That takes courage."

"Thank you." He felt pleased but embarrassed. "So, how are you? You seemed the other night like you were upset too?"

She nodded. "I'm better, but I had gotten overwhelmed by my own shit for a while."

"Claire, why?"

"I'd had a real shitty night on Monday and when I saw you, I was still in a crappy place."

"I'm sorry. What happened?"

"After Branham dropped me off—and that was awkward: he wanted to come in and I had to keep telling him no—I found Ryan's socks and shoes strewn across the living room and Josh's shirt in the sunroom. I was going to leave their clothes and remind them to pick them up, but I realized they wouldn't be back for a week because they're with Ted. And Ted won't be coming home with the boys."

"Uh-huh." He regretted the wooden tone in his voice.

"Don't you get it? We're no longer a family anymore," Claire said. "And we probably never will be again. It's dead."

Her last words churned up some feeling—he wasn't sure if it was empathy, sadness, or simply fear. "I'm so sorry, Claire. That must have been painful."

"It was horrible." She broke open the cellophane wrapping around a new pack of cigarettes.

"What did you do?"

"What could I do?"

"I see your point."

She pulled a green lighter out of her top desk drawer, lit a cigarette, and took a long inhale. "I tried calling Felice a few times, but there was no answer. So I sat in front of the wood-burning stove and planned to journal, but I didn't feel like writing. I didn't feel like doing anything. I just sat in our big house by myself—it was so quiet, too quiet."

John, too, had worried about living by himself. Aloneness would be the hardest experience. "I can imagine."

"I went to bed but I couldn't fall asleep for the longest time—and then I woke before dawn to this terrible crash, like the roof was caving in."

"What happened?"

"The top section of the trunk and the biggest branches from my favorite old oak broke off in the high winds and scraped against the side of the house."

"Jeez," he said. "I'm glad it didn't fall on your roof."

"For a while, I was wishing it had—right on my head."

"Claire!" He knew her comment was flippant, but he hated the thought. "Don't say that. I never want something like that to happen to you."

"I was kidding." She laughed. "You know, though, someday something's going to happen to all of us. But anyway, it actually scared the shit out of me at the moment. And it made a gigantic mess—limbs, branches, the tip of the trunk, and a sea of leaves across the patio and yard."

"Darn."

"I just stood outside in the near darkness, and I thought this is my life: one big, broken mess."

"No." Her words upset him. She was a beautiful person and woman of courage, even as he worried that his own life was now a huge and possibly hopeless mess too. "Everything's not a mess. You're doing something really important—living your own truth by separating from an unhealthy marriage while still caring for your boys and getting your Ph.D. That takes courage and strength to find your own path and not acquiesce to Ted's or your mom's and any social expectations."

"Thank you." Her eyes widened and she spoke slowly, as if from both surprise and gratitude. "I appreciate that. I sure didn't feel that way Monday night."

"I know."

"Last night I wrote in my journal and I feel better now."

"Good."

"No matter what happens in my life, I have a choice." She tilted her head back, the way she had a few times before when she seemed defiant or determined. "I'm not a helpless victim."

"Yep."

"I still have some big messes in my life to clean up," she said. "Like a broken marriage to figure out and now the tree mess to take care of."

"You'll figure things out in time," he said. "And as far as the tree mess in your backyard, I'll help you clean that up."

"No."

"Why not?"

"I need to do things myself."

"For God's sake." He laughed. "Lighten up, will you, and accept a little help?"

She snorted a deep laugh.

"What's so funny?" he asked.

"Becky—my best friend back in Ohio when Ted was in law school and the boys were toddlers—used to tell me to lighten up all the time. She said when I'd get stressed out, I'd slip into Superwoman mode, trying to do everything myself."

"Becky's a wise friend," he said. "So, take her advice and mine: lighten up and accept a little help from a friend."

"Okay." She smiled with an impish, almost arrogant grin.

"What's so funny?"

"I like you being direct. Usually you're so wishy-washy."

"I'll have to remember that." He wanted to lean forward and kiss her, but he knew he shouldn't even try.

"You're a good person," she said. "I've missed you, John, as a friend."

John stretched open the mouth of the black plastic garbage bag and Claire shoveled in a small collection of twigs and leaves.

"Looks like we got it," John said.

"Not quite." She scraped the rake hard against the ground, churning up tiny furrows of damp earth and harvesting a very small pile of broken leaves from a patch of melting snow. She scooped up the leaves with cupped hands, threw them into the bag, and plucked at the remnants of several remaining twigs. Her fingers were slender and strikingly long—longer than John could ever remember seeing on any woman. "Now we've got it."

She offered John a cold drink, climbed the back steps, and returned with two green Tupperware glasses filled with iced tea. She thanked John excessively.

"Glad to help," he said, sitting down next to her on the stair step. "Besides, it was a nice day—finally feels like spring—and the cleanup went fast."

"It didn't take as long as I thought."

"It's because of the way you work—like my grandmother, Nona: rapid-fire pace but jerky."

"Jerky?"

"Yeah, you know, jerky, choppy, like watching one of those old silent movies on fast forward."

"That's quite the contrast with you." A sneer mingled with her smile. "You move like my sons: slow motion. But I appreciate your pitching in. It was a big help."

"Sure, it was fun." Her blond hair was pulled back in a ponytail, and her face, smooth-skinned but broken by dimples, reflected the afternoon sun. "You look beautiful, Claire. With your blonde hair, you look like a Swedish movie star— except maybe for this smudge of mud. Here," he caressed away the spot of dried mud. "There you go. Now you're ready for that big screen."

"In your dreams."

"Definitely there."

Her eyes shone a brilliant blue—the gray slivers were no longer visible in the bright sun. He again felt the urge to kiss her, but the memory of her telling him she didn't want a romantic relationship resurfaced in his mind. Those words echoed at night on Phil's sofa when he was trying to sleep, like they had become seared into his brain, leaving him both confused and anxious. He would eventually get himself to sleep after telling himself Claire might come around, though he would have to be patient and it might take months to know how things would play out. In her backyard, he extended his hand now to Claire while feeling somehow both closer to her and also sad. "Good working together," he said. "Good teamwork."

She shook his hand. "Yes."

Some feeling—he wasn't sure if it was intimacy or regret—passed over her face. He let her hand linger in his for a moment longer, but then let go. He asked if he could use her shower before changing clothes and heading back to campus. She pulled a towel from a hallway closet and pointed him toward the upstairs bathroom. He stripped, climbed into the tub shower, and watched the streaming water wash mud from his body into the drain. He closed his eyes, soaking up the feeling of hot water running over his body.

A rattle startled him, but then he recognized the sound of shower hooks scraping against the metal curtain rod. He opened his eyes, twisted around, and saw Claire stepping naked into the back of the tub. Her large white breasts sloped toward her slender stomach.

"Don't be scared," she said.

But he was scared, excited, and happy all in the same instant.

She stepped toward him. Shower water splashed past John, raining against Claire's collarbone and cascading down her breasts. She extended her hand, cupping the back of his head, and then playfully twisted his wet hair between her long fingers. Her skin glistened under the shower water. He inched closer, leaning down, eager to kiss her.

"Wait." Her fingers caught his chin, holding him still. She stared into his eyes, pursed her lips, and blew a long breath across his face.

He laughed, and then closed his eyes, focusing on the sensation of her breath. The warmth spread across his face, and somehow merged with the heat of the shower water streaming over his shoulders and neck.

Her breath receded, and then she blew stronger across his face. Something wet and moist—Claire's tongue, he realized—pressed against the side of his neck. She licked away a bead of water from his body. Her tongue carved a warm path up his throat and across his cheek.

"Claire." He reached to hold her.

Her full, thick lips pressed against his mouth, and her hand gripped his engorged penis. She slid her body, slippery and wet, onto his flesh, and he felt aroused in some way that went far beyond his body.

PART TWO

CHAPTER 12

His body was weary after a long day of clinical work at the state mental hospital, but a lightness rose within John's spirit as he walked the curvy stone path to Claire's house. He liked her home—the dark brick and sloped tile roof reminded him of a gingerbread house—not only because of its style but also for the pleasures of being with Claire. As he knocked on her wood door, he remembered how beautiful she had appeared, dressed in boots and black, on their Friday night date of drinks and dancing at Laclede's Landing, and then the intensity in her blue eyes when she had brought him home and made love to him with a passion.

She answered the door with a wave. "Wait here." Her words were friendly but rushed. "I'll be right back."

She disappeared into the kitchen, and he thought he'd take her out in two more nights to celebrate the two-month anniversary of their first time of making love. But it was more than the sex that attracted John. On Saturday night she had invited him to a movie with her and her boys, and then Sunday she had him over for a family dinner of fried chicken and mashed potatoes. At first, she had been protective of her sons, not wanting them to know she was dating John, but now he realized with a sense of warmth, she was letting him into that part of her life.

Claire returned with a bottle of wine, and she took him by the hand and led him up the stairs to her bedroom where a red-and-white tablecloth covered the wood floor. Large throw pillows bordered the tablecloth, and a white candle cast a yellow light across a fondue pot and several china plates, which were covered with sliced French bread, wedges of apples and pears, strawberries, and chunks of dark chocolate. After a long dinner, eating so much that he felt his stomach expanding, John leaned over the tablecloth to kiss Claire.

Her lips touched his for an instant before darting away. "Do you know I love your smell?" she asked.

"My smell?"

"Yes."

"I've been hoping I don't smell."

"Everyone has a scent," she said. "But don't worry; yours is earthy and rich and I love breathing it in when we're kissing or you're holding me. Are you ready for dessert?"

"Dessert?" He found himself grinning from her comment about his scent. "I'm not sure where I could put it right now."

"This will increase your appetite before satisfying it."

"Okay," he said.

"Great. Undress."

"What?" he laughed.

She took his wine glass and set it on her chest of drawers. He tried to kiss her, but she dodged his kiss while unbuttoning his shirt. She touched her hand to his chest, and then traced a path with her fingertips in the valley between his pectoral muscles. The phone rang.

"Aren't you going to get it?" he asked.

"Absolutely not."

She pulled his shirt off and flung it onto a chair. When the telephone ceased ringing, she picked up the headset and buried it under the blue-and-white embroidered pillow on the floor.

"I almost forgot," she said. "No distractions."

She reached for his waist, unbuckled his belt, and popped open the top button of his jeans. She stared into his eyes, popping open one button at a time, leaned him onto her bed, and tugged the jeans off his legs.

"Claire . . . ." He reached for her, remembering the first time together in the shower when he had brought her to orgasm over and over with cunnilingus until the water had turned ice cold.

"Not now." She touched two long, firm fingers to his lips. "I want you to lay still, flat on your stomach."

John did as she said. From beneath the bed, she pulled out a plastic bottle, clicked open the lid, and poured a thick liquid onto his back. She rubbed her warm hands into his flesh, swirling the cool lotion across his back. She massaged the breadth of his back, pressing her palms firmly against his muscles, dragging her fingernails lightly against the surface of his skin, then digging deep into the tight muscles of his rounded shoulders.

He groaned. "Feels great."

"Enjoy." She swept her fingertips across his back to his shoulders, and then down to his buttocks. She pressed harder, rubbing deep into the flesh of his butt. His erection bore into the mattress. He turned to embrace her.

"*No,*" she said. "Wait. Hold still and *feel.*"

He lay back down and she touched the back of his thighs. She kneaded her hands into his legs, releasing soreness in muscles previously unknown to him. When she rubbed the balls of his feet, he felt tension dissipate in a way that was nearly orgasmic; he imagined melting into a pool of liquid as malleable as the body lotion.

"Turn over," she whispered.

As he did, he tried to kiss her.

She gently pushed him onto his back.

Claire squeezed out more lotion, squished it between her palms, grabbed his foot, and tugged gently on his little toe. She worked each toe on both feet, and then rubbed her way up his shins and thighs. She pulled his underwear down.

"I love you, Claire." He reached for her. "I want you."

She grabbed his hand, returning it to his side. "I don't want you to *do* anything right now," she said. "Close your eyes. Just feel."

He flickered his eyelids shut and felt a tingling pleasure where Claire's fingers danced. She touched him with light, teasing strokes, her fingers skittering across his abdomen. She rubbed his chest, kneading, touching, releasing fatigue deep in the muscles. She paused; he felt nothing and waited. Then he felt a soft sweeping, like a faint breeze, across his chest. Peeking through half-closed eyes, he saw Claire leaning her head upside down, her hair falling onto his chest, swishing her hair back and forth. She caressed him with the tips of thousands of long, blonde strands.

He closed his eyes. Warmth again pulsated across his chest.

He felt her breath, a slow and gentle exhale, blowing across his chest, his lips, his eyelids.

Her warm lips pressed against his mouth, and then her tongue thrust against his own. He felt her body grinding firm against his flesh.

Just feel, she had said.

"Claire, I feel . . ." He was scared but her passion gave him the courage to say the words aloud. "So alive."

He called Claire the next afternoon. After she answered the phone, he hesitated, but he felt too brimming with feeling to contain his words. "I love you, Claire."

"I love you today too."

"Today?"

"Yes, today," she said. "Sometimes I feel confused in this crazy world, but not today. Today, after making passionate love with you last night, I know I love you."

"Well, good."

"This afternoon after I got home, I sniffed my pillow and smelled your scent again."

"And tell me again, that's a good thing, right?"

"It's a wonderful smell and it was a wonderful night."

He found himself smiling so wide that he was glad Claire couldn't see him. "This may sound corny to you, but I was almost sorry when morning came. It was so good to sleep with you last night."

"Nights come and go, and lots of times the feelings go with them. But not last night's feeling today. I feel like a giddy teenager, oozing with romance. I love you, today, John Arthur Anderson, and you can come over again tonight if you want to."

So he did. It was late when he arrived after conducting a psychology testing battery at the university clinic.

"You're tired," she said.

"I'm okay."

"Be honest," she said. "I can tell."

"A little tired. It was an awful long day."

"Come." She took him by the hand to her bedroom, pushed on his shoulders until he sat on the edge of her bed, unbuttoned his shirt, and announced that she was going to give him a back rub.

"A back rub after last night's full body rub?" he asked. "How come you're being so good to me?"

"Because I'm in love with you today."

"You're going to spoil me."

"No, I won't." She rubbed his upper back. "Just enjoy it now."

"I am." He twisted, rising up to kiss her. "And I loved last night too."

She pushed him back to bed and massaged harder into his trapezius muscle. "Do you know I love our lovemaking?"

"Good to know." He grinned. "Me too."

"No, really," she said. "Sex has been a painful part of my life. When I was a girl growing up, my mom would sometimes catch me masturbating and she would always slap me and scold me harshly, saying that was a terrible thing to do."

"I'm sorry." He remembered his mom catching him touching himself once when he was very young and telling him that was nasty. "Not exactly the healthiest message for a parent to give their child about sexuality."

"It would happen a lot, actually. It wasn't really about sex, but something I'd do when I felt tense and pressured." She paused, as if waiting to see if he was judging her. "She got to the point where she would fly into a rage when she would catch me masturbating and hit me harder and harder."

"Oh, Claire. You didn't deserve that." He wondered if her mom was sexually repressed—and was his mom?

"Sex was a troubled area in my marriage too," she said. "I really didn't feel much pleasure with Ted, and I wasn't very interested in having sex with him. Of course, Ted was hypercritical of me, saying something was wrong with me and my libido."

"There's nothing wrong with you, Claire." He loved saying her name; it came easily to his voice with a lyrical sound, unlike the plodding tone of Joanie. "Making love with you is wonderful."

"Before you, I felt bad about myself as a woman. I believed there was something wrong with me sexually."

"You, Claire, are a passionate, sensual, sexual woman."

"And with you, sex is a delightful pleasure." She paused, and then in a low voice, whispered, "It's healing for me."

Her lips nuzzled the corner of John's cheek. He craned his neck to meet her in a kiss. They made love—intercourse that John imagined was like a huge wave: swelling, mounting, rolling and then finally crashing onto the shore.

He spoke softly later, his lips close to her ear, stroking her back as she lay naked on top of him. "It's more than just sex," he said. "You've touched me at some deep level. After years of being caught up with school, of doing exactly what I'm supposed to do, of going through the motions of life with Joanie, it feels like I'm emerging from some huge shell."

She nudged his cheek. "Come out of the shell, John. Come out and play with me and live."

He slept with Claire, dreaming dreams he couldn't remember but which left him happy.

He tried to hold onto the feeling even as he longed for more close times with her. The next afternoon he planned to stop by her house with a bouquet of flowers to surprise her for their two-month anniversary. Before he left his apartment, his phone rang, and he hoped it was Claire, perhaps calling him with an anniversary greeting of her own?

Instead he heard his mother's voice on the end of the telephone.

"Hi Mom." It was unlike her to call him in the middle of the day, especially lately, as she had fluctuated between being standoffish and judgmental since his separation. "How are you?"

"Disappointed."

He tried to sit with the following silence and though he knew better, he couldn't stop himself from asking. "What about?"

"You know what," she said. "You left Joanie."

He did know, and he dreaded the lecture that was coming, expecting it to be little different than several other conversations in the past two months. "I've told you, Mom, Joanie and I were having problems and we just needed some time apart to think about things."

"*You* wanted the time," she said. "I spoke again with Joanie last night and she's very upset."

"Separation is hard on everyone, Mom, including her, me, and also you. I get that."

"She said she's willing to go to marital counseling." Her tone was moral and haughty. "But you're not even willing to do that."

The thought of going to marital counseling with Joanie was inconceivable given his feelings for Claire. "It doesn't really fit for me right now, Mom."

"A marriage therapist on the Phil Donahue Show said that any marriage can be saved."

John bit the inside of his lip so he wouldn't respond.

"He's written a book about it." Her voice rose in pitch, as she started to sound flustered as well as angry. "You need to at least give it a try for twenty sessions."

"I know you're trying to help, but I'm not going to do that now."

"Why can't you just try? You're being selfish."

"And why can't you just accept me and my decisions?" He knew his next comment would land as a low blow, but he was angry. "Nona does." His mom had long harbored feelings of inferiority in comparison to her own mother and was jealous of the closeness between John and his grandmother.

"The hell with you then," his mom said. "If you are too selfish to even try marital counseling, the hell with you."

Her words stung and left John with a mix of anger and hurt after she abruptly hung up. She had said before John and Joanie's wedding that he was too young to get married. True, she had always been polite toward Joanie, but in a reserved, stiff way and she had never really embraced her. Since the separation, however, his mom had elevated Joanie to near saintly status. It was as if his mom had reacted to his separation from Joanie personally, like he had boldly taken one more act in his own separation from her sphere of influence. Her "the hell with you" words rattled inside his mind, but he wanted to forget about the conversation and enjoy the anniversary celebration with Claire.

When he pulled into Claire's driveway, he saw her two doors down, reaching into the backseat of a faded, 1960s station wagon, unloading bags of groceries while an elderly man watched.

Claire shot John a sideways glance as he walked over. "Earl," she turned toward the elderly man. "This is John—a classmate."

John reached out and took the man's frail, liver-spotted hand in his own, saying it was nice to meet him.

"My pleasure." Earl was a short man—stooped shoulders added to this appearance—but a broad grin lit up his wrinkled face. "She's quite a gal."

"She is," John nodded. "Helping unload your groceries—that's nice."

"Unload them? She takes me grocery shopping every week."

"Really? That is nice."

"Takes me to the bank to deposit my check and to pay my bills first of every month too."

"I didn't know that." John looked at Claire. "She is sweet."

"Oh, she's a real sweetheart." The pride in Earl's smile made it look like he was talking about his girlfriend or daughter.

"And you're a character, Earl." She patted his arm. "Let me get the last of these groceries. John, wait here."

John mumbled a good-bye to Earl.

"Good to meet you, young man." Earl took one small, stutter step behind Claire, turned back toward John, and winked.

As he and Claire walked back to her house, John felt the churning of agitation and anger about his mother's call. He considered telling Claire about the conversation, but worried then she might agree with his mom and say he should go to counseling with Joanie. "Earl looks like he's getting up there," he said instead. "How old is he?"

"Ninety-one," she said.

"Did he lose his license?

"No, but he drives terribly. I have a bad feeling he's going to get into an accident someday—kill himself or somebody else."

"I didn't know you were helping him out."

"He lost his wife a few years ago," she said. "No kids—he's all alone."

"You're a sweet person, Claire."

"Sometimes," she said. "Sometimes not."

When they reached her walkway, he turned toward her. "I've got something for you."

"What?" She gave him a quick glance that seemed stern.

"It's in the car."

"I'll be in the house," she said.

He found her in the kitchen, rinsing dishes, and he raised up the bouquet of orchids.

"What for?" she asked, glancing away from the sink.

"Our anniversary," he forced a smile as a vague anxiety crept over him.

"What are you talking about?"

"Two months today since we first made love." He extended the flowers toward her. "Happy anniversary!"

"They're pretty." She brushed her hands quickly against a kitchen towel. "You shouldn't have spent the money but thank you."

"I wanted to."

She pulled out a vase from underneath a cabinet and took the flowers.

"These past two months have been so good for me." He watched her clip the ends of the orchid stems. "I'd felt like I'd been dying—suffocating with Joanie and drowning in grad school. It's been a special time with you."

"It has been special," she said.

"So," he paused, not completely sure how Claire would react. She was giving off some strange vibe. A conflicting mix of anxiety and exhilaration about his plan stirred in his gut, and he was unable to completely dismiss his mom's reaction from his mind. "I've been thinking we should plan a getaway trip to the West late this summer to camp and canoe along a mountain river. It can be our way of celebrating being done with all of our course and clinical work before the final push of getting our dissertations done and our Ph.D.s in hand"—and of being together for five or six months by then, he thought, but didn't want to say that aloud. "What do you say?"

"No." She set the flower vase on the dining room table.

"Why not?"

She whirled about. "I don't want to think about some vacation plans together months from now."

"Why?"

"Because," she said. "That's *too intimate*."

He remembered the night before, curled next to each other but laying upside down in the 69 position, each kissing the other's sex parts. After nights of knowing and embracing each other's bodies in the most private of places, how could talking about a trip together be too intimate? "Claire, a trip like this is something you've wanted to do for a long time, and it's something I've imagined for a long time too. It's like it's meant to be for us—it's synchronistic."

She shook her head, walked into the sunroom, pruned a yellowing leaf from a hanging philodendron, and sat in her rocking chair.

At first, he hung back, upset now with Claire and still angry with his mom, but then he followed Claire into the next room. "At least tell me what's going through your mind, will you?"

"John," she paused, staring at him as if she was preparing to remember how he looked. "It is nice to have some time together, and I do care about you, but this is a temporary relationship."

"A temporary relationship?" Something thick and heavy sank inside him, but he refused to believe her words.

"It's good we have each other at times right now," she said. "This is a crazy, transitional period—for both of us, just out of marriages. But the last thing I need is planning another long-term commitment."

The arguments formed quickly in his mind: now was the time when they needed something to look forward to, at least a trip together. That wish had taken shape after being in Claire's arms but now it was intensified by the stirring of guilt and even panic as he thought about Joanie and his mother's disapproval. His longing to travel with Claire was fed by more than negative emotions, however, for the reality he felt in his heart (and he sensed it in Claire's, too, when they lay together) was that their feelings for each other were so strong that their relationship could be permanent. He started to argue the points, but he stopped himself after seeing the hardness in Claire's chin line and feeling his own vulnerability— a feeling he wasn't sure if he wanted to fight against or run away from. "Okay, Claire. We don't have to plan the summer now."

"I wasn't expecting you today," she said. "You didn't ask to come over."

"Thought I'd surprise you." He guessed his next request would probably be shot down, too, but he wanted it so much while convincing himself that it might work out, that he asked anyway. "With our anniversary and all, I thought I could take you out for dinner."

She shook her head.

"After feeling so close the last two nights, I thought we could make it three nights in a row, you know?"

"No."

"Okay, then." He felt himself withdraw—it was an automatic reaction to her distancing, but he forced himself to try to stay with her. He waited, but she said nothing, so he kept talking. "How come? Are you mad?"

"No."

"Did I do something to upset you?"

"*Stop,*" she said. "It's not all about you."

"That's good to know," he said. His parents used to withdraw from one another when his mom was upset or his dad angry. "But what's going on? I'm still feeling close to you after the last two nights, but you're obviously in a different place."

"Feelings pass. I told you they would."

"Yeah, you did." He thought he should let the topic go but he couldn't stop himself from trying to talk her into being together, even as he felt a twinge of self-contempt. "And feelings resurface, too—and maybe they would for us if we were together again tonight."

"You don't get it, do you?"

"What?"

"I need space and you're crowding me."

"Sorry," he said.

"I need to be alone tonight," she said. "Don't make this into a huge deal."

"Okay," he said. "I won't."

⁓

John forced himself not to call Claire the next day—he was wanting her to make the next move, but he broke down late Friday afternoon, asking her over the phone if she wanted to go out for dinner on Saturday. But Claire said Ryan and Josh were going to spend Saturday night with her.

"I thought they were going to be with Ted this weekend?"

"The boys have been missing me big time," she said. "So, I worked it out with Ted for them to stay with me until Monday."

"I see. That makes sense," John said. "Hey, I got an idea. If you want, I'll take you all out for pizza."

"No," she said. "They need time alone with me."

"I understand," John said. But he didn't understand when he called Claire back on Monday and she said she didn't want to get together.

"Then how about something later in the week?" he asked.

Claire refused to make plans—saying she needed space after having the boys—and ended the call abruptly. John wondered what she meant by "needing space?" He hadn't seen her in five days! He knew that she sometimes fell into pockets of grief, sinkholes of loss that opened up out of nowhere, swallowing her. Perhaps having her boys had triggered more sadness? He just hoped she would climb her way back out. But then he wondered if the two nights together last week had been too much for her—that it felt "too intimate" and she was trying to back away from him? He fretted this was the case—perhaps she was plotting an end to their relationship? The idea saddened him, and then he was scared when she didn't return his calls for the next three days. It bothered him, too, that he hadn't heard from his mom since their last call. Undoubtedly, she was upset and ostracizing him too (his dad would be more open and accepting, but it was unlikely he would take a strong stand against his wife).

When Claire finally called back, he hoped she would be emerging from her self-imposed absence with offers of a fun date, perhaps drinks and dancing again at Laclede's Landing, but she only invited him to her house for a talk.

He worried when she had him sit on her sofa alone on her sofa, half-expecting she'd announce she and Ted were moving back in together or that she was going to stop seeing him for one reason or another.

"Claire, how are you?" he asked as soon as he sat down.

She grimaced and shook her head. "Sad."

"What?" Bart the beagle nudged John's knee and fixed a brown-eyed stare at John. John rubbed the dog's head. "Why didn't you call me?"

"Ted called." She brought a coffee cup to her lips.

"What?" John asked.

"He's moving another woman in with him."

"That's a shock." But he felt relieved. His worry that Ted and Claire would get back together evaporated. "Who is she?"

"Some woman." Then she shook her head as if correcting herself. "Rebecca—I need to get used to calling her by name if she's going to be living not just with Ted but with my boys half the time. He only met her six weeks ago on a spring skiing trip to Colorado."

"That's sudden, isn't it?"

"He told me that they're planning to get married as soon as we can get divorced."

"Oh, Jesus."

"She has three girls, about the same ages as Josh and Ryan. They want to have one big, happy family, he said."

"How are you doing?"

She swallowed a sip of coffee. "It's awful. It's the end of a dream."

"Oh, I'm sure."

"I tell myself it's probably for the best about Ted, but it's still a huge loss."

John scratched behind one of Bart's ears. "It has to be."

"I feel so sad, especially for the boys, about the family."

"Claire, I'm sorry. What did you do?"

"I just sat here the first couple of nights thinking. Then last night it hit me that it's really the death of a family. That's when I started to panic. I called Felice a bunch of times, but she wasn't home. I started to feel really scared and alone when she didn't answer."

"You could have called me."

"I started to, but I told myself, 'Claire, this is one of those times when you need to stand on your own two feet, like it or not, and face the feelings.' But I still felt like shit and cried. By then, the whole thing had become one of these experiences you just want to survive, you know? Just hang on until it's over. I decided then to sleep it off. I went to bed, but I fell into another crying jag. I missed Ted and the boys and the life we used to have. I cried so much that I didn't know what to do or how to stop, and by then, I just wanted the pain to end. So, I was lying in bed, crying, smelling my blanket—I smell the fringe of my blanket when I feel bad, I have ever since I was a little kid, did I ever tell you that?" She looked at him with darting eyes, and he wasn't sure if it was from shyness or pride.

"I didn't know that," he said gently.

"I felt utterly miserable and I wished I was dead. And then I noticed my nose was running, with snot dripping all over my blanket as I smelled it. I suddenly thought how funny I must look: a thirty-four-year-old woman crying and sniveling with snot running all over her blanket while she's desperately trying to smell it like a little child. I thought it was pretty funny—and then do you know what happened?"

"What?"

"I started farting. Just the loudest, smelliest farts you can imagine. I started roaring with laughter: I'm in bed, miserable with grief and crying, and I'm sniffing and farting nonstop." She laughed from her belly.

"I'm sorry it was such a hard time. But," he forced a chuckle. "I'm glad it all came out for you in the end, so to speak."

"I knew once I got to sniffing and farting, that I was going to make it through the night just fine."

John blinked and realized he felt embarrassed, though he wasn't sure if the embarrassment was for Claire or him. But he slid across the loveseat cushion and hugged her. Her cheek, splashed with droplets of tears from her laughter, pressed warm against his face. "I'm glad you made it through all of that."

"Me too. And do you know what I need to do now?" She grimaced.

"What?"

"Poop." She laughed. "Don't you sometimes just suddenly have to poop?"

John felt himself flush and Claire hurried into the half-bath at the end of the sunroom. He rubbed the beagle under his throat. Bart's cocked head dangled toward John's hand, the dog's eyes glazed, mesmerized by the scratching.

Claire yelled out something from the bathroom.

"What Claire?"

"Do you want more coffee?"

"No, thanks."

"Help yourself if you do."

John shook his head. She was so different: if he felt a bowel movement pressing, he'd try to hold it until he was home alone. But not Claire. She not only announced her intentions and initiated a bowel movement, but also then carried on a conversation throughout her pooping.

The toilet flushed. Claire swooped by the coffee table, swept up her cup, and returned in a minute from the kitchen. She sat back down, gazed at John, and smiled.

"It's been good to talk with you," she said.

"It's been good to talk with you too," he said. "And it's good to see you again. I've missed you."

"You're a good friend. I appreciate your support," she said. "But it's getting late. I need to kick you out now so I can get some sleep."

"It's not that late." John checked his watch. "9:05."

"You know me, I like to get to bed early."

"Yeah." He hesitated. "You still can, though. I was hoping maybe we could sleep together."

"No."

"*No.* Just like that huh?" He faked a laugh. "That's one of the things that I love about you Claire. You know your own mind, no hesitation. Can I ask why?"

"I'm too raw. The loss of the family feels too fresh."

"I meant I could just hold you."

"No. I need to be alone." She stood up. "But I'll walk you to the door."

John took a last sip of coffee, letting the warm liquid linger in his mouth before swallowing, and then he ambled into the living room. He picked his jacket from the coat-tree but struggled with connecting the zipper. Claire's long fingers interlaced his, threading the zipper, pulling it up.

"Thanks," he muttered.

"Sure."

"Well, bye. It was good to see you." He backed away, toward the door.

"Come here, screwball," she said.

Claire opened her arms and he stepped into her hug. She held him tight, her arms crisscrossing his back like girders. Neither spoke, but John felt warmth flow—almost jump, like electrons between atoms—where their bodies touched.

"Claire," he pressed his moist lips against the top of her blonde head. "I love you."

"I know." She cinched her arms tighter against his back.

She seemed content in this embrace, so he didn't move. "I love you, *lots*, Claire."

She cocked her head back and gazed into his eyes. She reached up, stepping up on tippy-toes, and pressed her lips against his. They kissed in one long embrace, her tongue pressed into mouth and her fingers slipped between their bodies. She unzipped his jacket, and her hand found his top shirt button, deftly popping it open. She undid each button in sequence and spread open his shirt. She traced her fingertips across his chest, unraveling the curly hair of his chest. Her mouth, warm and moist, slid down the side of his neck and chest.

He massaged her long blonde hair. The closeness he felt swelled—a feeling that was well worth his mother's disapproval and the loss of Joanie. "You mean so much to me."

She scooted up his chest, thrusting her lips onto his, gnashing teeth in a rush to kiss. She pulled him away from the front door, toward the living room sofa. She yanked off his jacket, shirt, pants. She pulled her sweater over her head and slipped off her pants. She leaned him onto the sofa cushions.

"Let me caress you," he said.

"Shh." She pressed her fingers against his mouth, and then replaced it with her lips. She gripped his penis, inserting it inside her. They rolled together, synchronized and rhythmic, like waves. She sat up on him, thrusting harder, her hair dangling into his face, her eyes closed to narrow slits, her forehead creased in concentration. Her white breasts, long and full like gourds, hung toward him.

Her breathing grew more rapid, and then jagged.

"Claire," he whispered.

She sang out a deep, long cry.

Her voice broke as she cried out once more. She fell onto him, and wetness trickled against his chest. For a moment, he was unsure what was happening, and then he realized tears were streaming onto his flesh as she sobbed.

CHAPTER 13

Claire wiggled out of John's arms and slipped out of bed. "We should go for a run," she said.

John rolled over and stretched. "You mean now—first thing in the morning?"

"Yes, silly."

"I hate running in the morning. Besides, I don't even have any running shorts."

Claire yanked open her desk drawer and pulled out black cotton shorts with wide white stripes on the side. "Here."

He planted his feet on the wood floor and held the shorts next to his hips. "I don't know. These look pretty girly."

"It'll just be me looking." She reached out and cupped his testicles in her hand. "And I know you're all man."

"Hmm." He leaned forward to kiss her. He wanted to make love with her this morning—it was their eight-month anniversary, but he had judiciously decided not to speak the words aloud. The last two times he had told her it was a monthly anniversary, she had withdrawn from him, as if the recognition that their relationship was evolving into something long-term was more than she could consciously accept. "Maybe we could go back to bed for our morning exercise instead?"

"C'mon you." She slapped his chest. "We're going for a run now—at least I am."

They stretched their hamstrings on Claire's front porch in the chilly October air, and he admired her firm thighs. "You're beautiful," he said.

"Stop! We're going running."

"What? I'm just saying you're beautiful." He tilted his head, trying to look innocent. "Really. And you're kind and caring. I appreciate how you've been there for me." She had comforted him the week before when his divorce had been final. He had known a divorce was what he wanted, and now it was necessary: a few months after the separation, Joanie had gotten pregnant by Steve and they planned to marry. Still, John had been surprised by the grief that had overwhelmed him. On the worst night, he'd been crying in an uncontrollable way that had frightened him, but Claire drove to his apartment and held him, singing soft folk songs until he fell asleep. Her tender comfort had deepened his appreciation for her. She was a blend of empathy and passion that he had never experienced before in one woman.

The telephone rang from the house and Claire scurried back to answer it. John peeked at the sky from the covered porch. A gray mass—if it was more than one cloud the distinctions were imperceptible—had settled over St. Louis, and it had rained almost daily for two weeks. He grieved again the passing of summer into fall, a season that left him tired and with a vague sense of dread. He had loved their summer together. They had had fun playing softball and taking her boys on picnics and to water slides, but they had been too busy with prelims and dissertation proposals to do what he most desired: a trip to the mountains for camping and canoeing. He knew, though he didn't want to fully admit it to himself, that he wasn't ready for such a trip yet, but he hadn't given up on the idea. He'd convinced himself they could make the trip next summer after they had hopefully finished their doctorates and he had more time to prepare himself.

John was bobbing for his toes, trying to loosen his tight hamstrings, when Claire's next-door neighbor clamored through her front door with her five children. Mary's brown hair, speckled with gray, was bunched tight around her head, and she was wrapped in a pastel floral bathrobe. He found it hard to believe, but Claire insisted Mary was only three years older than herself. Through her thick, brown-framed glasses, she was staring at John. He waved, mumbled a good morning greeting, and realized he was smiling sheepishly. Mary gave an abrupt, stiff nod, said something sharply to her oldest daughter, and herded the children into her gray, submarine-shaped 1960s Plymouth for safe passage to their parochial school.

Out of the corner of his eyes, he watched Mary start her car, and he wondered what she thought. Disapproval, maybe even disgust, he thought that two unmarried people—worse yet, Claire was still legally married to a different partner—would be sleeping together. Mary was very Catholic—like John's mother, and he knew his mother would also be disapproving. In fact, apparently his mother already was. He had told Nona during the summer about Claire, and then Nona had told his mom, who reportedly was very upset he was seeing someone else, especially an older woman with children. His mom had not answered his calls in two weeks—she was a pro at the silent treatment when she was upset. She had never approved of premarital sex, anyway, lecturing him about the immorality of it while he was growing up and reacting with an aura of personal woundedness when she found he and Joanie had snuck away for a weekend together at the age of eighteen. But that was his mom's view and he recalled the joy of making love with Claire the night before. If that was sinful, then something was wrong with whomever was making up the sin list. He decided he had no use for Catholicism, no idea what God was about, or if He even existed. On an impish impulse, he grinned and waved wildly at Mary as she maneuvered her gray bomb away from the curb.

"Ready to run?" The front door slapped shut behind Claire and her dogs.

"Who was on the phone?"

"Ryan. He wanted me to see if he'd left his library book here—of course he did. I'll drop it by Ted's later. Come on."

Claire pranced down the porch steps and broke into a run. Bart and Serendipity scampered past her, their toenails clicking against the sidewalk, and John raced to catch up. The dogs exuded boundless energy on the run. A dozen times on the three-mile loop, Bart and Serendipity streaked off behind houses or onto the golf course, only to soon return to Claire's and John's side, or at least Serendipity did. As they entered the final block before Claire's house, Bart strayed further away, trotting down a side street. Claire called several times, but Bart ran out of view, around the next corner while Serendipity raced back.

"Good girl—you come when you're called." John reached down to pat her head. Serendipity, her yellow tail curved like a scimitar, trotted just ahead. "Do you want me to go after Bart?"

"No, he'll show up, baying at the front door to be let in when he's good and ready."

"I love Bart a lot," John said. "But Serendipity listens much better."

"Bart's a stubborn stinker," Claire said.

They rounded the corner, surprising two rabbits squatting behind a large oak. Serendipity streaked toward them, stretching out the stubby legs of her short body as she galloped. The rabbits froze for a microsecond, before darting in different directions, one zigzagging toward shrubs, the other rabbit into the street where a car approached.

"Stop!" John yelled. But Serendipity chased the rabbit and John ran after them both. The car driver was late seeing them, but then braked hard. The rabbit, a yard ahead of the dog, ran head first into the side of the car's front tire; the rabbit's head recoiled, a grimace crossed its face, before blood sprang from the side of its head. The rabbit fell to the street. Its body twisted in a spasm, and then lay still.

Serendipity, who had stopped with the car, poked a curious nose toward the bleeding rabbit before John grabbed the dog by the collar. "Bad dog!" he yelled, yanking her back.

After they jogged the half-block to Claire's house, after she had taken a black trash bag back for the rabbit's body, John sat fidgeting in the sunroom while Claire brewed tea. He eyed Serendipity critically as she stole toward him, her potato-shaped head lowered and trembling side to side. Her tail drooped toward the floor but wagged slightly.

"That was a bad thing to do," he scolded. "What are you doing, attacking a poor rabbit? Was that rabbit doing you any harm? *No*. It was just trying to live its life."

Serendipity slunk back into the dining room.

"That's right: hang your head and think about what you've done."

Claire smirked as she handed him a cup of tea.

"It's not so funny," he said. He realized he was playing up his admonishments of Serendipity for Claire's benefit, but he also felt an agitation churning inside that he didn't understand and that his humor couldn't placate.

"I know," she said. "I hate seeing animals hurt or killed. It really bothered you, too, didn't it?"

"Yeah, I've always liked watching rabbits. It's one of my favorite things about St. Louis—you don't see them like that in California neighborhoods. Plus, can you imagine the terror the poor thing felt—being chased by a dog that wanted to tear it apart and then the shock as it ran headfirst into the car?" Another image broke into his mind then—of the young Vietcong being shot in the head by a South Vietnam official. John had only seen the photo once as a young teen when he opened the morning newspaper, and though he had not thought of it for years, the image had imprinted deep in his mind: the recoiling of the head, the grimace—it was the same look for rabbit and man. The image had made him sick then and so did the memory now. He suddenly wished he could go back to bed with Claire for the day.

"It's sad," Claire said about the rabbit. "But I had to laugh, listening to you scold Serendipity like she could think about the things you were saying."

"I know." He had worried as a boy about how his mom would react to the execution photo—she was very sensitive about suffering. He hid the front page behind the sports section, but later he found his mom looking at the front page, shaking her head. "I'm sorry," he had told his mom. "Life is cheap in the Orient," she said then. "People can be so cruel—look at this." She pulled from the kitchen table an envelope with pictures of dogs, cats and rabbits strapped onto operating tables at research laboratories, saying a solicitation letter had come in the mail from an animal rights group. "Vivisection. How can people be so horrible to innocent animals? They are all God's creatures—look at this poor bunny's big brown eyes. I hope those scientists burn in hell."

Claire grinned over her teacup. "And the things you said! You sounded like a parent. I thought, John probably doesn't know it, but he's practicing for the day he'll have a child instead of a dog to discipline. I won't be there to see it, but you'll be a good father."

The sick feeling spread inside him and was followed by something desperate. It was less about having a child together—he wasn't even sure what he felt about having children, other than it had been expected of him by Joanie and his father—than about being with Claire permanently. "Who knows—maybe you'll be there to see it as a coparent."

"No." She took a sip of her tea. "But maybe we'll be able to stay as distant friends or colleagues by then."

"You never know." But she seemed to know, he thought, and that deepened his desperation. "I could see us getting married someday."

"John, I'm nearly a decade older—"

"Actually, it's only six years and a few months or so."

"I have two adolescent boys and I'm in a different life stage. This is good, but it's only for now, for this crazy, transitional period in both of our lives."

"It is good, and it is a crazy and transitional period in both of our lives, but I don't know what lies ahead." Anger swelled within him, which he preferred to the other feelings. "Neither do you really, so I'm not sure how you can sit there sounding so certain."

"John, listen to me." She slowed her words down. "It's *not* going to happen."

"It's not so impossible or crazy to imagine that we'll transition together and be married someday and maybe even have a child together."

"Stop!" She slapped her cup against the coffee table. "Why do you do this?"

"What?"

"You don't want to accept this, I know, but this time hear me: I've got my own life, and it's separate from yours. I have a separate future, a separate direction. I'm *not* something you can just latch on to and hold. Do you understand me?"

"So, you have what?" He knew they were way past a rational conversation, but it felt better to argue than to accept her position. "A fucking crystal ball? You know in advance how everything is going to turn out?"

"I do on this one."

He changed his clothes and left, neither he nor Claire saying anything more. It was juvenile, he thought afterward, giving each other the silent treatment. He considered calling her, but he didn't want to be the first one to reach out after a fight, at least not this time.

That evening he debated giving Claire a call. Twice he went to the telephone, but both times he put it down before dialing. He read until past midnight, but he still couldn't sleep. He tossed and wrestled with his sheets, thinking about Claire. He wished she had called. She was as aggravating as she was wonderful.

John pulled himself out of a dream—he was on a speedboat with Claire and her boys, and then Josh was banging driftwood against the hull—when a sharp crack resounded against his window.

"What the hell?" He stumbled from his bed to the window. Claire stood directly below, next to the first-floor apartment. Her arm was cocked, a small rock wedged against her fingers.

Seeing John, she smiled, waved, and dropped the rock. She pointed toward his front door. John nodded and waved back. He checked his alarm clock—it showed 6:14 a.m. He shook his head and laughed.

When he unlocked the front door, Claire stood at the top of the stairwell.

"Want to call a truce?" she asked.

"Sure." He opened the door wider. "Come in."

She sat on the love seat, motioning for John to join her.

"You have your perspective on the future of our relationship," she said. "And I have mine. I want you to know mine, John, and to have no false illusions. I want you to know what I *know* will eventually happen."

"I know *your* view." He had been glad to see her, but he felt upset at the certainty in her voice.

"Yes—my view. And I know your thoughts. They're different, but we don't have to force one on the other. And since our time is limited—*actually*, I guess everyone's time is limited." The corner of her mouth sank into a crooked smile. "But knowing that, I'd say let's enjoy each other today and not fight over tomorrow."

"Well, good, but I still think it's important for us to recognize the possibility of a future. Otherwise, you can block yourself from actualizing it." He caught himself trying to convince Claire and realized that would start another argument. "But, yeah, okay—I hear what you're saying, and I agree. I'm in favor of this truce."

To his surprise, she hugged him. Then she pulled back just as quickly.

"Let's go on that canoe trip we've talked about," she said.

"To the mountains?"

"No, silly. We don't have time for that one—to the Ozarks."

A surge of adrenaline pulsed through his chest. "When?"

"Today. Today and tomorrow, actually."

"Today? Just like that?" His chest tightened and he remembered the sensation of being squeezed too hard as a child in a bearhug by an older boy in the neighborhood. "Something like that takes planning, Claire. I've got a lot to do today and tomorrow."

"Like what?"

"Like working on my research. I planned to do another analysis and get it written up tomorrow." Those tasks were more ambitious that he'd previously planned, but they sounded convincing and necessary when he heard his own words.

"You'd really choose that over camping and canoeing?"

"I also have a meeting at eleven this morning with Crebs on my dissertation."

"That's a problem." Her eyes darted. "I'll tell you what. Let's leave after your meeting—say twelve thirty sharp, camp this evening, canoe all day tomorrow and camp out again tomorrow night before coming back really early the next morning. I have to be back by two Thursday for the class I'm TAing, but that'll give us enough time. It'll be a good couple of days away. Can't you see us out there, gliding through crystal clear water?"

Instead, something like nausea rolled through his stomach. "I'd like to go, I just feel like I'm falling behind and want to get some things accomplished."

She laughed. "I love you, John Anderson, but have you ever considered that maybe you're a tad bit rigid? Wait—let me see how I can put this in a different light that's not critical. Is staying here and working on your research today—this special day of your life that will never pass this way again—is that what you most want out of life? Or would you rather reach out and embrace a new adventure—and in so doing, embrace this *woman*?" She drew out the last word slowly, exaggerating the o vowel. "This woman who is opening her heart to you?"

"I love it when you get theatrical," he said.

"And so?"

"So." He didn't want to go, not today. He needed more time to work up to a trip like that, but the enthusiasm in Claire's eyes inspired him. And he worried about telling her no. She had surprised him by this turnabout in her attitude, reaching out to him instead of withdrawing, and he didn't want to sabotage the moment.

"Yes, my love: I will do this with you today—how's that?"

"Ah, wonderful. A partner for a leap into a new adventure."

"Have you ever thought of becoming an actress?"

"As a matter of fact, yes. I might still do that in my life."

He kissed her.

"Umm, nice." She broke off the kiss. "But no more now."

"Why not?" He had visions of returning to bed with her.

"Too much to do before we leave. I've got to go."

"Oh, rigid, huh?"

"Meet me at my house at 12:20 sharp. Be ready, and we'll be on the road within ten minutes. And don't be late—as usual."

She rose from the love seat, started out the door, but circled back and kissed him with an open mouth, and then she left.

John had a hard time concentrating while prepping for his research meeting and he didn't mind the distraction of a ringing phone, wondering if Claire was calling with a last-minute request for him to pick something up for their trip?

"Hello, my dear boy." His grandmother's rich voice resounded through the line.

"Hi, Nona, how are you?"

She said he was fine and asked him about his studies. They talked for a few minutes over typical topics—the weather, Emerson, how John was eating and whether he was taking his multivitamins—before he sensed that she had an ulterior motive.

"Anything else going on?" he asked, trying to flush out the issue. "I've got to run for a meeting with my research advisor in a minute."

"Have you talked to your mother recently?"

He suspected Nona already knew the answer and that was her reason for the call. "Not in a while."

"You should give her a call."

"I've tried a couple of times last week and the week before. But she either hasn't called me back when I left a message or dad said she was busy and couldn't come to the phone, but then she never calls me back. So, the ball is in her court."

"She's been a little upset about this divorce business and your dating another woman."

"You know, Nona, it's my divorce, not hers, and yet she's been the one acting hurt and withdrawing."

"Your mother is overly sensitive, believe me, I know—"

"My divorce is my business and it's also my business if I'm dating and who I see." He felt blood starting to rush to his face. "She's being ridiculous now, anyway, since Joanie is pregnant by someone else and getting married."

"She can get on her high horse. Always has. But I think with Joanie getting married again, she's open to talk now. Why don't you give her a buzz again?"

"She can call me. When she's ready to talk, I'm open."

"Blood is thicker than water." It was one of his grandmother's favorite expressions. "She's your mother and she needs you to reach out to her."

"Not sure that's going to happen. Sorry, I got to get to my meeting with my professor."

"Don't be mad," she said. "I love you."

"Love you too." He dearly loved his grandmother, but she pampered his mother's moody ways too often. They had a strange relationship in ways. His grandmother was clearly the stronger one, something his mother resented, and though Nona could be dismissive of his mom's complaints at times, Nona also would do whatever it would take to ensure his mom's happiness. In many ways, John had also tried over his life to make his mom happy, but he told himself he was no longer willing to sacrifice his own happiness.

After his dissertation meeting, he pulled into Claire's driveway at ten past noon. Her car was missing, and he wondered why she wasn't home, but after he let himself in, he saw next to the door she'd piled a tent, sleeping bags, a grocery bag packed with cooking supplies, and a stuffed Army-green duffel bag. He carried these items to his trunk where he'd stored a bag with his clothes and a cooler with a bottle of wine and a six pack that he hoped would help calm his nerves on the trip. He brewed a pot of hot water in her kitchen, and then sipped tea in the sunroom. Without wanting or even intending to do so, he imagined himself on the river. Tightness pinched his lungs.

The dining room clock chimed half-past the hour. He wondered where the hell Claire was. He fixed more tea, returned to the sunroom, and saw in the backyard a rabbit sitting in the sunlight along the bushes. Claire's black cat crouched in the grass, stalking the rabbit.

He threw open the back door. "Go on! Damn cat—go!" He grabbed one of the boy's boots from the porch step and hurled it at the cat. The cat fled to the side of the house and the rabbit scampered into the bushes.

Saved that one, he thought, retrieving the boot. But not the one that Serendipity chased into the car. That one was dead. Dead—and what? He didn't know and pushed away the question, remembering again his mom and the photos of the Vietcong and the rabbits on the research tables. She had complained bitterly another time about a neighbor who had taken a job with an optical research company that performed research on rabbits. He liked that his mom was sensitive to animal rights, even if she tended to tread on his.

It was nearly one o'clock. It wasn't like Claire to be late, especially this late. The image of a car crash seized his mind. He tried to dismiss the worry with contempt for his own anxious nature.

A few minutes after the dining room clock chimed one, the front door swung open.

"Where have you been?" He heard the edge to his voice.

"Talking with Lyle," Claire said. "I ran into him right as I was leaving campus, and I wanted to visit a minute."

"More than a minute, I'd say."

"He was almost killed this morning."

"*What?*"

"He was driving on the interstate and just a mile before the campus turnoff, a big truck moved in front of him—and smashed the car in front. The truck and this car went sliding across the highway while Lyle slammed on his brakes, just missing them. Less than an inch, he said. The truck rolled over, and the car was crushed between the truck and the center divider." Claire stared at him.

"Lyle's okay?" John asked.

"Yes, but shaken up. He could have been crushed to death if he hadn't swerved in time." Claire plopped herself into the rocker. "Less than an inch and he could have been killed."

"I know—you already said that, but he's okay, thankfully."

"He's afraid the driver of the other car was killed. He doesn't know for sure—he got off the highway and called the police. But he said all he could see in his rearview mirror was crumpled, twisted metal. He's afraid the other driver was crushed to death."

"I hope not."

Claire lit up a cigarette and rocked back.

John fidgeted, unsure of what to do or say. "I loaded up the car. We're ready to go."

"Life is so fragile."

He left her, walking into the kitchen. Next to the toaster, he spotted a plastic grocery bag with hot dog buns, potato chips, cookies, and a can of beans. He grabbed the bag, checked the refrigerator, and pulled out a pack of hot dogs.

"I think I got everything." He held up the grocery bag as he walked back. "Claire, are we going to go?"

"I want to sit awhile." She looked away. "This shook me up."

"I'm sorry it did," he forced himself to say, though he felt agitation, not empathy. "But the plan was to go, so unless we're going to forget the whole thing, let's follow the plan."

She stiffened in the rocking chair. "Plans get interrupted sometimes."

"I know it must have been scary for Lyle, but he *wasn't* in the car crash, and chances are 9 out of 10 he wouldn't have gotten hurt, and 99 out of a 100, he wouldn't have gotten seriously hurt, and 999 out of a 1,000 that he wouldn't have gotten killed."

"It upset *me*. That's not some ridiculous probability statement—it's my emotions. *I'm scared and sad.* Do you understand that?"

He knew immediately he'd acted like an ass. "Yes. Now I do."

She said nothing, her nose flaring, as she glared at John.

"I'm sorry," he said. "I didn't mean to sound so insensitive. I just wanted to get going if we're going, rather than sitting around here wondering, but that's okay. We can sit and talk. We don't even have to go if you don't want to."

She crushed her cigarette into a ceramic ashtray. "Let's go."

"Really, we don't need to go right away—or at all. It's up to you. I'm sorry for being impatient."

"*No.*" She told him she was going to pee, pack the rest of the refrigerated food, and then they'd go.

Once they were on the freeway, Claire stared out the window.

"Sorry if I got uptight," John said. "Sometimes I get a fixed idea of what I'm going to do and then I get frustrated if plans get up in the air. Plus, when you were so late, I worried that something bad had happened, you know?"

"I understand."

"How are you feeling about Lyle and all that now?"

"I don't want to talk about it anymore."

They drove without speaking. He hated the silent treatment—when he was growing up, his mom wouldn't speak with his dad when she was upset and she also used it selectively with John—but he understood Claire being mad. He'd been a jerk. He was surprised and somehow both relieved and disappointed she still wanted to go on the trip. Claire pulled a paperback from her backpack, curled her legs up Indian style on the passenger's seat, and became engrossed in the book. John stole glances at her and after another half-hour, ventured another question.

"You can read in the car—doesn't make you sick?"

"Usually doesn't bother me."

He sensed she had thawed, so he engaged her in brief conversation, first about her dissertation research, and then about camping and the river. But mostly they traveled in silence. In the vacuum of conversation, he sorted out a lingering mixture of annoyance and defensiveness about his grandmother's call. She could be bossy, but he had learned long ago that he could still follow his own mind and she would love him nonetheless, and he, in turn, loved her with his whole heart. Nona was accepting, not judgmental, and she did not hold grudges, unlike his mom. True, his mom could be very compassionate for those suffering—he had probably learned this from her—but it dawned on him she often reserved her compassion for those she thought were most deserving, like her dogs who always listened to her or at least didn't talk back.

After ninety minutes, Claire directed him to turn onto a two-lane country road. The road rose and fell and twisted through hilly pastureland. After a few miles, he became nauseated, but he dismissed it as the normal queasiness that sloshes in the pit of your stomach after too many winding curves. Fifty miles later, after the farmland had given way to oak and dogwood forests, they turned off for the campground. There were few campers in the park, and they picked a spot near the end of the campground, away from the handful of other cars and trailers and close to the river. They pitched the tent—Claire directing and laughing at his outdoor ineptness—and then she settled under a sycamore with her book. He sat next to her, gazed at the autumn sky, which was lustrous blue and expansive, wider somehow here than over the city. Claire scooted back, leaning herself against the chalky white-and-tan sycamore trunk. From her big, orange backpack, she pulled out her journal and turned to an open page.

"It's beautiful out here," he said. "I'm glad we came."

"It is." She had nested her paperback inside the journal and was skimming its pages.

"I'm surprised the leaves are changing colors here already. It seems so soon."

She flipped through her book.

"How deep did you say the river is?" he asked.

"John, listen to me. I need uninterrupted quiet time to write about some of the ideas from this book."

"Okay, sorry." Talking helped the uneasiness that he was feeling, but he told himself to relax, to just enjoy being outdoors and next to Claire. He leaned back against the sycamore, just around the curve of the trunk from her. A breeze severed a handful of shriveling leaves above his head. He watched the leaves, which were the color and shape of huge corn flakes, float to the ground. Soon he caught himself playing a mindless game, trying to guess which leaf would fall next.

He tired of the game. Claire was writing fervently in her journal and he whispered that he was going for a walk. She nodded without looking up. He walked without thinking about the direction, following the trees that burned with color, and he found himself at the river's edge. The river was only twenty yards wide and the bottom was visible all the way across. The water was still, peaceful. Nothing to be afraid of, he thought, but his chest tightened as he unwillingly pictured he and Claire falling from a canoe into the river. He closed his eyes tight and urged himself to *stop*.

He jogged back to the campsite. Claire smiled at him.

"Sorry if I was ornery," she said. "I wanted to get my ideas down on paper while they were fresh."

"That's okay. Is this for your teaching assistantship?"

"I was reading the assignment for the Death and Dying class I TA, but the writing is for me, personally—not the class. It was the chapter on Kierkegaard in Ernest Becker's book, *The Denial of Death*. Ever heard of it?"

"No, but I like the title."

"Most people do," she said. "And that's the problem, but it's a brilliant book about issues we should all face—not just as psychologists, but as people."

She waved her hands for emphasis as she spoke, and he realized he loved how Claire loved ideas. "Like what?"

She described in detail Becker and Kierkegaard's analysis that depression resulted from people trading away their own authentic self-esteem while avoiding existential truths in exchange for social approval and a sense of comfort and security. John muttered the theory could be helpful in therapy with depressed clients.

"But it's not just depressed people—that's the power of this." She spoke quickly, the pitch of her voice higher. "Becker says normal people are also afraid to stand at their own center. We ingest our sense of right and wrong, our meanings, even our self-image from people around us. We become trapped in characteristic patterns, and these patterns prevent us from seeing ourselves as we truly are and from experiencing life fully. Most people are 'Philistines' as Becker and Kierkegaard described, settling for the security of living a culturally-approved but narrow life while 'tranquilizing' themselves with the trivial or with feeling they are special in some small way. And most of all, people deny their existential nature—their freedom, their need for personal meaning, the inevitability of death. Fascinating, don't you think?"

He wasn't so sure. "It's interesting, but kind of dark."

"Life is kind of dark, John."

"I know," he said. "But I mean what are his recommendations?"

"There's no simple, quick fixes, like out of a cheap self-help book." A sneer passed over her face. "Becker says people can live more free, open, and deeper lives, but to do so you have to break down your normal cultural routines, your own character defenses, and then recognize the existential truths. It's not easy, that's for sure. Do you want to hear what I wrote about this part and my own personal plan?"

He was much more interested in her ideas than Becker's. "Sure."

She opened her journal and read aloud:

"This realization of the inevitability of our personal death often results in a 'flood of anxiety,' as Becker writes. The flood of anxiety, however, can be a school, an education, a pathway for self-transcendence, breaking down a person's normal character defenses. The person may feel lost, and yet this is the beginning. For at this point, as Becker quotes from Ortega, the individual:

> looks life in the face, realizes that everything in it is problematic, and feels himself lost. And this is the simple truth—to live is to feel oneself lost—he who accepts it has already begun to find himself, to be on firm ground. Instinctively, as do the shipwrecked, he will look round for something to which to cling, and that tragic, ruthless glance, absolutely sincere, because it is a question of his salvation, will cause him to bring order to the chaos of his life. These are the only genuine ideas: the ideas of the shipwrecked.

She glanced at him, and then back to her journal:

"I have much yet to experience in life, some of which will be painful and some, like death, terrifying. How all this will affect me I do not yet know. But I do know that I will live my life different than the Philistine. Many people falter at the chasm between fear and courage, as Becker describes, but I want an intense, courageous life, one open to new experience. I choose to live my life by using 'anxiety as an eternal spring for growth into new dimensions of thought and trust,' and I choose to embrace life as an 'adventure in openness to a multidimensional reality,' as Becker said. But for me, I want that adventure based on a centeredness in myself, not as a surrender to a man or a family, not a capitulation to an institution nor a religion. I will not falter at the chasm of terror and authenticity. I will leap into a multidimensional reality from my own center."

Claire clapped her journal shut. Her eyes looked strange, perhaps wet, but he was sure the moisture was not from sadness but from intensity, a fire that radiated through her. She looked beautiful.

"Claire, it's great. It's really brilliant stuff: The analyses of Kierkegaard, Becker, and Claire Evers, though personally I still prefer the approach stated in the title: *The Denial of Death.*" He chuckled but saw Claire frown. "No, really, Claire, it's good—really good—what you've written and I'm inspired by your words. I don't remember it all exactly—it all runs together in my head—but some of what you wrote about using anxiety as an eternal springboard and leaping across the chasm into the adventure of a multidimensional reality—that was moving."

She spoke of her personal striving for "a multidimensional reality" amid her separation and her struggle to be free from the tugs and pushes of obligations placed on her from her estranged husband, her mother, her former church, and her socialized self. She said she wanted to be free to be herself, to experience all of life. She and John talked long after darkness had replaced the faint glow of sunlight.

Claire started a fire and they cooked a meal of hot dogs and beans. She pulled a hooded, black parka tight around her and huddled close to the fire while John shivered, drinking cold beer in the crisp night air. After dinner, she announced she was going to bed. John protested the early hour—it was only 9:05—but they were soon zipped tight in interlocking sleeping bags. He reached across the fluffy padding for Claire, inching his body tight against hers, and slipped his hands under her thermal undershirt.

"Ay! Your hands are freezing!" She pulled his hands from her back and brought them to her mouth. She blew over his fingers and palms until they were warm, and then tucked his hand back under her shirt. She kissed John, and they made love with their long underwear yanked only partially down.

Their sweaty bodies were sticky, and the goose-down sleeping bags radiated back their body heat. John felt hot—an absurd image crossed his mind of himself wrapped inside aluminum foil like a potato baking—but he still cradled Claire's warm body tight against his legs and chest. He caressed her hair with his fingers.

"I love you, Claire."

"Mmm. I love you too." She was falling asleep quickly after their lovemaking.

"But it's more than that, Claire. I respect you a lot."

She squeezed his hands between her fingers.

"I respect the way you are as a person," he said softly. "How you think, how you bring so much passion to life, how you want to live fully."

Claire's body jerked into sleep.

"You're a good person—good for me," he whispered. You help me grow, he thought, be open to life. He hoped then he was up for the task.

As he gazed through the dark at Claire, he felt something catch in his chest. He didn't have precise words for the feeling, but suddenly he felt very small and inexplicably bad. The feeling was familiar, he often felt that way as a child, but he understood its nature and origins no better now than then.

The faded brown-and-tan Jeep Wagoneer lumbered toward the river. The winding road was pocked with potholes, and the truck rattled as if it would fall apart. John leaned forward and grabbed the vinyl front seat to steady himself, but nausea still swirled in his stomach. Claire didn't seem fazed by the bouncy, swaying ride. She sat perched on the edge of her seat, talking nonstop with the driver about fishing. The rearview mirror showed leathery furrows that ran across the driver's forehead beneath his John Deere's cap, and down his cheeks. The driver probably looked older than his age, as if he'd spent his life outside and was prematurely wrinkled from the sun and elements. He was a quiet man but answered Claire's questions about hunting and fishing with a trace of enthusiasm in his Southern Ozarks twang.

"Excuse me," John said. "Do you think we'll have time to complete the canoe float before dark?"

"You won't have a lot of time to dilly-dally, but you ought to make the shorter run by dusk."

John leaned forward. "You're sure?"

"Sure as sure can be. The river's running fast. It's higher and rougher than usual from all the rain."

"But safe?" John asked.

The driver looked at John through his review mirror. "Should be."

"We wouldn't have to worry about the time if we hadn't gotten such a late start." As he spoke, John glanced at Claire, but she ignored him. In the morning, Claire had delayed the float plans, wanting to read more of Becker under the sycamore. John had asked her repeatedly if they were still going to canoe the river, but she'd only said she didn't want a time schedule dictating her actions. Shortly after one thirty, she said she was ready to go canoeing. John told her it was too late, that they could get stuck on the river in the dark, but Claire replied there was enough time and *she* was going to run the river, with or without him.

The driver slowed the Wagoneer and turned onto a narrow, bumpy dirt road. After a quarter mile, he swung the truck into a small clearing. Across a rocky beach ran the river. It was wide and calm.

John offered to assist the driver with the canoe, but the man declined. He grabbed the aluminum canoe, lifted it effortlessly from the truck roof, and carried it to the river's edge. John took the life jackets from the driver while Claire reached for the paddles. She wished the driver good fishing. He smiled a thin grin, the wide gap between his two front teeth glistening, and bid them a good float.

Claire pushed the canoe further into the river while John fastened his life jacket. She sat in the front and told John to shove off. His stomach pitched. He examined the river again—the water seemed peaceful enough—and told himself everything would be okay. He tightened the strap on his life jacket and shoved the back of the canoe from the shore. It barely budged. Claire scampered out and they shoved the tip of the canoe deeper into the river. Claire climbed back in and John gave the canoe a good push. The canoe slid into the water and he leaped in, but his tennis shoe dragged against the river's surface.

"Ay!" He yanked his foot into the boat, but the canoe wobbled mightily.

"Steady!" Claire yelled.

He centered his weight and the canoe stabilized. "Damn, that water's cold." His hand trembled, but looking at the river, he saw it was shallow, only about waist deep. John paddled on the left side and so did Claire, and the canoe curved back toward the bank. He paddled right but Claire did the same, and the bow swung back toward the opposite shore.

"Pick one side and stick to it," Claire said. "I'll take the other. We can both paddle on the same side if we want to change directions."

"Good idea."

It took a few minutes, but they found a stride. John dipped the paddle deep into the water, watching the wood spawn clear bubbles that rose to the surface as he pulled the paddle back with a long, full stroke. He felt a power in the stroke; the water swirled off his paddle like a miniature underwater cyclone beginning to spin. His paddling was much stronger than Claire's, but he learned to balance their flow, dipping his paddle occasionally on Claire's side to keep the canoe headed straight downstream.

"Are there many deep spots?" he asked. "The river's been pretty shallow so far."

"It's mostly like this. There are a few good swimming holes where the water is over your head, but not many."

"If you fall in, I'll save you," he told her.

"Well, thanks." She laughed

"And you'll do the same for me, right?"

"Definitely—I think."

"Be serious."

"Of course. I wasn't a lifeguard in high school for nothing."

"I know. I'm counting on it."

He checked the sun in the west; it was squatting toward the horizon, but still cast an intense white-yellow glow. He scanned the rest of the expanse to gauge the distance the sun had traveled. The sky appeared huge, like someone had grabbed it at each horizon and tugged; the air was crisp and clean, as if you could reach up and pierce the atmosphere. John guessed they had two-and-a-half to three hours of light left; not much time, but he figured it should be enough to make the float.

Claire rested her paddle and he laid his own across his knees, allowing the canoe to glide with the current. He leaned back, the metal rim of the canoe pressing warmth against his lower back. He gazed upward into a vast blueness, thinking nothing, only observing. The horizon gave way to treetops. Like plumes of fire, the trees lined the river, leaves ablaze in red, copper, gold. He found it beautiful—the sky, the trees, but especially the river. For a hundred yards, the river cut a thin strip beneath the October sky and the fiery stands of autumn color, before it bent and disappeared behind trees. The river flowed without even seeming to move, the surface placid and reflective like a mirror. He leaned over the edge and peered into the river, seeing the wavy reflection of his long, hooked nose over his black mustache.

"It's beautiful here," he said. "Peaceful too." For the first time all day, he felt relaxed, like it was right for him to be there.

"It is."

He dipped the paddle back into the river, pulling a long and powerful stroke, and the canoe glided forward. A large maple leaf, submerged a few inches beneath the surface, flowed in the current. The maple's scarlet color was still vibrant, not yet washed out by the water. The leaf twirled and tumbled end over end, traveling at the same speed as the canoe.

A rushing sound surged toward them.

"What's that?" John asked.

"Sounds like rough water ahead."

The surface of the river was changing, no longer placid but rippling. Ahead, a fallen tree pinched the river in two, creating a shallow pool along the left bank and a steep channel to the right. The river splintered into a thousand churning white caps in the right channel, dipped into a hollow, and reappeared downstream in rapids that swirled around a bend and splashed against a huge boulder.

"What do we do?" He heard the high-pitched edge to his voice.

"Well, first off," she laughed. "Don't panic."

"C'mon—what?"

"Just keep paddling us toward the right. We'll shoot through that channel and when we get closer, I'll read the current and call out to paddle left or right. We'll slip around that bend and boulder easy, like a knife through butter."

John stared at the opposite bank. "Can't we just go to the left? It's shallow through there and we can avoid the rough water and that big rock?"

"Yes, we *could* do that, but that would be no fun. Look—it's so shallow there we'd probably have to drag the canoe in places. Let's shoot through that right channel."

"I don't know."

"Come on." She looked at him over her shoulder. "It'll be no problem."

"Are you sure?"

"Well, there's no absolute guarantees in life, you know."

"What are you saying?"

"It should be fine, fun—an adventure."

"Okay."

"*Okay.*" She mocked his tentative tone. "Oh, my cautious adventurer. Don't be scared. Let's do it."

Claire paddled easily and he followed her lead. He looked for the trolling maple leaf, but it was gone. The speed of their canoe increased, traveling faster than the propulsion of their paddle strokes, as they passed the fallen tree into the channel.

The thought that they should have gone around the rapids sank into his gut, but he knew it was too late. Claire had sounded confident, even cocky, but the canoe could capsize, and they would be thrown into the water, thrashed about, dragged under the surface. They could bang their heads on the rocks and drown.

An urge to swear, to scream at the top of his lungs, swelled inside, but he bit the inner flesh of his lip instead. The water bounced toward the peak of a rapid.

"Paddle left!" Claire yelled.

He dug his paddle deep into the river and yanked it backward. The canoe bucked and rolled, tossed by the rapids, but the bow pushed through the white caps. He paddled hard left again, and so did Claire. His shoulders and arms churned under his chin, and he concentrated on the river.

The current swept the canoe around the bend and toward the boulder. Rapids hit the canoe at crosscurrents; they could overturn at any moment.

"Claire?"

She called out a path to the left of the boulder and John paddled quickly.

A bang echoed from the bottom of the canoe where they'd hit a submerged rock. The boat rocked, knocking John from his metal seat. He scooted back, paddling hard.

"Left," Claire yelled. "More left!"

The river steered them toward the boulder. Water smashed white against the huge rock, but Claire shoved them away with her paddle.

"Made it!" John yelled.

"Left John! Now!"

Another boulder reared from the river bottom. It rose in a long, knobby ridge, like a massive spine, just below the surface.

"John, paddle!"

He hesitated, but then shoved his paddle into the water and pulled back, rotating the paddle like a rudder. Their bow swung left. They veered past the backbone of the rock. They floated on by, and the rapids faded into riffles.

"*That* was exciting," Claire said. "We got closer to that boulder than I thought, but we maneuvered our way through nicely. Good job."

"Thanks, but I hate to think about what would have happened if we didn't do it right," John said. "But we did, and that's what counts."

"No." She turned around again in the canoe. "What counts is that we tried."

The canoe glided downstream while Claire and John paddled quietly, effortlessly. The blueness of the sky seemed deeper, particularly in the east as the sun slunk toward the horizon. He rested his paddle on the shiny steel canoe bottom and dangled his hand above the mirrored river surface. He touched a fingertip to the surface, watching the water spew into a "V," a miniature wake spewing from his finger. The water did not feel as cold as when his foot dragged against the surface. He sank his entire hand into the water and opened his fingers, sensing the flow of the river around him. It felt refreshing, not so cold, he decided, and there was something more that was invigorating and good but for which he had no words.

A leaf floated past his hand. It rolled gracefully, end over end, traveling at the same speed as the gliding canoe. The leaf was broad with five points, a maple like the last one, and he wondered for a moment if it could have been the same leaf, having made it through the rapids and reconnected with them, but the color in this leaf had faded and he quickly dismissed the idea as a silly notion. He lunged for the leaf, grabbing it in his hand but rocking the canoe.

"Hey! Steady!" Claire yelled.

"Sorry."

"What are you trying to do? Tip us over?"

"I was just playing around."

"Well, be a little more careful or you're going to dump us both in the drink."

He opened his fist. The current swept the leaf from his hand. He liked drifting in the current. He felt full of the beauty of the place, of the autumn-colored trees, the translucent blue sky, and the river. He felt serene, then expansive, and then the feeling faded. In its place, something bad appeared, small at first, but it grew, and then it threatened to overtake him. He didn't know what to call the feeling—it was vague but strong, damning. He suddenly felt flattened and little, and he felt bad in some overwhelming way that he couldn't shake. The feeling was like guilt, but more personal and pervasive. It seemed like something was wrong—or, more to the point, that there was something bad not only surrounding him, but so close to him, so much on the inside, so much a part of him, that it felt like the badness was *him*.

His chest tightened and he wanted to scream like a child. A sound rose in his throat, but he chocked it back.

"John." She looked back over her shoulder. "You okay?"

"Yeah."

"Sounded like you were choking or something."

"I'm okay."

"Yeah?"

"Just something caught in my throat." He didn't know for sure what had happened, but it made him feel small and scared. He tried at first to analyze the feeling, but then he dismissed it, chiding himself for his obsessively anxious and episodically morose nature. He told himself to let go of worrying—the bad feeling seemed childish and out of sync in being with Claire. He directed his attention to the autumn leaves, to the flaming scarlet colors, and then to the river. It was smooth, beautiful, and it simply flowed. Relax and just go with the moment.

The river eased into a long stretch of calm water. Later, they hit a series of rough passages, but they were less turbulent than the earlier rapid. John realized their process had changed too. Claire still called out the way, but he was already paddling in the right direction. He had learned to read the river.

He grinned. Shooting rough water had become exciting. The river was challenging, but no longer scary. He found the long stretches of calm water peaceful and—with the sky, the trees, and the water itself—beautiful. But the rapids and the long smooth passages were not so separate. They were strung together, tied by the river into one long stream that felt singularly good.

"Claire, this is great."

"Do you like it?"

"I love it."

"What's your favorite part?"

"Hmm, tough question. I like going through the rapids. But I also like just floating along, just being out here and taking it all in. I don't know what my favorite part is—I can't dissect it into pieces. I like the whole thing."

She twisted around in the canoe to face John. "If you like this, you ought to go up river sometime."

"What's that?"

"You paddle upstream and when the river gets too rocky or shallow or rough, you portage your canoe, and when you can no longer float anywhere, you hike along the edge of the river."

"Paddle, portage, hike. Sort of a river triathlon, huh?" He laughed but noticed Claire did not. "Sounds fun, but why would you do that?"

"Everyone goes down river. This is great today, because it's a good river with a few small rapids and because there's no one else out here. But some Midwest rivers are slow and during the summer there's so many people yelling and thrashing about and drinking beer—it's like being bumper to bumper on the highway during rush hour. I hate it." She downed a long sip from her water bottle. "But going up river, that's a different story. It's a lot more work, paddling up current, portaging around rocks and rapids. But if you go far enough, you go where few people ever go."

"You've gone up river before?"

"When I was a girl, I used to go hunting and fishing a lot with my dad, and occasionally we'd go canoeing." She dipped her hand into the river and then spread apart her fingers, letting the river run through them. "Usually we went downstream, but twice on longer summer trips up north, he took me up river."

"What was that like?"

"Wonderful, special times. I loved them—having that time alone with my dad and nature with no one else around. He told me when I got older and stronger, we'd go all the way up, to the source of a river."

"Did you?"

"No."

"How come?"

"I used to ask to go, but he said I needed to get a little older and stronger first. But then he died when I was fifteen before we ever went."

"Oh, Claire," he said. "I'm sorry."

She turned back to the bow.

"I can't quite imagine."

"I vowed to go up river to the source for him and for me," she said. "I wanted to go the next summer after he died, but my mom wouldn't let me. I decided I would go as soon as I was old enough to do what I wanted without my mother's permission. But then I got engaged and married right after high school and had the boys right away. Ted and I were supposed to go when they got older, but we never did—and now we won't."

"Do you still want to go?"

"As much as anything. I don't feel compelled to make the trip immediately, but it is something I will definitely do someday."

"I hope you do, Claire. That would be great." He saw her nod. "What's at the source of a river?"

"My father used to say a melting glacier, but I don't know if he was serious or spinning a yarn."

He shoved his paddle deeper into the river. "You forgot to tell me about this before—when we first started hanging out, back along the Missouri River, talking about things we really want to do. Remember?"

"No, I didn't."

"Yes, you did. You didn't tell me."

"I didn't tell you, but I didn't forget."

"Why didn't you tell me?"

"It's private, a sacred kind of experience." She dipped her paddle back into the river. "I didn't tell you before because I didn't trust you as well then."

She surprised him by her comment—she often did, but he liked this about her. "Well, I'm glad you trust me now."

She nodded.

He thought there was something very special, maybe even mysterious, about her past, about her dreams, about her, and that no matter how close he got to her, there was still more to discover. Their being together suddenly seemed synchronistic to him in some way that he didn't rationally understand, but he knew he felt a deep connection with Claire, and a joy in being together that seemed simple, almost childlike. For a moment, he thought they were soulmates, even though he wasn't really sure if there was such a thing. "That's something I'd really like, too—going up river to the source," he said. "I'd be happy to do that with you sometime."

She glanced over her shoulder before turning back to face the river. He was puzzled by the look in her eye, unsure if it was appreciation or anger.

"Claire, you okay?"

"Yeah, but I don't want to talk anymore about it now."

He started to ask her why but stopped himself. "Okay." He wondered what Claire was feeling, but she said nothing more. She puzzled him—the way he could feel so close to her, and then suddenly she could push him away or disappear. He worried he had said something wrong, or perhaps intruded, but he tried to let go of the worry. He wanted to recapture the feeling of simply floating, of enjoying the trees, the sky, and especially the river. But it was difficult to recreate those feelings.

The blueness of the sky drained away. The sun had slipped behind the treetops. A golden pall cast over the trees, into the edges of the sky. It was a strange light, faintly yellow, and the air was quiet, still, the way it sometimes becomes at sunset.

Ahead a large bird swooped across the river to the west bank. It was unlike any bird he had ever seen. It was large, sleek, but gray in color, and it glided with wings outstretched. The creature emitted a deep, haunting cry just before it dropped into the shadows of the forest. He had never heard any sound like it before. It was more a cry than a chirp or a caw. The cry echoed along the riverbank, resounding strangely primeval.

"That was incredible," he said. "A beautiful bird."

"It is."

"Do you know what kind it is?"

"No," she said.

"Are we getting close to the end?"

"Yes, pretty close." She pulled her paddle from the river. "Are you glad?"

"No. Not necessarily."

Soon the river quickened. He had longed for another passage of fast water before their trip ended. They approached a sharp bend where the water became choppy. The current swept them around the curve.

"Quick!" Claire yelled. "Go left!"

The river was narrow and pocked with boulders. Claire yelled out more directions, picking a course through deeper water close to the limestone cliffs on the left. They paddled into this channel.

"Oh shit," she hollered.

A huge boulder peeked just above the surface, blocking their way. The rock split the channel in half, and then the river dropped several feet. Claire yelled to go left. They paddled hard but the canoe caromed off the boulder and bounced into the air and over the cascading eddy. As they descended, John saw a tree trunk rising from the river below. The top of the tree, grotesquely withered and knobby like a skeleton's arm, reared out of the water, stretching to the point just beyond where they would soon fall.

Thud. The canoe slapped the river's surface.

"Duck!" Claire yelled.

John instead raised his arms, trying to shield himself, but the fallen tree jabbed at him. He grabbed for it, trying to hold on, but he was yanked from the canoe like a plaything.

Cold water encapsulated John. He opened his eyes to murky darkness, and his body burned with a familiar, freezing sensation, like he was pressed between sheets of ice. He thrashed wildly, flailing beneath the surface. For an instant, he worried about his father—no, Claire—and then saw light above him and struggled to swim upward.

His head popped above the surface. He gasped, choked on water, coughed, and spat out the river. He sucked in a deep, rapid breath and then another.

"Claire!" He saw neither her nor the canoe. The current propelled him downstream. His knee slammed into a boulder. "Goddamn it! Claire!"

He stared downstream but saw her nowhere.

He heard her yell. He twisted around and saw her sitting in the canoe along the bank. She was laughing.

He swam out of the current, banging his shin against another boulder, swearing, before finding his footing in the rocky riverbed. He strode upstream, stubbing his toes against river rocks, making his way in the shallow water that had opened up along the bank. The back of the canoe was beached against stones on the shore. Claire sat in her spot in the front, bent over, roaring with laughter.

"What's so damn funny?"

She gasped for breath, the whites of her eyes growing huge. "You looked comical, sailing rapidly downstream but without the canoe."

"I don't think it's so fucking funny."

"What's wrong with you?" She frowned and shook her head. "God, can't you laugh at yourself just once?"

"I was worried about you."

"Me? Why?"

"I couldn't see you anywhere." He shook water from his hair. "I thought you'd been thrown into the river, too, and something bad had happened."

"I was fine. You're the one who got launched out of the canoe by trying to grab onto that tree trunk."

"I couldn't see you were so fucking fine when I was under water and getting swept downstream, now could I?"

"People fall into the river all the time—I didn't know it was such a big deal to you. It just struck me as funny, watching you float away, but I'm sorry." Claire extended a hand to pull him back into the canoe. "Here."

When he stepped in, the canoe wobbled, and they almost tipped over. He stabilized the canoe with his weight and by balancing his arms. He settled back in, trying to wring his shirt dry. They pushed off and paddled back downstream. Claire was trying to be nice, he realized, no more sarcasm or laughter, but he said nothing more.

He felt like he was freezing. The sun had disappeared, and his clothes were drenched, tight against his body. He shivered, and his trembling grew worse in the breeze. Within a quarter-hour, they found the put-out place. The outfitter sat in his Wagoneer at the edge of the rocky beach, smoking a Marlboro. He surveyed John's wet clothes, started to say something, but then stopped. He flicked the gold cigarette butt onto the river stones, loaded the canoe atop of the Wagoneer, and drove them back toward John's car. Claire asked no more questions and they rode in silence.

It was dark when they arrived at camp. Claire started a fire from twigs and driftwood and soon it was raging. John changed his clothes and then huddled close to the fire but the chill lingered. He uncorked the wine bottle, filled a paper cup with chardonnay, and held the bottle up for Claire to see. She shook her head and fixed dinner.

"Are you ready to go home now?" she asked after they ate.

"No." He looked at her. "Why?"

"You haven't said two words since I laughed at you. Obviously, you're still pissed at me."

"I don't know what I feel." He poured himself another cup of chardonnay.

"For God's sakes, be honest at least, John."

"Maybe a little pissed," he said.

"Well, get it off your chest. Don't just sit there and brood."

"What?" He was lightheaded from the wine and felt freer to speak his mind. "It's okay for you not to talk about things until you're good and ready, but not me?"

"Okay. What's fair for the goose is fair for the gander."

They went to bed late. Their sleeping bags, zipped together from the prior night, felt uncomfortably close. John and Claire lay at opposite corners. The ground was hard yet lumpy, and he shivered.

"It's really not about you," he finally said, pushing himself to talk. "I don't mean to be taking it out on you. I really loved being on the river together. I just panicked and freaked out. It was almost a phobic reaction."

"How come?"

He shook his head in the dark and wished he had just gone to sleep.

"What's the matter, John?"

He said nothing. The ground seemed too cold. Claire reached over and found his hand under the sleeping bag. She gripped his clenched fist.

"It's damn stupid," he said. "But it's probably left over from when I was a kid."

"What?"

"My dad and I went ice fishing when I was eight and we ended up in the middle of this frozen lake and . . . goddamn but we fell through the ice. It happened so quick. One minute we're standing there, my dad punching out the fishing circle, and then the next second, 'boom'—everything was different. I was freezing and sinking and at first my dad was trying to lift me out of the water but then suddenly I didn't see him anymore. That's the last thing I remember."

"What happened?"

"Apparently, a couple of other fishermen saw us. They pulled us out, but by then my dad and I had both passed out or something. We had hypothermia and my dad had a seizure afterward—lack of oxygen, apparently he had almost drowned."

"How traumatic," Claire said.

He shrugged inside the sleeping bag. "Anyway, after that we were both fine."

"I'm sorry." Claire squeezed his hand. "I had no idea. That had to be so scary."

"I guess it was scary then, but I don't really remember much."

"You blocked it out," she said. "Did your parents take you to therapy afterward?"

John snorted. "My family's never been to therapy, and besides, we had a bigger problem soon afterward."

"What?"

"Afterward, my parents argued more than ever, and then one day my dad got fed up and left."

Claire rubbed his back. "They separated?"

"I don't know if that's really what you'd call it. It was only like for a week or so, and then when my grandmother was staying with us, my mom just freaked out—crying nonstop, sitting on the kitchen floor, unable to get up. She ended up in the hospital."

"The mental hospital?"

"I don't know. Maybe—no one talks about it."

"What was wrong?"

"I think she was just really nervous and depressed—maybe a nervous breakdown as they used to say. I just tried to keep my head down as the whole thing felt really bad."

"I'm sure."

He knew she didn't understand what he meant. He was tempted to just shut up, but he needed to finish what he started to tell her. "No, it felt like it was my fault."

"How was it your fault?"

"I was the one who wanted to go way out to the middle of the lake and that's what caused the whole mess to begin with."

"And you were a child." She shook her head. "It wasn't your fault, but children always want to take responsibility, as if they really did have that kind of power—and so they don't have to be angry with their parents."

"I don't know about that," he said. "But I got to stay with Nona for a few weeks, and that was good because we're very close, but I still missed my mom. Anyway, when I came home, my dad and mom were both there, and everything kind of went back to normal."

"And what about you—about what you went through?"

"Everything seemed forgotten."

"I doubt that."

"It all seemed fine until a couple of years later when my dad took us to this mountain river he used to go to as a kid, and suddenly I got terrified. My dad kept telling me to get in—it was his family's favorite swimming hole once they moved out from Vermont—but I just couldn't do it. I didn't know what was happening—I was just scared and froze up. He started yelling but my mom was pleading with him to stop. Finally, he did, and I didn't go in."

"You were scared from the ice fishing."

"I didn't realize that then. I just felt awful, like a little scaredy-cat, who couldn't do what his father wanted. I knew it was pretty stupid—my parents had made me take swimming lessons at the city pool since kindergarten and I could swim—but the prospects of swimming in a lake or the ocean or a river—anything other than a shallow pool—terrifies me."

"And it still does?"

"I guess some. It's weird, because as I got older, I found that despite my fears about getting immersed that I like being around water—a lake or river—as long as I don't have to get in. It's strange."

"It's scary for you."

"But it's a silly, irrational fear. When I took my first psychology class in college, I realized it was just a matter of conditioning. A simple phobia, that's all. I decided then to try to recondition myself. When Joanie and I went to the beach, I'd relax by the waves and gradually got my feet wet. That helped some, but I never got past knee deep. The beach wasn't that close and we were always busy with school and other stuff, and then I moved here and there's no real body of water to speak of for miles. It's really not that big of a deal. An aversion reinforced into a simple phobia."

"John," her voice was lower. "You need therapy."

He forced himself to laugh. "It's not that big of a deal."

"Your parents should have taken you then, but they didn't, and now you should go yourself."

"It was a difficult experience back then, but it's long over, Claire. I'm just telling you because maybe it got touched today, being in a somewhat similar situation. That's probably why I was so upset and then moody afterward. It touched old stuff, but just for a minute."

Claire reached her arm around his shoulder. She pulled him close, cradling his head against her breasts. He felt both good but also uncomfortable, like she was holding him too tight and he felt constrained. He wiggled in her arms so he felt freer but he kept his face near her breasts.

That night he dreamed of falling through the ice again. He panicked, yelling and thrashing in cold water, but Claire was there, pulling him from the ice.

His dream had awoken Claire. She whispered it was okay and pulled his head back to her breasts. He heard rain pelting against the canvas tent. He asked if they needed to leave, but Claire said that the tent was waterproof and that they would be fine.

He woke again later. It was still raining but the tent was repelling the water. He smiled and cuddled close to Claire. She felt good, warm, and after a while the rain subsided to a light patter against the tent, and then it ceased altogether. There was a chill, but it was the good kind of crispness that leaves you feeling snug in a warm sleeping place. He listened to the birds singing in the predawn and he felt marvelously happy for a long time before he fell back to sleep. But in the morning, he woke to wetness. The rainwater had soaked through the ground and risen up beneath their bodies.

Despite the rain, it was a great trip. He loved the canoeing and being on the river, and he felt very close to Claire. Where the road was straight, he held her hand driving home. They talked some, but mostly they were silent. The next day, after they were back, it came as a shock when Claire told him over the phone that she definitely didn't want to see him that day or any other day for a month, and that they probably needed to break up for good.

CHAPTER 14

Claire greeted him at the front door with a forced, tight-lipped smile, and then ushered John into the sunroom. She poured two cups of steaming tea that smelled of orange spice, stoked the glowing embers within the wood-burning stove until they flamed red, and crammed three split logs into the fire. She settled into the pea-green, cracked vinyl rocking chair and stared into his eyes.

"Claire, it's been so long." The month apart she needed had turned into six weeks by her choice, and he spoke quickly now, worried she was going to immediately announce the coup de grace to their relationship. "What have you been up to?"

"Dissertation proposal." She frowned. "Working. Parenting. And visiting Earl in the nursing home."

"Oh no. What happened?"

Claire said her ninety-one-year-old neighbor had suffered a stroke a few weeks before. She'd been visiting him at least twice a week, three times when the boys were with their father all week.

"That's very sweet of you." He found himself wishing she'd shown him the same level of kindness. Her abrupt decision to cut off after their canoeing trip had surprised and confused him. He wasn't even sure what the problem was and when he had initially telephoned to ask, she had told him she needed space and to stop calling. He worried now she would break up with him for good.

"And you?" she asked. "How have you been?"

"I've missed you a lot."

Claire flushed, and heaviness sank inside him; he'd hoped for a smile.

"It's been an important time too," he said. "I've realized a lot of things, first and foremost, how important you are to me. I know on the camping trip I got pretty uptight, and I apologize. Some conflict is inevitable in any relationship, and I need to be more patient, not so damn tense and irritable. And I realized even more clearly how much I love you, how much I want to commit to being with you, even without any guarantees about the future."

"John." She lowered the teacup from her lips. "It's not going to work."

He breathed deeply. "Why?"

"You're a good man. I appreciate the caring and kindness you've shown me and the boys. That means a lot to me." She blew on her tea and drew in a small sip. "I'll miss you, but a romantic relationship isn't going to work between us."

"Why do you say that?"

"I've always said this would be a temporary relationship."

Panic swelled inside. He then grabbed hold of the thought that if he could keep her explaining her reasons, maybe he could talk her out of breaking up. He remembered one of his favorite clinical questions. "Why now, Claire?"

"There are some serious differences and problems between us."

"Like what?"

"You want a permanent relationship, someone you can marry someday and have children with, and I don't."

"I don't know." The heat from the stove had become oppressive. He leaned away. "I always assumed I wanted children someday—that was part of the plan with Joanie and something my dad encouraged." His dad had grown up with four brothers and used to talk about wanting a big family, but his mom had often acted like children were a near-unbearable stress. "But I really don't know what I want. Maybe I do, maybe I don't. But definitely not any time soon."

"John, don't lie to yourself about your own feelings. Having children—there's nothing like it. It's an important part of life."

"What I said is true: *I* have to figure it out. But what about you? You're a great mother. Are you so sure you don't ever want more children?"

"That time of my life has passed." She stood up, reached for the black iron poker, and tapped open the vents to the wood stove, letting the fire draw more air. "A couple of years ago, I wanted another child. Ted didn't, and while we were talking about it, he had an affair."

"I'm sorry," John said. "I didn't know that."

"It's done. That time is over."

"It's more than about having kids, anyway—I love you. Like you said before we left for the canoe trip, we'll figure out tomorrow when it arrives, but let's enjoy being together right now."

"Right." She shook her head. "You saw how well that worked on the camping trip."

"What?" He knew what she meant. It had been the best and worst of times. Being together on the river had been a wonderful adventure but falling out of the canoe had triggered an old and awful fear, and telling her about the fishing accident was nearly as bad, making him feel like a scared little boy again. Still, she had comforted him in her arms after they argued like she accepted him and he felt deeply connected.

"We couldn't even make a camping trip fun without getting all heavy and arguing."

"It's usually not like that for us." Despite her kind words that night in the tent, she had probably found him weak and now she was pulling away. "I'm not sure what came over me, but I'll work on being stronger and more patient."

"It's more than that."

"Like what?"

"I'm a lot older and at a different stage of emotional maturity."

"*Emotional maturity.*" He repeated the words with contempt, though inside he felt something more like shame. "What do you mean by that?"

"It's the way you handle things sometimes," she said.

"For example?"

"Like how upset you were when I wanted to read the morning we were camping. You kept pressuring me to go, hovering around like an anxious child, making me feel guilty. It's things like that." She raised her cup to her lips. "Plus, other problems."

"Like how irritable I was later? I realize that and I apologize. That's not like me normally. I'll do better managing my emotions in the future."

"That's only the surface problem. It goes a lot deeper."

"To what?" He recognized he'd lost his strategy; now his questions spewed out from defensiveness.

"I'm not comfortable with this conversation."

"Why?"

"You're putting me in the position of pointing out your problems," she said. "They're your issues to recognize—not for me to be the critical parent or confronting therapist."

"Don't patronize me." He caught himself glaring. "If there are problems threatening to break us up, I have a right to know."

"All right." She shoved two more logs into the fire before sitting back. "Think about the canoe trip, about your falling out and how you were afterward."

"Pretty unreasonable, I know. And then I pouted for a while. I'm sorry."

She shook her head. "It was more than that."

"I was scared for you."

"You were scared for *yourself*!" She rocked forward. "That's *exactly* what I'm talking about."

"What?"

"You're not straight about your own emotions, either with yourself or with me."

"I don't understand." He lifted his arms, more as a plea than a shrug.

"Your 'phobia' as you called it. You haven't dealt with it in therapy, you didn't talk with me about it before we went on the river, and I don't think you're even aware of all of the emotional issues under the surface."

"It's not that big of a deal." He thought he had actually shared too much with her, and now she was making him pay. He felt ashamed and looked for a way to hide the feeling. "And I don't really get what you're saying anyway."

"You've got issues left over from childhood. I don't blame you for that—we all do. But you're choosing not to be aware and you're definitely not straight in dealing with this—you deny it, you minimize it, you put it on me, and I become the focus and the one who's supposed to make it all better." The lines in her face seemed firmer, harder.

"You're twisting and exaggerating what I shared."

"You're denying, John, and projecting your unrecognized, unexplored baggage on me to take care of. I don't need that from you or anyone. I've been through that sick dynamic in my marriage and I'm not going to be part of that kind of relationship again." Her voice rose and she talked quicker, like she was winding herself up. "On the camping trip, it became clear that dynamic was operating again with you. It's like you needed a lot of attention and reassurance. Way too much of my energy went toward giving you attention, responding to you, meeting your hidden agendas. I felt totally drained—and I was losing myself to you. You needed so much—and more than that, you weren't upfront about your needs. You played them out on me and a web was spun."

"In your theatrical style, you're not being very fair or accurate." He tried to pick his words carefully, to slow down and quell the emotions roiling inside. "First of all, I was scared for you. Yes, I was scared for myself, too—maybe it touched old stuff—but it wasn't such a big deal for God's sake. Second, I did talk with you a lot that night about my feelings."

"You *talked* a lot, yes," she nodded, but rolled her eyes. "You *said* a lot of words. There were no feelings there. Yet underneath the surface, you pulled on me ferociously. When you told me about your accident as a boy, you needed me to comfort you, to reassure you, to tell you everything would be okay. You were like a little boy, needing the good mom to pull out her tit to comfort you, to make it all better—"

"Claire—"

She waved him off. "Do you know what I felt? I didn't feel anything. *Nothing.* And that felt horrible—not to feel for you, for anyone who had gone through a trauma. I felt bad then and I responded as I should have—sympathetic, comforting, reassuring. I felt guilty and blamed myself for not genuinely feeling compassion for you. But when I thought about it later, I stopped blaming myself. Do you know why?"

She stared at him with intense, almost crazy eyes. Beneath that look, he feared she was enraged—or was it hurt and disgusted? He struggled to find words, but she didn't wait for him.

"I didn't feel for you because I didn't feel anything *from* you when we talked," she said. "Where was your pain? Your fear? I didn't feel any emotions from you—it was just words. Instead, you acted out the feelings on me: afraid for me, enraged with me. Then it was like nothing happened. I didn't feel anything from you, except this melodramatic presentation of an intellectualized analysis—sorry, but that's how it was—of this awful story from childhood, and then this pull, this huge tug from you to me to be the good mom, to reassure you and tell you everything would be okay. And I did that, but down deep I really didn't want to. I didn't have any more to give you. I felt empty, my tit sucked dry."

"Did I want your reassurance? Hell, no." He let his rage build. "And I'll be goddamned if I wanted your pity. Do you understand me?"

"No, I don't. That's how it felt to me."

"Maybe that's what you needed to put on me. Where was my pain, my fear? That's really none of your business, is it? But I wasn't feeling it. It's past history. And want your pity? Fuck no."

"Really? I almost asked you in the middle of your monologue that night why you were telling me all this? What did you want from me, anyway, a mother?"

"Stop saying that, will you?" He was sick—and embarrassed—hearing her saying he was looking for a mother. "I was telling you so it would make some goddamn sense to you, but you're blowing everything I said way out of proportion. Maybe you're projecting your old stuff with Ted? Have you thought about that?" He saw her open her mouth to respond but he cut her off. "And even if you've stopped doing that for Ted, you're still in a similar pattern with your sons. Maybe you're projecting your own mother stuff—your solicitousness with your boys, rushing in and pampering their every whim? No wonder you feel your tit's sucked dry, but don't put that on me. That's probably your projection, and now you're the one who's afraid—afraid to be open to intimacy."

"And you're denying. I told you what I felt. I trust my gut."

"Damn you! Who the *fuck* are you to tell me how I'm feeling?"

She stood up. "Get out."

"What?"

"I'm *not* someone to be sworn at in my own house. I'm not going to be verbally abused anywhere. If that's the way you're going to talk, then get the hell out."

John jumped up. Swear words crashed against the back of his clenched teeth. An urge to kick over her coffee table nearly overwhelmed him, but he brushed by her shoulder instead. Walking through the living room, he felt dizzy. The wavy designs in the beige carpet swirled. He grabbed his coat, which hung stiffly on the rack, and reached for the brass knob to her front door. It was cold in his hand, and he felt then like he could scream like a crazy person. She was the most important person in his life—and he was walking away? She brought him intensity and frustration and passion and bewildering feelings, but at least he felt alive. "Claire." She had followed him into the living room. "I'm sorry for swearing."

"That pissed me off."

"I know—I apologize. I was pissed, too, and confused—I still am—but I love you. You're the most important person in my life. I don't want things to end."

"Everything ends eventually."

"I don't want this to end. Not now, not like this."

She said nothing.

"Claire, I love you. I want things to work out between us."

"It's not just things between us," she said. "There's deep, personal things you need to look at."

"I heard what you said." He was still confused and disagreed with most of her comments, but he didn't want to win the argument and lose her. "I'll look at it more."

"It scares me you'll keep playing out your issues on me—or the next woman you get close to."

"I'm pretty insightful." He saw her frown. "And I'll go to therapy, if that helps."

"I hope so," she said. "But do it for yourself—not for me."

"I know." He wasn't sure he believed his own words, but he felt like he was beginning to persuade her. "Let's give the relationship another chance."

"You know, it's not going to work in the long run," she said, but she glanced away, like she was considering his proposal.

"It might in the short run."

"I don't know," she said.

"Claire, I love you, I care about you, I'll go to therapy and deal with my stuff."

"I care about you too." She sighed. "But I'd feel bad, like I'm using you for companionship and sex, knowing things aren't going to work out in the long run."

"First of all, it's not using me if I know up front and I agree. Second, who's going to say for sure it won't work out in the long run? Maybe we just need time and the vision."

She shook her head. "I don't think so."

He did, but he realized it was foolish to push his point now: he needed to find common ground with her. "You're so important to me—and at least we have the present. You've become my best friend."

"Mine too." Her lips curled, a mixture of sadness and affection, it seemed.

"I don't want to lose this, Claire. Let's just hang out and be together—no guarantees. You know, conduct an experiment, see how things go."

She leaned against the back of the living room sofa. She blinked, her eyes wide.

"I'm willing to commit to a new way of relating," he said.

"I can't commit," she said. "But I am willing to hang out and see how it goes, one day at a time, if you are."

"Maybe that's what I need, anyway—fewer guarantees."

She nodded, then a small, crooked smile crossed her lips. She extended her open arms toward him. He stepped forward and embraced Claire in a long hug.

"Feels good to be held again," she said.

"Yes."

She pulled away then. "But I'm scared."

"About what?"

"About sleeping together tonight," she said. "I don't know if we should."

"Why?"

"I separated myself from you emotionally over the past six weeks," she said. "I needed to. It feels good to hug, but I'm scared about being too close, too soon, especially to have sex."

"I'd love to sleep with you tonight," he said.

"I don't know if that's a good idea."

"We don't have to make love." He circled his arms gently back around her. "We could just snuggle. It's up to you." He held her gaze as she stared into his eyes, saying nothing but obviously weighing his offer.

"I want to sleep with you—to hold each other." She pointed her finger at him. "No sex."

He agreed, but as they cuddled together in bed, her body felt hot and pressed against his. He kissed her, and as her mouth opened to his, he pulsated with a sense of energy at each place their bodies touched. For an instant, he worried whether she wanted sex, but her pelvis nudged against him, and he let the question fade away as he slipped her nightgown over her head. He held her tight after he climaxed, stifling an urge to cry.

In the morning, she brushed her teeth at the bathroom sink. He drew aside her hair, still damp from the shower, and kissed her on the nape of her neck. She pulled away.

"How are you this morning?" he asked.

She spat toothpaste. "Fine." She stepped around him, walking out of the bathroom.

Downstairs, around the coffee maker, he tried to engage her in conversation about her day. She answered in brusque monosyllables.

"How are you?" he asked again.

"Fine. I already told you."

"Good, but you seem upset or something." He brought the coffee cup to his lips, taking in the smell of the French roast. He debated with himself, but then asked the question worrying him. "How do you feel about making love last night?"

She clanked their breakfast dishes against the countertop. "You really want to know?"

He wasn't sure. "Yeah."

"Pretty mixed. I desired you when we were lying close, but then I felt torn. I wanted to make love, but I also didn't want to. Immediately after you were inside me, this thought stuck inside my head: 'John's reclaimed his territory.'"

"For God's sake! I wasn't reclaiming *territory*." He wasn't sure if he was hurt or angry or some mixture of the two. "You're not real estate to me."

"Like it or not, that was how I felt." The firmness of her jaw was an expression he'd seen many times before, but he still wasn't sure if it was defensiveness or defiance.

"I made love with you because I wanted to be close to you—you're the most important person in my life. I thought you wanted to be close too."

"I did at first, but then I felt mixed emotions," she said.

He couldn't believe they were arguing again. He didn't want to be fighting with her, and he didn't want the distance. And yet there it was. Perhaps after their big argument, it was something they had to go through, like aftershocks, he thought.

He didn't call her for over a week, and they saw little of each other over the next six weeks. They only slept together once, and when they did, she jumped up from bed when he was in the middle of pleasuring her, dressed in the bathroom, and left for her house. At first, he was tired of being the one to reach out after a conflict and he accepted the diminished contact with Claire as a necessary cost for preserving his self-esteem. By early February, he felt like a prideful fool and feared his relationship with Claire was irretrievably broken. He peppered her then with phone calls, hoping to get together, but Claire told him he was crowding her and she needed space. He mourned not seeing her, feeling both abandoned and aggravated, but he was glad she was willing, albeit ambivalently, to meet him for dinner on Valentine's Day. He plotted to make the most of it.

$$\backsim$$

John greeted Claire with a grin when she walked through the restaurant doors wearing a tight-fitting tan dress with a wide red belt with a golden buckle that complemented her hair. "You look beautiful for Valentine's Day. A new dress?"

"I didn't have time to change after work," she said. "I have to dress up for the West County school district."

"Whatever the reasons, you look beautiful." He gave her an enthusiastic hug.

Claire wiggled out of his arms, turned to the hostess, and followed her to the table for two. John walked behind Claire, admiring her long legs, the fullness of her butt. For a moment, he delighted in the fantasy of making love to her again, but he knew he'd have to be careful not to press her about their relationship during the meal. Claire had agreed to his invitation to Valentine's Day dinner with the greatest of reluctance. He'd wanted to pick her up for dinner at her house after his intramural basketball game, but she insisted that would be too late and she wanted to drive separately to dinner. He wasn't thrilled by the arrangements, wishing instead to return with her to her house late at night, but he was pushing himself to enjoy the time together without conflict. Throughout the dinner, he asked her about her job, a new thirty-hour-a-week position while she finished her dissertation. He listened to her describe the psychological testing duties, but he lost the content of their conversation while gazing at her blonde hair, with more of a curl now, and at the dimples that flashed as she smiled.

After dinner, she clanked her coffee cup back onto its saucer. "You don't have much time left before your basketball game. Here," she reached into her purse and pulled out a sealed, white envelope. "I want to give you your card before I go."

"Thanks, but you know, if it's too rushed, we could get together after the game."

"No."

"I was afraid you'd say that." He picked up the shopping bag at his feet and handed it to Claire.

"You didn't need to get me a gift." She said this more like criticism than from humility. "I only got you a card."

"A card's fine." He'd wondered if she'd get him a present, and while he told himself it didn't really matter and he was glad he'd bought her the gift, he was dimly aware of some uneasy feeling—he wasn't sure if it was hurt or numbness—that spread inside him. "Go ahead, open yours."

She sliced open the purple envelope with a butter knife. Her blue-gray eyes skimmed the card's verse and his handwriting. At home, he had stared at the blank space on the card for a long time, unsure what to write. He finally chose to state what he felt: She was wonderful, a special person whom he appreciated more than anyone, and he would continue to learn how to step back and allow her space, even as he hoped they would always remain close and in love. She laid the card on the table. Her lips parted, but she said nothing.

"Open your present," he said.

She unraveled the wrapping paper and pulled out the department store box, opening it to find a black sweater with a narrow, purple band woven into the fabric. "It's beautiful." She actually looked pleased. "My two favorite colors."

"I know."

"But you shouldn't have gotten me anything." She folded the sweater and put it back in the box. "I shouldn't accept it."

"Don't be ridiculous." He tore open the envelope she had handed him. The front of the card had a picture of pastel flowers in a wooden basket, and the words, "To A Dear Friend" printed across the top. He skimmed the inside verse, a rhyming passage about a friend who is always there, who can always be counted upon. Underneath, Claire had signed her name.

That's it? John thought. No hint of a reunion. No deep professions of love. Just a singsongy verse of appreciation for being a friend in the kind of card his mother would give to a neighbor lady. He had hoped their Valentine's Day dinner would reignite their romance, but now he wondered if she was simply trying to make a transition to friends.

"Claire," he said. "What's happening to us?"

"We're in very different places."

"Yes—because we've had way too much going on that's gotten in the way. Me working long hours trying to finish up my dissertation while working full-time for the state, you doing your dissertation and working thirty hours a week while going through a divorce and being a single mom and everything. It's been an incredible amount of stress."

"Yes, but—"

"You know what? What we need is time for ourselves, a good break so we can get away from everyday hassles and do something renewing. We ought to go into the country and go camping and canoeing again soon. And this spring let's take that trip to the mountains, to where you used to go as a kid, and go all the way up the river, all the way to the source."

"No."

"Why not?"

"For one reason that should be obvious, in case you've lost all touch with reality, it's winter and it's freezing out there."

"I know." He leaned over the table. "But I researched this yesterday—there's subzero sleeping bags, snow tents, and cold weather survival suits—we'll be fine."

"Fine, huh? Just like last time we went in the fall? That didn't turn out so fine."

"I know—because I overreacted. But I've been dealing with my phobia in therapy."

"Okay." Claire paused her coffee cup before her lips. "That's good. What have you been working through?"

"I've been learning relaxation techniques—deep breathing—and we've been doing desensitization for being around open water."

"*Behavior therapy*?" She spat the words.

"Yes—he's a really good therapist."

"My therapist says behavior therapy is like water skiing—you're just skimming the surface, not dealing with the deep emotional issues."

"And the research says there's not much evidence to support the efficacy of psychodynamic therapy, such as your therapist does."

Claire shook her head, as if she was unimpressed.

"But tell me, Claire—if we put aside all of our theoretical arguments—what's your first reaction at a deep, emotional level—doesn't it sound good to return together to the river and camping?"

"My first thought is that you've gone crazy. This is no time to think about us going canoeing and camping."

"Okay, so it's winter, it's not practical, I'm crazy, but realize if we really want to, nothing can stop us." He heard the pace of his words accelerate, a product of excitement and passion, he thought, while a desperate feeling crept up on him. "But tell me, if you just allow yourself to *imagine* the possibility, what do you *feel*?"

"That it doesn't fit for me." Her words were slow and measured. "I don't want that kind of time—that kind of *intimate* time—together. That's not where I'm at and that's not the kind of relationship we have now."

John pushed back from the table.

"I'm sorry," she said. "I shouldn't have gotten together for dinner tonight—I was afraid you might get the wrong idea."

"You need your space, I know, Claire. I respect that, but don't lose sight that things can be different, that I love you and we can be together when it does fit for you." He realized he was speaking softer, and he felt a distance grow between his words and himself. He tried, too, to push away a sense of desperation that was chased away by self-loathing.

"You say that as if I only understood, then everything would magically be wonderful between us. Well, listen: I do know that you love me and you want us to be together, but that doesn't make it all better. I'm not doubting your love for me—I'm changing. I'm at a different place. I don't want to be that close to you—or probably any man right now. I need to be alone. I'm sorry if it hurts you, but it's true—it's what I need. So if you respect me, then respect this: right now, I'm not at a place to make any plans to be together. And I have serious doubts about whether I ever will be again."

Without intending to, he looked out the window at the street.

"John, I don't want to hurt you, and I don't want to argue. I'm sorry, but I need to go now."

He tossed his cloth napkin onto the table. "I've got to go too."

He offered to walk Claire to her car, but she declined, pointing to her yellow VW Bug a half block away. He walked two blocks in the opposite direction, watching Claire as she passed him without a wave. He slammed shut the door to his Mustang, turned the music on the hard rock radio station way up, and shoved the accelerator toward the floorboard. He sped along Kingshighway, searching for and then spotting the bumblebee yellow of Claire's car a quarter-mile ahead. The light at the intersection turned red; he swore and braked hard. He cursed the long light, watching Claire disappear out of sight, and then burned rubber when the signal turned green. He soared to sixty, then sixty-five miles per hour, more than double the speed limit, but he was afraid he'd lost Claire. On North Kingshighway, he spied her car again. He pushed his car faster. He worried for an instant, but threw that thought aside, feeding on the adrenaline that mixed with the music and the speed of the car.

As he gained on Claire, the traffic signal between them flashed yellow. He hesitated for only the slightest of instants, and then accelerated, rushing through a red light at seventy miles per hour. As he approached Claire, he braked hard, slowing to her speed as he came alongside her in the next lane. He stared at her through the dark, having a hard time seeing her clearly in the night. He honked his horn, and she looked over. He wanted to hold her gaze, but she looked at him for only a second. He pressed his gas pedal hard once more, sped ahead, and then cut ahead of her. She blared her horn, but he turned onto the entrance ramp to the interstate and accelerated his car to ninety miles per hour by the time he swerved onto the freeway.

He pulled into the gym parking lot right at game time. He imagined running hard, driving the ball to the hoop, pulling down rebounds rattling around the rim. He changed in the locker room, clanged shut the metal cage locker, and ran to the court. The guys gave him shit for being late, but they whistled him into the game at the next foul.

John raced the length of the court on a fast break and scored on a layup. He grabbed two rebounds and ran up and down the court with a fire the other players didn't possess. He took a pass at the top of the key, and fed a bounce pass to Phil, who missed an eight-foot bank shot. The opposing center snagged the rebound and threw a quick outlet pass to their point guard for a breakaway. John caught up to him in the backcourt, edging in front and veering away from the center lane. Their guard pulled up, then dribbled behind his back, and slipped past John. The move fooled John, and he lost a step, but then recovered. He waited until the player started his layup, timed his jump, and smacked the shot out of bounds. The referee's whistle shrieked and he pointed at John.

"I didn't touch him," John yelled. "That was a clean block."

The referee ignored John and pointed the other player to the foul line. "Two shots."

"Where did I foul him?" John asked.

"With the body," the referee said.

"Bullshit!"

The referee blared his whistle again, calling a technical foul and warning he'd throw John out of the game if he swore again. Frank Crebs, his dissertation advisor and team captain, walked John to the side of the court as if to scold him but instead he whispered it was a terrible call.

"The ref's an idiot," John said.

After the technical free throw shot, the other team threw the in-bounds pass back to their point guard. He dribbled to the top of the key, then drove the lane, straight at John, but he pulled up just inside the free throw line and shot a jumper. The ball caromed high off the back rim, arcing toward their center. John leaped high, grabbing the ball with one hand, but coming down he hit the back of the opposing center, jostling John off balance. He landed on the side of his foot. His ankle wobbled, and then twisted over; the top of his foot jammed against the hardwood floor, his full body weight pressed on top, and his ankle seemed to explode. Something like fire flared across his ankle, down to his foot, and up his leg. John yelled and crumpled to the floor, cradling his body in a ball around his ankle.

Claire surprised John the next evening at his apartment. He'd called her that afternoon, leaving a message on her answering machine about his ankle: The doctor had diagnosed his ankle—which had swollen to elephantine proportions and turned a deep purple—with ligament and tendon strains and microscopic tears. He was supposed to rest in bed with his foot propped up for three to five days and then use crutches for two weeks. Claire carried a get-well balloon and a pizza box, but she scolded him as soon as she saw him.

"I ought to clobber you," she said, brandishing the pizza box.

"Why?"

"Why?" She gave him an incredulous look. "Because you were driving like a reckless madman last night."

"I didn't want to be late for the game."

"You could have killed someone," she said. "I was watching you in the mirror—and then you cut right in front of me."

"Sorry, but I was in control."

"In control, huh? Look where that got you." She nodded at his swollen ankle, and then handed him a slice of pizza.

She worked at the desk in his bedroom on the data analysis for her dissertation as he edited a draft of his dissertation. At 8:30, she excused herself to go home. He almost asked if she wanted to spend the night with an invalid, but he decided not to push his luck.

He didn't expect it, but Claire returned the next evening carrying a large Pyrex dish containing a cheese macaroni and ground beef casserole mixed with a thick tomato sauce. He ate until he was past full and after dinner Claire sat at the edge of the bed, flipping through computer printouts. John read, but sometimes when she wasn't watching, he just looked at her.

He glanced at the clock, swearing silently when it turned 8:30, expecting she'd soon announce her departure. He told her how much he appreciated her company. "It's felt really good—not just you helping out while I'm laid up, but spending time together."

She stretched and yawned.

"I dream of us being like this again," he said. "Not just for a few days while I'm stuck in bed, but for everyday life."

"I don't think that's a good idea."

"Why?"

"I need to be alone—without a man." She stood up.

"Why?"

"Because I was starting to lose myself to you. That's what I did with Ted. I end up giving away my needs for what the man wants, and then I hate myself for it."

"That doesn't mean you need to be a hermit," he said. "We all have our issues to deal with."

"Yes—*deal* with in a deep way—not behavior therapy."

"Claire . . . ." He really didn't want to reopen that issue now, but he offered it up as a necessary sacrifice. "I'll think more about my ice fishing accident."

"Good—do what you need to do. And I need to be alone." She shoved the computer printouts into her backpack.

He saw in the purse of her lips that she was determined, like she had already decided the matter, and then he recognized a hole in her argument. "That's really important: to be yourself—not to lose yourself with a man," he said. "But you can't really accomplish that by isolating. Your challenge is not whether you can be yourself *without* a man—you've already proved that by all of these weeks when we weren't seeing each other. The real question for you is, 'Can you be yourself *with* a man?'"

She pursed her lips. "Say that again?"

He tried to give his most persuasive analysis—without being too forceful—that her psychological growth hinged on being herself in a relationship with a man—not to give away her needs to meet the explicit requests or the covert tugs a man might present. "Being alone at times—yes, that's absolutely important, and I really respect how you take time to be alone on occasions. That proves you don't have to always be with a man. But to avoid being in any relationship because you're concerned you won't be yourself with a man—well, wouldn't that just be a phobic response, evading your own personal challenge for growth? You need to practice being yourself with a man."

Claire laughed, first a nasal chuckle, then a deep belly laugh. She stood up and walked to the bathroom. When she returned, she pulled on her coat.

"Well?" he asked. "There's something to that, don't you think?"

She leaned over the bed. He smiled, and reared up to kiss her lips, but she turned her head and kissed him on the cheek.

"Maybe," she said. "We both have things to think about."

He heard little from Claire over the next three weeks. At first, he tried to be patient, thinking she needed space to think things through. He convinced himself that Claire was still badly hurt from Ted leaving her and that this needing-to-be-alone business was really an attempt to protect herself from getting hurt again, but she would come around in time. But then he grew aggravated, considering her self-centered when she didn't return his phone calls (other than quickly once to check on his progress in physical therapy for his ankle). His annoyance turned to worry, and then fear, when he concluded her silence meant she was indeed ending the relationship to be alone. He made a flurry of phone calls but was only greeted by her answering machine (he only left messages twice) over two days, and he felt despair encroaching. He was battling his funk when Claire called him in his campus office on a Thursday evening, asking him to go that night with her and Felice to a poetry reading by a Black feminist. He had plenty to do on his research, but he wanted to see Claire. She and Felice picked him up on campus within an hour.

They slipped into the old, gray stone library in North St. Louis just before the reading was to start. The room was crowded, predominately with Black women. They found a place to sit on the spiral staircase leading to the second floor. Their view was partially obstructed; they had to lean forward, craning their necks around the black rod-iron railing to see the poet. Even then, they could barely make out her face, which was partially hidden by the stairs and a turquoise scarf wrapped over her hair and forehead. But she made up for the poor view, filling the air with ripe images of Black women struggling with White society, with Black men, and with themselves. She refused to read from her play, *For Colored Girls Who Considered Suicide When the Rainbow Isn't Enuf*, a commercial and critical success from years prior; it was too draining emotionally, she said. But she read poems, including a recent piece that she said was a favorite, of a Black woman that included a long stanza about a man who seduced her, and then during intercourse, slammed his penis into her anus just before coming, his semen too good for her pussy, the character in the poem said.

On the drive back, John tried to discuss the poem, which he feared would have only reinforced Claire's notions of being alone without a man. "It was powerful but disturbing," he said, glancing at Claire. "A sad reflection of how the power dynamics between men and women can become sick, if both parties aren't aware and communicating openly about the relationship."

"It's just like a man," Felice replied. "He seduces, he gets you to open up, and then bam—he fucks you in the ass."

Claire laughed, so did Felice. Felice complained she was getting sleepy. After dropping Felice off at her apartment, Claire asked if she could drive John home. She made herself at home in his apartment, taking the glass decanter of cheap chardonnay from the refrigerator and pouring two glasses. She sat next to John in the loveseat, swiveling toward him.

"So, what are you thinking?" she asked.

"About what?"

"About anything."

He figured it was a trick question. "I have thought more about things, like you asked." She looked at him quizzically, saying nothing, and he decided she wasn't going to let him skate by. "About our canoe trip and my ice fishing accident. I think you're right, to some extent: falling in the river did touch old issues that were scary." The truth was that he hadn't thought deeply about the accident so much as it had hovered around the edges of his mind. But the whole affair felt like a sinkhole that made him feel small and helpless and confused, so he tried to just push it away and move on. But all of that seemed too much to expose and he hoped he could dance around the issues now.

"What did you say?" she asked.

"Are you messing with me?"

"No," she laughed, and pointed up. "I wasn't sure I heard you with the plane overhead, and you were mumbling."

He hadn't really noticed the airplane engines until her comment. Living under one of the flight paths to Lambert airport—they varied with the weather—he had become nearly oblivious to the sound of planes. "I said that I think you're partially right—my falling in the river probably touched old issues that were scary."

"Is that it? You already told me this before when we first talked at my house."

"There needs to be more?" He shook his head. "Yes, it's also true that I felt scared and crappy because of the accident itself, I felt guilty about how it inflamed my parent's arguments, and I felt terrible about my mom's problems afterward. Honestly, at times I still feel bad about all of that, but that was a long time ago, and that experience rarely, if ever, gets stirred up now and my parents and my mom are doing okay now. And even if the past does occasionally rear up, then what do you do?"

Claire looked him in the eye. "What do *you* do?"

"You don't get lost in the muck. What's important is trying to accomplish something positive in life—like helping others, which is why I persevere with all of the demands of graduate school. And I want to open up and love again, but this time in a way that is more fresh, intense, and real. That's what's important, that's what my life is about. And despite some tough times between us, I realize how much I love you. Maybe you'll break up with me for good someday, but for now, loving you is what I want most."

"Your words of romance are a sweet song, John Anderson, but I still think you're in denial."

"About what?"

"The extent of the old pain. And more than that, about your childhood family dynamics, your own vulnerability, and the fragility of life."

"You must still be reading Becker."

"I didn't bring this up—you did. I was simply asking how you were. But now that you've opened it up, I can tell you the threat is not confined to the pages of a paperback. Life is full of trauma and vulnerability. And we're all going to die—you, me, everyone—sooner or later."

"Well, I know—"

"That fact is something we each know at some level, yet we try to deny. But we can't rid ourselves of it. It affects us profoundly. Becker says—*actually*, I am rereading him—the threat of death is an unresolved dynamic that perverts life for most people."

"That's obvious that we're all going to die eventually, Claire." He was tired of both her digging into his past and her annoying existential lectures. Every time he opened up to her, she seemed to still want more. "But life is *not* all about death and trauma and living in fear of that. I fucking refuse to believe that. Life is about a lot of other, more positive things."

"Yes, but life is full of tragic, terrifying things that are easy to deny."

"And sometimes it's easier to run and hide from love and intimacy when closeness is scary."

"Perhaps sometimes. But not tonight." Claire smiled. In the bright light from the reading lamp, her hair shone golden.

He was proud of himself. He had hit her square with his belief that their problem was not his issues but Claire's running away from intimacy because she was scared. But her reaction to his words puzzled him—she seemed neither surprised nor defensive. "So, are we agreeing? It felt for a while like we were arguing again."

"Just a spirited discussion," she said. "I like a challenging conversation on occasion."

"Ah, so that's it." He wondered about her wanting to be alone, without a man—had she really decided to be with him after all? He stopped himself before he spoke. Better not to ask directly.

"Besides, in my therapy I've been working on two things," she said. "One is trying not to take responsibility for your past and your emotional issues but to let you deal with those while focusing on my own issues from the past."

"Well, I appreciate that," he said, though he was sorting through his own mixed reactions. Her words made it sound like he was in denial or irresponsible, characterizations that disturbed his self-image. He also appreciated Claire's insights to a certain extent; it was just that she pushed too hard even after he had made himself vulnerable. "So, what's the second thing you are working on?"

"Reclaiming my own body and pleasures as a woman." She glanced away but then quickly looked directly at him while taking a breath. "I've told you before about how harsh, even abusive my mom was to me as a child when I masturbated. That was her problem, I'm sure now. There's nothing wrong with me as a sexual woman, other than I was made to feel bad about it as a child."

He found himself nodding. "That's good, Claire. I've said that before, but you are wonderful, sexually, but I'm glad you are feeling that way now about yourself."

"I am." She smiled. "And you've helped me realize that about myself. I appreciate that and I want to own my own sexuality as a woman." She leaned forward, pressing her warm lips against his. Her tongue forced its way into his mouth.

His body tightened; he broke off the kiss.

"What's the matter?" she asked.

"Nothing."

"Feels like something."

"There's a little something. I don't know what." He fidgeted, trying to find a more comfortable spot on the loveseat. So, it seemed she'd decided to be with him. But was that still what he wanted—after she'd backed away and kept him wondering and worried for weeks? "Maybe I'm a little preoccupied with all of the hard times we've had lately."

"Dealing with the conflicts is hard. But I'm glad we do."

"Plus, some of the talk was a bit morbid. It's still kind of bouncing around in the back of my mind."

"Death and trauma do have a way of sticking with people."

He felt himself frown. Why did she have to be so obsessed with death? "Are you disappointed?"

"No. Well, a little."

"I'd like to put this behind me."

"I'm glad you're thinking about those things," she said. "Don't lose it. Recognize it and use it instead."

"What?"

"Know what I said about vulnerability and death are true. But don't despair. Accept it, let it give you a passion. Tonight, think of it, but enjoy our being together even more. Make love with me knowing we won't live forever, hold nothing back, give me all your passion."

"I'll make love with you. But my passion will have everything to do with loving you and nothing to do with death."

"And I will make love to you knowing that we will not live forever but choosing to embrace my sexuality and my life." She took John by the hand and led him to the bedroom. Her fingers popped open his top shirt button, then the next. She touched her hand—it was warm and soft—against his pectoral muscles. She leaned him onto the bed, finished undressing him, pulled her black sweater over her head, and dropped her jeans and underwear to the floor. She climbed on top of him, her naked body over his, strands of her long hair dangling onto his cheeks. She peered into his eyes, and as he tried to hold her gaze, she blew a long, slow breath across his face.

After they made love, he found her staring at him.

"I could feel your pulsations when you climaxed," she said. "They were like concentric circles of explosions: boom, boom, boom." She opened and closed her fist to emphasize her point.

He laughed, pulling her to his chest.

"I wanted you," she said.

"I'm glad you did. I wanted you too."

"I could tell."

She let her body relax into his. He caressed her back, and her breath danced light and warm on the faint hairs of his chest. Her arm jerked abruptly. She raised her head, droopy eyes trying to focus. "I was starting to fall asleep."

"I know."

She clambered off John and walked to the bathroom. When she returned, she exclaimed it was cold. Standing naked, blonde hair falling almost to her shoulders, she looked beautiful. She rummaged through his closet, pulled out a red-and-white flannel shirt, and slipped it over her arms and shoulders. The clock next to her shone 11:52.

"Sometimes it feels like you're going to drive me crazy, but you're an amazing, one-of-a-kind woman." He had never been with anyone who would withdraw—no, it wasn't withdrawing, but more like shoving off and running away, like an emotional hit-and-run—but then return so intense and fully present. She was still an enigma to him, but there was something about her he needed, something that restored him to feeling alive. "I love how passionate you are."

"There was plenty of passion tonight, and it wasn't coming just from me. You made love to me like it would be the last time."

"I hope not."

"You never know." She sat on the bed.

"Now what?"

"I don't mean another upset between us."

"Oh, another existential lecture then?"

"Everything is existential at some level," she said. "But it's not a lecture. It's news. I almost forgot. Tonight is when the world is supposed to end."

"I heard two disc jockeys jabbering on the radio about something, but I thought they were just bullshitting. What is it?"

"Some religious sect is predicting the galaxy will explode tonight because of the alignment of the stars and planets."

"That's crazy. I wouldn't lose any sleep over it."

"I don't know. I felt an explosion just a few minutes ago: boom, boom, boom."

He grinned. "Come here."

Claire climbed under the covers and John wrapped his arms around the flannel shirt, cuddling her close to his body.

"Have you ever read *Humboldt's Gift* by Saul Bellow?" he asked.

"No."

"There's a scene in there where the protagonist, Charlie Citrine, fantasizes about a woman he once loved. He thinks if he only could have had ten thousand nights in her arms, he'd be satisfied with his life. That's how I feel about you, Claire, but I want even more."

"Even more? What—10,001 nights?"

"At least."

He stroked her hair again. After a few minutes, her arm jerked. He was amazed at how quickly she fell asleep and wished he could do the same. He caressed the back of her head, watching her sleep.

He woke to a thunderous noise. The room was dark—the alarm clock showed 3:12—and he recognized the loud, groaning sound as airplane engines. He'd never heard a plane this close—it was as if he was seated next to the tail-mounted engines of a MD-80 jet airliner. The whining of the engines grew louder. He found Claire—she had rolled to the edge of the bed—and cradled her sleeping body in his arms. He waited, thinking the plane was going to crash nearby, perhaps through his apartment roof. It was too late to try to run away. He hugged Claire tighter, savoring the warmth, thinking if the plane crashed, if he was going to die, he'd die happy in her arms.

The roar reached a crescendo, and then lessened. The plane passed overhead and flew past. The world was not coming to an end tonight, but he kept Claire tight in his grasp.

◗ CHAPTER 15

Everywhere Claire's skin touched his, John felt warmth. The midday sun and her body radiated heat, and he had the sensation of baking like a loaf of bread dough, rising in the oven. He nudged Claire, scooting even closer across the red-and-white bedspread as they lay together on the beach. The Southern Illinois lake was not pretty compared to the mountain lake that John vaguely remembered in the California Sierras, but the water, a murky green-brown, was thick with bodies on Memorial Day. Swimmers bumped into each other, and the sand beach, coarse and dark like brown sugar, was covered with blankets, sunbathers, and castle-makers.

He closed his eyes to the glare glistening off the water. Winter had refused to relinquish its dominance to spring until the last few weeks, and John reveled in the afternoon sunlight. The months of gray and cold had seemed endless, but he had passed some invisible barrier with Claire. She no longer actively pushed him away; if anything, she seemed to be slowly opening up to him.

Raucous laughter clamored nearby. John and Claire sat up and saw Josh buried up to his head in a mound of gravelly sand. His brother and their two friends had excavated a shallow grave on the beach, burying Josh in the sand like an unlucky pirates' captive.

"Oh, my word," Claire exclaimed, carefully praising the work of the sand diggers as well as Josh, who remained patiently still. She clicked one snapshot with her instamatic camera and then took several more photos as directed by her boys. Josh giggled his way up and through the sand. He ran into the lake, dove beneath the surface, and rinsed away the caked sand clinging to his flesh. He returned to the beach and, after a brief caucus with his brother and friends, the four guys trudged along the shoreline in search of adolescent girls. Claire yelled after them to go no further than the dam.

"Look at them," Claire laughed. Ryan pushed Josh into the water, toward two bikini-clad teenagers. "They're half-boys, half-men, and they can't decide which they like better, playing in the sand or looking cool to girls."

"That's adolescence," John said.

"It's good to see them laugh again."

"It's good to see *you* laugh again."

Claire and Ted's March divorce court date had been hard on her boys. Josh was suspended from school for fighting and most days at home he hit his brother and yelled at Claire; Ryan retreated to his room and read fantasy novels. The boys had also been staying most of the time with Claire, as Ted said they were fighting constantly with Rebecca's daughters and causing trouble there. Claire talked about dropping out of graduate school—she admitted she was completely overwhelmed—but John pitched in, twice a week watching the boys after school, helping with the homework, and cooking the family dinner. Claire had started the boys in therapy, and just the prior week she told John that she thought the boys were healing. John agreed, thinking Claire's passion was reemerging, too: to his delight, they had slept together each night of the prior week while her boys had been at Ted's and he was enjoying the fruits of her labors in her own therapy, as she was reclaiming her sexuality with a new level of abandonment. He interpreted the week as a good omen for the summer, and perhaps for a new season in their relationship.

"It's hot," Claire said. Sweat beaded just above the miniature chicken pox indent on the bridge of her nose.

"Feels good after such a long cold spell."

"Too hot for me. Let's get in."

"No thanks."

"Are you scared to get in the water?" she asked.

"Not really." It was a half-truth. He wasn't scared in his *thinking*, but her invitation had sent a flash of adrenaline surging through his chest that preceded any rational thoughts. "It's going to be too cold out there."

"I wasn't being hostile, asking if you were scared."

"I didn't take it that way."

"Good. Then there's no excuse." She bounded to her feet, tugging on his hand. "Come on. I'll make it worth your while. Promise. Plus, we'll only go chest deep and I'll hold onto you the whole time."

"I don't think so." He'd finished his therapy, and in his mind, the systematic desensitization had been successful—he could imagine himself swimming in open water without fear and panic. He just wasn't sure that he actually wanted to do it.

"Nothing's going to happen in a few feet of water. Nothing bad anyway."

John surveyed the swim area. He wanted to prove to Claire, and perhaps himself, that he could get in the water. He rose into a crouched position.

"Wonderful!" Claire grabbed his wrists, pulling him up. She held his hand and walked him to the lake's lapping edge.

"Let me just feel it," he said. The water swirled around his ankles, cool but not as cold as he expected.

"Good! You're in. Now another step."

He inched forward. "Let me acclimate, Claire." His head felt light, dizzy. He resisted an irrational impulse to run and remembered to focus on breathing from his diaphragm.

"You're doing very well," Claire said. "Just a little further now."

He walked baby steps into the lake, Claire holding and gently pulling on his hand, coaxing and encouraging him with her words. Soon the water sloshed against his belly button and he could no longer see his knees, which had disappeared into the murky green-brown lake. A small boy gripping a yellow-and-green air mattress collided with John's hip. Clear mucus rolled from his left nostril as he stared at John.

"Hi there." Claire grinned. The boy asked if Claire would give him a push toward shore, and she obliged.

Claire tugged on John's hand, pulling him into deeper water. The boy soon looked small and far away.

"That's far enough." A wave flopped against John's collarbone, emitting a fishy smell.

"No, come on. You're okay and I've got you." Claire touched her nose to his, wrapping her arms around him. She blew a long, warm breath on his cheeks and embraced him as if they were in slow dance, leading him further out, a small step at a time.

"Not too deep. Really, Claire." He scanned the water. Children and adults were splashing and playing everywhere. No one seemed to be watching. Water covered half of his rib cage. "This is far enough. *Really.*"

"Okay, good." She cinched her arms tighter around him, holding him close for a long time, and he felt his body relax in her arms.

"How are you?" She asked.

"Better. I was petrified a couple of times walking out, to be honest with you, but I practiced the relaxation breathing therapy and I feel a lot more at ease now."

"Good!"

"But let's not go any further."

"No, we won't go any further out. This will be fine." She slid her hands the length of his back, and then rubbed, long and hard, the small of his back.

"Mmm," he murmured. "That feels good."

"I know that's your favorite spot. Let me correct that—it's your second favorite spot." She planted her moist lips on his neck. "I'm proud of you for entering the lake. I wasn't sure if you would."

"Me either. I mean, I thought I could, but to be honest, I still thought of turning back a few times."

"I'm glad you didn't. You're much safer here than driving on the highway, you know."

"So, you're what, trying to transfer my phobia to driving?"

"Turn this way."

"Why?"

"So I can keep an eye on the boys. They're splashing each other way down there." She pointed to a bend where the beach curved back in a half-moon.

"I'm surprised you could spot them so far away with so many other kids in the water."

"A mother's instinct." Claire intertwined her legs with John's.

"That feels nice."

"Umm." She massaged his lower back, then slipped her hand under his swim trunks. Her fingers stroked the naked flesh of his butt, then slid across his hip, finding and holding his water-shriveled penis in her warm hand.

"Claire! For God's sake—what are you doing?"

"Just helping you fully relax."

"There's a hundred people per square yard in this lake."

"So many, that they don't even notice what's going on a few feet away," she whispered, her moist lips tickling his ear. "Besides, with the murky water, who can tell the difference? We just look like a couple of lovebirds snuggling close. You're a romantic, you'll like that." She stroked his penis while she explained.

"Claire, I don't know."

"Oh, look." Her hand gripped his swelling penis. "I'm holding hard proof that you do want this."

He kissed her. Her wet nipples prickled his chest. She tugged on his trunks, yanking them toward his thighs, but they caught on his hips.

"Hold on."

"Claire . . ."

She dove under the surface, her hand and shoulders disappearing in the brownish water. She pulled his trunks down around his knees. She bobbed up, spewing lake water, smiling.

"Now, where were we?" she asked. She embraced him, her wet nose bumping against his. Beneath the murky surface, she gripped his penis and slipped it under the edge of her swimsuit, sliding him inside her. A boy and a girl wedged inside a huge black inner tube bumped into Claire on a wave.

"Hi kids," Claire said. "Having fun out here?"

The boy, about eight with a ban of freckles across his nose, nodded.

"Me too. Here, want a little push off?"

Claire gave the inner tube a gentle shove, then rocked against John. They nudged groins, a slippery slide into each other. Claire stared into eyes, smiling a crooked grin. He laughed, closed his eyes, and felt overwhelmed by her.

He held Claire's hand for a long time, long beyond the point in which it was comfortable since he had to awkwardly rotate his shoulder to reach her, but he wanted to stay connected. "Claire, I love you."

"I love you."

"Thanks for taking me out in the water."

"Umm, it was my pleasure, and *erotic*."

"I lost all fear out there." An expansive feeling—he wasn't sure what to call it but it included lightness and happiness—swelled inside.

"You experienced a stronger emotion, one incompatible with fear, which inhibited the anxiety."

"Huh," he said. "I've never thought of you before as a behaviorist."

"I'm not. But sometimes you need the right tool for the right job. Besides, I didn't conduct a behavioral analysis beforehand. I just suddenly felt sexual."

He found himself grinning. Not only had he conquered his phobia, but also Claire's heart was healing from her divorce and opening to a new level of intimacy—emotional as well as sexual—with him. He imagined again a great summer, a season of daily encounters, lots of sex, and weekend trips. He wished for another chance for he and Claire to camp and canoe; it would be different this time, without secrets, without old fears to mess them up. By the end of the summer, he should be finished with his dissertation, finished with his long over-due paper to resolve a delayed grade, finished with his doctorate, and they could plan a longer journey together out west. They could travel upstream on the trip she'd always wanted to take and search for the source of the river.

"Claire?"

"Hmm?"

"The boys are with you until Friday afternoon?"

"Yes."

He rolled onto his side and propped himself up on an elbow. "What do you say we leave then and go camping and canoeing for the weekend?"

"I can't."

"Darn it. How come?"

"I have a date."

He felt himself pull back. "You're getting together with Felice before she moves?"

She sat up, faced John, crossed her legs Indian style. "I've decided I want to date other men, too, for the experience."

"What's that supposed to mean?"

"I'd been with one man—Ted—from high school until last year—every year of my adult life. And since then, I've only dated you. I want to keep a relationship with you, but I need the experience of dating other men too."

"The *experience* of dating other men?" He glared at her.

"Yes. How do you feel about it?"

"Scared. Bad. How did you think I'd feel?"

"I'm sorry—it's not about hurting you. It's something I've realized I've needed to do for myself."

"I don't get it, Claire. What's wrong?"

"It's not about you. It's about me. I intended to date other men when I first separated from Ted, but I haven't. I've only been with you."

"So?"

"Don't you see? I've restricted myself to the same one-man pattern all my life. And as much as I love you, I don't want to suppress myself for any man—or feel a sense of obligation to a man. It's my issue, not yours, but I need to do this for myself."

He groaned. "And so you just suddenly decided this without even telling me?"

"It just happened."

"What?"

"I just decided in my therapy and then serendipitously I got asked out on a date yesterday. I was going to tell you tonight after the boys went to sleep." There was a defensive edge to her voice, like she felt guilty, but it was unlikely that she would apologize, at least right away.

"Who are you going to date?"

"I don't think it's helpful to say."

"It's someone at the Unitarian church, isn't it?"

"I'm not going to say."

"I bet it is. You're beautiful and you're bright and you sit in those book groups and talk and guys see how attractive you are . . ." And they want to fuck your brains out, he almost blurted out but he stopped himself. She had been working in therapy on freeing herself from the negative messages about her sexuality from her mom and even Ted, which John was glad about, but now he worried she wanted to experiment with other men too.

"Maybe you want to date too?" she asked.

"No."

"Don't you ever feel that way?"

"I used to imagine that it'd be nice to date more women, but I haven't wanted to since we've been together."

"But at least you understand why it's important to me."

"I can understand the feelings but not the action. I don't understand why you want to mess with a good thing."

"Because life isn't made to live safe all the time." She picked a small rock out of the brown sand and tossed it into the water. "At least not for me. It's important for me to do what I feel, even if it's scary for me and the people I care about."

A catamaran whipped across the middle of the lake, banking in the wind on one pontoon. "Are you going to have sex with someone else?" John asked.

"I don't have that planned."

"That's not exactly a 'no,' is it?"

"I'm not planning to go out Friday night or any time in the foreseeable future and jump in bed with anyone else. That's not what this is about. But—and I know this is difficult for you—I have to open myself to the experience of dating and trust that in the process I'll find out who I am and what fits for me."

"So, that leaves you wide open for having sex with someone else in the future, doesn't it?"

"If you want a guarantee, I can't give it," she said. "I can't promise you anything other than I'll be true to the adventure of being myself."

"The adventure of being yourself, huh?" He hated the idea she was going to act out her newfound freedom for sex with other men too. "I guess that's a fancy way of saying you reserve the right to fuck whomever you want whenever you want."

"Fuck you."

"Sorry," he said.

"That was really shitty." She glared. "I thought you would understand. I put up with my mom and Ted both being critical of my sexuality and trying to control my choices around my body, but I'm not going to accept that from anyone ever again, including you."

"I'm sorry," he nodded. "That was a shitty way for me to say it, but this isn't what I want, Claire. I want it to be just you and me."

"You know, I suspected this conversation would be challenging for you to accept, but I thought we could make it work. Maybe I was wrong, John. Maybe we just can't make it through this one."

"Don't jump to conclusions." If she was forced to choose, he figured Claire would stop seeing him before she'd let go of her desire to date other men. "If dating is something you have to do, then that's what you have to do, but it's a shock. And it's hard on me. I need time to adjust."

She said nothing.

"Okay?" he asked. The wind had whipped up, carrying the smell of barbecue and leaving goose bumps on his arms.

"Okay."

"You still mad?"

"Don't worry about it."

She lay back down, but he felt a gap where their bodies once touched.

John slammed the tennis ball toward Phil, but it caught the middle of the net.

"Set point." Phil grinned from the far side of the court. "Second serve."

John pulled another tennis ball from his pocket. He told himself to lob the serve and play the volley. But he reared back, catching the ball high above his head. He hit it as hard as he could, but the ball pelted the white strip atop the net and fell back into his court.

"Shit."

"A heroic attempt," Phil called. "Stupid, perhaps, trying a power serve for the second serve, but heroic. Let's play another set."

"No thanks. I'm through."

"Come on, you won the first set. Don't be a sore loser."

"I'm not."

"Then play. This is the rubber set."

"I gotta get going or I'll be late to Claire's."

"Still at the end of her leash, huh?"

John walked out the gate.

Phil followed. "Let's have a quick beer anyway."

"I'd better run."

"Come on." Phil pulled two green Heineken bottles from a small Styrofoam chest in his trunk, popped the caps, and thrust the cold bottle into John's palm. They leaned against the fender and drank.

"That was fun," John said. "Some good volleys, a lot of running around, a good couple of sets."

"Better if you'd play that third set." Phil wiped his sweaty face on a white tennis towel. "How's Claire?"

"Okay, I guess. I'm not seeing her that much, once a week, sometimes twice."

"She's still dating?"

"Afraid so."

"How do you like that?"

"Doesn't bother me."

"Yeah, right."

"Really. Except every night when she's not with me and I'm going crazy at home imagining she's fucking some guy's brains out."

Phil laughed.

"I don't know if she is or she isn't," John said. "But either way, it sucks. Even if she's not sleeping around, she just isn't available much." He didn't want to admit it to Phil, but he'd found himself in his calmer moments actually admiring Claire in a confusing way—that she was willing to overcome her childhood issues and push her own edges, to choose adventure over security, even while he hated the particulars. "It's not the summer I imagined, for sure, but what can you do?"

"Be a monk."

"Now there's a helpful thought. Got any more great suggestions?"

"Not at the moment, but I'm sure they'll come."

"That's what I'm afraid of, but luckily I got to run."

John showered quickly at his apartment, then drove to Claire's. The last time he'd seen her, they'd gotten into another argument about her dating. He chided himself, thinking that when they were apart, he missed Claire, but when they were together, he felt resentful and they argued. He remembered his mother's saying about the neighbors across the street, the Petrallis, who separated, got back together, separated, got back together, ad infinitum, ad nauseam: can't live together, can't live apart. He worried for a second that he and Claire fell in the same category, but the thought was disturbing, and he pushed it away.

Claire told John to come to the sunroom. She propped herself against the corner of the loveseat, her legs crisscrossed over the cushions, and she swiveled her neck to stare out the back window.

"What's the matter?" he asked.

"Ted called this morning." She paused. "He wants to take the boys with him to South America for the rest of the summer."

"Why?"

"He's taken a job with a prestigious firm in Chicago for a lot of money—"

"I thought he loved working for the poor as a public defender?"

"He said he's paid his dues and he's tired of being poor himself, but I think maybe it's because he and Rebecca broke up and he's just trying to run away and get a fresh start. Anyway, he wants time to reconnect with the boys after Rebecca and he's going to get away to his brother's cattle ranch in Argentina before he starts his new job in September. He wants his boys with him for the summer, working on the ranch."

"What did you say?"

"No, at first. I don't think it's good for the boys to be away from their mother for such a long time. But he got angry, saying they were old enough, and that I had always been overprotective and that I'd never let him parent the way he should as their father. He said it would be good for the boys to see the world, to work hard on the ranch and earn wages, and for all of them to be together before his move. He'd already told the boys about Argentina—which pissed me off—and he said they were excited about the trip and making money and riding horses. So, I said yes." She shrugged and shook her head.

"You're going to miss them, aren't you?"

She nodded. "I miss my boys when they're with Ted for more than a few days—I can't imagine them being gone for the entire summer. But it's more than my missing them. It'll be hard on them to be without their mother for seven weeks, and it'll hit them all over again about the divorce. It's too late now, but how much have I damaged my sons by not staying married?"

He found himself agreeing in part with Ted—Claire often *was* overprotective of her boys, even as he admired the way she loved and supported them. "You listen to your boys," he said. "You support them, you encourage them, you love them. You don't make them appendages of yourself—you nurture their development into individuals. It may be hard for them to be away, but you've given them a lot to sustain themselves."

"Thank you." A corner of her mouth curled up for a moment into a mournful smile, but then she shook her head. "But it's also the loss of family all over again—for them, and for me."

"It hurts, I know. I'm sorry."

"I thought I'd finished grieving, but it's still there. It feels like a terrible hole."

"Grieving is like traveling down a road full of potholes—you never know when you're going to fall into a rut," he said. "If there's anything I can do to help, I will."

"Ted's going to bring the boys over soon. They're going to stay with me until they have to leave on Wednesday. I need that time alone with them."

"I understand." He didn't fully, but he wanted to be supportive.

"I also need to be alone while they're gone."

"Take the time you need. We'll get together in between times."

"No. I need these seven weeks to be truly alone, without any man, including you."

"What?" He tried to read her face and saw she was serious. "Why? That's crazy."

"It's *not* crazy."

The fierceness in her eyes *looked* crazy and almost scared him. "Sorry," he said. "But I don't get it."

"I haven't finished grieving. I was dependent on that old life and meanwhile I've become dependent on you—another man—for a new life."

"You're hardly even with me." He exhaled forcefully, like a short laugh, but it was more out of exasperation.

"When Ted said they'd be gone for seven weeks, I immediately panicked—it felt like an eternity of empty nights and weekends. I didn't know what I'd do, and I automatically thought of spending that time with you—I even thought of asking you to move in for the summer."

"I'd love that," he said. "That's a good thing, Claire. Embrace it."

"No—that was the clutching response, grabbing for something known and familiar. Don't you see? It would be a mistake for me to be with you—with any man—right now. I need to face my aloneness first."

He groaned, flooded with memories of how she wanted to be alone, then wanted to be close and sexual with him, and then she wanted to experiment with other men. He wondered if she knew what she really wanted and he debated in that instant whether he wanted to try to persuade Claire to stay together or to give into his impulse to tell her to shove the whole idea of a relationship. He felt about done, fed up with her back-and-forth dance of intimacy and avoidance. "I don't see it the same way," he said. "Your boys go away, you miss them, and you're going to stop seeing me? That sounds a little reactive, a little displaced to me."

"That's the way it's going to be."

"Jesus, Claire. Sometimes I don't know what to say."

She looked through the window to the backyard.

"So, what are you going to do with all of your time?" He wondered and worried at the same time.

"There's a dog rescue shelter in the country that I heard about. I'm going to volunteer there some on the weekends. And I need time to be alone."

There was another question that he wasn't sure if he wanted to ask. "You've been dating another man—or other men—and yet you say you're dependent on me? I'm confused."

"I've felt guilty all along about dating someone else—like I belonged to you."

"Well, that's good to hear." He felt some relief, though he wondered if she had slept with another man, and then he tried to figure out how he could change her mind about being alone. "You know, though, like we've talked about before, the issue is about how you can be yourself *with* a man, not without a man."

"*No.* You're not going to talk me out of this again," she said. "If you understood me, you'd respect my need to be completely alone now."

"I'm not so sure, but I'd like to understand."

"Not now. The boys will be here soon."

"And the other men?" Self-loathing surged inside him for even asking, but he felt compelled. "What about you dating?"

She shook her head slightly in a look he'd never seen before, like she was disgusted or maybe going to scream. "That's over. You need to leave now."

In some ways, John's discussion with Branham was the kind of conversation—a debate about clinical approaches—that John had imagined he'd engage in frequently in graduate school. But the content, at least on Branham's part, was not what he expected. Branham was anti-academic, clearly suspicious of intellectuals, although he deftly censored himself whenever faculty was nearby. Why Branham had chosen graduate school had puzzled John and also Phil, who had once put forth the question directly. "That's easy," Branham had answered. "Money. Seventy-five bucks for fifty minutes to start—and then up from there—to listen to people's problems and do a little hand-holding. *That's* easy money." But John didn't completely believe his mercenary remark. Branham was practical, a problem-solver, not theoretically sophisticated; but beneath his bravado, burly frame, and frequent reminders about being a Vietnam vet, there seemed to be a heart of genuine caring (he had once gotten in trouble with the faculty for surreptitiously volunteering, after permission had been refused because of the heavy graduate load, twenty hours a week as a counselor at the Vet Center). But whatever the source of their differences with Branham, John and Phil were having little success persuading him on the necessity for specialized clinical approaches with minorities, which they found unfortunate, since it was the topic of the group paper they jointly owed a professor from two years prior to resolve a delayed grade.

"I'm telling you, it's pretty fucking simple," Branham said. "People are people, full of neurotic problems, and you don't need a lot of silly-assed concepts and techniques. It's like all this stir over post-traumatic stress disorder. You know what that is? It's some nervous Nelly junior faculty trying to guarantee himself tenure by coming up with an elaborate scheme for the fact that a lot of people go fucking bonkers after they've been in a crazy war."

"I'll grant you that it's essential to view people from a humanistic frame," Phil responded. "But PTSD is a complex phenomenon and if psychology is truly going to develop itself as a science, it needs—"

"Cut the bullshit, will you?" Branham said. "For Christ's sake—psychology as a science. It's about people making enough money to drive BMWs and live in places like Ladue. This post-traumatic stress disorder shit for Vietnam—I'm all for there being more money for vets—but I can tell you it's a lot of words made up by some prematurely balding associate professor with wire-rim glasses who doesn't dare fart in front of anybody but himself."

Phil argued back, citing research and diagnostic criteria, but Branham disagreed all the more. They looked to John like they were in for a long debate.

"What was it like over in Vietnam anyway?" John asked. He figured they needed a neutral diversion if they were ever going to get back to their paper.

"You want to know what it was like?" Branham eyed him.

"Yeah, I've always wondered."

"It was fucking crazy. They knew it—Washington, the Joint Chiefs. Joint Chiefs—what a name, as if they're a bunch of Indian Chiefs who ride into battle. Ha!" Branham had long claimed that his great-grandfather was the head of a tribe, and with that heritage and some connections, he'd finagled a Native American scholarship to go along with his Veteran's college funding. "They're a bunch of stodgy assholes who didn't give a shit about guys like you and me. You two think *I'm* sociopathic, I know, but our system, the military-industrial-political complex, is fucking sociopathic. They didn't give a flying fuck about wasting sixty-thousand guys and mind-fucking a couple million more because they had to keep the military—and the corporate defense contractors—*strong*." Branham snorted. "I learned a lot over there, not what they wanted me to think. Not myths, but how things really are. But I went in green. You should have seen the recruiter's eyes light up when he saw me—this big-as-an-ox, gung-ho, hungry, eighteen-year-old farm boy. I was gung-ho, I admit it. It was like being pumped up for a Friday night football game, except we had guns to shoot the Commies and a wild-assed, nonstop party with all the drugs and booze and whores you could imagine on the sidelines. *Fuck.*"

"So, what changed your thinking?" John asked.

"Experience. I had this platoon buddy, Burt—how's that for an All-American name?—as green and naively enthusiastic as I was. A regular little cannonball, short but with stocky arms and legs, a high school football star, like the pint-sized halfback I used to block for back in the Bootheel. The first week out we get pinned down with lead screeching over our heads, and one of our buddies caught it bad in the leg. He's screaming, sixty yards ahead, and this little showdown is going fucking nowhere with night starting to fall. We know if it gets dark, the VC are going to find a way to slit this boy's prick, not to mention his throat. So, Burt and I charge after him like fucking Teddy Roosevelt up San Juan Hill, bullets fucking flying everywhere. We pull him back and kill a couple of VC who tried to stop us in the process."

"Heroes," Phil interjected.

"Fucking heroes." Branham eyed Phil. "The lieutenant, a college boy, says he's going to put us up for the Silver Medal."

"Did you get it?" John asked.

"Burt didn't."

"Why?"

"A few weeks later there's a similar deal, only this time it's a bigger fight, more assholes shooting at each other, and it's the fucking middle of the night. Some guy gets wounded, stranded out there, and is screaming for help. Burt and another grunt volunteer to go get him. I wanted to go again but I'm back protecting a flank and this other GI really wants to be a fucking decorated hero too. Only problem is that Burt and this guy don't come back. Finally, just before dawn, the show's suddenly over and we search for them, hoping they just got pinned down somewhere. They got pinned down all right—right to the fucking ground. I find Burt first—I can tell right off its him by his pint-sized body—lying there, and I turn him over. You know what I see?"

"What?" Phil asked.

"His face half-blown off. You ever seen anyone with his face blown half-off?"

"No," John said. "Thank God, no."

"It's ugly. It's like bloodied, ground beef, except there's a shattered skull sticking through it."

"I get the picture, at least enough of it," John said. "That had to be awful."

"I'll tell you what was awful. Listening so fucking many times after that to people screaming at night. I never went out again, never wanted to be a hero again, but I used to lie there during firefights at night, listening to people scream, never knowing if it was really a buddy you could bring back or a trap with a VC waiting to blow your face off. Try to sleep through that shit."

"How'd you cope with that?" John asked.

"Same way everyone else with any brains did: get high and stay high. It was the best way to get through it."

"Your Silver Medal—did it come through?" John asked

"Nope."

"What happened?"

"Who knows," Branham said.

"You didn't ask?"

"Why the hell would I?"

"I see your point," John said. "Guess getting a medal pinned to your chest didn't seem to matter much after your friend was killed."

"Fuck no," he shook his shaggy head. "There was way too much crazy bullshit going down."

"That was a lot of shit to live through."

"Yeah, but I lived through it. The fuckers didn't get me killed and they didn't make me crazy, even if it seems like it to you. But I got a hell of a lot smarter."

"How is it," John asked, "talking about all of this?"

Branham eyed him. "So, what—you're practicing being a fucking therapist with me?"

"I didn't mean it that way. I just wondered—it sounded like a lot of old, painful, crazy stuff."

"Relax. I'm not jumping your case. Hey, you guys want to smoke some shit?"

"It's a little early in the day for me," Phil said.

"Not me, either, thanks."

"I was kidding. Had you guys going, though, didn't I—thinking ol' Branham is still a doper? No, sir, I've given that up. I'm all about academics these days."

"Right," Phil said.

"And women," Branham winked. "So, tell me, John, how are things with Claire?"

"She's all right, basically." He hesitated. "Of course, there's always some ups and downs."

"Most of them in bed, I hope." Branham's blue eyes twinkled.

"Not all." He worried Branham might pay Claire a visit, if he thought she was a lady in distress. "But you know Claire. She bounces back strong. She's fine, really."

"We're going down to the lake this weekend, just me and Karen—she'll have her kids at their dad's. What do you say you and Claire come down?"

"I don't know."

"What kind of answer is that?" Branham gave a crazy-eyes stare. "Say yes, goddamn it. It'll be a good time."

"What are you going to do?"

"Just kick back and enjoy life. Lie on the beach, float a little on the blowup mattresses, drink a lot of beer and a bottle of Jack. Swim if you want."

"I'm not big on swimming, thanks."

"Me either. But you can float on a mattress or just lay out on the beach. We'll have a wild time."

"I can ask Claire. I'm game, if she is, but I don't know if she'll want to go. She's a little asocial these days."

"Well, shit, ask anyway."

"I will," John said. "But I'm not very optimistic. She's kind of running away again."

"Listen," Branham said. "Seducing certain women is like reeling in a big fish—you gotta let them have some play, not fight them at first, and then when they've tired themselves out, you reel them in, nice and easy."

"Thanks, but unfortunately, I've never been much of a fisherman." John had intended to say the words with dry humor, but they sounded hopeless, not funny, to his own ears. Branham peered at him for a moment, not speaking, which was unusual for him. "What?" John asked.

"Claire's complicated," Branham said. "She's a really big fish, and she's going to give you a run for your money, but down deep, she loves you. She's just scared of getting hurt again. Hang in there."

Branham patted John on the shoulder, which felt both awkward, like a guy hug, but also caring, even intimate. "Thanks, Branham." Some emotion—John had felt moved by Branham in a way that caught him by surprise—pitched a warble to his words.

"Sure, just stand tall." Branham nodded. "And just don't be a pussy."

John laughed. It was like their moment of intimacy had been too uncomfortable and Branham had to take it partially back.

"Ask her about the lake," Branham said." And even if she says no, then just come yourself."

"But don't be a pussy about it," Phil joked.

Branham swiveled his desk chair toward Phil. "Speaking of pussies, you can come too. Now that Felice has departed for her Hawaiian internship, are you panting again after that South American senorita with the tight ass?"

John wondered if Claire might actually go. The last time he'd called, she was friendly, saying it was hard being alone, especially at night, though she refused his offer to get together. He thought about being at the lake, swimming and floating with Branham and Claire. The image made him nervous, but it would be worth it, he thought, if Claire went.

He called Claire that evening to ask her about Branham's invitation, but she didn't answer the phone then or with any of his other calls over the next two days. John worried something had happened to her—or perhaps she'd met someone new? But on the third day she answered the phone, and while John was glad to hear her voice, her tone changed when he said he'd been trying to reach her for a few days.

"I was gone for a couple of days."

"Oh." John paused. "Where did you go?"

"Camping and canoeing, if you need to know."

"Who'd you go with?"

"Myself."

"I see. Where did you go? The Ozarks, where we went?"

"Yep."

"Sounds fun." John felt something bad sink in his gut—he took her going without him as a sign she was withdrawing even further away from him. He wanted to say he would have loved to have gone with her, but he didn't want to get her on the defensive at the outset of their conversation.

"It was good," she said. "I wish I had more time—I would have gone canoeing out West, but I could only get a couple of days away from work and the dissertation. But someday I'll go."

"I'm sure." He resented that she hadn't thought to invite him. "Hey, this isn't nearly as exciting, but Branham invited you and me to go with him and Karen this weekend to the Lake of the Ozarks. You know, lay out, take it easy, maybe do a little floating. What do you say?"

"No."

"I was afraid you'd say that but maybe just think about it. It would be fun."

"Then why don't you just go?"

"It wouldn't be as much fun without you."

"I've told you—I need to be alone."

"You have been. You can feel proud about that. But how about taking a weekend respite from your self-imposed summer of solitude? You know," he wanted to make her laugh, "think of it as time off for good behavior."

"I said 'no.'"

Her tone was angry and he was tired of it. "Okay, but you don't have to sound so cranky."

"I do when you refuse to give me the space that I've repeatedly asked for, and I have to keep telling you no."

"I've called you a few times in three weeks—that hardly seems like I'm badgering you."

"Badgering isn't the right word—it feels maybe like you're clutching for my skirt. Whenever I need to be alone, you try to latch onto me."

"I called because Branham invited you and me to go to the lake this weekend."

"You know I want to be alone."

"Jesus, Claire. Why do you have to sound so mean?"

"I know this is scary for you," she said.

"What?"

"To be alone. And going to the lake touches your unresolved fears and death issues, but you need to get into depth therapy and deal with that stuff, not expect me to fill the holes."

"Are you done? Because I don't need to listen to your hostile, pseudo-intellectual existential psychoanalysis of me."

"Then don't."

John fumed a long time after hanging up. He preferred the anger to missing Claire, especially over the weekend when he worked long hours on the minority mental health paper instead of going to the lake. On Monday morning, he shoved copies of his sections of the paper into Phil's and Branham's boxes in the psychology department mail room. He pulled out papers from his own mailbox. A mimeographed notice, strong with the smell of fresh purple ink, lay on top:

IMPORTANT NOTICE

To: All Psychology Faculty, Staff, and Graduate Students.

From: Edward Lerner, Ph.D.

Date: Monday, August 6

Re: Sad News

It is with great sorrow that I must inform you that Branham Taylor died this past Saturday. He drowned at the Lake of the Ozarks.

Funeral services will be conducted this Wednesday at 11 a.m. at the Hope Lutheran Church of Manchester. The family has invited Branham's faculty, peers, and friends to this service but requested that internment be private.

Having known and worked with Branham closely in the past five years, I can only say I know that we will all deeply miss Branham. His death is as tragic as it is premature.

John ran across the hall to the psychology department office. Nina, one of the secretaries, sat alone at her desk.

"Is this true?" John waved the memo in the air.

"I'm afraid it is." She was in her late forties, with dyed red hair covering gray roots.

"How did it happen?"

"Apparently he fell off a rubber air mattress."

"Oh, God, no. Why didn't he swim to shore?"

"He didn't know how, I don't think."

"*Shit*," John swore. "Sorry. Wasn't anyone with him?"

Nina said she knew little other than what Dr. Lerner had given her to type fifteen minutes earlier. John wound his way through the cavernous hallways that crisscrossed the building to Lerner's office. His door was half open.

"Dr. Lerner?" Papers, folders, and books were stacked several feet high on the desk and similar piles rose like hoodoos from the floor.

"Yes?"

John peered around the door and saw the elderly professor crouched in the rear corner of his office, going through a folder. John stepped carefully into what appeared to be a narrow path carved between the spires of folders and books. "Sorry to disturb you, but I just read your memo about Branham. I can't believe it."

"Neither can I, but I fear it's true." He stood up.

"What happened? I just spoke with him on Friday."

"He drowned." Lerner repositioned his thick black frame glasses further down his rubbery nose. "He was floating on an air mattress at the Lake of the Ozarks and he slipped or something off his raft."

"Couldn't he swim?"

"Karen said he didn't know how. She'd been floating on another mattress next to him, but she'd come in to use the bathroom and when she returned, his raft was floating out on the lake but he was missing. She searched for him and finally saw him on the bottom. She called for help, but it was too late."

"Oh my God. What was he doing way out there if he couldn't swim?"

"That's the tragic part. They found him only thirty feet from shore. It was only seven feet deep."

"God."

"I'm sorry, Mr. Anderson, but I need to leave shortly to meet with Karen and Branham's mother to help with the final arrangements. In fact, I should have left already." He slipped his glasses back up the bridge of his nose. "But I was just looking for my last student evaluation of Branham—you know, to work into his eulogy."

John wandered back across the building, searching for someone to talk to, but the wide hallways were empty. He walked into the winding complex of hallways within the clinical students' office area, which surrounded the psychology clinic like catacombs. No one was in the corridor. He checked his watch. It was almost nine in the morning—still early for grad students, especially in the summer. The doors were all closed. Adjacent to John's office, Branham's name glistened in brass on his shut door. It looked like an executive's nameplate, shiny and bold. Phil had once teased Branham about it. "Where did you get that?" Phil had asked. "Brookstone's or the Sears catalog?"

"Just getting used to the good days ahead." Branham had stood up and wagged a long, thick finger at Phil. "If you don't think big, you'll never be big. Know what I mean?"

At six-foot-six or so, Branham towered over Phil, who had a dubious claim of being five-foot-ten. Branham always seemed so big, so strong—how could he have drowned? Especially in seven feet of water? He was nearly that tall. He envisioned Branham thrashing in the water, gasping for air, the water freezing. *Goddamn it.*

Dear God in heaven, John prayed while wondering if there was even a God. Still, he commanded himself to finish: *Dear God, please let Branham live on, somewhere. He is a good person, he cared a lot about people.*

John questioned himself for praying, like a little child. He felt guilty then, like he was sabotaging his own prayer. He stared at Branham's name in brass. He felt like throwing up. He hurried out of the building, thinking of Claire. She had a fondness for Branham, for his independence, for his odd sense of humor, for his big heart that lurked beneath his bravado. When John arrived at his apartment, he called Claire at her office at the VA hospital. There was no answer at her extension. He called back, time and again, trying unsuccessfully every five minutes over the next half-hour. The operator sounded disgusted and so he asked her to connect him to the unit nursing station. The ward clerk said she didn't know where Claire was and to call back later, but John told her it was very important and asked to speak to the head nurse. After a long delay, the clerk returned, reporting that Claire had gone with a group of patients and the recreational therapy staff on a day-long out-trip.

"Where?"

"Hermann, Missouri."

"Where in Hermann? What are they doing?"

"I don't know."

"Can you try to find out, please? It's an emergency."

The telephone clanged against the desktop, and the clerk's voice echoed in the background.

"A tour of the city," she reported tartly. "And the local VFW is sponsoring a barbecue for them."

"At the VFW hall?"

"No, at a local park."

"Which one?"

"Look, we don't know."

"Well, what time will they be back?"

"About 4:30."

"Will you please leave a message for Claire to call me as soon as she gets in?"

"And who are you again?"

"John Anderson. We're . . . good friends."

John tried to work on his dissertation throughout the day, but his thoughts drifted back to Branham and to Claire. He called her office several times in the afternoon in case she had returned early, but there was never an answer.

He called the nurse station at 4:20 but Claire wasn't back yet. He called four times in the next forty-five minutes, but the staff person told him with mounting irritation that the rec trip was running late, and that they would pass on his message to Claire. John worried something tragic, like a bus accident had happened. He tried to dismiss the thought as complete paranoia, but he couldn't get the worry completely out of his head. When he called back at 5:25, the clerk said the patients had gotten back ten minutes before but Claire wasn't there.

"She must have left already," the clerk said. "You should call her at home."

John silently cursed the clerk's passive-aggressiveness and then called Claire at her house several times over the next hour but without an answer. He decided he needed to do something productive to calm down. He read his sections of the minority mental health paper with an eye for revisions. He picked through the pages, remembering how difficult it had been for he, Phil, and Branham to get started on the assignment two years prior when they were attending the class and before they had to take a delayed grade. John and Phil had wanted to request a computer literature search from the library, but they were struggling to identify keywords. When they talked about asking the instructor for suggestions, Branham snorted.

"You don't need all that shit," Branham had told them. "Everything I've learned in college that's worth remembering is something I've learned by myself, by reading or by doing, not by being directed by some Bozo professor—that's a joke."

"So how do you propose we get rolling on this paper?" Phil had asked.

"Easy. All you have to do is go to the library and pick up a book, any book, off the shelf, and just start reading through it and you'll find something you can bullshit about."

"Five bucks say you can't do just that," Phil said.

"Shit," Branham laughed. "Be like taking candy from a baby."

"And since it's any book," Phil said, "you should be able to go to the library and be back in say, ten or fifteen minutes tops."

"No fucking big deal." Branham strode out of the office. John and Phil watched from the second-floor window as Branham charged up the hilly cement path toward the library. His huge head and shoulders slouched forward and his long arms hung low, swinging back and forth as he took stiff strides, lumbering ahead on his giant feet.

"Look at that big lummox," Phil pointed and laughed. "He looks like a gorilla on cross-country skis."

Fifteen minutes later, Branham burst back into the office carrying a thick, black bound volume of a research journal.

"Hmm, the *International Journal of Mental Health*," Phil said. "At least you're in the right subject area, Branham. You know, just picking one off the shelf, you could have just as easily come back with the *Journal of Mechanical Engineering*. How fortuitous that your random draw was one on mental health, huh?"

Branham sat down, ignoring Phil, and flipped through the journal. "Aha," he said within a few seconds. "Right here: 'A taxonomy of personality structures in Sub-Saharan Africans: a preliminary investigation.' Pay up, you doubting Thomas."

"Not so fast," Phil said. "We need more than a title. What's the relevance of their findings for our paper?"

"Jesus," Branham glared at Phil and then shook his head. "Never had to work so hard before for a lousy five bucks. Give me a minute." He remained uncharacteristically quiet, skimming through the papers of the journal article.

"Well?" Phil asked after a few minutes. "What does it say?"

"It doesn't say shit." Branham tossed the book over his shoulder; it smacked the floor with a huge clap. "Fuck it." He had swiveled in his chair, staring first at Phil and then at John. "We'll just make up whatever we need."

John redialed Claire's number. Still there was no answer. He flipped through the course paper again, skimming for content and typos. Then he flung it against the wall.

Much later, after the sun had slipped depressingly early in late summer and the night had turned black, Claire answered her phone.

"Claire—I'm glad I finally got a hold of you. But I'm afraid I've got some bad news."

"I know about Branham." She sounded tired.

"How'd you hear?"

"I stopped by the department on the way home and saw the notice."

"I'm sorry you had to find out that way. I've been trying to get a hold of you all day so at least you could hear from someone, instead of just reading it." John waited. Claire said nothing. "I was in early this morning and found out myself by reading the memo—it just seemed so cold and so bizarre. How are you doing with it?"

"How do you think? It's shitty."

"It is terrible. It's such a shock."

"It is a shock," Claire said. "Even when you know death can happen at any time, it's still a shock when it hits. At least there were a few people sitting around the clinic. We went out to Whalen's for a drink and to talk. That helped."

"Good." John pictured Claire at the pub while he sat by the phone trying to get a hold of her. He felt hurt and like an idiot at the same time. "Claire, do you want to get together, just tonight, just talk for a bit?"

"No."

"All right. I'm going Wednesday to the funeral. Do you want to drive together? I can swing by and pick you up?"

"Nope. I'm going to drive straight to the VA from there. Look, John, I'm upset about Branham. That's what I need to deal with now—not talking with you about getting together. Good night."

John spotted Claire as soon as he walked into the church. The sanctuary was packed but the sun, filtered by the church window, glistened off the back of Claire's blond hair. She sat near Peg, and John eyed the empty space between them, but he joined Phil several rows back. The minister and Dr. Lerner spoke at the service, but John had little idea what they said. He tried to listen, but his mind wandered amid a myriad of thoughts. More than anything, he thought about Branham—disparate incidents, some remembered, some imagined partying and bullshitting together in the future, but he was dimly aware that he wasn't really *feeling* anything as far he could tell, other than an annoying, dull ache over missing Claire. He felt disgusted with himself then for numbing out as he often did when overwhelmed by loss, but he wasn't sure how —or even if he wanted to—to make himself feel differently right now. Instead, he forced himself to try to concentrate harder on Branham and the sermon.

After the service, as people filed out of the church, Claire nodded at John as he and Phil stood on the landing outside the main door. John muttered hello, and Claire hesitated, as if she might join him, but she and Peg were caught in a stream of people and trickled down the steps into the parking lot. Several other graduate students joined John and Phil, but they all left quickly; no one seemed to know what to say, and the words that were spoken about Branham, about the service, about his death, all echoed of funeral clichés. He and Phil stood in the August sun, not saying much, but the silence felt better than memorial platitudes.

"I hate this heat," Phil finally spoke.

"Me too." The heat and humidity had been oppressive for three days straight. John's white shirt clung to his body in patches bonded by sweat. "It's pretty sad about Branham, huh?" He knew it was sad even though he wasn't really feeling it.

"It is. It's fucking sad."

"You know, it still seems pretty weird, pretty fucking strange." A throbbing dulled John's head. "Remember the time when we were first trying to write that damn minority mental health paper and he charged over to the library and grabbed the book off the shelf to find something to write about?"

"Yeah." Phil laughed. "I've been thinking a lot about that since Monday."

"He always seemed so full of life, almost bigger than life," John said. "At times, I thought he was crass, but down deep, I think I envied his rebellious spirit and passion."

"Yeah. Not sure I have the balls to act that way, but he did whatever the fuck he wanted to do without worrying about it—though he was often sly about it."

"Wish I could be like that." John nodded. "But it's still hard to believe. We spend all that time with him last week, he even invites us to the damn lake, I call him on Friday to say Claire and I won't be coming, and then—boom, he's dead on Saturday."

"I know."

"This is getting morbid," John said. "I got to go."

Phil invited him to lunch, but John didn't feel much like eating. He said he needed to work on his dissertation, but the rest of the day at home he accomplished little.

John was swinging his softball bat over and over in his living room to the sounds of a Santana album when he heard the loud pounding on his front door. When he opened the door, Claire stood in the hallway, her fingers tucked into the front pockets of her jeans. She peered into his eyes, and then her gaze fell to the bat in his hand.

"What are you doing?" She nodded toward the bat. "I was knocking for a while."

"Just trying to groove my softball swing." He didn't want to share that when he was missing her, he often swung his bat listening to Santana with the stereo turned up in his apartment. "So, you came over to check on my swing or what?"

"No." She looked at him funny. "I came to talk."

"So, how are you?" he asked.

"Sad. I miss Branham."

"I know." He opened the door wider and stepped back. "Come in."

She sat on the loveseat. "And you? How are you?"

"It feels really strange." He perched himself at the far end of the loveseat, away from Claire. "You know, I'd just talked with him on Friday and he's such a big man. It's hard to believe he could die, especially by drowning in seven feet of water."

"He shouldn't have been out there in the first place. He probably thought he was invincible—part of his macho shit—but he had no business being out in water over his head if he couldn't swim."

"He probably fell asleep, drifted out, and then slipped off."

"He was probably shit-faced from drinking and drugging."

"Maybe." He noticed her chin tightened. "You mad at him?"

"Yes. He was reckless, and now he's gone. I miss him."

"I miss him too."

She scooted forward and wrapped her arms around John. She smelled faintly of perfume. "It's good to feel you again. I'd like to spend the night together, if that fits for you."

He moved away. "I don't know."

"What's wrong?"

He couldn't tell if her expression was one of surprise or hurt, but he said nothing and only shrugged.

"What is it? I was pretty shitty when you called last week, wasn't I?" She took his hand in hers.

"Yep."

"What bothered you the most?"

"I don't know. I guess the hot-and-cold treatment. I should have given you more space, but it makes me mad how flip you sound, like you're the expert on my emotional dynamics while psycho-existentially-analyzing me to death."

She nodded. "I was out of line. I'm sorry."

"Sometimes I don't know what you want from me when you say stuff like that."

"Probably for you to see things like I do."

"Well, I don't. Not completely anyway. I agree that falling through the ice as a boy was traumatic, more than I recognized, and it probably left me with some fear and anxiety, but overall, I'm handling it, and even if I don't, I defend against it pretty well. And defenses aren't such bad things—don't you remember Dr. Whitson saying that in our very first psychotherapy seminar? I have a fear of heights, too, but I don't have to stand on top of the World Trade Towers to prove anything. But it's more than that, anyway, Claire. I just don't want to get lost in negativity, in fear, in hurt. I want more out of life."

"What do you want?"

"I'm tired of you pushing me away, running away, criticizing me."

"I needed space, but I never meant to hurt you. I'm sorry," she said. "But what is it you want now?"

"Like I said before, I want, for starters, a relationship with you that is honest, authentic, and intimate. I want you to accept me for who I am and as an equal partner in a struggle for a vital, growing, close relationship, for as long as it lasts."

"I respect that." She paused, looking him over. "John, I have such strong feelings for you, and that scares me. You are the kindest, most loving man I have ever met."

"Thank you." Her words surprised and touched him, and he felt his guard lower.

"I'm not done yet—let me finish. Ted of course meant so much to me—as a young mother and member of the LDS church, my husband and family defined my identity. But I was so young, so naïve, and he broke my heart long after his was empty. And now I feel your love and my own love for you and that scares the shit out of me."

"I know you're scared, but thank you for sharing it directly," he said. "I am too."

"My therapist told me that I'm not just grieving Ted and our family, but I'm running away from you and from being vulnerable again. I can't make any promises, but I want to stop running away. So, yes, I'll engage in this struggle for as long as it lasts, though no one knows how long anything lasts."

He found himself smiling for the first time all day. "I will engage you in the struggle too."

They retired to bed. Claire cuddled against his chest. With soft, short strokes, she ran her fingernails across his back.

"I missed you," he said.

"I missed you, too, screwball."

John didn't expect it, but they made love.

He woke later from a nightmare: he and Branham were floating on air mattresses, and Branham saluted him with his beer can, taking a swig, but then slipped off the mattress into the water. Branham thrashed wildly, hollering for help; his eyeballs rested just above the water's surface, staring at John. Branham sank then, but he grabbed John's air mattress on the way down.

John's heart beat fast when he woke and he gulped a desperate breath. He checked the clock; it was just before 3:00 a.m. He forced himself to take slow, deep breaths, and he scooted next to Claire. She slept soundly, even as he wrapped his arms around her. He tried to remember the sensations of their lovemaking earlier, though he hadn't been able to get lost in their sex like usual; it was an uncomfortable awareness, which he soon tried to forget with sleep.

PART THREE

CHAPTER 16

John picked his way across his messy bedroom to answer the ringing telephone. Claire's voice resonated with a warm hello on the other end, though he heard an edgy undertone.

"Did you get the boys settled with Ted?" he asked. After a tumultuous past year with Josh and Ryan staying with Claire but acting out at school after Ted moved away, they were going to try having the boys live with Ted and attend a private high school in Chicago for the next academic year.

"I did."

"How are you feeling about it?"

"Don't ask," she said. "I'm trying not to think about it."

"I know," he said. Claire had talked often about the plan for her sons. She had initially resisted the idea of them moving to Chicago, but wore down with Ted's insistence and the boys' frequent arguments, especially as they each failed several spring semester classes and looked to be in danger of repeating their grade levels. Claire had seemed tired, too, in a way he'd never witnessed before, but she was working late four nights a week in private practice on top of a full-time job at the VA.

"I have some bad news," she said.

"What?"

"I'm not going to make it out of Chicago and to your place tonight—there's violent thunderstorms up here that are creating huge traffic jams. I just heard on the radio news there's another accident—this one fatal—and that they've closed the highway for a couple of hours. They're recommending people stay off the roads, between the accidents and more heavy rain."

"Sounds like a mess."

"I'm really disappointed," she said. "I wanted to be with you on your last night of being in your twenties and to wish you Happy Birthday as soon as you wake up tomorrow."

"That's sweet." Claire had settled into their relationship over the past year—there had been no more major conflicts between them, though they were each busy and stressed launching their careers after finishing their doctorates. He'd felt fortunate there was no more turmoil with Claire, but he'd been dimly aware there was less passion too. He'd heard this was normal for long-term relationships, but this alarmed his fears of a mundane existence. "But it's okay."

"I'm really sorry. I could wait awhile and see if the highway and weather clear."

"Don't worry about it." It wasn't like Claire to be so apologetic, and it was better for her to stay put for the night anyway. He didn't want her to try to navigate a long highway drive late at night during a torrential Midwestern thunderstorm, especially since she wasn't the most attentive driver to begin with. "Better to play it safe."

"I'll make it up tomorrow night with a special birthday dinner for you," she said. "It's a big birthday."

"Don't remind me."

"Thirty is a rite of passage," she said. "And a lot can happen in any one year."

After they hung up, John kicked off his shoes and plopped onto the loveseat, which was losing its spring and becoming lumpy. He was tired from the week, or maybe it was the past year. He'd written a grant for the state that drew on his dissertation to develop and evaluate a drop-in center for homeless and runaway youth. He'd considered himself extremely fortunate that the grant had been funded and he'd been asked to direct the project. He'd been working sixty-plus hours all summer to set up the program. The center had only opened four weeks before.

He felt himself drift toward sleep and forced himself to get up and reheat a plate of leftover spaghetti. As he ate, he flipped through the TV channels; the network shows rang with raucous but inane laughter to contrived sitcom lines. He pressed the remote power button off. He wished Claire had been able to make it back to his place for the night. He missed her in some dull but confusing way—they'd been seeing each other nearly every day, but it was only after long days at work and dealing with Claire's boys. Although he and Claire slept together regularly, they rarely made love anymore. But it wasn't just the lack of sex, he thought—they were falling into some rut, missing both the passion and the sense of adventure that had originally drawn them together and enlivened him. This was the summer—their first since completing their degrees—they were supposed to make the trip to the mountains and journey upriver, but the topic had not even come up in months, which triggered both disappointment and relief.

He grabbed a cold Michelob bottle, flopped back onto the loveseat, and rolled the rubber band off the *St. Louis Post-Dispatch*. He read through the front page and the sports section. He thought about going to bed but felt too tired to move. He skimmed the inner news sections until the death notices seized his awareness: fine print, cryptic reminders, a few sentences long, about the life and death of Mary Antonio, Thad Brown, John Dietz. He read each notice about a named but faceless dead person. And Branham Johnson, he wondered, had there been a death notice for him? He hadn't checked the paper last August for Branham's death notice, but he wished now that he had. It was almost exactly a year since Branham had drowned. He wished he could call Branham up, bullshit for a while, maybe even agree to get high together. But none of these things were possible. A year didn't sound so long, but it seemed like an unfathomably long time to be dead.

⟡

Like most days, John was running behind schedule. He worried he might be late for his birthday dinner with Claire. It was 4:50 and he still needed to meet Amy, the new practicum student, for supervision, when he heard a din of shouting. He ran from his office to the drop-in center area. One of the newer clients, Andy, a young man of seventeen, stood at one side of the long cafeteria dining table, brandishing a small knife and swearing at Dennis, a teenager with carrot-orange hair, who stood at the opposite side of the table. Bennie, one of the counselors, stood next to Dennis, barking orders for Andy to put down the knife; a dozen other clients and two other staff stood further back.

"Andy," John walked closer. "We don't want anyone to get hurt. Do everyone a favor, including yourself, and put the knife down, will you?"

"Fuck off!" Andy's long, stringy brown hair fell past his boney face and toward his shoulders. A purple-blue bruise and a small, crusty scab covered his left cheek.

"What's the problem, Andy?" John stepped in front of Bennie and Dennis, nudging them backward.

He pointed toward Dennis. "This fucker called me a cock-sucking fag."

"Pissed you off big time, huh?"

"I'm going to cut his dick off and shove it in his mouth. Then we'll see what the asshole has to say."

"That's one way of dealing with the problem, but if you stop and think about it, what would happen to you?"

"I don't care." Andy lifted his head, his chin jutting out.

"Well, I do. I care about you and I don't want to see you rotting in jail for the next forty years," John said. "That's no place for you."

"I still want to cut his dick off."

Police sirens echoed in the distance. Andy glanced around, swore, and glared at John and the others. John inched backward, bumping Dennis and Bennie further away.

"You trying to trick me—calling the police?" Andy said.

"Not a trick—it's a rule for everyone's safety. If anyone has a weapon here, one of the staff will always call the police."

"Fuck your rules," Andy said. "And fuck you."

"We'll talk to the police together," John said. "Put down the knife and we'll see what we can work out."

"You think I'm fucking stupid?" He looked over his shoulder. There were a dozen kids, but they had backed up near the walls. He had a clear path to the door.

"Andy, put down the knife. You don't want it in your possession when the police arrive."

Andy glared at John, then whirled his arm over his head, lunging his fist straight down. His knife sank into the tabletop. Andy laughed and pulled it out. He pivoted and ran out the door.

"*Shit,*" Bennie swore.

The police asked a slew of questions, scribbled a few notes, and said to call again if Andy returned anytime soon, but when pressed, one admitted they probably wouldn't do much, as they were busy with more serious crimes. John and his staff pulled the other kids together, trying to reassure them the center would be safe, and then talked in private with Dennis, who was scared and then angry, saying what he'd do to Andy if he bothered him on the streets. After Dennis calmed down and left with friends and a safety plan, John debriefed with the other staff.

"Whew," Bennie exhaled. "That was close, Dr. Anderson."

"I thought things would be okay," John said. "As long as we stayed clear but firm without backing him into a corner. I thought he might leave with a flair though."

"I don't know, chief." Bennie was in his early fifties, a tall Black man who had served a stint in the army as a drill sergeant. "All I could think of while you were talking with him was this movie I saw years and years ago about this priest in New York City, I think it was, who worked with juvenile delinquents. He started up Boys Town, or one of those places, I don't remember for sure. But to make a long story short, at the end of the movie, his favorite boy has a gun. He's held up a store or something, and the priest walks up to him, inching closer and closer, telling the boy to give him the gun. And right as he gets to him and reaches for the gun, *bam*." Bennie pointed his finger at John like a pistol and closed his thumb like a hammer falling on the chamber. "The boy shoots him. Yes sir, kills him dead."

"Thanks for sharing, Bennie," John said. "That's really comforting."

"What?" Bennie asked.

"So, how are you feeling?" John asked.

"Me?" Bennie said. "I'm good."

"You looked so calm," Amy, the new practicum student, said to John. "Weren't you scared?"

"A little, but not too bad. I just focused on defusing him. I didn't think he'd actually try to hurt me."

Bennie waved his hands. "If he'd tried anything, sir, believe me, I would have been there. I was watching him close. I knew right away he wasn't going to try anything. Did you see how he gripped the knife? It was from the topside. He couldn't have lunged into you as far away as you were with that grip. Now if he'd switched to the underside—I'd have jumped up next to you."

"Thanks, Bennie."

"You bet, chief. I got your back."

"There's more to talk about," John said. "But let's do it tomorrow at the morning staff meeting. Amy and I need to meet and it's already after five."

"And it's your birthday—thirty years old, I hear." Bennie let out a low whistle. "Yes sir, that's *old*. Got big plans tonight?"

"Just dinner out."

"We can reschedule," Amy said. "Supervision is important, but not compared to your birthday celebration."

John said he had time and insisted they meet. Amy was a second-year graduate student in clinical psychology at Washington University and the drop-in center's first practicum placement. She'd only started the week before but had already impressed John as being incredibly bright and clinically sophisticated, way beyond her twenty-four years. John finally shooed Bennie out of his office— Bennie had asked three consecutive "one last question" questions—and closed his office door.

"What will happen to Andy?" Amy asked. "Will he be terminated from the program?"

"No. Bennie's already lobbying for that, but Andy and kids like him are exactly why we started the center."

"How so?"

John briefed her on the case history. Four different agencies and his grandmother had referred Andy to the program within the first week of opening. He had a schizoaffective diagnosis in addition to the conduct disorder that most of the program's clients carried, and on occasions he heard voices, though it was possible the auditory hallucinations were secondary to him using a plethora of street drugs, including toluol. It was clear, however, that his ability to relate was unambiguously impaired. He'd burned bridges not only with his working-class South St. Louis family, including his mother, stepfather, and father—all of whom had abused him as a child—but also his grandmother, a sweet and caring woman who'd taken him in for several years before his behavior had become unmanageable. He was also prone to suicidal thinking, and indeed his grandfather and uncle had both taken their own lives years before. "He's been through multiple traumas, from an early age, starting with his twin brother who fell into the toilet as a toddler and drowned while his mom was drunk."

"That's horrible," Amy said. "I can't imagine."

"I know. Me either. But it happened," John said. "And so the question is now: What can we do? He's already been in the state acute psychiatric hospital repeatedly and has run away from or been thrown out of a half-dozen community homes and institutions."

"Have you admitted him to the crisis shelter?" Amy asked. "I'm sure he'd pose a behavioral challenge, but has that been tried?"

"We offered him shelter after we first outreached him, but he refused. He said he was nearly eighteen and didn't need 'a fucking social service agency' for a place to stay, pardon my language in quoting him. As far as we can tell, when he isn't in the hospital, he sleeps in the streets or abandoned buildings or with so-called friends, usually in exchange for sex, but often he'll get into a fight and so that housing doesn't last long either."

"So, what will you do?" she asked.

"I don't know yet." He looked at Amy as he thought. She had full lips, a slender if sharp nose, and long, golden-red hair with a sensual radiance that belied her professional skirt and blouse. "His pattern after a confrontation is to stay away for a while, but then he comes back around. I think we need to keep him out of the building for a while—the other kids need to feel safe—but I can meet him outside, give him a sandwich and soda, talk with him for a while, and try to build a stronger therapeutic relationship. You know, people see Andy as the aggressor—and he often is—but I think with his history of severe abuse and trauma, he doesn't feel safe inside; he feels threatened and scared, and then acts out. We need to build a relationship so he feels safe here with us. Does that make sense? What do you think?"

"It makes a lot of sense." Amy's lips parted in a faint smile. "And it feels safe here with you."

Claire drove John to a candlelight Italian dinner for two on The Hill, not displaying the slightest aggravation, as far as John could tell, for his tardiness. Afterward, she brought him to her house where she unveiled a German chocolate cake—his favorite—with thirty candles. She sang, "Happy Birthday" and presented him with gifts, including new dress shirts for work. After she held one of the shirts up to his chest, she kissed him full on the lips, sliced the cake, and pulled a half-bottle of champagne from the refrigerator. Claire, who rarely drank, raised her glass in a toast.

"At the milestone but still tender age of thirty," she said with a wink. "I wish you a happy birthday, with an amazing year—and decade—ahead, that brings you continued success in your remarkable start as a psychologist and founder and director of a new program for homeless youth."

"Thank you—"

"I'm not done yet. I also wish you a remarkable year of personal growth, one of deepening happiness, and a special year for us, that includes both fun and memorable times—next summer maybe we can finally make that river trip to the mountains—I'd like the boys to go with us, too—and a year of growth for us as a couple, with a whole new, deeper level of love and sharing, including, perhaps—who knows?—even our exploring the possibility of a formal commitment as mates."

He set his champagne glass on the table. "What did you say?"

"Maybe we could finally take that trip to the mountains. I was thinking I'd like for the boys to go, too, before they get any older and will never want to go on a family vacation again. Of course, they'll slow us down and get bored and we probably won't make it all the way up to the source, but it'll still be a fun family vacation."

Something unpleasant sloshed in his stomach, but he pushed that sensation away as it seemed secondary to surprise about her comments about commitment. "No, the other part."

"I said I hoped this would be a year of growth for us as a couple, too, and that we explore the possibilities of deeper, formal commitment."

"You mean like marriage?"

Claire fidgeted with her fork, sliding it around her plate. "Yes, possibly even including marriage."

"Wow, Claire. That's a shock." He couldn't quite believe she'd spoken about marriage. "When I used to mention the remotest possibility of marriage, you'd throw me out and refuse to see me for days."

"I know. That's why I'm telling you now."

"What's changed?"

"We've been monogamous for over a year now. It just seems like maybe it's time to grow, that maybe marriage is the next step and a way to honor and deepen our relationship."

"'Deepen the relationship?' You used to tell me that marriage dulls intimacy and provides a false security."

"That was a long time ago, after I separated from Ted."

"True, but back then you were adamant about the cost of marriage. It was 'a charade of intimacy,' you said, an out from having to experience and work through the real thing."

"I don't remember that," she said.

"You did. In fact, you said a lot more, too, like that marriage was a cheap cultural contrivance to give the illusion of intimacy, but that too often it impedes living an open, vital life and forging an authentic relationship."

"If you're not interested in the possibility of marriage, just say so." She clanged her fork against the plate. "Don't hide behind my words from years ago."

"It's not that, Claire. It's just a shock to hear you say this—it's so different from what you used to say."

"Stop using the past against me." She slid her slice of birthday cake back to the platter without taking a bite. "So, are you against it?"

"No, not necessarily," he said. "It just takes some time to get used to that as a possibility between us or something that's even okay to talk about."

Claire said nothing more. John picked at chocolate cake crumbs. "Claire, I'm sorry. I'm glad to hear that you're open to possibilities."

"I don't want to talk about it anymore now."

She left the table at the first ring of the telephone. John heard her voice lighten, talking cheerfully for a minute in the kitchen before returning, pulling the long phone cord with her, to the dining room. "I know you want to talk with that birthday-boy grandson of yours," she said. "Yes, it was nice talking with you again too." Claire handed the phone to John. "It's Nona." She said in a dull voice to John she was going to bed.

"Happy thirtieth birthday my dear boy," his grandmother said.

"Thank you." He watched Claire disappear from the room without a look back. "That's sweet of you to track me down at Claire's and call for my birthday."

"I wouldn't miss it for all the money in the world. I wish you a year of good health and wealth." Her voice cracked as she spoke.

"What's the matter, Nona?"

"Oh, brother. I'm just getting too sentimental in my old age." Her words sounded moist with tears. "Stupid, huh?"

"No, not stupid." He guessed from her tendency to get choked up at past family birthday celebrations, she would be sad as well as sentimental as she mourned time passing. He didn't particularly feel like getting into that conversation but felt compelled to ask more about her feelings. "Why are you crying?"

"I feel so old—ancient—with you turning thirty."

"You're not so old. In fact, you looked pretty darn good at Christmas, I thought."

"I looked like an old hag," she said. "A lot older and fatter than when you turned ten and even twenty. Those were good times," her voice trembled again. "But this is the last milestone birthday of yours that I'll live to see."

"Don't say that. Don't even think that."

"It's true. I'm already seventy-six."

"And you're in great health. You're going to be here on my fortieth and fiftieth birthdays too. In fact, we'll get together for dinner then—at Bartolli's for steak and pasta, and how about a glass of your favorite burgundy?"

"I'll be long gone."

"Stop with that kind of talk, will you?" All of her life, Nona had been prone to make occasional, darting references to aging and death, but she talked about those things much more frequently now, though John wished she didn't. He tried to divert her attention and asked if she'd gotten together with any of her friends; she had always had good friends.

"No," she said. "Harriet from the switchboard at the hospital—do you remember her?"

"No."

"You met her when we were working together, but you were little. A heavy-set girl with brown hair, and funny."

"What about her?"

"She died Tuesday of a heart attack."

"I'm sorry," he said.

"She'd been widowed for five years, and her only daughter died in a car crash years ago. It's no wonder her heart gave out."

John said nothing.

"I check the obituaries every day in the paper," she said. "All my old friends are dying out."

"I'm sorry." He had grown weary of the topic. "How about you and Emerson? Are you getting out for dinner? Things going okay?"

"Oh, everything's fine," she said. "Just boring."

"What is?"

"Life here." She lowered her voice. "Ever since Emerson turned sixty-seven and retired, all he wants to do is sit around the house and watch TV, like an old man."

Sixty-seven was old, John thought, but he had the fleeting, uncomfortable thought that he was almost half-way there himself, and that time was scurrying by. "What about you two taking a little trip—like to Monterey or Tahoe?"

"He doesn't want to," she said. "He'll still play a little golf around here now and then—just the nine holes now, but other than that, all he does is eat, sleep, and watch TV."

That was pretty much all that John had ever known Emerson to do, but he held that thought to himself. "I'm sorry that's got you feeling bad tonight."

"Oh, it's not really that bad," she said. "I was just complaining like a cranky old woman."

"You've earned the right to complain now and then," he pushed himself to say, though he was growing tired of hearing complaints on his birthday. "Hey, I love you, but I'd better get to sleep soon. A workday tomorrow, you know. I'll call you this weekend. Give my best to Emerson too."

John climbed the stairs, quickly brushed his teeth, and gargled, trying to rinse away his annoyance from the call with Nona. She had been available and good to him all his life, especially when he was little when he needed her the most, but now he wanted to celebrate turning thirty by having sex. Claire's room was dark, and he slipped under the covers. He scooted next to her, nudging her body with his, but she didn't move. He cursed his luck that she once again had fallen asleep so quickly.

He witnessed some dissatisfaction rising within him, and then he admonished himself—Claire had taken him out to a fancy restaurant, baked him a cake, given him sweet and thoughtful presents, and yet still something felt bad. Perhaps he was just being a selfish man, wanting to have birthday sex. But it was more than that—the excitement that had been rekindled when she had talked about them going upriver in the mountains was immediately downgraded when she spoke about making it a family trip with her boys. Not that he didn't care about them, because he did, but he could see them bringing friends and soon they'd all be complaining or jacking around like city boys at a summer camp. He didn't blame the boys—they were just teenagers. But they'd never make it all the way up—how could Claire settle for that?

◗ CHAPTER 17

Claire's idea for the Fourth of July the following summer was to take her boys and John to Johnson's Shut-Ins. John tried to talk her out of the plan. He reminded her he'd been working long hours—Andy in particular was presenting a series of escalating crises—and John had traveled two out of the last three weekends; homelessness had become a *cause célèbre*, and at the request of the federal government, he had presented his dissertation research at conferences. He was worn out from all the travel and presentations, and, to his unpleasant surprise, he had become anxious about both flying and public speaking. It sounded good, he told Claire, to sleep late, take it easy, and grill at her house—his IBS symptoms had flared up for the first time in years. He yawned as he said this— he'd been having trouble sleeping. After receiving a few, late-night crisis calls in past weeks about Andy, John worried that something awful was going to happen to the young man with his out-of-control drinking, drugging, and fighting. John had his staff fooled about his own emotional state—Bennie and a few others had said multiple times how John had appeared as cool as a cucumber in a client crisis, but at home he was awakening around 3:00 a.m. with nightmares about Andy, expecting another middle of the night call that Andy was in jail or in the hospital again—or worse yet, dead.

But Claire was insistent—Ryan had just gotten his license and he'd be off to college in two years, and Josh would be right behind him. She was relishing having her boys living back with her—the experiment of their living with their dad in Chicago for the school year turned into a contentious failure with their father—and she seemed to want to make up for lost time. She wanted a family trip over the Fourth. There wouldn't be many if any more times that she could hold them together for a holiday celebration, she said, and she wanted them all to go away for a fun day, like when they were younger. Her argument reminded him of the idea she had presented on his last birthday: that they should take a family trip to the Western mountains *after* making a marriage commitment. They had successfully avoided talking any more about marriage for nearly a year, and, not wanting to trigger that discussion again, John grudgingly conceded to the Johnson's Shut-In trip for the Fourth.

After they reached the state park, John told Claire that his IBS was acting up. He needed to stay close to a bathroom, he said, plus he was afraid of venturing away from his crisis pager. He knew it was an improbable wish, but he longed to prevent something really bad from happening to Andy. Claire changed into old jeans cutoffs and a baggy T-shirt and then he walked with her and the boys along the tree-shaded, hilly path to the river's edge, listening to the rushing river water. He said to Claire he'd fire up the grill and have lunch ready after their swim.

Claire kissed him. "It's beautiful here."

"It is."

The Black River had cut a rocky canyon gorge. The river ran clear and bubbly white over rhyolite boulders and fell frothy into potholes and still pools. Scores of nearly-naked young people sunned on rocks like turtles. The boys clambered over boulders and splashed into the river.

"Sure you don't want to join us?" Claire asked.

He decided not to tell Claire he also felt anxious about the prospect of swimming in the river. He figured it was just his old anxiety resurfacing because he was tired and stressed, and he could talk himself through swimming if he had to. But he didn't feel like it, not with the IBS, the worries about Andy, and feeling exhausted. "Like I said, I'd better stay close to a bathroom."

"That's the shits."

"You could say that."

She grinned, and then kissed him again. He watched her climb over rocks and after her boys. Josh, then Ryan, slid down a chute, over the smooth face of a red boulder, into a deep pool. Two young women with voluptuous bodies bulging from bikinis sat on an adjacent boulder. The boys glanced at them, but they were in their mid-twenties, closer to John's age than Josh and Ryan's. Claire hoisted herself over the side of the boulder, planted her butt in the cascading water, let out a whoop, and slid into the pool with a splash. She bobbed up, laughed with her boys, and waved at John. Her wet T-shirt billowed upward at her belly with air trapped beneath. He stood watching Claire, her sons, and the young women, but his intestines cramped, and he walked back up the path.

Ryan wanted to drive home and Claire was hemming and hawing in her response, about to say yes, John thought, when he said—with apologies—that he'd stay behind the wheel. A scowl turned the corners of Ryan's mouth at the edges of his wispy mustache.

"Tonight, after we're safely home, you can borrow my car to take Janice to the movies." Through the rearview mirror, John saw Ryan's frown relax but it didn't totally disappear. "Sorry, but the traffic is just too heavy today with all of these big-butt campers and boat trailers, and the crazy holiday drivers out."

"It's a good thing," Josh said. "In driver's ed, they said the Fourth of July is the biggest day of the year for highway deaths. And with Ryan driving—I'm just too young to die."

Claire stifled a laugh, but Josh's words triggered memories for John of news reports about Fourth of July accidents. He suspiciously eyed each car and truck speeding toward them on the two-lane highway. During an open stretch, he pushed the throttle. Josh exclaimed from the back seat that they were going eighty-five miles per hour. Claire squinted at John.

"Eighty-four," John told her. "Just trying to get us safely home before it gets too dark." He didn't tell her he'd had an ominous feeling all day that was growing stronger.

A panorama of red sky lit the horizon, which faded to an ash gray as dusk overtook day. They made good time until Interstate 55 crossed the Meramec River into St. Louis County where the traffic thickened. The lanes slowed and then clogged as they approached downtown. In the nightlight, the stainless-steel legs of the Gateway Arch shimmered like a mirage; it was hard to perceive which leg was in the foreground and which was in the background.

"Look at all of the traffic," Claire said. "It's probably the last-minute rush of people trying to make it to the Arch for the fireworks."

"Fireworks!" Josh said. "Let's go."

Ryan told him no way. He said he was taking Janice to a movie at nine thirty and the fireworks were juvenile anyway. The brothers argued, then Claire told them to stop: they were headed straight home.

"Go ahead—take Ryan's side like you always do," Josh said. "I never get to do anything fun."

"We just spent all day at Johnson's Shut-Ins," Claire said.

"Big fucking deal," Josh said.

"And now you're grounded tomorrow for that," Claire said.

"God, I hate you."

"*Stop*," she said.

"This family sucks." Josh slumped back in his seat.

"Idiots," John said.

"What?" Claire asked.

"These stupid drivers—slowing down in the middle of the lane. I guess they're trying to slip over at the last second to exit at the Arch, but it's dangerous. Somebody could get rear-ended."

He lurched to a dead stop amid a logjam of cars at the confluence of interstates 44, 55, and 70. Humid air that smelled of hot asphalt wafted in the window. Cars on the left from I-44 tried to merge. John let a station wagon slip ahead, but then he rolled up to their bumper when a Chevy tried to squeeze in. They crept several yards ahead but squeaked to a halt.

In the next half-hour, they progressed less than a mile. Claire turned on KMOX radio, which described the highway near the Arch as a massive parking lot.

They rolled slowly into the depressed section of the highway, adjacent to the Arch. Several cars had parked on the narrow shoulder against the cement wall, drivers peering through open windows at the night sky.

"Fools." John pointed to them.

A shrill whistle vibrated through the humid air. John looked heavenward and a rocket exploded—compressed air rushed past, spreading a palette of colors across the dark sky.

"Bitching," Josh said.

The fireworks paralyzed the traffic.

John pounded his palm against the steering wheel. "This is madness."

"Be patient," Claire said. "Sometimes you just have to take life as it comes."

More cars slid onto the narrow shoulder. A Chrysler and two big Buicks loomed fat fenders into the highway lane, but a line of cars trickled forward on the left. John cut in and they began to roll. Josh protested; he wanted to watch more of the fireworks, but John kept driving. The traffic remained thick, then slowed again to a crawl, as cars tried to merge from an entrance ramp.

"Check out the pickup," Josh said.

The driver revved his engine, roaring a few yards forward, and then slammed on his brakes at the back bumper of the Toyota in front of him. The Toyota inched forward, and the pickup waited, and then repeated this pattern of racing forward and slamming on his brakes a second, third, and fourth time. The exploding fireworks illuminated a young man, baseball cap turned backward, frozen for a moment in the flash of artificial light that poured into the truck cab; John felt something awful catch in his chest, perceiving the pickup truck driver as Andy. But fireworks sparked again, revealing a stocky build to the driver—it couldn't be Andy—who was chugging from a bottle; a young woman with long hair sat at his side. The driver steered his pickup sideways, nosing his way into the right lane of the highway.

The traffic remained congested but picked up speed, reaching forty miles per hour. The pickup raced alongside John's car, nearly ramming the back bumper of a Honda sedan. Just as it was about to hit the Honda, the pickup's brakes screeched, and the pickup fell way back in the lane at a much slower pace.

"What is that fool doing?" Claire stared out her window; the pickup had been right next to her.

"Don't know. He's crazy or something." It was the kind of absurd acting out that Andy would do, but he didn't even drive, and John wondered if he was the one who had lost his mind for misperceiving the driver as Andy.

"Or drunk," Claire said.

John kept a close eye on the pickup in his rearview mirror. The driver repeated his pattern of speeding ahead and, when on the verge of ramming the car in front of him, slamming his brakes. Josh and Ryan thought the driver was probably buzzing a friend as a joke, but John pointed out that the cars he targeted varied as he cut back and forth between lanes. Three times as they drove through North St. Louis, the pickup roared past John's car in another lane, but each time the pickup lost speed, falling way back and slowing up the cars behind him.

"He worries me," Claire said.

"Me too," John said. "Doesn't seem to be any rhyme or reason to his driving."

John watched the pickup closely and changed lanes when the pickup did, but in the opposite direction to create more distance between them. He exhaled deeply when they rolled down the winding freeway hill to their exit. As he steered toward the exit ramp, he watched the pickup driver in the fast lane. The pickup tailgated another car. He then heard a screeching of brakes and tires as the pickup slid horizontally across the highway.

"Fucking-A!" Josh shouted.

The pickup was sliding across four lanes. The truck driver appeared frozen in John's rearview mirror for an instant; John saw the shadow of the young man with the backward baseball cap, and the girl. Then they were gone. The pickup toppled sideways off the highway and down the overpass embankment.

The sound of something like thunder exploded nearby. Josh and Claire screamed and John realized they'd heard metal being crushed. He hit his brakes hard and inched down the exit ramp. Across the cloverleaf highway exit and halfway down the overpass embankment he saw the pickup. Its headlights shone like a spotlight in the night but the truck had flipped upside down.

"Let me out," Josh shouted. "I'm going to help them out."

"Sit still and be quiet," Claire told him.

"I'll pull over at the 7-11 and call the police," John said. "That's the best thing we can do to help."

They crept off the exit ramp and under the highway overpass and into the 7-11 parking lot where two Cool Valley police cars were parked. John met the policemen, gigantic Coke Icees in their hands, walking out the door. John told them a pickup had rolled halfway down the embankment and overturned on the other side of the highway.

"He'd been driving crazy since the Arch, speeding up and tailgating, then slowing way down, over and over again. It didn't make any sense." John gulped an anxious breath. "He suddenly tried to go from the fast lane to the off-ramp, like he realized he was missing his exit, and he slid sideways across all four lanes. But he just kept sliding and—boom—disappeared and then there was this terrible crashing sound."

"We'll take care of it," the short policeman with thick forearms said. They slurped their Icees and sauntered to their cars.

Red-and-blue lights flashed and the police cars sped across Florissant Road. The police charged up the eastbound freeway ramp and slowed.

"What are they doing over there?" Claire asked. "That's the wrong side."

"I don't know. I told them the other side, at least I'm pretty sure I did."

The police cars idled on the ramp, then raced onto the highway.

"Now where are they going?"

"I don't know," John said. "Maybe they've figured it out and are going up to Bermuda road to turn around and get back to the westbound exit."

"I wish they'd hurry," Claire said.

"Let's go help," Josh said.

John rolled his car to the exit from the 7-11 parking lot but braked to a stop at the street. "The police are going to help."

"Yeah," Josh said. "By speeding off in the wrong direction they'll be a huge help. *Stupid* cops. Come on—aren't we supposed to be like the Good Samaritan?"

They could drive back under the overpass and be at the accident in a minute. John imagined prying open a mangled pickup door and finding the young man—he looked like Andy again—impaled through the chest by a dislodged steering column. "No—the police will be there any second."

"I bet they're dead," Josh said.

John glanced over his shoulder at Josh. "I hope not. Let's not even think about it." He turned his car onto the road, driving away from the accident and toward Claire's house. "They're probably just banged up, maybe with some cuts and bruises."

"They're dead," Josh said.

"*Shut up!*" John shouted.

Claire stared at him—he'd never yelled at her boys before—but she said nothing.

He saw in the mirror Josh's sullen pose—the pouting lips made him look more like a small boy than a fifteen-year-old. John thought he should apologize, but he didn't feel like talking. No one in the car spoke, and John listened to the shrillness of the sirens, but they soon faded as he drove away. He expected to feel relieved when he could no longer hear the faintest echo of sirens, but he realized then he didn't feel anything.

Claire left John a message at his office, asking him to come over after work. He did most nights, anyway, and he drove toward her house after working late while thinking again about Bennie's message that had been waiting for him first thing in the morning. In a quivering voice, Bennie had said that he needed to take at least the next week off and probably longer. His brother, Bennie had explained, had been stabbed and killed during a fight at a Fourth of July barbecue. Bennie broke into a sob, apologized to the voice mailbox for crying, then hung up.

Clients were asking repeatedly where Bennie was. Although his authoritarian personality clashed with the most rebellious youths, most of the clients had formed a strong attachment to Bennie. By midmorning John told the group that Bennie was off on emergency leave, that his brother had died unexpectedly. That afternoon a spate of arguments broke out and several shoving matches erupted; the most psychotic client withdrew, talking to himself in the corner. At the afternoon staff meeting, Amy said even as grief twice removed, Bennie's loss seemed too much for the clients to bear.

Claire wasn't home yet when John arrived at her house. He plopped himself into a lounge chair on her back deck. The massive oak tree at the back of Claire's yard blocked the setting sun and John closed his eyes. Humidity hung heavy on his body and cicadas hummed from the trees like electric power lines. John considered driving up to Chicago for Bennie's brother's funeral, but it was a long drive and he'd miss too much work when they were already shorthanded. Bennie would need his support more when he got back, John figured. The screen door squeaked.

Josh stepped onto the deck with a Coke can.

"How's it going?" John asked.

"Good but guess what?"

"What?"

"Danny's brother knows the guy driving the pickup on the Fourth. Matt Tristan."

"And what happened?"

"He totaled the pickup. It's toast. And he's in the hospital now with broken ribs and a punctured lung."

"That's bad." John felt himself exhale deeply. He was glad this Matt wasn't dead. "But it could have been worse."

"He's going from the hospital to jail."

"For what? Drunk driving?"

"That and because his girlfriend was killed in the crash."

John hoped Josh was wrong about the girl being killed. He told himself maybe it was like a story whispered in the telephone circle game—that the details were distorted into grotesque, exaggerated proportions at each retelling. That was easier to accept than the girl being dead.

Claire brought home angel hair pasta and chicken cacciatore, compliments of the drug reps visiting her office, and spread the food out on the dining room table. Josh told his mom about Matt Tristan and his girlfriend, grabbed a drumstick slathered in tomato sauce, and left for his friend's. John told Claire about Bennie.

"I'm sorry," Claire said. "That's tragic."

"It is," John said.

She glanced at his full plate. "I thought this was one of your favorite meals?"

John picked at his chicken. "Yeah. I'm just not that hungry." He asked Claire about her day.

"Good, busy. I saw seven therapy clients in a row this afternoon and tonight."

"That's a lot."

Claire fidgeted with her cigarette and then lit it. "I've been thinking and wanted to ask you tonight," she said. "Where are you at with our relationship?"

The abruptness of her question startled him. He had been thinking of the girl in the pickup. He'd seen her only for a second in the light of the exploding fireworks. She was beautiful, long hair draped around her face, as she snuggled close to the idiot driver.

"John?"

He glanced back at Claire. She gripped her coffee cup tightly. She was often abrupt, saying whatever was on her mind without preamble, but she seemed both serious and vulnerable now. "Sorry. I was in my head."

"What are you thinking?"

"Nothing, really, except about Matt Tristan's girlfriend." She was hard to forget—young, attractive, full of life and possibility. An image of being with her for fun and romance passed quickly through his thoughts before he labelled it as a ridiculous fantasy: he did not even know her and now she was dead.

"Sad, I know," Claire said. "What are you thinking about her?"

For a second, he saw himself next to her in the pickup seat, tumbling down the overpass embankment right before the final collision. "I wonder what it was like for her, you know, in that instant after she realized they were going to crash and that she was going to die?"

"She was so young—it's tragic," Claire said. "But it's like Becker said, death can strike at any moment, you know?"

John stood up from the table. His annoyance was a convenient distraction to the anxiety that was gnawing within him, but he was okay with that. "What I know, is that I'm fucking sick of hearing about Becker."

CHAPTER 18

While writing a therapy chart note, John noticed a faint but familiar scent of roses. When he looked up from his desk, he saw Amy standing with a wide smile just beyond his half-open door. He greeted her with a hug, savoring for a second the smell of her perfume, and ushered her toward his office couch.

"Are you sure you have time now? —it's late already." she asked. "I should have called but I was driving by and took a chance."

"For you, absolutely, I have time." He sat across from her in his therapy chair. "It's good to see you."

She brushed back a long strand of her golden-reddish hair from her face. "It's great to see you."

"We're looking forward to having you back soon for another semester of practicum," John said. He had missed their supervision meetings while she was gone for the summer. She was insightful and skilled well beyond her years of clinical training and her youthful energy infectious. During her past semester, their meetings had frequently extended beyond the particulars of her clinical work to deep personal sharing, at first by Amy but eventually in moments by John as well, about their families, relationships, and lives. They had become confidants (almost intimate friends, he wanted to say, though this was uncomfortable to admit as he was her clinical supervisor) and they had finagled together to get a third practicum semester approved from her university.

"I can't wait to start back. I love it here. I've learned so much."

He felt himself smiling back in a way that felt both good and awkward. "Your summer vacation—how was that Greek isles cruise with your parents?"

"Beautiful and fun—and I survived yet another family vacation."

"How'd it go with your dad?" Amy and her father, a prominent Ivy league professor, had a complicated relationship.

"As usual," she said. "He held court every night at dinner with the other guests at our table, which included a radiologist and a corporate lawyer, engaging them in stimulating intellectual conversations and after they had spoken their piece, he'd say, 'We're missing the most important point here,' and then explicate his view. And you know the most annoying thing?"

"What?"

"His point was always indeed the most perceptive insight and everyone else would see that too."

"Your dad is very intelligent."

"Yes, he is," she nodded. "And he can also be such an arrogant ass."

John laughed. "And very annoying to his daughter in his arrogance." He knew from the past year that Amy wrestled with conflicting impulses, ranging from admiration to rebelliousness, toward her dad.

"But the worst thing is that while we're on this incredible vacation, he'd spend most days in his stateroom working on his new book." She spoke quickly as she often did when describing her irritations with her father. "We'd put into a port for the day and he'd have my mother and me go off by ourselves, saying he had a deadline to meet. I'm sure that's why my dad insisted I go with them on the cruise: so I could entertain my mom while he did his own thing ninety percent of the time."

"He must have missed out on a lot."

"He did. There were such unique, colorful places. It was an adventure for my mom and me, but most of the time he sequestered himself in his stateroom, writing his latest book, which for all of it academic brilliance, will eventually be like toilet tissue blowing in the wind to all but a handful of academics while he's missed out on really living."

"Of all the things to miss, really living is the worst," John said. "I'm sorry."

"Me, too, for him." Amy said. "Despite his intelligence, he hasn't figured out there's more to life than work."

Amy had chosen psychology not physics like her father, but she, too, was both brilliant and driven to excellence, qualities she undoubtedly drew from her dad, but John liked she also wanted more for herself than achievements. "So, how are things going otherwise?" he asked. "Most important, how are you?"

"All right," she nodded. "But it's been stressful."

"What?"

"Tim broke up with me."

"Oh, Amy." He started to say he was sorry but hesitated. "I feel for you."

Tears slipped down the smooth skin of her cheek. She waved her hand as if trying to make the crying vanish. "Err!" she growled, chastising herself.

"What?"

"I didn't want to cry."

"Amy, it's okay. That just means you feel deeply—and that's a good thing. I know it's sad, too, though. I'm sorry you're feeling bad."

She managed a pained smile. "Thank you."

He leaned toward her. "Breaking up with a significant other—it's one of the hardest things we ever do. How are you doing?"

"Sad," she said. "But good too. Something had gone sour in our relationship, even more than I'd let myself know. I love Tim a whole lot, and even though he's the one who broke us up, I realize now something was wrong: we were just hanging on to each other out of habit. Do you know what I mean?"

"Yep." Something sad shifted in him as he worried that he and Claire might be slipping toward something similar. "I do."

"I loathe to say it, but my parents have seemed to hang on to each other more out of habit than intimacy and passion. I'm selfishly glad my parents are still together but they seem to go about their lives in parallel orbits and they don't seem very happy together. I miss Tim but I want more for my life than that kind of relationship."

He looked into her green eyes. "What do you want?" Years ago, his own parents had seemed to settle into a similar peaceful co-existence.

"Love. Intimacy. Passion. Playfulness. Authenticity. Does that sound selfish?"

His mom would say yes it was selfish, especially if it meant breaking up a relationship, but he had wanted those experiences for himself, too, when he separated from Joanie. Now he wondered if those feelings, which had once been so strong with Claire, were decaying? "No. It sounds healthy. I wish that for you too."

"Thank you." She nodded. "When I get through all of the sadness, I'll be better off."

"Yes, you will."

"It's a therapist's cliché, I know," she said. "But it feels like it's going to be a growth experience."

"'No pain, no gain,' my high school coaches always used to say. But even then I hated that expression and they never mentioned that feeling the pain sucks."

She laughed. "It does."

"Actually, Amy, it says a lot about you—that you want to grow and make something more, something positive out of this."

"I appreciate that."

"I respect how you're handling all of this."

She hesitated. "Even though I cried? I didn't want to cry in front of you."

"Why? Because I'm so mean?" He winked.

"Just the opposite." She flipped her hair back, off her face. "Because you're so caring."

John jogged from his car into Claire's house, clutching the entertainment section of the *St. Louis Post-Dispatch*. The door was unlocked but the house was dark.

"Claire?"

He flipped the light switch, calling Claire's name again. He walked through the living room, dining room, and back sunroom, turning on lights as he searched. The back door was ajar. "Claire?"

"I'm here."

She sat in a lounge chair on the back deck. The cigarette wedged between her fingers glowed in the dark.

"Sorry I'm so late—another big crisis in the community with Andy right when I was trying to leave." He decided not to mention his hour-long visit with Amy; he had stayed at the office talking with her longer than he had intended but it was good to see her again.

She nodded and inhaled on the cigarette.

"I checked the paper." He waved the entertainment section. "There's a late show out in West County. If we hurry, we can make it."

"It's too late."

"I'm sorry. I tried to call once—but there was no answer."

She sucked another long drag from the cigarette.

"Plus, Nona called me when I was changing at my apartment and she needed to talk for a long time too."

Claire glanced over. "They okay?"

"Yeah—she was just complaining again about Emerson, about how he never wants to go anywhere or do anything." He watched for Claire's expression, but she had turned away. "She was feeling down about it and, anyway, I can see her point. Emerson has pretty much always been a bump on the log, even if he's usually a benign one."

"You're too critical of him."

"I'm not sure that's true." John's self-defense was immediate, but then he wondered. "Why do you say that?"

"You just are. You take him for granted. He's always been very nice to me on the phone and he told me a few months ago how proud he is of you, but you always seem to have a little snide comment about him."

"I'd forgotten he'd said that." His mom had long said Emerson was a stick in the mud, but then she'd had plenty of critical things to say about Emerson over the years. He'd come to realize her jabs probably had less to do with Emerson per se (though his lack of social graces did make him an easy target) and more an indirect way to criticize Nona, whom his mom both depended upon and resented. While it was unfair, John knew he had lazily absorbed over the years some of his mom's negativity toward Emerson.

"You do that."

"What?"

"You take people for granted after a while."

A gust of autumn air chilled John. "Claire?"

"What?"

"Are you pissed off?"

"Why do you say that?"

"Well, at first you didn't say much, and then you were critical of my being critical of Emerson, and you're smoking again—that's never a good sign. I'm really sorry about being so late, but I'd prefer if you'd just yell at me."

"I'm disappointed, but not so much about the movie—I was pretty tired anyway."

He sat on the edge of the other deck chair. "What?"

"I've been rereading this." She took from her lap the hardback notebook that served as her journal.

He felt a little sick in his stomach. "And what did you read?"

"How much I've been hoping we'd commit to a permanent relationship—how much over the past two years I've wanted that."

"I know—"

"And nothing's happened, not even any real conversation about it. Every time I've brought it up, you've just avoided the conversation. That's what I'm tired of waiting for—not the movie."

"It's an important possibility for me too."

"*Possibility,*" Claire drew out the word in a hiss. "Yes, you like *possibilities*. But what have you *done* about it?"

"Thought about it some."

"Ah, yes, I should have known you've been *thinking* about it," she said. "You're a great thinker. But tell me, John, so what do you think?"

"I think it's a really good possibility—you know, there's potential for us, and that's nice to know." The newspaper movie section fluttered in the wind but he clutched it tighter. He really didn't know what to say--he wasn't sure he felt happy and alive with Claire the way he once had been, but he couldn't share that with her. He thought of Amy's parents and then his own—couples who had settled for going through the motions with the legal credentials of intimacy rather than the vital substance. Then he wondered if he was overreacting in a negative, unfair way toward Claire "You know, Claire, for a long time, I dreamed about us being married, and you kept pushing me away."

"Not now. Not in the past two years."

"I know," he said. "But I think we need some more time to think about things, to sort things out, and to focus on our relationship too."

She whirled in her seat to face him. "You know what I think?"

"What?"

"That's a crock of bullshit. You don't need time, you just need to shit or get off the pot."

"Now there's a romantic analogy."

She glared. "I mean it, John. You need to choose."

"Claire, I love you. But it's a gigantic step to think about marriage again. I need more time to think everything all the way through."

"Ah, the great contemplator, thinking once more."

"Make fun of me, if you want, but this is important for both of us, after being married and divorced before. And you know what? We need to be doing more fun things together."

"Like maybe on a Friday night we could go to the movies together?"

"Okay, I had that one coming. But yes, despite my messing up tonight, we need to get out more—yeah, go to the movies, but also get out to bars and clubs and hear some music, cut loose, go different places, and really live," he said. "We've both been working so much and then we're drained. Sometimes I feel so tired and used up."

"Fine. Let's do it. Anything else?"

"Yeah . . . ."

"What? Spit it out."

"We need to talk about the possibility of having a baby together."

"That's a biggie." Claire ground the butt into an ashtray and yanked another cigarette from the pack. She flicked her lighter, a spark flittered in the night, and she took a drag. "You want to have a child?"

"I don't know. I have mixed feelings. Children are a lot of time, work, and worry, I've always heard. But some days it seems like a child might be very nice. And you?"

"No, thanks."

"You wanted another child when you and Ted were still together, just before his affair."

"That was a long time ago, John. Those days have passed." She sucked on her cigarette. "You've been like a father to my boys for years—you really have: doing things together like a family, taking them places, hanging out with them. But that's not the same as having a biological child since birth. I understand you wanting a child."

"I'm glad you understand, but I don't know for sure what I want," he said.

"This will be what breaks us up for good."

"Claire, stop!" He shook his head. "God, I hate it when you get so pessimistic."

"I wish it was different for us, but it's what I feel." The corners of her mouth curled slightly, as if she was trying to smile. "I knew a long time ago you wanted a child, but I've been denying it because I love you so much and hoping things would work out."

"This is why it's so hard to bring up issues with you, Claire."

"What?"

"You shoot things down immediately. It's like, boom—you automatically think you know what's going to happen with some negative, fatalistic clairvoyance. But I said I'm not even sure what I want."

"I've always been clearer about my feelings than you."

He shook his head again. "Will you slow down, please? I just need some time to think and we need time to talk things through."

She peered into his eyes, said nothing, and then nodded. "All right."

"Good. Thank you."

"But I don't want things to drag on forever, John. I need to know where we're headed."

Claire pushed the idea of having a time limit to decide on their future. John suggested a year, but Claire balked at this as way too long, as she did at his counteroffer of nine months. He protested that their relationship was way too important to be rushed by some artificial deadline. He suggested then their anniversary date, the annual celebration of their first kiss at Phil's party, about five months away, as a compromise.

"All right." Claire said.

In the moonlight, the crow's feet around her eyes gathered in a deep crease as she nodded. She looked older, he thought, but still beautiful. "I love you, Claire. I don't want to lose you."

"Then don't blow it. You don't have to lose me," she said. "But you have to decide what you want."

CHAPTER 19

The last Monday of November was the end of Amy's advanced clinical practicum, and John organized dinner and drinks as a going-away work party. Amy, John, and a half-dozen of the other staff met at a Soulard restaurant and bar after an evening group therapy session. They gave Amy a new book on therapy that John thought she'd enjoy and a purple T-shirt with the name of the outreach and crisis residential program, *Our House*, lettered in black on it. They ate a light dinner and talked until late about her graduate program and their favorite stories about the *Our House* clients. The other staff left by 11:00 p.m., Bennie last among them, leaving John and Amy alone at the bar table. Bennie slipped out the door, reappeared on the other side of the wide bar window, and walked with his head down into Soulard.

"He's so quiet now," Amy said.

"I know. Before at happy hours he used to sass and tease and talk nonstop. He's reeling still from the murder of his brother—not just the grief, but it was so sudden and insensible," John said. "I think that shattered his sense of a just, orderly, controlled world."

"And for Bennie, that's paramount: order and control."

"He's a bit on the controlling side."

"Just a bit," Amy laughed. "Not to mention authoritarian, arrogant, and egotistical."

"He's good with the kids." John fidgeted in the hard, wooden chair. "Most of them have really formed strong attachments to him."

"I'm sorry," Amy said. "That was really catty and insensitive. He does have a knack for getting kids to open up and bond with him—and what happened to his brother was terrible. I can't imagine what that would be like."

"Me either." He fumbled around in his coat pocket for the small present he'd been holding for her. For the past month, he had been counting down the days until the end of the practicum, not out of eagerness, but with a sense of sadness and longing. Most mornings this month he woke, often next to Claire at her house, but with an ache deep in his solar plexus, thinking of Amy leaving. His early morning fantasies about being with Amy seemed impossible to achieve because she was his practicum student and six years younger, and, most of all, because he was with Claire. While he knew in his head there were major barriers, he also realized he was certainly infatuated and maybe even falling in love with Amy—she was beautiful and smart but also sophisticated, feminine, and youthful in a way that Claire was not. He suspected that beneath her professional demeanor, Amy had fallen in love with him too. They had been emotionally and intellectually close for months because of working together but anticipating the end of her practicum had somehow seemed to intensify their attachment and created a desire for something more. He pulled from his pocket a small package, bringing it under the table and holding it lightly. He tightened his grip, debating himself for a moment longer whether he should actually give it to Amy, and then he handed the gift-wrapped present to Amy.

"What's this?"

"One way to find out." He worried she might consider the present as too personal and he tried to think of something he might say to minimize the gift.

Amy carefully removed the wrapping paper and opened the box, which revealed a gold, herringbone necklace. "It's beautiful! But you shouldn't have."

"Why not?"

"It's too expensive."

"Not really, especially not when you think of all of the time and caring you gave to so many of the kids." Falling in love with Amy, his first practicum student, was a dubious start to his supervisory career, but he told himself her practicum was now officially over, and he knew plenty of professors who had gotten involved with graduate students. Besides, it wasn't something he'd planned—it had grown organically on its own inexplicable accord out of some strong if unspoken connection between them. For the time being, he gave himself permission just to have strong feelings toward her, even as he was uncertain and cautious about doing anything with the emotions. "I'm sorry we couldn't pay for your practicum, but your being with us was really special."

"Your gift is special. Thank you so much."

"Do you like it?"

"Love it." She slipped the necklace around her neck and deftly clasped the hook together. The gold shone against the faint freckles on her flesh, beneath the curls of her long, reddish hair. There was something he found incredibly sexy about the rolling waves of her hair, but then the unwelcomed image of Claire's new hairstyle—clipped straight and blocky with thick bangs, she looked like the image for the Dutch Boy paints—crossed his mind before he shoved it away.

Her lips parted. "Guess what, John?"

"What?"

"There's a present here for you too." She pulled from her leather satchel a thin, rectangular present wrapped in blue and green paper. "I'll give you a hint: It's not a necklace, but I hope you like it."

He unwrapped a coffee table art book containing photographs of Renaissance masterpieces with brief, educational narratives. "This is great. I was expecting a therapy book when I saw the present, but I'm pretty ignorant about art—unfortunately—and I've been wanting to learn more."

"I remembered you saying that once, so I found this book for you."

"That's very sweet—thank you."

"I've learned so much from you about therapy with teenagers—especially the really troubled ones who no one else seems to care about."

"Well, good."

"But it's more than clinical techniques—you have a personal warmth that comes across as someone who really cares about each client, each staff member, too, in a very deep way."

"Thank you." He picked at the paper label on his beer bottle and forced a laugh. "Flattery will get you everywhere."

"You probably know me well enough by now to realize I'm not one for empty flattery." She tilted her head and looked up at him with a partial smile in a way that he had come to know meant she was letting her guard down. "You are pretty remarkable, you know?"

He felt both pleased and awkward, and rushed to remind her of her final practicum evaluation where he had commented on her excellent clinical skills, professionalism, and a confidence that belied her graduate school status. "Plus," he winked. "Beneath that polished, professional presentation, there's a personal spark that's pretty delightful when you let it out."

Amy smiled at him with a shine in her eyes that he'd seen a handful of times in recent weeks at the end of supervision. He wasn't sure what to say next—or if he wanted to say anything more.

The blues-rock band playing at the bar started a new set, belting out a loud song. Amy swiveled in her chair to watch. Her profile was beautiful: a slender nose, small but full lips, and the waves of long, red-golden hair that fell gently against her shoulders. Her foot tapped rhythmically to the song.

"Do you like the band?" John asked.

"Definitely. They've got a great beat."

"Would you like to dance?"

"Yes!"

They stepped onto the small wooden floor just in front of the band. A half-dozen other couples were dancing and John found a spot to the side, dancing with

Amy, but the song ended abruptly. After a momentary pause, the band slipped into the soulful music of George Bensen's "Masquerade." Amy looked him in the eye tentatively, a half-smile on her face as she recognized the slow dance music.

"Shall we?" she asked.

"Absolutely."

He opened his arms and slipped them around her back. He hugged Amy gently, feeling the contours of her toned body against his. She nudged closer, finding a resting place for her cheek against his chest. He remembered dancing with Claire years before at Phil's party, of how she had blown a breath across his face. That was Claire—bold, exuberant, even outrageous, and he had needed that then. It felt different now with Amy—not so outlandish, but more comfortable and with a sense of connection that felt very deep. John leaned his chin against Amy's soft hair and closed his eyes. He smelled a sweetness, a faint perfume that he'd sensed before when they'd huddled in his office for supervision. At odd times, long after supervision had ended and when he was working alone in his office, he had caught the rose scent of her perfume. She exuded an aura of youthful femininity that he savored. He found himself smiling, happy for an instant.

Amy rocked her head away from his chest, her long hair dangling gently against his cheek, almost as if in a caress. He imagined making love to her: he would run his fingers through the curls of her hair as they kissed and surged into one another. But to become lovers with Amy would mean having to leave Claire and that thought seemed as horrible as it did terrifying. He opened his eyes; the music had stopped. Instinctively, he cinched Amy closer for a second, and then stepped away. An ache—it had become familiar, rising with him every morning for the past two weeks when he woke and thought of her leaving—returned. He forced a brief smile and motioned to their table.

"Are you okay?" Amy asked.

"Yeah."

"You looked sad suddenly."

"You're too good of a clinician." He tried to laugh.

"What is it?"

"Oh, different things."

"It's okay if you don't want to share," she said. "But you can trust me with your feelings, John—I'll never hurt you."

He blinked twice, sat back in his chair, and leaned toward her. "I'm really going to miss you." He debated himself even after he'd spoken, wondering if he should have said the words aloud.

"I'm going to miss you too," she said. "But this doesn't have to be goodbye."

"I'd like that. I really enjoy talking and spending time together."

"That makes two of us." She smiled. "So, that means we should still get together."

"Good," he said. "I want to hear how you're doing with your program and, you know, everything."

She blinked and pulled back slightly. "Yes, I'll let you know about my progress in the program. You'll have to update me on my therapy clients too."

He gulped another swallow of beer as he sensed his formality had unwittingly distanced her. He still felt unsure and hesitant but he pushed himself. "So, if I was going to be genuine —and therapists are supposed to be genuine in real life and not just in the therapy office, I'm pretty sure—I'd disclose that I want to see you not just to talk about your graduate program and how your old clients are doing, but because I care about you deeply and I have a lot of strong feelings for you."

"And if I was to be genuine back, I'd say that sometimes I feel overwhelmed by my strong feelings for you." Her eyes grew large and moist, as if she was suddenly brimming with affection.

She slipped her hand across the table. John opened his fist, accepting her hand in his. Her warm fingertips stroked his palm, and a tingle shivered across his flesh.

"Feels good," he said. He guessed by her mien she was opening to him even as she felt exposed and vulnerable.

"I've been imagining holding your hand for a long time."

"Amy?"

"Yes?"

"I'm sorry, but it's complicated."

"Claire?" she asked.

"Yes."

"I don't mean to complicate or mess up your life," she said.

"It's already complicated and a bit messed up."

She held his hand tighter. "What's happening?"

"I don't know." He shrugged, but Amy looked at him with a casual gaze, comfortable with the silence, even though he wasn't. "We've been together for a long time now," he said. "Even though that's what I wanted at first, it just hasn't felt the same the past couple of years. I don't know—does that make any sense?"

"A lot," she said. "That's what it was like for me with Tim, even though I didn't let myself realize it at the time."

"I still care about her a lot, but something's been different—it's like we've been going through the motions for a while, but it's hard to even think about letting go."

"I know exactly what you mean."

"How did you let go of Tim?"

Amy reached for the necklace box, and fiddled with it for a second, before looking him in the eyes. She said that even though Tim had broken up their relationship and had become seriously involved with another woman—a woman he intended to have a future with—that she and Tim still saw each other once a week on the side. "It's just a temporary thing between us," she said. "Something I needed to do because I miss him and it's been too painful to think of closing the door forever."

"It's hard to say goodbye to someone you love, even when you know being together is not for the best in the long run." He wondered if they were still having sex.

"I know I need to end it to be with someone else—and for myself," she said.

He nodded.

"You looked surprised when I said I'm still seeing Tim. Does that worry you?"

"No." He wasn't really worried about Amy being unable to end things with Tim; he was worried whether he could ever do that with Claire. The very thought seemed unimaginable. "I just didn't know that."

"I'll be able to end it with Tim," she said. "What about you and Claire?"

"What about us?"

"Can you see yourself ever letting go?"

"I don't know."

"I'm sorry," she said. "That was intrusive."

"It's okay. I'm the one who's sorry," he said. "I said I want to see you—and I do—but I am conflicted about what to do with Claire."

"I understand."

There was a vacuum, not only in the conversation but in his feelings, so he forced himself to say the thought in his mind, even though he wasn't sure if it was true. "Maybe it's like you with Tim. It's hard to say goodbye, but I have the sense that's exactly what I need to do someday. I just need for us to go slow, I think."

"Going slow can be a good thing." She smiled.

They talked and danced until one in the morning. When the bar closed, he walked Amy to her silver Audi, a gift from her parents. She leaned against the driver's door and they struggled to continue an idle conversation about her graduate program that had grown awkward. A cold wind whipped around John's pants legs.

"Thank you," he said.

"For what?"

"For being so understanding about everything I said about my feelings for you and my relationship with Claire."

"You don't need to thank me," she said. "I wasn't trying to be nice—I don't normally try to be—it's just genuinely how I feel."

"Well, I'm glad. I was afraid it was a funny message: saying I'm attracted to you and I want to see you, and then saying it's complicated because of Claire and that I need for us to go slow."

"It sounded true." Amy brushed a long strand of blowing hair behind her ear. "I want you to be real with me."

John worried he was making a huge mistake. Amy was beautiful and wise beyond her twenty-five years. He knew it could complicate his life even more, but he was suddenly tired of worrying about things. He leaned close and kissed her. Her lips were warm, moist, and they kissed smoothly, not struggling, but joining tenderly and with ease, as if they'd had been kissing for years. His heart pounded and he felt breathless and giddy. The thought that he was being silly and romantic, like he was very young again, passed through his mind, but he didn't care—he felt light and happy.

A car blared its horn and a raspy male voice yelled an obscenity. John broke away from the kiss. A white Olds Cutlass with a black vinyl top sped away. A long-haired young man laughed out the window.

"Jealous jerks," John said. He pressed his cheek against Amy's and then kissed her again, feeling almost as if in a trance.

When he opened his eyes, her green eyes were staring into his.

"It feels so good to kiss you, Amy."

"Wonderful." Her voice was a low, hushed whisper.

He held her close, her body warming him against the chill of the November wind.

"I love the way you take things slow," she murmured.

He laughed, kissed her again, and marveled at the passion that roiled inside—a feeling, he knew, that he had not felt in a long time with Claire. He tightened his arms around Amy after they kissed. He didn't want to let go. But leaving Claire would be like closing a chamber to his soul. He felt sick in his stomach. He wanted to be with Amy, and the thought of not seeing her again left him with a sadness that seemed bigger than he was. Maybe, he thought—even while knowing it would be an impossible situation—he could somehow be with both Amy and Claire? He felt then like a coward, but the sense that all of this was too much to think about overtook him. He'd figure it out later. He wrapped his fingers in the waves of Amy's hair and leaned forward, waiting for the sensation of her kiss to overtake his worries.

▶ CHAPTER 20

Emerson had grunted only a few words during dinner, but this was his way. He had transfixed his vision on his plate, slicing his T-bone steak into thick chunks that he stabbed with a fork and hoisted into his mouth. After devouring the steak, he ate his baked potato—skin and all (something John's mother had told him never to do in a restaurant—you couldn't trust how well the kitchen staff had scrubbed the peel)—and then polished off his green beans. From the first family dinner that Nona had brought Emerson to years before, shortly before they were married, John's mother had complained to Nona about Emerson's lack of mealtime conversation. Nona was quick to defend him (initially and in the running conversations that had been repeated episodically over the years), saying Emerson had been raised in a poor Oklahoma farm family where his parents had worked all ten children hard like farm hands, but there was little food, and dinner was a time to eat, not talk. Emerson's table manners, John's mother had retorted, were less like a farmhand and more like a farm animal.

Nona made up for Emerson's silence, peppering John with questions and sharing her own stories. Now that he'd finished eating, Emerson leaned back in his chair, smacked his lips and slushed his tongue around his mouth like he was clearing away any remaining morsels of food. Behind his thick bifocals, his eyes were big and brown with a bovine quality. He jiggled his empty highball glass at the waiter who was setting the bill in the middle of the time. "Another of these. And the coffee's cold."

Nona and John both reached for the bill, but she grabbed it first.

"Why don't you let me get this?" John asked. His hand hovered above hers.

Nona snatched it away. "My treat. Save your money to pay off those student loans."

"Sure?"

"Yes, my dear grandson." She fixed her reading glasses onto the bridge of her nose, and then shook her head. "$1.95 for a cup of coffee! That's highway robbery."

Emerson nodded. "And they're slow on refills."

She leafed through the green bills in her wallet, and then glanced at her third husband. "Do you want to leave the tip?"

Emerson scoffed at the suggestion. "They get an hourly wage, plus the coffee was lukewarm."

John wasn't sure why his grandmother even asked Emerson. He'd been out to dinner enough times with the two of them to know the routine—she'd ask him for the gratuity, he'd say he didn't believe in tipping while finding some fault with the service, and then his grandmother would scrounge through her purse for some minuscule tip. John wondered if her repetitive requests represented some subtle resentment in his grandmother—she had worked hard all of her life and saved up her "small nest egg" for retirement, but as far John could tell, she paid for all of the bills for the two of them without complaint, although the lack of reciprocity annoyed John. She seemed to consider herself fortunate to be with Emerson after being widowed twice (which John realized had something to do with why she had married a man almost nine years younger), although as she had said on more than one occasion, after two divorces and a failed business, he had "barely a pot to pee in."

"I'll get the tip," John said. His grandmother was generous to him, but she was hardly a big tipper. He remembered being out to lunch as a boy with her and his mom: the waiter stood at the table as she dug through her purse for loose change, saying, "You people make more than I do with your tips." The memory still embarrassed John.

"I can get it," Nona said now.

"No, you got the meal. I insist." He decided to wait to leave the tip until they were walking out. Nona and Emerson had been horrified once before at his leaving twenty percent.

"You are a sweet boy. Tell me," she said. "How are your pupils?"

"They're called clients, preferably, or even patients, remember?" He knew though she wouldn't remember—she invariably referred to his therapy clients as pupils.

"You ought to hear how she brags to her friends about her grandson, the psychiatrist," Emerson said. He drank deeply from the new whiskey and water, his fourth, that the waiter set down with an updated bill that his grandmother seized.

"I'm a psychologist, not a psychiatrist," John said, already a little weary of the topic, which they had discussed multiple times before.

"What's the difference?" Emerson asked.

"One of my first professors in graduate school said to explain it this way: 'As a psychologist, I can talk with you to help you understand yourself and feel better, whereas a psychiatrist wants to deal with your problems by giving you a lobotomy.'"

Emerson shook his head. "The nut jobs I know need a psychiatrist, not a psychologist."

John laughed. At times, maybe despite himself, he enjoyed Emerson's cynical humor.

"How's your love life going, my dear?" Nona asked. "Are things getting serious with Clara?"

He corrected his grandmother on Claire's name, but dodged her question about the seriousness of the relationship. Even as he told her that Claire was fine but working long hours in her private practice, he thought of Amy. He was seeing her twice a week without telling Claire and he didn't want to tell Nona either. He was finding a joy and closeness with Amy that fulfilled some deep longing in him, even as seeing her brought guilt and anxiety. In an attempt to assuage his guilt, he was keeping intercourse off-limits with Amy, but maybe because they were enjoying almost every other sexual intimacy, his guilt had not abated.

"It would be good for you to settle down soon," Nona told him.

John laughed. "Okay, thanks."

"Let him have his fun while he can," Emerson turned to John. His head was square and thick with loose jowls, which gave him a bulldog countenance. "Once you get married—pht! The fun pretty much evaporates, replaced by a daily diet of nagging."

"Oh, quit joking," Nona forced a chuckle. "Don't scare him off from getting married again."

"Who's joking?" Emerson asked.

"*Testa quadrata,*" She shook her head. "*Testa dura.*"

"Can you believe her?" Emerson asked John. "Born in Italy and didn't speak a speck of English when she started first grade here—and now the only Italian she remembers is a few insults and cuss words."

"It's true," she said.

"Except when she's sleeping—you ought to hear her. She gabbers away in her sleep in Italian like she's never left the place," Emerson said.

Nona laughed, a pleased look crossing her face like a schoolgirl being teased by the boy she liked. John remembered his mom saying once she came home early from school one day and found a peddler inside the house, his hand resting on Nona's shoulder after he had pinned a brooch to her blouse. Even when his mom had told that story to John years later, she spoke with a certain moral indignation, saying Nona liked to flirt. He wondered if his mom was implying that Nona had had a sexual indiscretion, though he suspected his mom's story might have been in part a jealous ploy to discredit Nona in John's eyes, given their close relationship.

"I didn't know you dreamed in Italian," John said. He, too, had learned to be a flirt when he was young, and his mom had always seemed to approve, giving him an impish smile and calling him devilish while saying that when he was older he was going to be a heartthrob to women someday (when she wasn't envisioning him as a priest). Apparently, though she wanted him to act like Cary Grant in the 1950s movies, exuding charm and good looks but keeping his pants on until after marriage. "What do you make of that?"

"They say everything we do now is because of our childhood," Emerson said.

"He heard that on TV," Nona said.

"Maybe she had a traumatic childhood," Emerson said.

"It's more about the choices we make now," John said. "All that about childhood dynamics gets overblown."

"Or maybe she needs to see one of those psychiatrists," Emerson said.

"You didn't answer my question," Nona said to John.

"What?"

"When are you going to settle down?"

"Look out—she's got a one-track mind," Emerson said. "Like a junkyard dog with a bone. She's not going to let this go until you answer her."

"I don't know," John said. "What's the worry?"

"I just want you to be with someone," Nona said. "Not all alone."

He felt something sink inside. He didn't want to be alone, either, and he thought then about Claire. He could be with her. She wanted that, but something was missing. In a few years, they could end up like Nona and Emerson, wrangling over trivial matters to mask a deeper boredom. "Don't worry."

"I do worry about you. I'm not going to be here forever, you know, and I want someone to look after you."

"No, that's not true." He hated whenever his grandmother alluded to her eventual death. "You're staying here forever with me."

"I wish." Two tears crept from the corner of her eye. "Oh," she waved a napkin at John and Emerson, and then blotted it against her eyes. "I'm such a silly old woman!"

"It's okay," John said. "You have a sweet and tender heart, that's all."

She teared up again for an awkward moment, but she shook her head. "Are you and Claire planning any fun trips?" she asked. "Emerson and I used to love to go to Monterey and Carmel—bring the sticks and play a round, though I'm a terrible golfer, have a nice dinner, stay the night in a motel. Remember? We should do that again."

Emerson grunted, and she patted her hand against his, but he grabbed his coffee cup, raising it to his lips, and her hand slipped away.

"We've both been so busy with work we haven't had time to think about a vacation lately," John said.

"You should. We've taken some nice exotic trips, haven't we?" She turned to Emerson. "Mexico, Panama, Bahamas." She had been the planner—and financier, John suspected—of their trips, but it had been years since they had traveled further than Monterrey or Reno. They had lost energy in recent years, especially Emerson. Despite his being younger, he seemed like a balloon slowly leaking helium. "Where else? Oh, Alaska, Miami Beach, and Las Vegas, of course, plus Italia."

"Out of the country sounds great, but that's beyond our budget right now," John said. "But Claire and I have talked about taking a nice long trip to the mountains near where she grew up. Maybe this summer."

"That sounds nice."

"Yeah, and we'd like to make a long canoe trip on a remote mountain river she knows about."

"*No!* Don't you do that."

The abruptness of his grandmother's words surprised John. "Why? It'll be fun."

"It's not safe—being on the water," she said. "I almost lost you once that way."

"What? You mean when my dad and I fell through the ice?" He scanned her face; her worry lines tightened. "That was a long time ago, and not such a big deal. Nothing to be scared about now."

"I heard you died and came back to life." Emerson leaned over the table, clasping his hands together. "Just like Jesus Christ."

"Shush!" Nona flashed him a cross look.

"What?" John forced a laugh without trying.

"Where's our waiter?" Nona asked. "Come on, let's pay up front."

"What's he talking about?" John asked.

"Oh, nothing to worry about."

"Nona, tell me." She looked incredibly uncomfortable, like the time she had the gallbladder attack at dinner. "Come on," he said. "Is this about the ice fishing accident?"

"That was so long ago—no need to dredge up ancient history."

"Tell me," he repeated, but this time in a voice so stern it surprised both him and his grandmother.

"When they got you out of the ice, they couldn't feel your pulse—that's all."

"What?" He stared at his grandmother. "For how long?"

"I don't know. A couple of hours, maybe." she said. She rearranged her dirty silverware on the table.

"Are you kidding me? I don't remember any of this."

"You were unconscious and so was your dad," Nona said. "But they could always feel his pulse and he was breathing."

A sense of incredulousness swarmed over John. He felt then like he was observing their conversation from some place far from their restaurant table. "I wasn't breathing either?"

"That's what the hospital nurse said, but it must have all been a big mistake," she said. "Or a miracle. When the hospital called, I started reciting the rosary—I hadn't in years—and by the time we drove to the hospital, you were breathing again with a pulse. It was like a prayer had been answered."

"I think you were frozen and just thawed out," Emerson said. "Just like a goldfish in those science experiments."

"*Stop*," Nona told him.

"Why didn't anyone ever tell me this?" John asked.

"You were little and didn't remember what happened—so why worry you?" she asked. "Plus, it was horrible. You should have seen your poor mother on the drive up to the hospital—shaking like a leaf and sobbing, not knowing if you were dead or alive."

"Yeah, your poor mother," Emerson repeated but it sounded thicker with sarcasm than empathy. "Heard she lost her marbles after that."

"Of course it was hard on her." Nona said.

A sense of guilt about his mom's problems stirred, but the shock of what John heard overtook the bad feeling. "So, I was dead and came back to life?" His words sounded distant, like someone talking from across the room. "Don't you think someone should have told me before now?"

"You weren't dead," Nona said. "The doctors said you were just unresponsive—but it's a miracle that you survived. My miracle boy." She tried to smile.

"Someone should have told me."

"It was a long time ago. There's no need to dwell on the past. We just all wanted to forget it."

"Still—"

"Be glad you're alive—that's the important thing," she said. "Be thankful for that—I am. Every day in my prayers."

Emerson clanged his coffee cup on the table. "Coffee's cold and you can't get a warm up around here."

"Let's go home." Nona clutched her purse.

John wandered behind them. He was dead and came back to life? Was that even possible? He didn't remember any of that. He felt lightheaded. Someone should have told him. "Shit," he said as they reached the parking lot.

"What's the matter?" Nona asked.

"I forgot to leave the tip."

"Forget about it," she said. "It's not important."

"No." He turned and walked back. When he grabbed the restaurant door, he heard the high-pitch protest in Emerson's voice.

"*What*? Why are you giving me that dirty look?" Emerson said.

Nona tried to whisper, but the bite to her words carried across the parking lot. "You're a donkey's ass."

CHAPTER 21

John jiggled the airline plastic cup, hoping to discover more of the amber-colored whiskey, but the cup was empty, save for ice cubes that seemed to stare back at him. It was probably just as well—he'd already had four 7-and-7s (two was his normal limit). A numbing feeling swelled over his head, and he blamed this on the alcohol, even though he dimly realized the self-deceit, for he'd felt detached and dull all day.

The plane pitched as it descended through dark cumulonimbus, bouncing the heavy-set businessman in the aisle seat against John's side. John had been wedged tightly the entire flight from California between this man and the severely obese, young man with bad facial acne who was squeezed against the window seat. It was a good reason to drink, John thought—he'd always hated feeling crowded, and now this situation bordered on claustrophobic, and he had tried to drown his occasional, panicky impulses in alcohol. He had the impulse to unbuckle his seatbelt and run amok down the aisle, but he knew there was no place to go and the plane would soon be on the landing strip. His stomach felt queasy as the plane pitched and rolled through bumpy air. He closed his eyes and breathed deeply, trying to talk himself past the surging anxiety that pressurized his lungs.

The airplane touched down smoothly, but then lurched to an abrupt stop at the St. Louis gate. The passengers clambered into the aisle and John slipped out of his seat. The man from the aisle seat swung his bag from the overhead compartment, banging John on the shoulder, and then from across the aisle, his thirtysomething business companion with slicked-back, raven hair in an expensive suit and shiny black shoes stepped on John's little toe as he positioned himself for the march to the exit. But no one was going anywhere immediately. The ground crew was slow in opening the plane door and the long queue of passengers, packed body to body like cattle crowded in the chute, waited with no exit.

John hated feeling swaddled by the swollen line of passengers. He longed for fresh air, and felt his chest tighten again. He wanted out, but there was nothing he could do—a fact that again stirred a crazy desire to scream. Finally, the plane door popped open and passengers spewed into the narrow gangway leading to the gate.

John peered around an obese man, searching for Claire in the small crowd that waited inside the terminal. He saw grandparents, wives, husbands, children and a man in a black suit with a thin black tie holding a sign with "Mr. Frank Sextro" printed across it, but not Claire. For an instant, John mistook a blond woman standing at the edge of the circle of waiting people for Claire. Her hair was golden like Claire's, but she was younger with a pretty face and a slightly upturned nose, prominent breasts that also turned up, and a shapely body clad in a short dress. A towheaded girl, no more than four or five, let go of the woman's hand and ran toward the man in the expensive suit. The woman smiled, watching her child and husband embrace, and she leaned into the man and kissed him full on the lips.

John looked down the long, congested concourse, past the moving sidewalk, searching as far as he could see. The last stragglers wandered off the plane and the circle of family and loved ones drifted toward the baggage claim. John waited at the gate, wondering where Claire was. She had picked him up a handful of times after his business trips, giving him instructions to call after he had landed and retrieved his luggage, and then she would drive over and meet him curbside at the terminal. He had initially acquiesced, but he told her last month (after Amy had offered to meet him at the gate), that he felt like a stranger being ferried by a taxi. He had asked Claire three weeks earlier, when he was returning from grant meetings in Washington DC, if she'd meet him at the gate. She was resistant, but he told her that was what most couples did, that was what he'd like, and she had reluctantly agreed. But when he had returned from DC a fortnight before, she was not there; when he'd called, she was still at home, saying she'd forgotten. He was sure she'd forgotten him again now.

He walked toward the baggage carousels, thinking he should have accepted Amy's offer to pick him up. She would have met him at the gate, taken him home to a gourmet dinner, and been intimate with him in some wonderful and passionate way, while still keeping intercourse off-limits as a bargain he had made with himself to keep his guilt in check. But if Amy had picked him up, how would he have explained to Claire that he wouldn't be seeing her after being gone for more than a week? His intestines cramped. The anniversary of their first kiss at Phil's party was two days away, and by then, they were supposed to determine their future. He shook his head. They hadn't even talked in weeks about marriage, much less having a child, and he hoped that Claire, who had a terrible memory, had forgotten about the whole thing.

He jammed a shiny quarter into the pay phone and called Claire. Her phone rang ten times without an answer. He hung up, worrying something bad had happened to her. Carousel 4 was motionless, its sliding, interlocking metal plates devoid of baggage. He questioned an airline agent, and the man pointed John to the lone suitcase that had been set to the side.

A blast of February air numbed John as soon as he stepped outside. He looked around for a cab and heard a honking horn. Two headlights glared at him, and a boxy new Toyota Corolla swung curbside. Claire, in silhouette against the dome light, waved. Her hair was now even shorter with a lopsided cut—a new hairstyle, but it looked silly, almost buffoonish.

John shoved his suitcase into her backseat. The Corolla had more room, but John regretted that Claire had given her VW Bug to her boys who were running the aging car to death.

As he climbed in, she planted a sideways kiss against his cheek and lips. "How do you like my hair?" she asked.

"It's interesting." The short hair made her head appear huge and square. "Nice, but you know I always like your hair longer."

"I'm getting too old to wear it long."

He frowned at her. "I hope not. Old is Nona and Emerson's age."

"We're getting old too. Middle-aged—at least I am," she said. "Better get used to it."

He said nothing, but she chattered about her boys and then the cold weather as she pulled away from the terminal. She talked nonstop about trivial matters, which was unlike Claire. At the next stoplight, she turned toward him. "What's the matter?"

"What?"

"You're not very talkative. Are you mad because I was late picking you up?"

"You forget again?" he asked.

"No. Carol Burke." Claire had talked previously about her, a private practice therapy client with an underlying personality disorder who was in the throes of grief and guilt after her husband had died suddenly of a heart attack while she was carrying on an affair. "Another crisis—I had to see her for an emergency session. Sorry—thought I'd be here in time."

"I understand."

"You're mad," she said.

"No. I was worried—I was afraid you got in an accident or something."

"I'm sorry I was late, but you're pissed too. Why don't you just say it?"

"I'm not pissed—just disappointed."

"I hate that," she said.

"What?"

"Disappointment masking anger. At least be straight about it."

"I told you, I'm not pissed." John cracked his window—Claire had been smoking—and frigid air rushed in. "I'm disappointed and maybe slightly annoyed, but it's really not a big deal."

"I'd say get over it, but I know you had a hard week."

"Thanks—that's really sensitive." She'd been goading him to say he was angry, and now as soon as he admitted to feeling aggravated, she was telling him to get over it? "Guess you used up the last of your empathy with Carol Burke, huh?"

She glanced at him while merging onto the highway and nearly sideswiped a car; the other car honked, and she swerved back into her lane.

"Claire—for God's sake!"

"Shit," she said.

"Are you trying to kill us?"

"Sorry, but don't be overdramatic."

He said nothing.

"But I am sorry for being short," she said. "I know you've been through a lot—Emerson dropped a bombshell on you."

"I guess."

"He really broke open the family secret," she said. "How are you feeling about it?"

He still couldn't quite accept Emerson and Nona's account about his ice fishing accident, even while he was trying not to think about it. "I can't believe my family never told me before, and I can't believe that I don't remember it, either— I usually have a good memory." He remembered his parents arguing more than usual afterward and, even worse, his mom crying and not feeling good. And then she went into the hospital.

"You do," she said. "But maybe you don't want to remember. But those are thoughts. How are you *feeling* about it?"

She sounded like a therapist and this too aggravated him. He dimly realized that down deep he was far more upset about hearing he almost died as a child than about Claire's comment. But he tried to forget this, preferring to be annoyed with her. "I don't know." He heard the tartness of his words. "But I don't want to talk about it."

They drove in silence until she neared her exit from I-70.

"I rented us a movie from Blockbuster," she said. "Want to come straight over or shall we stop by your apartment?"

John said he wanted to change at home and he'd drive over later. By the time he had unpacked and climbed into his car, snow tumbled earthward in thick flakes. The snowflakes clotted the night sky with whiteness and slathered a slippery layer of wet snow onto the streets. For an instant, he wondered if as a boy he'd truly been dead or just unresponsive. He quickly dismissed the possibility that he had died and speculated instead about what movie Claire had rented. Watching a rented movie had become a Saturday night ritual. Claire was invariably dressed down in her worn pajamas and robe and she would routinely knit her way through the weekend date night. He'd complained a few weeks earlier to Claire that he'd missed going out and doing something more exciting, like going to a club or bar, but she'd said she was tired from the week and enjoyed staying home. He usually conceded—it felt more like a capitulation—but tonight he welcomed the opportunity to escape from the fatigue of flying, the nagging disbelief about his childhood accident, and the encroaching worries about the relationship. Driving through the flurries, he entertained a hope that he and Claire would slip back into routines and forget about their self-imposed deadline for a decision about their relationship.

Claire was dressed in her peach robe with her fluffy pink slippers pulled over her men's black tube socks, and she greeted him at the door with a dozen red roses. Her face looked pale from the long winter. Wrinkles framed her eyes and crisscrossed her cheeks. She smothered him with a wet kiss, but he pulled away, thanking her for the flowers though asking what they were for. A late Valentine's Day gift, she said, since he'd been gone to California. He reminded her they had celebrated before his trip, but thanked her again as he slipped past her, asking what movie she'd rented.

Claire slid *An Officer and a Gentleman* into the VCR and John plopped into the old green vinyl rocker, groaning as he sat back.

"Tired?" she asked.

"Dead tired."

"Do you want to just go to sleep?"

"No. Sounds good to watch a movie."

He watched Debra Winger, young and beautiful, in lusty pursuit of Richard Gere. He glanced at Claire. She sat with crossed knees on the loveseat, her large-framed reading glasses positioned halfway down her nose as she knitted in the dim light. The actors on Claire's small television screen struggled with commitment as the plot unfolded and his mindless escape into entertainment dissipated. He silently cursed the three-dollar rental movie for dredging up the issue of commitment that he and Claire had been successfully avoiding for months.

They watched the movie in silence, but John was sure Claire, too, was thinking about the question of their future.

A dull ache sat in his stomach by the time the movie ended. Claire stood up when the movie credits scrolled up the screen. She punched the power button, the TV blinked green, and the light drained rapidly into a spot in the center of the screen, like water swirling down a drain.

Claire turned and faced John.

"Good movie," he said.

She walked back to the loveseat, flipped a cigarette from her pack, and lit it. She took a long drag and exhaled toward John. "Why did you pull away when I kissed you?"

"What?"

"When I gave you the flowers tonight and went to kiss you, you flinched."

"I wasn't really aware of it."

"But you did. Why?"

"I don't know."

"I'm tired of the silence, John." She stared at him with her serious, aggravated face. "Tell me, and I want you to be straight."

"I don't really know for sure."

"Then give me your best guess."

He thought about telling her all of his doubts about their relationship, about how the sense of aliveness that had attracted him to Claire in the first place had faded, about how he felt those passionate feelings more now with Amy, and about how with Amy he had a sense of wide-open possibilities versus a future with Claire that seemed plodding and predictable, one that would pen him into the banal routine that had become their norm. But none of those feelings seemed possible to share with Claire—or, maybe he just didn't want to hear himself speak the words aloud. Plus, he was still preoccupied. "I don't know, Claire. It's hard to even think about all of this now, after hearing that story about the ice accident from Emerson and Nona."

"I know." She nodded. "That had to be a shock."

He wondered if she understood the weight of that story even better than he did? He'd almost died—maybe he even had? It was too much to consider, and now the threat of Claire breaking up with him seemed likely—maybe even inevitable—and the prospect of that felt terrifying though simultaneously, somehow, like it would also be a relief. "A huge shock. It's just hovering in the back of my mind now, overshadowing everything."

"I'm sorry," she said. "But what about us?"

"What?"

"Where are you at with our relationship? In two days, we're supposed to decide about our future."

"I just said it was hard to even think about anything right now because of this bombshell from Emerson." He hoped her sympathy about his childhood accident would provide him a shield.

"You've had months—years—to think about what you want with our relationship before you heard that story."

He didn't know what to say, and found he was watching the thick snowflakes falling in the night in Claire's backyard.

"John, I want you—I need you—to be really honest with me. What are you feeling about our relationship?"

"I don't know." Her stare seemed to harden. "I guess I worry sometimes about what's happening to us, like I said months ago."

"What worries?"

"Sometimes I get the feeling we're going through the motions. I miss the passion we used to have, and so that makes me wonder about the future. And what about having a child together? If I'm honest, sometimes there's a desire to have a child—though I'm not sure about my feelings—but I don't know if that's even a possibility with you." He had been having fantasies of being with Amy—they were only fleeting images, but they were delightful ones of romantic intimacy and even the possibility of being married someday and having a child. "So, all of that's been churning inside me, along with knowing how much I love you, but sometimes that leaves me with doubts. So, there it is." He couldn't believe he had told Claire all of those feelings. He tried to figure out if he felt relieved or scared. "Where are you at?"

She said nothing. He leaned forward, started to say something, but she shook her head. "I think it's time for us to say goodbye, John."

"*No*," he said. "Why?"

"The differences between us are irreconcilable."

"Not necessarily."

"We're at different life stages, John. I definitely don't want another child and you do. I was hoping it'd be different, but there's a fundamental difference we can't bridge."

"We might be able to."

She looked at him for a long time without saying anything, as she often did in serious moments. "When you were talking, I realized I'd been avoiding talking about a child—and even hiding myself from thinking about it—because I didn't want to face it. I haven't wanted to admit it—especially to myself—but our relationship has to end."

"Claire—"

She held up her hand. "I appreciate you so much over all of these years. I want to honor that, John, and celebrate our being together, but I need to accept the basic difference and let go, soon."

"Claire, I don't know. That sounds so final."

"It needs to be final."

He shook his head. "No, it feels too sad."

"You always used to get angry at me for saying we're in different life stages and we'd only be together for a time. We've been together a lot longer than I thought, and I've wanted to believe over these past two years that we'd be together for the rest of our lives, but that was living in denial. We're not going to make it." She seemed to force a wry smile, but moisture gathered in her eyes. "Oh, jeez," she said, shaking her head at herself. She tried to stifle the tears but broke into a sob.

He slipped next to her on the loveseat and took her hands. "Everything's moving way too fast," he said. "There's a lot I'm not sure of right now, but I know I love you and I don't want to let go."

"I dread being all alone," she said. "Especially without being able to look forward to being with you. I'll miss you, John. It already feels like a light has gone out of my life."

"I'd miss you, too, but maybe it doesn't have to be that way."

She wiped her eyes and then stood up. She crammed three more split oak logs into the wood burning stove and then sat alone in the green chair he had been in. "I don't want this to drag on and on. You're going to want more time, and more time, and still more time, and I'll start to withdraw." She paused, and then raised her chin as she spoke again. "I want time together to celebrate our love, and then I want to let go and grieve alone."

"What? What are you thinking?"

"We'll take a week together to celebrate and then we'll say goodbye."

He shook his head. "That's awfully sudden."

"Anything longer would be unbearable."

"A part of me thinks you're right." He paused until she looked up from the floor and made eye contact. "And a part of me thinks we're making a terrible mistake."

She glanced away, but her eyes had softened, like some strong emotion—affection, perhaps, and sadness—had passed over her.

"This is going to sound corny," he said. "But thinking of not being with you is more terrifying than anything in life, except death."

"That's not corny. It touches me."

"I only wish we could be together past death."

"Maybe we will be," Claire said. "Maybe we'll be reunited after life, as spirits that play together. That helps me, imagining that."

"It would be nice. There's only one thing," he said. "I would miss your body. I enjoy it so much."

"Maybe spirits have sex."

"Yes, maybe they do, like the alien in *Cocoon*."

He imagined holding her, kissing her, going upstairs and making love together. But she stood up and walked to the bathroom.

When she returned, she stood at the far side of the coffee table from him. "I need to be alone now."

He tried to smile. "I was afraid that was coming."

"I need time tonight to feel this and write about it in my journal. But then I want to take next week to be together to celebrate—then to say goodbye."

"Don't you have doubts?" he asked. "That we're moving too fast? That things are too final?"

"No."

"I do." He exaggerated his words, partly as a ploy to get her full attention, partly to try to steady himself. "Sometimes I imagine us together without a child and happy. And I feel better now, like we've reconnected by talking tonight, instead of avoiding the issues. I have more hope we can work things out."

She looked at him for a long moment. "I don't know."

Claire called late the next morning. "How are you?" she asked.

John said he woke up in a weird mood and then felt sad. "How about you?"

"Similar," she said. "But then I realized we've been thinking about this the wrong way."

"How so?"

"We need to put our relationship first," she said. "We should be committing as partners for the rest of our lives—not first trying to decide about having a child. Once we're committed and married, then we can decide as a couple about having a child. I might feel differently then."

As she spoke a sense of panic swelled within him, like he'd felt back on the airplane. "I don't know, Claire."

"What?"

"I mean I'm glad to hear there's possibility," he said. Instead of relief, he felt trapped. Claire was giving in some, saying she might be open to having a baby after marriage, but in return she was pressing him for a commitment. But what if he decided he wanted a baby and then she reneged about a child after they wed? She had gone back and forth about her wanting to be with him countless times over the years. Might she not do the same about conceiving a baby? "I still need time to sort stuff out." He heard himself talking as if he were from a distance.

"Like what?"

"This issue about having a baby seems too important to leave up in the air for a decision later." Or what if they did have a child and *then* she regretted it? Wouldn't she be depressed and withdraw from him and the child? "I think we both need to think through more of what we really want individually, you know, to make sure we are on the same page later."

She was silent, and he had the sense that across the telephone lines she was withdrawing from him.

"Having a little more time for both of us to think about all of this is probably a good thing—we've been so busy with work and everything's so complicated." The complications included Amy too. He didn't want to lose Amy, but he couldn't tell Claire about that relationship. He wasn't sure he could tell her anything.

The telephone line communicated only silence and that made him more anxious.

"Or worse yet, we could bring a child into this world and something tragic could happen—we could lose the child" he said. "I almost died as a boy. Or maybe I did—it's mind-numbing to even think about that. You know? Claire?"

"I'm listening."

"It's a hard to even think about a decision right now, after hearing what Emerson and Nona told me." He sounded to his own ears like he was babbling. He had the sense he should just shut up, but he couldn't stop himself. "It's a lot bigger than I ever knew. It makes me question everything in life. I know it's hard to wait and I'm sorry, but we'll work it out. I just need time to figure things out."

John hoped she was considering his points, but he wondered if she'd realized he'd been dancing around what was essentially her marriage proposal. She said she needed to go, and he quickly confirmed their dinner plans for 6:00 p.m.

He drove that evening to pick up Claire, shivering inside his Mustang despite the heater blasting away. An Alberta Clipper had blown in, dropping the temperature to near zero and freezing the snow into a thick, hard crust. The exhale of his breath rolled past the steering wheel; tiny crystals formed a lattice of ice on the inside of his windshield. Without knowing where the memory had come from, he remembered being in a hospital bed as a boy. Someone had given him a red toy airplane that fired plastic rockets, but he had shot off the missiles at the snowy pane of glass and lost the pieces in the hospital room. He tried to remember before that, about what had happened after he had fallen through the ice. There was no memory.

It was unpleasant business to think about, and he shoved the whole topic away. He thought instead about Claire. He didn't want to lose her—not now. He imagined returning to her house after dinner, and he pictured them making love, and then falling asleep in an embrace. Perhaps that was all they needed. The talk about ending the relationship was too sad. If they could just have more nights of going out, of making love, of sleeping together, then maybe things would be good again. Yes; 10,001 nights of making love together. The questions about what to do about Amy and having a child and his perhaps having died as a boy would all drift away.

When he arrived at Claire's house, she met him at the front door dressed in old jeans and a faded blue sweatshirt. He hoped she was just running late.

She told him to follow her into the sunroom. Her face was ashen and stern.

"What's the matter?" he asked.

She sat in the rocking chair and shook her head. Her long fingers gripped the wooden knobs of the armrest. "It's over."

"What?" He knew what she meant but the thought was too terrible to accept.

"It's time to end our relationship," she said.

"When?"

"Now."

"No." He heard the tremble in his voice. "Just last night you said it might be close to that time, but at the very least, you wanted a week to celebrate being together. And today, on the phone, you were talking about us committing and then deciding about a child."

"Right—and then I realized what a terrible idea that was. I really don't want another child. I was offering having a child as a possibility for you, but it's an awful idea to sacrifice myself for you—for any man—especially when you don't know what you want."

"Claire—"

"You know, you surprised me. I thought you really wanted a child and the only obstacle to our commitment was my reluctance to have a baby. But hearing your intellectualized ambivalence—or maybe it was just bullshit avoidance—about having a child this morning and needing more time—that made it clear: you really don't know what the hell you want. Or, if you do, you're too afraid to muster the courage and responsibility to embrace it."

"Things are complicated, Claire, and confusing. But with time, I can figure it out."

"You're scared of commitment," she said. "I think you stay ambivalent because it saves you from having to commit. You act like you have forever, avoiding decisions and postponing life, but you don't. You know, you're way too old to be so immature—you're not ready to be a parent or even a partner."

"Maybe I am a little scared of commitment, but it's also complicated. It's a big decision."

"I think you're afraid to make a decision because you're a chickenshit coward."

"That's not fair."

"It's true." She paused, like she was pacing herself. "This morning I practically asked you to marry me, and all you could do was to give this long, rambling excuse about how you're not sure about bringing a child into this world, and needing more time, and then all of this mental masturbation about whether you'd already died or not. You know what, John? Maybe you already have."

"That's not funny."

"You're right. It's not funny. It's sad. You're so wrapped up in your cocoon of worries and pseudo-existential bullshit that you're afraid to open up and risk embracing me or anything else in life."

"That's your opinion," he said. "Your *biased* opinion."

"It's my *experience*."

He gulped a breath. "Claire, I don't want to fight you on this. It's natural for me, for us, for anyone to have some doubts. It takes time to sort things out—plus it's not just all me. We have problems communicating sometimes too."

She shook her head.

"Listen, I also have hope for us," he said. "Even driving over here, I felt like we could turn things around. I would like that—I just need time to be sure."

"No," she said. "That's no longer what I want."

He felt his energy draining away. His perception changed, too—Claire suddenly looked older, her wrinkles ran like deep gullies across the hollows of her cheeks. And then, somehow—it felt crazy; *he* felt crazy, like he was looking through a kaleidoscope—she looked beautiful again. He felt strange, as if he was about to come unglued. It felt like too much pressure. "Claire, this feels really confusing and weird to me. I know I've said this before, but it's different now and I just need us to take a bit more time to talk this through so we can make a clear decision."

"It's over now," she said.

"Why?"

"There's no longer a point to it."

"No, there is," he said. "I don't want to lose you."

"You already have," she said. "I'm really pissed at you tonight, but don't think this is coming just from my anger. I realized as much as I had dreams of a future together, things simply are not going to work out between you and me. I don't want to get into this, but I will miss you, and I wish you a good life."

"That sounds so final." Something very heavy like an unbearable sadness settled inside his chest.

"It is. This isn't like those other times when we stopped seeing each other for a while," she said. "This time it's for good."

"Maybe this doesn't mean much to you right now because you're so angry, but I'll always love you, Claire."

She nodded. A sad smile cornered her mouth.

The possibility of not being with Claire sank deeper. "This is too sad," he said. "To think of losing you is so—"

"*Stop!*" She stood up. "I can't talk anymore. I can't be there for you in this. I know this is scary and sad for you, John, but you'll be okay. Come. I'll walk you to the door."

His body felt heavy, almost immobilized. He thought of just sitting there in front of her wood burning stove, but he noticed he was following her.

She unlocked the front door. She pivoted, facing him, gazing into one eye and the other as she had so often done. He tried to hold her gaze, but without intending to, he looked away.

She hugged him and he wrapped his arms tight around her.

She broke away. "Goodbye, John."

She pulled open the door and the frigid February night air swept over him. He stepped past her, onto the porch. He held the screen door open and tried to fashion a smile.

"I love you, Claire."

She nodded, and then closed the door. The metal lock clicked inside.

He stared into the night sky. The clouds had passed over, and now the sky was very dark, save for a few faint stars that shone through the city glare. He took a deep breath—the air burned a chilling sensation against his lungs—and coughed. He stepped from the porch to the cement steps, hit a thick patch of ice and slipped, but caught himself on the rail.

Gusts of wind whipped across the lawn of snow. He huddled his arms tight across his parka.

As much as he had considered the possibility, as much as he thought at times it was necessary and occasionally desirable, Claire being gone from his life seemed unreal. A sinking sensation settled into a pool of sadness. He felt scared.

He looked at the sky, and as he did so, he pictured—he *felt*—himself being hurled out of Claire's neighborhood into the sky, into the vastness of the universe like an astronaut without a rocket ship. He saw the blackness of space, massive against tiny spots of light, rushing past without end.

PART FOUR

John flipped back through his notes for his presentation on homeless youth that he was to give to the state mental health commission. It was material he had presented before in other talks, but his notes now seemed fragmented. He needed more prep time, but when he glanced at the clock on his bookcase, he realized he should have already left work for his afternoon date with Amy. He considered calling her and cancelling their plans—there was still considerable preparation necessary for the presentation and no other time for it; he had to be at the Chesterfield airport by 6:30 a.m. for the flight to Nevada State Hospital for the meeting. He debated himself about cancelling plans with Amy. They had gotten together about twice a week in the two months since his breakup with Claire. Amy was easy and good to be with, but things seemed to be moving fast, even as he was still wondering what had happened between him and Claire.

"You fucker!" The shouting was far away but the words were distinct. John ran toward the drop-in center lounge. He heard more swearing, this time not only Andy's high-pitched teenage voice, but also the unmistakable, excited tenor of Bennie. They stood face-to-face in the center of the room, Bennie waggling his long, index finger under Andy's nose, yelling to sit down or get out. Andy slapped Bennie's hand out of his face.

"Stop!" John shouted. "Both of you."

Bennie stepped back while still yelling at Andy, telling him he was a baby with a big attitude problem. Andy erupted into a stream of cursing interspersed with insults. His left eye was nearly swollen shut, shiny and blackish-blue.

"I said stop," John said. "Bennie, stand down. Come on, Andy—let's talk outside."

"Go to hell," Andy said.

"Come on," John said. "I want to hear what you have to say."

Andy glared at him. John's nose tingled, his flesh remembering the sensation of getting punched in the nose during a grade school fight. John watched Andy's hands out of the corner of his eyes. Andy flipped around, kicked a plastic chair across the linoleum floor, and stomped outside. John followed him into the street.

"What happened, Andy?"

"That fucking asshole was bossing me around again."

"Tell me what he said, without calling names if you can."

"To sit down and shut up."

"Why?"

"You got to ask him that. I was just seeing if I could get something for lunch and he said I knew it was too late—I didn't know—and then when I was talking to him about it, he told me to shut up and sit down."

"He said shut up to you?"

"I said he did. You got a cigarette?"

John shook his head, saying he didn't smoke. "Staff need to enforce rules, but not by saying shut up. I'm sorry about that."

Andy shrugged and pulled a crumpled package of smokes from his pocket. He pulled out the last cigarette, crumpled up the package and tossed it against the drop-in center door.

"What happened to your face, Andy?"

"Nothing." He took a long drag from the cigarette.

"Looks like something." The eye was puffy as well as bruised, and an open scrape oozed a whitish pus. "Looks like it hurts."

"Not a big deal, but I'm going to kill the fucker who did this."

"Who's that?"

"I don't remember his name—some fucking Hoosier I met outside a tavern last night. I stayed with him last night and then the fucker rolled me this morning. He kicked me in the face while I was waking up, otherwise I'd have beat the shit out of him."

"I'm sorry." John shook his head in sympathy and wondered if he legally needed to warn the man that Andy might try to retaliate. "That sucks. You stayed at his apartment?"

"No, just a place in an old building that he knew about."

"Where's that?"

Andy looked at him suspiciously. "Doesn't matter. I don't know if I could even find it again anyway."

"You're right," John was glad the threat didn't sound serious and he didn't have to break confidentiality. "Doesn't really matter where, but it's tough staying on the streets or with someone you just met. You never know when someone is going to turn on you and steal your money or beat you up."

"Fuckers," Andy snorted.

"You know, we got an extra bed open right now in the shelter program. Why don't you stay here?"

Andy's glance shifted, taking a furtive scan of the brick building that adjoined the drop-in center and held the twelve-bed youth crisis shelter program. His eyes glistened with a wild look that seemed to hold both longing and fear.

"What do you say, Andy?" John nodded, hoping to encourage him to stay. "How about you just try it for tonight?"

"Fuck you, man." Andy turned his back and strolled down the street.

"Andy, come on back. Let's talk."

He kept walking, holding his fist high in the air, and flipping the bird as he left.

"Stop apologizing already, will you?" Amy squinted, as if she was trying to look cross, but it was only for an instant; she delicately flicked her red hair from her cheeks with a motion that John found seductive.

"Okay," he said. "I was just feeling bad about being so late after you'd fixed us a big picnic lunch and then had to sit around waiting in my apartment parking lot."

"Err! You're not apologizing again, are you?"

"No," he said. "No, no, no, of course not. I wouldn't dare."

"Smart move."

They loaded his car with picnic supplies and drove toward Sioux Passage Park.

"You're still thinking about Andy, aren't you?" she asked after a few miles.

"How'd you know?"

"You wear this serious, absorbed look—your eyes look faraway and you purse your lips—when you're thinking about clients, especially Andy. I saw that look a lot during my practicums."

"Come on."

"You do. Trust me. It's quite charming. What were you thinking?"

"I was just thinking Andy's such a challenge. I don't think I've ever worked with a client with so many issues and yet you could glimpse such potential down deep. But the progress has been *so* slow. It's been more than a year and a half since we first started working with him."

"Good thing for Andy you're extremely patient," she said. "Plus, I think you like the challenge."

"He was so close to saying yes to staying at the crisis shelter tonight for the first time," John said. "I could see him thinking about it, wanting to say yes."

"Why do you think he didn't?"

"Fear. It seems crazy, because there he was: black and blue, his flesh oozing pus from being kicked in the face by some guy who'd picked him up for the night, and yet I'm sure he didn't stay in the shelter because that was subjectively more scary to him than sleeping in an abandoned building with some older guy he just meet at some crappy little bar."

"But those places are familiar to him."

"Exactly. He retreats to those places and ways of coping to make life feel safer. He's afraid of breaking out, trying something new, even if it looks appealing. He wanted to say yes. I could see it, but there was fear—no, terror, and he shut down and told me to fuck off."

"Why do you think he's so scared?"

John remembered how Andy's twin had drowned in early childhood and the suicides of his grandfather and uncle, but he didn't feel like talking again about all those morbid events on the way to their picnic. "I don't know. Maybe he's just stuck in a homeless way of life, and he's afraid of trying something different."

"Hmm." Amy waited, as if she knew he was thinking more.

"Or maybe because his childhood was so abusive, painful, and traumatic that the idea of staying around other people is too frightening and he can't imagine saying yes yet," John said.

"*Yet*," she repeated.

"A part of him wants to overcome the fears and rut he's stuck in. I just hope we'll be able to reach him."

"You will," Amy said. "You really care about the kids most people have forgotten about—Andy most of all."

John mumbled a thank you as the thought crossed his mind that perhaps he and Andy were not so very different. John was thankful he had not gone through the multiple severe traumas that Andy had, but maybe they were different more by degree than kind.

After a minute of silence, she said, "You're still thinking about Andy, aren't you?"

"It's not just about Andy or runaway, homeless kids," he said. "It's everyone. We're all too afraid, too confined to old habits and narrow little boxes that shut out new experiences and more life."

"Including you?" She reached across the car's console. Her fingers felt small to John, yet they snugly gripped his hand.

For years he'd wanted to be with Claire, and then when the opportunity came to commit, he'd missed it. Maybe the relationship wasn't the right one and it was simply time to let go? Or maybe he'd gotten so tangled up in his head with his mélange of worries and fears about marriage and passion and children and his near-drowning that he'd simply froze up, too afraid to decide anything? Or maybe—and he hoped not—it was the sad reflection of some deeper flaw in his character: perhaps in some core part of his being, he was simply afraid to really live, to embrace life? He didn't know. "Sure," he said. "Everyone, me included."

"Anything you want to share?"

He thought of the frozen lake and his near-death and his growing cornucopia of anxieties, but that all seemed very complicated and too difficult to explain— even to himself. He glanced over as he drove. Amy's blue eyes gazed at him and he felt a different hesitation inside. Amy was young and passionate and in love with him and he didn't want to saddle this relationship with another retelling of his unpleasant childhood history and his difficulty figuring out what he really wanted in terms of a relationship. "Like everyone, there are different things, you know. But mostly I guess I feel a little vulnerable about feeling close to someone again after breaking up with Claire." It was true, he told himself. He did feel an uneasy vulnerability about being emotionally close to Amy after Claire (and his unhappy marriage to Joanie). He gladly leveraged this awareness to push aside the events of his childhood.

"I understand," she said. "And I won't hurt you emotionally—that's the last thing I'd want—but I want to be close to you."

"I want that too. I just feel a little raw."

"It's scary, I know. So, I won't overwhelm you and I won't push you away or abandon you. I just want you to be open and honest with me, and I'll be here for you."

He came to a stop at a red light. He felt something—he wasn't sure what to label the emotions, but he knew it included a sense of gratitude. He squeezed her hand while thinking Amy was denying the fact that she'd be leaving for her internship in less than five months. He wondered if her move was going to function as a barrier or a facilitator for their relationship? He decided then he was engaging in way too many obsessive worries. He should take a break from his typical mental masturbation and just embrace the day with Amy.

"What are you thinking?" she asked. "You look serious again."

"It's not about Andy this time, it's about you," he said. "I'm thinking you are so beautiful."

She laughed. "You are so sweet—and I'm glad you haven't been to the ophthalmologist recently." She leaned across the console and he met her halfway, her full lips joining his. "Umm," she said. "Maybe we ought to go back to your place."

"Absolutely—but later. You're not getting out of our little softball practice that easy."

After they arrived at the park and ate a five-course picnic lunch, it was Amy who insisted that they play softball. John accused her of simply trying to humor him (for weeks, he had been extolling to her the joys of playing softball). But she insisted, so he slung the equipment bag over his shoulder and walked with her, hand-in-hand, to the empty field. She provided a running, self-deprecating commentary on the quality of her play, and he coached her first on her skills and then on her attitude.

"It's wonderful to be outdoors," he said. "To be able to play softball on the first warm day of spring—it doesn't get much better than this. Just relax and enjoy."

She stuck her tongue out at him. "Easy for you to say, Mr. Softball."

"You can do this." For all of the confidence and competence she projected professionally, he understood she was afraid to look silly or inadequate. "Before long, they'll be calling you Ms. Softball."

"Yeah, right." But she creased her brow in concentration and during batting practice, more often than not, swatted the ball through the infield. He eventually talked her into a one-on-one game he played with his best friend during childhood: he'd pitch, and she'd hit and run the bases while he fielded the ball and tried to beat her to the base. He spotted her ghost runners once she safely reached a base so she could bat again before he recorded three outs.

He chased down a ground ball she'd hit into right field, sweeping it up and pivoting to run back to second base. "Oh, come on," he said, seeing her perched on the flattened twelve-pack soda box they used for first base. "You could have easily made it to second."

"Sure, so you could run back and tag me out before I got there," she called out over her shoulder as she trotted back to home plate.

"No, you could have made it. Where's your daring sense of adventure?"

"It's already out of control or I wouldn't even be out here."

"Really—you can get more than one base at a time." He'd never met her father, but from Amy's accounts he was an incredibly accomplished if too often annoying parent. Although she postured independence and even at times a certain rebelliousness toward her father, she often talked about him with a respect that bordered on awe and with a hint of intimidation. John wondered if her father's large personality had left Amy with well-guarded insecurity. "You've already hit a few balls that could have been doubles and at least one triple."

"You're setting me up."

"I wouldn't do that to you."

"Go ahead, then." She tapped her bat against home plate and waggled her hips. "Pitch the ball."

He dangled the ball in front of his body, giving her a good view, and tossed a flat pitch toward the middle of the plate. She smacked a line drive into left-center field.

"Damn!" He watched the ball sail into the gap. "I'm the one who's been set up!"

He chased down the ball, her longest hit of the day, and when he turned back, she was already past second base. He trotted back toward the infield and to his surprise, she rounded third and headed for home.

"You'd better run fast!" he yelled. "I'm going to catch you!"

He was gaining ground, but she was faster than he thought and already halfway home. Her short legs kicked way up, almost hitting her round butt. She was then just a stride from home plate. He lunged for her, but her foot hit home just before he wrapped his arms around her. They fell together to the ground.

"Are you out of your mind?" she asked, but she was laughing.

"No, but I think I've just been hustled."

"Beginner's luck," she said. "I'm not an athlete."

"Not true," he said. "I've experienced you as very athletic, but of course that was in an indoor sport."

She leaned her lips gently into his, and they kissed a long time, lying on the grass like two teenagers. Early in the evening, they returned to his apartment, changed clothes, hurried to a movie and then ate dinner out. Back at his apartment, they kissed more and then made love in his bed. He lay afterward, with his arms cradled around her bare shoulders, sensing himself falling asleep as her fingertips lightly stroked his chest.

He woke later with a start; she was pulling back one of his eyelids.

"What are you doing?" He heard the annoyance in his voice.

"Just looking at your peepers, trying to see if you're still asleep." Her voice had a playful, almost childish quality.

"For Christ's sake." He raised his head from the pillow to look at the clock. "It's 2:10, Amy. I have to get up in less than three hours."

"That gives us just enough time to play again!"

"Let me sleep, please." He rolled over, worried about being exhausted for his morning presentation to the state mental health commission. For a moment, he kindled his aggravation with indignation about her waking him up in the middle of the night, but his annoyance faded as she tapped on his back and spoke in a lyrical voice.

"You-who." She raised up, leaning over his shoulder. "Peek-a-boo."

He contemplated snapping at her, but he laughed instead, more amused than irritated at her childlike playfulness. He rolled back toward her. "What is it with you?"

She grinned, and then kissed him. She slid her hand between his thighs and caressed him. They made love again, and his passion swelled, consuming the last of his aggravation.

Sometime later, it was still dark and the alarm had not yet sounded, he woke, feeling her body cuddled tight against his backside. He felt both happy and comforted, and for a drowsy instant, he thought it was Claire holding him—they had often slept this way. As his consciousness cleared from sleep, he realized it was Amy, not Claire. An ache stirred deep within him, and, in a way that made it impossible to return to sleep, the thought intruded that this was Claire's space.

CHAPTER 23

The panel moderator flashed John a card with "2 minutes" inscribed in bold black ink. John scanned the audience of about seventy-five people, mostly St. Louis State Hospital staff who probably wanted to get off the wards for a while. The psychiatrists, a half-dozen foreign doctors in white coats, slumped in their front row seats like frail trees bowed in the wind. After five presenters, and an hour and a half, most of the audience appeared bored.

John looked at his notes about outreaching and engaging homeless and runaway youths, shuffled through the three remaining pages, and then dropped them to the podium.

"We're running out of time and I'm getting the hook here, but let's take a few last minutes to conclude. I spoke at length about research data and broad clinical concepts—but probably said too much in abstract words that obscure the essence.

"The heart of this new mental health service is about caring for and building connections with young people who have been seriously wounded emotionally. These teens and young adults carry a multitude of mental health diagnoses, but almost all have endured multiple traumas, from early childhood abuse to violence on the streets to a mental health system that at first ignores their needs and then too often tries to lock them up against their will.

"Any effective mental health program must begin by reaching out to these youths, by making the clients feel safe, by treating them with respect, by being responsive to their needs for food and shelter, and most of all, by providing constant caring, even when that caring is tested and rejected time and time again. This way of reaching out is an important start, but it is not easy. What seems simple to us constitutes a huge request to many youths when we ask them to come in for shelter to join a rap group or to talk with their parents again—if they have any. In each case, we're asking the young person to trust once more, to open a part of life that has been closed because it was too painful in the past.

"Andy is one such young person. He is a survivor of a plethora of traumatic experiences who has not lived in a familial home since age fifteen. During his teenage years, he was hospitalized at least thirteen times and had a long string of unsuccessful residential placements. By age sixteen, he was staying regularly in St. Louis' streets or abandoned buildings or with adult males who used him for sex.

"Andy's grandmother is a very caring woman, but she has been unable to provide him with a home since he was fifteen because of his escalating problems. She also reported a group of neighborhood youths have teased, bullied, and beaten Andy for years. He became the target for their abuse not only because of his proclivity for insulting people and provoking fights, but also because of community intolerance for his unusual behavior, such as occasionally talking to himself, his drug abuse, his bisexuality, his disheveled homeless appearance. Although Andy now wanders far from his childhood roots, he often returns to his old neighborhood during times of crisis, trying to survive there by modifying his typical in-your-face posture by keeping a low profile, staying in back alleys, or only coming out after dusk. His pattern of avoidance became so distinct that neighborhood children now call him the "shadow man." Unfortunately, his defenses are not always successful, and his grandmother first called us for help after a group of teens had beaten him one night with pipes.

"Despite his serious needs, Andy has not been an easy client to engage, especially for housing. Persistent street outreach, aided by sandwiches and sodas, helped coax Andy to visit the drop-in center, but he quickly alienated others by threatening another client with a knife. In time, however, we were able to engage Andy in therapeutic one-to-one conversations and later in recreational activities at the drop-in center. But he continued to react to any suggestion of shelter with a quick rejection of swearing, yelling, and stomping off.

"After more than eighteen months of engagement, Andy stayed in the crisis shelter last month. It is the first time he has stayed in any residential program in several years. His stay has presented its challenges, especially for managing his anger, but he has resided successfully in the program for more than a month. During this time, he has begun to open up in individual sessions about past, painful events—such as at age seven when he accidentally broke a beer glass and his mother's boyfriend dripped scalding water on his wrists—but also about his hopes for the future.

"Andy still has much work to do on his recovery from mental illness, from substance abuse, and from life on the streets. But he has started a fundamental journey to be open, to trust, to risk living more fully, instead of lingering in the shadows.

"Thank you."

The inside of his car was sauna hot and John cranked down the windows. He scanned the early July sky, a humid-smoggy gray, and hoped it wouldn't rain. Our House had a one o'clock softball game against another youth treatment center, and he was going to have to hurry to get to the field by game time. After his presentation, the psychiatrists filed out of the auditorium without a word, but a couple of the hospital social workers had peppered him with questions about referrals. He caught himself wearing a smile of satisfaction about the presentation, but his smile faded as he thought about Andy being beaten with pipes. It was hard to imagine what that was like, and then he remembered another hot summer day in the third grade when his friend, Robby Roberts, had stomped across the garage and slugged John over and over in the shoulder, giving him a dead arm. Robby was at least a head shorter, but John had simply passively accepted the beating without even trying to fight back. But why?

He wanted to dismiss the memory—everyone takes some licks growing up and getting slugged repeatedly by Robby Roberts was way less serious than Andy's beatings. But he realized that wasn't the point, and the word hypocrite intruded his thoughts. John regularly pushed Andy; therapeutically, yes, but it was something more personal than that—he wanted Andy to open up and take a risk, to really live again. But was that more than he expected for himself? Hadn't he been passive most of his life in a multitude of ways, from social shyness to tentativeness in sports to relationships—holding himself back, afraid to really live? Isn't that what Claire was talking about—he was a chickenshit, afraid to be open and celebrate being alive?

John pulled into the ball field parking lot and walked toward the field. The kids were warming up and it was a beautiful field, the manicured grass outfield set against the edge of a forest and the perimeter of an old cemetery that crept along the left field line. He tried to get excited about the game as he quickly stretched, but something gnawed at him. He was angry at himself for turning the good feeling about his presentation into self-doubt. He tried to dismiss the concerns. He was prone to neurotic self-deprecation, but he also knew, as much as he didn't want it to be the case, that his worries contained some unpleasant truths.

"Blind old man!" Andy shouted from the batter's box. The softball umpire took a step back, but Andy immediately closed the gap, wagging his finger in the umpire's face, yelling again: "How much did they pay you? That was a ball!"

John slipped between Andy and the volunteer umpire, a silver-haired administrator from the other youth program, who was telling Andy he'd better cool down and get back to the bench after being called out on strikes. "Living with the ump's call is part of the game, Andy," John said. "You gotta let it go."

"Traitor!" Spittle spewed into John's face as Andy hurled his insult. Andy spun around then and stomped toward Our House's bench, kicking the empty equipment bag. "This team sucks."

"He's right, you know." Jeffrey was one of the program's first clients and the most cynical. "It's only the first inning and we're already behind 10-2. They're going to slaughter us. What's the fucking point?"

John asked the umpire for a timeout. "Come on, gather around." He wiped sweat from his forehead. "Everybody."

The kids meandered toward him, Bennie and Loretta cajoling the stragglers like sheepdogs nipping at the wayward members of the flock. Only Andy refused to join the circle. John shook his head at Bennie, who was walking toward Andy, to undoubtedly issue an authoritarian ultimatum.

"I know it's hot out here and it's discouraging to be behind, but you know what? I'm a lot more concerned about you guys and your attitude than I am about the score." From a quick, sideways glance, John saw Andy scoff, a scowl affixed to his face. John intentionally spoke softer. "Are you just going to give up because you're behind? I hope not. I hope you keep going and focus on playing your very best in a good, clean way that upholds your dignity. That's what it's all about. If you do that, you can hold your heads up, and we'll celebrate by going out for pizza afterward, win, lose, or draw."

Andy stepped closer.

"But that's secondary," John said. "What counts most is that you give it your best and have fun. Now let's go."

"Thank you, Knute Rockne," Jeffrey said. "Absolutely inspiring."

John laughed and so did the kids, but they took their positions in the field, except for Andy. He tugged his red Cardinals baseball cap tighter over his long hair, mumbling it was fucking stupid to play with a bunch of losers.

"Hey, Andy," John called on his way to center field. "We really want you back at first base, but it's your choice, of course. If you don't come out by the time Matt finishes his warm-up pitches, I'll assume that means you've decided not to play and we'll put Loretta at first. And you know, Andy—no offense, Loretta, you're a great nurse—but the team would much rather have you as our first baseman."

Andy snorted another explicative and kicked his glove, but it was toward first. He sauntered after the glove, kicked it up into the air, caught it, and stood near first base, his arms folded.

Our House held the visitors to two runs and then scored three in the bottom of the inning. By the bottom of the third, after the opposing team had scored two more runs, Anthony, one of the other counselors, arrived with Deon from a juvenile court hearing. "What's the score?" Anthony asked.

"15 to 5," Jeffrey said. "And, of course we're not the 15."

"All right, all right." Anthony rubbed his palms together, his white teeth bright against cocoa-colored skin. "We're within striking distance. Got them right where we want them."

Bennie, who warned all week that he wasn't very athletic and had already proved his point in the field, begged Anthony to replace him as the third staff player each team was permitted. Anthony batted for Bennie, and on the first pitch, launched a long, majestic fly ball that carried fifty feet over the left fielder's head. Anthony had gone to the state track finals in high school and he circled the bases before the outfielder had relayed the ball back to shortstop. Three batters later, John hit a line drive to left center for a double and two runs batted in.

"What I tell you?" Anthony high-fived players and even Jeffrey cracked a thin smile before announcing they still trailed by seven runs.

Andy fouled out to the catcher to end the inning. When the other team came to bat, he cursed vehemently at Loretta and Ben after a pop fly dropped between them in short left.

"Ease up, Andy!" John shouted from centerfield. "We're here to have fun. Get it together now!"

Andy grumbled but wandered back to first base. Loretta trotted closer to John as they backed up in the outfield. "You okay?" she asked.

"I just get tired of his negativity sometimes," John said.

"I know."

"He should just enjoy the game and not be so serious, cursing out some-one if the play goes bad." John had his first start in the majors division of Little League at age of eleven. His nervousness had exceeded his excitement, but he had played okay—nothing remarkable, but nothing embarrassing—until the last inning. The coach's son was pitching and their first-place team was unexpectedly losing by a run in the top of the last inning. A fly ball looped toward John in left field. He got a good jump, charged the dying fly ball, but then inexplicably stopped at the last second. The ball fell at his cleats. One more step—if he'd only kept moving—and he would have caught the ball. Instead, the batter was safe at first with a single. The coach immediately called time and yanked John out of the game. "You should have caught it," he growled, pointing John to the bench. "You should have at least tried."

It was total bullshit, John thought now. You don't humiliate a kid, especially in front of his peers and family. You build them up, let them develop skills and confidence—not tear them down. But when he had sat on the bench, tears had slipped onto his eleven-year-old face and now he wondered if his failure to go after the ball then was just one more symptom of a lifelong anxiety about allowing himself to let go and live passionately?

The next inning, when he was batting, John heard Jeffrey's gravelly voice call out Amy's name. He had expected her at some point—she had said she would stop by and they had plans for dinner later at his apartment—but he was still distracted knowing she was there, and he let an inside pitch go by for a strike. He had come to love Amy—she was intelligent, beautiful, sexual—qualities he also loved in Claire, but Amy possessed an ease in being together plus a feminine allure that escaped Claire. Near the bench, Jeffrey and a small swarm of older kids gathered around her, though Andy kept his distance. John stepped back into the batter's box, took a mighty swing on the next pitch, and sent a weak pop-up back to the screen. Jeffrey hooted and more kids laughed at John. He took a deep breath, concentrated, and drilled the next pitch on a line deep into the gap into right center. He sprinted around the bases for his second home run of the game. The kids high-fived him after he crossed the plate and Amy stood behind them. "Give me some skin," she grinned. He resisted an impulse to kiss her in front of the clients.

The opposing team scored two more unearned runs in the top of the seventh. Anthony and John sang out positive chatter, but John mumbled to Loretta, after the errors that this could be one of those interminably long innings. There were two outs, but the other team had runners at second and third and their big kid dug in at the plate; he'd hit a long home run his last time up. Anthony had taken over the pitching and he tossed the first pitch extra high toward home. The batter took a huge swing, but the ball popped weakly toward short left. Ben backpedaled and Loretta loped in; John raced toward the spot, but it was a long way off. He saw that neither Ben nor Loretta would get there in time, and the ball would fall for two more runs.

"I got it," John yelled. He wasn't at all sure that he did, but he envisioned the ball falling for a hit and more runs amid a three-player collision if someone didn't call for the catch. He dove for the ball, remembering in midair another game in his men's league when he dove and caught the ball, only to see it slip out of his glove when he fell against the ground.

The falling pop-up landed in John's outstretched glove but when he hit the ground, the ball popped loose. The white softball floated up and away from him as he tumbled in an unintentional somersault on the outfield grass. He grabbed the ball in the air with his bare hand, pulled it against his chest, and flipped over. His shoulders and knees plowed to a stop in the short grass, and he cradled the ball against his breastbone. He thrust his arm into the air, holding the ball in his bare hand for the umpire to see.

"Out!"

Ben helped pull John to his feet and Loretta inspected his scraped knees and elbows, asking if he was okay. Anthony sprinted over and flashed his pure white smile: "Way to be, chief." The kids were whooping it up and Andy was going crazy. He squeezed John in a huge bear hug—the first time he'd ever hugged John—and slapped him on the back.

"What a catch!" Andy said as they ran back to their bench. "Best I've ever seen. Better even than Ozzie." Andy's room was plastered with red-and-white Cardinals paraphernalia. Ozzie Smith was the only person that Andy unabashedly adored. "How did you catch that?"

"I don't know. It was a blur. I just knew I wasn't going to let that ball slip out once I got to it."

"Did you see that, Amy?" Andy asked. "That was amazing—just like Ozzie!"

"Yes," she said. "He's pretty amazing."

Anthony chattered at the kids, pumping them up to come back with a big at-bat to overcome the seven-run deficit in the bottom half of the last inning. The middle of the lineup scored three runs and the bottom of the order scored one more while making two outs. Ben, the leadoff hitter, came to the plate and he blooped a single to left. Anthony batted next and a murmur rumbled through the kids that they could actually win. Anthony belted a towering drive to left-center over the outfielders and he skipped around the bases grinning. The other team's second baseman yelled at the outfielders, their lead cut to one run, 22 to 21.

Donnie was up next. He was one of Our House's best players—not a home run hitter, but scrappy and a hustler. On the first pitch, he hit a line drive to right center. Donnie sprinted around first toward second, but he didn't stop: head down, he ran toward third. The second baseman relayed the ball from the outfield over to third, and the ball arrived way before Donnie. Our House's bench screamed, and Donnie looked up and saw the third baseman waiting with the ball. A look of horror crossed Donnie's face and he skidded to an abrupt stop. The third and second basemen had him trapped in a rundown. Donnie scampered back and forth, but he slipped near second. The third baseman fired his throw, but it was low, bounced in the dirt, and kicked away. Donnie scrambled to his feet and sprinted toward third. He slid safe, just before the throw. Donnie popped to his feet, faking a run home.

"Stop, you idiot!" Jeffrey yelled.

John stepped to the plate, taking a deep breath and telling himself not to swing at a bad pitch. Wait for something you can hit hard and on the line, he told himself. Doesn't have to be a home run; just relax and enjoy.

Barney, their staff player-coach, called time out. The Our House kids had snickered and teased about his name, but he was a good player who knew his baseball. He talked with their pitcher, patted him on the shoulder, and trotted back to center.

John waited for the first pitch, but it came in way low and short. The next pitch came in the same way and John realized Barney's trip to the mound was to tell his pitcher to intentionally walk him. After he'd hit two home runs and two doubles, Barney didn't want to give John the chance to drive in the tying run or maybe even win the game. Andy was up next, and he was only one for four. Even if he managed to get a hit, John was only at first and Loretta followed Andy and she'd made outs every time. The intentional walk was a smart strategy.

Jeffrey howled as the next pitch bounced over the plate, calling the other team cowards and cheaters. A couple of other Our House kids immediately picked up the name-calling chorus. John yelled for them to stop; intentional walks were part of the game. The next pitch hit three feet in front of the plate. Jeffrey mumbled curse words from the bench.

John leaned his bat against the cyclone fence backstop while Andy picked up another bat, grinding it in his hands.

"All you, Andy," John said before trotting to first base. "You can do it. Just relax and concentrate."

The first pitch came in high and inside, but Andy took a mighty tomahawk chop at it. The ball tipped straight back, clanging against the metal backstop.

"You don't have to kill it, Andy," John called. "Just relax and focus, just meet it."

Andy's face was red, his neck muscles bulging like he was going to burst a blood vessel.

"Take a practice swing, Andy," John called to him. "There you go. Again, nice and easy this time. That's it."

The pitcher stared in, grinned, and tossed the pitch a foot outside. Andy reached out and swung, bumping the softball off the end of his bat like a cue ball spinning off a pool stick. The ball squirted foul along the first baseline, then spun toward the bench. Jeffrey emitted a loud groan as it rolled to his feet.

Andy stared at John while digging in deeper in the batter's box. John called timeout and jogged toward home. Andy met him part way down the first baseline.

"What?" Andy said.

"Hey, relax," John told him. "You can do this. But just by being out here and not giving up, I'm proud—"

"I'll hit." Andy's voice was high-pitched.

"Good confidence, but don't put a ton of pressure on yourself. This is a great game, but it's for fun. Give it your best effort and enjoy—"

"Shut up," Andy said. "And you'd better fucking score when I get a hit." Andy whirled around and stomped back to the batter's box.

John braced his back foot at the side of first base and leaned like a sprinter toward second. Donnie, Jeffrey, and the other kids were yelling a hodgepodge of batting tips to Andy. "All you, Andy," John sang out while drawing a deep breath. "Just you and the ball—just look for a strike. You can do this."

The pitcher grinned again. He started his underhand windup and let loose a low, flat pitch. Anthony yelled not to swing. But Andy did. He chopped at the ball, nicking the pitch with the bottom of the bat handle. The ball dribbled along the third baseline. Andy hesitated, watching the ball as if shocked by the puny result of his mighty swing.

"Hustle, Andy," John yelled. "Run hard!"

Andy was off, running with his funny gait—his knee had been kicked in once during a street fight—his elbows hitched high, his arms chugging back and forth like pistons. The third baseman had been playing deep, but he charged the ball, which trickled just inside the foul line, and the pitcher scampered off the rubber. John was nearly to second, watching the third baseman and pitcher converge on the ball. Donnie streaked past them to home plate and Andy strained toward first. The third baseman and pitcher looked at each other, as if trying to decide if the ball would roll foul or who was going to field the ball. Third base was wide open and John rounded second without breaking stride. The third baseman gloved the ball and threw toward first, but his throw sailed wide. The first baseman came off the bag, caught the throw, and scrambled back to the bag, but Andy's foot descended on the base first and the umpire yelled safe.

The pitcher saw John streaking toward third and he ran to cover the bag, screaming at the first baseman to throw him the ball. The first baseman, double clutched, and then let loose a loopy toss across the diamond. John stopped safely on third, way before the throw arrived. He grinned, but then saw Andy running toward second.

The shortstop ran to cover second and shouted at the pitcher, who threw him the ball. Andy was only halfway to second. He stopped, frozen for a second, and the shortstop ran toward him. Andy headed back toward first; they had him trapped between the bases and soon he'd be tagged out.

John broke for home. "Hey," he yelled at the fielders. The shortstop hesitated; he was about to throw the ball back to first where they would tag out Andy, but the shortstop whirled toward home. He wound up and heaved the ball toward the catcher.

John put his head down, focusing on home plate. Loretta grabbed Andy's fallen bat and scurried away from the plate. The catcher stood at home plate, crouched, and jumped for the high throw. John leaned into his slide before the batter's box. He slid through the dirt and safely across home plate just before the catcher came down with the late tag.

"Out!" the umpire yelled.

"What the fuck!" John jumped to his feet. "I was across the plate before he tagged me."

"No." The umpire started to walk away. "Your leg was up and he tagged you first. That's it—out of time. Game ends as a tie."

"That's bullshit!" John threw his hands up and stepped toward the umpire. "Come on, don't do this. Be fair."

The Our House kids came running to home plate, most of them swearing and all of them yelling at the umpire.

"You'd better get your players under control." The umpire pointed a finger at John, but his eyes had widened. "And I'm about an inch away from filing a complaint with the state about your cursing and inappropriate modeling in front of these young people."

Jeffrey led the pack of kids, screaming insults about a fixed game, swearing at the umpire. John wanted to tell the umpire he was going to report the program administrator to the state for cheating on the last call, but he knew the man was right about one thing: he needed to get his clients—and himself—under control.

"Over to our bench now, everybody." John yelled. None of the clients turned back, but they stopped at home plate as John stood in front of them and the retreating umpire.

"Total bullshit!" Jeffrey spat the words. The whites of his eyes loomed large behind his thick glasses, the way they appeared when he was enraged.

"I agree—he missed the call." John took a step to the side to block Jeffrey, who seemed intent on confronting the umpire face-to-face. "But the ump's calls—even the bad ones—are part of the game and something we have to accept."

"Fuck that!" Andy had run in from second base.

"Learning to accept things—even bad things—is part of how we cope with life," John said.

"Maybe you have to accept that bullshit," Andy said. "But I don't."

Jeffrey eyed Andy with a quick, sideway glance, and then turned on him. "You shouldn't even be opening your mouth after your dumbass play."

"What the fuck are you talking about? I got a hit to win the game, just like I said I would."

"Yeah, big hit—what it do? Dribble thirty feet? But never mind that—running to second?" Jeffrey said. "What was the fucking point of that? Your run didn't matter. The game was tied when Donnie scored and we only needed one more—not two—to win. John was the only one that mattered—not you."

For a moment, there was silence. Andy looked surprised, and then something else, like shame or despair or maybe a combination, crossed his face as he grasped Jeffrey's point. He glanced at the ground.

"Idiot," Jeffrey said.

"Shut the fuck up." The self-blame had passed from Andy's face, which now showed only anger. "I should kick your ass, four-eyes."

"Stop, both of you, and everyone, stop swearing." John nodded at Anthony, who slipped next to Andy while Bennie stepped in front of Jeffrey. "The ending was frustrating for sure, and we all have a right to feel disappointed and angry. But sometimes in life, shit just happens and it's normal to feel mad, but don't take that out on the people around you—on each other: you're teammates. It's a challenge but learn to let the bad stuff go and look at the positives." A few of the kids looked at him, and John felt like perhaps he was starting to reach them. "You guys have a lot to be proud of—the way you rallied from a huge deficit and tied the game. That says a lot about you—you don't give up. You're resilient."

"Yeah, go ahead, spin your psychobabble now," Andy said. "You lost us the game. I told you to score when I got a hit and instead you got tagged out."

"Hey," Anthony said. "That's not fair. John had no choice but to break for home when you got caught in a rundown, and he almost scored the winning run. In fact, he did score with his hustle, but it was the bad call that cost us winning the game."

Andy didn't seem to hear a word that Anthony said. He was transfixed on John with a look of rage that bordered on hatred, but wetness shone in the corner of his eyes. "I didn't come here for a fucking tie. A tie don't mean shit. I wanted to win. I never fucking win."

"I understand, but watch your language." John said. "It's disappointing. You did your part—you got us a hit—and you expected us to win. It's frustrating."

"I don't want to hear your fucking therapist bullshit." Andy was screaming now. "I don't need you or any of this." He turned and walked away.

"Andy," John yelled, but he detested the desperate tone in his voice. "Come on back—you're an important part of this team."

"Fuck you, man. Fuck all of you." He ran then, across the ball field, and away from John, the other counselors, the other youths, his elbows hitched high in his funny gait until he disappeared into the woods next to the cemetery.

John declined Amy's offer to help, telling her to relax with her glass of wine while he set a crystal vase with two vibrant red roses in the middle of the white linen tablecloth.

"That was quite the game." Amy sipped her wine.

"I couldn't believe what an asshole that umpire was," John said. "It was obvious he called me out because he didn't want his program to lose."

"I've never seen you that mad. You looked like you were about to punch him out."

John shook his head as he put a dish of cheese raviolis in a creamy red sauce on the dinner table. "Probably wasn't the best modeling for the kids, huh?"

"Not a textbook intervention," she said. "But I've heard it said that sometimes when therapists uncharacteristically lose their tempers for a moment—within bounds—it shakes clients out of their normal defenses, and things begin to change because you're showing you're human too."

"Showing my humanity, huh? That's a nice reframe." John transferred to the table garden salads, a bowl of sautéed green beans with almond slivers, sourdough bread, and a platter of sirloin steaks. "Andy doesn't have much trouble showing his humanity—did you see that look he gave me before he stomped off? He was beyond angry—it was like he hated me."

Amy leaned across the table to kiss him. "Andy idolizes you. He also has unrealistic expectations sometimes—like you could magically win the game after he messed up."

"I just hope he'll come back around. I called Bennie before you got here—"

"Of course you did." Her smile was set in a square, knowing, almost jealous expression.

"Anyway, Andy hasn't shown back up at the residential program. He's probably back out on the streets, getting high again."

"He's a survivor," she said. Amy liked Andy, but he had never been one of her favorites and Andy displayed a palpable coldness toward her. Amy had told John once that Andy was jealous of her—that he had sensed the unspoken affection between her and John.

"He is a survivor, but I still worry a lot about him."

"Why so much?"

Perhaps Andy was jealous of Amy, but months before he'd met Claire twice at program events and he had taken an immediate shine to her. "He's been through a lot already and he's a good kid. I don't want him to just survive—I want him to really recover and live a good, full, happy life."

"That's one of the things I love about you," she said. "You always want the best for people—especially those who need it the most."

"Enough about Andy." He raised his wine glass for a toast. "To you—your beauty, your playfulness, and especially to your sweetness."

"You're too sweet." She lifted her glass toward him. "And to you—especially that you aren't cured of your delusions about me any time soon."

"As my Nona would say, 'Manga, manga. Eat hearty.'"

There was plenty to eat, and Amy complimented him on his cooking even as she wondered aloud why he had fixed such a large and fancy meal. He shrugged off her question, saying simply he wanted to serve her a nice dinner, and they talked more about the softball game, then about John's morning presentation, Amy' part-time therapy job, and a band they wanted to see. They spoke of many things, but by the end of the meal, it seemed disingenuous to John that neither of them spoke of her upcoming internship and move from St. Louis. He had appreciated theirs was an easy as well as loving relationship. On occasion, they had each made vague and fanciful references to a distant future together, but there had been no talk or pressure about commitment. Now, he was increasingly clear he did not want to see her go. He could bear their collusion no longer. "It's hard to believe you'll be moving in just twenty-nine days."

"Shush," she scolded. "I'm trying to deny that."

"How are you feeling about it?"

"What?" She feigned a look of innocence.

"Honestly," he said. "How are you feeling about moving away for internship?"

"Excited when I think about the internship itself—I think I'll learn a lot that will help me grow professionally. And it'll be nice to be closer to my family." She scooted two remaining green beans to the perimeter of her plate and then let her fork clatter against the tableware. "But I don't want to leave you."

"I know," he said. "But it's definitely not goodbye."

"I'm glad." She smiled in a sad way. "I don't think I could go if it was."

"I'll come visit and you can come back when you have time too."

"I love you, you know," she said.

"I know. I love you too."

"I also know that long-distance relationships are hard to sustain. I tried one once, as an undergraduate, and it didn't last long—but I want us to try."

"Absolutely." He sounded tentative as he wondered where she was headed.

"You're free to date other women, if you want." She swallowed more wine. "I'll hate that, but I can accept it, if that's something you need, as long as you are honest with me about it and if you keep loving me."

"I haven't even thought about dating anyone else." He scanned her face, trying to figure out what she really felt. "Is this what you want?"

"It's not what I want," she said. "But maybe it's a realistic accommodation for the miles? I mean, we've never talked about an exclusive commitment before, and now probably isn't the time to start. As long as you don't start seeing Claire again—that would feel too threatening, plus I don't think she's good for you."

He was confused and took a long drink of water while trying to think. Was an exclusive commitment what Amy really wanted, but she was afraid to ask for it? She hated appearing vulnerable. Or did she want to date other people? He doubted she was looking for someone new, but Tim's internship was in Boston, too, and though they had broken up months ago, their history ran deep and he sensed she still loved him. For a moment, he considered proposing an exclusive commitment—but that would feel like closing all the doors to possibly getting back with Claire, and he wasn't sure he was prepared to do that though he didn't want to lose Amy either. "You're free to date, too, if that's what you want."

She nodded. "Okay if we don't talk anymore about this now?"

"Yeah," he said. "What do you want? For dessert, I bought a strawberry-glazed cheesecake, which looks delicious."

"What I want," she said without hesitation, "is to make love with you right now."

"Well," he said. "That would be even more delicious than the cheesecake."

He stood up, deciding to let the leftovers sit on the dining table, and reached for Amy's hand. His phone rang.

"That," he nodded at his phone. "I'm going to ignore."

Amy stood and he embraced her. As they kissed, the ringing ceased and gave way to the recorded message on his answering machine, and then the quivering voice of his grandmother.

"John? John, are you there?" she asked. "Call me back as soon as you can, my dear boy." Her strained voice cracked.

"I better get that," he said to Amy.

"Of course."

He picked up the receiver. "Nona, what's the matter?"

"Emerson," she said. "He has cancer." She cried then, emitting a broken sob that she tried to smother.

"Nona, I'm so sorry Emerson has cancer," he said, looking at Amy. He told his grandmother that he knew it must be scary for both of them, and he pressed for more information, hoping to find evidence for the optimism he wanted to convey. But a tightness pinched in his stomach when he heard that Emerson's cancer was stage D2 prostrate cancer, a cancer which the doctor suspected had been present for at least five years and had already metastasized into his bones. John talked about scientific advances in cancer treatments, sensing a boost in his grandmother's morale as he spoke, even though the words sounded like empty recitals to his own ears.

"You know what they say?" he asked his grandmother.

"What?"

"You gotta believe."

"You're a good boy."

"You're a good Nona," he said. "And I love you, very much."

"Love you too." She cried again.

"It's okay."

"I'm sorry—what a big crybaby I am, huh?"

"It's normal to be upset. This is scary, but let's hold on to hope in science and the doctors and see what happens, okay?"

"All right."

"I can talk with Emerson if you like."

"He's sleeping in front of the TV," Nona said. "He never wants me to wake him up when he's napping, but I will if you want me to."

"No, that's okay." A sense of relief passed over John—he didn't know what he'd say—but then he felt guilty. "Tell him I'm thinking about him, and I'll call him back tomorrow or sometime soon. So, Nona?"

"Yes?"

"How are you feeling now?"

"All right," she said in a deadened voice.

"Yeah? What's going through your mind right now?"

"Nothing."

"Come on, talk to me. A penny for your thoughts."

"God punishes."

It was a saying Nona's mother had often used; it had been passed down from his great-grandmother through Nona and to his own mother. They each recited the phrase when bad events occurred. "Nona, that's superstitious. What do you have to be punished for anyway?"

She was silent.

"Nona?"

"Nothing, I guess," she said. "And plenty of things."

"Nona, Emerson's cancer isn't about God punishing you. You are a good person, a wonderful grandmother. Cancer is a disease, and diseases just happen."

"Maybe you're right."

"Can you think of something more positive, more realistic, to tell yourself, if you find yourself thinking again that 'God punishes'?"

"I don't know."

"Come on. Think of something."

"Dear God in heaven," she said. "Have mercy on our souls."

After he hung up, Amy said how sorry she was about the cancer. "I can only imagine what it's like for your grandmother and step-grandfather," she said. "But I was impressed by how reassuring and positive you sounded with her."

"Emerson's going to die soon," he said without intending to.

She cocked her head. "Why do you say that?"

The bluntness of his comment still surprised himself. "I don't know. Doesn't sound good, medically. But more than that, I just have a sinking feeling."

"I'm sorry. Do you want to talk about it?"

"Not really."

Amy stood up and walked around the table. She rubbed his shoulder. "I'll get the cheesecake—this probably has taken you out of the mood."

She cut two pieces of cheesecake and slipped the thicker slice onto a plate and in front of John. She leaned down and kissed him tenderly on the cheek.

"Thank you." He took a bite, chewing it slowly, savoring its richness. He pushed the plate away, trying then to forget his dread about Nona's sadness and Emerson dying. He rose from the table and kissed Amy fully on the lips. He interlaced his fingers with hers, lifted her to her feet, and stepped her toward the bedroom.

"A nice surprise." She smiled. "I didn't think you'd want to make love after the news."

He tried to smile back. "I do now more than ever."

▶ CHAPTER 24

After dinner, John retreated to his Bethesda hotel room. The meal with a half-dozen of other researchers from the federal grant meetings had been pleasant enough with intellectual conversation and a platter of cheese enchiladas, rice and beans, a margarita and two Mexican beers that had left him full. Still, John resisted the invitations from his colleagues to join them in the hotel lounge for more drinks. Tony, a long-haired and bearded anthropologist who was as witty as he was brilliant, had tried to cajole John into coming into the bar. John had hemmed and hawed, saying eventually he had to finish a report before morning for his boss back in St. Louis—it was a white lie to provide him cover to call Amy before it got too late.

Tony had become a long-distance friend and he had asked at dinner about John's trip to see Amy over the weekend. John felt self-conscious as the other researchers also looked at him. He said simply it had been a good but short trip—he had flown into Boston Sunday morning before flying to DC this morning. He diverted the conversation then, asking the Johns Hopkins professor about his grant project. This man took the bait and started in about his research, but Tony shot John a penetrating look out of his blue eyes, as if he knew there was more to the story. John glanced away, not wanting to say aloud that Amy had told him three weeks prior she was seeing Tim again. She wanted to continue the relationship with John, too, but an awkward strain had been palpable between them when he arrived on Sunday. A wound had burrowed inside him and it festered when they slept together Sunday night without sexual intimacy. She had always manifested a strong desire for him and sleeping together without sex for the first time worried him. Even worse, he knew their relationship had lost its ease and yet her distance made him desire her even more.

But early Monday morning, before she drove him to Logan Airport, they had unexpectedly made love. He had the sense then that everything was going to be okay, even as he wondered if he unknowingly made relationships overly complicated over time (or did relationships invariably become that way)?

He called Amy from his room phone, telling himself as the phone rang in her apartment that he shouldn't have been surprised that she and Tim had started seeing each other again. Amy had told John during his trip that it wasn't supposed to happen, but she had come to love them both and didn't know what to do.

He hung up the phone after the twelfth ring. Amy was routinely working twelve-hour days at her internship. He glanced around his room, looking over the king-sized bed, the end table, the oak dresser supporting a TV, and shook his head at the princely sum the hotel could charge at nongovernmental rates for the sterile room.

He peered into the miniature refrigerator and grabbed the cold neck of an imported beer. He checked the price list—five dollars for the beer—and snorted. Still, he popped off the bottle cap and let the cold beer splash down his throat. He fluffed the pillows against the oak headboard, turned on the TV, and surfed across sitcoms, talk shows, and weather programming. In some ways, he couldn't blame Amy. The truth was even though he hadn't seen Claire in months—they had talked briefly on the phone a few times, mainly about his taking her boys out for a pizza or a movie—he still loved Claire as well as Amy. He wished he knew what he really wanted, though he dreaded that would mean giving up one of them for good.

He muted an inane sitcom and went back to the phone. He weighed asking Amy to join him in California over Christmas, though he felt both too vulnerable that she would say no and too uncertain about his long-term commitment to Amy to ask this early about Christmas. The phone rang again in Amy's apartment and he decided for now to chicken out and keep it simple, just telling her how good it was to be with her again. He let the phone ring for a long time and then hung up, forcing away the thought that she might have gone to Tim's apartment for the night.

He gazed out of his fourth-floor hotel window at Wisconsin Avenue, which bustled with cars. The sidewalks, despite the rain, were spotted with pedestrians. He strained to see their faces but they were indistinguishable from the distance and hidden beneath umbrellas. He thought about calling Claire, but what would he say? That he harbored hopes—even while he was pursuing Amy—they might still get back together someday? Doing so would only expose to Claire, once again, that he was pathetically conflicted. He gulped the remainder of the beer, grabbed another bottle from the squat icebox, and punched into the phone the numbers for Nona's house.

"Hello?" His grandmother's voice wavered unevenly, higher pitched than normal.

"Nona, are you okay?"

"Horrible news."

"What?"

"Dr. Banez told us Emerson's bone scan results: the cancer's spread throughout his body," she said. "He only has four to six months to live."

John stuttered in his reply. The news was somehow both shocking and expected. He told her how sorry he was but added that the doctor could be wrong. Maybe, she said, in a flat voice. She asked John to talk with Emerson. When he agreed, she told John that she loved him and walked into the living room and told Emerson to pick up the other phone.

"Emerson," he said, clutching for words. "I'm sorry about the doctor's report. How are you?"

"Don't believe it." Emerson's voice was different—not monotone and plodding as usual but animated and forceful.

"I don't want to."

"That Filipino is more of a witch doctor than a MD," Emerson said. "Who the hell does he think he is, telling me how long I have to live? Those doctors think they're God."

"You're right."

"How does he know? I could be alive in twenty years."

"Yes, you could be. He could be wrong." John doubted it, but there was something infectious in Emerson's voice. John wanted to believe Emerson more than the physician. "Doctors are wrong all the time."

"You're damn right. I'm going to fight this. I'm not going to roll over and play dead."

"Good for you. That's so important. If you try and fight it, well, that's a big plus—that'll help right there."

"You know what he said to me?" Emerson's words were indignant, but an anxious undertone colored his question.

"What?"

"He had the balls to say, 'You're sixty-nine and have lived a good life. What do you want to do? Live forever?'"

"Sounds good to me," John said.

"That's exactly what I told him," Emerson said. "My dad lived to be ninety-one and my mom to eighty-nine, and there's better medicine now than in those days. With a little luck and a good doctor, I could live to be that old—even older, maybe."

"I hope so," John said. "I really hope so." He admired Emerson's will to live, even as a sense of shame crept in. While growing up, John always avoided one-on-one conversation with his step-grandfather, but at least he wasn't overtly critical toward him like his mother was. He had had some vague sense of this before, but only now he understood that the biggest barrier for his mom accepting Emerson was simply he wasn't her own father, who had died years before, and that Nona had the audacity to marry again ("How could she possibly sleep with another man after being married to such a wonderful man as my father for thirty years?" his mom had often railed). Of course, all of this had seemed a little confusing to John, as his mom had also once confessed she wasn't close to her dad growing up; her dad had worked long days with a two-hour commute each way, leaving before she got up and returning around her bedtime, when she was a child. She was much closer to her maternal grandfather, Papa Marco, who lived upstairs. Still, John's mom had said she developed a better relationship with her dad as a young adult—though perhaps that was only after Papa Marco had died?

Whatever the family dynamics, it was clear now that his grandmother loved Emerson. John appreciated that and it was unbelievable that Emerson could be dead by spring—that certainly wasn't what John wanted for Emerson or his grandmother. He told himself that perhaps the prognosis *was* grossly inaccurate, the byproduct of a haughty physician, but a sickly feeling settled deeper in his gut.

After the telephone call with Nona and Emerson, he tried Amy's phone number again. He was about to hang up after the seventh ring, but she answered with a muted hello.

"Hi there," he said. "How are you?"

"Fine. I can't talk now." Her words were stilted. "Tim's over."

"Gotcha," he said.

"Is everything okay?"

"Don't worry about it." He told her they'd talk after he got back to St. Louis and hung up. He realized she hadn't said she was sorry that she couldn't talk. He would have felt better if she had, but then Amy was never much of one to apologize. She said once that most people were too quick to apologize—that it wasn't genuine and a sign of insecurity, but he wondered if her attitude wasn't something she had learned from her supercilious father.

He shivered, realizing the cold was penetrating the window, and glanced around the room. Despite its pricey rate, it seemed more like a drafty tomb than a comfortable hotel. He wished he could call Claire—she was always empathic about Nona and Emerson, but he couldn't do that either. He rode the elevator to the lobby and joined his colleagues in the hotel bar. Tony, the anthropologist, greeted him with boisterous laughter and pulled another chair up to their lounge table. He was holding court, telling stories of his travels across the country for a book he was researching on homelessness, weaving in a mix of anecdotes from the streets, sociological theory, and cynical humor punctuated by well-placed swear words. John was thankful that Tony had seemed to forget about the weekend trip to see Amy. John listened to Tony's stories—they were compelling and also funny—and forced himself to laugh at the appropriate times. A brown-haired woman sitting alone at the bar stared at John with a smile. Without thinking, he returned her smile and added a lingering look.

Near the bottom of another beer bottle, his attention drifted from the conversation and his occasional glances at the woman to the bar TV screen, which replayed the highlights from the prior night's World Series game. Tony's chatter, the laughter of his colleagues, the clanking of bottles against the wood table receded into the background; as a boy John had accompanied his dad for his company's recreational outing to a noisy restaurant and bar before a Giants game. The dinner and drinks had seemed to last forever. Most of the men had brought their wives—not a child—but John's mom was away at Nona's house. Nona had taken her the day before to the doctor, who said his mom should get away and rest her nerves. There was another child at their restaurant table, an older girl with small breasts budding. She yawned throughout dinner as the married couples laughed over things that didn't seem funny and rolled her eyes when John looked at her. The clanging of silverware against plates, the clicking of ice cubes in cocktails, and the laughter over a babble of adult conversation John didn't understand—it all made John want to scream. He whispered to his dad, but he was busy talking about engineering-sounding things with two men from his work. John tugged on his dad's sleeve twice without a response, and then John yawned loudly, emitting a tiny yelp at the height of the yawn. His dad looked at him. John said he wanted to go home.

"*Why*?" his father had snapped. "We're not even to the game yet?"

His mother had been crying while running naked down the hall from the bath before she had gone to the doctor. She had been crying a lot for as long as he could remember since Grandpa Shea's funeral—but something about this time, about seeing his mom's bare butt while she ran away with a towel draped around her front and her shower cap on, made him feel very bad. He knew he should do something, but he didn't know what. He didn't think he should tell his dad about his mom crying and running naked, though the image was stuck in his mind. He shrugged at his dad's question, and his dad stated firmly they were going to the game—this was a once-a-year opportunity he had already paid for and it was going to be fun. John tried to sit through the rest of the dinner, but while his dad was talking engineering again, John started to cry. His dad excused the two of them and pulled John from the table to the parking lot. "What's wrong with you?"

John didn't know what to say, and a look of rage overcame his father. "Get to the car while I tell the others you're sick."

"Dad." He sucked in a breath, trying to stop crying and trying to make himself look strong, stronger than he felt. "I want to go to the game."

"Make up your mind, will you?" His dad shook his head. "You're always changing your mind."

"I want to see the Giants play," John said again.

"It's okay." His dad exhaled deeply and then patted John's shoulder. "We can go home."

"I really do want to see the baseball game."

"Sure?" A thin smile crossed his dad's lips. "We're taking a charter bus from here, so once we leave, we're there for the entire game."

"I'm sure."

"Okay." His dad rubbed his hand over John's buzz cut. "But you need to be a man there. No more crying."

At the game, he sat next to his dad and his engineer friends who talked more about work than the game. The girl was nearby, but she stared crossly at John when she caught him staring at her. By the fourth inning, John was thinking again of his mother and Nona. They were probably watching a TV movie and eating a snack that Nona fixed—she always had cake or ice cream or salami sandwiches before bedtime and she would sit next to him on the sofa. He wanted to be with them, but this made him again feel like crying, so under the sleeve of his jacket he dug his fingernails hard into the bottom of his palms.

Tony and the others were laughing hard but John had missed the joke. The brown-haired woman sat propped at the edge of her barstool, chatting with a man who had sat alongside her. John realized he must have been staring, for she caught him looking at her and responded with a dismissive glance before smiling seductively at the man next to her. A vague sadness sucked at John's insides. He abruptly excused himself, leaving over Tony's admonishments to stay for one more beer. He returned alone to his room, belittling himself as weak and stupid as he fought a crazy impulse to weep.

CHAPTER 25

John had saved Andy for his last home visit on Christmas Day. This new service of home visits on holidays was something that John had proposed to his staff a few weeks prior, arguing as their program matured and more of their clients eighteen and older graduated from the group home to independent apartments scattered across the city, many of the clients needed extra support in the community. Many of the young adults had no close family but they shouldn't have to be alone on holidays. The Our House staff team was supportive of the plan, at least until each pulled a slip of paper with the name of a holiday out of paper bag, and then Bennie began to howl. "*Christmas!*" he exclaimed. "*God Bless America.*" He said as far as his second wife was concerned, this would be grounds for divorce if he wasn't home with her and his stepdaughters for church and Christmas dinner. John guessed his wife might actually be relieved if Bennie was working—it was clear from his other recent complaints that the couple was having conflicts—but John switched his Memorial Day pick with Bennie for Christmas Day.

John waited at the back of a long line at the fried chicken franchise to order a takeout Christmas dinner for Andy. "I owe you a huge favor," Bennie had said, whistling and then shaking his head in the overly dramatic style that typified his interactions with people in authority. "If I'm not home to carve the goose, my wife would take the carving knife to me after cooking my goose. Yes, sir, phew!" John had repeated he was glad to help, but he didn't share it was also good for him, as he didn't have better plans for Christmas. True, his parents and Nona had offered to buy him an airline ticket to California, but he'd imagined feeling even lonelier in California without Amy, who had turned down his offer to come for a visit. It wasn't fair, Amy had acknowledged, but saying she couldn't risk upsetting Tim and having him break up with her again. John had told his family he'd visit them sometime soon in the New Year. Nona in particular was disappointed, which he hated, but he found it easier to be working over the holidays than licking his wounds in California over Amy, especially as he sensed that relationship was nearing its last breath.

John usually avoided fast food, but as he drove toward Andy's apartment on the state streets of south St. Louis, the strong smell of fried chicken made his mouth water. John planned to leave the food with Andy—he'd bought a huge family pack—but if Andy offered, he'd sit down with him to greasy, fried chicken for Christmas. John looked forward to seeing him, but then he felt a twinge of some uncomfortable sensation—perhaps it was self-pity or a sense of being pathetic?—that he tried to brush off. He'd spent Christmas Eve with good friends, who had invited him for Christmas dinner, too (he'd declined), and the prior night he'd taken Ryan and Josh out for pizza and a holiday movie. Claire had answered the door when he had picked up the boys—she had smiled and been pleasant, which felt both casually comfortable and concerning to John, making him wonder if she'd adjusted fully to these new roles of being without each other.

The Christmas weather was more like California's climate than St. Louis, with temperatures near sixty from an unseasonable warm front and a blue December sky that was now fading into dusk. John parked curbside in front of Andy's small, two-story apartment complex. Andy had almost seemed to turn a corner. He was doing better—true, he was still doing some drinking and drugging with occasional angry outbursts, but he was staying out of the hospital and jail and had his own place for the first time. More important, he seemed to let himself open up and get closer emotionally in therapy. John carried the sack of food up the hooded stairwell, which smelled of stale cigarettes and the sickly, malodorous scent of cockroach spray. When he entered the second floor, open-air gangway, John heard hard rock music blaring from Andy's efficiency unit. Andy's window was wide open and so was his front door. Andy, bare chested and dressed in floppy basketball shorts, grinned from his chair inside the apartment. "Hey, you came."

"Absolutely, Merry Christmas." John stepped inside and cast a lingering look at the open window and door. Cold air would soon be rolling in and Andy was already behind on his heating bill. "Airing the place out?"

"I love the outdoors," Andy flipped down the radio. "Feels like summer."

"Yeah, I get that." John wondered if the years Andy had spent sleeping on the streets still made it hard to be confined to a tiny apartment. "But a cold front is supposed to be rolling in this evening. Might turn your place pretty cold and raise your gas bill."

"Cold is a state of mind."

John laughed. "You sound like a psychologist."

"Fuck that!"

"Hey," John grinned. "You got something against psychologists? I'm one, remember?"

"Every other psychiatrist and psychologist I've ever met has been an ass-hole, trying to mind fuck me. Besides, I think of you as my friend, not a psychologist." Andy glanced into John's eyes, and then averted his gaze. "Have a seat."

The efficiency apartment was decorated with furniture they had cobbled together from a thrift store, with a small love seat that was soiled in places, a worn blue fabric chair, a fifteen-inch TV and a boombox on a vinyl stand, a single bed that was shoved between the wall and the window, and a small kitchen table with three chairs.

"How are you?" John set the bag of food atop of the kitchen table and sat down on one of the chairs.

"I didn't think you were coming," Andy said.

"How come? I said the other day I'd be here."

"People say a lot of things they never do." Andy's eyes appeared glassy and his pupils dilated.

"Yeah, I guess they do." John figured Andy had been smoking pot, but he decided not to confront him. He'd already been pushy about the open window and door. Besides, it was Christmas, and at least Andy wasn't smoking crack. "But I'm here for you—no way I'm forgetting about you, especially on Christmas. I was just running a little late from the other home visits and the chicken joint was backed up."

"Fried chicken smells great." Andy peered in the direction of the bag. "Rolls too?"

"Yup, and mashed potatoes with gravy and corn on the cob. Plus," John pulled the pie from the bag and held it out to Andy. "Apple pie for dessert. Go ahead, help yourself."

Andy grinned and dug into the bag, pulling out the carton of chicken. "Have some."

"That's okay—that way you can have plenty of leftovers for yourself."

"*No.*" Andy jerked his head to the side, flipping his long brown hair out of his eyes. "I want you to have dinner with me. It's Christmas."

"In that case, I'm glad to," John said. "Thanks."

"John?"

"Yeah?"

"Alright if I invite that girl next door to have dinner with us?"

"Who's that?"

"Patty. You've seen her around here—you know, she wears glasses and is retarded or something."

Andy had been seeing a different young woman, Ashley, in a stormy, on-and-off again relationship for a few months. John had been starting to ask Andy in therapy if this relationship was healthy for him, but so far Andy had remained stuck on her. "Sure," John said. "Fine with me."

"I'll be right back." Andy pulled on a baseball T-shirt; the Cardinals red had faded to a dusty rose from what looked like years of wear. Claire's sons had both worn Cardinals' gear when they had gone out two nights before. John had liked seeing them and he didn't want them to feel abandoned after the breakup with Claire. He tried to take them out every month or two, but it felt strange—and sad—not to have Claire there too. He had been tempted to ask her boys if Claire was seeing someone new, but he knew that wasn't right.

When he returned, Andy said the neighbor would be over for dinner in a few minutes.

"I didn't know you were friends with her," John said.

"She gives me cigarettes sometimes and we talk over a smoke." Andy popped the plastic lids off the mashed potatoes and gravy and arranged the containers on the table next to the chicken and corn. He moved the pie to the middle of the table like a centerpiece.

"You like her?"

Andy was setting out paper plates, but he looked over, sneered, and shook his head. "Not like *that*. She's fat and old."

"Just wondering," John said. "Well, that's kind of you to invite her for dinner."

"She doesn't have anyone, except a daughter in foster care that they won't ever let her see." He tore open the small carryout packages of tableware, placed the napkins next to the paper plates, and arranged the plastic forks and knives neatly on top. "No one should be alone on Christmas, you know?"

"Yeah, not if they don't have to." A sadness shifted in John. "What about you and Ashley?"

"I'm done with her."

John had seen them break up and get back together multiple times in the few months they had been involved, and he wondered if this time Andy would be resolute. "I know it's been a hard relationship for you, but I'm curious: what led you to that decision?"

"Every fucking thing." The pitch of Andy's voice rose. "I mean, she tells me she wants to be together, and everything's fine for a few days, and then boom—she blows up over some little thing." He motioned with his hands something like a volcano exploding. "Or she just fucking disappears and I have no clue where she's at or what she's doing."

"That must worry you."

"Pisses me off," he said. "Like where is she now? What has she been doing for the past three days?"

"What do you think?"

"She's probably out fucking someone else."

John couldn't help himself from thinking of Amy being with Tim. "That's a tough thing to have to worry about."

Andy shook his head. "She's a bitch, you know what I mean?"

"Yeah." John caught himself. "I mean, she hurts you by distancing or being with some other guy. But you still care about her, don't you?"

"Fuck her," Andy said.

His neighbor walked in, complained it was cold, and shut the door behind her. They sat together at the small table and John contemplated asking if anyone wanted to say grace. He wasn't sure how he felt about it, but it was a family Christmas tradition. While he hesitated, Andy and his neighbor, Patty, dug into the food. Patty talked loudly while she shoveled mashed potatoes into her mouth. Listening to her, John realized she wasn't retarded, as Andy had called her; she probably had a bipolar disorder, given the push of her speech. She wasn't so old either—John figured she was maybe in her late thirties—but the lines in her face suggested she had lived a hard life. She was a bit plump, not really fat, but then Andy liked women who were thin almost to the point of anorexia. She told John over a chicken breast that she had twin daughters. "One of my girls is in foster care, but they won't let me see her," she said. "The other is with their father, David Letterman."

"Isn't that something?" Andy said, looking at John like he believed it.

"Yeah," John said. "It's pretty remarkable."

"It's true," Patty said in a loud and pushed voice. "He's going to come on New Year's Eve in a limo to pick me up and because he's David Letterman, they'll let us get Mary out of foster care."

"I'm sorry they won't let you see your daughter now," John said. He figured his initial diagnostic impression was off. Patty must have schizophrenia, or maybe a schizoaffective disorder, rather than bipolar, given the David Letterman delusion.

"I met him when I was twenty and a dancer in a club he was performing at," she said, her mouth full of potatoes. "I told them I was twenty-one."

"Where?" Andy asked.

"New York City. I lived there after high school before the twins were born." She looked up from her plate and smiled, but one corner of her mouth turned down. "I was beautiful back then. A lot of people told me that."

Her large breasts nearly flopped out of her loose top, and John realized she had been attractive once. You could still see a shadow of beauty in her face. He wondered if maybe she really had met David Letterman—perhaps they even had a one-night stand—or was it all the product of delusional thinking?

Andy dropped a drumstick gnawed to the bone to his plate and pushed away from the table. "Got a cigarette?"

"I already gave you one today." Her words were stern, almost angry. "I only have two left to last me all night."

"Come on, Patty," he said. "That was this morning. Please?"

She eyed him for a moment. "Is your girlfriend coming over tonight?"

"Ashley?" he snorted. "*Forget her.*"

With a grudging nod, Patty pulled a wrinkled pack from her pocket and flipped out the last two cigarettes. She put one to her lips and handed the other to Andy. "Got a light?" She smiled at Andy.

The two of them took deep drags and blew smoke out over the Christmas leftovers.

After a few minutes, she drew her cigarette down to the butt. "Now I'm not going to have any more cigarettes tonight." Her voice was accusatory and a frown settled in the wrinkles around her mouth.

"What kind of things do you like to do?" John asked. He'd seen plenty of arguments erupt in the drop-in center after the last cigarette had been smoked, and he hoped to divert one here.

"*What*?" She looked at him like he had two heads.

"I mean, you know, what do you like to do for fun or enjoyment? Just curious."

"Oh. I thought maybe this was the Dating Game." She laughed loudly, revealing a missing tooth along the side of her mouth.

"No," John said. "I was just making conversation." He figured she'd soon be hitting on Andy and wondered how that would play out.

"TV. I like to watch TV."

"Any show in particular?"

"David Letterman," she said. "I like to watch Dave."

"Of course."

"And sex," she said.

John hesitated, unsure of what to say. Andy looked at him from across the table with an impish grin.

"I mean, who doesn't?" Patty said. "I like sex when I can get it, but it's been so long, I'm starting to crave it, you know?"

Andy looked at John, raising his eyebrows suggestively.

"Well, sex is a basic human desire," John said, trying not to look at Andy who was winking at him. John reached toward the center of the table. "Who wants apple pie for dessert? This looks *really* good."

A loud bang rattled the front door.

Andy startled, and John's first thought was that a drug dealer was pounding on the door. Andy had often got behind in paying for his drugs after buying them in advance against his next SSI check.

Another loud bang boomed against the door.

"Want me to get that?" John asked.

"Andy!" A high-pitched female voice screeched out. "For fuck's sake, let me in."

When Andy opened the door, Ashley swept into the room. Her hair was freshly dyed a peach color, though it didn't completely cover her head; a large, mousey brown patch showed in the back. She yanked off her jean jacket and tossed it onto the love seat, revealing a low-cut blouse. A push-up bra squeezed her breasts two-thirds of the way out of her top. She laughed, then kissed Andy at the doorway. By the convulsions of her mouth, it looked like she was trying to shove her tongue down his throat, and she touched her hand to his chest. "Merry Christmas," she told him after the kiss.

"Hey, Merry Christmas." Andy laughed. "Good to see you." He pulled the fabric chair to the table, squeezing it next to his chair while asking Patty to scoot over. He pointed Ashley to the open chair. "You hungry?"

"Maybe just a smidge of the mashed potatoes." Ashley was very thin, almost bony looking. She nudged her chair even closer to Andy, lifted a small spoonful of potatoes out of the plastic container, and ran her other hand along Andy's inner thigh.

Patty scowled at both of them. "I thought you said to forget about her?"

"What are you talking about?" Ashley gave Patty the briefest of glances before turning her attention back to Andy. "He's my boyfriend." She leaned over, touching his chest again.

"Where you been?" Andy asked.

"My mom's," Ashley said. "Wanted me home for Christmas but she turned into quite the bitch for the holiday. I wanted to call you but her phone is turned off."

"Good to see you," Andy repeated himself.

"I missed you." She laughed, and then whispered into his ear.

Andy grinned. He looked at John and then motioned with a nod toward the door. "That was a good dinner," he said. He glanced from John to Patty. "Thanks for coming over."

"*What?*" Patty said. "You mean you want us to get out?"

"Not get out," Andy said. "Just, you know, go. It was a good dinner, but we're finished."

"That's bullshit," Patty said. "When you invite someone over, you let them enjoy the meal. I'm not even full yet."

Ashley whispered to Andy, but loud enough for everyone to hear: "Looks like it would take a lot to fill her up."

"Bitch!" Patty spat the words.

"Hey, let's all get along," Andy said.

"Tell her that," Patty said.

"It was a good Christmas, but dinner's over," Andy said. "It's time to go."

"You took my last cigarette." Patty glared. "And then right away you want to kick me out?"

"I gave you dinner," Andy said. "Besides, John can probably run you to the gas station for another pack."

"I don't have any money," she said.

"John can loan you the money, I bet." Andy gave John an imploring look. "Can't you?"

Patty glanced at him, too, an angry scowl still covered her face, and then she looked back at Ashley with a beady, almost violent stare.

"Yeah, okay," John said. "Come on, Patty, let's go get you a pack of cigarettes."

"I didn't even get a piece of apple pie," Patty said.

"Jesus," Andy said.

"I'm not leaving until I get pie for dessert."

"Here," Andy stood up and swooped the pie from the table. "Take the whole goddamn pie."

After John and Patty had walked out and Andy had shut the door behind them, they heard Ashley laughing in a high-pitched voice, almost like a hyena.

"She's a whore," Patty said.

"I know that was upsetting, the way the dinner ended abruptly, but I thought that was really nice of you to share your last cigarette with Andy. Anyway, I'll take you to the gas station." The wind had sprung up and the temperature was falling. "You want to get a coat? It's getting cold."

Patty shook her head. "She's crazy. They're both crazy. One day they're yelling and throwing things and she stomps out, slamming the door. The next day they're banging his bed against my wall, moaning and screaming like they're going to die having sex. Drives me crazy."

"That 7-11 a few blocks away is open, I think," John said.

"She's got him pussy-whipped." Patty suddenly looked up at John as they walked to his car. A gleam had replaced her angry expression. "Do you think they have one of those cans of whipped cream there?"

"I'm not sure."

"If they do, can we get one?" She smiled. "You know, a topping for the pie? Plus the cigarettes?"

John bought her whipped cream and cigarettes. When he drove back to the apartment, he pulled up to the curb and wished her a merry Christmas. "Enjoy that pie," he added.

"Walk me to my door?"

"Why?" John felt bad as soon as he'd spoken.

"Bad things happen around here at night," she said.

"I know," he said. "Sorry."

She stepped out of the car. "It's freezing."

"Yeah." He walked a step behind her. She ran her hand over her head, like she was trying to brush her hair, and glanced over her shoulder, smiling in a way that revealed her missing tooth again.

When they emerged from the hooded stairwell, a woman's cry echoed from down the hallway. John worried something bad had happened; then he recognized Ashley's voice as she yelled out God and Andy's name—all run together, as if they were one long word. As they walked closer, he could hear, too, the squeaking of bedsprings.

"See what I mean?" Patty said. She slipped a key into the lock and pushed open her door. "That drives me crazy."

John caught himself exhaling deeply. Not knowing what to say, he only nodded.

"Come in." She motioned inside her apartment. She flipped on the light. Roaches skittered under the clothes and plastic bags that were strewn across the room. One small path cut between the clutter led to the kitchen, and another path to the bed in the corner. "Have some pie with me."

"No thanks," he said. "But I appreciate the offer."

She ran her hand quickly through her long hair again, and then stepped closer. She raised her hand, resting it on his chest. "You're nice," she said softly. "And I'll be nice to you."

He stepped back and her hand fell off his chest. "No, thanks."

"*Why?*" She spoke louder, though it wasn't clear if she was angry or trying to be heard over Ashley's cries that were reaching a crescendo. "You think I'm not good enough for you?"

"No, I don't think that," he said. "But you're already in a relationship."

"What are you talking about?" She cocked her head and displayed the same scornful look she had cast earlier at Ashley.

"David Letterman," John said.

"Oh," she said. "David would understand—it's Christmas. He'd want me to be with someone tonight. No one should sleep alone on Christmas, right?"

A sad feeling turned over in his stomach. "You have a point, but I need to go."

"Are you?" She gazed into his eyes. Her angry look disappeared, replaced by deep brown, mournful eyes.

"What?" he asked.

"Married or have a girlfriend or something?"

He thought of Amy, picturing her with Tim at his house for Christmas. And Claire? Was she with someone new too? "No."

She reached her hand to his chest again. "Then come in."

Andy was moaning now, too, and his bed pounded against Patty's wall. John imagined himself having sex with her. He could close his eyes, lose himself in her fleshy body, picturing her at twenty and a club dancer. Or he could imagine himself with Amy—or Claire. He felt his penis swell as he considered taking Patty to bed. Maybe it would be good to lose himself in her.

"No." He turned and hurried back to the stairwell.

"Come back," Patty shrieked. "You bastard! You led me on!"

He ran to his car, knowing he had come irrationally close to doing something he would have later hated himself for, the imagination of which now filled him with self-disgust.

CHAPTER 26

Nona was crying. It wasn't a full-hearted weeping, but the crying choked her words and a tear gullied a smudgy trail through the rouge on her olive-skinned cheek. John hugged her, noticing as he patted her back that she seemed shorter. He wondered if she was shrinking.

"Look at me." Her voice began in pain and ended in self-contempt. "*Silly old woman.*"

"Nona, it's okay that you're crying," John said.

"I shouldn't." She brushed away the tears with a brusque sweep of her hand. "It's weak."

"It's okay. You've been the strong one in this family for years."

"I want to be strong now."

"You are, Nona. It takes strength to feel sadness and let yourself cry." He didn't want to say it aloud, but he knew it also took strength—perhaps more than she could muster—after being widowed twice to face the prospects of another husband dying. Emerson's hormonal therapy had stopped working and the doctor wasn't recommending any more chemo after a brief trial, saying it would do little to prolong his life while destroying the quality of it. John kissed his grandmother. Her cheek felt soft and wrinkly, like an over-ripe apricot.

"It's hell to get old." The expression had become her frequent lament.

John leaned against the oven door, which was still warm from dinner. "What bothers you the most?"

"We don't do anything anymore."

He had begun to feel the same way. Amy had consistently declined for months to make any new plans to meet, even as she still said she loved him and was trying to come to a decision about relationships, and so he'd even stopped asking. "How so?"

"We don't go anywhere."

He had heard this complaint frequently in past months. He anticipated her saying next that they used to take trips to Tahoe, Monterey, and Pebble Beach.

She mentioned each of these places and continued. "We'd bring our sticks and shoot a round of golf. We'd eat at a nice restaurant and stay overnight. Now, we don't do anything. He just sits there all day." She shook her head in the direction of the living room. "Watches TV all day and night."

She had always been the motivating force behind their trips, but Emerson used to go along, probably even enjoyed them, but left to his own devices, he would have just sat around and watched golf on TV, especially as he became more sedentary—or was it depressed?—after his retirement. "Do you ever ask him to go out?"

"Yes."

"And?"

"He says he's too tired. No energy for anything, he says."

"I'm sorry. That's got to be frustrating." His own frustration with Amy came in swells, at times overwhelming him, and yet so far he'd been reluctant—maybe afraid—to completely let go, even as he told himself there was still hope for the relationship. "I guess, though, the cancer drains away some of his energy."

"I don't think it's the cancer." One corner of her mouth curled up, the way it did when she was feeling disapproval. "I think he sits in that room and does nothing because he's so afraid of dying that he won't do anything, except fart his time away."

John almost laughed—it was the first time he could remember his grandmother saying fart—usually she preferred a more subtle word, like "putt" or "toot"—but then it seemed more sad than funny as he understood how the prospect of dying could immobilize Emerson with despair. "I wish it was different for both of you."

"Me, too, but you have to face the facts." She shook her head and drowned a dinner plate under the suds in the sink. "I need to stop being a selfish brat about all of this."

"You're not being a brat."

"Selfish. Damn selfish. He's dying and I'm whining like a child about not going anywhere."

He saw her point but resisted it, not liking the notion she was selfish and not wanting her to feel bad. "You've been a caretaker your whole life. It wears you out sometimes. It's okay to be aware of your own feelings and needs too. Instead of feeling bad, I think you need to have more compassion for yourself."

"I need to just snap out of it."

He found himself without an immediate reply and knew he wasn't going to persuade her. "Here, let me do the dishes. You cooked a good dinner—as always." He tried to smile.

"I'll do it." She rinsed a plate off and shoved another into the sink. "But go talk to him."

"What do you want me to say?" He dreaded what she might ask.

"Whatever you think is best," she said. "You're the psychiatrist."

Emerson had settled into his corner recliner with the television on.

John sat on the adjacent sofa. "Great dinner, huh? Her steak and raviolis have always been one of my favorites."

Emerson grunted while he stared at the TV. The newspaper was spread across his lap, but he wasn't reading it; for an instant, John pictured the way Claire used to drape her knitting across her lap while sitting in front of the TV.

"How are you feeling?" John asked.

"Full," Emerson said.

"I mean, how are you feeling with the cancer and everything?"

"My bones ache," he said. "They hurt, on the inside."

"I'm sorry."

"I'm out of breath easily. And I'm tired all the time."

"I'm sorry it's so painful and draining." John let his gaze linger, hoping Emerson would make eye contact. "You mean a lot to me, you know?" He had come to this realization gradually, almost begrudgingly, after being influenced for years by his mom's negative feelings and also, he knew now, by his own apathy to seeing Emerson as something more than an appendage to his grandmother.

Emerson seemed to give a slight nod and, as he often did, he made a clicking noise from swishing and sucking on one side of his mouth. He looked back at the television, aimed the remote, and punched the volume higher.

"I know it must be hard to want to do anything when you're not feeling good, but I was thinking—you know how it helps to get out sometimes? Well, I could take you and Nona on a drive, somewhere pretty, or we could get some dessert, or whatever you like."

"TV sounds good," Emerson said, without looking over.

John remembered Emerson's anger back in October when the doctor had said he only had six to nine months to live. Emerson was full of fight then, but none of that energy was apparent now. John hoped Emerson was still holding onto his will for more life but it seemed he had given up. "I understand, but we can go another day while I'm here, if you want."

"Lawrence Welk is coming on in a little bit. He's always got a good show."

"I thought he died." John immediately regretted his words. Nona had said for years that Emerson was afraid of dying. He didn't seem scared now, but his dry, smartass nature seemed deflated, replaced by numbness. John wondered if beneath the surface Emerson was terrified.

"Reruns," Emerson said. "We watch him every Saturday night. We don't know the difference and I'm afraid he doesn't either."

Nona and John sat next to each other on her sofa, watching Lawrence Welk with Emerson. John forced himself to put the newsmagazine back on the coffee table and to watch the program he detested. He shook his head but censured himself from making critical comments about the show's glitzy and gay skits so far removed from the reality of the poverty and pain of the homeless youth he worked with in St. Louis. He glanced at the clock, grateful that the show would soon be over, and looked back at Nona and Emerson. They both stared emotionlessly at the television framed by a dark walnut box. A mix of feelings tumbled inside John: a rising (though probably unreasonable) frustration with Emerson, not so much for his retreat to the recliner since the cancer diagnosis but because it seemed like Emerson had been detached most of his life—a withdrawn cynic, never really engaged except for occasional sarcastic quips or when Nona had arranged some fun trip for them, and now he was dragging Nona with him down this rabbit hole of retreat. At the same time, John felt a welling of sympathy, sensing how frightened Emerson must be—perhaps had been all of his life? John argued with himself to the point of a no-decision as to which of two feelings—contempt or empathy—he should be feeling.

"Look Emerson!" Nona exclaimed. "A harmonica."

"No kidding," he said. It was the kind of smartass comment that Emerson frequently jabbed at Nona, but a thin smile split Emerson's bulldog face as he watched the man playing the harmonica on TV.

This was the last musical act of the program, and after the show ended, John asked about the harmonica.

"Emerson used to play," Nona said.

"Really?"

"Used to play a lot," Emerson said.

"When was that?"

"Long time ago," Emerson said. "I was a boy."

"You used to play all the time after we were first married," Nona said. "I loved it, but you just stopped for some reason."

Emerson gave a slight shake of his head but said nothing.

"Will you play?" John asked. A sense of guilt stirred. He had probably been too judgmental and critical of Emerson. John was protective of Nona and didn't want to see her suffer because of Emerson's despair, but he was a decent man, too, in a terrible spot. Besides, it was John's problem that after almost twenty years, he still wasn't completely sure how he felt about this man. "I'd love to hear you."

"Maybe sometime."

If not now, when? John stopped himself from blurting out the statement, realizing the implications were too harsh. "How about now?"

Emerson frowned, his large jowls sagging over his small mouth, yet lightness seemed to pass over his face.

"It'd be great to hear you play, Emerson. Please." It would be good for Emerson to be active, but John also heard the tremor of something needy in his own voice.

It took two more requests from John—on the second time, he realized *he* needed to see Emerson fight his despair about dying—and some prodding by Nona, but Emerson eventually nodded begrudgingly and told Nona to fetch his harmonica. Nona readied herself to climb atop a kitchen chair she'd dragged to the hallway closet, but John stopped her. He stretched high on his tiptoes and grabbed the forest green case from the top shelf. Emerson powered his motorized reclining chair back to a sitting position, leaned forward, and popped open the box. He pulled the harmonica from its red velvet casing, inspected it like a jeweler with a gem, blew out some faint dust, and brought it to his lips.

Emerson's cheeks puffed full, and the harmonica whistled rich and melodious. He blew and it wailed long, soulful notes with a twang, like bluegrass, and John remembered a similar, haunting sound at a country fair long ago as a boy. Emerson's cheeks filled with air and then deflated rhythmically, as his mouth pressed firm against the harmonica. He played for a long time, and then stopped abruptly.

"Out of breath," he gasped. But he twisted his head over his shoulder to eye Nona and John. He was grinning, his large blue eyes bigger than normal, with an innocence to his smile.

"That was fabulous!" Nona clapped and turned toward John. "Isn't he good?" Her smile showed the wide gap between her front teeth, a facial feature about which she had long made self-deprecating comments.

"He's great. Emerson, I had no idea you were so good."

"Thanks." His grin remained.

"How did you ever learn to play like that?"

"His whole family played music," Nona said. "The entire tribe of them. Go ahead, Emerson, tell him."

"My mom and dad and us kids, eight of us all told, used to play one instrument or another and sing. My mother taught music on the side and Sunday after church we'd play in town. 'The Singing Burnhams' they used to call us, except I didn't sing since I played the harmonica and neither did Ben because he played the flute."

"The Singing Burnhams. That's great."

"It was," Emerson said. "A long time ago now, but it sure was."

"You might have made the Lawrence Welk show, if it had been on back then," John said.

"We might have. Of course, they would've had to invent TV sooner too."

"Play again." Nona said. "Please."

Emerson eyed her, hesitating. "You ask the impossible, woman. I'm out of breath and my mouth is bone dry."

"I'll get you a glass of water," she said. "*Please.*"

Emerson glanced at the muted television and then back at Nona. She shuffled herself on the sofa, starting to rise.

"Stay," John told her. "I'll get the water. It'd be great to hear an encore, Emerson."

"One more time." Nona reached over and patted his thigh. "You can do it, Em."

By the time John returned with the water, Emerson was already playing. His elbows were planted over his knees, the harmonica cupped in his hands and clamped against his mouth. He played with passion, oblivious it seemed at first to Nona's clapping, but then he glanced over, a shimmer of wetness glistening as he looked at Nona, who kept the beat with her hand against his armrest. John set the water on the edge of the coffee table and then he backed away. He paused before leaving the room, watching his grandmother laugh while Emerson closed his eyes. He was lost in his music like a little boy with his harmonica again—or perhaps like a groom serenading his newlywed bride. John wasn't sure which of the two it was—or perhaps it was a conflation—but he was distracted by some strange mix of his own emotions—of sudden gratitude for both of them but also a disquieting sense of shame as he had failed for years to accept Emerson or to commit to Claire.

CHAPTER 27

John stayed busy at Our House on the day of Claire's thirty-ninth birthday, but he left word with the receptionist to put through any calls from Dr. Claire Evers. By late afternoon, he had not heard from her and, after double-checking with the secretary for messages, he called the florist who confirmed the dozen roses he'd ordered had been delivered before noon to Claire's work address. John hoped Claire was waiting until evening before calling him at home about the flowers.

When he arrived home late from work, the message machine showed a steady green indicator light—no messages. He had not talked with Claire in weeks but he thought of her daily. He missed her now even more acutely since things were obviously over with Amy. He scoffed thinking about how pathetically things had come to an end with Amy. As much as he loved her, he wondered now if he had been driven more by fantasy, turbocharged by hormones and the satisfactions of sex, which were fading with time? He stopped himself then, knowing he was reducing his cognitive dissonance and protecting his ego after her withdrawal. The truth of the matter was that their relationship, at least over time, had evolved to a deep affection that mirrored genuine love, though it was difficult to say for sure how much was romantic infatuation and how much was true love. In any case, their breakup had been anticlimactic: there had been no big scene, no major proclamations, no emotional farewell. Rather, malnourished by a lack of contact, their relationship had simply, unceremoniously faded over the months. They had been talking over the phone a few days prior (for the first time in weeks) when she mentioned a vacation she had taken with Tim, and John realized then he and Amy had already gone through a de facto break-up months before, even though neither had had the courage to admit it.

John stayed in his apartment the rest of Claire's birthday night, working on his conference presentation, and hoping for a phone call from Claire. The phone rang only once with a call from a sales representative wanting to sell him a life insurance policy. John picked at his leftover steak—the meat had a rubbery consistency—and worked late over musty-smelling, supermarket-brand coffee. He climbed into his bed, dead tired, but had a hard time falling asleep. He convinced himself his missing Claire was not simply a displaced reaction to the relationship ending with Amy. As much as he had come to desire Amy, perhaps she had always been a convenient distraction from his facing a deeper confusion about what he really wanted with Claire?

He wondered how Claire's birthday had been. Once for a previous birthday, after they had woken up together, he'd given her presents: tickets for two to *Evita* that night, with dinner reservations at an elegant restaurant, and diamond earrings. She said she'd never seen a professional musical, and on the front porch, her hair still damp from the shower, she broke into a cancan dance, kicking up her legs, pulling her skirt high onto her thighs, and then twirling and lifting the back of her skirt, showing off her panties. He realized then that perhaps Claire hadn't even seen his flowers yet—maybe for her birthday she had gone to Michigan to visit her sister?

Late the next afternoon, he called the mental health clinic where Claire worked. The receptionist answered on the second ring and John recognized the secretary's voice as Joyce. He had talked with her scores of times over the years when calling for Claire. "Is Dr. Evers in?" he asked.

"Yes." The secretary's voice changed, becoming both more personal and simultaneously more serious. "But she's in with a patient. Would you like me to take a message?"

"That's okay, thanks." John forced a slight cough as he spoke, an unplanned but feeble attempt to disguise his voice. He figured Joyce had recognized his voice, as well as his awkward attempt to sound like someone different. He felt incredibly ridiculous while also wondering if she would tell Claire he had called.

He held onto a shard of hope that Claire might call him that night to acknowledge the flowers. At home his phone rang three times—once from Nona, once from a car salesman, and once from a funeral home agent selling prepaid burial plans.

He fought drooping eyelids to finish his presentation. It was after midnight and his plane to Indianapolis left early in the morning. He packed his bag and lay down to sleep, pushing away thoughts about Claire. He was exhausted and his body sank heavily into the hollow of the mattress. He knew he was going to lose consciousness quickly and he took comfort in the thought that he could escape further worry about what—if anything—he really wanted with Claire by soon falling dead asleep.

John hurried across the hotel lobby, looking away from the lounge and out at the parking lot. He crossed the opening to the bar without attracting attention from the other researchers having drinks, but as he turned the corner, he nearly bumped into Tony, his anthropologist colleague and friend.

"Ready for a beer?" Tony asked.

"Unfortunately, not." John tried to portray a disappointed look on his face, though inside he was relieved, not disappointed, as the happy hour invitation made him remember how awful he had felt at their last bar get-together in DC in October.

Tony peered intensely with his deep blue eyes, as if he was trying to read John. He glanced down at the suitcase clutched in John's hand. "Where are you going? You just got here this morning?"

John explained a client at Our House had slit his wrists at lunch. The staff had called the ambulance and hospitalized him. The teen would survive, but his suicide attempt rippled a wave of suicidal threats and crises across the other clients. He told Tony he needed to get back to the program to help, now that his presentation was over.

He extracted himself from the conversation, feeling guilty for telling Tony a half-truth, and took a cab to the rental car office. The airline had wanted $270 to change his return ticket but John found a rental car special for $69. He wasn't sure that the state bureaucrats would reimburse him for the rental, even with the crisis, but he wanted to be back at Our House in the morning, he wanted to sleep at home for the night, and he wanted to drive—not fly. On the trip out, he had been unable to get crazy thoughts out of his head that the plane was going to explode.

Armed with the small map from the rental agency, he negotiated Indianapolis' city streets and found his way onto the twisting metropolitan freeway. He stared through the car's narrow windshield at the last of the day's light, which lingered in the western sky beyond the unfurling interstate. He regretted missing the sunset. Just past the airport, the evening shadows slipped into a darkness that grew blacker as he drove west.

An ache, dull but constant, grew deep in his abdomen. He pressed the gas pedal harder, his car hitting eighty-five miles per hour, but within a half-hour, yellow bulbs blinked "Highway under repair next 17 miles" on a portable orange highway sign. "Expect long construction delays," the next electronic sign stated. A half-mile ahead, brake lights shone bright red, and cars lurched to a dead stop at the end of a backup of vehicles that stretched as far as the eye could see. John cursed and saw an exit sign calling out the two-digit number of a back road. He swerved onto the off-ramp.

A gas station anchored the far side of the exit. The rental car's tank was nearly full, but John stopped anyway. He plucked a pack of gum from the gas station shelves and asked the clerk if the two-lane road could take him west, past the highway construction. The young man grunted, and John quizzed him, getting directions for a series of turns and roads to avoid the construction and reconnect to I-70, west of the repairs. John thanked him. The man nodded with a smirk.

John followed the two-lane highway south. He was surprised there were no other cars, other than an occasional pickup whizzing northbound. He drove straight for a few miles, and then the road banked a wide curve and wound its way into a small town. In the town center was a public square, a park hemmed-in by old, three-story white wood buildings along the perimeter. He drove in short, right angles around the square until he found the numbered road sign on the far side of the square. He turned right, followed the road out of the town, past a cemetery pocked by tall tombstones and angel statues, and back into the country. He drove for twenty minutes, the pain inside growing stronger, but it was a different sensation than his IBS cramping, more of an ache than intestinal cramping. He missed—he *ached* for Amy, and for Claire, and yet the sensation simultaneously seemed older and more familiar, like he felt sometimes lying in bed as a child. Then it seemed even deeper, more primal, an inner ache of being alone that no person could fill.

He made three more turns as the gas station attendant had directed and drove for several miles. He didn't see any other cars and the faded asphalt road narrowed. He whizzed by two farmhouses in quick succession, but their fields of corn gave way to shadowy images of an encroaching forest. He sped seventy miles per hour into the night, though he had the sense that he was racing toward nothing but more darkness. He checked his odometer again and calculated that he'd already driven five miles further than the gas station clerk had estimated.

He wondered if he'd missed a turn or mistaken one poorly marked road for another in the night? Or had the clerk played a country boy's joke on a passerby from the city? He thought of turning around, but worried that as he attempted a Y-turn in the middle of the narrow country road a pickup truck would barrel out of the night at eighty miles per hour and strike the tiny compact broadside. And even if he did turn around, where would he go? Backtrack all the way to where he veered off I-70 to complacently join the back of the massive traffic jam?

He figured he was probably lost but he kept driving straight. It was a dumb idea, he chided himself, to venture off the freeway and attempt to find an alternate route. It was impulsive and foolish to have even left Indianapolis at dusk after a crack-of-dawn flight and a long day of meetings. But he wanted to drive, not fly, and to have time on the open road, to take in the scenery, to hear his own thoughts. And he wanted to be in his own bed tonight, not in an alien, aseptic hotel.

The pain grew sharper, as if a blade of steel was lodged inside him. He wondered about Claire again, about how her birthday had been, and if she had been alone. When they had been together, her birthday had always been an occasion for celebration. Dinner, movies, picnics—and once he had thrown her a small party with her boys and a few friends, everyone wearing birthday hats and blowing horns. He remembered then, for the first time in years, a birthday party of his own, when he was only about four or five. He guessed it was his oldest memory, though he couldn't recall his age for certain, but Grandpa Shea and maybe Mama Clara were there, and so were neighborhood kids, but not Papa Marco, as far as he could recall—had he died already? John had wandered away from the kids table, set with paper plates loaded with hotdogs and chips, and searched for his mom and Nona. Down the hallway, his mom cried, and he snuck closer to his parents' bedroom. "What are you crying about?" Nona had asked his mom. "You'd better snap out of it."

He understood now his mom's problems had started long before the ice accident. He had already known this, sort of, but his brain had not clearly grasped it before. There was another time, when he was older and watching TV in the next room, when he overheard his mom talking with a childhood friend who had just married. The friend, who had married late, said she was afraid she was too old to have a child. His mom had retorted that she had wanted children when she had first married, too, but a child was a lot of worry and her depression had started after John was born. She had even said this directly once to John, when he took his first psychology class in high school and had asked about her depression: "My problems started after you were born." She had not spoken out of meanness— she stated it more as a fact—and though John had laughed initially with surprise, he had also known there was truth to this, a fact that simultaneously felt both terrible and incredulous, though he had not wanted to think about it.

Whenever her problems started, his mom had not really been there for him when he was growing up. His dad was, sometimes, but he wasn't very comfortable with emotions and struggled with his own frustrations. Nona loved him whole-heartedly, but she lived an hour away. As an adult, Claire had been there for him for years. Well, she used to run away intermittently, but she always came back, and when she did, she was fully present emotionally in a manner he had never experienced before.

Now was he the one who had run away? Perhaps he had taken her for granted—or was he too scared to be truly close? He should have appreciated her more. He should have celebrated every day with her like it was a birthday. He should have overcome the banality and staleness that crept in over the years. He should have taken her away for times that were more special, like canoeing and camping in the Ozarks again—or even to the mountains in the west. To the source of a river. Yes—he should have done that; should have given her the time of her life, something remarkable that she'd never forget.

Why didn't he? He was always too busy, always had too much to do, with the dissertation or work. Or maybe he was just a chickenshit. Afraid to break out, to do something really different. And now, perhaps, it was too late?

He should go alone to the source right now. Just find the fucking freeway and go west. But he couldn't just leave with the kids in crisis. That would be crazy. He needed to be there for them. But why not be crazy?

◗ CHAPTER 28

When he saw Emerson, John tried to mask his shock. Emerson's hair was sparse, his face drawn, his zygomatic bones protruding above hollow cheeks. Emerson looked like he had aged twenty years in the few months since John had last seen him. It was not just his face, but his entire body: once weighing more than 250 pounds, Emerson's frame was now gaunt like a concentration camp prisoner. Most striking was the whiteness of his skin. His coloring triggered a childhood memory of John seeing a white worm writhing within freshly spaded earth.

John reached through the steel railings of the hospice bed to hold Emerson's hand. Emerson's fingers were frail and bony, and some horrible feeling passed over John as Emerson tightened his grip on John's hand. Emerson's lips creased into a narrow smile.

"It's good to see you, Emerson."

"It's good to be seen," Emerson whispered in a faint, hoarse voice. He lifted his head, hovering it a few inches above the pillow, as if taking a long, close look. "I was hoping you'd come."

John squeezed Emerson's hand tight, then worried it was too hard. Yellow and purple veins protruded from the back of Emerson's hand. They talked for a few minutes, Emerson saying he felt better. Then he closed his eyes and was quiet. When John asked, Emerson admitted he was tired and needed to rest.

"I love you." John couldn't remember ever saying he loved Emerson before the cancer diagnosis, but this was the third time in the past few months he'd said so. True, he felt self-conscious saying the words aloud, but he regretted never telling Emerson sooner—or even knowing himself—that he loved him.

"You're a good boy," Emerson croaked, and he managed a sad smile.

John laughed, but seeing the moisture well in Emerson's eyes, he understood this was Emerson's code for saying he loved John too. He patted Emerson's hand. "I'll let you rest," he said. "Love you."

Ricardo, the stocky, young hospice aide, walked John out of the bedroom.

John waited until they had rounded the corner in the hallway and were out of earshot. "How is he?"

"He's stronger this afternoon," Ricardo said. "He's been saving his strength since he heard you were coming."

John looked at him. "Really?"

"His lifting his head off the pillow—did you notice? He hasn't done that in a few days. He was showing off for you."

Nona steadied herself, gripping John's arm with her liver-spotted hand, as he helped her into bed. "I've lived too long, if I need my grandson's help to get into bed."

He scolded her gently for saying such a thing and pulled back her blankets and sheets.

"Wait, almost forgot." She touched her fingertips to her lips, kissing them, and leaned toward the nightstand with the small marble replica of the Pieta, touching her fingers to the top of the Virgin Mary's head while mumbling something in Italian that John didn't understand. The small marble figurine was her most prized possession and, as a boy, John had thought there was something holy about it. Perhaps there was, but he had come to realize that more than any religious significance, she valued the figurine because it had come from the marble mine that her maternal grandfather had supposedly owned back in Italy. "I pray for her to look after you too" she said.

"Thank you."

"Especially after I'm gone."

"Shush now. Here, let me get these." He pulled off her thick, nylon stockings that her doctor had ordered to improve the circulation in her feet. She looked very tired. He kissed her cheek, her flesh mushy against her lips, and pulled the covers up around her. He tiptoed into the next bedroom where Emerson was sleeping, his mouth ajar. In the corner, beneath a cherub-figurine lamp, Emerson's niece read a thick paperback; the cover art depicted a busty brunette in a low-cut gown being kissed by a soldier.

"Do you need anything, Angie?" John whispered.

"No—other than you taking care of Mary. Him," she said, tilting her brown frame glasses at Emerson, "I can handle. But she drives me crazy."

"I just helped her to bed."

"Take her somewhere tomorrow, will you? I don't care where—just out of this house. She's always hovering, telling me what to do and fussing over Emerson—then in the next breath, she's complaining she never gets to go anywhere anymore. It would do her good to get out—it would do me good. She's a pain."

John started to snap back a defense of his grandmother, but he stopped himself. True, his grandmother paid her, but Angie watching Emerson at night was indispensable. John said he'd take Nona to lunch, bid Angie good night, and walked out to the patio for fresh air. The air was cool and light, so different from St. Louis' humidity. Despite Angie's venomous spirit, he was glad he'd come. After the phone call that Emerson was weakening, he'd been conflicted about immediately flying out. The airfares were outrageous, work was busy, and he was still grieving Amy, though he had started to question himself if he was glorifying the relationship in her absence? Perhaps he had even taken refuge in the type of relationship they had—the enjoyable fantasy of a *possible* future together but without the hard work of having to forge an actual commitment that Claire demanded? He missed Claire too. He had just heard from Josh that Claire was dating some new guy. Josh said the guy was a jerk and he hoped his mom would break up with him, but John worried that Claire was gone now for good. When the hospice nurse had said Emerson could rally and live for weeks, John had thought he'd wait and fly out in two weeks so he could get a cheaper fare, but when she added he could also die any day, he decided to come see Emerson without delay.

Emerson was much weaker and thinner than John had imagined. His grandmother, too, seemed older and weaker. The moon rose beyond the hills that encircled his grandmother's subdivision; it appeared huge, hanging on the horizon just above the hilltop. The moon was luminous—a brilliant white against the black night—and he watched for a long time with an unexpected sense of gratitude.

$$\sim$$

"We're lucky to get a corner table." John motioned toward the San Francisco Bay. A loose-knit armada of sailboats spotted the blue-gray water and the Bay Bridge stretched its way to Treasure Island. "It's a great view. Do you like it?"

"It's cold," Nona said. "I don't know why they make these restaurants so drafty these days."

"You want me to help you with your sweater?"

"No. It'd be too hot," she frowned.

Nona had tried to back out of the lunch trip, saying she didn't want to leave the house. John had encouraged her gently, and Angie pushed Nona hard, saying she had been complaining for weeks about never going anywhere and she'd better take advantage of the opportunity. Nona had talked with Emerson and he'd told her to go. That was why she'd come to lunch, John thought—not because of his encouragement or Angie's nagging.

"It's beautiful here," John said. "I'd never thought of the Berkeley side of the Bay as particularly scenic, but it is. Look at the sailboats, how the sails carry the wind so full, like peacocks strutting with their tail feathers fanned out."

"I can't see them."

"Really? How come?"

"Can't find my glasses," she said. "Must have left them at home."

John thanked the waitress for delivering the sushi appetizers and hoped they would interrupt his grandmother's stream of complaints. "These are great. Try one."

"Let's go." She stirred in her chair.

"Go? Why Nona?"

"I've got a bad feeling." She creased her brow, with an expression that looked both sad and panicky. "Let's go home."

"You're worried about Emerson," he said. "That's natural. You've been by his side for weeks."

"I shouldn't have left him." Her forehead tightened, like she was in pain.

"Sometimes you need a break from the caregiving to take care of yourself," he said. "It's a lot of stress on you too. Tell you what—let's call and ask Angie. I'm sure he's okay."

She clung to his arm walking to the pay phone between the restaurant restrooms. Angie said Emerson was resting comfortably. She told Nona—the aggravation in Angie's voice resounded from the telephone receiver—to just relax and take her time. Back at the table, John again offered his grandmother sushi.

She curled the corner of her mouth in a sneer. "You have to be very careful eating raw fish. They say it's full of bacteria that can make you deathly ill, even kill you. You shouldn't be eating it."

He laughed. "I'm sure they're fine. I've eaten sushi a bunch of times. Here, try this one—it has crab and avocado."

She sneered but took a small bite.

"Good, huh?"

She turned down the corners of her mouth in an exaggerated frown that he'd seen hundreds of times. "Not bad."

"There you go." He smiled at her. "You're quite the yuppie at seventy-nine."

"You're not seeing anyone now?" Nona asked.

"Not really."

"What about Clara? She seems like a nice girl."

"*Claire* is, but we're not dating now."

"Maybe you should." A grain of white rice dangled from her lower lip. "I worry about you all alone."

"I know. You've only told me this, oh, about fifty times before." He winked at her, hoping to generate a laugh or at least a smile, but none was forthcoming. She looked sad.

"Being alone is the worst thing," she said.

He didn't quite understand it, but he sensed that Nona dreaded being alone after Emerson was gone more than anything, more even than her own eventual death. "Don't worry. It'll be okay."

"We should go now." Her face was serious, determined.

"Why?"

"Emerson. I shouldn't have left him."

"Nona—you've complained for months about never being able to go anywhere, but since you've got here, you've done nothing but complain about wanting to go home." He heard the irritation in his voice, and then he felt guilty as well as exasperated. She gave him a sheepish but sad frown, and he softened his tone. "It's natural to feel anxious being apart, but everything's fine—Angie just said that. I love you, Nona, but you need to learn to relax."

She stuck out her tongue at him.

He laughed. "That's better. At least you can be playful. Here, try the shrimp tempura—I think you'll really like it."

She was calmer and ate most of one large shrimp. Then she said again she wanted to go home. He talked her into staying until the meal was over, but she ate less than half of her dish, asked the waitress for the bill, and then complained at the total. John quickly paid and they left.

San Francisco's TransAmerica Pyramid and Bank of America buildings and other skyscrapers dominated the horizon across the choppy water and the long span of the Bay Bridge. He remembered countless car trips as a boy, riding home from Nona's, feeling a thrill while seeing San Francisco across the Bay and the Sherwin Williams neon sign in Emeryville showing a bucket spilling over and paint covering the earth. Now they drove in silence, John stealing glances over his shoulder at San Francisco, and he found himself thinking about Amy. He knew that relationship had been going nowhere—she was locked into some deeper, older bond with Tim that he couldn't penetrate. Still, he missed Amy, even as he had the strange sense that missing her was only a brief interruption in a larger stream of longing for Claire that both preceded and would persist beyond his feelings for Amy.

He pulled into Nona's driveway, punched the remote control, and the garage door began its jerky ascent. Before the garage door was all the way open, the kitchen screen door swung open and Angie stepped out. The car was still rolling but Nona flung open the passenger door. John lurched the car to a stop as Nona took a shaky step onto the concrete driveway.

"What's the matter?" Nona's voice was tight, high-pitched.

"Nona—be careful," John yelled. "Watch your step."

"Emerson's gone, Mary," Angie said.

"What?" Nona asked.

"It was painless. He had a bowel movement in bed, right after you called, and he was embarrassed, but I cleaned him up, and he rested. He closed his eyes, and then he was gone. Be thankful, Mary. He died peacefully."

Nona, perched on the kitchen barstool, slouched over the breakfast bar counter, propping herself up by her elbows. She wedged the phone handle against one ear, but the mouthpiece dangled well below the bag of skin drooping beneath her chin. Wrinkles ran deep in all directions on her olive complexion face. "Lillian?" she said into the phone. "It's Mary. Emerson passed today."

She had removed the rubber band binding together the loose pages of her address book—the spine had broken—and was systematically going through the book, stopping here and there, letting each person know at the outset in the same phrase, "Emerson passed today." She talked only a few moments, each time telling the story of being out to lunch while Emerson died at home. She hung up the phone.

"*Que miseria, que miseria.* Oh, dear God in heaven, have mercy on us." She rubbed her hands into her face.

John rubbed her shoulder. "Done making calls?"

She nodded.

"That was a lot of calls. You have a lot of good friends."

"Only a few are left. Most have died. I've outlived most of them."

"There's still a lot of people," he said. "Lillian, Peggy, Josephine—I don't even remember them all, but you made well over a dozen calls."

"I've lived too long."

"Don't say that."

"I have. In three days, I will have buried my third husband. I'm tired. There's nothing to look forward to but death."

"*Please* stop saying that. You're sad and tired, but you need to keep up your will to live."

"Why?"

"Because I love you and I would miss you more than I could say."

A thin smile broke her lips. "You're a good boy."

"You're a good Nona."

"I am *tired.*"

"Why don't you rest?"

"Lying down for a few minutes might do me good."

"You've had a draining day." He helped her off the barstool, held her arm, and led her to bed. There he pulled off her thick nylon stockings, leaned over, and kissed her cheek. Out of the corner of his eye, he saw the marble Pieta. She had forgotten to kiss it.

"He's a good husband," Nona said.

John nodded and was careful to speak in present tense, as she had. "He's a good man too."

"He is a good man, but sometimes he's as stubborn as a donkey's hind end," she crinkled her nose, making a face.

John laughed. "It's good you can keep your humor up."

She gazed at John. "I don't know what I would have done without him these past twenty years."

"I know." John realized he probably didn't know—probably couldn't know— the full extent of her loss. "He's been such a big part of your life. But you're a strong person too."

"I probably would have died by now."

"Stop. You're stronger than that." He pulled up her covers. "But it's time to get some rest."

He retired to the backyard, settling into a patio chair. He remembered how, after a big family dinner, everyone would sit together outside: him, Nona, Emerson, his dad and mom and whatever friends or relatives his grandmother had invited. Years later, when he was older, sometimes just him, his dad, and Emerson sat together on the patio, drinking beer. They had talked little, certainly nothing of real substance, but he had enjoyed those moments then. Now they seemed more special than he had ever acknowledged, even to himself.

The sky was a deep, brilliant blue—vivid and clear, as if you could reach out and rub your fingers into its blueness. He sat watching, letting it in. Emerson had been a good step-grandfather too—more than he'd appreciated for years. Claire had been right—John had taken Emerson for granted. Then John had another, more horrible thought: that a critical flaw ran deep within his character, like an underground fault line, making him never quite satisfied with the people close to him and thinking he needed someone or something else. He hated the possibility and tried to dismiss the thought, but it bubbled back up, leaving him wondering if this was what had destroyed the relationship with Claire too?

The color drifted out of the sky, then passed into a glow of gold that radiated from the edge of the sky beyond the bordering hills. He wondered about where Emerson was, if he still existed in any form, other than the dead body being embalmed at the mortuary. He breathed deep, staring into the darkening sky. A puff of wind caressed his cheek, as if someone had patted him, and he felt a warmth rise in his chest. He thought of Emerson. It *felt* then like his presence was near, touching him with the breeze.

John scoffed then at his own sensation. It was sentimental, magical thinking. Emerson was dead. He had joked once that John had been resurrected as a boy, like Jesus Christ, but it was clear that Emerson was not coming back to life now. An itch burned on John's back. He tried to scratch it against the patio chair but found no relief, and the sense of peace and connection he had felt a moment before was replaced by restlessness.

He scrambled to his feet and left the patio to grab a beer from the refrigerator. Instead of returning to the patio, as he had intended, he changed direction at the sliding glass door to the backyard. Without really knowing why, other than to try to avoid some vague sense of agitation that was gnawing at his gut, he diverted himself to the living room, turned on but muted the television, and called a young stewardess who had been chatty and flirtatious with him on the flight out.

The droning airplane engine made John want to scream on the flight back. He chose to sit in the last row because he'd read once that the safest seats were in the very tail of the plane. His dad had even said that once: look at the pictures of plane wreckages—the fuselage is usually smashed to pieces, but the tail section is almost always intact. John heeded his dad's advice, but the engines on the MD-80s were mounted on the tail and they screamed and whined in his ear.

His dad was sensible and even-keeled most of the time, but he had been irritable with John's mom when they came to Nona's house after Emerson's death. The negativity was undeserved—his mom had done nothing wrong as far as John could see, but aggravation seemed to be the way his dad responded to loss. To John's surprise, his mom did not retaliate with wounded or snippy comments. Instead, she was genuinely upset about Emerson. "I'm so sorry, momma." She had cried and hugged Nona, holding onto her mother for a long moment, as soon as she entered the house. John's mother had her issues—he had grown much more aware of them in recent years, but beneath her emotional problems, she possessed a compassionate heart, especially for loss and suffering. She had not been much of a support to him as a child—indeed, she had often needed John to comfort her—but it seemed like her shortcomings were not out of meanness but simply she had been underwater for years with her own anxiety and depression.

John studied the river below as he flew east. It was wide, snaking back and forth through green-and-brown earth, seeming to run without beginning or end. He was confused about which direction it flowed. But the plane journeyed alongside the river. The sun was setting behind the tail of the plane. He figured the sunset would be beautiful: a burnt orange glare spreading across the sky and reflecting on the water.

After Emerson's graveside service, as John helped Nona up the hill and back to the mortuary limousine, he watched his dad and mom hold hands as they walked. Their irritability had evaporated, replaced by a quiet tenderness that surprised John, though he then remembered witnessing similar times over the years.

His hamstrings ached in the narrow plane seat. The trip seemed to be taking forever. He tired of craning his neck to glimpse the sunset in the narrow slot outside of the porthole and beneath the bottom of the engine. He closed his eyes, deciding he'd look again later.

John visualized Emerson in the hospice bed, and he felt again the skeletal-like touch of Emerson's bony fingers, like the flesh was already decaying. But there had been an emotional bond at that moment that rivaled in strength the sense of impending death. And later, on the patio after Emerson's passing, he had felt in the wind on his cheek a deep connection with Emerson. John had figured the sensation was his mind playing tricks on him. Still, after a long, vacuous talk on the phone with the chatty stewardess, he had hoped to recapture that sense of Emerson's presence. He had returned to the patio and stood in the breeze, waiting, but there was nothing—only his own unfulfilled longing and a feeling of emptiness at the encroaching night.

He hadn't slept well that night. Claire, Amy, even Branham—were on his mind and he missed them all, but he felt the worst about Emerson. As much as John had hated seeing Emerson emaciated and barely able to move in his hospice bed, it was far better than not ever seeing him again. For weeks, John had anticipated the loss that Emerson's death would bring, but it was stronger now than he had imagined, pulling him into a sinkhole of sadness. True, he had taken Emerson for granted for years, but there had long been a comfort from his presence in the background of the family, and now John missed him in a way that ached inside. The grief was intertwined with self-disgust, for John had allowed himself to embrace Emerson only once he was dying; it was a problem that seemed sickly similar to his mom's pattern, of valuing the deceased more than the living. In any case, his sadness extended beyond Emerson, for John acutely missed Claire again.

When he had taken Nona to the mortuary to plan the funeral, he noticed a statue of a crane staring at him from across the marbled lobby. Years before he and Claire had seen a crane flying over the river as they canoed, and later she had said they were her favorite birds, that they seemed magical. As he and Nona waited for the funeral representative, he missed Claire with a longing that resonated deep in his core. It had been seventeen months since he and Claire had been together, but the truth was that he had missed her every single day. She had remained a huge part of his life, even in her absence. It came to him then, with a sense of horror, that he had grown accustomed, maybe even comfortable, in his grief over Claire. Perhaps it had even become an alternate way to relate, but in a way that permitted him to avoid the risky business of actually having to face commitment to her? This thought made John feel both terribly anxious and like a coward.

He realized then he was being self-indulgent in his ruminations. Whatever grief he felt could only be a small fraction of the loss Nona must be experiencing. It was difficult to imagine the depth of her sadness, being without her mate and knowing her own death could be any day. For all of Emerson's faults, Nona loved him; he was the centerpiece of her life. John had been critical of their marriage—it often seemed replete with banality and convenience, not unlike his parents'. But he realized, seeing again in his memory as if it was just happening, Emerson's pride when he had played the harmonica for her and the joy in Nona's smile. An intimate connection bonded them and transcended their tensions; it was probably even deeper than their passion. (Seeing his parents hold hands, he sensed this was maybe true for them too). Had they exercised some courage that John lacked?

For a moment, he wondered if he had cloistered himself so tightly over the years—because of his ice accident or trying so hard to make his mom feel better or just generalized anxiety or guilt, he wasn't sure. But it seemed now that he had withdrawn not only from commitment to Claire but also from much of his own life. He sensed for years he had stumbled through life half-asleep and numb, too afraid to know what he really wanted, including in terms of authentic intimacy and commitment. That was not how he wanted to be. He wanted to be open and to live with courage.

But now he was incredibly and suddenly tired. Perhaps the heaviness of Emerson's death and funeral had caught up with him, or maybe it was his own incessant self-questioning? In any case, he was exhausted and too tired to think any more. He rested with his eyes tightly closed, trying to clear his mind.

The stewardess' command to fasten seat belts startled John. The pilot announced they'd soon be starting their descent. John stretched and brought his seat upright. He twisted around to look for the river through the porthole; he was disappointed, mainly with himself, as the sunset was gone. There was nothing but darkness behind him and he could no longer see the river.

PART FIVE

⏵ CHAPTER 29

John rested on Claire's new sofa with his eyes closed, remembering the prior night of lovemaking with Claire. The memory left him satisfied but sleepy, even as he enjoyed the fantasy of more sex tonight. Their reunion three weeks before had sparked a series of passionate nights together, but he savored even more just being with Claire again. Being back together had felt not only familiar but also right, like coming home. Still, he had noticed nascent doubt the past two days creeping into the corners of his contentment.

Her hair brushed across his face. He opened his eyes, seeing the entrenched crow's feet wrinkles around her eyes as she planted a firm kiss on his lips. He flinched and pulled away. Claire hesitated, standing in silhouette in front of the reading lamp, before retreating to the rocking chair in the corner of the sunroom.

"What is it?" she asked.

"What?"

"You know what. You pulled away when I tried to kiss you."

"You startled me," he said. "I was daydreaming."

"Bullshit," she said. "You looked repulsed. It's like when we split up the last time, isn't it? You have a wall up and if I try to cross it, you pull away."

"That's not true." It *was* true about erecting a wall, but he wasn't sure why and he didn't want to hurt her. "I was just startled, and actually I had just been thinking about how good it's been to make love with you again."

"There's more to a relationship than sex."

"I know." He scanned her face, trying to gauge her mood. "I love you, too—you know that."

"Where are you at with commitment?"

"I don't know, Claire."

She shook her head. "When you asked me to get back together, I told you this would be the last time, one way or the other. I'd hoped we would make it."

"For God's sake, Claire, don't give up. After being apart for more than a year, there's bound to be some issues."

She walked out of the room.

"Where are you going? Claire, come back."

She reappeared from the kitchen, clutching a pack of cigarettes in her slender fingers. She lit a cigarette, took a deep drag and sat back down. She tucked a strand of hair behind her ear. She'd stopped highlighting her hair in the time they'd been apart and now the gray was more striking than the blonde, aging her appearance. She looked at him but said nothing.

"I'm making progress," he said. He hated that she still smoked. He had asked her to quit multiple times over the years, but she stubbornly clung to her unhealthy pattern. If she did that to her own health, what might she do to him over years in a marriage? "But you know, commitment is kind of scary."

"Why?"

"I guess the responsibility. That and maybe the finality."

"What?"

"The finality—you know, you choose a partner for life, hopefully. I want you to be happy and I want to be happy." He wanted his life to be more than happy. He wanted passion, adventure, and he wanted her—or some woman—to be a partner for that adventure. But he wondered if that was really how it worked. Does marriage turn the adventure into something bland and banal—a monotony of sameness? It bothered him that soon after getting back together he and Claire were bickering again; it reminded him of his parents when he was a child. "It's a lifelong commitment and we're talking about possibly having a baby right away."

"You think too much," she said.

"No, it's important. Most people would—or should."

"Then people think too much. We should be like wolves—they pair off and mate for life. It's natural, no obsessing."

"Now there's something to think about." He winked, hoping to elicit a smile from Claire, but she turned stone-faced.

"You get scared of the finality, of committing to someone and making the decision to be a father?" she asked.

"Yeah, something like that." Her hurt was unspoken but writ large across her drawn face and somehow her feelings extended from her to him. He felt bad, and then an urge swelled inside to ask her right then to marry. He toyed with the idea—it would make her happy. The words rose in his throat, but then he fought the impulse, and said nothing.

"Still the chicken who's always afraid of something," she said.

"That's a cheap shot." Now he was angry and that helped dissipate the impulse to propose.

She flicked her cigarette into the ashtray. "It was. Sorry."

"Thanks," he said. "I appreciate you acknowledging that."

"But I want you to leave now."

"What?"

"I want you to go home now."

"Claire, no."

"What do you mean, 'no'?"

"How are we going to handle arguments if we get married?" John reached toward her, opening his hands, as he spoke. "You won't be able to send me home then—like you've done too many times in the past. We need to figure out a different way of handling things—as if we were married."

"Okay," she nodded. "You're right. But this is hard."

"I know, Claire. What we're talking about is hard, but I really feel like I'm making progress. I just need a little more time to sort—"

"*Stop*! I'll scream if you keep talking." Wildness glared from her eyes as if she truly would burst into a banshee howl. "You can stay, but I need space. I'm going to read upstairs—by myself."

Claire pattered away. It was better than being sent home, but he hated that Claire had left alone for the bedroom. How many times growing up had he watched his mom withdraw to her room after a disagreement with his dad? He had felt bad then too.

He sat on the edge of the sofa, realizing after a moment he was staring through the window without really seeing anything. His ambivalence about their relationship confused not just Claire but also himself. He remembered the prior night, of lying in her bed, listening to the shallow waves of her breath beneath the oscillating window fan. He'd drifted toward sleep, blissful with the lingering sensations of their preceding passionate embraces. There had been a dozen times in the few weeks since they'd been back together when being with Claire had again filled him with joy and comfort. And yet there were other times when they seemed separated by an insurmountable abyss, and he wasn't sure how to reach her, though she sat only a few feet away.

He wondered why they rapid-cycled through periods of intimacy and emotional distance. For all of her pressure about a commitment, there were unbearable moments when she seemed inexplicably distant—or, worse yet, unknowable. He wasn't sure why. His lack of a proposal upset her, but he guessed at times there was something more in Claire—it seemed like sadness or wariness—that kept her at arm's length.

And then again, perhaps it was his fault—maybe she was reacting to him, for at times, he, too, felt distant. Perhaps she sensed this? Although he had not shared those feelings with Claire, there were occasions when he had felt himself withdraw while critically observing her annoying little habits, like rubbing her face and blowing her nose at the dinner table—small things, he knew, yet they grated against his sense of romance and he couldn't help himself then from comparing Claire to Amy's femininity.

He tired of his own worries and felt nagged by work that he should be doing. He pulled from his briefcase a new federal grant announcement to fund integrated outreach and case management services for homeless people, including youth. He flipped the pages, highlighting passages to focus his attention, but he drifted back to the idea of marriage. He had come close to blurting out a marriage proposal when they had argued—but wouldn't that be falling back into his old pattern with his mom? That was how he had proposed to Joanie and that turned out to be a colossal mistake.

Maybe marriage was only a cultural contrivance, anyway—a way to delude couples into a sense of security while paying off thirty-year mortgages; a way of distracting oneself from the deadening monotony of life that accumulated over 360 monthly house payments until you realized, with crushing despair, that you were now old and the opportunity for a life of adventure had slipped by. Since John was little his dad had talked about getting his private pilot's license and flying across the country, but his mom was always too critical of the expense and too scared about his flying. His father was no closer to doing so now than he ever was, though they had paid off their house.

It was late when he checked the clock. He turned out the lights in the sunroom and the whole downstairs blinked to darkness. As he stood for a moment, letting his eyes adjust, he remembered the terrible ache of missing Claire when they had broken up the last time. He hoped she was ready to talk.

He climbed the stairs to the second-floor bedrooms, but hesitated, halfway up, gripping the wood banister. Relationships are so complicated—that's what Amy used to say. She was right. He could write a book on it, using himself as a case study: A phenomenological account of relationship fucked-upness. Maybe then he'd make sense of his life.

He found her sitting in bed, reading a book. He watched her for a moment before knocking on the half-open door. "Can I come in?"

"Yes."

"How are you feeling?"

"A little better."

"Good."

She motioned for him to take a seat on the edge of the bed. "Sometimes you confuse me, John, but I understand what you said about being scared. I'm scared too. And when I'm scared, it usually comes out by lashing out at you. Sorry."

"Thanks," he said. "That means a lot."

She nodded.

"What scares you the most?" he asked.

"I'm opening my heart to you, to the possibility of marriage and family again, and I'm afraid you'll break my heart."

"That's the last thing I want to do." Some feeling passed over him, but he wasn't sure if it was empathy or guilt. "You have a precious heart. I never want to hurt it. I love you, a lot."

"I know. I love you a lot too. That's what's so scary."

She extended her hand, and John took it in his. She squeezed his hand and they sat in silence for a minute. He glanced around, anxious to change the topic, and pointed to the book on her lap. "What are you reading?" he asked.

"A book on dream interpretation. I heard about it from a dream group I was in when we were apart."

"A dream group?"

"There were eight people and we met every Friday night for eight weeks. Each week one person shared a recent dream and the rest of the group interpreted the dream. Then, at the end of the hour, the person told the group her own interpretation of the dream."

"Not sure I could do that," he said. "I usually have a hard time remembering my dreams."

"I used to never remember mine, either, but they train you to remember your dreams."

"How?"

"You instruct yourself before falling asleep, 'I'll remember my dreams,' and then you put a pad of paper and a pencil by your bedstand so you can write it down as soon as you wake."

"Hmm, that works?"

"Yes, it's fascinating. They're more the exception, but I've had a few incredibly lucid dreams."

"What dream did you tell the group?"

Claire tugged the blanket to her nose and sniffed it.

"Do you want to tell me?"

She swiveled her hips to face him. "I dreamt one night that I was leaving my home, and immediately there was someone following me. I walked faster but the person—it was a man—picked up the pace. I turned down different streets, but he turned after me. I kept walking, faster and faster, and still he followed me. I knew he was after me, and he was trying to kill me. I started running and he chased after me. I turned again, trying to lose him, but he followed me, and I ended up in a dead-end alley.

"I knew he was going to kill me then. So, I turned to face him. I wanted to face him as he killed me. He stopped and pulled a gun from his pants. He raised his gun, pointed it at me, and fired three bullets. I suddenly wasn't scared. I wasn't even *in* my body anymore. I was outside of my body, watching. I watched each bullet hit my chest and burrow right into my heart. After the third one penetrated, I watched my body fall. I lay on the ground and gasped. I saw my body shudder once, a really big convulsion, then twitch, and then it ceased moving. I was dead."

"Oh, God," he said. "How awful. That must have been a terrifying dream."

"It was strange, because I was frightened at first when I was running from him. But once I knew he was going to kill me and I turned to face him, I wasn't scared anymore. But watching each bullet hit and explode into my heart, I felt terrible sadness and pain. Not physical pain, but emotional."

The dream sounded horrible but he wondered about its meaning. "What was your interpretation?"

She sniffed her blanket again, but then turned back to him. "Each bullet represented a man, or rather the loss of a man in my life. The first one was my father, the second one was Ted, the third one was you. Each loss broke a piece of my heart and drained away my life energy."

John reached for Claire's hand. He held her long fingers in his own, squeezing them tight, guessing these losses were the source of the sadness he sometimes sensed in Claire. "I'm glad we're back together. I really am. And I'm sorry my indecisive and cautious nature is so frustrating for you."

She gave him a sad, half-smile.

"I don't want you to lose me or me to lose you," he said. "I'm not just saying that, I really feel it."

"I hope so, but we will see."

"You will. I love you, Claire."

"I love you too." She pulled her hand away. "But it's about more than love at this point—it's about commitment."

"I know." His tone sounded defensive, but beneath that he felt fear. He didn't want to disappoint or hurt her, and he didn't want to decide something that would leave him trapped and unhappy. But why should he worry about being trapped and unhappy? He loved her and there were certainly moments of joy together. "I want to be able to commit again, too, and I'm working on it, in my own way. It's just harder to change than it seems."

"Why?"

"Why? I don't know, exactly, but probably in part because I obsess and worry so much."

She said nothing.

"I don't know why I worry so much, though it seems to be a family trait on my mom's side, part of my Italian heritage."

"So that's it, huh?" She pursed her lip in the same expression she had used before when she had said he was full of shit. "Your DNA is to blame?"

It was more than that, he knew. Growing up with a depressed mom, he had witnessed ample anxiety and avoidance, and it was his job to try to make her feel good, even at the expense of his own desires, especially after the ice accident had pushed her over the edge of sanity while leaving him with his own heightened if largely submerged anxieties. He had learned as a child how to be exquisitely sensitive to the needs of a woman, but he wondered if he even knew what he needed to be happy himself, beyond the impulse to placate and please a woman: first his mom, then Joanie—and perhaps now Claire? But he loved Claire immensely and he felt such passion together, sometimes. He felt lost in a thicket of confusion and contradictions, but it was one of his own making. He wanted to figure his way out. He also needed to say something more now to Claire. "I think sometimes I'm scared of getting married because I'm afraid I'll end up like my parents. I know they love each other but they don't seem that happy."

"Marriage is not a guarantee for happiness," she said. "You still have to work for it."

"I know." Still he found himself wishing marriage would bring a certainty for happiness. "But I'm not sure I can completely trust myself either. I got so stuck in a pattern of pleasing my mom as a child that I worry sometimes I fall into the same rut of focusing on pleasing the woman and not even knowing what I need to be happy."

"It's good you recognize your childhood patterns."

"Thanks." He nodded.

"But I'm not your mom."

"I know that."

"And as much as I would miss you," she said. "I don't want you to be with me if you won't be happy."

"Thank you." From the way she had spoken, something about the firmness in her voice, he knew she was sincere. "I appreciate that. You either."

She nodded but said nothing.

"I appreciate how you've been hanging in with me, not just suddenly giving up and disappearing like you used to," he said. "I hope you can be patient awhile longer."

"I'll try. I just don't know how long I can stay open."

He feared he could lose her again, but he was weary of the topic. He reached out for her, though he wasn't sure if she would respond in kind or pull away. When she opened her arms to him, he nuzzled his face against the hollow of her neck. He held her for a moment. He wanted to redirect the conversation away from the issue of commitment. "I'm sorry you had such a terrible dream. What a nightmare."

"It was so vivid, so real. A man in the group—he had traveled throughout the world and seen many things—said the way I described my death was exactly how he'd seen so many creatures—including people—die, right down to the shudder. 'The final twitch of life before death,' he called it."

John woke in darkness to terror. He listened carefully but heard no sound other than Claire's breathing and the whirl of the window fan.

What had woken him up? He worried he had heard in his sleep someone breaking into the house.

The thought that someone was creeping toward them, trying to kill him, seized his mind. Adrenaline surged through his chest as panic overtook him. His eyes adjusted to the darkness, but still he could see no one in the bedroom, only the shadowy outline of her furniture. He strained, listening for sounds beyond the room, but heard nothing. He got out of bed then, peering into the hall and trying to muster his courage.

He inched into the hallway and fumbled with the light switch before flipping it on. It cast a harsh, glaring light from a bare bulb against the white enamel walls. He stared down the stairs and after seeing nothing out of the ordinary, tiptoed in the other direction and entered Josh's bedroom. His long body stretched straight out beneath a blanket, his mouth open, whistling soft snores into the air. He checked Ryan's room, but he was gone for the week with his father looking at colleges for the fall, and the bedroom was empty. So was the bathroom, even behind the shower curtain.

He slipped downstairs, turning on lights as he went. The doors and windows on the main floor were closed and locked. He crept down the basement stairs, but then stopped himself. Claire had stored a plethora of boxes and pieces of old furniture in the basement—it would be difficult to search safely. He left the light on and walked backward up the stairs, closing and locking the basement stairwell door behind him when he reached the main floor.

He left all the downstairs and hallway lights on and retraced his steps to Claire's bedroom. He looked around, saw nothing unusual, and crawled back into bed. He listened to Claire's breathing and told himself to relax. He realized Claire's bedtime account of her dream, of being stalked and killed, had undoubtedly triggered his own night terror. But then again, someone could be breaking in—the evening news reported people getting robbed or burglarized and killed for paltry sums of money almost nightly in St. Louis. It wasn't likely, but someone could be lurking in the house, waiting to murder them.

John slipped out of bed again, pressed the bedroom door tight against its frame, and turned the old skeleton key to lock it shut.

He lay back down but couldn't fall asleep. He scooted next to Claire and tried to find comfort in the warmth of her body, but the thought intruded: there could be a killer and then he'd be suddenly dead. *And then what?* He hated to think about it, but he forced himself to try to remember being on the lake as a boy. He tried to remember what happened after he fell through the ice, but there were no memories, other than thrashing in the frigid water. There was no light, no tunnel, no grandparent, no God to meet him that he could recall. Maybe he was just dead; maybe there was just nothingness.

It was impossible to conceive. There would be no feeling the softness of the bed, nor the warmth of Claire's body. There would be no thinking. Nothing.

He could not stand the thought. He wanted to scream—or to pull up into a ball and pretend none of that had ever happened. He rolled onto his side and yanked the cold sheets up to his chin.

Claire jerked upright. "What's the matter?" she asked.

"I can't sleep."

"Darn it."

She flopped back onto the mattress. Then she threw back the covers, mumbling she was going to the bathroom. She struggled with the door. "Why did you lock the door?"

John didn't answer.

When she returned from the bedroom, she slipped back into bed and scooted close to John. "How come you can't sleep?"

"I don't know."

"Something on your mind?"

"I just woke up terrified."

"Why?"

"I thought I'd heard something, like someone was breaking in. But I don't think so—I checked the house. I was just scared of being killed—of dying."

She snuggled closer, wrapping her arm over his shoulder. "That's frightening."

"Yeah, it is. I think your dream of being killed upset me."

She massaged her fingers against his neck. "What's the scariest part, when you think about dying?"

"It's not dying per se. It's not the physical condition or pain." He reached for her hand. "But I'm terrified of nothingness, of not being. I can't even imagine it, but it's a horrible thought."

"It is frightening."

"When I was little, I was afraid of a slow, painful, and helpless death—of knowing you were dying but being powerless to do anything about it. I wasn't scared of death itself—maybe because I always believed there was a heaven and I'd go to it. Now, as awful as it would be, I'd choose a slow, helpless, or even painful death over nonexistence—at least then you'd still *feel*, you know?"

"You're really facing it."

"What?"

"Death. It's not easy."

"No, it isn't," he said, his voice soft and low. "It's like I'm finally starting to wake up, wanting to be fully alive, you know? It's a struggle a lot of the time, but at least I'm trying—and now death is staring me in the face."

She squeezed his hand.

"How can you go from being totally alive—living intensely, trying to live fully aware—to being totally devoid of any perception or feeling or thoughts, and having no awareness of anything for the rest of eternity?" he asked. "It's awful to imagine."

"I don't think there's an easy answer, at least that I can give you, but you'll find your own answer." She snuggled him closer, pulling his face against her breasts. She stroked the back of his head. "But I know it's good to hold you again. I missed your scent."

John cinched her tighter in his arms. Soon, her body twitched, and her breathing rolled in and out softly, like gentle waves on a lakeshore. Her breath fluttered against the faint hairs of his chest, feeling warm, almost ticklish. More than ever, he suddenly wanted to feel their bodies intertwined and passionate, not so much in denial of death but in the face of it. Instead, she slept, and though he took some comfort in her breathing, he still had a hard time falling back asleep.

Driving to her house, John worried what Claire would say. She'd been sullen in the morning. He had sensed something was wrong and he had pushed her to talk. Now he cursed himself for not just letting her be. She had lashed out, angry that in three months of being back together he hadn't proposed. It was the same as last time, she had said—the more she opened up, the more he withdrew and closed down. A chickenshit, she'd called him again.

He argued that she lived in a world of her own misconceptions, filled with fears about him and the relationship. She'd walked out, slamming the front door. He followed her, saying he didn't care if they were late for work—they needed to talk.

"See how it feels?" she said. "How do you like feeling vulnerable and left hanging?" She glared at him and said they'd talk that evening. She slammed her car door, a tinny sound reverberating between them.

No one answered his knock at Claire's front door that evening. He let himself in. The house was nearly dark, and he could not see her anywhere. He wandered through her house, calling her name.

"Back here."

She sat on the deck in the dark, her back to the house. Oak branches and drab green leaves framed streaks of grenadine—the last vestiges of the day's sun—that dissipated at the horizon.

"Sit down," she told him.

He worried what she might say. "Beautiful sunset, Claire."

"It has been."

"How are you doing?"

"Okay."

"How are you feeling about our words this morning?" he asked.

"It's hard to stay open."

"I know," he said. "It's really hard to stay open and wait for the other person to commit when you're ready, I know. But I want to say it feels like I'm making progress and we're moving ahead."

"Nice words, but it's hard to trust."

He tried to think of some way to help her stay patient with him. "I understand, but you know our situation makes me think of this scene at the end of *Manhattan* when Hemingway's granddaughter, Margo or Marietta or Muriel or whatever her name is, is leaving for England for a year of studies. Woody Allen is convinced their relationship will never survive the trip, but she tells him it'll be okay—he just needs a little faith in people sometimes. Now it's a lot easier for me to say this than for you to feel it, but I feel like I'm in the shoes of the Hemingway actress: I wish you could have a little faith in me about this."

She hesitated. "Okay."

"That's good." He forced a smile. "Thanks."

"But it's not just about proposing, John. I'm scared about what it'll be like over time."

"What do you mean?"

"I'm scared you'll have a hard time with all of this someday when you're older—that you'll get bored and act out your issues about commitment and everything by divorcing me, or having an affair with some young, fresh-skinned beauty." She stared into his eyes like she was trying to read his soul.

"That must be a scary thought," he said.

"Do you deny it?"

"What?"

"That you'll have a hard time with commitment over the years and you'll become bored or afraid of growing old and dying someday, and you'll run from all of those feelings by finding some new, exciting young woman to be with."

"Geez," he said. "That's quite a story you've concocted, Claire."

"How will you deal with those feelings if they come up?"

"Come on, Claire—this is all hypothetical."

"No. It's looking inside your character. I want to know."

He fidgeted, uncertain what to say. "I'd sit with those feelings and hold your hand until they passed." He realized he was telling Claire what she wanted to hear. "And then I'd go upstairs and make love with you."

She gave him the slightest of nods, and he saw some wariness in her eyes like she wanted to believe him, even as he himself hoped but wasn't sure if it would be true.

John heard Claire talking but he didn't know what she was saying. He was looking at the small hills, one giving way to another, as he sped toward the lake. He thought the Ozark Mountains belied their name: more mounds of broken earth than mountains. Millions of years had worn them down.

"It's wonderful to get away." As she spoke, Claire waved her arm out of the window, her hand floating in the wind like a seagull soaring in air currents.

"Yeah." He forced his attention back to Claire.

"I've been looking forward to this all week."

"Great," he said.

"And you?"

"Yeah, it's good to get away, but I feel really drained."

"What's the matter?"

"You know, just normal work bullshit you've heard me complain about before: mental health bureaucracies and politics—psycho-politics, really, which are always insane, but seem to be more so right now, and long hours with good but needy kids. Sometimes it just sucks me dry."

John bit his lip for telling a half-truth, but how could he have told her the real reason for his stress? This was the day he'd planned to ask Claire to marry him, but he woke alone in his apartment with a single thought: *I am scared shitless and witless.* Like a banner headline in the morning paper, the words had spread across his mind.

As he drove, he worried about things he'd already been over in his mind a thousand and one times. He knew unmistakably that he loved Claire deeply, but was marriage really the right way to go—a way to truly deepen love and vitality, or a cultural trap that dulls feelings over time? Was it really what he desired to be happy or was he just trying to give Claire what she wanted, just as he had with his mom and then Joanie?

He glanced at Claire, her hand still bobbing in the wind. He wanted her to be happy, as he himself wanted to be happy, but would he be so with Claire? If not with Claire, then who? What was he looking for anyway? A perfect relationship with a beautiful woman who was mature and worldly and insightful and scintillating and full of life and who would passionately fuck him back to life every time he started to find his existence stale or depressing? *Get real*, he thought.

A sickening feeling came over him, but it wasn't about Claire. He had the sense that something was seriously wrong with him. Was it that he couldn't ever quite allow himself to be happy in a relationship with someone who wanted him in return? Maybe he felt so bad about his mom's unhappiness after the stress of the ice accident—and, even more, because her problems started after his very birth, as if his very existence was a blight on her happiness—that he couldn't let himself simply be happy? There seemed to be something to that notion, and a heaviness sank into his gut. He worked to shove the feeling away.

"Mind if I try to catch the Giants' game?" he asked.

"Go ahead."

San Francisco was playing the Cubs and on a good day the team's Chicago station or a local affiliate could be picked up most places in the Midwest. He fiddled with the tuning knob, discovering the Cardinals, Royals, and White Sox games along the dial, but he heard only one scratchy account of the Giants-Cubs game. He listened for a few minutes, hearing a clear signal for a fleeting instant, but Harry Carey's and Steve Stone's voices crackled and faded away. He tried to fine tune the reception and turned the volume up high, but the static grumbling became unbearable. He flicked off the power.

"Damn it," he said.

"Can't get it?"

"Not really. I wanted to listen to the Giants. I hoped they would say something about Dave Dravecky. He was supposed to make another start for their minor league team in Phoenix."

"Who's he?"

John told her about Dravecky's surgery to remove a cancerous tumor on his deltoid and about his comeback that defied medical and major league predictions. "I saw a TV interview where he talked about not passively accepting defeat or limitations from his cancer or surgery. He said it was important for him to try to live fully, not just for himself but out of a sense of purpose, almost an obligation, he said, to live that way as a Christian."

"Sounds like a strong person," Claire said.

"Yeah, he is, and not just as a ballplayer, but also as a man with his determination to overcome a life-threatening illness and still live with a sense of direction, meaning, and intensity. That takes courage and purpose."

"You really respect him." She sounded like she was reflecting the emotions of a client in therapy.

He slowed the car. A line of trucks and pickups towing boats and trailers chugged up a hill. "Yeah, I guess I do."

"I respect him, too, from what you said."

He spotted another armadillo on the side of the road. He had never seen armadillos in the wild before today and this was the third one he'd seen on the drive, but they were all roadkill. "As much as I admire what Dravecky is doing, I wonder if in some ways it isn't easier for him than for most people. I mean, cancer is a terrible disease—something I hope I never have—but it is a single, dramatic problem to focus upon. And his solution is simplified because he's chosen to accept an encompassing, religious belief system that provides answers to all questions, directions for all uncertainties. Compare that to most people, who instead are dealing with multiple situations that are less intense, more mundane, less clear."

He glanced at Claire, wondering if he would actually follow through and ask her to marry him. And if he did, was it really what he wanted or just acting out his childhood pattern of trying to please the significant woman in his life? "We get confused by our own family dynamics, other people's issues, crazy institutions, and worn out from everyday living, the daily grind of work and even the oppressive heat and humidity of a St. Louis summer. We tend to get buried beneath all of that without a clear idea of what we're living for. In a way, perhaps it takes as much—maybe even more courage and awareness—to face the everyday, small moments and problems that compose the fabric of life and to still choose to live honestly and with openness and purpose. Does that make any sense at all or am I just rambling on in a psychotic stream of consciousness?"

"Yes."

"Yes, I'm sounding psychotic?"

"No, you're making sense."

"Don't get me wrong. I'm inspired by Dave Dravecky, by his facing the threat of cancer and even death and coming back to play baseball, to really try and live and not just give up. But maybe the underlying issues are there for everyone—just not illuminated so starkly, you know?"

She said she did. They rode in silence for a dozen miles before John turned the radio back on. As they traveled, he heard coherent but brief streams of the game, interspersed with long stretches of static.

John told Claire he was too tired to play hearts. He plopped himself into the wood-slatted deck chair under the awning of the cottage porch and tried to rest. The smell of barbecue from a distant cabin wafted in the breeze.

"What's the matter?" Claire asked, putting the card deck back into her bag.

"I'm suddenly so exhausted."

"How come?"

"Just drained from the work week, I guess, plus the long drive here and our round of golf in the afternoon heat."

"I'll get you a cold soda with ice."

He murmured thanks, but he knew his energy was sapped not just by the heat but by his continuous internal debate about whether he should propose to Claire tonight as planned, or to wait until tomorrow, or to forget the whole thing. He knew she wouldn't wait much longer, but he couldn't predict how much longer she'd stay open. She could suddenly end things, this time for good. He berated himself for his indecisiveness—he was exhausting himself with ruminations—but he didn't want to think about it now. Indeed, he didn't want to think any more about anything. It felt good to just melt into the wooden chair and watch the tall oaks darken in the fading light.

"Here you go." Ice cubes clinked as Claire handed him the soda. "How are you feeling now?"

"I'm just kind of dying."

"Maybe we shouldn't have played golf in such heat."

"No, it's okay. It actually feels sort of good. I just need to sit here for a while and vegetate."

"Let me know if you need anything." She pressed her soft lips against the bristly whisker stubble on his cheek.

There was a comfort to her kiss. It wasn't passionate or seductive, but kind, empathic. She was very different from his mother, he thought. She was able to be emotionally present, at least much more so. Still, he felt exhausted and said nothing.

The cabin door squeaked open and then clanked shut. He slouched in the chair. His long legs stretched across the rough pine deck. He lay motionless, listening to the hum of cicadas and watching the sky, juxtaposed against the dark green mat of tree leaves, turn deep purple. He closed his eyes and felt himself fade.

⌥

John woke the next morning feeling both drained and distant. Claire must have noticed immediately. "Are you still exhausted or are you feeling withdrawn?" she asked, cocking her head and waiting for his answer.

"Just really tired," he said. The truth was that he felt more distant from himself than her. "Some good restaurant coffee and food will probably help."

After breakfast, he complained that he still felt fatigued and he asked Claire to drive them back to the cabin. Travel along the two-lane road soon came to nearly a dead stop and he grumbled the traffic was unbearable. The road was jammed with RVs, vans, buses, campers, sedans, and cars pulling boat trailers. He watched all of this with a certain disinterest, and then he glanced again at his watch. In thirty-five minutes, they'd crept past a bizarre mélange of miniature golf courses, T-shirt stores, trinket shops, strip malls, fast food restaurants, and country music halls. The traffic lurched again to a complete stop, and the bleach smell of chlorine from a sardine-packed water park wafted through the open car windows. He felt his detachment crumble, giving way to an overwhelming agitation. He felt like screaming.

"Let's get out of here," he said.

"What?"

"I gotta get out of here. This overly congested, chintzy, neon strip is driving me crazy. Let's turn around, get away from all of this for the day."

"Why?"

"We didn't come here for this. This is like Saturday morning at K-Mart during a two-for-one sale. Come on."

"And where would we go?"

"I don't care—just out of this mess."

"Just drive? No plan?"

"Back to the main highway, away from all of this touristy crap, and we can take that road south into Arkansas. There are supposed to be some great rivers down that way. We can go canoeing. That's it!" His own impulsiveness startled him, but he liked the idea. "What do you say?"

She gazed at him; he was expecting her to say no, but she grinned. "You're on."

They drove for nearly two hours into the backwoods of Arkansas. John talked about enjoying a float down a pristine river, far from the hassles of tourists and the commercialized glitter of Branson, but as he spoke, a sense of dread floated in his chest. He wasn't sure if this apprehension was the product of his obsessive debate about a marriage commitment, or if he was beginning to feel anxious about getting back on the water.

They found a small canoe rental company, and as they put in the river, he found himself lightheaded. His hand trembled as he reached for the paddle. He thought of turning back to shore, but he knew that idea was completely crazy and he couldn't give into it.

He instructed himself to relax. He focused on the brown tree limbs that bent over the river and the clear water below. He practiced cleanly dipping the paddle, so it didn't create a wake. He commanded himself to think no more this weekend about the pros and cons of marrying Claire. He would defer the decision and return to therapy to sort out his feelings.

The river ran faster. Clear water churned white edges and crashed against the rocks. This was a faster, more complex river than they had floated before. They had not seen anyone else on the river, which ran clear beneath the thick Ozark forest. The back of Claire's head shone golden in the sun.

"I'm glad we came," Claire said over her shoulder.

"It's beautiful here."

"There's something peaceful about this place. Do you feel it?"

"Yes," he said. But he was also aware something else, fear or worry, crowded the edges of his mind. He tried to dismiss the feelings as vestiges of his phobia about being on water.

The river narrowed, bending around a steep granite boulder. Ahead the river fell in a series of cascades.

"Nice!" Claire said, staring downstream.

"Yep." White water danced visibly ahead as far as John could see.

They paddled in strong strokes toward the rapids but did not speak, not out of conflict but as if they were both readying for the moment. The bottom of the canoe slapped rhythmically against the quickening water.

"Yahoo!" Claire shouted as the canoe slid into the first rapid. "Here we go—"

Her words were swept away in a swirl of turbulent water. A thundering clap, like cars colliding, resounded, and the bottom of the canoe bounced skyward and rolled toward its side. The moment unfolded as if in slow motion. John could see the canoe was going to tip, but there was nothing he could do to prevent it. He glimpsed Claire startle in her profile, as she fell and disappeared into the river.

The water slapped him, and the river opened. Swallowing him, its coldness flashed through his body like an electric shock. The river current seized him and tumbled him over and beneath the surface. When he opened his eyes, he felt lost. Water surrounded him, and he was uncertain which way was up. For an instant, he felt like a boy again, searching for his father, and he panicked.

His head bobbed above the choppy surface. He gasped for air. A burning sensation, like ice, pinched his lungs. "*Claire!*" White water splashed against his face. He gulped water, spat, and coughed. "Claire?"

He did not see or hear her, and the memory of being in the lake as a boy, afraid his father had drowned, made him scream her name louder.

Please God, he thought. *Not her. Not yet.*

He slammed shins first into a boulder. He yowled with pain, but it was more in his soul than his shins, as the current swept him away. He struggled against the river, fighting to pull his knees together and to point his feet downstream. He yelled again for Claire.

He heard her shout. Her head bobbed above the caps of white water twenty yards past him. The rapids propelled them both swiftly downstream, past boulders and overhanging branches. The sensation seemed strange, as if they were floating through space in free fall.

Claire swam toward a flat boulder. She grabbed on, pulled herself up, and reached out toward John. He maneuvered himself in the current toward the rock and took her hand. She helped him up.

"You okay?" he asked.

"Yes—just a few shin bruises, plus I'm ice cold." She shook water from her hair and laughed. "That was quite a ride!"

"Yes, quite a ride." It was more than a ride; it was a flashback and a reminder of how quickly even a simple adventure could turn dangerous.

She shivered, a field of goosebumps springing up across her shoulders. Her hair glistened with blond streaks in the sunlight that found its way through the tree branches.

Seeing her in the diffused light, he was struck by how precious Claire was to his life—a feeling that matched and then overtook his sense of vulnerability. "I love you, Claire."

"And I love you."

He kissed her. He clasped the back of her head with his hand, water dripping from her hair and through his fingers. For the first time all day, for the first time in a long time, he no longer felt afraid. He broke off the kiss and leaned back, looking into her eyes.

"Claire, will you marry me?"

"What?" She blinked but then smiled.

He grinned. "Will you marry me?"

"Yes!" She laughed and kissed him. She pressed her moist lips full against his. They held each other, kissing. Claire caressed his neck and then his chest, and he found her wet, hard nipples with his fingertips. She unbuttoned his shorts and climbed on top of him, her wet body pressing firm against his. She pressed her tongue into his mouth, and then he was inside her, their two bodies intertwined on the hard boulder. They made love with a passion that swelled and expanded, and after hearing her rapid cries, he let himself climax.

CHAPTER 30

John woke scared. He didn't know where he was, and the room, cast in faint light, looked unfamiliar. A dank, sickly-sweet scent assaulted his nostrils. He remembered the smell from the night before. The scent had greeted him and Claire when they had entered the garden courtyard and it permeated the *pensione*. They were traveling in Europe, parlaying John's conference presentation into a belated honeymoon four months after their wedding, and had arrived by train last night along the Italian Riviera.

He reached across the lumpy mattress for Claire but she was gone. He realized he had been dreaming just before waking—he and Claire had been inside a gigantic cave with stalagmites that looked like huge melted waxed candles while water dripped from somewhere high above onto the rock floor. He had looked up in the dream, trying to find the source of the dripping water, but the cave was dark and rose like a vaulted cathedral ceiling beyond his sight. He couldn't see where the water was coming from and then he realized that Claire was gone. She had suddenly disappeared; that was when he woke scared from the dream.

John figured Claire was gone now for another early morning walk. He tried to recall but couldn't quite catch the beginning of the dream. Or was there even a beginning, he wondered? Before their trip, he and Claire had seen a segment of a documentary showing the cave in France with the prehistoric paintings. He'd told Claire he wanted to see that cave, but there was no time on this trip after his presentation at the international children's mental health conference in Vienna and their subsequent, whirlwind honeymoon tour of Berlin, Salzburg, Venice, and Rome.

John tumbled out of bed and peered through the cloudy pane of glass in the room's single, square window. Branches of an orange tree sprawled beyond the window and the courtyard was thick with tangled green plants badly in need of pruning. When they'd arrived the night before, Claire had marveled over the garden and the orange trees with limbs that hung low with heavy fruit; other oranges rotted on the soil. More striking to John than the garden was the smell: it was pungent and nauseating.

He pulled on gym shorts and went in search of Claire. The hallway was quiet and barren, but in the front parlor a huge dog with shaggy red hair was curled up on a chair. The dog's head drooped over the chair. The dog's brown eyes peered at John from beneath his reddish bangs.

"*Buon giorno, cane,*" John said.

A deep-throated growl resonated from behind John. Near the opposite wall, a smaller, black dog lay on a loveseat.

"Easy boy," John said.

The dog raised its muzzle and growled again.

John scurried across the room to the next hallway.

The bathroom door was closed and the sound of running water splashed inside. He guessed Claire was in the shower and though his bladder pressed tight, he slipped past the guard dogs again and returned to the small bedroom. He flopped onto the uneven mattress, waiting for Claire, and closed his eyes. A memory from the Sistine Chapel—it was packed with tourists, heads raised, looking at God and His angels on the ceiling—flooded his mind. He'd been struck by Rome: the Sistine Chapel, the Forum, the Colosseum—by the incomprehensible expanse of history of Romans and gladiators and Christians being fed to lions. He was glad he'd talked Claire into taking time off from work and turning his conference trip into their belated honeymoon, but after crisscrossing Europe on Eurail and shouldering a stuffed backpack for the past thirteen days, his body ached and he felt exhausted.

The door squeaked open. Claire stood at the threshold, her hair wet and once again a golden blonde. Despite an initial protest at his request, she'd re-colored her hair to cover up the creeping gray before their trip.

"There you are." He struggled to sit up from the lumpy mattress and leaned forward to kiss her. "*Buon giorno, bella biondina.*"

"*Buon giorno.*" She kissed him a second time and smiled.

"I'm glad you're out of the bathroom. I was about to pee my shorts."

"You could have handled it like the dogs." Claire tousled her hair with a towel.

"Huh?"

"That's the odor we've been smelling—dog pee."

"You're kidding?"

"No. I saw the big red one whizzing in the corner of the living room on my way to the bathroom," she said. "And then the black one was lifting his leg in the hallway on the way back."

"Tell me you're joking."

"They're great dogs that the old man has, but they've been peeing inside the house and the patio garden for a very long time."

"Shit. I was trying to tell myself that it was some sort of exotic Mediterranean fragrance wafting from the garden."

"Not so exotic," she said. "But it is wafting from the garden, not to mention the living room and hallways and probably the bedrooms too."

"Gross. Well, I'm going to be old-fashioned and pee in the toilet and then wash off the travel grime with a good, long shower too."

"I don't think so." She giggled.

"Why's that?"

"The shower head doesn't work."

"Great. That's just great."

"And the bathtub doesn't either—the stopper's missing. But you can do as I did: sit in the cracked tub and splash water on yourself."

After using the bathroom, John found Claire sitting in the garden, talking to the old Italian man. The two dogs were sprawled at their feet in sunlight. The *pensione* owner had to be at least eighty, John figured, with tanned, wrinkled olive skin and thick, white chest hair that sprang from his open collar. There was something familiar about him, and John recalled a white-haired, wine-making Italian neighbor of his great-grandfather, but the memory was vague. When John and Claire had arrived the night before, the *pensione* owner had taken Claire's hand and kissed it gently. "*Bambinos*?" he'd asked after Claire had introduced John as her husband. No, Claire had said, telling him they'd only been married four months. "Ah, soon," the old man said, winking. "I'll give you my finest private bedroom." John had immediately diverted the topic, asking the old man about the town, for he wanted to avoid any awkward conversation about a possible pregnancy. He was still indecisive about having a child. He worried Claire might react with postpartum depression and would then withdraw both from their child and from him. But now he wondered if *he* would be the one who would be depressed—that having a child would make for one more person he needed to take care of while eliminating possibilities for more freedom and adventure? He wasn't sure but he felt pressure to decide. Claire had given him a year to determine if he wanted a child—after that, she would be too old and it would be too late, she had said.

Now he greeted the old *pensione* owner and told Claire he was going to grab some food—did she want to go? No, she said; she was going to sit in the garden and visit with Signore Falcioni. John returned to their room, tucked *Let's Go Europe* under his arm, and found a pay phone within a few blocks. He called another *pensione* listed as modern with three stars, confirmed they had individual showers, and reserved a room for that day. When he returned, he found Claire sitting alone in the tattered rattan chair on the patio.

"Wait until you hear what I got: Fresh *Italian* bread—not French bread, as my great-grandfather Papa Marco used to say." He pulled a loaf from the bag. "And Italian pastries, grapes, apples, coffee with steamed milk, and," he lowered his voice to a whisper, "a room with a shower in a modern *pensione* in town that's available by noon."

"Why?" She looked crossly at him.

"I want to leave."

"I don't," Claire said. "I like it here."

"I don't—not enough to stay a second night anyway."

"I like the old man and his dogs and garden," she said. "It's quaint and homey."

"And dirty and reeks of dog pee."

"For God's sake. It's not the Hyatt Regency, but it's full of local ambience—isn't that why we came to Europe?" She pointed a pastry at him. "Besides, I enjoy talking with the old man. He's delightful."

"I like him too. But we decided to stay an extra night instead of pushing on so we could relax after running through half of Europe in the past thirteen days."

"So, let's stay and relax."

"I can't here—it's smelly and dirty and cramped and there's no shower," he said. "I want to go."

"I want to stay."

"I already paid for the new *pensione* with my Visa—it's nonrefundable."

She glared at him, a wild look burning in her eyes. "I don't have much choice then, do I?"

They lied to the old man, telling him they'd decided to travel north a day early instead of staying a second night. Oh no, he had said in his thickly accented English, he was sad they were leaving so soon. John asked if he would pose with his dogs and Claire for a picture in the garden. He agreed but they found only the large red dog, the black one had slipped away. The old man kissed Claire's hand once more, asking them to stay with him again on their next trip to Europe. *Familiare*, he said, kissing Claire on the cheek this time.

In the afternoon, after showering at the new *pensione*, John lay with Claire on a pier that jutted into the Mediterranean, their backs against the warm stone. He thought of the old man. John regretted lying to him and leaving his home. He was a nice man—simple, at peace. He exuded warmth—like how family should feel. John imagined seeing him again, but a feeling of sadness quickly passed over as he realized by the time they returned to Europe, the old Italian would certainly be dead. He thought of his great-grandparents, Mama Clara and Papa Marco. They were only memories now: old figures, wrinkled and stooped with thin, gray hair, living with Nona. Emerson was gone, too, now, and someday, before too long, so would be Nona.

Stop. He told himself to think no more of such things. He tightened his grip around Claire's hand. She had given him the silent treatment when they were packing to leave the *pensione*, but he had apologized profusely for not talking over the decision to leave, and she seemed to have forgiven him. "It's good to be here with you," he said.

"Mmm." She squeezed his hand. "Sun feels good."

Someday we'll be old, too, he thought. Completely gray with thin hair, and wrinkled flaps of flesh sagging from their necks like turkey throats.

He admonished himself for thinking such things. He told himself to focus on the warmth of the sun hitting his face and the comfort of Claire's hand in his, as he listened to the Mediterranean Sea lapping on the rocks below. In a day they would be in the small town in the foothills of the Italian Alps where Nona, Mama Clara, and Papa Marco were born. The town was supposed to be beautiful, but he could not escape the thought crowding the border of his awareness, that as good as the trip might be, as much as he wanted to hold onto everyone and the good times just as they were, that time passed quickly and his family was dying out.

After a train ride and car drive the next day into the Piedmont, John woke to a rooster crowing, but he realized it was still late afternoon, not morning. He felt Claire's shoulder next to his. She was still napping in the new *pensione*. Footsteps clacked against the cobblestone street below, and the church bells clanged from the village where his grandmother and great-grandparents had been born. He closed his eyes, listening to the bells until the chiming faded and disappeared, and then he heard a swishing noise, almost like water rushing in a stream, and he realized a car was passing on the street. Soon a dog barked, followed by the yapping and yammering of smaller dogs. There was so much to hear—it was almost overwhelming—if you listened.

Through the open window he saw fuzzy, apple-green trees on the rising slope of the mountain. The trees looked small, like miniature plastic trees in a model city. He wondered if they were the same trees as when Papa Marco grew up in the village? Maybe not, he thought—it was over a hundred years since his great-grandparents had been born, and the trees of his boyhood were probably gone now too. But the hills and mountains were still the same. They had been here tens of thousands, maybe millions, of years.

Snow topped a distant mountain peak like vanilla ice cream atop a cone. White clouds billowed heavenward above the mountain and he remembered God and the cherubs sitting in clouds on the ceiling of the Sistine Chapel. Beyond the *pensione* window was a different scene—of hills and trees and mountaintops and clouds—and yet it was just as beautiful as Michelangelo's fresco. He considered getting the camera, capturing the image on film, and holding it forever, but he realized it would not last.

His mom had often spoken about being a girl and Papa Marco cooking her a poached egg for breakfast and giving her red wine cut with water for dinner while telling her stories of his growing up in the village. She would say with a smug smile how much her grandfather loved her, that she was the "apple of his eye." But at other times, his mom and Nona would also talk about how Papa Marco was so incredibly superstitious: he wouldn't leave the house on Friday the 13th or walk under a ladder or cross the path of a black cat.

As John got older, he used to scoff at the stories of Papa Marco's silly superstitions: he was so afraid something awful would happen. But now John remembered that Papa Marco's brother had died in a mine cave-in and later his sister killed—decapitated—in a horse carriage accident. Maybe those traumas were where his great-grandfather's superstitions came from? Undoubtedly, his mom had absorbed some of his anxieties, too, given how close she had been to him as a child, even before her emotions imploded as a young adult, first with what must have been postpartum depression; then with the deaths of Papa Marco, her grandmother, and her dad; and then with the ice trauma. In a way, though, Papa Marco's and his mom's fears were not just irrational anxieties: Accidents happen, and life can suddenly disappear. But does it really matter? John, too, could get lost in fears about accidents and what might happen in life, for he had picked up anxiety from his mom and the ice accident, and for too long he had bound his fears by narrowing his world to pleasing his mom or some woman. He had distracted himself so well that he avoided having to face not only his own vulnerability but also figuring out what he really wanted in life. But he was changing and right now, John thought, looking at the gray gathering of clouds for a thunderstorm in the mountains, he was very much alive. He wanted to savor the moment.

Claire jerked in her sleep, her hand grasping and tightening around his hand.

"*Bella,*" he whispered. He saw God again in the ceiling of the Sistine Chapel, reaching out, touching Adam's finger, giving him life. The painting had stirred him in some way he couldn't quite describe, and yet in this moment, looking through the open window, he felt something even more beautiful, more intense in the clouds and the mountains and in the feel of Claire's hand resting on his own. For an instant, he had the sense—not just the memory, but a sensation—of Papa Marco, as if he was close by. Without knowing why, he remembered his dream of Grandpa Anderson from years before, of his grandfather catching a salmon in one hand and beckoning John to come up river with the other. His grandfather was dead at the time of the dream, and so were Papa Marco and Mama Clara. They were all long dead now, but *something,* a sense of connection, was with him now, even if it made no rational sense and sounded crazy to his own thinking.

"*Bella,*" he whispered. Claire's head rested on his shoulder. Her beautiful blonde hair was almost golden in the filtered light of the *pensione* bedroom. "*Bella biondina,*" he said softly. "It is so good to be here with you now." It was a glorious moment and he wanted it to last. Nothing lasts, his mind retorted. He conceded the point, but he knew he wanted more and more of these times.

He gently caressed her head.

"Hmm." Claire stirred, cuddling tighter against John's body.

"*Bella biondina.*" He fluffed her hair.

She raised her head, sleeping eyes looking into his. "I was sleeping."

"Yes." He smiled and then kissed her.

"Mmh," she murmured after the kiss, and then she kissed him again, opening her mouth to his.

As they kissed, he rolled over, pulling her on top of him. He knew she liked to make love after waking up. He savored the press of her body and the warmth of her flesh against his skin. She grasped his fingers as they kissed, and he saw again God touching Adam, and he fantasized of making love with Claire, of being inside her and of conceiving a baby together. He kissed her passionately and pulled away her clothes.

She sat up on him and smiled. "I'll be right back."

"Where are you going?" he asked.

"To the bathroom—to put in my diaphragm."

"No." He pulled her back down on him.

"Why?" she asked.

"I want to make love with you now—without it."

"You are sure?" She smiled.

With her question, there was a rustling of doubt, but it passed quickly, and he rose to kiss her. "Yes, my love. It is time."

CHAPTER 31

John stirred the polenta while he watched Josh peering into the refrigerator. "Have you heard from your mom?"

"Nope." Josh shut the refrigerator and sniffed at the oven-stove unit where John was baking chicken cacciatore and cooking spaghetti in addition to the polenta. "Smells good. Is it done? I'm starving."

"We're waiting for your mom." John twisted off the heel from the French bread loaf, slathered it with butter, and handed it to Josh. "She should have been home forty-five minutes ago, so I'm guessing she'll be home any second. We're going to have a nice, sit-down dinner together."

"What's the big deal?" Josh asked. "I'm not leaving for college for two weeks."

"Our wedding anniversary—nine months today."

"Nine months, wow." Josh grinned. "You two could have had a baby by now." He laughed.

John worried Josh would be horrified if he knew that his forty-one-year-old mother and John were trying to get pregnant, though they had no luck yet. "We'll celebrate your starting college with a fancy dinner next week. But here," John tore off another chunk of warm bread, slapped on butter, and handed it to Josh, who took a bite and disappeared into the sunroom.

John lowered the oven door. Heat blasted his face and he worried something bad had happened to Claire. He tried to dismiss the thought, admonishing himself for even imagining such a horrible thing. Still, he could not completely assuage the worry that she was so late because of an accident. He silently cursed his anxious nature, and then distracted himself by draining the spaghetti, mixing the noodles with olive oil, and stirring the tomato sauce. Soon he heard the front door crack open.

"I'm home." Claire's face was drawn and pale. "Finally."

"Let's eat," Josh shouted from the other room.

"Why are you so late?" John asked.

"Carol Burke. Another emergency call."

After John carried the dishes to the table, he leaned down and kissed Claire. "Happy anniversary."

"Anniversary?"

"Nine months today since our wedding."

"You're sweet."

"Yeah," Josh said. "And you two are such wild newlyweds, too, lying around in your pajamas watching those hot movies on Friday nights—what was the name of that last one with all of that singing and stupid dancing?"

"*Fiddler on the Roof,*" John said. "That movie and the one we watched the Friday before—*Zorba the Greek*—were really good."

"I bet." Josh laughed.

"Really," John said. "They both had great main characters who showed how a man should live. You should watch them sometime."

"Yeah, sure," Josh said. "I'll invite Ben and Matt over this Friday for a big pajama party while we watch these movies about how to be a man."

"By the way, it's your mom—not me—in pajamas."

"They're comfy." Claire's shoulders hunched over the table.

"You had a long day, huh?" John leaned over and rubbed her shoulders.

"Too long, too busy. And scary too."

"Why?"

"I was tooling along Highway 40 to the office when there was this terrible boom—and then broken glass sprayed through the open window and splattered across my lap."

"What happened?" Josh looked up from his pasta.

"Two cars going in the opposite direction collided at high speed, sending shattered glass over the divider and onto my lap."

"Yikes—you okay?" John asked.

"Yes, I was lucky, though, that the glass landed on my lap and not in my face. And some of the glass landed across the hood and scratched my paint something terrible."

"What happened to the other cars?" Josh asked.

"I couldn't see very well, but they looked all mangled and crushed."

"Bet they were killed," Josh said.

"Hope not, but they might have been," she said.

"I saw a guy killed last night," he said.

"*What*?" John asked.

"I saw a guy killed," he repeated. "It was after midnight when I got off work and on the way home, this guy on a Ninja motorcycle flies by at a hundred miles per hours, then on the ramp for 70, he veered just a little and aimed straight for the divider pole. He looked like he was on a kamikaze mission, and then, bam—he smacked dead into the pole."

"God, no," John said. "That's awful. Did you stop?"

"No, two cars ahead of me did, but there was no point. He was dead."

"Was he wearing a helmet?"

"Yeah, but there was no way he survived that crash. He hit that pole like a guided missile. It looked like he wanted to self-destruct, like something was driving him crazy."

"That's sad," John said. "Terrible."

"Cars and motorcycles speed along all the time," Claire said. "And we take life for granted, but death can strike in an instant. Life is so fragile."

"God, you two are great dinnertime conversationalists, you know that?" John grabbed the long wooden spoon and whipped the spaghetti around the bowl. He wasn't surprised by Claire's comment: ever since she'd read Becker, she interpreted every mishap as a signal for the precariousness of life. He had become wiser because of her perspective, and yet sometimes he was sick of hearing it. "I cook this sumptuous Italian meal so we can eat hearty and celebrate, and all you two morbid personalities can talk about are fatal highway crashes and the fragility of life."

"It's true, but sorry." Claire raised her wine glass to John. "The food's great. Thank you."

John lifted another spoonful of spaghetti onto his plate. "I was kind of teasing," he said while wishing they would drop the subject.

"So, can I tell you one more thing, then?" she asked.

"What?"

"The broken glass flew into my shoe too. I didn't even know it, and then when I stepped out of the car, a piece cut me."

"Really?"

"See?" She lifted her foot to the edge of the tablecloth, easing her foot out of the shoe; a crescent-shaped cut adorned the corner of her big toe.

"Geez." John shook his head and passed the pasta back around. "Remember some of the dishes we had in Italy? Like the risotto, *futura d'orso*, polenta, and fettuccini? Amazing dishes."

"*Delizioso*," Clare said.

The phone rang in the kitchen and Josh popped up from the table.

"Let it ring, please," Claire said.

"Matt's going to be calling. We're making plans to go out."

Josh returned quickly to the table and nodded at John. "It's your grandma."

John left the dining room and leaned against the kitchen counter to take the call. "How are you, Nona?"

"Terrible."

"What's the matter?"

"Everything."

"Well, what's the worst?" John asked.

"My back—it hurts. And I'm so tired and bored."

She had taken to complaining on nearly every call. When he was growing up, he never remembered her complaining. She had always been the strong one, especially for him. She sounded different now, her voice tiny, weaker. He could barely hear her. He remembered her sitting on her kitchen barstool, calling her friends to say Emerson had passed, and how the speaker unit of the phone had drooped well below her chin. John had wondered how her friends could even hear her.

"Nona, can you put the phone all the way up to your mouth?"

"It's miserable." Her gravelly voice intensified. "Can't even drive myself to the bank or the dime store when I want."

"I'm sorry. I'm sure it's frustrating when you can't do the things you used to be able to do so easily."

"You know the worst part?"

"What?" As soon as he uttered the question, he guessed what she was going to say.

"There's no excitement in my life anymore," she said. "No weekend trips away, no nice restaurants, no dancing. There's just no fun anymore."

"I'll talk to mom and dad," he said. "The next time they come up, they can take you to that nice seafood restaurant that you like."

"That place is too drafty and the service is so slow."

"You can take a sweater. Come on, Nona, it would be fun for you."

"So what if we get out to a restaurant five minutes away? That's not really living."

"That's a pretty negative attitude," John said. "You have to think positive and do some things to make life better."

"It's not going to get better," she said.

"And why do you think that, Nona?"

"I'm too old."

"Age is partially a state of mind," he said. "There's people much older than you who are doing a lot and still enjoying life."

"I'm tired and don't feel good, John," Nona said.

"I'm sorry you don't feel great, but the way you're thinking is a big part of the problem."

"My body's giving out," she said.

"You're giving up, aren't you?" It was more an accusation than a question. "The problem is more your thinking than your body."

Claire was starting to clean up the kitchen. She gave John a funny look from the stove where she was scrubbing away dried splotches of splattered tomato sauce.

"No, it's my time," Nona said. "I want you and Claire to have my china cabinet after I'm gone."

"Nona—"

"And I'm leaving you my china and silver," she said. "I want you to have the marble Pieta figurine too."

"Will you please stop already? I don't want to be talking about this, Nona. I want us to be planning where we're going to go play a round of golf the next time I'm there, not about inheriting your dang dishes."

Claire had gone upstairs by the time he ended the call. He found her in bed, propped against two fluffy pillows and reading a paperback. He recounted the conversation with his grandmother.

"It's sad," he said. "She's giving up."

"It's hard to hear Nona talking about her own death, isn't it?"

"Well, yeah," he sniffed. "I think it would be for most people."

"*Yes, exactly.*" Claire lowered her paperback to the blankets. "Most people can't be there for people they love when they're old and preparing for death. I'm sure your parents can't be there for her like that, but can you imagine how difficult it must be for Nona?"

"No thanks."

"She's the one facing her own death. It's not an abstract, far-off philosophical thing for her. At eighty, with health problems and not feeling well, she probably knows death might truly come any day. That's a lot to come to terms with, especially when you have to face your death alone."

"I guess."

"That's the hardest thing for a lot of old people—not the prospect of dying per se but feeling all alone in facing it."

"Now I feel like a schmuck," he said.

"Don't. But she needs you to be there for her, John. She needs you to listen to her putting things in order, to make plans for her china, to ask her how she's feeling about dying."

"I hate this," he said. "And you're probably right."

"I know it's difficult. You love her so much and you don't want her to die."

"Of course not."

Claire leaned forward and wrapped her arms around John.

"It's not just the talk about dying," he said. "When people I love are depressed, I try to talk them into feeling better. I'm pretty good at it, usually, but if they stay stuck in despair, I feel bad and so I try harder again to talk them out of it."

"I know. I've experienced that a lot with you over the years." She laughed.

"What? Why are you laughing?"

"I was just thinking what a terrible fight we'll have forty years from now if I'm the one preparing to die and you're pestering me, trying to plan a vacation to go to the mountains or golfing or some damn thing."

He yanked a pillow out from behind her back.

"Hey, give it back."

"Want it?" He smacked her over the shoulder, and then tossed the pillow like a huge Frisbee at her.

Claire repositioned the pillow behind her back, stuck her tongue out at John, and reached for Salem Lites on the end table. She tapped out a cigarette, put it in her mouth, and reached for the lighter, but John snatched the cigarette from her lips.

"Give me back my cigarette."

"No way. I don't want to be sitting here in forty years, listening to you moan day after day while you're dying from emphysema and I'm trying to plan our trip to the mountains."

"My cigarette back," she said. "Now."

"Nope. I want you healthy and strong forty, forty-five years from now, and I want to be making wonderful, passionate, tender love with you even in your eighties."

"You did through most of the eighties."

"That's not enough," he said. "I want more."

John returned to the kitchen and called Nona back. She immediately asked him what was wrong that he had called back on the same night. He said he'd realized, with Claire's help, that he hadn't been a very good listener earlier. "I'm sorry about that," he said. "I think you were trying to tell me how hard this time is for you right now, and I was being pigheaded, trying to divert the topic to golf. How are you, really?"

"I'm okay." Her voice quivered, and she quickly added: "How are your pupils?"

"Actually, right now, they all seem to be doing pretty well. You know, they've had some ups and downs and hard times, for sure, but all my clients seem to be working through stuff and feeling better right now, knock on wood. But tell me, how are you feeling—really?"

He had to probe again, but she said then she was missing Emerson and their trips to Tahoe and Carmel—*the good life* they had, she called it. Now, she said, she had nothing to look forward to, and it was her time to die. Those were all things she had told him multiple times before, but this time he just listened to her, trying to be patient. Soon she began to sob and immediately criticized herself for crying. He interrupted her, telling her it was okay to cry. It took strength and courage to feel those emotions, he said, and he loved her very much. They talked for a long time.

John sat in the dark in the sunroom after hanging up. When he got up and climbed the stairs, he saw the lights were out on the second floor too. He walked to their bedroom and stood in the threshold until he could make out Claire's form in the darkness. She had the sheets and blankets pulled high, over her chin, and a pillow flopped over her forehead, her long nose protruding for air like a snorkel. He took off his clothes and slipped beneath the cold sheets.

He remembered Nona picking him up after school and putting him in the back seat of her big, blue Mercury. John's mother had gotten out of the hospital months before, but she still wasn't feeling good and needed quiet at home, so Nona drove John for the weekend to her house, via Fisherman's Wharf in San Francisco where from a sidewalk vendor she plucked a huge crab with red and orange claws out of the ice. She fed John crab for dinner and let him stay up late with her to watch a Friday night movie on television. Before bedtime, she fixed him a salami and cheese sandwich for a snack, followed by a bowl of strawberry ice cream. He remembered the chunks of strawberries, frozen and hard against his teeth.

She had been strong, very strong, for him when he had needed it. He found it hard to believe that she was in her eighties now, old and weak, and now he needed to be strong for her.

Twenty-five years were gone, and those experiences as a boy felt important to him in some way he couldn't put into words, but now they were only memories. He inched closer to Claire, snuggling against her shoulder and side. She stirred, and he reached to hold her, but she stayed asleep. He knew that someday they would be old—and then one of them would be gone.

He tried to fight off that thought, but it stayed with him, even though he only wanted to savor the warmth of her body.

CHAPTER 32

From thousands of feet in the air, the Mississippi River appeared different at dusk to John. At first, as the plane lifted off from Lambert Airport and flew southeast toward the Arch, the river was partially hidden. But the 727 banked wide, toward the northwest, making a semicircle. From that vantage point, peering through his porthole, John could see the river broaden, and then a second river, the Missouri, joined with the Mississippi, swelling its banks.

It was strange, John thought, to live so close but not to know the shape of the Mississippi. The river twisted and contorted north of St. Louis, and there were droplets of land, thick with trees, plunked into the middle of the river. The islands looked pristine, probably as they had been in Mark Twain's time and long before, wild and primeval. And yet adjacent to the trees, the islands, and the river, hundreds of electrical lights flickered surreally like luminescent fireflies.

The river is unknowable, he thought. It twisted and meandered like a ball of string dropped against the earth. The river continued to unravel, to run so far ahead that he could no longer see its dark outline. He knew neither its path nor its source, where it began or ended.

It was helping to let his thoughts wander mindlessly about the river. Waiting on the runway, a heaviness, like a suit of armor, hung thickly on his heart and soul.

The river disappeared in dark shadows, as the plane traveled west. He still found the phone call hard to believe. He knew Nona for as long as he'd existed. He could always count on her, definitely more so than his mother, and more even than his dad.

He'd known it was coming for months, but now it still seemed unfathomable, and his feelings numbed while his thoughts constricted to only one fact: Nona was dead.

PART SIX

CHAPTER 33

Bart's beagle bay resonated through the study.

"Hey!" John startled and looked up from his papers. "How am I supposed to concentrate and get this done?"

Bart scooted forward, pressing his black nose close to the desktop where the last half of John's turkey sandwich sat untouched. Serendipity sat next to Bart, her narrow-set, dark brown eyes shifting her beady stare from the sandwich to John's eyes. With her head cocked slightly, neck craning toward the desk, and her short ears creased at the midpoint, she looked in posture and shape like the RCA dog.

Bart howled again.

"Shush! You need to be quiet for a minute so I can give you a bite without reinforcing your obnoxious behavior." John reached down to pet the bony top of the dog's head, but Bart shied away. "What? Am I disturbing your begging concentration?"

The shine to Bart's black, tan, and white coat had faded, his fur worn and dull, his muzzle tipped with white. Bart had nearly died from a seizure two months back. After conducting laboratory tests, the vet had diagnosed the beagle with a rare and terminal neurological disorder. The medication had thus far prevented any new seizures, but it seemed unfathomable to John that six weeks prior the vet had said Bart had only one to four months to live. John tore the remainder of his sandwich in two, tossed the larger portion to Bart, who snatched it out of the air, and dropped the rest to Serendipity.

After the dogs devoured the turkey and bread, John held his plate vertically; a few tiny crumbs slid toward the bumpy black knob of Bart's nose. "All gone, see?" John scratched Bart behind his floppy ears. "You're a good boy. Hang in there, huh? Don't want to lose you too."

John checked the desktop clock. Claire was late again by nearly an hour. He figured she'd be tired after a long day of seeing therapy clients. He planned to warm up a bowl of soup for her, she was never very hungry late in the evening, and draw her a bath. He wanted to get her to bed before it was too late, wishing to make love. Fourteen months after stopping birth control, she was still not pregnant, and though Claire was growing discouraged, at least he knew unambivalently that he wanted them to have a child. He was hoping for a girl, and he'd been lobbying Claire to call her Maria, at least the middle name, after Nona's Italian birth name.

"Berrrouu!" Bart arched his muzzle upward as he bayed again.

"Bart, damn it! There's no more food—I told you that."

He bayed again.

"You old beggar. I shouldn't give in, but one more hot dog and then that's it. Come on."

Bart and Serendipity scampered down the stairs after John. Serendipity bumped into Bart rounding the corner into the kitchen, snapping then at the beagle as if it were his fault. Bart appeared unperturbed, his sight transfixed on the refrigerator. Two wet noses nuzzled against his hand as John reached for a hot dog from the deli bin. He broke the hot dog in two, and as he flipped the halves through the air to Bart and Serendipity, the door to the garage creaked open. He called out to Claire. She appeared in the kitchen in her black-and-white dress. Her neon green backpack, which she used in lieu of a briefcase, was bloated full and strapped over her slumping shoulder. He embraced her in a giant bear hug, lifting her off the ground.

"Put me down."

He complied, planting a kiss on her lips as she reached the door. She pulled away.

"Something wrong?" he asked.

"I'm tired."

"How many clients did you see?"

"Eleven in a row. They all came, and I ran behind with phone calls to return."

"Yikes! That's too many, Claire! You must be worn out."

"Yep."

"I don't know how you do it—or why. That's a lot of therapy sessions for one day."

She shrugged.

He tried not to pepper her with questions, knowing sometimes she needed space after a long day of providing therapy. After a few minutes of silence, he asked if she wanted to go for a walk with the dogs before the sunlight faded. She declined.

By the time he and the dogs returned from walking the empty golf course, it was dark and the cicadas were humming from the oak trees like transformers. He fixed Claire a bowl of clam chowder and made himself a salad. Claire slouched over the bowl, yawned, and rubbed her face in her hands—it was an annoying habit, rubbing her face, but she did it frequently, especially at night, even though her mother on a recent visit had told her she should stop because it caused premature wrinkles. "Really?" Claire had said to her mom, and then she rubbed her face again, harder this time, and laughed, saying she didn't care. She yawned again now at the table.

"Tired?" John asked.

She nodded.

After dinner, she cleared the plates while he took Bart and Serendipity outside and then put them in the downstairs laundry room for the night, filling their bowls with the dog chow burger that was ground into small, worm-shaped strips. He patted Bart an extra turn, and then found Claire upstairs under the covers, propped against three quilted pillows, reading a paperback novel.

"You okay, Claire?"

"Tired, I said."

"Sorry you're so tired." He unlaced his cross-trainers. "But don't get smart with me, Claire Elizabeth Evers Anderson."

"Sorry."

"Apology accepted," he said. "Now roll over and I'll give you a good back massage."

"No."

"Claire, roll over. I need to therapeutically rub that lactic acid out of your body and soul after you saw eleven clients in a row so you're not so exhausted—not to mention so ornery with your husband who loves and worships you."

She hesitated, and then rolled over, hitching up her nightshirt. He rubbed his fingers deep into her shoulder and back muscles. Her neck was tight, and he massaged along the top of her spine and onto the back of her head. She sighed, her sides falling with a deep exhale. He drummed his fingertips across her body, pressing rhythmically into her flesh as if he was playing an instrument. When he was finished, he leaned down and kissed her skin between her shoulder blades.

"That was wonderful." Her voice was soft. "I could fall right asleep."

He hoped not, wishing instead that they would try again to conceive.

"Oh, sorry, almost forgot—did you hear the message on the answering machine from your mom?" He had indeed forgotten, but he also hoped the news would wake her up. "She wants you to call her back tonight."

"Already talked with her. She called me at the office this evening."

"That's different." He looked at her. "What's the matter?"

"My grandfather had a stroke."

"Oh, no! I'm sorry. How is he?"

"Paralyzed on the right side and unable to talk, but he's in stable condition and expected to live."

"Good. I mean I'm sorry about the stroke—that's got to be very upsetting—but good that he's going to live." He sat up, agitated, and leaned against the headboard. "Claire, why didn't you tell me earlier?"

"Didn't want to talk about it."

"Really?" He cuffed at a pillow, fluffing it up and putting it behind his back. "Claire, I wish you'd at least said something."

She shrugged. "Sorry."

"I'm sorry, too," he said. "About your grandfather. How's your grandmother taking it?"

"Mom says it really hasn't registered with her. Her mind is slipping so fast with the dementia—she's living fifty, sixty years back most of the time. Mom's afraid they'll have to put them both in the nursing home."

"Damn it, I'm sorry, Claire. I know you're close to both of them."

"I'd hoped my grandfather would live to one hundred. He's always said he wanted to see his one-hundredth birthday."

"But his birthday's only six weeks away and he's physically stable, right? He should still make it."

"Some celebration—paralyzed and unable to talk, a prisoner in his own body." She tugged at the blankets, pulling them higher. "He'd be better off dead."

"Claire, don't say that."

"It's true."

"I don't think so, but I'm sorry he's paralyzed."

Claire threw back the covers and walked toward the bathroom. When she returned, she flipped off the lights and returned to bed on the far side of the mattress. She was withdrawn and cranky because she was upset about her grandfather—it wasn't personal about him, John told himself, but just her pattern. Still, he had to give himself a pep talk to reengage her instead of withdrawing himself, for it invariably left him with hurt feelings when she remained distant despite his efforts at reaching out. He made himself inch closer to her in the dark, but she leaned toward the nightstand where she kept the dental floss container. She snapped off a piece of string and in the dark vigorously worked the floss between her teeth, a repetitive clicking and sawing sound that made John think of a beaver gnawing on wood. The noises finally ceased, and she flung the dirty floss to the carpet.

She rolled onto her side, her back to John. He inched closer to her, and slipped his hand under her nightshirt, rubbing her back again.

"Don't do that—you already gave me a good back rub."

"Quiet."

He traced his fingertips over her skin in slow, teasing strokes. He imagined them overcoming the evening's irritability and distance and regaining a sense of intimacy and, perhaps, even making love. Indeed, he wished they would conceive a baby, and he planted a wet kiss on the nape of her neck. He nestled closer, but felt her hips rise up from the mattress. She pushed out a fart.

"Claire!"

"Just getting a little gas out so it doesn't hurt my stomach."

"That's totally unromantic." He rolled over.

"I don't want to be romantic."

He bit his inner lip and wondered if this was the way it was going to be—no baby, no lovemaking, just he and Claire in petty arguments and feeling distant, even as he remembered how their bed used to be for lovemaking and cuddling, instead of flossing and farting.

"I hope I die first," Claire said.

"What?"

"I said I hope I die first."

"Now why would you say such a thing, Claire?"

She rolled onto her side. "I don't want to be put into a nursing home."

He thought about reaching for her hand, but he still felt upset with her. "I know it's sad about your grandparents."

"What do you want?"

"Pardon?"

"Do you want to die first or be the one left behind?" she asked.

"Claire, please. I'm not in the mood for a morbid conversation."

"Tell me."

"I don't know. I haven't thought that much about it."

"I want to die first. I probably will, being older." She scooted further away, pulling more covers with her. "I hope I do anyway. I don't want to be old and alone, losing my mind and shuffled off to a nursing home."

Claire left for work early the next morning. John had slept through the alarm and woke after she was gone. He looked in the kitchen for a note—Claire usually left him a smiley-face love note if she went to work while he was still sleeping—but today there was none. Of course not—she was still upset about her grandfather, and in her brooding, distancing from John. He detested her displaced reaction—it made him anxious and aggravated himself—but that was her way.

On his way to work, he turned the car stereo up extra loud when a Foreigner song came on the radio and he sat listening in in the parking lot until the song was finished. As he walked into the center, he found Bennie and Anthony waiting for him.

"Whew!" Bennie shook his head. "Your boy's in a bad funk this morning."

"What?"

"Andy," Anthony said. "He was here early this morning, talking about how he's going to shoot himself in the heart."

"I'll talk to him," John said.

"We were hoping so—he's waiting in your office," Anthony said.

"I told him what to do to feel better," Bennie wagged his finger. "But that one never listens."

Andy slouched over the edge of the sofa in John's office. He took a long drag from his half-smoked cigarette, holding the inhale for a long time in his lungs.

"Hey, Andy." John pulled out the chair from behind his desk. "How are you doing?"

Andy blew smoke across the small room and shook his head.

John leaned closer. "I hear it's a tough morning for you."

"Bennie thinks he knows everything, but he doesn't know shit."

"You're the best expert on you," John said. "What's going on?"

"What's going on? Life fucking sucks." Anger radiated in his eyes, and then he looked away. "It ain't worth it anymore."

"Life can be very challenging sometimes. What's the hardest part for you right now?"

Andy shook his head. He sported new chin whiskers that were sparse but growing long, and their color matched the mouse-brown hair that fell beneath his red Cardinals cap.

"Have you been thinking of hurting yourself?" John asked.

"Why do you want to know? So you can try to shove me in the hospital? I ain't fucking going there. I'll tell you that right now."

"I want to know because I care about you and I want to understand what you're going through." John eased back in his chair. "If you're honest and talk with me, I'm pretty sure we can work our way through this without worrying about any hospitals—that's not where I want you either. So, have you been think-ing of hurting yourself?"

He stared at John for a good minute. "Yep."

"You know, you've been making a whole lot of progress, Andy. You've got a really nice apartment that you've had for six months now. You're not drugging any more, you've cut way back on drinking. That's a lot of impressive changes, but sometimes when good things start happening, it scares and overwhelms us. I wonder if something like that is happening to you?"

"That's not it."

"So, what do you think is stressing you now?"

"Ashley," Andy said. "She's pregnant."

For an instant, John felt jealous, wishing Claire was pregnant before he rec-ognized that was a ridiculous reaction as a therapist. He silently chided himself for being narcissistic instead of empathic. "That's a lot of responsibility all of a sudden, isn't it? A lot of pressure?"

"No—she's going to have an abortion."

"Oh, I see."

"My baby is going to be dead before I ever see him."

"I'm so sorry." John sensed Andy's sadness as well as some of his own, though he knew Andy loathed to ever admit any emotion but anger. "So, you want the baby—have you talked with her about it?"

"She doesn't hear anything. She says she doesn't want anything to do with me anymore—that it was all just a big mistake."

"That hurts," John said. "You care about her."

"*Fuck* her." Andy tugged on the bill of his baseball cap.

"Maybe she's talking out of her fear now, saying things she doesn't mean."

"She means it. So, I say, fuck it. Why put up with this shit? Why even bother, you know?"

John nodded. "She's hurt you, so now you feel like hurting yourself."

"I just feel like killing myself."

"I know—it's an automatic reaction for you. It's part of the pattern you learned in your family, with your grandfather and uncle taking their own lives. The challenge for you is to break that self-destructive family pattern."

"Doesn't matter." Andy stared at him. "I'm not having a baby."

"I know this is really rough. Children give us hope, and through them we see that life can be better," John said. "I'm very sorry, Andy, it's a painful situation, for sure, but I have lots of hope for you and your life. Things will be better."

"Doubt that."

"And who knows? You may have other children in the future. Plus, think about the family you do have, especially your grandmother, but also your mom. How do you think they'd feel if you took your own life?"

He scratched his scraggly goatee. "They'd be upset for a while. But then they'd forget. Nobody would care."

"So, you *feel* like your family wouldn't care."

"No one would care."

"Really?" John leaned forward. "Not even your grandma?"

"Maybe for a bit, but she'd forget. You don't know them like I do."

"Let's say you're right about them. But I know I would care. I care about you a whole lot, Andy. I don't want to see you die."

"You'd forget too."

"Andy." John paused, waiting until Andy made eye contact. "Is it really so hard to believe that I truly care about you and your life?"

"You'd forget."

"Out of sight, out of mind, huh? Maybe other people have been that way with you," John said. "But that's not me. You, your life, are important to me."

"That's what you say now, but you wouldn't feel that way after a time."

"Suicide sticks with the people left behind—family, the people who care about the person who kills himself. It leaves an "emotional skeleton" in the lives of the family—that's how one researcher described it."

"People always forget about the dead. It's been seven years since my uncle killed himself and ten since my grandfather did. Everybody in the family was real upset when they died—but you know what? Nobody is now. Truth is that nobody thinks much about you after you've been dead for a while."

Something sickening twisted inside John's stomach. He remembered Emerson—then Nona. As much as he loved them, especially Nona, he didn't think about her every day the way he had for the first few weeks after she'd died. He felt both horror and self-disgust. He didn't know what to say.

A long silence passed over them—Andy was staring at him—and then John let his clinical training take over. He asked Andy if he had a suicidal plan, and then suggested a safety contract and tried to convey empathy and hope. He sounded to his own ears like he was on therapy autopilot, but Andy agreed not to hurt himself for at least twenty-four hours and to stay overnight in the crisis shelter.

When they walked out of his office, Andy went to the bathroom. Bennie, who was hovering close by, flashed John a wide, white grin. "You work some of your doctor magic?"

"He agreed to talk more later and to stay here tonight in a crisis bed, but we need to watch him closely and provide a lot of support." John turned back to his office, biting his lip to fight an urge to confess to Bennie that he'd never before felt so impotent as a therapist.

John sensed Claire on the far side of the mattress. He raised his head, spying over the two fluffy pillows that lay end-to-end and separated him from Claire, and he saw the back of her head. He glanced at the clock, which showed 5:52—thirty-eight minutes before the alarm was set and more than six hours before his flight departed. He pulled away the barricade of pillows, scooted across the mattress, and gently cuddled Claire.

She stirred, stretching.

"Good morning, love," he whispered.

She grunted.

He rubbed her upper back through her flannel pajamas. "You awake?"

"Half awake. Been for a while. The damn birds woke me up early again."

He kissed the back of her neck. "I'm going to miss you on this trip."

"San Diego should be a nice trip for you," she said.

"Yeah, but I wish you could come."

"Too much to do at work." She threw back the covers and clambered toward the bathroom. "Good luck on your presentation."

He watched her disappear from the bedroom. He lay still, closed his eyes. She was still withdrawn, a radiating impact from her despair about her grandfather's stroke. He understood her despair, but her reaction felt all too familiar, both to their own history and to his childhood with his mom. He debated whether to try to engage her again or to fall back asleep. After a few minutes, he forced himself up.

The bathroom was filled with warm, moist air from the running shower. He took off his boxers, pulled back the shower curtain, and stepped into the tub behind Claire.

"What are you doing?"

"It's okay," he said, grabbing the soap bar and rubbing her back. "Just your friendly shower valet, giving you special treatment this morning." He planted his lips on her shoulder.

"Stop." Her tone was sharp.

"What's the matter?"

Claire turned, rinsed the soap off her back, and punched the shower knob; the water ceased. "I don't want to have sex, that's what."

"That's not very romantic," John said. "Not to mention a little abrupt."

"Sometimes being abrupt is the only way you hear me." She patted herself dry with a terry cloth bath towel.

"I just thought it would be nice to make love this morning before I have to leave town, that's all. You know, we haven't made love in over a week, almost ten days."

"I haven't wanted to."

"Claire, we're not going to get pregnant through abstinence."

"I'm so sick of that." She stepped out of the tub.

"What?"

"*Trying* to get pregnant."

"Claire, stop." He strode out of the tub, too, stepping next to her on the bathmat.

"Maybe you should have married a twenty-five-year-old with young eggs who would screw you every day and pop a baby right out."

"God," he said. She had this ridiculous theory that her eggs were too old and that's why they hadn't conceived. She had even asked her OB/GYN who replied there was no medical support for that possibility, but Claire still hung onto the idea. Her irrationality had puzzled John until he figured out she was feeling inadequate as a woman—an old insecurity for Claire that still lingered, despite all of her posturing as a confident female. "Why do you have to be so difficult?"

"Why do you have to be so persistent all of the sudden about having a baby?"

"Because." He thought of Nona, and then of other people he had lost. He did not want to pressure Claire—he knew she would react defensively—but still he needed something—or someone—to overcome his despair. "Because it's what we decided we wanted. But forget about the baby now. It would just be nice to make love, you know, to be close, before I have to leave town."

"You want to have an orgasm?" She flipped her towel back onto the rack and stood naked before him.

"Well, I did before we started arguing." He looked her in the eyes and swallowed. "Like I said, it would be nice."

"It's my body and I'll do with it as I feel. But here." Claire reached for his hand and pulled it to his penis. "Jack off then."

He jerked his hand away. "It *is* your body," he said. "But why do you have to act the part of the asshole so often?"

She slammed the bathroom door behind her on the way out.

CHAPTER 34

John searched again through the piles of folders on top of his desk for the recent review on teenage mental health problems. The article was rich with substantive findings that he wanted to anchor the introduction for his San Diego presentation but even a third time of flipping through the folders still failed to yield the paper.

"Shit!" He slammed the folder he was holding, thick with papers, onto the floor. Pages fluttered across the linoleum like pigeons scattering in a public square.

He was surveying the mess of papers, hands on his hips, when a knock tapped at his door.

"Come in."

Crystal, who worked on the grants as a research assistant, slipped into his office.

"Sorry to disturb you." She examined the strewn papers on the floor, a quizzical look on her face. "You okay?"

"Yeah. Just having a little temper tantrum, I guess."

"Hmm. Something you learned from one of our younger clients, like Gerald or EEJuan? They usually model temper tantrums daily." She managed a faint if sad smile. Crystal had worked at Our House for less than a year. She had a master's degree and was clearly very bright and competent, but she was quiet and hard to get to know. Bennie had complained once to John that she was stuck up, but John had pointed out she flashed a witty though ironic sense of humor on occasion and he said she was probably just shy. Privately, he thought she seemed wounded, and he wondered what had happened in her life to make her retreat.

"Not sure I can blame my acting out on them, but it was definitely juvenile."

She kneeled down and collected the loose papers on the floor.

"Thanks," he said, "but you don't have to do that. I can clean up my own messes."

"I got it. What's the matter?" she asked.

"Oh, no big deal," he said. "Just can't find a damn article I need for my pre-sentation and I'm running out of time to pull the talk together." He shook his head. "Guess I probably shouldn't have left this presentation to the last minute, huh?"

"You worked long hours last week talking Andy through his suicidal crisis. Not sure what else you could have done."

"That's true, thanks," he said. "At least he seems better now."

"A lot better," Crystal said. "I did a research interview with him yesterday and he actually sounded great."

"Good. Now all I have to worry about is what I'm going to say for twenty minutes in San Diego."

"Maybe this will help." She handed him a new file folder along with the one he'd thrown on the floor. Inside, John found four tables and corresponding overhead displays summarizing preliminary data from their current research project.

"Crystal, this is great. I was going to try to work up something like this before flying out but I'm not sure I would have had the time to pull it together. Thank you."

"Least I can do." She flipped a strand of her long brown hair away from her face. "What article are you looking for?"

John told her.

"Got it. Be right back."

She spun on her heels and walked out. John was glad a satisfied smile had slipped across her face. An aura of something like sadness seemed to surround Crystal, but she exuded a spark when she was engaged in her work.

He was looking over the data tables when she returned. She laid a copy of the article at his fingertips.

"Here you go," she said.

"That was quick, thanks."

"Had it right on my desk from when you copied it for the research staff a few weeks ago."

"Sitting in your 'to read' pile?"

"No, I read it right away." Her face blushed.

"Sure." Lately he liked to tease her. "Of course you did."

"Really. I just made you a copy from my copy. See." She leaned over his shoulder and pointed to a scribbled note in the margin. "There's your notes and . . ." She drew her fingertip to much neater handwriting beneath his. "And my notes from when I read it."

"I was just kidding." As he glanced up at her, a strand of her long hair fell across his cheek. "Thank you—I really do appreciate all of your help. Not sure I've told you this before, but you are a great addition to the research team."

She gazed at him, and her dark, brown eyes softened with a look of appreciation or maybe it was affection. A slight smile escaped her lips, but then she pulled away and her expression became serious or sad or maybe both. "You're welcome."

After she had left his office, he couldn't help himself from recalling the sensation of her hair against his cheek: it had felt almost like a caress, and her eyes had shimmered with some deep emotion—it was as if she had lowered a barricade, and for a moment an unexpected intimacy had connected them, but then she pulled away. He wondered if it was just his imagination—a fantasy fed by his frustration with Claire and his pattern of beginning to look around when a relationship felt stuck and boring? He turned to his work and scribbled a note for his presentation on a blank page. He remembered Claire telling him that morning he needed to be with a younger woman who'd have sex with him every night and pop a baby right out. Claire was wrong—it wasn't just about a pregnancy or even sex. He missed something else—a feeling of passion, or connection—he wasn't sure what to call it because the desire seemed beyond his words, but the sensation he longed for was seductive, and he'd sensed the feeling for an instant with Crystal. He enjoyed a fleeting fantasy of kissing Crystal, but then the realization intruded: she might just be an easy distraction from having to face the distance from Claire. He dismissed all of these thoughts; they were allowing him to procrastinate from the work he had to do. He glanced over the note he had written the moment before, but now it made no sense. He crumpled up the paper and threw it hard into the wastebasket. After years of baseball pitching, his shoulder hurt with the motion, but he knew he could no more think of leaving Claire for another woman than amputating his throwing arm.

After his San Diego presentation, John hurried back to this hotel room, stripped off his suit, changed into gym clothes, and headed to the hotel gym. He pumped out reps on the bench press, resting only for a brief interlude between sets. He felt a burst of energy, realizing he had no responsibilities for the next two days at the conference, save going with two Missouri state mental health administrators to tour a local residential program on Friday. He waited at the leg press for the blond woman to finish.

She stood up, turned around, and then smiled broadly. "Well, hello," she said in a British accent.

"Hello."

"You're here for the mental health conference, aren't you? A presenter, I believe?"

"Yes, John Anderson." He extended his hand.

She took it snugly in hers. "Anastasia Sokolov."

"Have we met?"

"Not formally, but we nearly bumped into each other in the conference ball-room. You wore a speaker's red ribbon on your name tag."

John was surprised he didn't remember her. She was young, probably late twenties, and strikingly beautiful. Her long hair was tucked along one side of her neck and draped down her tight, black workout top.

"Have you presented yet?" she asked.

"Yeah."

"How did it go?"

"Okay," he said. She looked at him with an inquisitive, sideways nod of her head, as if she wanted to hear more. "Not my best presentation to be honest—I didn't prepare as much as I'd wanted, but it was fine overall and there were a lot of thoughtful questions and comments from the audience, so that was good."

She asked the topic, and he said mental health services for runaway and homeless youths, and then asked if she was giving a presentation. She laughed, saying she was still finishing her undergraduate degree in psychology at Sussex in England, though she was hoping to go on for at least a masters and maybe a doctorate. She described herself as a "mature" student, and he took this as an English expression meaning she had previously taken time off from college and was a bit older than most undergraduates. She was attending the conference with her father, she said, a psychiatrist who'd emigrated from Russia the past year to Minneapolis to work for a managed care company.

"Your father is from Russia and you're from England?"

"Yes, and Russia. I lived there after I was born until I was fifteen, at least most of the time. My mother's British and we lived in England with my grandparents when my mom was pregnant with my sisters and then for a few summers after that. Then we lived permanently in England after my parents divorced. Do you mind spotting me?"

She stepped to the squat rack and shouldered the bar. He stood behind her, squatting as she bent at the knees. Her thighs and butt were firm and full, but not fat in the least. He watched her face in the mirror as she squatted the next rep.

She held her head high, concentrating, exhaling as she rose up. Her breasts were round, like taut balloons, under her workout top.

She thanked him for the spot, saying she'd like to return the favor. She sounded determined, and so he asked if she would hold his shoulders while he did lat pulls. She pressed strong hands onto his shoulders, anchoring his body while he pulled down the weight. They took turns spotting for each other, talking as they lifted.

"Are you liking the conference?" he asked.

"Yes. Especially the presentations on cognitive-behavioral therapy. It's a very effective treatment, don't you think?"

"Yes, for many clients."

"And you? Do you like the conference—you must go often, presenting and all."

"It's good to hear what other people are doing, but you know it gets kind of old, holed up in windowless conference rooms in the bowels of hotels where you never see blue skies or sun."

"I imagine so. We've been here two days and I've already begun to feel that way. I'm taking tomorrow off for an excursion into Baja."

"Sounds much better than more research symposia."

"Yes, absolutely. A Jeep drives into Baja, to a small village, and then you go on horseback to a secluded beach."

"Sounds really fun."

"Yes. Why don't you go too? It's just me—my father's attending more meetings."

John thought of reasons why he shouldn't go. He hemmed and hawed, starting to make an excuse, but then he gazed at her. To his surprise, he heard himself agree.

"Wonderful! I have to shower and meet my father for dinner in twenty minutes. But I'll meet you in the lobby at eight o'clock in the morning."

She was gone before he could change his mind.

The Jeep turned out to be an old Toyota pickup with metal scaffolding added to keep the tourists from bouncing out over the Mexican potholes. John worried about getting carsick, but his stomach felt fine and he figured the open air and sitting across from Anastasia were effective antinausea remedies.

"The fear of snakes is the most common phobia, isn't it?" She peppered him with psychology questions. He figured she was still decompressing from her recent term exams and there was an innocence and charm to her questions that made the conversation delightful.

"Yes, I think you're right. Fear of snakes and fear of public speaking are the most common, if memory serves me correctly."

"The fear of snakes, don't you think there is something ethological about that?"

"What do you mean?"

"Early men and women needed to fear poisonous snakes to survive, and it became an adaptive trait that self-selected over generations."

"I've never thought of it that way before, but it makes sense."

The pickup was cramped, filled by a German couple and their elderly parents; a thin, bookish health care economist from the Northeast with his sister; Anastasia and John; and the Mexican guide. The others banded together in their original cliques while Anastasia talked to John about Wolpe and systematic desensitization and the efficacy of behavioral therapies, especially with the inclusion of cognitive interventions. He listened and nodded, murmuring "mmm-hmm" intermittently, but his attention drifted from her words to her presence. She smiled wide and her hair—a pure, Scandinavian blond, not a dirty blond— glowed in the sunlight. She was beautiful, like a model, a Swedish model, he thought, remembering a public television documentary about early Viking tribes conquering and settling Russia.

The pickup rumbled down a hill and into a small village. Barefoot Mexican children ran in the road after the truck. "*Dulce, dulce,*" they cried. The guide, a tall and dark-skinned man in his early fifties named Eduardo, tossed a handful of hard candy wrapped in bright cellophane against the cracked asphalt road; the children scrambled after the pieces. The driver turned onto a dirt road and the truck's tires kicked up a billowing cloud of brown dust. He lurched to a stop in front of a stable constructed from wooden posts and rails and a roof patched together from scrap tin. The sweet stench of horse manure made John's nose and eyes itch.

Eduardo spoke rapidly in Spanish to a short man with sinewy forearms who barked orders to three stable hands who led horses out to the tourists. A teenage boy lengthened the stirrups for John's long legs, then held the brown stallion steady. John mounted the horse, glancing at Anastasia next to him atop a huge, elegant white horse. She patted the side of his long neck. "He's beautiful," she said. "Isn't he?"

The teenage boy jumped on a gray stallion and led the gang of tourists past the stable, four hens and a rooster, and up a hoof-pocked dirt path.

They rode past two adobe shacks, where black-and-white spotted pigs rooted through the brown dust, and then through an open field. The field was strewn with empty tin cans, an orange juice carton, and other debris that smelled of rotting garbage. Eduardo explained this was a shortcut to save time getting to the beach.

They rode for thirty minutes before the echo of the ocean rose above the brown hills. The trail wound around a ridge and emptied onto a white beach and the gray-blue waves of the Pacific smelled of saltwater. The teenager led the riders to the damp sand where the tide had receded. The ocean, enormous, broken in white caps, spread out into the horizon.

"Our guide," Eduardo's high-pitched voice broke the moment, "says you can run your horses down the beach."

"What do you say?" Anastasia grinned.

"I don't know." John looked at the rest of the group. The Germans and the economist and his sister were all declining.

"Let's do it," she said to John. "Come on."

She laughed, gently prodded her horse with her feet, and gathered the reins. She galloped across the sand, and he chased after her. He bounced wildly but clung tight to the horse. Sand flew up from her horse's hoofs, spraying onto his face. He guided his horse left, gaining ground on Anastasia, but she saw him and dashed the reins against her horse. Her laughter rolled over the surf.

The beach narrowed; cliffs pinched the sand against the ocean. Anastasia glanced over her shoulder, her horse a neck ahead. The cliffs were less than fifty yards away and outcrops pocked the sand. She banged her legs harder against the horse, and he galloped faster. John pulled up on his reins while Anastasia and her white stallion ran straight ahead, toward the rocks. He yelled for her to stop. She jerked the reins, running the horse into an ebbing wave.

"Good boy." Anastasia patted the neck of her white stallion, guiding him back to the strip of sand. The horse lowered his neck, sniffing a string of bulbous brown seaweed that had washed ashore. Anastasia leaned ahead, unfolding at her waist; she stretched across the horse's neck. "Wonderful, wasn't it?"

The Toyota pickup found a bumpy but faster road home. The wind had picked up and it was difficult to hear. Anastasia sat across from John and they shouted a few words back and forth, but mainly they watched the countryside and each other. Her long hair glistened pure blonde in the sun, her skin a light brown tan. The pickup crossed the border, entered the freeway, and left them curbside at the hotel as the clouds turned tangerine at sunset.

He offered Anastasia his hand to help her from the truck. She held his hand for a moment, squeezing it, but jumped on her own to the ground.

"I am so sorry," she said. "But I have to hurry. We're late, and I promised my father I'd go to dinner with him and some old friends from Russia. It's our last night before we fly our separate ways tomorrow."

"I understand."

"He leaves in the morning, but I don't have to check out until after one. We could go for a swim together and have lunch afterward, if you're game."

"I'd love to, but I can't." He told her of a site visit of a local residential program he'd committed to going on with two Missouri state mental health administrators who funded his own program.

"I see," she said.

"I really wish I could."

"Me too." She let her gaze linger.

"Yeah."

"If your plans change, I'll be free after nine thirty and at the pool or in my room until the airport shuttle comes at one thirty. Do you have two business cards?"

He pulled them from his wallet and she wrote her address, and phone number on one, handing it back.

"If you can't make it in the morning, look me up in Europe during your next international conference. And if not," she said, smiling, "then it's not our destiny." She raised up onto tiptoes, and kissed his cheek, her lips pressing tight and warm against his skin. She turned then, slipped into the lobby, and disappeared into an elevator.

The rest of the night, John was absorbed by thoughts of Anastasia. He saw her sitting high on the white horse, like the television commercial that had captivated him as a boy of an English lady riding up to a man with a bottle of British Sterling cologne atop a silver platter, leaning down in her low-cut gown, kissing him. Perhaps that was the attraction, he thought, but then he corrected himself: it was more than a childhood association. There was an allure to Anastasia, to her beauty and adventurous nature, which stirred something deep inside him. He imagined seeing her in the morning, swimming together, then ending up in her room, wet skin slippery and muscles taut against each other, grinding and pounding against each other in the intensity of sex. He wondered then, what he really desired? Was it affection and acceptance, or intimacy and love, or just losing himself while gleefully fucking with abandonment? He was confused, for all those things felt intertwined in a way that he could not separate. In any case, he returned to his fantasy, imagining Anastasia unfolding at the hips, lying across his chest after their orgasms, just as she'd stretched across the horse's neck.

She knew he was married—he'd mentioned it—but it didn't seem to bother her. In the pickup truck, she'd told him she used to ride a motorcycle with an old boyfriend until, after an accident, her mother had made her promise she'd ride no more—but then she'd taken up skydiving. "I'm a risk taker," she'd said, with a sly smile.

But what about Claire? If she found out he had slept with another woman, it would end their marriage for good. But how would she find out? She was two thousand miles away, he thought. But maybe Anastasia would call or write a love letter, and then what? And even if Claire didn't find out, it was wrong.

He told himself to stop fantasizing. It was absolute craziness to throw away years of a relationship with Claire over a sudden infatuation. Although it would be immature and self-defeating, the impulse to pursue Anastasia felt nearly over-whelming. It was an old pattern he realized, of wanting to find favor with some new, beautiful and exciting female, and he thought of how his mom used to tell him as a child he was going to be a ladies' man when he got older. Perhaps originally that was his mom's idea, but it had merit.

He flipped off the television and tried to sleep but he found he was touching his fingertips lightly to his cheek, sensing still the warmth of her lips against his flesh.

Despite his self-admonishments, he was haunted by dreamy images of Anastasia who he imagined was stretching across the horse's neck, and then lying across his own body, smiling down at him. There was something about her smile that was arresting. He lay awake thinking about it in the dark. Her smile lingered—no, it more than lingered—it penetrated him, opening him and touching something deep inside that was dormant but yearning to awake.

He slept fitfully, disturbed by the choices to be made and excluded, and was fraught with angst in the morning. In his mind, he changed his plans several times, but then joined the state administrators in the lobby for the visit to the community mental health center. They met with the local director, toured the residential program, and were making lunch plans when on impulse he announced he had to get back to the hotel to meet another colleague. He caught a cab, ran up the stairs, and stared at the clock shining 11:34. He dialed Anastasia's room extension. He let the phone ring twice, and then pressed down the receiver.

He changed into his swimming trunks. Then he yanked them off. He needed more time to think, he decided—and a clearer perspective. Perhaps he was misreading her, but he thought it was pretty certain that if he saw her now, they'd end up in bed together. He realized he could always rendezvous with Anastasia in Europe for an international conference—that was the safer course; it gave him more time to think. He pulled on his gym shorts and shoes and slipped back down the stairwell.

He ran across the downtown streets, jammed with cars, to the harbor. He ran along the wharf. The water along the pier was dark green, and a red-and-gold arched French fries box and a small white fish—dead and on its gill—floated together on the surface.

An impulse to turn around, to sprint back to Anastasia's hotel room, overcame him. He imagined her smiling at her door, him kissing her beautiful lips, feeling the tumble of clothes, the grapple of naked bodies, and the rapture of making love and feeling totally alive.

No, he told himself. Something had to be wrong with him for being obsessed with sexual fantasies about a woman he'd just met. But maybe the problem was really with Claire and their marriage? They had planned in their life together to do so much. In graduate school they swore to always live passionately, to go on adventures, to travel to the source of a river. But they had done none of those things. They had fallen into deep ruts, even having sex by the thermometer, and now Claire was tired and withdrawn.

He wondered if it was inevitable: relationships grow old and decay. He hated the thought, and then he blamed himself too. He had become too wrapped up in work, with grants and research papers and conference presentations, bustling about work in a frenzy like an insect flying around a light. He had been moving so fast he was losing himself and withdrawing from Claire. He was carrying on like he was on autopilot or like some fucking robot.

He remembered Zorba and Tevye. He and Claire had watched both movies twice. They were real men, he thought, men who lived with passion and purpose. They possessed the fire of life and they kindled the same flame in the people around them.

A deflated feeling descended over John. He was no Zorba or Tevye. He only watched them on video, lying in bed on a Friday night with Claire.

But he should be more like them, he told himself, instead of a coward, avoiding life. He wondered what they would do. Zorba would sprint back and make love to Anastasia, he knew. Tevye would pray to God.

John glanced at his watch. There was still time to race to the hotel and make love with Anastasia before she left.

But wouldn't that be one more retreat from Claire? Still a chickenshit, he thought. Wasn't Claire the one he needed to embrace in a passionate life—not some young woman he barely knew?

He spied a pay phone on the corner. He darted through the boulevard traffic and called Claire's office. The secretary said she was in a meeting, but John told her it was important and asked her to get Claire.

"What's the matter?" Claire's voice was rushed.

"Claire, I've been thinking. I've been thinking about how we've been lately, and well . . . The truth is that I've been an ass and I think you've been an ass sometimes too."

There was nothing, only silence, but then Claire's belly laugh roared across the telephone lines.

"You're calling me for this?" she spat.

"Yes, and to say I want things to be different. Claire, I love you, but we've been going through the motions. Maybe it's because we've been frustrated with trying to get pregnant. I don't want to try anymore. I want to make love, if that's what we feel, not breeding by the thermometer like animals."

"That's what I've wanted for weeks," she said.

"But it's more than that, Claire. We need more time together, time that's unique, that's adventurous, time to break out of the rut. We need to take that trip to the source of the river together."

"There's no time."

"There is. We can just add it to our trip for your grandfather's birthday."

"It's too hard to cancel private practice clients."

"Claire, we need to make the time. We can fly out Thursday instead of Tuesday—that's only missing two more work days, plus we'll have another weekend."

"I don't know."

"Claire, have you ever considered you're being a bit rigid? I mean, how can I put this differently, less critically?" He remembered Claire talking him into their first canoe trip years before. "I know," he said. "Do you really want to stay in St. Louis, working just like every other day? Or do you want to open up to life, to what's really important? Will you join me, instead, be my partner and embrace a new adventure—and in so doing, embrace this man who loves you passionately with a full and open heart?"

"That sounds theatrical," she said. "And vaguely familiar."

"Undoubtedly, it is a tad theatrical and it should be familiar, as that's basically what you asked of me years ago when we went canoeing for the first time."

"So, you're mocking me?"

"No," he said. "Just reminding you of who you are."

"You think so, huh?"

"Yes, absolutely. And this trip together to the source of the river is absolutely and definitely what I want—and you want it, too, down deep in your soul, Claire Elizabeth Evers Anderson."

There was silence for a moment before she finally spoke. "You drive me crazy sometimes."

"Better crazy and alive than sane and half-dead," he said. "What do you say? Will you join me as a partner in this adventure?"

She laughed in a way that was familiar, though he had not heard it in some time; her laughter was deep, but not so much rising from the belly as full-hearted. "I say yes," she said. "I'll be your partner for adventure."

CHAPTER 35

Northern Arizona, sculpted into cliffs of salmon and chalk white and broken by the thinnest of two-lane highways, stretched through the Navajo Nation as far as John could see.

"I'm glad we came, Claire."

She stared at the knitting needles and yarn on her lap.

"I had been obsessing over whether it was the right decision," he said. "But it feels good to see all of this. It's a wonder."

"Forty-one, forty-two, forty-three." She said nothing more, but her lips moved without sound.

He looked at her.

"Sorry," she said in a moment. "I was starting a new line and had to count stitches." She was trying to finish the sweater for her grandfather in time for his birthday.

"This is beautiful here," he said.

She surveyed the landscape and smiled. "It is gorgeous."

"I want us to see as much as we can," he said. "But I just wanted us to make sure we have enough time on this whirlwind vacation to canoe up river."

"I know. We should." There was a bite to her words and the knitting needles clicked sharper.

Even though his impulse was to keep talking when she seemed upset, he decided saying less was better than saying more this time.

As they drove west, a formation of red and white rock rose from the desert like a monument and stood stark against the surrounding flat land. At both corners of the butte, white talus slopes formed the shape of the legs of a sculpted lion.

"Claire, look at that. That's incredible."

"Amazing," she said.

"Get the camera and let's take a picture out the window."

"No, let's stop and explore."

"Claire, we don't have time."

"I'm not going to snap a picture out the window as we whiz by at eighty miles per hour. The picture would mean nothing. You can't capture it—you need to sense it."

He braked hard and veered across the empty highway, pulling her mom's car off the road. A protest was forming in his mind, but he suppressed the argument. They'd argued enough already for one vacation and they were only on their third day of the trip. After Claire had unilaterally told her family that they would go with them from Utah to attend her great-aunt's seventy-fifth wedding anniversary in New Mexico, John had complained bitterly that they wouldn't have enough time for their river trip before her great-grandfather's birthday party back in Utah, but Claire insisted that they go. They'd compromised by driving from Utah to New Mexico in a separate car from the rest of her immediate family and by leaving early for their canoe trip.

They walked across four hundred yards of desert under a slipping but still hot sun to the foot of the butte. Red and white colors radiated from the rock.

"It's beautiful, these colors," John said. "And it looks like the sphinx—see the corners are shaped like legs and paws. It's amazing."

"Even more amazing than the sphinx because nature, not man, carved it."

They walked to the lion's leg of white rocks. Claire peered at the butte, absorbed with a look of rapture.

"What are you thinking, Claire?"

"It's a magical place. I can feel the presence of spirits here very strong, can't you?"

"Not exactly." He could hear the undertone of sarcasm in his words, and yet simultaneously a childlike hope stirred that Claire's perception was accurate.

She strolled along the base of the rock, staring upward, engrossed. He wandered around the side. Toward the back, the shape of the formation changed from sheer cliff to a slope that was steep but gradual enough to climb. He considered hiking up with Claire; it would be a grand place to look over the land and see the sun set. For an instant, he sensed a connection with the place; maybe *there* was something more, something spiritual as Claire suggested, but he wasn't sure if he believed this or not.

"John," Claire yelled. "John?"

"Yeah?" He trotted back.

"I didn't know where you went. Ready to go?"

He debated whether to tell her they could climb the butte from the backside and watch the sunset. He worried they could slip on the steep slope. At the least, they would lose more driving time. He said nothing.

The image of the rock formation stayed in his mind as he drove west. The place was beautiful—but there was something more, something ineffable. He glanced at Claire. She was quiet and transfixed on her knitting, as she had been most of the drive. He worried then something was bothering her—was it about their relationship? Or maybe their upcoming river trip was touching old grief over her father? John wasn't sure—perhaps both possibilities were true—but he sensed she was distant and didn't want to talk.

Claire had acted very differently at her great-aunt's seventy-fifth wedding anniversary—flitting about, gabbing with a score of relatives he'd never met, laughing away. At the party she had exuded an energy, a spark that he knew she possessed, and he hoped her passion would extend to him when they returned to their hotel room, but then she was tired and just wanted to fall dead asleep.

He gazed through his car window at the distant mesa. This mesa was larger, continuous, not broken into a smaller sphinx-like formation like the butte they'd just left, but the land was still outrageous—its pink, deep red, and white colors splashed together as if they'd been spread across an enormous palette. He tried to lose himself, to be absorbed in the colors of the mesa, but gnawing inside was something disquieting. He tried to push the feeling away, but it kept pulling on him, and he wondered if he placed too great of demands on his relationship. Perhaps he was expecting Claire alone would fulfill him, satisfying his yearnings—not just for intimacy, but for meaning within the crazy chaos of life? He had a horrible sense that was, indeed, true. He tried to refocus on the grandness of the desert surrounding him, and yet inside he felt little and weak; something had left him inexplicably scared and feeling inherently deficient. He hated the feeling—it was so different than what he'd felt at the butte, where he sensed something expansive, maybe even magical. He wanted to shake the feeling of being small and weak. He wanted to lose it in something bigger, better than himself.

"We need to go back to that rock," he said.

Claire cocked an eyebrow high on her forehead. "Why?"

"I forgot something."

"What?"

"Something important."

"What's that?"

"Trust me."

"For what?"

"Come on," he said. "Just trust me."

"I do trust you—a lot."

"Good." John slowed the car, looping a U-turn on the two-lane highway. The tires crunched desert sand as they turned around. John sped back to the butte, parked, and led Claire to the rear slope. He took her hand and started to climb. She laughed but followed him. He picked a path up the rocky, steep slope, feeling Claire's hand on his back. When they reached the top of the butte, the desert spread before them as far as they could see, bathed in the yellow light of the setting sun. Claire stood in front of him, her back pressed snugly against his chest as he wrapped his arms around her, as they watched the day fade. Soon the sun torched the sky with streaks of red that leapt from one cloud to the next.

"I love you, Claire."

"I love you too."

"I'm glad you do. It's wonderful—to hold you and watch the sun set over the desert. I just wish we could make this day last forever."

The ruby red of the sunset soon drained away, leaving the high, thin clouds a charcoal gray. He muttered he hated to leave, but they'd better start back to avoid climbing in the dark. They picked their way down the back slope of the butte, watched the last vestiges of the sunset at the foot of the huge rock, and walked back across the desert to the car in the dusk. John noticed the shadowy outline of a pickup parked in front of Claire's mother's car, and as they drew near, saw two men hunched over at the passenger's door.

The men drew back, one removing a blackjack from the car window and holding it then behind his back where it was out of sight.

"Greetings, tourists," said a short and stubby man with a potbelly and a Jack Daniel's baseball cap. "Looked like you ran into car trouble out here in the middle of the desert."

"Yeah," said the other man, a tall Native American with long black hair falling beneath a blue Dodgers hat. "Wanted to make sure everything was okay."

"Bullshit," Claire said. "You were trying to break into our car and steal our things."

"*Claire!*" John said. "No, we're fine. Thanks."

"The lady's got spunk, all right." The man pulled his Jack Daniel's cap down a little further on his head. "You're right, too, but it'll be easier with your keys." He pulled a Bowie knife from his side and brandished it at them.

John gauged the distance between them. For an instant, he contemplated attacking the man—John was taller and probably stronger—but he decided the distance was too great and there were two of them, one with a knife and the other with a blackjack. He thought, too, of running back into the desert, but he was overtaken by the image of the men catching him and Claire from behind, clubbing them with the blackjack, and stabbing the knife into their hearts. John pulled the keys from his pocket, tossing them to the man.

"Wise decision," the short man said. "But I think you forgot something."

"What?"

"Your wallet."

"Here." John pulled his wallet from his back pocket. "It's yours."

"Good boy," the man in the Jack Daniel's cap said. "Now where's the bitch's purse?"

"Don't talk to me like that," Claire said.

"Yeah?"

"Claire—" John said in a low voice.

"Yeah." Claire glared back at the robber.

The short man flinched, and then he forced a mocking laugh. "I said, where's your goddamn purse?"

"It's in the car," John said. "In the red knitting bag. Look, we don't want any trouble. Take the stuff and leave us alone."

"That's better," he said. "And smarter than your old lady—she might get you in trouble yet." He pointed the Bowie knife at them while his partner rummaged through Claire's knitting bag. He pulled out Claire's purse and wallet, took the cash, and then grabbed the camcorder case.

John thought again of rushing the man with the knife. He was a good eight inches shorter than John, but he wore snub-nosed boots that could double John over with a solid kick. John remembered Bennie's brother who was killed in a knife fight. He looked at the highway, hoping to see a passing car, but it was dark.

The Native American emerged from the car holding the camcorder to his eyes. "Hey, I always wanted one of these."

The two men laughed.

"You got what you wanted," Claire said. "Now go on."

"Shut up, bitch," the White man said. "Where's the other set of car keys?"

"We only have one set," John said.

"Sure you do."

"It's true. We borrowed the car from her mother—we're staying with them in Kayenta," John lied. "And we're already late. They're probably worried about where we are. Her mom is such a worrywart—she's probably called the police by now, afraid we've had an accident or had car trouble, asking them to look for us. She only gave us the one set."

The man scowled and tugged at the bill of his whiskey cap. "Did you see keys in the bitch's bag?"

"No."

"Check again."

The partner again rummaged through Claire's knitting bag and purse. "Nothing."

"Fuck," the other man said.

"Really," John said. "There's just the one set."

"Let's go," the tall man in the Dodgers hat said. "Get in your car."

"No," Claire said. "We're not getting in."

A terrible image of people getting forced into their cars right before getting killed, execution-style filled John's mind. True, the image was from television shows, but it still terrified him. "We're not getting in," he said. "But we're not going to try anything. Go now, while you can, and we won't follow you."

"Oh, now the big man is getting uppity too." The White man twirled his knife. "He's been so cooperative. I guess the bitch is giving him some balls. Tell him again."

"Get in the fucking car." The taller man pulled a snub-nosed pistol from his back pocket. "Now."

John's heart thumped against his sternum. He glanced at the highway, but he saw nothing but darkness. His stomach felt sick.

"Get in the fucking car, I said."

"Okay, okay," John said. "We don't want any trouble."

"No trouble, just get in the car. Both of you, this way." The short man swung open the car door.

John and Claire walked toward the open door. He gripped her hand hard and she squeezed back. She scooted across the seat and he followed, a tightness clutching at his chest. He waited.

The white man stood at the open door. "You know," he nodded at Claire. "You're a real uppity bitch."

"Go on," Claire said. "You got what you wanted."

The man laughed. "You think?" He took the pistol from his partner. "What if I kill your man? How'd you like that?"

Something squeezed John's lungs; he felt like all of the oxygen was being sucked out.

"Leave him alone," Claire said. "If you have a problem with me, then deal with me."

"That'd be too easy." He shoved the barrel of the gun against John's head. "For fifty cents, I'd shoot him dead. You got the fifty cents for the job, uppity woman?"

"No, please." Her voice quivered. "Leave him alone."

"We'll leave that to fate." He glanced at his partner. "See if she's got fifty cents in her purse. If she does, you're dead, big man."

The partner grabbed Claire's purse and rooted through loose change. "Look at that," he said. "A quarter right off. Halfway there already."

"Good start," the man with the gun said. "What else?"

"Here's a dime, and there's a nickel. And another nickel. Here's a penny—what's that, forty-six cents so far?"

"Please, leave him alone," Claire said. "You're right. I was a bitch. You win."

"And here's another coin—huh, wonder what it is?"

Numbness overtook John; it was like he was no longer there.

"Ah, crap," the partner said. "Another penny. That's it—forty-seven cents."

"You know," the man with the gun said. "I'm feeling generous today. Maybe I ought to chip in the three extra cents." He laughed.

When John heard the gun chamber cock, terror replaced numbness, and then a warm, wet, sensation overtook him.

"Look at that!" The man with the gun broke into laughter. "The big man just peed his pants! Can you believe that?" He laughed hard. "He's so scared, he pissed himself!"

His partner roared with laughter too.

"That's even better." The man pulled the gun away. "We'll just leave you here, soaked in your own pee." He was still laughing. "I don't think you'll get too far with slit tires, anyway, but if you're lying about the keys and try to come after us, we'll shoot you dead, starting with you, pee boy."

From the corner of his eye, John saw something coming toward him. He jerked away, but the blackjack slammed into his face. His eye and cheek exploded with pain, and he screamed as blood flowed around his eye. The robber laughed again, and the car door slammed shut. Claire screamed and hugged John, holding his head as blood streamed across his face. The pickup rumbled to a noisy start, and then gunned out of the desert sand and onto the highway. There was a honking of a horn and a whooping sound, like a war cry, that soon grew faint.

John and Claire rolled the car into a stop at the fishing and outfitting shop in the small mountain town two-and-a-half days behind schedule. Claire had wanted to cancel the river trip after they'd lost two days dealing with the police, the doctors, and the insurance companies, but John insisted that they continue, saying he wanted the river trip now more than ever. Claire reluctantly agreed to keep going as long as they were back for her grandfather's birthday celebration. She'd taken over most of the driving, giving his swollen eye more time to heal, but they'd lost more time on the road as she wasn't comfortable driving as fast or as late into the night as John usually did.

Inside the sporting goods store, two men in their late fifties, one with artificial flies pinned to his green vest like war medals on a soldier, talked fishing with an older man who appeared to be the store's only employee. He nodded, saying to John and Claire he'd be with them soon, but the man continued to talk fishing for at least another five minutes. John peered at the older man. He was tall, about six feet five with a long-boned face that was creased in a series of deep wrinkles around his jowls. His right cheek bore a striated track of scars— four narrow but deep old cuts. John sighed loudly. The old man looked at him but said nothing, and John looked away in embarrassment. Claire browsed the aisles and marveled at a collection of trout flies entombed within the thick-paned window case.

The older man ambled toward them, introducing himself as Andy Stone. The two fishermen watched from the front counter. John told Stone he'd talked with him over the telephone several times about renting a canoe to go up river, the last time from Arizona after the robbery, saying they'd be at least another day late.

"Yep," Stone said. "Anderson from St. Louis."

"Yes, that's right. You still have one available, right?"

"Sure do." Stone gazed at John's black eye.

"I'm sorry we're running a couple of days late." John explained they'd been robbed and mugged, pointing to his black eye. He said at this point, they only had time to rent the canoe for two, maybe three days, instead of the five they originally planned. Stone nodded again and said to follow him to the back of the shop, where he pointed out the canoes. John said they looked fine and asked again how long it would take to go up river to its source, even though he'd already quizzed him over the telephone from St. Louis while planning the trip.

"Hard to say," Stone said. "I've never been all the way up."

"Well, how far do you think it is?"

"Depends on where you start."

"From where we talked about starting."

"Probably a good day-and-a-half of paddling and portaging and then hiking. That's a guess, and it depends on exactly how far up the river starts and how fast and strong you travel."

John worried they wouldn't have enough time to make it all the way up river. "Give us your best, fastest canoe then, please."

"You want the best one?"

"That would be great."

"I'll rent you the one I use. It's at my ranch, I just got done refinishing it, but it's along the way."

John thanked him, and Claire interrupted, asking Stone about fishing along the river. She picked out a rod, tackle, and some flies to purchase. Stone telephoned his wife, and she arrived in twenty minutes to mind the store. He loaded floating and camping gear into his pickup, and John and Claire followed him through town and across two-lane roads to his ranch where they picked up his canoe, and then drove for another thirty minutes. John stared at Stone alone in his truck cab, the top of his cowboy hat nearly touching the cab ceiling. A dull ache descended over John's head while Claire talked about fishing. His eye hurt, too—not badly, but a dull throb hovered over his eye as a fuzziness swelled over his scalp. It was a beautiful day with a pine forest lining the narrow road and a strip of blue sky above. John wished he felt better—he wanted to feel excited, but his body—his entire being—sagged with fatigue and dull pain.

"You okay?" Claire asked.

"Yeah, why?"

"You're awfully quiet."

"I'm okay," he said. "Just tired."

"Aren't you excited to be here finally?"

It wasn't excitement, but more like detachment he experienced. He was watching Stone's truck and the road ahead with a mindless stare and the growing sense nothing was quite real. He tried to fight those sensations. "Yeah, I am."

"You sound so animated." Claire chuckled.

"I'm just tired from the long drive and everything, smart-ass," he said. "You know, you haven't exactly been a ball of energy or enthusiasm on this trip either. How are you feeling?"

"Okay," she said. "But we've been through a lot these past few days."

"Yeah." He nodded. "We have. But that's behind us. I mean, how are you feeling about being almost back to the river after all of these years?"

"Okay." She glanced at her knitting, clicking the needles together again. "I'm glad to be here, but it's a lot to take in, and I don't want to overthink it."

"Does that mean you don't want to talk a lot about it either?"

"You got it."

The outfitter slowed his truck and turned down a side road. For several miles, the descent was steep and winding. The road ended abruptly at a small turnout, and through the pines the river appeared. The rhythm of flowing water gurgled into the forest.

The older man pulled the canoe from his truck and Claire asked him about fishing holes. He told her of a favorite spot upstream.

"How's the hunting these days?" she asked.

"Not like it used to be, ma'am." His scarred cheek protruded with a wad of chewing tobacco. "But deer hunting isn't so bad, and the elk are coming back."

"Not like years ago, huh?" Claire asked.

"Nope, used to be plenty of elk and bighorn sheep in the mountains. And bear too."

"Really?" John asked. "Did you ever get a bear?"

"Two. And one got me." He pointed to his scars.

"What happened?"

"I was a boy, hunting with my father. A grizzly got up on me. I froze, and he took a swipe out of my cheek. He would have killed me, but my father shot him dead before he could maul me."

Stone bade them a good trip and they shoved off, paddling up river. John had wondered if he'd feel anxious on the river, but he did not; after the gun and the long drive, his phobia seemed trivial. Puffy afternoon clouds had sprung up, nearly covering the sky, and a light breeze prickled the faint hairs on his arms. He felt something inside lift and soar, rising from him and then through the gaps between the clouds where sunlight flooded the earth.

"I'm glad to be here with you, Claire Elizabeth Evers Anderson."

"Me too."

"Good."

They paddled in silence for a long time. The river was shallow but clear and it flowed easily without rapids or rocks. It cut its way through thick forest on one side and a steep, tree-studded gorge on the west. Its pristine beauty was unlike any river John could remember, yet something struck him as familiar, and he imagined it was not unlike hundreds, perhaps thousands, of other mountain rivers.

After a bend, the river narrowed and dark slate rock rose in a precipitous cliff above the river on the west bank, spilling its shadow over the deep water. The old man had described this spot as a good fishing hole. Claire made them stop in the shade so she could cast her line. In twenty minutes, she caught two small rainbows, both of which she released.

"We should get going, Claire."

"A little longer."

He was about to urge her on again when she let out a whoop of laughter. Her pole looped toward the water, the small muscles in her arms bulging. She fought the fish for a few minutes before reeling in a cutthroat trout the length of her hand and forearm.

"He's a beauty, Claire."

"Yes." She grinned. "And he's dinner."

"You're not really going to eat him, are you?"

"Sure. What do you think you do with a big trout when you're camping, city boy?"

As they paddled, John wondered again if Claire harbored a resistance, probably unconscious, about returning to the river. He guessed that somewhere in her psyche she feared the journey would dredge up old grief, which was why she seemed to be undermining the trip, first with her insistence that they attend her great-aunt's anniversary celebration, and second by her reluctance to proceed after the robbery. He had been avoiding talking about her childhood trips with her father, but now he asked if the scenery seemed familiar.

"I think we were on a different stretch of the river," she said. "But I definitely remember being up here somewhere with Dad."

"What do you remember?"

"Different things, including the first time. I was so excited about the trip, and he told me how great the fishing was, but the first day out I didn't catch a single fish. I was so disappointed, but he told me not to worry, that they'd probably just taken the day off, and he said by morning they'd be jumping out of the river at me." Claire wiped her nose with the back of her hand. "So, the next morning, guess what I woke up to?"

"A new fishing pole?"

"A huge cutthroat, about the size of this one, stuck inside my sleeping bag. 'See,' my dad exclaimed. 'What did I tell you? Jumping right out at you.' He couldn't stop laughing. He loved practical jokes."

"How is it to be here again, going up river on the trip that the two of you talked about?" John asked.

"Good."

"Is it sad at all?"

"No. Not sad. It feels right—like a way to honor him."

They camped next to the river for the night and he made himself eat a little of the trout that Claire cooked over the campfire for dinner. The mountain air dipped to a very cold temperature and they zipped their sleeping bags together. Claire cuddled close, and he wrapped his arms around her. He nuzzled his lips to her cheek, kissing her softly, and she burrowed her nose deep into his chest. He found her naked ear, softly blew a warm breath into it, and whispered to her. "Do you want to make love under the stars?"

"No," she said.

"Why?"

"I started my period."

"Oh, that's okay."

"But it feels good to cuddle," she said.

He snuggled closer and rubbed his hands through her long, thick hair, kissing her forehead. He wished they could make love—he'd fantasized about conceiving along the river, but he understood. Perhaps it was better this way: bears can smell blood and sometimes attack women during their periods—it had just happened in Yellowstone. They didn't need that. No bears, no more traumas on this trip.

He felt Claire's body twitch next to his. He envied how quickly she could fall asleep, even as he felt himself drifting into a drowsy state.

He woke up—startled by his own snoring and gasping for breath—and terrified, like he was dying for lack of air. He realized his nose was clogged. Something in the mountains was triggering his allergies. He couldn't breathe on his back.

He rolled over on his side, but the memory of the pistol being cocked, its barrel pressed to the side of his head, intruded. He could have been shot. Wasn't he within seconds of being killed? He dismissed the thought and rolled over onto his other side, forcing his attention on the choir of frogs who sang along the river.

John woke early to the yellow light of sunrise. He looked around for Claire and saw she was gone. He pulled on his clothes, called her name, and found her sitting on a water-bleached log next to the river.

"Good morning," she said.

"Good morning." John sat on the log and rubbed his face.

"How'd you sleep?"

He remembered the shards of a dream, of a bear attacking him, but the old man Stone shot the bear dead and pulled its bloody body off John. He shook his head at the crazy dream, wanting neither to talk nor think about it. "Okay, I guess. What are you doing?"

"Watching the river, the trees, the sunrise."

"Nice."

"It's beautiful."

"Glad to be here?"

"Yes. Really glad. It's good to be back on the same river that Dad and I came to. It feels like a lifetime ago and also like yesterday."

John patted Claire's leg. She took his hand in hers, saying nothing more. He watched her watching the river, the placid surface slipping by like reflections glinting across mirrored windows. It was beautiful, peaceful, he told himself, but some discomfort roiled inside his gut as he glanced at Claire's profile. He loathed the realization, but after years together, after sharing a multitude of unspeakable intimacies, there were still times when he had no idea what she was really feeling. She possessed inner places that were private and inaccessible to him, as she held up some barrier—intentional or not, he wasn't sure—that at times kept him at a safe distance, though he longed to cross it. He hated the sense of distance when she seemed upset more than anything.

Claire rose, retrieved her fishing gear from camp, and waded into the river. He watched her for a long time, glad to be with her on the river but worrying about the time.

"Claire," he called out. "This is great, but we need to get going."

"Stop."

"Claire—"

"Err!" She waved her hand as if swatting away a black fly.

"Come on, Claire. I know it's fun to fish, but the river awaits us. It's time to find the source."

"Three more casts," she said. "And then we'll go. But if you don't stop hurrying me along, I'm going to clobber you with a canoe paddle."

They paddled until midafternoon when they came to a small lake that opened up from the river. The shoreline was thick with trees except for a rocky beach on the east side where they'd entered and an opening in the west where the river flowed through. The surface was serene until the bow of the canoe split the water and ripples rolled off. They stopped paddling, letting the canoe drift.

He dipped his fingers into the cool water. "It's really peaceful here."

She nodded.

He waited a few minutes, and then told Claire they should push on.

"No. I'm not ready to go."

"It is very serene, the kind of place you could really savor."

"Dad and I hiked into this same little lake. We fished here, just the two of us. There was no one else on the lake."

"Just like now."

"Yes. Just like now."

"When was that?"

"I don't know. But that's not what was important." Her lip curled slightly, as if in the smallest twinge of annoyance. "What's important is the experience."

"What was it like?"

"It's just a sliver of a memory, but I remember being by that big rock with Dad, and struggling with a huge fish on the line, trying to reel him in. I could see him break the surface of the water as I pulled him in—he was a huge rainbow trout, blue and red and purple, glistening in the sun. I screamed, wanting my dad to wade out with the net and snag him—but he was busy laughing at me and the fish."

Claire paddled the canoe to the shore near the salt-and-pepper boulder. She walked along the water's edge, without saying anything, as if she was searching or remembering.

"This must be the lake the old man mentioned," John said. "We must be getting close."

Claire returned to the canoe and pulled out her fishing pole.

"What are you doing?" John asked

"Getting my gear to go fishing."

"I hate to say this, but we should get going. The clock's ticking."

"No." She picked out a fishing fly.

"Claire, if we don't get going, we won't make it all the way up river."

She shook her head. "We don't have time now anyway."

"We do, if we push hard," he said.

"My grandfather's birthday party is the day after tomorrow. Even now, we have lots of hard paddling and driving just to get back in time."

"I know, but we can do it. If we push on now, we should make it to the source."

"No, there's not enough time."

"We'll make up the time on the way back. I'll drive all night if we have to so we can go all the way up to the source."

"I'm staying right here." Her expression turned stern, like she was both determined and aggravated but trying not to lash out. "I'm going to enjoy this place with the time we have before we have to turn back."

"And going to the source?"

"We'll do it together another time. Or, if you really have to, take the canoe and go by yourself. See if you can make it but meet me back here in three hours."

"Claire, that's not long enough—especially just with one person paddling."

"Best I can do," she said.

"I can't fucking believe this." He remembered the gun being pulled on them in the desert, and the barrel pressing hard against his skull, which made him even angrier. "We've waited so long for this. You've wanted to do this for so long, and now you want to hold back? I don't get it."

"John, listen. This trip is something I've wanted us to do together to enjoy."

"I have."

"I don't want to keep rushing and pushing—that kills the experience. But that's how you've become, like this is some task you have to achieve. But you know what? If you do that, you miss the whole point."

"But the source—it'll be a special place."

She cast her line. "So is here—just open your eyes."

"It's important to you, I know, having been here before with your dad."

"It's not just here—it's everywhere on the river, if you open to it. You don't have to rush ahead. John, stay and enjoy this place with me before we have to go back."

"But then we'll have to hurry back anyway."

"Yes, soon. I want to be there for my grandfather's hundredth birthday. I don't want to miss that."

"You confuse me, Claire." He kicked a stone; it twirled end over end and plopped into the lake. "You know, I almost think you don't want to keep going all the way to the source—like if we did, it would destroy your sense of mystery, which you seem to need to hang onto for some reason."

"Maybe." Her lips parted wryly. "But we'll find the source, if we're meant to, another day."

He hunkered down on the boulder close to her, annoyed beyond civil words but trying not to say anything more, and confused, too, wondering if she was perhaps right, but too frustrated to know for sure.

The vibration of the plane on the first leg of their flight back home almost lulled John to sleep, but he realized he was smiling underneath his drowsy demeanor. He didn't intend to tell Claire—his feelings were still too mixed after her reluctance to keep going—but he sensed that maybe saving the trip all the way to the source of the river had worked out for the best; perhaps another time they would need the journey even more.

"Despite the calamity in the desert and our not making it to the source, I'm really glad we made this trip," he told her.

"Me too."

"Thanks for taking me to the river."

"It was good to have you there with me."

He snorted a short laugh.

"What?" she asked.

"I remember years ago when I'd ask you about your trips here with your dad and you'd stop talking to me." He reached for her hand. "We've come a long way, eh?"

She squeezed his hand.

"You know what I wish?" he asked.

"Hmm?"

"That we could make love right now."

"You're always wishing that," she laughed.

"But now I really want to. I wish I could feel every inch of you against my body, and that we were making love, eyes wide open, peering into each other's souls."

She squeezed his hand again, but neither said anything more. They changed planes in Chicago, the jet rising from O'Hare, soaring above the great lake and then banking south. Through the right airplane window, the sky was brilliant, a red-orange sunset lit the far stretches of the western horizon; to the east, the sky was black through the left window except for a full moon glowing with a vanilla sheen. Claire and John peered out both windows, watching until the sky faded to charcoal and then blackness.

"I've never seen anything like that," John said.

"Nor I."

"This trip has had all kinds of unique experiences I've never imagined—most good, one terrible."

"It has."

The plane swooned, beginning its descent toward St. Louis. John interlaced his fingers with Claire's, and craned his neck, hoping to glimpse the full moon again.

"Where do you want to be buried, John?"

"Now hush." He shook his head.

"Seriously, where do you want to be buried?" she asked.

"What makes you ask that now, for God's sake?"

"Maybe seeing my grandfather at a hundred, knowing he doesn't have much time left, or maybe visiting my father's grave or being back on the river again. I'm not sure why, but we're all going to die sometime, you know."

"I know, but that can be a long time off. With your genes, you could live to a hundred, too—probably at least a hundred-and-one—and if I take care of myself, I could live into my nineties."

"I hope not—at least not me living to a hundred."

"Don't say that, Claire." His tone was more of a plea than an admonishment.

"That's too old."

"If we lived that long, we could make love ten thousand more times—at least."

She swiveled in her seat, looking him full in the face. "I'm serious. Where do you want to be buried?"

"Claire, please. I don't want to think about it."

"Come on," she said. "It's important to me. Where do you want to be buried?"

He gazed into her eyes and sighed. "Next to you."

CHAPTER 36

When he opened his eyes, Claire was gazing at him, her lips parted in a faint smile. "Good morning."

"Hmm," he groaned and stretched. He shut his eyes again, but the image of her hair glistening in the sunlight overtook his sleepy mind. He rolled over on the mattress, closer to her. "Morning."

"I'll let you sleep longer." Her lips brushed across his cheek and then she stood up.

"Not so fast." He grabbed her hands, pulling her back to bed.

"Hey!"

"Hey, beautiful," he said. "What were you doing anyway?"

"Watching you sleep. Your eyelids were flickering a mile a minute." She rapidly opened and closed her fist to demonstrate. "What were you dreaming?"

"I was . . ." He paused, pulling back shadowy images from the edges of his consciousness. "I was dreaming I was going to the source of the river."

"Really? What was it like?"

"Beautiful. There was this river, clear with blue water tumbling down a thick-forested hill. I wasn't all the way to the source yet, but I knew it was close, just over the top of the hill."

"Was I there?"

"I think you were going to meet me there."

She nodded. "Nice."

"Yeah." Something unsettling—an unnamed anxiety or sadness that bordered longing—turned over within him. "It's cool, but it's also strange. I don't know that the dream is identical, but from time to time I have what feels like the same dream where I'm hiking through a forest, following a stream uphill, and usually you or my Grandpa Anderson are in it. It's kind of strange. Have you ever heard of those before?"

"What?"

"Reoccurring dreams."

"I've had a few therapy clients who've talked about them."

"Hey—are you saying I need therapy?"

"Doesn't everyone?"

"Good point." He threw back the covers. "Speaking of which, I'd better get to work."

She frowned. "It's a bummer you have to work on Labor Day."

"Even though it's kind of weird, it's a good dream," he said. "It leaves me in a good mood."

"That's cool."

"But you know, the next time we have to make it all the way to the source."

"We will," she said.

"Really?" he said with a trace of an edge. "No backing out next time?"

"You aren't going to let me forget this last time, are you?" She made a face. "We didn't have the time to go all the way up—plus I needed to savor the river, not rush through it."

"I know." He tried to say this without irritation. "But I really want us to do that together someday."

"We will," she said. "It's a promise."

"Good. I'm going." He swung his feet over the mattress. "And I'm not going without you."

John was anxious to see Andy though he was the last client on his list for a home visit for the day. John worried about Andy after the latest breakup with his girl-friend—they had gotten back together after the abortion conflict once Ashley said she wasn't pregnant after all. John thought it was hard to know the truth, as Ashley often lied, but Andy believed her. This was their pattern, of breaking up and getting back together, ad infinitum, ad nauseam, in a way that seemed hard to understand and yet it reminded him of he and Claire from years before. When he had talked with Andy on Friday afternoon, Andy seemed okay, and he said he was better off without Ashley, but John suspected Andy would have a delayed reaction.

John rapped on the paint-chipped apartment door and waited, but there was no answer. He knocked again, and then called Andy's name, but there was still no response. Something worrisome clutched at John. Andy had been almost perfect in keeping his appointments in recent months and on Friday John had reminded Andy he'd stop by for the home visit and then give him a ride afterward to the drop-in center where Bennie was organizing a Labor Day holiday barbeque for the clients. John pounded the front door harder and then peeked through a gap between the window curtains, but he saw no one.

The thought that something bad—maybe something *really* bad—had happened to Andy invaded John's mind. He tried to shake the thought and when he could not, he reframed it: Andy's pattern after a breakup with Ashley was to embark on a rampage of drinking and drugging, which sometimes then triggered suicidal thoughts, and that was probably what he was up to again now. John cruised the streets around Andy's apartment, passing by a liquor store on South Broadway where Andy often got his booze, and then John drove down the state streets where drugs were easy to come by. Andy had gotten drunk or high hundreds—probably thousands—of times before, and while he sometimes ended up in a psych ward or even in jail for a few days, he always got out and landed on his feet. He was a survivor.

John turned the corner and slowed his car when he saw from the backside a man with long hair like Andy talking to a teenager with a buzz cut. As John passed, he peered at the long-haired man but it became clear that he definitely wasn't Andy, and John wondered if a drug deal was going down. The teenager returned John's stare, and then raised his hand, gesturing like he was shooting a pistol at John. John sped away toward the drop-in center and reminded himself that Andy knew the streets a lot better than he did.

At least thirty clients were hanging out in the drop-in center, most eating hot dogs or hamburgers with potato salad and drinking sodas. John worked his way through the dining area, stopping here and there to check in with some of the clients, before he made it to the back patio where he expected to see Bennie flipping burgers on the barbeque. Instead, Andy—sporting a tall chef's hat that rose from his head like a cylinder—stood next to the grill.

"Hey," John said. "I was supposed to pick you up at your apartment, remember?"

"Crap," Andy said. "Forgot. I took the bus down here for the barbeque."

"It's okay." John grinned. "You look, by the way, pretty official in that chef's hat."

Andy shook his head. "This thing looks stupid, but Bennie told me I had to wear it to grill. I was going to tell him, 'No fucking way,' but then I thought, 'What the fuck'—excuse my cussing—'Why not?'"

"It's great you didn't let a rule get in the way of doing what you needed— that's exactly what it takes to hold down a job."

"Bennie said he could probably get me a job with his cousin—he owns a restaurant—if I do a good job here."

"That's promising," John said. "Where is Bennie? I didn't see him inside."

"In the kitchen," Andy nodded in the direction of the building. "Said he needed to check on Adrian who was supposed to be making more salad. But don't bring him back here—he's always looking over my shoulder, bossing me around."

John laughed but stopped himself before agreeing aloud that Bennie was bossy. "So, how are things going for you about Ashley?"

"Haven't seen her." Andy rolled the hot dogs over on the grill.

"How are you feeling about that?"

"Fine." Smoke from the coals drifted into Andy's eyes.

"It's okay to talk about your feelings, if you want, Andy."

"I'm fine," he said. "I don't need a girlfriend now."

"Well, good." John still wondered if Andy was going to have a delayed emotional reaction of loss that he'd act out in anger or self-destructiveness.

Andy wiped sweat away from his forehead with the back of his hand. "How are you doing?"

"Pretty good." John forced a laugh. "Why do you ask?"

"You worry too much." Andy stepped closer to the grill, rolling the hot dogs over again. "I got it under control."

On the way home, John stopped by the grocery store. He picked out a sack of pears for forty-nine cents a pound and rolled his cart toward the lettuce bin, thinking Andy was right: he did worry too much. He loathed to admit it to others, but he'd been a worrywart most of his life and though he hid it well at work, he worried more now than ever. Perhaps it was a vestige of the robbery in the desert—some leftover, displaced anxiety?

An older woman loomed in front of him, half-blocking the aisle. Her hair, a pale orange-red over gray roots, puffed around her head like a lampshade. She pointed to the display stand where apple chunks skewered on toothpicks were neatly arranged around the plate like numbers on a clock.

"Try an apple with peanut butter-caramel dip?" A thin smile slipped across her moon-shaped face.

John twirled a green apple chunk in the dip and plopped it in his mouth. The gooey sauce tasted sweet on his tongue next to the tartness of the apple. "It's good," he said. "Do you know its fat and cholesterol content?"

She peered through silver-framed bifocals at the jar label. "I don't see it."

He was thinking again about Andy, wondering if he'd stay sober. "That's a bad sign," John said to the woman. Something about her looked familiar. "It's usually high if it doesn't specify on the label."

"It has peanut butter, so there's probably some."

"And I think caramel is high in cholesterol. It figures," he said. "It tastes too good to be without a lot of fat and cholesterol."

"You're right."

"But they've done a lot in the last couple of years with low fat and no cholesterol versions of cookies, crackers, and even cakes that taste good." An image of his mother, carrying on a long conversation with a perfect stranger, drifted into his mind. He had poked fun at his mom a number of times for this, and now he was doing the same thing. But this old woman, vendor of apples and peanut butter-caramel, was pleasant, almost familiar, and he felt compelled to talk with her.

"They needed to do something," she said. "Lots of people need to watch their diets."

The way she shook her round head, along with her loud orange-red hair color touched a memory then of his Italian great-grandfather's younger sister, an eccentric figure who had floated in and out of his childhood. "It makes good business sense," John said. "Plus, it's socially responsible to give people the foods that help them live longer lives."

"You'd think that you'd live a longer life," she said. "But you never know— you can walk outside and still get hit by a bus."

She sounded like his great-grandfather. His mom had often said how Papa Marco had been such an anxious man, so often afraid an accident would strike and bring tragedy unexpectedly. "No guarantees, I guess, but we can still try to live the best life we can, while we can, maybe."

"You think?" The corner of her mouth twisted, as if she was trying to put on a wry smile, but it looked more like despair that crossed her face. A young woman with three tow-headed youngsters wheeled her cart in front of the apple dip stand. The older woman managed a fuller smile, bid John goodbye, and barked her peanut butter-caramel sauce spiel to the new customer.

He glanced back at her from the lettuce bin. They were not so different, he realized. He had argued the other side—that eating healthy would give you a long life while she talked about getting hit by a bus—it was a ludicrous thought, something his great-grandfather would have said aloud, or maybe that John himself would think privately. Perhaps he and this vendor were related—distant Italian cousins? The idea intrigued him and made him feel uncomfortable at the same time. He felt then like he was on the edge of slipping toward something unpleasant: was it more worry or the start of despondency? "No," he muttered in the direction of a head of lettuce. "Not today."

Claire helped him put away the groceries at home, asking John about his holiday workday.

"Good," he said, telling her about the program barbeque and Andy working the grill. "Andy can be such a tough guy, but you should have seen him in that chef's hat checking the hotdogs every few seconds. He wasn't just trying to get a good job recommendation from Bennie—it was like he wanted to make sure the food was perfect for the other clients."

"He has a good heart," Claire said, but she seemed distracted.

"He does." John closed the cupboard behind the last of the groceries. "So, how was your day? You get a lot done in the garden?"

Claire nodded. "But Lindy called with terrible news."

"What?" John feared Claire's sister was the messenger of a death in the family. "Your grandfather?"

"No. Mark left her."

"Oh, geez."

"What a shock." Claire shook her head. "People used to say what a perfect couple they were together."

"Your aunt said that a couple of times at your grandfather's birthday." Mark was Lindy's second husband. Like Claire, Lindy had married young but after a few years and one child, she had left her first husband. She and Mark had married soon after her first divorce and had been together for years. Lindy and Mark were both lawyers, smart people with sarcastic wits, who had done very well financially. They were extroverts who were a little too loud for John's comfort, but they were family by marriage and Claire adored her sister.

"How can a relationship just dissolve like that?"

"I don't know," John said, but he did know that relationships, like everything in life, could suddenly implode. Or perhaps it wasn't so sudden—maybe Lindy's marriage had decayed from within over time, like his own marriage to Joanie? "Does Lindy know what happened?"

"Lindy said he just suddenly said he wanted a divorce and left."

"That's rough."

Claire fiddled with a knife on the counter. "Actually, don't tell anyone else in the family—Lindy doesn't want anyone else to know—but Mark told her he had been so unhappy in the marriage for so long—she had no idea—he had been contemplating killing himself."

"That's scary," he said. "And sad."

"He told her he had taken his gun to his head, stuck the barrel in his mouth, and was planning on pulling the trigger when instead he decided he had to leave—that if he had to sleep with Lindy one more night, he would shoot himself."

"Oh, my God. Well, at least he didn't kill himself. I mean I'm sorry he left Lindy and what a terrible thing to say, but can you imagine a suicide by your spouse?"

"No." Claire shook her head and then stared at him. "I never want you unhappy like that. If you are, tell me and we can work it out, and if we can't, then leave me, but never kill yourself because you're unhappy with our marriage."

"Claire." He exhaled. "It's the opposite for me. I love you so much and *not* being with you is what I would dread. But why are we even talking about this? You are precious to me, and this is about Lindy." He stepped closer, took Claire in his arms, and hugged her.

Claire wiggled out of his arms. "Yes, but life can change in a heartbeat."

He shook his head. "So, how is Lindy?"

"In shock, can't you imagine?" Claire said. "And she's devastated. She said it's like her whole world totally exploded."

"She's probably feeling pretty lost right now."

"Absolutely. She was sobbing and saying she didn't know what she was going to do. I'm worried about her." She loaded a glass into the dishwasher with the hurried motion she used when stressed. "I'm going to call her back."

Claire jabbed at the telephone buttons. John thought of the apple peanut butter-caramel vendor. Perhaps occasionally she was right—random, improbable, senseless events—like getting hit by a bus—can suddenly upend your life. He had allowed himself to see this fact before—Claire had often foisted it upon him—but more often it was the slow degradation of vitality that occurs in relationships over time, not a dramatic event, that destroys the sense of feeling alive. He felt the edges of despair creeping back toward him.

"Damn it, got the answering machine," Claire said to John. She left a warm, solicitous message, asking her sister to call back.

Despair was like an addiction, he thought, becoming not only familiar but something you looked for, maybe even turned to as known and dependable in your life. Still, he pushed the nascent feeling away. *Not today.* "Claire, let's catch that movie."

"I don't know," she frowned.

"A romantic comedy," he said. "It'll do us good to get out. We could use something light about now."

"There's still time?"

"There is if we make a run for it now."

They watched the theater movie and then grabbed a snack out. It was after 10:00 p.m. when they arrived back home, and Claire hurried to check for a message from her sister.

"Shit," she yelled.

"What's the matter?"

"I forgot to rewind the answering machine," she said. "Damn it—I wonder if Lindy tried to call back."

"Well, that's not the first time you've forgotten to rewind the answering machine, is it?" He had become frustrated with her for frequently forgetting to reset the answering machine, but he felt bad for the small dig as soon as he said it, given Lindy's situation. "I hope she's okay."

"I know." She looked more annoyed at herself than him. "I'm going to try calling her again. Will you take the dogs out?"

Serendipity trotted into the darkness of the backyard beyond where John could see while Bart ambled on weak legs, peeing by squatting instead of lifting his leg. As he waited for the dogs to return, John found himself worrying again about Andy, fearing—or was it *sensing*?—that something really bad had happened. John tried to convince himself that the worries were just part of his obsessive and anxious nature, especially after the apple peanut-caramel vendor's chatter about random, tragic events.

He walked the dogs into the house where Claire was wiping down the counters. "How's Lindy—pretty upset?" he asked.

"I imagine so, but she didn't pick up." Claire scrubbed the sink harder, and then said she'd feed the dogs if he wanted to take his shower before bed.

Upstairs, John chided himself for his worries about Andy, telling himself he was being both superstitious and ridiculous. Still, he decided to give Bennie a quick call at home. Bennie answered the phone with a wary hello.

"Sorry to call you so late," John said. "I just wanted to check in to see how the barbeque ended up?"

"Oh, man." Bennie gave an exaggerated exhale. "I wondered who'd be calling so late—that usually means bad news."

"Sorry," John repeated. "We can talk tomorrow if I'm disturbing you."

"Oh no, it's okay." Bennie's voice climbed an octave. "Always glad to do whatever the program needs."

"So, how'd it go?"

"Went okay, but some stragglers need some extra close supervision." Bennie went on in detail about a few clients who wouldn't clean up their dishes and his impromptu counseling of a client who frequently asked the twice-divorced Bennie for relationship advice.

"Sounds like you handled those situations well," John said. "How was Andy doing?"

"Your boy's doing all right. He did a pretty fair job grilling but I had to get on him twice to clean up the grill—he was gung ho to cook but didn't want to clean up, but he eventually did when I kept talking to him. I need to give him more supervision in the kitchen, but there's hope for him yet."

"Thanks, Bennie. You're making a difference for him."

"I have a cousin who manages a restaurant," Bennie said. "I told Andy I might be able to get him a job as a short-order cook, but I need to see more progress before I vouch for him."

After John showered, he found Claire sitting in bed, a frown crinkling the corner of her eyes. "Did you get a hold of Lindy?" he asked.

"No," she said. "I tried again but there was still no answer. She probably went to bed and turned off the phone."

"You worrying about her?"

"Not right now, though I was earlier," Claire said.

"I know," John said. "It's upsetting."

"I can't imagine." She reached for John's hand. "I'm glad we have each other."

Something about her words—*have* each other—made him uncomfortable. She made it sound like he was an object being possessed for security, and he wanted something different—a relationship that was loving and intimate but where he also felt like he was being seen in a very personal way, as a unique individual. Whatever her words, though, and no matter what occasional, old insecurity they might reflect in Claire, he was more clear than ever before that he loved her. That is, he *truly* loved her, in a way that felt authentic, even if less intoxicating, and the thought of being without her seemed unimaginable, so he only said, "Me too."

"I was actually thinking about Bart and Serendipity right now."

"Something wrong?"

"Bart moves so slow now. He's getting weaker and his little elbows jut out like chicken wings when he walks. I know you don't want to think about it, but he doesn't have much time left, John."

"You never know."

"I know. And I worry that Serendipity will be lost without Bart after all those years."

He slipped between the sheets. "I worry about Serendipity too."

"Sometimes I hope she dies soon after Bart—you know, so she doesn't have to live without him."

"Do you really?"

"Yeah. I even give her fattier food than Bart, thinking that might clog her arteries and even out their life spans."

"Claire!"

"Sounds terrible, doesn't it? But it's hard to imagine what her life would be like without Bart."

She reached across the mattress to turn off the lamp, groaning as she stretched, complaining her back hurt after a long day in the garden. John figured this was his cue to give her a back rub. Moonlight shone into the room and he swung his legs over her body, sat on her butt, and massaged his fingers deep into her back muscles. After a few minutes of silence, she asked what he was thinking.

"You talking about Bart and Serendipity made me think of an article I was reading yesterday about Konrad Lorenz."

"What about him?"

"He used to say that people who didn't relate to animals like humans missed so much in life, that each animal is unique and special, but most people don't see that. Instead, they treat animals like objects, rather than as beings."

"What do you think?"

"I believe that. I don't mean that you should treat them behaviorally as humans—can you see Bart sitting down at the dinner table with us?"

She turned her head to the side. "He'd love it, but his table manners would be beastly."

"I mean you can relate to them as something—someone—more. Animals definitely have personalities and some people say they possess spirits."

"Do you think so?"

"Bart does. And Serendipity does. You can connect with them, not just as 'master' and 'pet' but as two beings. Do you remember that passage from Martin Buber that Dr. Whitson quoted in our psychotherapy seminar?"

"No."

"I don't remember it exactly, but Buber tells a story of when he was a boy and as he was grooming a horse, something magical happened: he and the horse connected and flowed together, as 'I-and-thou,' like two spirits in union, rather than as horse owner and horse as object. I feel that way with Bart sometimes."

"You really love that dog."

He laughed. "I used to make fun of my mom, of how she fawned over her miniature poodles, but yeah, I love Bart and sometimes I feel some sort of spe-cial—almost spiritual—connection with him."

"It's the way you relate to him—as another being."

"If you take the time, you can *see* him—not just as a dog, but you can glimpse the being between his floppy ears and beneath that tan-and-brown-and-white baggy fur—and then there's an intimacy, a connection, that sparks."

"Not everyone sees that."

"Nope. And even for people who truly see and connect with dogs—well, that's not how we relate most of the time either. It's more the exception. It's strange—it's such a fulfilling way to relate, and yet we're rarely in that way of being."

"Why do you think?"

"I don't know." He rubbed her back harder. "Maybe because we don't value that way of being very much culturally. We recognize making money or achieving something external that we can point to." He pulled her nightgown higher, bunching it up around her shoulders so he could massage her upper back and the base of her neck. "But that's probably only the most obvious factor. Maybe also life seems too intense, too awesome in its experience, and we feel puny by comparison. Maybe we're too inhibited by our low self-esteem and we fear sticking out in life, or maybe it's from our sense of vulnerability. Maybe it's just hard to stay open and so we shirk from life, from really living." He paused, noticing as if for the first time how the black moles that ran in a line next to her spine crossed with a row of moles across her lower back.

"We close down," he said. "We cut life back to a smaller, more manageable piece, to something that's familiar and routine, even if it's shredded of vitality. Perhaps we close down to the grandness and splendor of life, to the threat of loss and death and the unknown, and then we distort and compartmentalize and objectify everything, making them concrete and empirical. But then that distorts people and animals and experiences out of their spiritual context into something safe but empty." He leaned down and gently kissed the small of her back. "Did you know, by the way, and incredibly this is the first time I have ever seen it this way, that the shape of the moles across your back almost form an upside down cross, if you just fill in some of the space with your imagination."

"No," she said. "But do you know you have quite the imagination?"

He laughed and patted her back, as he always did at the end of her back rub.

"I didn't know you had that philosophy," she said.

"I didn't either. Maybe it's that way, maybe not—I was just indulging in some wild ass philosophizing." He pulled her nightgown down and slid off her, back to his side of the mattress.

"Thank you. That was a lovely back rub."

"You got me blabbering on again in order to extend your back rub, didn't you?"

"Yep," she laughed. "But it was wonderful. Massage therapy with philosophical musings—you've invented a new service."

"A big seller, I'm sure."

"With me, it will be."

John's thoughts drifted back to Bart and Konrad Lorenz, but after a moment, he sensed Claire was breathing shallow and falling asleep.

How many times, he wondered, had he sensed Claire fall asleep next to him? Hundreds, maybe thousands. He still marveled—with envy—how quickly she could slip from intimate conversation or passionate lovemaking to sleep. He recalled the first time, years before, after sex at her house as clandestine graduate school lovers, when he had been intoxicated by her sexual passion, and then he startled, realizing she had fallen asleep next to him afterward within minutes. He remembered, too, how tumultuous those early months—even years— had been: the relationship was off and on, off and on, a confusing mélange of intimacy and sudden breakups that Claire had initiated. Once he had arrived at her house to take her to the movies only to find she had his belongings—a few clothes, textbooks, a tent that he had stored at her house—waiting at the door while she told him she needed to end the relationship. He had been so devastated—and then so needy, apologizing and asking her again and again for another chance, though he wasn't clear that he had done anything wrong.

John rolled over in the bed, disgusted with himself for how dependent he had once been. He had been so fragile, so terrified that their relationship might end at any moment, and he desperately clutched at her, like a scared little boy, as if everything hinged on having a relationship with Claire. How narrow he had whittled his life!

He tugged on the covers, pulling them up over his chin. He told himself he had done the best he could then, and though he never wanted to be so insecure and needy again, he was glad that Claire lay in bed next to him now as he listened to the rhythm of her breathing. He wanted to love her now—not from neurotic neediness, but in wonder and joy.

Dreams of being old and dying treaded across his restless sleep and then the sleep vanished to the blackness of night. The red-numbered alarm clock showed 3:12, the moonlight had disappeared from the room, and he knew death would happen. It is not just the fate of other people, he thought, but it would be Claire's fate someday, and his own too. He prayed that it would be a long way off, but he knew it was not something that could be avoided by being careful and avoiding fatty foods. Death will come to the old woman hawking peanut butter-caramel apple dip, and it will happen sometime to everyone. Life is a slow progression toward that morbid conclusion. *And then what?*

He told himself to shut up. There was no point in being paralyzed by that awful dread. He should make the most of life—it can be full of joy. Why couldn't he always remember that?

John swung his legs over the bed, landing bare feet on the grainy wood floor. He walked downstairs and out onto the deck. High clouds had blown in to the south and a luminescence in the western sky showed the moon was hidden but not completely dimmed. How many nights, he wondered, had his sleep been broken by death worries? Perhaps the reoccurring, nocturnal chatter was just his morose neurosis, a transgenerational transmission of anxiety from growing up with superstitious great-grandparents and a mom so overwhelmed by nervousness that she was mentally disabled rather than a functional mother? And maybe their fears had become etched deeper into the recesses of his mind after falling through the ice? He was not the only one, though—lots of people are anxious about death and afraid of happiness, whether they know it or not.

He thought this fear of death was peculiar to humans among all animals, a species-specific anxiety. Bart doesn't worry about death—he just lives. Perhaps the dread of death—the human element—is the worst part. It is terrible to think of nonexistence *now*, he thought, but it is painless *then*.

Light flickered in the southwest sky as lightning leaped from one high cloud to the next. He wondered if people—and animals, too—were like electricity, having souls in an invisible dimension that could rarely be seen but which materialize every now and then? Maybe we appear and reappear every few eons, flashing off and on like cosmic fireflies. Or maybe this life is the only part that's visible of something deeper, like the tip of an iceberg. Maybe we sleepwalk through this world, unaware of an invisible dimension that subsumes birth and death.

He leaned back and gazed into the open sky above him. His eyes adjusted to the darkness and he saw there were more stars than he could count. He knew, too, that there were millions, maybe billions, of stars in the sky. He shivered, feeling something. It wasn't coldness, but more like energy touching him. He wasn't sure what, but he had felt *something* invisible. God? He wondered, and then scoffed at himself while simultaneously hoping God and an afterlife existed beyond his wishful thinking. And if not?

He shuddered. That was the worst of his fears: not to exist, to cease consciousness. But he tried to reassure himself that even if there is no consciousness, there's still something. There's matter, broken into minerals and molecules; eventually, that becomes part of the earth. Even after the sun burns out and the earth dies in darkness billions of years from now, there's still matter, there's some energy, some life force that grows and collapses and reappears in some new form, in waves of big bang cycles. There's something, and we exist as part of it, whatever *it* is.

In the southern sky, the thin edges of a high cloud, shaped like the top of a valentine heart, grew iridescent. The celestial light intensified, and the moon peeked back into the open sky. A delicate wind fluttered across his cheeks and rippled the hair on his bare chest. The breeze brought coolness, a hint of autumn, and he knew death would eventually come, but still at this moment—amazing for the beauty of the world and the intensity of his experience—he wanted to just live. He felt an explicable happiness pass over him. He had held his happiness hostage for so long, out of guilt—a penance of sorts—for his role in his mother's problems and out of his own anxiety over what terrible thing might happen next in life. But he could choose instead to embrace life, whatever it might bring. He wondered for a moment if he was being foolish, but then he dismissed the question. It did not really matter.

John slipped back into bed, wrapping his arm over Claire's side, squeezing her firmly. It was good to feel her body against him. Someday he would lose her—or she would lose him—but he was with her right now, feeling every inch of her warm back against his chest, and he told himself that was what mattered.

She stirred, and he kissed the back of her head softly. She rolled over.

"I love you, Claire. I am so happy you are in my life."

"Mmm." She burrowed her nose into the cleft between his pectoral muscles.

He cinched her tighter in his arms. She snuggled closer, then pulled her head away from his chest, looking at the radio clock. She moaned that it was 4:11 and asked him what was wrong.

"Nothing," he whispered.

"Why are you awake?"

"I was just contemplating the inevitability of death while trying to focus on living life to the fullest and in the process, I began to marvel at the warmth and comfort of your body and how much I appreciate and love you being in my life."

"Oh my."

"I love you, Claire." He cuddled her closer, smelling the earthy scent she gave off when she slept, and as he did, his lips found hers, and they kissed. His body tingled, even trembled. He laughed, and so did Claire, and they were fully together in some marvelous way that was almost like a trance—yet it was not one of drunkenness but of full consciousness—and they made love with a playfulness of being in the middle of the dark night.

John and Claire climbed the trail in silence, except for the scuffing of shoes against the earth and the splashing of the stream over rocks. He listened to the churning of the water like a mantra, but it was broken by the cry of a bird deep in the woods.

"I feel like Garp today," he told Claire.

"Hmm—I'm supposed to know what that means?" she asked.

"Remember that scene in *The World According to Garp*? The one where Robin Williams is sitting around the dinner table with his family?"

"No."

"He says in just that one day, he lived a full life. That's how I feel today."

"Why?"

"For a multitude of reasons. I woke early but refreshed and eager to write on that essay about homeless youths and society for Tony's edited book. Remember when Bart was younger and we'd let him out of the basement in the morning— he'd prance at the back door with Serendipity, then he'd just race outside to start his day, sniffing and baying away? That's how I felt this morning—not to sniff and bay, mind you, but just glad for a new day."

A sideways, bemused smile crossed her face. "That's cool."

"Yup. And it was good to write. I got ideas down on paper about the kids, about their humanness and worth, despite their being neglected by parents and society. And I was able to write something about the formal systems of assistance, which are too often encrusted bureaucracies that respond with rigidity to the pain, confusion, and multiple special needs of youth. It's like the systems don't really see the kids, not as people, anyway, with their own unique needs, strengths, and potential. And it's bigger than that too. Sometimes I think that as a collective of individuals, as a society, we don't really see other people's suffering—that it might be too disturbing to our own comfort or maybe comes too close to our own pain."

"I get that," she said. "That's so frustrating when our systems are like that."

"Yes, sometimes," he said. "But today I didn't feel so frustrated or bitter. Writing about it, I felt like I could see the kids' needs and the system problems without being consumed by them. I felt happy to see you when you got up and excited to get to the park and play softball this afternoon. It's a gorgeous day, the sky is clear blue and expansive with that crisp feel of September. It was a great day to play softball, to hit the ball out to the fence, seeing it soar toward the smattering of yellow in the trees just beyond the fence, and to circle the bases in full stride. It was great. A great day to be alive, and it's beautiful here, serene, cool under the canopy of green leaves turning gold and yellow and rust.

It's beautiful, and it's good to be with you, Claire—and I love you, a lot. I have for a long time."

"It's nice to be loved by you." She smiled. "Seems like you are more loving lately—or maybe you're more open with your love?"

"Maybe I am. I always have been, down deep, but we've been through some crazy, hard times together, you and I, Claire Evers Anderson. There were a lot of ups and downs you put me through."

"Me!" She slapped his shoulder playfully. "At first, yes, but then it was you—unwilling to commit, keeping me waiting."

"We certainly had our struggles, didn't we? But I'm glad to be with you now. I'm happy with our life. It feels like a golden period in life."

She smiled, and then laughed. "Maybe it's a short one, if we do end up having a baby."

"Now, don't be pessimistic."

"You have no idea how much work a baby is."

"I'm sure we'll adjust and figure it out," he said. "Then it'll become another golden period."

"Right—with a lot of poopy diapers," she said. "We'll see if the gold tarnishes with the poop."

"Shush—it'll be great. *Today* is a great day."

"It is." Her blue eyes shone in the fall light.

"I can think of only one more thing to make the day complete."

"What?" She looked at him, and then laughed. "Oh, no! You sexy man." She turned, glancing down the trail.

"We haven't seen anyone for a good mile," he said.

Her laughter was gentle, like the flutter of falling leaves. He picked her up, and like a new groom fawning over his bride at the threshold of the honeymoon suite, carried her through the bushes to a small clearing of moss that crept upon pebbles cast out by the creek. He held Claire on top, sensing the warm but shivering flesh of her partially naked body, listening to their exclamations of rushed breathing as the stream tumbled and splattered over the rocks.

CHAPTER 37

Claire flopped herself onto a patio chair and scooted closer to John. "Ah," she said. "Feels good, finally, just to sit, huh?"

"Yep." John slouched, trying to ease his sore back. With the help of a handful of friends, he had carried in the past two days an assortment of beds, sofas, dressers, and even a piano among countless other pieces of furniture and boxes as he and Claire moved from her old house to a home of their own. "Really good, but I can't sit very long—I'd better get something done on that presentation."

"It's crappy you have to work after moving all weekend."

"I agree, but it's got to be done." He glanced at her. "Feels good, though, just to sit with you for a moment in silence."

She rested her hand in his lap. "I'll be quiet."

He took her hand in his and peered into the high blue sky. The blue began to fade and two barely discernible pinpoints of light emerged in the pale gray dusk of the eastern sky. These tiny flecks of light were the harbingers of night, and he wondered if they were planets or stars; with streaks of scarlet still spread across the western sunset, the presence of distant suns seemed miraculous to John. More stars sprang into the sky, and a slice of moon shone its vanilla glare through the prickly needles in the pine tree. The trail of puffy clouds caught the glow from the rising moon.

"It's beautiful here," he said.

"A gorgeous night."

He squeezed her hand. "This is going to be a good home for us."

"I love it."

"Sorry," he said. "I'd better get working on that talk."

She held onto his hand as he tried to let go. "I wish we could just sit here all night."

"Me, too, but there'll be plenty more nights here together."

"Too bad you couldn't have gotten your presentation done at the office this week."

"That was my intent, but those client crises scattered those plans to the four winds."

"I know."

"But at least Andy's doing well. I meant to tell you about seeing him Friday afternoon." John described how they'd been reviewing Andy's progress—keeping his apartment for a year, no fights or legal trouble for months, starting a healthier relationship with a new girlfriend, plus interviewing for a part-time job as a short-order cook. "The best part was that Andy was telling me all this—all I had to do was reinforce and celebrate it. And then when I'm leaving, he's standing outside, his Cardinals cap on backward, saying—"

A female voice yelled out their names from the side of the house. Claire called back, and a short woman, attired in a woman's business suit the dark blue color of a police uniform, emerged from the corner of the house. Claire greeted their real estate agent.

"Sorry to interrupt," Denise said. "I was in the neighborhood, so I thought I'd stop by and see how your move went." A fine layer of makeup covered her late forty-something face.

"Busy," Claire said. "But it was fine."

"Actually, it was a lot of damn work," John said. "Even with five friends and the biggest truck that U-Haul rents, it took us three-and-a-half loads—you wouldn't believe how much stuff Claire has. And putting everything away—geez!"

"I wanted to come help, but I had to show another house" Denise said. "I don't ever help clients move, but I've come to see you two more as friends than clients. But I'm so glad you got this house. It's beautiful and it's perfect for you."

"Thank you," Claire said.

"It will be a lovely home for you and your family." Denise feigned a smile that was too wide to be natural.

"Thanks." John repeated, wondering if Claire had told her they were hoping to have a baby?

"When will your boys be home next?" Denise turned toward Claire.

"We're hoping for Thanksgiving, but maybe not until the Christmas break."

"Well, that will be so nice." Denise typically projected a chatty, upbeat persona, but the corners of her mouth always sagged slightly, belying her self-presentation, and now the edges of her forced smile drooped sadly.

John had a sick feeling she was going to talk again about her deceased son—she also had two daughters—who had died seven years prior in a car crash in his early twenties. He felt bad—it was a terrible loss, but she had already told them the story three times, each time starting from the beginning and repeating the same details, as if she didn't remember she had already shared the story.

"I do imagine that would be so wonderful to have all of your children with you for the holidays." A thick tear cut a soggy gully through the makeup on her cheek. She blinked, swallowed a deep breath, and stepped back. "Oh, geez, I'm sorry. I don't know why I do this."

"It's okay." Claire stepped forward and gave her a hug.

"You know, I still miss Chad, my son. I lost him seven years ago."

"I know," Claire said. "And I'm so sorry about your loss."

Denise pulled away from Claire's arms and then repeated her story about the old accident. New tears welled around her brown eyes.

John glanced at this watch. He felt inconsiderate and selfish, but he didn't want to hear about her loss again. He needed to escape the conversation—Denise could talk about her deceased son for a long time, and John had work to do.

Denise apologized for crying, admonishing herself for her lack of self-control, but Claire hugged her once more, telling her crying was a necessary part of grieving and there was no deadline for dealing with losses of those we love.

John watched for a lull in their conversation, and then told Denise how sorry he was about her loss, but he had to excuse himself, explaining about his presentation. He closed the door to his new study—he liked both having a room for his work and the way he had decorated it—and turned the stereo on to try to block out Claire and Denise's conversation, even as he chided himself for leaving instead of staying and be supportive. He busied himself with a stack of articles and folders, reading through the notes he'd scribbled down in the past week. There were a number of good points, he thought, but they were without organization: a collection of disparate ideas that begged for a synthesizing structure and a meaningful conclusion. He searched through the folder and found the outline of a presentation he'd given at a conference in Chicago eighteen months earlier. It was a similar topic, a review of the existing empirical literature, highlighting the lessons learned from prior projects and their implications for further research and treatment. There'd been an explosion of new research in the past year, and so it would be time consuming to update before Tuesday's talk, but it might be feasible. He drummed his pen against the desktop, thinking of the possibilities, but unsure where to start. He exhaled forcefully and gazed at the print of Michelangelo's The Creation of Adam that he had bought after their Europe trip and hung on the wall.

A light knock tapped against the door and Claire entered the study.

"Did Denise go?" he asked.

"Just a minute ago."

"Sorry I deserted you."

"It's okay."

"I feel for Denise but it's hard to hear her talk about her son every time."

"It's a terrible loss." Claire slumped into a chair in the corner.

"As soon as she started talking about your boys coming home, I knew she'd bring up about her son's death again. You can see it start to happen—it's almost like she starts leaking, a little bit of loss drips out at first, before the floodgates open."

Claire's eyes narrowed in a sharp, almost angry look, as if he was being insensitive rather than insightful. "There's some losses I don't think you ever get over. I can't imagine as a mother having a child die."

He hesitated. He'd been reactive to Denise, withdrawing rather than listening to her, but he knew people could get too bogged down with life's losses. "Sorry if I was a bit of a jerk about Denise. But at least Josh and Ryan are both doing well. They're safe and sound and away at college."

"Thank God," she said. "I hope I die long before my children."

"I didn't mean to be callous about Denise's son—I know it's tragic," he said. "But I don't think you have anything to worry about your boys."

She nodded. "How's your presentation coming along?"

"Like pulling teeth."

"A lot to do?"

"Yeah, plus I'm not excited about it." He dog-eared a page in an article he was reading. "I'd like to make it more than one more regurgitation of the research literature, but I don't know what to say."

Claire nodded. "I used to hate organizing presentations, especially at the last minute, but I bet you'll figure something out."

John considered asking her to go back and sit together on the porch, but the sky was now pitch black; it wouldn't be the same. "What are you going to do?" he asked.

"Straighten out my closet and iron a couple of things for tomorrow."

"Sounds fun."

"Sure." She rolled her eyes. "I'm going to turn in soon."

"Already?"

"It's almost nine."

"Oh, yeah, that is super late." He furrowed his brow, making a feigned serious expression. "And by the way, it's only eight forty-five, not nine."

She stuck out her tongue. "I'm tired. Are you coming to bed soon?"

"I wish, but I have miles to go on this damn presentation, and I have a lot of meetings tomorrow before my plane leaves at four thirty."

"I'm sorry you can't come to bed with me."

"Me too." He kissed Claire. "Come back before bed, okay?"

She nodded.

He read more articles, jotting down notes. Claire reentered the study in her nightgown, announcing it was nine thirty and time for her to go to bed, but she lingered, leaning against the corner of his desk. "I love the new walk-in closet. And the cedar smell—it brings back memories of playing in my grandmother's closet with my cousins when I was a girl."

"Good memories?" he asked.

"Good, and a little sad, too, you know?"

He nodded, familiar with the melancholy of remembering good times with grandparents gone by.

"How's it going?" she asked.

"Ugh. It's a slog, and I hate to say it, but I'd probably better get back to this presentation."

She crumpled her nose, making a childish face of disappointment, and then nodded. He kissed her good night, noticing as she walked out of the room the roundness of her butt beneath her flannel nightgown. He returned to his stack of articles, shuffled through a reprint, and realized he had little memory of what he had just read. He forced his eyes back to the paper, but then rolled his chair away from the desk.

He figured his concentration was hopelessly broken. He'd wanted Claire to stop by, but he realized her visit had violated his unspoken expectations: that their interlude would be sweet, perhaps with a hint of passionate longing, but it would be brief, not exceeding a few minutes. He chided himself, thinking he had internalized the management seminars his new boss had made him attend: he was now acting at home as the six-minute manager of intimacy, or maybe it was intimacy by the micro minute.

He would be gone to Washington for just one night, but already he missed Claire. He wanted to sleep with her, to hold her close, perhaps even to make love for the first time in their new house.

He decided to go to Claire, leaving the work for the morning—he'd get up early and skip a meeting or two. John brushed his teeth and hurried to bed, making his way through the dark room. He climbed onto the mattress, discerning Claire's nose sticking out between the blankets and the pillow situated over her eyes. He cuddled close and her hand stirred, but he realized this was an unconscious reaction. He nestled his nose against her flannel-clad shoulder, breathing in the warm sweet scent of her body, and smiled, as he gently caressed her shoulder with his nose. He laughed at himself—though he wanted her to wake up and make love, she was dead asleep.

He fantasized about the next time they would make love. He imagined cradling her warm flesh against his own body, wrapping her legs over his own, feeling her fingertips caress his chest as she leaned her dangling nipples against his moist lips. He relished the images, hoping they would consummate the fantasy—perhaps they'd even conceive—in the morning, or at least the night he returned from Washington. He scooted closer to Claire and let his fantasies subside into sleep.

John awoke to wet lips against his cheeks. He startled, noticing Claire sitting on the edge of the bed, smiling, clad in a black dress. He glanced at the alarm clock, which showed 7:42. "*Shit.*"

"That's quite a greeting for your wife who just gave you a big, good morning kiss."

"No—it's not you." He sat up in bed. "I wanted to get up early to spend time together before you left and then work on that presentation, but here you're about to leave."

"The alarm clock went off at six, but you didn't budge."

"Damn it."

"You must be tired—it was probably the move."

"I guess," John said. He rubbed his face into the pillow. "I still feel dead asleep."

"I would have let you sleep in but I figured you needed to get up for work." She hesitated and then leaned forward. "Plus, there's something I want to tell you before your trip."

"What?"

"I'm late." She smiled. "Two weeks late."

"Late?" He repeated the word and didn't know what she meant until he heard himself say it again. "You mean you think you're pregnant?"

"I do."

"Claire!"

She said she didn't have medical confirmation, but her body felt different. She had been fatigued and nauseated the last few mornings, and she was fourteen days late for her period. She smiled. "My body is telling me I'm pregnant."

"Yes!" He wrapped his arms around her, kissed her, and pulled her atop of him as he laughed. "I'm so excited. Do you really think so?"

"It's a feeling more than anything, but yes, it *feels* like I'm pregnant."

"Yahoo!"

"I almost didn't tell you because I'm not sure yet, and I don't want to let you down if I'm not, but I figured you have as much right as me to know how it seems."

He squeezed her. "I'm glad you told me."

"You won't be disappointed if I'm not?"

"Well, I guess I'd be disappointed, but if that's the case, we'll just have to keep up the baby-making activity, you know? When do you think we conceived?"

"That afternoon after the softball game, off the trail in the park, next to the stream."

"Yes! How romantic. I couldn't have wished for a better place."

"That's my husband: a romantic."

John kissed her again. "Claire, what do we do next? I mean, shouldn't we go to the doctor or something?"

"I'll call for an appointment."

The phone on the bedroom dresser rang.

"Maybe that's the stork calling now to schedule a date," he said.

"More likely, it's your work, as usual, Dr. Anderson. Speaking of which, I should get to mine."

"Wait, please. I'll call them back. I want to talk a bit more before you go, since I won't see you before I fly out."

She nodded, and he picked up the receiver.

Bennie's high-pitched and rushed voice came across the phone. "Sorry to disturb you, chief."

"That's okay," John said. "But let me call you back in five minutes."

"I apologize, chief, but you need to hear this as soon as possible."

John held a finger up to Claire, motioning for her to give him a minute. Bennie often became overwhelmed by clinical crises and turned to John for supervisory support. "How about you tell me very briefly in a minute or two, and then I'll call you back."

"I don't know how to tell you this," Bennie said, and hesitated. "But Andy's been critically shot."

At the hospital, John found Bennie and Loretta, the program nurse, in a waiting area; Andy was still in a coma.

"What happened?" John asked.

"I don't know much, chief." Bennie's hands flailed more wildly than usual. "When I got to the center—I was the first one in, as usual—I found a message from the police and also Sonny." Sonny was one of Bennie's favorite clients and he often hung out with Andy. "So, I knew something bad had happened. I called the police back first—a Detective Long, but he wasn't in. I wasn't sure if I should wait for him to call me back, since the police are in charge, or call Sonny. But then Sonny called again."

"Bennie." John was typically patient in listening to Bennie's palaver, but now his long-winded style was making John want to scream. "Get to the point: what happened to Andy?"

"I was getting to that." Bennie scooted his chair back, but he spoke quicker. "Sonny told me that they were walking back to Andy's apartment late Sunday night—he said they'd been over at some other guy's place, watching TV and eating pizza—I bet they were smoking some of that dope too. It's hard to trust what the guys say."

"And what happened?"

"Sonny said they were just getting back to Andy's apartment when some man steps out from a pickup parked right in front of Andy's place and shoots Andy three times with a handgun. Andy didn't have a chance to say or do anything: the man suddenly swung open his truck door, jumped out, shot Andy in an instant, and then sped away."

"God—." John stopped himself from swearing.

"God Bless America," Bennie said, shaking his head. "Sonny said he didn't recognize the shooter, but I wonder about that—he's probably scared if he says something, he'll be next."

After two hours of waiting, the surgeon, a man in his late thirties with wire-rimmed glasses and balding brown hair, emerged, saying they'd removed three bullets, but Andy remained in a coma and critical condition.

John quizzed the doctor about Andy's prognosis, but he responded with vague answers. "So," John asked, "is he going to live?"

The surgeon looked tired and he glanced at the wall clock. "Like I said, he's in critical condition. He came through the surgery well, but he suffered extensive internal damage. We'll have to wait and see."

"Well, what do you think?" John pressed him.

The surgeon returned John's stare. "I think it's hard to wait with uncertainty. Excuse me, but I have other surgeries. We'll keep you informed about his progress."

"So, can I see him?"

The surgeon walked toward the waiting room door but glanced over his shoulder. "Not now. He's in too critical of condition."

"Geez." Bennie scowled as the doctor left the waiting room. "He didn't say much, did he?"

"No." The surgeon was just keeping his professional distance, but John felt pissed off: "hard to wait with uncertainty"—who the fuck did the surgeon think he was? A therapist?

"It's unbelievable," Loretta said. "Andy's been doing great, and now he's shot outside of his apartment?"

"It's hard to imagine," John said, but his words sounded hollow and false to his own ears. It wasn't so hard to believe. Tragic and absurd—even crazy-making—yet it was understandable, and even something that he should have seen coming. Andy had made a lot of enemies on the streets over the years. He was incredibly impulsive, quick to explode and start a fight, and he could be a royal smart-ass even when he controlled his fists. He was a likely target, especially with his past drug use—and yet underneath the hotheaded bluster, there was a good, even lovable kid, though the people who were closest to him had wounded him emotionally for years. "What do the other kids at the house know?"

"Nothing so far," Loretta said.

"That won't last long," Bennie said. "Sonny will be talking and word travels fast on the streets."

"We need to pull a community meeting together right away," John said. "Then we'll need to follow-up with some clients individually—this is going to put some of our more fragile clients like Brandon close to the edge. After that, I'll come back here this afternoon and see if I can talk someone into letting me see Andy."

"Excuse me," Bennie said. "But you've got a plane to catch."

"I'll cancel my trip. This is more important."

"There's nothing you can do here but wait, chief."

"I'll get a doctor or a nurse to let me see him. Even if he's still in a coma, I can talk to him—they say a person can still hear what's being said to them in a coma."

"What do you want to say?" Loretta asked.

John hesitated, and Loretta looked at him with her blue eyes. He felt Bennie peering at him, too, from behind his thick-lensed glasses. Loretta and other staff had told John more than once that he had a way with words—that he knew just what to say during a tense clinical confrontation or in a staff meeting when morale was sagging. Bennie had teased that John was the only person he knew who could talk longer than himself. But in the hospital waiting room, John was suddenly at a loss for words. He grew self-conscious as Loretta and Bennie both looked at him. "I don't know," he stammered.

Loretta and Bennie exchanged a quick, uncomfortable glance. "How about we tell him to hold on," Bennie said.

"Yeah, thanks," John said. He suddenly felt emotionally impotent and he hated himself for the feeling.

"We'll tell him that you're thinking of him and can't wait to talk to him in person, but that Bennie and I made you go to DC for a grant, but you'll be back real soon," Loretta said.

"Do it, chief. He'd want you to. We'll tell him we'll even buy a new pool table with the next grant you get—he'll like that."

It was a lie, John thought, about going for money—it was a state-of-the-field review and planning conference that would inform future funding directions, but no new grant money was going to be handed out at this meeting. He started to explain but realized that was irrelevant. He told Bennie and Loretta he'd think about going, but he was still embarrassed by not knowing what to say.

He called Claire to let her know about Andy's condition, and asked her advice about going to the conference. She didn't say what to do, telling John to follow his own gut, but she offered to go by the hospital and see Andy for him while he was gone; with that, and a painful though familiar sense of ambivalence, he made his flight.

The black-tinted mirror panels made the crowded elevator seem tiny, like an overstuffed box. A chime—a sickening sound, like the doorbell at his dentist's office—dinged at four lower floors and the other hotel guests disappeared behind the sliding doors, leaving him alone. The elevator doors parted again, revealing the pewter candelabras and ebony-smoked glass flanking the hallway of the thirty-first floor.

He stepped from the elevator, wandered the hallways, searching for his room, and then slipped the magnetic card into the doorknob's metal box. He twisted the handle quickly as the buttons flashed green, but the door remained locked. He tried again several times, cursing, wishing for a simple metal key, before realizing the door needed to be pushed open after the card had been pulled out. He entered and found a narrow corridor next to the bathroom that opened to a large bedroom. A wall of windows behind the drapes revealed a plethora of neon lights dotting the skyline. It was a grand view—a nicer room than the standard government fare—but a palpable emptiness permeated the room.

He unpacked his dress shirt and slacks and hung them in the bathroom with the shower turned to its hottest setting to steam away the wrinkles. He lingered in the moist heat before closing the bathroom door and returning to the main room. He gazed out the window again, peering heavenward, into a black night. He wondered why it was so dark—perhaps it was because the hotel windows were tinted or had the moon already set? In any case, he hated the dark night and the emptiness of the room, both of which felt oppressive.

He called home. Claire answered in a sleepy voice.

"Hi. I'm sorry—did I wake you?"

"Mmm, I was reading in bed, waiting for your call, and must have dozed off. How was your flight?"

"Oh, you know."

"What? Anxiety-provoking?"

"A little, yeah," he said. "But the worst part was the damn plane got delayed nearly two hours on the tarmac before taking off and then we circled Washington for forty-five minutes before they let us land. Have you heard anything about Andy?"

"Bennie called an hour ago—same condition, no changes. He did say there was a rumor spreading among the kids that a drug dealer had gotten out of prison and was settling old debts."

"Shit."

"I know," Claire said. "I keep praying. How are you doing?"

"Worried." John twiddled with the phone cord. "You know, it feels so sad."

"I know."

"I should have stayed."

"You did what was best," she said. "But it's hard not to be here now."

He caught himself staring into the night. "I guess."

"I'm going to run by the hospital tomorrow in the afternoon between clients."

He smiled. "I love you."

"Me too you."

"How are you?"

"Fine, but I miss you in bed with me," Claire said.

"Anyone else there with you?"

"No—I sent my other lover home five minutes ago," she snickered. "You're silly."

"I mean, do you still think you're pregnant?" he asked.

"Yes, sweetie."

"Will you call tomorrow for an appointment?"

"It's a busy day."

"Please try."

"I'll try," she said.

"Thank you. You know, I miss you."

"Do you already?"

"Yes, I wish I was home tonight," he said. "I hate being in this hotel."

"What's wrong with it?"

"Oh, nothing. It's sleek, elegant, modern—and cold. I feel like an alien in the middle of the next century, and all alone at that. I wish I was home in bed with you. You know what I'd like to do right now?"

"I can guess, knowing you," she said.

"Lay my head on your belly and try to feel the baby."

"You couldn't feel the baby yet, silly."

"I know. But I'd still do it."

He called the hospital after he hung up with Claire, got disconnected twice while being transferred, and after a long wait, talked with a brusque nurse who said Andy was still in a coma and critical condition. He forced away the unwanted image of Andy hooked up to IVs and replaced it with the memory of Andy at the end of their talk on Friday afternoon, grinning, his baseball cap on backward, his thumb up, saying, "I'm doing good." John murmured something—he wasn't sure if his own words were a prayer or a plea—that Andy wouldn't die.

He forced himself to read back through his presentation notes, trying to commit the structure, major points, and transition statements to memory, but he felt bored by his own material. The information was what the conference organizers expected: a review of empirical findings and research recommendations. But it was sterile academia—like reading an encyclopedia, lifeless. He wanted something more, but now there was no time. Or maybe it just didn't matter.

He wished he'd never left home. He'd run over to the hospital, and even if the doctor denied him access, he'd slip into Andy's room. He shouldn't be alone now. John thought if Andy was going to recover was now up to Andy—that somehow, even in his coma, he was still deciding, albeit in an unconscious way, whether to live or die. John hated himself for having the thought, but considering all the chaos, losses, and pain that had been ingrained in Andy's psyche, John couldn't blame Andy if he decided to give up.

John jerked awake, terrified. Something like thunder had woken him. He listened in the dark hotel room, hearing the rumble of a plane, but it was not so close. The Crystal City hotel was close to the Potomac and just off the flight path into Washington National and it was not unusual to hear a passing airline, and then he remembered the nightmare that had woken him up: he was on a hijacked plane, a baby crying behind him, while a man with a scraggly beard had thrust a gun into John's face. The plane started to fall, and John screamed along with the baby. That was when he woke up.

He told himself it was just a bad dream, but he was short of breath. His nose was clogged—perhaps he had trouble breathing while he was asleep? He wondered again if he had sleep apnea as Claire had once suggested? He told himself to relax. He gulped a breath, but as he did so, he thought the dream was not necessarily the crazy irrationality of his sleeping mind. A plane *could* miss its approach into National Airport and crash into the top of the building, and the hotel—so glitzy and expensive—could become his tomb.

He breathed faster, sucking air, but it left him breathless. His panic swelled. He told himself to breathe slower, knowing he was starting to hyperventilate. He rolled over, trying to find a comfortable position, but he was afraid if he went back to sleep, he might die. A plane could crash into the hotel, or he could die suddenly for any of a thousand and one other reasons. He could be alive one moment, but then—without even waking up and knowing what was happening—be gone forever.

How can anyone ever sleep, he wondered, knowing that?

❧

John tried to gauge his timing to call home to be late enough that he didn't wake Claire up but early enough that he didn't miss her in case she left early for work. "Ah, caught you," he said when she picked up. "Good morning! Glad I didn't miss you."

"Almost love—just walking out the door," Claire said. "I only answered because I thought it might be you, but I've got to run. I've got a seven-thirty client and a busy day."

"Well, I'll let you go," he said. "But I wanted to call and say how much I love you, Claire."

"I missed you this morning," she said.

"Did you?"

"Yes, I smelled your pillow after waking up."

He laughed. "How come?"

"Because I was missing you and it has your scent."

"Well, if you really want, I'll let you smell me in person tonight, even as I plan to kiss you all over."

"You're silly. And seductive as usual."

"Did you start your period?" he asked.

"Nope."

"Yes!"

"Are you going to love this baby more than me?" she asked.

"Never," he said. "But I'm going to love this baby a whole lot and I'm going to love you even more."

"Good answer. Hey, I've really got to run. Have a good presentation."

"Thanks," he said. "See you tonight."

"Bye love."

John showered, dressed, and called the hospital. He waited on hold for several minutes before a nurse picked up the line and said there was no change in Andy's status.

John gathered his notes, descended in the elevator, and nearly bumped into Jackie, who was coordinating the conference, on the crowded promenade leading to the ballroom. She smiled and touched his arm.

"John, there you are! As a dutiful conference organizer, I was beginning to worry you weren't here. How are you?"

"Tired, but good. How are you?"

"Fine and looking forward to your presentation." She glanced toward the grand ballroom where the conference was being held. "All set?"

"Finally. I didn't finish until last night's flight here, but I wasn't very satisfied with it, and then I woke up in the middle of the night and couldn't sleep, so I completely rewrote it. A last-minute effort, for sure. We'll see how well it goes over."

"I'm sure it'll be fine. Every presentation I've heard you give has been."

John thanked her and stepped outside, letting a fall wind brush across his face for a few minutes before reentering the hotel and making his way to the podium. As the facilitator introduced John, he watched for the momentary stir of anxiety in his stomach that he felt before most speeches, but there was none, and he knew in his gut this talk wasn't about him: it was for Andy.

"Thank you, Dr. Bierman, for your very generous introductory comments about my work in this field." John looked into several faces in the crowded ballroom. "As kind as your words were, and as gratifying as they are to a part of the ego that propels me at times, my own contributions are but an infinitesimal speck in the constellation of issues surrounding homelessness and youth.

"I'd been asked to talk with you about what we know about homeless and runaway youth, based on the burgeoning empirical research of the past five years. This research has provided data for a rough guesstimate to the question of the number of homeless and runaway youths in the United States and a number of studies detail the common demographic characteristics of homeless youths, such as their age, race, and education. Other research describes the significant mental health and substance abuse treatment needs of these youths, and a few projects examine the disturbingly high prevalence of trauma, especially the all-too-frequent experience of childhood abuse—sexual, physical, and emotional. Several studies also examine family characteristics and predictors, with recent works highlighting the transgenerational nature of these patterns and problems. And a handful of pioneering studies have begun to examine what services help youths who runaway or are homeless.

"Clearly, there has been an explosion in research in the past five years and a concomitant advance in our knowledge. This research is important, and so are many of the unanswered questions that remain on the research agenda for the field. I had intended to review this research and summarize what we know about homelessness and youth while highlighting critical questions that should be addressed in the next generation of research. But as important as these topics are, it struck me at three thirty this morning that what we know from the empirical literature is not the most essential issue for us to think about during these fifteen minutes.

"I was thinking about many things in those late hours of the night, but especially about Andy, a twenty-two-year-old with a history of conduct disorder, schizoaffective illness, polysubstance abuse disorder, revolving-door institutional admissions, and reoccurring homelessness, with whom I and other staff have worked with over the past five years. There is, of course, no single representative person; heterogeneity is one of the hallmarks of the data. Any attempt to simplify reality into a single modal case would do an injustice both to the research and, more important, to the unique humanity of each homeless youth. Yet there are common characteristics, experiences, and themes, some of which are evident in a description of Andy and his life, although the generalizability of Andy and his life now seems less important to me than his unique story."

John described Andy's early school difficulties, the drowning death of his twin brother as a toddler, and the chaos, violence, and dysfunction of his family. He summarized Andy's extensive treatment history, which began in third grade, and of the long and challenging process to successfully outreach, engage, and serve Andy in the homeless youth program. Treatment progress often stalled, he said, but in the past eighteen months, after forging a deeper therapeutic alliance, Andy had made substantial progress, albeit on an uneven course.

"Although several goals remain on Andy's current treatment plan," John said, "he has improved overall and, in some areas, in quantum leaps. His steady growth is reflected quantitatively on measures of days housed, mental health symptoms and coping skills, alcohol and drug use, social support, and interpersonal relationships. While significant, these measures of improvement pale by comparison with seeing Andy Friday afternoon as he stood on the deck outside our drop-in program. After we'd reviewed his progress in treatment, he stood on the steps and waved goodbye for the weekend, his red Cardinals baseball cap turned backward over his long, golden brown hair that reaches nearly to his shoulder. He grinned his broad smile and flashed me a thumbs up, and said, 'I'm doing good.' I agreed, and he repeated to me, or perhaps more to himself, 'I'm doing good.' It was an image that stayed vivid for me over a busy weekend. I'm not clear why, but perhaps it was because at that moment, he seemed infused with genuine happiness about his life.

"Whatever the reasons, I'm glad Andy had that experience. Early yesterday morning, I received a phone call that Andy had been shot Sunday night. He was walking home with a friend when a man stepped from a pickup truck and shot him three times at short range. Andy was brought to the hospital in critical condition and in a coma, a status in which he remains, at least as the last time I checked, thirty minutes ago.

"I don't know why Andy was shot. I don't know a lot of things, it seems. I am suddenly flooded with questions to which I don't know the answers. And those questions, with all due respect to the scientific literature and the investigators themselves, seem far more essential than the findings I could cull from research journals.

"I don't know why Andy, like five hundred thousand children each year, had to suffer serious abuse as a child.

"I don't know why, at an early age, he has had to suffer the ravages of mental illness and chemical dependencies.

"I don't know why our schools and our treatment and social service agencies failed so completely that Andy had to become homeless in the first place.

"And I don't understand why there has been such a lack of compassion and sensitivity to Andy; why in the wealthiest nation in the world there were no better alternatives for Andy than homelessness.

"More than anything else, I don't know why he had to be shot.

"When an event like his shooting happens, we are outraged and saddened. It shocks our moral sensibilities, as others have said about homelessness in general. And yet the greater tragedy is that we permit these children, these adolescents, these young adults to become homeless and to remain homeless.

"I don't know why we permit this unacceptable condition to exist for hundreds of thousands of our children and youths, for millions of people of all ages.

"Perhaps it has something to do with the way we view young people who are homeless. I say people and yet our language dehumanizes them. We refer to them as: troubled teens, runaways, street kids, and even occasionally as bad boys.

"Our language refers to these clients as a 'them,' as if somehow they are very separate from us. These labels mask their basic personhood. We dehumanize them. We ignore their childhood, and even our brotherhood and sisterhood—the kinship through humanity we all share.

"Closing our eyes, we permit inhumane conditions to persist, conditions that not only reduce the quality but also the quantity of life. The annual mortality rate of homeless youths, of all people who are homeless, is far greater than their same-aged peers in the general population, or for you and me. People who are homeless too often fall victim to physical illnesses, to pneumonia, to AIDS, to drug overdoses, to terrible street violence, and even to their own hand when the despair of their current living situation suffocates their hope for what life might be.

"How can we change these conditions? How can we recognize that life is often short and certainly precious? It is precious not just for Andy, who is fighting for his life, but for all runaway youths and homeless people, service providers, policy makers, administrators, and researchers, indeed, for us all, since this is an essential fact of being human.

"And how can we react then, seeing that? Are we seduced by intellectual explanations, seeing the young people primarily as victims of deep-rooted, structural-social problems, or as disturbed children, diagnosable entities of pathology? Do we simply treat these individuals in prescribed ways from our narrow professional perspectives, treating them solely as research subjects or even clinical patients, closing our eyes to all but the thinnest and most superficial facets of their existence?

"Can we choose to be different? Can we stay open to their pain from so many traumas and losses, to their vulnerability of living on the streets—a condition that is imbued with an anxious sense of the fragility of life itself? Can we stay open to such a mosaic of pain and fear—not just theirs, but to the sources of fear and grief that spring within ourselves as their stories touch our personal histories and our own sense of the unpredictability of life? Can we live with an awareness of those feelings, with knowledge of future pain in life and the inevitability of death while reaching out with welcoming hands and embracing hearts, not just to homeless youths but to everyone, including ourselves? Can we live openly and compassionately as full human beings?

"I don't know. I think we can, but I don't know if we will. Sometimes it seems too difficult, too taxing to our sense of a fragile, inner reservoir of courage and confidence. I hope we will, but I don't know.

"I do know the schism that we draw between us and them is fundamentally false.

"We are all human.

"We all struggle to fashion some solution to survive our personal history of pain, trauma, and fear while trying to live our dreams.

"And the sources of our troubles are more similar than different.

"We are all vulnerable and we will all die.

"It will happen eventually to Andy.

"It will happen to all the children, adolescents, and young adults who are living without homes in St. Louis and every other city.

"It will happen to me.

"And to you.

"I don't know if Andy will live or die from these gunshot wounds.

"And I don't know what happens to him when, eventually, inevitably, he does die.

"I don't know what will happen to me, either, or to you.

"I wish I did.

"I pray to God—if there is a God—that Andy recovers. I pray that he will live now because this is the only life we know for sure we have. I pray that he is able to resume his life and grow, that he will have a better existence. I pray that others, that each of you, will do the good work that needs to be done to serve the thousands of boys and girls, of young men and women like Andy, who are still living without families and homes, and to prevent trauma like this incomprehensible shooting from ever occurring again.

"This is what I pray, even though I don't know for sure if there is a God, or if Andy will live or die.

"And if he dies, I don't what will happen to him—if his spirit lives on, as much as I hope it does—or if he simply ceases to exist, except in the fading memories of those who know him, people who will surely also die themselves someday.

"But I do know that Andy has lived with courage in facing the traumas and pain of his life and in weaving a thread of hope to try to overcome his hardships. And I know that his life has enhanced mine, and that if he dies . . . that if he dies, that my life—and I suspect all of our lives in some way that defies precise articulation—though perhaps John Donne came the closest—will be diminished.

"Thank you."

The cab ride to Washington National was only a few miles but John left the conference late and the taxi stalled in traffic. John cursed under his breath, hoping he wouldn't miss his flight; he wanted to be home in bed with Claire by nightfall. He weaved through the congested terminal, running down the long concourse tunnel while gripping his briefcase in his hand, an act that conjured up unwanted images in his mind of the old O.J. Simpson rental car commercial. The gate area was crowded and the monitor showed his flight was delayed. He waited in a long line at the check-in counter before reaching the agent.

"Why's the flight delayed?" John asked.

"Bad weather in St. Louis," the agent said.

"Snow and ice storms already?" John joked.

The agent looked at him with surliness rather than a smile.

"Sorry," John said. "That was lame."

"Heavy thunderstorms." She seemed humorless and turned back to her computer terminal.

"How long of a delay?"

"At least thirty-five minutes but it could be considerably longer. You should stay in the gate area and listen for announcements."

John leaned back in a hard plastic chair. He closed his eyes, hoping to relax, but a pain tightened across his chest. He straightened up, opened his eyes, wondering why he suddenly felt anxious? His presentation had gone well—a half dozen people had stopped him afterward, saying they were touched by his talk and were praying for Andy, though Jackie said with disappointment that the assistant director of the sponsoring federal research institute had complained he'd wanted science, not sentiment. Still, John dismissed any concern about disappointing the bureaucrats, but he suddenly flushed with worry. He wondered if Andy had taken a turn for the worse? John joined the line of men and women in suits, waiting for an open pay phone.

He asked the hospital operator to ring Andy's nurses' station in the critical care unit. The nurse said he was no longer in the unit.

"Why?"

"He's stabilized," the nurse said. "He was moved this afternoon to another floor."

"He's out of a coma?"

"Wasn't my shift, but I suspect so or they probably wouldn't have moved him."

"Thank God." John asked to be transferred to the new room.

"Hello?" Bennie's voice was high-strung, as usual, but spoken in a hushed whisper.

"Bennie, how is he?"

"He's going to make it, chief. He pulled out of the coma a few hours ago, and the doctor said it's going to take a while for a full recovery, but he's going to be okay."

"Oh, man. Thank God. I was afraid we were going to lose him."

"I had a feeling this whole time he'd pull through," Bennie said. "I knew he'd make it. He's a survivor."

"Yes, he is. Can I talk with him?"

"He drifted back to sleep a bit ago. He's pretty doped up with pain meds. You want me to wake him?"

"No, let him sleep. But if he wakes while you're still there, tell him I'm thinking about him. It may be too late by the time I get there—the damn plane's delayed because of St. Louis' bad weather—but if visiting hours are still on, I'll be in. Otherwise, I'll be over early tomorrow morning."

"Sure, chief. You just missed Claire by fifteen minutes. She got to see him for a few minutes before he fell back asleep. She didn't stay long—said she had to hurry back to see a couple more private practice clients, but that she wanted to run over during an hour break. She told Andy you're really pulling for him—and so is she."

John found himself smiling. "Well, good."

"What time do you get in?"

"Supposed to be 5:50, but they said it would be at least a half-hour delay because of the weather."

"It's raining cats and dogs here—might hold you up longer."

"Damn it. Claire's going to pick me up, and if there's time, we'll come straight over."

"Probably won't be—they've got him on a very short leash now for visitors, saying he needs plenty of sleep. Plus, you're entitled to a little time with the missus after being gone."

"We'll get to that too. Bennie, how are you holding up?"

"Phew!" Bennie exhaled loudly into the phone. "It's been something, chief, but you know me—I'm here and I'm holding up. It'll be good to have you back though."

"Thanks for looking after him while I've been gone."

"I wanted to," Bennie said. "Me and Andy don't always see eye-to-eye—he's as hard-headed as a mule—but he's my boy too."

"I know. But thanks."

John sank deeper into the cushion of the window seat, the Washington metropolis drifted away, and the plane climbed into the aqua sky, piercing thin cirrus clouds. He felt tired but decided it was a good tired—a product of the late-night prepping for the presentation and the emotional intensity of the past forty-eight hours. It was a crazy couple of days, and he'd struggled with sleeplessness and anxiety—but who wouldn't? After the move, after the presentation, after Andy was shot and it wasn't clear if he was going to live or die—who with an aware mind would be able to sleep?

At least, John thought, he didn't let the shooting and the uncertainty stop him: he'd shared Andy's story with four hundred other people, and he did that without shaking like a scared little boy. He had nurtured himself, overcoming his anxiety, treating his inner child like a good father would. And now, he hoped, he was going to have a child of his own to father. He felt ready.

Through the airplane window, he saw the clouds below and the sunlight glint off the plane wing. From somewhere in the universe or another dimension, a new life would be entering the world. He nodded. There'd been too many losses, it was time for a new life.

Claire had said a baby would cause much stress and sleep deprivation, but he knew it would still be joyous. He wanted to appreciate everything in life, even the poopy diapers. He wanted to make the most of these next seven-and-a-half months. He pictured himself patting Claire's belly as it grew, talking to the baby, and then he imagined he and Claire in a canoe for one more river trip. He worried for an instant if a canoe trip would be safe for Claire's pregnancy—they could check with the OB first, make sure it's okay for the fetus. *Fetus*—it sounded impersonal. They'd check to see if a river trip was safe for their baby-to-be. He thought a canoe trip should be fine—and even better than fine—what an excellent start for their child: floating inside Claire in the embryonic sea while mom and dad floated on the river so in love with each other and their baby-to-be! They wouldn't even need to go upriver to the source—it would be good just take an easy float before winter to celebrate their new life.

The pilot's voice cracked over the intercom, updating the passengers on the weather. St. Louis was cloudy, he announced, but the heavy thunderstorms had passed to the northeast. They were going to start a long descent.

John repositioned his tired hips and leaned close to the window. A huge and puffy white cloud vaulted upward. He strained for a better view out of the small window. The cloud rose thousands of feet toward the heavens. He remembered being with Claire in the Sistine Chapel and the sense of awe seeing God in the clouds, surrounded by cherubs, reaching out to give life to Adam.

The stewardess announced it was time to fold up the tray and bring the seatbacks to their full, upright positions. His ears clogged on the slow, deepening descent into the West, and as the plane dipped into a thick band of clouds, the image of a sudden crash fell into his mind. Something surged in his gut, rose into his chest, but then passed over like a wave. It was just a symptom of his unmet need for control, he told himself, for he had no control now as the plane passed blindly through the clouds at hundreds of miles per hour. It was old stuff, feeling vulnerable, afraid, helpless. *Cyclotherapy* Yalom called it: a recycling of old fears, over and over. But it was nothing to obsess about—he could just let it pass.

He picked up the *Washington Post* on his lap. It was a good paper, with well-crafted writing about important events, not the town crier of the prior night's murder, like the St. Louis paper.

From the corner of his eye, he saw a glitter outside the window. Gold shone off the pond surface that spotted the farmland below. The glint of gold disappeared—and then it flashed in the next pond, as the sunlight seemed to follow the plane, skipping and shimmering across the farm ponds.

He craned his neck, peering up through the portal. A lattice of clouds stretched across the sky. The sun was not visible, but the trailing edge of a cloud was illuminated, glowing like a thin, incandescent wire. Whether the plane continued to fling itself airborne (and this thought surprised him, emerging unexpectedly) or whether it fell, and especially the worry about either, seemed insignificant, compared to the magnificence of the sky.

Fields stretched unbroken beneath the descending plane, save for the archipelago of ponds, the smattering of scattered houses and barns, and the small roads that joined at neat right angles. He figured they were flying further south than usual, probably dipping down to avoid the passing storm, and somewhere over southern Illinois.

The farmlands gave way to a highway dotted by cars, and soon to the worn buildings of East St. Louis. St. Louis' skyline dominated the view to the west, while the Arch was reflected in the Mississippi River; the reflection disappeared quickly, as the plane passed over factories, highway lanes, and soon a long stretch of cemetery where neatly arranged rows of white crosses reeled below. The engines groaned as the plane squatted its heavy body toward earth. The cars on I-70 looked like fragile playthings, and then the freeway curved, exposing a field of tall grasses and gray tombstones in the old and unkempt graveyard that was split by the interstate just before the airport. He glanced away as they passed by a tombstone splintered in half; landing lights replaced grave markers and the plane dropped closer to the earth. The aircraft skimmed over the asphalt runway and the ground seemed to rise up for a meeting. The plane bumped hard but slowed to a safe stop.

John grinned while walking off the plane, anticipating seeing Claire's smiling face and her imperceptible but hopefully pregnant body. He surveyed the individuals waiting at the gate, but Claire was not among them. He checked the time. The flight was a half-hour late. He wondered if the flight delay had thrown Claire off?

He waited until the rest of the passengers left the gate, thinking he wasn't the only one prone to regressions. Perhaps this was cyclotherapy for Claire, too— back to her old habits of forgetting to pick him up at the airport?

He hung around the gate for another five minutes, looking for Claire. She was neither walking down the long hallway nor at the baggage claim, where his suitcase circled in solo orbit around the shiny metal carousel. He dragged his luggage to the pay phone and called home. The home phone buzzed a busy signal and he shook his head, thinking Claire was on the phone. He called back in two minutes and waited for her to answer, preparing his sarcastic question: Forget something or someone?

But she didn't pick up. The answering machine came on after the fourth ring, and Claire's recorded voice told him to leave a message.

"Claire? Claire! Can you hear me? Claire, pick up the phone, please. Claire! Ah, damn it," he said. "I'm at the airport and already picked up my suitcase, but lo-and-behold, you're not here. Did you just leave? You probably just called the airline and found out we got in earlier than expected after the rain delay and ran out the door to pick me up. Up to your old habits, eh, forgetting about picking me up? I'm going to pinch your butt when I see you, but I'll forgive you with hugs and kisses when I get you home. Hey, you probably won't get this message until we're home together, but I'll wait for you by the baggage claim entrance. Love you."

He sat near the baggage claim, watching two of the terminal entrances and checking his watch. John figured it would take about ten minutes for her to reach the airport, maybe another five to park and walk in. He waited fifteen minutes, then another five, before lugging his suitcase upstairs to the curbside pickup zone to see if Claire was waiting there. The sun had set, it was growing dim, but he didn't see Claire's car. He ran back inside, looking again for Claire at the baggage carousels. He waited ten more minutes, shuffling twice more between the passenger pickup zone and baggage claim. He called home, but again only the answering machine picked up. He figured Claire had the arrival time completely messed up. He'd written the information on a scrap of paper but wondered if she'd misread his messy scribbles. Or perhaps, he thought, she was responding to yet another client crisis.

He found a courtesy white phone and had Claire paged. He waited five minutes without a call back. He called home once more, talked again with the answering machine, took a last look at the baggage claim and pickup zone areas, and then hailed a cab.

The cabbie was an obese man in his late forties with a bulbous throat and gray stubble growing over his sallow skin. He was carrying on about football. John only half-listened, worrying instead about Bart, wondering if something bad had happened. Six months back he and Claire had rushed Bart to the vet, who'd said the old beagle only had one to four months to live. He was a good dog, a damn good dog. The cabbie repeated a question about Saturday's Mizzou game. John replied he no longer followed college football closely.

The taxi driver shrugged, pointing a stubby finger at the standing puddles on the side of the road that glistened against the black tar. "Hell of a storm this afternoon."

"Pretty bad, huh?" John asked.

"Jesus! Good thing you missed it. Caused a goddamn mess on the highways. You couldn't see shit in front of your face. Some cars pulled over to the side of the road. Me, I just kept hauling ass. But it was bad. One of those goddamn torrential downpours."

John directed him off the highway, down several side streets, and into his subdivision. He peered ahead, hoping to see Claire's Toyota rolling down the street, but the road was empty.

John tipped the cabbie ten dollars on the inexpensive fare, unlocked the front door, and called out for Claire, but the house was silent. He checked the garage; Claire's car was gone. He figured either they'd missed each other at the airport or something bad had happened to Bart. John hustled downstairs, hesitated, and then opened the laundry room door. Serendipity emerged, sniffing at his pant leg, and wagging her yellow tail. Around the corner, Bart struggled to his feet, stretching his neck and limbs. He waddled stiff-legged over to John, his tail wagging. John kneeled to pet him, and then hugged the old beagle around the neck. Serendipity brushed against him, and John petted her too. She growled at Bart.

"Stop, Serendipity." He pointed a finger at her long snout. "It's good to see you two, especially you, old beagle boy. I'm glad you're okay. But where's your momma, huh? Is she out looking for me at the airport while I'm looking for her at home? Or did she have to work late? You don't know, do you? You just like being petted. Come on, outside to pee, you old scoundrels."

John let them out to the backyard and searched the kitchen for a note, but there was none. Serendipity and Bart barked at the back door. John let them in, but they whined and he gave them each a hot dog. They devoured the meat in a nanosecond and followed John upstairs. He hoisted his suitcase onto the bed, reached onto the dresser to replay the answering machine, but found the lever was on playback rather than record. He lifted the cover; the incoming message tape had run all the way to the end.

"Damn it, Claire." He shook his head—she had once again forgotten to reset the machine. He rewound the tape, pressed play and listened, but the only messages were from the previous day. None of the messages he'd left from the airport had been recorded. He figured the busy signal he'd heard from the airport was Claire calling out to check the flight time—but maybe she was calling in from the office, leaving him a message that she was dealing with a crisis? In any case he realized that at this point, there'd be no messages from Claire, even if she had been trying to let him know what was going on.

He wished she'd come home soon. He checked the clock. There was barely enough time to see Andy at the hospital this evening even if Claire walked through the door in the next minute. He swore, but decided it would eventually make for a good laugh, once she was home and they worked through the aggravation. As he unpacked, Bart howled, his dark black eyes round and full.

"What is it, boy?"

He howled again, a soulful cry emanating from deep inside.

"You sound inconsolable. Ah, inconsolable for another hot dog, I bet." John rubbed Bart's floppy, brown-and-tan beagle ears. Bart stared back into John's eyes, and then howled once more.

"Stop, Bart, please."

A car door slammed outside.

"That's probably your mother," he told the dogs. "Home after a wild goose chase at the airport, looking to see if I'm home. She's going to be mad, but it'll serve her right for not being there on time."

John skipped down the stairs, Serendipity and Bart chasing at his heels. There was a knock against the front door, and John wondered if Claire had misplaced her new house key. He unlocked the door and opened it wide. Two St. Louis County policemen stood in their brown uniforms at the threshold. Bart growled and tried to push past John's legs. He clutched at the dog's collar. One of the policemen asked if he was John Anderson.

"Yes." John spoke automatically but with the immediate sense the moment was unreal.

"And is Claire Evers Anderson your wife?" The policeman was stocky and muscular like a bodybuilder, but his voice had a high-pitch whine.

John nodded, seeing things now as if he was watching from a great distance. The policeman darted a quick glance at his partner.

The officer looked back into John's eyes. "I'm sorry to inform you, sir, that your wife was killed late this afternoon in a car accident."

BOOK III

THE SOURCE OF A RIVER

John lay in bed listening to water drops plunk intermittently into the porcelain bathroom sink. He'd discovered the house he and Claire had bought together had lousy plumbing. Twice in less than three months he'd called plumbers to repair the leaks in the main stack that had turned the white plaster ceiling in the living room to a droopy vanilla pudding. They'd promised after the second repair call that they had fixed the problem, but water still dripped from a plethora of slow, leaky faucets. The leaks were annoying, not serious. Unlike his mechanically-minded father, John had never been particularly handy, and he'd always deferred minor house repairs to Claire.

He rolled over the heaviness that was his body, propped a cold pillow against his ears, and looked out the bedroom window. Gray pervaded the sky, the continuous cover making it impossible to distinguish a single cloud. It seemed to be raining again, not a heavy rain, but a light, steady drizzle.

He forced himself to look at the bedside clock, which illuminated 10:08. He cursed himself: this would be the fourth time within the week that he'd arrive ridiculously late to work. Loretta had told him the last time to take some time off, saying she and the rest of the staff were glad to pick up the load for as long as it took. She was a good person, they were all very supportive, but it was still hard—hard to wake up in the morning and even harder to fall asleep at night. And when he did finally fall asleep, it seemed like he'd sleep forever; it was almost impossible to wake fully when the alarm sounded. He was too lethargic to rise. After slapping the alarm clock silent, he'd lie there, sometimes falling back into a dead slumber, sometimes fully awake but too immobilized to stir. He hated himself for being so late to work but he felt neither the energy nor the motivation to get out of bed.

He made himself get up and call work, asking Loretta how things were going. Fine, she said, and suggested that he take the day off. He told her he'd be in after lunch. He pulled on gym clothes, including a heavy cotton sweat suit. He let Serendipity out the back door and snuck out the front; he felt guilty, but she was getting too old and slow to run with him. The next-door neighbor, a thirtysomething mother, who had the family dog in the passenger seat and her little girl in a car seat in the back, waved at John as she backed out of her driveway. The neighbor had taken care of Serendipity when John had flown to Washington for grant meetings and she'd offered to do so again any time he needed to travel. She waved a second time, and though he appreciated her kindness, he was sure she pitied him. He nodded back and ran off through the neighborhood, across the four-lane road, and onto the golf course. He'd expected to feel good running, but he was flooded with memories of walking on the golf course with Claire and Bart. John's body felt like it was made of clay, and he stopped running, trying to catch his breath. The light rain was more of a mist than droplets, but his sweat suit absorbed the moisture like a sponge, soaking his skin. A damp coldness bit the air and the temperature was dropping. He turned toward home.

An old man, crouched under a black umbrella, hobbled across the broken sidewalks. "Good morning," John said. The old man glanced at him with dark, listless eyes, and bobbed a slight nod. John nodded back as he ran past, but the image of the old man stayed with John, and for a moment John thought he could somehow sense that the old man would soon be dead. He quickly dismissed that thought as grief-induced, morbid thinking. Still, there was something familiar about the elderly man's gaze—dull, lifeless. It was the same look John had seen in middle-aged men at meetings and fifty-something women at the supermarket: drawn and ashen faces, a ubiquitous pallor, people moving about as if they were the walking dead. He wondered if that was the way most people lived—half-dead, trudging through life?

He took a long, hot shower. The curtain-lined tub filled with moist steam that he inhaled deeply. He backed further into the shower, closing his eyes, the hot water pouring over his head and streaming down his face. The water warmed the chill that had penetrated his flesh. He tried to think of nothing, though memories of Claire slid into his consciousness. He remembered making love with her for the very first time, her sneaking into the shower and then their slippery bodies slapping and sliding against each other in passionate embraces until the water turned freezing cold. What he wouldn't give for more times like that.

The red light on the answering machine stared at him. It had last night, too, after he had gotten home late from work but he hadn't bothered to listen to it then. He played it back now, hearing his mom's recorded voice.

"John, how are you?" she asked on the recorder. "Call me back. I'm worried about you. I'm praying for you, and for Claire too."

He scoffed at the message. What good would her prayers do now? But he had heard compassion as well as anxiety in her voice. She was always compassionate about loss. She had been at Claire's funeral, too, and he had appreciated her presence, though it was more of a hollow mental recognition as his gut had fallen numb to any feelings.

He pushed himself to fix a big lunch. For weeks he'd been eating next to nothing and he was losing weight. He microwaved three small red potatoes and warmed up a filet of orange roughy. While broiling the fish the night before, he'd been struck by the awareness that it was the flesh of what had been a living creature killed for his appetite. And then a horrible thought about Claire had invaded his mind: he imagined her flesh decaying within that $3,000 mahogany coffin he'd bought for her. He blocked the thoughts of Claire's body out of his mind while he sat down to lunch, but the sight of the dead fish tormented him. He ate the potatoes first, and then forced himself to stick the fork into the orange roughy; a chunk of white meat flaked off and he gagged. He shoved the fish back into the refrigerator.

He worked late, a self-imposed penance for his habitual tardiness and there was plenty to do: mounds of papers and folders cluttered his office desktop, file cabinets, and credenza. He picked at the top layer of mail and memos on his desk. There was a gentle knock at the door. He thought of saying nothing, pretending he was gone. The kids had left for the day or were in the transitional shelter in the next building. He figured the janitor was about to barge in. "Come in."

Crystal slipped into the doorway. The corner of her mouth turned up in a brief, shy smile. "Am I disturbing you?"

"It's okay."

"Looks like you're up to your old tricks, working late again." She fiddled with a strand of her long brown hair before brushing it behind her ear.

"Just trying to excavate the layers of paperwork on my desk."

"You're one of the most dedicated people I know. Even working late on a Friday night."

"Either that or I just don't want to go home." He grimaced, for his own words sounded pathetic as well as sad.

"It must be so painful." Crystal frowned, but with a look of sadness rather than disapproval. "How are you doing?"

"It's hard sometimes."

"I can only imagine," she said. "Loss and change are so wearing."

He managed only a slight nod for her.

"Well," Crystal said. She shifted her weight to her back foot. "I just wanted to say hi and wish you a good weekend."

"Thanks. You have a good weekend too."

"Bye." She raised her hand, folding her fingers down in a forlorn wave good-bye. She turned to leave but hesitated at the door. "Are you hungry?"

"Not really."

"But have you eaten dinner tonight already?"

"No."

"I've got an idea: why don't you come over to my house and I'll fix a good home-cooked dinner?"

"That's sweet of you, but I don't want to put you to any trouble."

"No trouble—I'm going to cook dinner tonight anyway. Besides, what are you going to eat otherwise?"

He pictured the orange roughy in the refrigerator and a wave of nausea rose in his stomach. "I don't know. I'm not very hungry these days, and I think I'm turning into a complete vegetarian."

"I'm already a vegetarian. What do you like? Spaghetti? Pastas?"

"Spaghetti is the one thing I still like."

"Fantastic. Spaghetti it is. Do you like vegetables? I can fix pasta primavera."

"Crystal, thanks for being so thoughtful but I don't think I feel up to it."

"John, I know it's hard. But you need to take care of yourself. You look like you've lost twenty pounds in the past couple of months. You need to take good care of yourself and you need to let your friends and colleagues be supportive of you too. I want to and so do the other staff here. Let me fix you a good dinner, as a friend who cares," she said. "Please."

There was an assertive edge to Crystal he hadn't seen before. He shrugged. "What can I say?"

"You can say, 'yes.'"

"Okay, yes."

"Good! Listen to me—I'm sorry." She shook her head as if gently scolding herself. "I can't stand being around bossy and intrusive people. I hope I'm not coming across that way. I just want to be supportive."

"It's okay. I need a push now and then," he told her, but he regretted the decision to go before he finished the sentence.

Crystal set the pasta and salad bowls on her small dining table. She sat next to John, smiled, and raised her bulb-shaped red wine glass in salute. "I'm glad you came."

He felt uncomfortable being at her apartment but thanked her for cooking dinner and diverted the topic, asking her first about her plans to return to graduate school for a doctorate, then about growing up in the South, and finally about her work at Our House. She spoke with passion and humor—much more than he'd seen at the office—and he listened with interest, asking more questions, and devouring the pasta. The spaghetti sauce was rich with tomato paste and Parmesan cheese and had a strong basil and garlic flavor. The garlic initially bothered him—Claire hated spicy foods, especially on his breath—and he'd grown accustomed to a bland diet over the years, but to his surprise, the meal was the first thing that tasted good to him in weeks. He complimented Crystal again on her cooking.

"Thank you, again." She displayed a lopsided smile as if she was embarrassed. "And how about you?"

"What about me?"

"You kept me talking about one thing or another about myself—I usually hate being the center of attention, but I'm comfortable with you and so I've been blabbering on about me. Look at my plate. I'm not even half done, because I've been so busy talking the whole time when you're the one who's been going through so much. What about you?"

He fidgeted on the hard wood chair. "Like what do you want to know?"

"I don't mean to be intrusive." She flapped her hands like she was flustered. "But, like, what are you thinking about our work?"

"You know, we've talked about this some at recent staff meetings, but I'm afraid our innovative little program is coming under increasing bureaucratization by the state. So, yeah, it concerns me that we're being pushed to adopt standardized clinical and administrative procedures that are used across the rest of the system, even though they are a procrustean fit for our clients and staff. Plus, now there's financial worries too."

"I thought we were doing okay." She cocked her head, looking both quizzical and worried. "You know, with the grants and all."

"We are. Or we were. The problem is that the rest of the region had a revenue shortfall, and now they want other programs that are in the black to help make that up, so they've redirected some of the core state funds that had been dedicated to the homeless to mainstream programs, which is leaving us in a bit of a hole."

"Can they do that?" Her Southern accent sparked as it did at times when she seemed excited.

"They are. It's all political, and homelessness is starting to become passé, while prevention of youth substance abuse is hot. Certainly, that's a worthy need, too, but it doesn't seem right to ask the homeless and runaway kids to pay for it."

"Can you do anything about it?"

"So far my pleas have fallen on deaf—even resentful—ears. But I think there's a couple of more political tactics we can try."

"That's good." She raised her wine glass. "Thanks for advocating for us."

"Yeah, except I'll probably piss off the administration even more." He tapped his fork against the plate. "And that's part of the problem. We're being charged more for overhead admin costs that keep growing to exert more control over our ways of doing things while we have less and less autonomy."

"How frustrating," she said. "You catch grief for all of this, don't you, from the new regional manager? What's her name, Phyllis?"

"Yeah, sometimes."

"That makes me mad," Crystal said. "She ought to consider herself lucky and appreciate you."

"Thanks. She's gotten under my skin a few times, to be honest with you." He pushed his plate away. "But at this point I don't really care what she thinks."

"What's her problem?"

"She's not a clinician, so she doesn't have a good feel for what we do, which is part of the problem. She's also into control management and loyal—if some-times buffoonish—underlings who blindly applaud and follow her ideas. But then again, she probably sees me as rebellious, arrogant, headstrong, and a gen-eral pain in the ass."

"She sounds like a bitch," Crystal said. "Excuse my language—I usually hate using that word for women."

"She's smart and knows a lot of business practices, but she doesn't under-stand the clinical implications of what she's doing. And sometimes she goes around like she has a corncob stuck up her ass, pardon the expression."

"I bet that's not so fun for you, working with a boss who has a corncob stuck up her ass."

"No, sometimes it's not."

She paused, scanning his face, and then gave him a smile that seemed both sad and warm. "How are you doing, with this, with everything else?"

"Okay."

"John, you always say that—'okay,'" she lowered her voice to a deeper tone, trying to imitate his voice. "I imagine you could be standing in the middle of a hurricane and you'd still say, 'okay.'"

"Probably so. It's a rote reply."

"How are you, really?"

"It's been hard."

"I'm so sorry." She grimaced. "I wish I had a way with words like you do—I don't know the right way to say this—but I feel so much empathy and caring for you. I can't really imagine what it's been like."

"Thank you." He hesitated, but only for a second. "You know, when I was first told about Claire, there was this flash of unimaginable horror and then I had this unreal perspective on what the policeman was telling me and everything that happened afterward. It was like I was observing things at the far end of a long tunnel." He hadn't intended to share that experience. For an instant, he was reliving the experience, and he told Crystal things he'd kept private, but he couldn't—or didn't want to?—stop. "I saw myself doing things, like making funeral arrangements in this quiet, sterile mortuary with white marble steps and a stained-glass window designed with a peacock whose brilliant colors had been properly muted; listening to a slick-haired casket salesman say empathic-sounding comments while he tried to sell me the most expensive casket; picking out the gravesite while Claire's ultrareligious brother was jabbering on about how peaceful the cemetery hillside looked—and the whole time I just wanted to scream. But I didn't. I just kept going through the motions, even while the whole thing felt completely unreal. And it got worse, with her family, my family, our friends all around. Good people, but too many. I didn't want our house to be crawling with so many family members, I didn't want to be at a funeral parlor or church or cemetery, surrounded by all sorts of people. I wanted to be off somewhere by myself, in the woods or on a mountaintop or near a river—it didn't matter. I just wanted to be alone with my grief for Claire. But I didn't do that. I did what was expected, listening to other people's sympathetic words, consoling more than a few people myself, but it became overwhelming and then do you know what I felt?"

"What?"

"Nothing. It was like I wasn't really there anymore—not my heart and soul. I was numb."

"You really needed time for yourself." Crystal frowned and an expression of pain—John wondered if it was empathy or a stirring of painful experiences from her past—passed over her face. "I'm sorry you couldn't get what you needed."

"Thanks, but maybe it was better that way—maybe being there with all those people and tasks helped ground me—maybe I would have gone crazy if I was off somewhere by myself."

"Maybe," she said. "Or maybe what happened—to lose your partner so young—feels crazy, no matter what. It's not what we expect, not what should happen in life."

Maybe not, he thought, but it is what happens. He looked at her, deciding whether he should keep talking or shut up. Something about the look in her eyes seemed both safe and caring. "You know, I've thought a lot about death all my life, even sometimes as a little boy, lying in bed and trying to fall asleep, and I've had lots of sleepless nights as an adult, trying to break through my own personality defenses and the cultural denial to really understand and come to grips with the facts—that we die, that it's inevitable, that it's unpredictable, that this crazy life is fragile and fleeting. I fancied myself a lot more aware of all this than the average person. And yet all existential pondering notwithstanding, it seems like a total fucking shock that Claire is gone. " And where did she go—did she still exist in some form? The question tormented him, but the worry felt both too intimate and too obsessively neurotic to share.

"I know," Crystal said. "It's unimaginable and horrible at the same time."

He blinked hard, holding his eyes tight for an instant.

"John, it's okay to cry now," she said. "I cried my way through so many nights after my divorce."

He shook his head. "That's good for you," he said. "But it doesn't fit for me."

"I understand. But do you give yourself permission other times to cry or be sad?"

"I'm sad every day."

"I'm sorry." She winced and leaned forward, touching her hand to his arm. "That was so insensitive."

"Don't worry about it."

"It was a stupid question," she said. "I know it's had to be very sad."

"This probably sounds really stupid," he said. "But it's been harder since Claire's old beagle died. Claire had him for sixteen years and she really loved that dog—and so did I. He had this strength of character, of presence, that I've never seen in an animal before." John told Crystal about the vet's prognosis the prior spring, saying that Bart had only one to four months to live. "I was hoping the vet didn't know what he was talking about—it had been six months—but Bart went downhill immediately after Claire died. It was like he knew she was gone and he lost his will to live. He died six weeks to the day after she did."

"I had no idea," Crystal said. "You needed him and he was gone too. I'm so sorry."

"Me too. I loved that dog and I sure didn't want to see him die, especially then, but I had no choice about that either. You know it's strange, but Bart's death hit me even harder in terms of my own sanity and emotions. I don't know why, but I'm sure it's related to Claire somehow."

"What have you been feeling?"

He scanned her face; she looked at him without judgment. "Sometimes I just feel so stressed out on the inside that it feels like I'm going to come apart at the seams. It's really hard to be around people sometimes."

"You need time for yourself."

It was more than that. There had been a few occasions when he felt like he was going crazy in meetings and had wanted to run amok out of the room, but he had held on, telling himself he was just on the verge of a panic attack from the grief, though it felt more like he was going psychotic from the loss. "Yes. And it's hard to sleep. There's a double whammy. I can't fall asleep at night and then in the morning I can't get up. I just lay there most mornings, like I'm immobilized, not wanting to do anything. It's like what's the point? What's the fucking point?"

"Loss makes us question everything," Crystal said. "But there's a point to what you do with the kids. Your work makes a difference."

"I try to tell myself that—that there's meaning to working with the kids, even if there's nothing else that matters. But you know what? It doesn't feel that way now. Maybe it's because I see the program slipping away, getting slowly chewed up and swallowed by the state bureaucracy—or maybe it's just me. All I know for sure is that work, like everything, feels dead to me. I'm just going through the motions."

"John, I don't pretend to know everything you're going through. But I know the grief I went through after my husband suddenly left me was awful. I felt so sad and depressed and anxious for months. It'll get better, but it's terrible when you lose someone you love. I'm so sorry." She said this with a look of discomfort like it was her fault. "I really care about you. I wish I could make it better."

"Thank you." He tried to scoff a laugh. "I'm sorry. I must sound like a real basket case."

"No. You sound like you are a really good, caring, sensitive person who's in pain."

"I don't know about that, but thanks."

"It's true," she said. "And you've also been through a terrible trauma that must hurt a lot. How are you feeling now?"

"Umm." He shook his head and a tear slipped onto his cheek. He blinked his eyes shut.

"It's okay." She rested her hand on top of his and squeezed it.

John closed his eyelids tighter, but tears slipped past. He cried aloud, trying to stop himself at first, but then breaking into a series of sobs. Crystal wrapped her arms snugly around his shoulders. She held him, patting his back, nuzzling his face against her breasts. He cried for a long time.

He remembered times when he and Claire had broken up over the years. He'd felt so sad then, but he'd always had the hope they'd be back together again. But no amount of self-examination, planning, and plotting would bring Claire back this time. He'd never see her face again. He heard himself emit a deep wail, a howling cry—like some wounded animal. He had no words for his feelings. He only knew he felt a deep, aching pain way inside, like a knife was lodged within his solar plexus.

He wasn't sure how long he'd cried, but at some point, he found there were no more tears. He heaved a dry sob, and then caught his breath. He noticed the warmth of Crystal's arms encircling him. He pulled his head back, opening his eyes.

"How are you?" she asked.

"Oh, better. Better for now anyway. Thank you."

"Do you want to talk about it?"

"No, that's okay. Not now anyway. I just want to enjoy feeling better for a minute."

"I'm glad you let me hold you."

"It helped, thank you."

"You're welcome. You know, I've noticed something about you."

"What's that?"

"You thank me every time I'm nice to you." She laughed. "You don't have to, you know."

Brightness shined in her large, brown eyes and her face flushed with color. He was lucky that she was there, so nice to him. She smiled, a slight upturn of her lips, with a look of kindness or caring or intimacy or flirting or something. He wasn't sure how to describe it, but he responded with a similar expression. She said nothing, but gently lifted her fingertips to his face, caressing away a lingering teardrop. She drew closer, looking into his eyes. With a mixture of excitement and incredulousness, he felt himself move toward her, losing the detail of her features in a blur and finding her lips with his own.

Her kiss was fleshy, warm, moist. He felt lightheaded, but passion swelled through his body.

He thought of Claire and felt guilty. It was too soon to be with another woman. But maybe this was exactly what he needed? A respite from his mourning. Claire would understand; more than that, she would want him to go on, to allow himself some comfort.

He told himself not to feel guilty, and then he imagined Claire was the woman he was embracing. He kissed her with fervor, sensing a roiling within of both pleasure and pain as they fell to the floor. He unbuttoned her blouse, unhooked her bra, and moved down her body. He cupped her breasts, kissing them, and then traced his tongue down her flat abdomen. He unbuttoned her jeans, pulled them away from her hips, and slipped them off her legs. He found her vagina, warm and wet, with his lips. He lost himself then, kissing and licking her; it was like being with Claire again and he let the sensations overtake him. He swirled and pressed his tongue against her while caressing her bare hips with his hands. She moaned and pressed herself against him.

Crystal grabbed him by the side of the head and tried to pull him, but he resisted, intent on licking her. "Come here," she whispered. She tugged harder, pulling him up to her face. She kissed him, grabbed his penis, and inserted it inside her.

He held his eyes shut, picturing the intensity of Claire's face when they used to make love, as he thrust himself in and out of Crystal.

Her mouth pulled away, breaking the seal of their lips. "Oh my God." She exhaled rapidly, her fingernails digging into his back. She gushed the words, "My God," over and over again as her body tensed under his. Her words were almost the same as Claire's as she orgasmed.

But it wasn't Claire. The voice was different, a tiny, high-pitched Southern accent instead of Claire's deep-throated exclamations, and the body convulsing in spasms underneath him was fuller than Claire's. Claire's body, he knew, was sealed within that mahogany coffin, under a ton of earth; her body was black and blue and probably beginning to decay. He swore silently and tried to push the image out of his mind.

Stop, he told himself. Just forget it. Be here now with Crystal. Lose yourself for a few more minutes.

He sensed his penis deserting him. It faded into a rubbery stump. He tried to excite it, to stroke his penis teasingly within Crystal, but it popped out of her. He tried to find his way back inside her; he humped and pressed, but it was hopeless. He was impotent.

"Are you okay?" Crystal asked.

"Yes," he said. "I just suddenly got distracted."

She kissed him. "Here, let me help."

She slid down his chest. She took his crumpled penis in her hands and licked it. She opened her mouth, sucking him, swirling her tongue around his penis. He closed his eyes and tried to focus on the pleasure he normally felt from oral sex.

But there was no excitement, no pleasure. There was only the image of Claire—and her decomposing body—overtaking his mind. He tried to block the image. He felt Crystal's breasts dangling against his bare thighs as she sucked him and he ran his hands through her thick hair. He pictured himself having intercourse with her again, lost in fervor, melting inside her. But his penis, small and shriveled, mocked him.

"Stop." He pulled Crystal off.

"I'm sorry." She brushed back her hair from her face. "It was too soon, wasn't it?"

"Yup."

"It made you think of your wife, didn't it?"

"Yes."

"I'm sorry," Crystal said. "I should have been more sensitive."

"It's not you. I'm the one who's sorry."

"It's okay." She tried to smile. "It happens."

"Not to me."

"Don't feel bad," she said. "It was still very sweet and nice. You gave me a wonderful orgasm—I just wish I could give you one." She stroked his chest with her fingers. "Maybe later."

"I got to go." He tried to slip out of her arms.

She lingered, holding onto him for an awkward moment, hugging him in a tight squeeze. He hugged her back, but just for an instant, and wiggled free of her arms. He politely refused her offer of ice cream for dessert and left quickly before he screamed.

Light snowflakes fell on John's drive home. It was the first snowfall of the winter, all the prior storms had passed to the north, but the snow wasn't heavy and the ground wasn't cold enough for accumulation. A flake splattered wet against his windshield. As he watched the snowflake melt, he concluded he'd been an idiot for trying to have sex with Crystal. It was stupid to think that he could have replaced sorrow with sex. He'd been temporarily insane, expecting he could have lost himself in the frenzy of flapping flesh, and the marvelous quickening of an orgasm. Yet it was an insanity that he had succumbed to time and again in his life, he realized, as if the arms of a beautiful and adoring woman could make him feel whole, and that pleasing a woman would make him happy too.

The telephone was ringing when he opened the house door. He reached for the phone and then hesitated, knowing it was not Claire, nor even Nona, the two people he most wanted to talk to. He didn't want to speak with anyone else, but his work might be calling about another crisis. He picked up the receiver and mumbled hello.

"I'm sorry to bother you." Crystal's voice, tiny and meek, like a child's, whispered across the line. "I just wanted to check and see how you are."

"I'm okay."

"'Okay,' like in the middle of a hurricane?"

"Yeah, probably."

"How are you really?" she asked.

"I don't know." He wanted to get off the phone. "Upset, but I'll be okay. Don't worry."

"I'm sorry," she said.

"You didn't do anything wrong."

"I wasn't very sensitive to you," Crystal said. "See, I care about you a lot. I have for a long time, so I wasn't thinking very straight. I wasn't planning we'd be sexual—it just happened. I just wanted to be your friend, but I should have been more thoughtful about your feelings and how upsetting it would feel to be with someone else right now."

"Well, thanks. But it really wasn't your fault. It's me—I'm just pretty screwed up right now."

"Do you want to talk?" she asked.

"Not really, but thanks."

"I understand not wanting to talk," she said. "But what do you need now?"

"Pardon?"

"What do you need now?"

"Probably just to be alone for right now."

"I understand," she said. "Take good care of yourself, though, okay?"

"Yes, thanks."

"See you Monday?"

"Yes."

"Bye," she said. "Call me over the weekend if you want. Take care of yourself."

Though the phrases were not uncommon, he thought she sounded like Claire, saying similar things as Claire used to tell him when he was upset: "What do you need?" "Take good care of yourself." It felt strange to hear someone say those words to him again in such a caring and intimate way.

For a moment, he wasn't sure what to do. He went to his study, telling himself he should journal, but he didn't feel like writing. He remembered years before when he'd felt the terrible ache inside—like a hole that couldn't be filled—after Claire had broken up with him. He rummaged through their record collection and found the old Santana album. He shoved aside the furniture, grabbed his silver-and-red aluminum bat from the closet, and swung to the chords of Santana. He swung the bat slowly at first, and then harder and harder, remembering years before, grooving his softball swing through winter nights while listening to Santana and grieving Claire after a breakup. It used to help. But then he'd always harbored hope that he and Claire would get back together. And now? Now there was nothing to count on. He'd never see Claire again in the flesh, maybe never again in any form—maybe death was only a portal to nothingness?

As he swung his bat, he eyed God hanging on the wall, pointing his long arm and finger toward Adam in the framed poster of Michelangelo's creation. The feeling was vague, but something churned inside, something that felt very small and scared, and yet also angry. He begrudgingly prayed to God. He prayed that death was not final, that Claire and Nona and Emerson and all of his grandparents and great-grandparents still existed and that he would see them again. He remembered then Nona and her mother, Mama Clara, saying multiple times after bad things had happened in someone's life, that "God punishes." He entertained for an instant that Claire's death was his punishment—or hers—but then he dismissed that notion as pure bullshit. But he wondered why God, who is supposed to be omniscient and all-loving, would let Claire die? Maybe, he told himself, because he doesn't want to over function in our lives?

Or maybe there is no God, he thought. He cranked up the stereo and gripped his bat tighter. No God who is cruel or insensitive or omniscient. Maybe God is just our unconscious, collective fantasy to fill our infantile need for a perfect, all-knowing, all-powerful father? A self-created solution to satisfy our need for security? Maybe God is a shared delusion to deny we are anything but meaningless plops of protoplasm in a random, chaotic, uncaring universe—a mental fabrication to alleviate our dread about not existing after death, about being gone forever, without consciousness, only flesh rotting, eaten by worms, dissolving into dust, like Claire.

He took a huge, uppercut swing. Or maybe there is a God, and He giveth and He taketh away. Or maybe God just doesn't give a fuck.

John lunged toward the wall and swung the bat like a tomahawk at the poster of God and Adam. His swing shattered the glass cover into a thousand pieces and hurled the poster off the wall and across the room. He tossed the bat to the floor and walked to bed.

He could not sleep. He felt both stupid and awful. Claire had been dead barely three months. It was wrong to be screwing around with Crystal—it would have been wrong with anyone. He had dishonored Claire, and he felt disgusted with himself.

His stomach was queasy. An unsettled feeling rolled inside his stomach and then pinched his intestines. Gas cramps, he thought, remembering the garlic in the pasta. He pushed out a blaring fart. He remembered Claire farting, one after another in bed. He'd complained about it. Just getting a little gas out, she'd say innocently. Sometimes she'd even announce her intentions ahead of time: I need to lay flat and get some gas out, she'd say. No embarrassment, simply au natural. If anything, she wanted a little empathy about her hurting stomach. But he'd turn off, her farting a killer to the sexual fantasies he was harboring for the night. He remembered withdrawing to his side of the bed, turning his back to her, ignoring her while trying to sleep. He wondered how many nights he'd squandered? Nights when he could have held her close, even if she blew the covers off. He'd give anything to be with her now, to hear her squeaky farts, to make love. But that life was gone.

He saw Claire in his sleep, dreaming he was making love to her, but she pulled her lips away, saying she had to run to the bathroom. It's okay, he told her, leaning in to kiss her again, but she said she had to throw up.

He woke up then, disoriented by fleeting and fuzzy images, recalling the dream but realizing he was alone in bed, his stomach nauseated and cramping.

He ran to the bathroom, kneeled in front of the white porcelain toilet bowl, and tried to quell his stomach. He closed his eyes, breathing deep, but lost control. His stomach contracted, and his head felt compressed, like a gigantic vacuum was sucking on his skull; half-digested noodles erupted from his stomach and mouth, spewing into the toilet bowl. He closed his eyes again and took several quick breaths. His stomach rolled, and then contracted, and he threw up again. He lingered on all fours in front of the toilet, and then trudged back to bed.

His stomach hurt less, but it was still irritated. He remembered having the flu once years before, right after he and Claire had broken up when he was seeing Amy. At the time, he had been reading Alan Watts, who had written we should not judge vomiting but instead open fully to the experience. John had found Watts' words provocative then, but now he thought himself pathetic. But wasn't that his characterological M.O.: always caught in his head, perseverating on some idea or worry, rather than truly being present to life and to Claire?

Even after they had married, he hadn't fully embraced her. He was always too busy with work or too caught up in this worry or that one. There was so much more they should have done, more places they should have gone, but they didn't. They never went all the way up river to the source.

They should have gone, but they didn't. Why not? Maybe because Claire had always been right about him—that he was a goddamn chickenshit, too afraid to really live?

Why not go now? He should go to the river, he thought, instead of moping around, remembering philosophy books, trying to fuck his employees.

He decided to wait no longer. He rinsed the remaining vomit particles from his mouth, put on clothes, scribbled a note for his neighbor, and left.

CHAPTER 39

John found the old man's fishing and sporting goods store in the predawn shadows and pounded the door with his fist, hoping to rouse someone. Peering through the window, he saw only darkness. He stood in heavy snowfall and banged the door again to no avail. Across the street he spotted a man leaving a coffee shop. John raised his arm to hail him.

The man was big, with a barrel stomach, a chest and shoulders like a pro wrestler, and a large, almost square head with a matching jaw beneath a red trucker's cap. John asked him when Stone's store would open. The man looked John over as if he was sizing him up for a match.

"Usually not at 6:55 in the morning," the man said in a rumbly voice that sounded more like a growl. "But Andy Stone keeps his own hours this time of year. If he feels like it, he'll be in most any day or time. If not, he'll be at his place."

John remembered the route from summer, but the road looked different in winter under falling snow. He worried on the drive that Stone wouldn't be home, but a light shone from a downstairs window and Stone answered the knock almost immediately, his lanky frame filling the doorway in silhouette. John apologized for the early hour and reintroduced himself, saying he'd rented a canoe in August.

"Yup. You did." Stone leaned into the doorjamb.

"I want to rent another one."

"When's that?"

"Now."

"Too cold now." He raised his coffee cup to his thin, birdlike lips.

"I'm not worried about the cold."

"The lake's already frozen," Stone said. "And the river's probably starting to freeze up north too."

"Doesn't matter. I'll paddle as far as I can and then hike along the river like before."

"Not many men travel the river in winter." Stone gazed at John as if he was trying to get a measure of his mettle. "Could be dangerous."

"I'm going."

"Your wife with you?"

John had hoped Stone wouldn't ask about Claire—it was too raw. "She died." He hated himself for the warble in his voice.

"Real sorry to hear that," Stone said. "She was a special lady."

For an instant, John wanted to tell him off: Who the hell was he to be talking about her? Stone didn't know Claire—how could he after a couple of brief encounters? John stared at the old man, but his resentment gave way to appreciation as he remembered Claire's affinity for the old outdoorsman. John decided Stone's comment was a tribute to Claire and the way she immediately impacted others. "Yes," John said. "I knew she was special from the day I met her."

"Tell you what," Stone said. "Come back early this summer and I'll let you use the canoe and camping gear for free."

"I drove all the way from St. Louis to get here to go up the river *now*, and that's exactly what I'm going to do."

"Not a good idea."

"Well, if you're not willing to rent me a canoe, I'll find another, even if I have to drive back to Denver and buy one, but I'm going up that river." The snow crunched under John's heel as he pivoted from the doorway.

"Hold on, young man," Stone called. "If you're so bound and determined to go, and I see you are, I'll get you cold weather gear down at the shop to go with the canoe."

Stone was good to his word, outfitting John with gear and supplies he'd not even considered, but it took a long time to travel from Stone's shop to the river in the snow. Stone said the winding, downhill road they'd used in July would be impassable with the fresh snow. He backtracked south of town, crossed to the west side of the river, and eased down a less steep but still slippery road to a put-in that was twelve miles further northwest. When they'd finally reached the river, the outfitter reached for the canoe on top of his truck, but then paused.

"Sure you want to try this?" Stone asked.

The frigid wind whipped tears from the corner of John's eyes, and he had the passing thought that his plan was insane. He remembered then lying in bed sleepless for hours but unable to get up, showing up to work hours late, and trying to have sex with Crystal—all those things seemed crazier than going up river. Even after a wearing sixteen-hundred-mile drive to the mountains over two days, he sensed a purpose in his actions for the first time in weeks. He deemed himself sane—not crazy—and if he was wrong, well, he didn't care. "I'm sure."

The old man cautioned to stay dry as he launched John into the icing river.

The wind slackened, and large snowflakes parachuted through the air. They clumped together on the ground, masking the bank in white. More snowflakes fell into the river. Their plumpness melted when they hit the water, exposing underlying crystal skeletons for an instant before they too dissolved. John shoved his paddle deep into the water and pulled a full stroke alongside his body. He found a rhythm, gliding his paddle through the icing water as if in a trance.

The river grew thicker with ice as he paddled north. The bow of the canoe broke a thin layer of ice midstream. He steered toward shore, ramming through thicker ice, and then jumped onto shore. The shoreline was too rocky and irregular to pull the canoe on the ground upstream and it was too heavy to portage alone for any distance in the snow. John dragged the canoe onto shore, lodged it between a rock and a tree, secured some supplies in the nose of the canoe, and lugged a backpack and another pack with gear over his shoulders.

He walked the shoreline north for an hour then paused, out of breath and fatigued. The cold air nipped at the eye openings in his ski mask and he felt light-headed, almost dizzy. He worried if he'd have enough energy, if the snow and rising wind were too cold—and then he dismissed the thought as one of weakness.

Ice soon sealed over the river and he debated whether to walk on it. The ice looked solid and the river shallow, but he continued hiking along the shore until he reached the lake.

The small lake lay at the feet of the canyon. Covered with snow and ice, the lake looked like a huge oval skating rink. The snow reflected a white sheen against the granite cliffs to the northwest. He kicked a clearing in the wet snow and peered into the lake. The water appeared frozen clear to its rocky bottom. He lightly pressed one foot against the ice. The surface felt solid, so he put more weight on his leg, and then stepped fully onto the ice. It was thick and firm, but he stayed near the shore and walked around the lake's circumference, past the rock where Claire had fished.

The wind had died but snow still cluttered the sky with wide, hoary flakes. The new snow plummeted to earth, laying down a cover on the preceding flakes and nearly hiding the ice. White-crested ridges of ice rose above the new snow. He walked further and came upon strange protrusions of ice that rose from the frozen lake surface in small, gnarled cylinders. They looked like the knuckled ends of sawed-off tree branches. He stepped carefully along the edge of the frozen water. The air was now still, and the whiteness of the snow and ice made the world seem desolate.

He wished for company and looked about, hoping an eagle or heron would soar over the treetops. But there were no birds, no animals, no people.

He remembered another January day, years before, when a winter storm had dumped six inches of fresh snow on St. Louis. Claire had roused him out of bed, eager to go for a walk in the snow, and she had taken him down the hills of the deserted golf course near her house. The weather had been freezing cold, the wind gusting across the barren course, but when he had complained about the temperature, she reached her hand into his coat pocket and held his hand.

The ice groaned a low sound and he jumped back to shore. He had the strange image of huge birds flapping their great wings to soar into flight. *Whooam*, the ice bellowed again. He scanned the lake. Nothing moved and the ice was solid. He figured that somewhere deep in the lake the ice was straining as it thickened. Still, despite his reasoning, he felt lightheaded. He had only been three feet away from the shore, and yet he moved back onto the rocky ground while admonishing himself for being a coward.

He followed the shoreline around the lake. The river, frozen solid, split the cliffs. He gazed upstream to a place he'd never been before. The cliffs descended sharply, straight into the river on the west side of the gorge, but crumbled on the east side into a narrow, rocky shore. He picked his way past the boulders along the eastern edge. It had stopped snowing and a thin band of wispy, gray clouds hovered near the cliffs and close to the earth.

The frozen river led into the gorge. As he hiked north, the canyon narrowed and the path he was following ended. There was no longer a bank or a shoreline, only the cliffs and frozen river. He tested the ice, gently tapping a single foot onto the frozen river; it felt as solid as the lake and yet a swell of anxiety mounted within him. He had the impulse to turn back—indeed, to run away, but he breathed deeply and told himself not to panic. He stood on the ice with both feet—he wasn't sure for how long, but he sensed it was for longer than he knew—and then he found himself striding ahead on the frozen river.

He hiked upstream on the ice for an hour and worried then it would be dark before he could reach the source. He walked faster, hearing again the flapping sound of giant wings as the shifting of the ice rumbled through the gorge. He felt nervous but told himself to relax. The ice still felt solid. He vowed not to be a coward and to make it all the way to the source.

He wondered what he would find—the leading edge of a glacier? He imagined icicles hanging from the glacier like long, thin fingers. Instead of melting and feeding the headwaters of the river like in the spring, the icicles would be frozen solid now. He had brought wooden matches and pictured himself striking the matches and holding the flame to the icy stalactites to melt the ice.

He quickened his steps, determined to find the source before nightfall. After he had reached the source, he would find a place nearby that was blocked from the wind and pitch the tent for the night. It would be freezing but he'd be okay. Stone had outfitted John with layers of specialized clothing, gear, and extra supplies, as if John was a soldier in the Icelandic Army. He'd be safe within the down sleeping bag. He pictured himself watching a black sky chockfull of stars. He would be missing Claire—he already was, but there was nothing he could do about that other than to keep going and hold her in his thoughts.

Ahead the river opened to the left, as if a tributary flowed from the cliffs. As he neared, he saw a cave opened from the base of the cliffs into the iced river.

Whoom. John stopped. The groan was louder, sharper than back at the lake. He told himself it was only the ice straining as it thickened.

He stepped upriver. The ice whined again. He berated himself for feeling scared and told himself to keep going and not to be a chickenshit. A silvery sheen reflected off the ice in front of him. He figured it was especially slick ahead. He removed one of the packs from his back to reduce his weight, stored it atop a boulder, and strode ahead.

The ice cracked, sounding like a giant bone breaking. The footing beneath him collapsed.

He fell into the river and coldness seized him. His skin burned, as if a huge flame enveloped his body. He felt himself sinking toward something unseen.

He thrashed beneath the surface, and then instinctively, without realizing for an instant what he was doing, he looked for his father. John wanted to scream but he couldn't.

Whiteness glared from above. He propelled himself toward the surface, but ice sealed the river. He looked about, trying to find the hole where he fell through, but could not find it. He pushed at the ice overhead but it didn't budge. He flailed at it with both fists, but the ice held solid and he sank downward again. His entire body burned badly as if he was in hell.

He remembered—he *felt* again—thrashing through the rapids after he and Claire had once capsized into the Arkansas river. He had been so scared then to ask Claire to marry him. But he did ask her, and she said yes, and he made love to her with complete presence on the boulder that split the wild river. It had been wonderful, but it was gone.

He realized then he could die. He should join her now. Maybe it was only endless sleep. Perhaps he had already died once years before. He entertained the thought of giving himself over to death, *choosing* it for an instant. He drifted deeper. His feet scraped against a rocky bottom.

Without conscious reasoning, he rejected dying. He struggled again in the water and slipped off his backpack. He swam to the surface, but the ice still trapped him.

He searched again for the opening where he fell through the ice, but he couldn't find it. He punched at the ice above him. It remained unbroken and he sank again.

His lungs screamed without sound. He felt ready to implode. He parted the river with a frog stroke, forcing himself back to the ceiling of ice. He struck it with short jabs. A thin line cracked across the ice. He smashed it again and more cracks ran across the ice like spider webs. He kicked his legs rapidly to stay close to the surface, and he threw a series of jabs until the ice broke cleanly.

He tore away chunks of ice and thrust his head through the opening. He gulped rapid breaths of air and spit water. He tried to pull himself on top of the ice, but it cracked wider. He slipped back into the water.

He grabbed again for the ice. He lifted himself out of the water, flipping his chest and stomach onto the frozen surface like a seal. He dragged his legs out of the water, watching to see if his weight would shatter the ice and plunge him back into the river. He raised himself to all fours. He crawled away from the open water as the ice held.

He kneeled at the river's edge. The skin across his body burned and then turned numb.

Keep going, he thought, to the source. But he realized then the idea was ludicrous—his whole plan had been. He could die of hypothermia or fall through the ice again, his body trapped in the river until spring. He debated himself. He did not want to give up his search, but then, almost instinctively, he crawled on the ice, full of self-contempt, toward the cave.

His knee cracked through the ice at the mouth of the grotto and splashed into the water, but he caught himself with his hands. The ice was thin where the river joined the cave, but the water was shallow beneath. He clambered to the side of the cave and steadied himself by grabbing onto large rocks.

A gusting wind picked up, lashing at him through the cave opening. He picked his way deeper into the cave, but stumbled over a rock, which sent an intense pain like his flesh was on fire flaring up his leg. The ceiling of the cave rose higher. He stood up and walked deeper into the cave for shelter. The stream narrowed, the ice changed to slush, and then the water ran clear and free of ice. His wet clothes had stiffened; it felt like dry ice pressing against his skin.

He stripped the layers of wet clothes from his body, and then rubbed his wet skin dry. He shook with cold and knew he needed to raise his body temperature. He sprang naked into a jumping jack alongside the small cave spring. He smacked trembling hands against each other and then against the sides of his thighs. The motion sent loud claps resounding through the cave. He repeated naked jumping jacks in the near dark, and he remembered how Claire had once flopped onto the new snow next to the golf course pond, her arms and legs waving rhythmically back and forth through the fresh powder as she sculpted angels in the snow. Seeing her then, her legs gyrating around the fulcrum of her crotch, had suddenly excited him. He had climbed atop of her then and they had made love in the snow in the dead of winter on the deserted golf course.

The sensation of his skin being on fire intensified as he clapped out another jumping jack, and he recalled how his skin had burned under the hot shower back at Claire's house after sex in the snow. He had figured then that it was a good sign though painful, that he was thawing out and the numbness was wearing off.

But that was then and what he wanted now was impossible. He could no longer make love with Claire any more than he could take her to the source. Nor would he be able to continue on his own up river through the snow and ice. It had been a deranged idea to even try. He had pretended like nothing could stop him, but now he knew the idea had been delusional. He shivered, half-frozen in the bowels of the cave as the light faded, wondering if hypothermia had already set in. He would be lucky not to lose a toe or fingers—he hoped not a limb—to frostbite, but he swore he would not die on this trip. He savored a momentary satisfaction from his angry vow, but soon that was eviscerated by the knowledge Claire was dead and no amount of determination, no fantasy trip of his, would ever change that.

He stopped the jumping jacks. He huddled himself on the ground and cradled his knees alongside his cheeks. A rock pressed sharply against the burning flesh of his bare ass.

He shifted his weight, closed his eyes, and curled his shivering body as tightly as possible. He had shivered when he and Claire had made love for the very first time, when the shower water had turned freezing, but he hadn't cared about the cold then. He heard in the cave what sounded like the plunk of water somewhere close by. He opened his eyes, searching about in the dim light, but he could not see water falling. He closed his eyes again and listened. There was another drop.

After a long interval, he again heard the sound of falling water. He wondered if the water was dripping from the ceiling of the cave into the spring. He wasn't sure, but as he listened, he soon heard, to his surprise, a sob break from his lungs. The sobbing transformed from a solitary cry into a crashing wave of tears. He wailed unfettered then, and as he did, the cry lifted from him and rose and rose and rose, an echo clamoring upward through some opening in the cavernous ceiling that he could not see.

CHAPTER 40

He was miles beyond the lake and the canyon passage, past the cave, and further upstream on the river than he'd ever been before. The warmth of the late July sun penetrated the flesh of John's bare shoulder as he dipped the paddle into the river. The paddle scraped bottom; the river had opened wide but here it was very shallow. Clear water flowed over glittering stones.

He was glad he'd returned to the river and being only one week into his month-long leave of absence, he had no sense of being rushed. He was lucky, he knew, that Stone had come after him in January, that he had survived that sortie with only two frostbitten toes that had to be partially amputated. His family had been incredibly upset that he had attempted such a trip alone and in winter—his mom in particular had scolded him while saying she couldn't bear to lose him—and his friends had told him on multiple occasions how stupid he had been. He'd confessed to his closest confidants that it was less stupidity than a raging but impotent protest against nature, against life's limits. But the trip had been a futile railing. He'd changed nothing.

The canoe scraped bottom and ground to a halt. He used his paddle like a gondolier's pole and rocked the canoe back and forth, but his attempts to set himself free were in vain. The river had transformed into a shallow brook, water rippling like miniature waves over a thousand small rocks. He could paddle no further. He stepped out of the boat and cold water seeped into his boots. He dragged the canoe to shore, fought with spindly and sharp-toothed bushes, and lodged the canoe securely between a bush and a large rock. The bushes grew thick along the shoreline, so he returned to the creek. He picked his way over the rocks in the brook as water streamed past his ankles.

He waded in the brook until the water ran fast over rough, angular rocks and slipped past two boulders that stood like sentries above the narrowing creek. After a quarter mile, a steep hill covered with thick, green brush rose in front of him while the water tumbled down the slope in frothy, white cascades. The falls were steep and slippery, so he switched back into the brush and scrabbled up the hill at alternating angles, steadying and pulling himself on bush branches. The tips of the branches were sharp. The bushes scraped thin, red scratches against his arms, but he felt no pain as he pulled himself higher. He broke into a sweat climbing the hill and removed his Cardinals baseball cap—a gift from Andy after his first paycheck—to wipe his brow.

Within a dozen steps, he saw the crest of the hill. He imagined reaching the top of the ridge and seeing a glacier melt into the headwaters of the river. He pushed himself a step higher, then stopped, pausing for breath. For the first time all day, he hesitated.

He remembered when Claire had refused to push ahead at the lake the prior summer. He'd angrily chastised her, accusing her of faltering in courage at the chasm of adventure—something years before when she was telling him about Ernest Becker that she vowed she'd never do. He'd been frustrated and disappointed with her, but now he wondered if she was right: maybe it was better not to advance.

The surging of falling water interrupted his thoughts. He cut through the brush until he reached the stream tumbling down the hill. He stared into the falling brook, watching the series of short falls burst from the earth as glistening white water. An urge swept over him to lie down on the moist earth, to fall asleep alongside the cascades, amid the small rocks quilted with moss. He inched closer to the falls, extending his hand under the spraying mist. He watched the water fall past his hand, descending toward the valley in the briefest of instants.

He focused on a single drop as it slipped off the rock. He followed its path as it stood out boldly, isolated and suspended for a prolonged moment, before accelerating and crashing on a rock below. He watched another drop pour over the ledge: it leapt out, swelled in size, and dove downward, falling gracefully at first, as if in slow motion, then it picked up speed, and splattered on the rock, rejoining the stream. He picked out drops, one after another, as they slid over the edge, and watched until they collided against granite and disappeared back into the cascading brook. He leaned further over a wet and slippery boulder, watching the flow of the cascades while the question of whether to continue to climb faded from his mind.

When he turned around, he stepped toward the ridge. He climbed to the top, expecting to see a glacier, but he saw only the rising slope of the mountain, split by the tumbling creek and scarred by outcroppings. He hiked for more than an hour, until he reached a place where the creek puddled into a small pool at the base of a sharp incline of boulders and rocks. He paused to catch his breath and glanced further uphill. The creek was no longer visible. He clambered over the boulders, looking for water trickling down the hill, but he saw only earth and stones. He ran further uphill. The land was flat and dry, bereft even of a dry creek bed.

He scrambled back downhill to where the creek ended in the small pool. The pool was only several feet across and a couple of feet to the bottom, though it deepened against the rocky embankment. He kneeled on a flat rock, braced himself with an arm against a boulder, and leaned over the pool. The image of his own bearded face shone back and he flinched with surprise. After his vision adjusted, he saw through his own reflection on the surface to pebbles glistening below in the refracted sunlight.

The creek seemed to seep out of two large boulders that were wedged solidly together on the uphill side. Beneath the surface, another boulder served as a buttress, though a gaping crevice ran between the rocks. The water receded into the shadows of this opening. John stared into the pool, searching unsuccessfully for the place where the crevice and the water ceased.

He lay over the hard stones, hovering his head close to the water's surface, but still he could not see an end to the pool. He removed his cap, pulled the tank top from his chest, and plunged his head into the pool.

Cold water sucked at his breath and he opened his eyes to try to see between the rocks. The space narrowed and darkened and the water ran into the fissure between the rocks for as far as he could see.

He wondered if he was staring into a joint between boulders—a small crevice that receded only a few inches beyond his vision. It was probably nothing remarkable. Then he wondered if it was a narrow passage into a vast underground cavern.

He pulled his head from the water, shaking the cold drops from his hair. He yanked off his boots and jeans, entered the small pool, and gulped another deep breath. He forced himself toward the opening, but the space was too small and the boulders blocked him from getting much closer. He could see nothing more than the crevice between the rocks and the water flowing into darkness.

He had found the source, though it didn't start from a melting glacier. Perhaps it was fed from an underground spring, but if so, where did the spring come from—a labyrinth that spread for miles under the surface? A slowly melting glacier trapped underground thousands of years earlier by the rising and falling of the earth? Or perhaps it was merely the simple accumulation of rain and melting snow into a small, insignificant crack between boulders. He couldn't tell.

He pulled himself out of the water. He didn't know where the source began. A swear word flashed through his mind, but he stopped himself. Instead, he emitted a raucous belly laugh that reverberated off the rocks and water and echoed back.

He pulled his paddle from the river. The current was slight but enough to carry the canoe downstream. The afternoon sun rose high in the sky and radiated warmth onto his bare skin. He thought of the source of the river—if it was that—behind him.

He missed Claire—he'd missed her all day—but the feeling transformed from a vague numbness to a sharp ache, like a cut that bled from his soul. He wished Claire could have been at the spring. She would have sensed its mystery long before him, even while he was confused and frustrated, and she would have loved the place. He wished after a lifetime of longing she could have completed her journey. He wondered again where her spirit had gone—if there was indeed heaven or some other, invisible dimension? Perhaps so; perhaps she *had* even been able to see the source of the river. He wasn't sure. It was only a musing, but he pictured her again on the boulder in the river when he had proposed—her blond hair wet, her eyes glinting blue-gray, when he'd asked her to marry him. That image, he decided, *was* real and it was something he could hang on to.

The canoe drifted against the west bank. He beached the canoe and stepped out to urinate. He climbed over rocks, away from the river, and as he stepped toward the ground, he saw beneath his descending foot a snake trying to swallow the top of a frog's head. John pulled back and the snake and the frog both recoiled. The crown of the frog's large head was gnarled and bloody—the snake had begun to devour the frog alive. For an instant, both animals stared at John. Then the frog leaped into the bushes; the snake slithered under a rock.

The look of terror on the frog's face stayed in John's mind as he floated downstream. He hoped the snake hadn't caught the frog again and that it was still alive. He realized then that every day thousands, maybe millions, of snakes were eating thousands, maybe millions of frogs, and there were also thousands of snakes being eaten by bigger snakes or eagles. He also knew at each moment there were thousands of animals and more than a few people being killed or dying. Death was a constant in life—he didn't understand why, but it was true.

John forced his attention on the river. A cutthroat trout wiggled past the canoe, his orange stripes flashing in the translucent water. He watched the fish swim by, he heard the surging of the river and the cawing of a blue jay, and he sensed something he didn't quite have the words for. He felt *something*—maybe a sense of connection?—to the fish, to the river, to the bird, and to the granite-faced mountain. The feeling grew bigger, as if it could not be contained by the river, and it filled him with a sense of peace.

He knew the feeling would fade, but he still vowed to try to keep that sense of peace within himself every day for as long as he lived. And how long would that be? It could be fifty more years, but then again, he could die that day—not that he was going to act reckless again, but death would arrive, perhaps without notice, on its own timing.

He thought again about Claire, and as he did, the thoughts were followed by a sense of her. He felt something—a presence, an energy—he didn't know what to call it. He did not see her, but in the stillness of the moment, he *felt* her presence as clearly as he saw the mountains, the pines, and the river. He sensed she was very near, and he felt then his own heart open, and expand, like his heart was growing beyond his body; for an instant, he felt something within him join with her presence, as if they were a part of each other.

The feeling soon passed. It was like she had been with him for a moment and then was gone. He still thought of her, but he no longer felt her presence. Now it was only a memory. Perhaps that was all it had ever been, but he didn't think so.

He drifted in the canoe. The day had become very hot. As he leaned over the side of the canoe, his sweat dripped into the river. A school of trout languished in a deep pocket of the river under the shade of aspens. He stood up, and the canoe rocked, threatening to tip him into the river, until he found his balance. He gazed at the mountains and the pines and aspens, and then he laughed. He leapt into the river. Coolness surrounded him and he searched for the trout. He could no longer see them, but he let the flow of the river carry him downstream.

WITH GRATITUDE

I am immensely grateful to the many individuals whose support and contributions have helped make this novel possible.

Susan Meecham-Reidhead Morse provided helpful comments and encouragement through the early stages of writing. So, too, did fellow writers and friends John Newsham, Mark Mueller, Mary Koyn Burke, Joris Miller, and the late Robert Calsyn.

Lindsay (Shadwell) Smith worked diligently and thoughtfully on later drafts of the manuscript as a literary editor, providing excellent (if sometimes difficult to hear) formative comments and skilled copy editing. Whatever strengths this novel may possess as a work of literary fiction are owed in no small part to Lindsay's skillful guidance.

The late Bonnie Barbareck helped with both early production details and encouragement. I also appreciate the sage advice, creative design, and production assistance of the team at 1106 Design. Their work made this book a reality.

I offer a very special thanks to Susan Lee-Goss Morse, whose generous support, encouragement, and editorial comments helped to bring this book across the finish line.

Although the book is a work of fiction and all characters creations of the imagination, I have nonetheless been inspired by many diverse individuals who have faced trauma, loss, fear—and yet still found the courage and will to create lives of love and interpersonal and spiritual connection. In the final analysis, this book is dedicated to all those who struggle against life's hardships to bring meaning, joy, spirit, and love to the world.

Thank you for reading *Source of a River*.
I hope you enjoyed the novel.

If you found the book to be of interest or value, would you do me a favor? Online reviews and ratings are critical for encouraging additional readership and book sales. Will you take a few moments now to share your assessment of my book at the review site of your choice? Your opinion is invaluable!

Thank you very much!

ABOUT THE AUTHOR

Gary Morse grew up in Northern California before living for years in St. Louis. He is the author of published literary short stories, newspaper and magazine pieces. Gary, who holds a Ph.D. in clinical psychology, has also published more than eighty articles and book chapters on mental health and psychology. *Source of a River* is his first novel. He is currently at work on two non-fiction books and a new novel. He lives in the Pacific Northwest and St. Louis with his wife and their three dogs.

https://drgarymorse.com

https://drgarymorse.com/books-and-fiction/

9 798989 278305